WILLIAM FLEMING AND FRANK MACOMBER

Musical Arts & Styles

UNIVERSITY OF FLORIDA PRESS / GAINESVILLE

Printed in the U.S.A. on acid-free paper

Library of Congress Cataloging-in-Publication Data
Fleming, William, 1909–
Musical arts and styles / William Fleming and Frank Macomber.
p. cm.
Bibliography: p.
Includes index.
ISBN 0–8130–0961–8 (alk. paper). ISBN 0–8130–0990–1 (pbk.)
1. Music appreciation. I. Macomber, Frank. II. Title
MT6.F619 1990
781.1'7—dc20 89–4951

Cover illustration: Hans Memling. *Angel Musicians*, 1480. Oil on wood. By permission of the Koninklijk Museum voor Schone Kunsten, Antwerp. Front, right panel: busine (long trumpet), folded slide trumpet, portative organ, harp, fiddle. Back, left panel: psaltery, tromba marina (marine trumpet), lute folded trumpet, tenor shawn.
Frontispiece illustration: Canon in a circle with a rose "for Henry VIII." Anonymous, 16th century. By permission of the British Library, London.

Excerpts from the following compositions have been reprinted in this volume with the permission of the copyright holders:

Le marteau sans maître, by Pierre Boulez, © 1954 by Univeral Edition London, used by permission of European American Distributors (see p. 453).

"Six-part Ricercar," from *Musical Offering*, by J.S. Bach, scored by Anton von Webern, © 1933 by Universal Edition, used by permission of European American Music (see p. 315).

War Requiem, Op. 66, music by Benjamin Britten, text by Wilfred Owen, © 1962 by Boosey & Hawkes Music Publishers Ltd.; copyright renewed. Used by permission of Boosey & Hawkes, Inc.

Appalachian Spring, © 1945 by Aaron Copland; copyright renewed. Reprinted by permission of Aaron Copland, copyright owner, and Boosey & Hawkes, sole agent.

Music for Strings, Percussion, and Celestra, by Bela Bartók, © 1937 by Universal Editions; copyright renewed. Copyright and renewal assigned to Boosey & Hawkes, Inc., for the U.S.A. Used by permission.

American Tune, © 1973 by Paul Simon.

The University of Florida Press is a member of University Presses of Florida, the scholarly publishing agency of the State University System of Florida. Books are selected for publication by faculty editorial committees at each of Florida's nine public universities: Florida A&M University (Tallahassee), Florida Atlantic University (Boca Raton), Florida International University (Miami), Florida State University (Tallahassee), University of Central Florida (Orlando), University of Florida (Gainesville), University of North Florida (Jacksonville), University of South Florida (Tampa), University of West Florida (Pensacola).

Orders for books published by all member presses should be addressed to University Presses of Florida, 15 NW 15th St., Gainesville, FL 32603.

Musical Arts and Styles

CONTENTS

PART III: COMPONENTS OF MUSIC

PREFACE

Musical Arts and Styles is addressed to general readers and inquiring students seeking a deeper understanding of the musical experience. Music in these pages is considered variously as an art in its own right, in its relationship to the allied arts, and in its larger historical, humanistic, and stylistic context.

Part I discusses music in its alliance with poetry in the art of song, with steps and gestures in dance and ballet, with narrative and drama in opera and oratorio, with architecture in diverse spatial and acoustical surroundings, and with various types of imagery associated with the visual arts and literature in programme music. Part II presents the development of music in the context of Western civilization from ancient to contemporary times. Each period is viewed as a distinctive style where music shares trends with other intellectual, social, and artistic developments. Part III is a review of the basics of music itself: notation; the elements of tone color, rhythm, dynamics, and melody; the complexes of harmony and counterpoint; and the art of form, ranging from simple sectional structures to the cyclical sonata and symphonic forms.

All of the musical arts are presented as interactive dimensions of human experience. Music can never exist in a vacuum. It is absorbed by the senses and the mind with all the powers of association, imagination, and thought that can be brought to bear on the experience. In approaching music, the work itself must come first and foremost. There is no substitute for continuous and attentive listening, for words are powerless to bring about a full understanding of music. But they can point to various levels of understanding, through the use of images and metaphors and appropriate parallels to the other arts.

Words can also invoke the spirit of a time and can surround the musical expression of an era with the aura and atmosphere in which the work was created. This book is thus based on two assumptions: first, that words can be used meaningfully and relevantly in relation to experiences that are essentially nonverbal; and second, that the nonverbal experience derived from actually listening to music is nowhere duplicated in these pages.

A composer addresses listeners just as an author writes for readers. Neither composers nor writers, however, expect their audiences to know how to write sonatas or novels. The forms they use reveal themselves as they unfold, and the expectation is that the alert listener or reader will perceive them in the course of the musical or reading experience. With an art so abstract and complex as music, it is inevitable that technical obstacles will be encountered. Every attempt has been made to explain these technical terms as they occur, or to cross-reference pages where explanations may be found. The reader may also consult the ample index.

Above all, the objective of the book is to illuminate the art of music in its broader aspects, and to enhance the pleasure and enjoyment of the listening experience.

Abbreviations of the catalogs of various composers' works used in this book include:

Johann Sebastian Bach: *BWV. Thematisch-systematisches Verzeichnis der musikalischen Werke Johann Sebastian Bachs: Bach-Werke-Verzeichnis*, edited by W. Schmieder.

George Frideric Handel: *HWV. Verzeichnis der Werke G. F. Händels*, edited by B. Baselt.

Franz Joseph Haydn: *Hob. Joseph Haydn: Thematisch-bibliographisches Werkverzeichnis*, edited by A. van Hoboken.

Wolfgang Amadeus Mozart: *K. Chronologisch-thematisches Verzeichnis sämtlicher Tonwerke Wolfgang Amade Mozarts*, edited by L. von Köchel.

Franz Schubert: *D. Franz Schubert: Thematisches Verzeichnis seiner Werke in chronologischer Folge*, edited by Otto Erich Deutsch.

Antonio Vivaldi: *RV. Verzeichnis der Werke Antonio Vivaldis, kleine Ausgabe*, edited by P. Ryom.

Op. is used for opus numbers of works by composers who so designated their own compositions. Titles in italics are works named by the composer; roman type is used for descriptive titles of works that were not formally named. Roman type with quotation marks denotes shorter sections within longer works.

Acknowledgments

The authors take pleasure in extending their heartfelt thanks and gratitude to their many friends and colleagues who have contributed so much to the cultivation and fruition of this study: at Syracuse, to George Nugent, David Tatham, and Eric Jensen for their cogent readings of various parts of the manuscript, and to Abraham Veinus for many illuminating ideas; to the Photo Center staff, Stephen Sartori, David Broda, and Richard Pitzeruse, Jr., for their photographic prowess; at the University Presses of Florida, to Walda Metcalf for her wise guidance and support at every stage of the production, Deidre Bryan for her editorial expertise, and Alexandra Leader for help with the illustrations. Farther afield, thanks go to Margaret Freeman of the College of William and Mary, to Alice Anne Callahan Russell of Baker University; and finally to the many generations of students who have taught their teachers more than they will ever realize.

William Fleming and Frank Macomber

Syracuse University

PART

I

Music and Its Companion Arts

INTRODUCTION

The Related Arts

MUSIC, FROM ANCIENT TIMES to the present, has always been found in the company of the other arts. Originally the word *music,* as coined by the Greeks, included all the arts cultivated by the Muses, those mythical maidens who presided over the destinies of poetry, drama, dance, and the tonal art itself. Today the play of step, gesture, and sound point to the dance and ballet, the union of word and tone to solo and group singing, the fusion of liturgy and music to solemn church ceremonies. The conjunction of drama and music occurs in opera and oratorio, in plays calling for incidental music and song, and in films and television productions. Opera also incorporates most of the other arts since, in addition to solo and ensemble singing, instrumental overtures and interludes, there is dramatic dialogue, dancing, scenic design, stage decor, and costumes.

On still another level, music is allied with the art of descriptive and narrative imagery in what is called programme music. Sounds from nature are the most obvious, with the flute that can imitate bird songs and the drums that can simulate thunder. On a more sophisticated plane, in works inspired by poetry and prose, an instrumental ensemble elucidates the mood of a poem or re-creates in sound the incidents of a story. Composers have also been inspired by the pictorial arts in consciously seeking to project the spirit and meaning of a painting.

Even when forms of instrumental music—fugue, sonata, concerto—seem relatively self-sufficient, separated as they usually are from any literary text serving as a programme, there is nevertheless an inescapable relationship between the music and its architectural and acoustical surroundings. Works meant to be played outdoors clearly differ from those intended for indoors. Music for church worship differs from that written for the ballroom and concert hall. Hence the art of architecture is allied with music by providing the setting where the music is performed. These physical and social conditions impose a mind-set that strongly affects both listener and performer.

This union of music with its allied arts is deeply rooted in human experience. Long before any of the arts became independent entities, they existed side by side in tribal festivals, war dances, work songs, magic rites, and ceremonial processions. Shouting, stamping, clapping, and miming expressed the group emotions of a society. War whoops, battle cries, love calls, shouts of joy, and outbursts of grief eventually became epic chants, heroic ballads, love songs, and laments. Out of the rhythms of group efforts associated with hunting, harvesting, threshing, and mowing came the work songs that relieved the tedium of labor. The emotional responses to the milestones of family life—birth, childhood, maturity, love, marriage, and death—crystallized into lullabies, children's songs, love songs, courtship dances, and songs of mourning. Magic incantations and ceremonial rites for the propitiation of the gods find more modern expression in a wide range of religious music.

Dance represents the union of physical movement and music. Gesture, mimicry, and pantomime are modes of visual communication that convey shades of meaning beyond the power of words. Folk dances of ancient origin survive, and the art of choreography dates from the time of classical Greek drama. As in former days, dancing gives delight, relaxation from the burdens of the day, and promotes social companionship. Through formal choreography dance rises to the level of an art form. The range of choreographic practice is vast and varied. It includes mass community rites, such as invoking rain and a good harvest, or celebrating the installation of a new ruler. At the other end of the spectrum, dance can project abstract studies in free form and motion to captivate a diverse public audience.

In addition to dances that are performed physically and presented as spectacles on the stage, there are the imaginary dances created only to be heard in the home or concert hall. Here the steps and movements of the dancing experience take place on the stage of the listener's imagination. Such works include the baroque instrumental dance suites, the minuet and waltz movements of symphonies, and the virtuoso instrumental dances written for concert performance.

Song merges the arts of poetry and music. In Western culture, religious chants and secular folk songs of considerable antiquity are the products of anonymous creators, passed down orally from generation to generation. Masterful songs, composed and set down in writing by acknowledged poets and musicians, flourished during the eras of the troubadour and Minnesinger during the Middle Ages. Much earlier examples of song survive from ancient Greece.

Music also joins with all the arts in religious worship, where it promotes feelings of unity within the congregation, inspires the spirit of prayer and praise, and helps to intensify the feeling of communion with a higher power. Out of synagogue, temple, and church have come the sacred services, masses, and cantatas that occupy a lofty position in the art of music through the ages. From the psalm singing in the ancient Jewish temple, through the rhapsodic plainsong of the medieval Christian church, to the chorales and anthems of Protestantism, religious music extends deep roots in the musical family tree.

Music and drama have always been closely related. Though the music of ancient Greek drama is now virtually nonexistent, it is well known that the tonal art played an important role in every presentation. The surviving terminology is enough to illustrate the point. A *melodrama,* for instance, originally meant a drama with melody. The circular space in front of the proscenium of the Greek theater was called the *orchestra,* and it served as the place where the *chorus* performed round dances with gesture and song. In all dramatic production, as Aristotle notes in the *Poetics,* "Melody holds the chief place among embellishments."

This association of the two arts continued through the medieval miracle and mystery plays performed by itinerant musicians and strolling players in castle and marketplace. Later, the plays of such great dramatists as Shakespeare, Calderón, and Molière often made liberal use of music, and today no cinema or television production would be complete without music.

In the final analysis, when composers write songs, they are setting poems to music; when they write religious music, they must be conscious of its place in the liturgy; when they write music for a ballet or an opera, they think in terms of the theater; and when they write orchestral works, architecture and concert hall acoustics command their attention.

Thus from spontaneous folk songs to sophisticated song cycles, from artless group singing to mighty choral symphonies, from folk-dance festivals to formal classical ballets, from primitive religious rites to grandiloquent masses and oratorios, from simple hymn tunes sung by an untrained congregation to complex polyphony sung by skilled choristers, from rustic narrative ballads to cosmopolitan music drama, and from Cro-Magnon bone whistles to the modern symphony orchestra, music is associated either explicitly or implicitly with one or more of its allied arts.

CHAPTER

1

Art of Dance

DANCE—WHETHER PERFORMED as a manifestation of emotion, group unity, religious exercise, or theatrical spectacle—is indissolubly associated with music. Even when musical instruments as such are absent, the human body itself takes over and functions percussively with rhythmic stamping of feet, clapping of hands, snapping of fingers, as well as melodically with shouting, crying, or singing. Since both dancing and music-making have a common source in the rhythmic impulse as well as in the natural enthusiasm of the human spirit, dance rhythms and musical rhythms serve to keep the participants in step, while psychologically they suggest appropriate moods and emotional states. Such rhythms achieve physical manifestation when danced formally on a ballroom floor or informally in a disco. They may also function nonphysically, projected by one's imagination while listening to dance-based music at a concert or folk festival, or to an instrumental suite—an unseen ballet meant only for listening.

Just as the union of word and tone in song results in all the complex forms of vocal music, so the joining of measured body movement and sound in the dance leads to a host of forms, ranging from simple and complex folk expressions to sophisticated commentaries on the dance heard in suites, sonatas, and symphonies. It would be impossible to overestimate the influence of the dance on the course of music. Whether a composer uses a primitive war chant or an aristocratic minuet as subject matter, one of the principal resources of instrumental music will always be the dance. Such music thus accounts for a considerable segment of the concert repertory, and unless a listener can establish some historical, social, national, religious, or expressive frame of reference, much of its significance will be lost.

Specific dance forms and patterns intended for active participation are found in all countries, at all social levels, and at all times past and present. Such dances are continuously cultivated in the countries of their origin, and often are performed by touring troupes that bring the flash and fire of Spain, the pounding percussive energy of Africa, or the dash and color of a central European country to international audiences. In refined forms these ethnic dances find their way into operas, ballets, and concert music.

In such piano music as Chopin's mazurkas, polonaises, and waltzes or Liszt's Hungarian rhapsodies, as well as Dvořák's orchestral Slavonic dances and Bartók's Romanian dances, there is a reflection of the characteristic spirit of the people. Contemporary composers find dance elements useful and often liven up their scores with waltzes, fox-trots, tangos, jazz, and rock rhythms in various guises and disguises, just as past composers transformed popular dance tunes and forms in their works. Surveying the contemporary scene, one finds the composer of today liberally injecting dance sequences in operas, musical comedies, and revues, as well as in incidental music for plays, motion pictures, and television.

The Dance Suite

The fountainhead of the instrumental suite and the ballet can be traced to the aristocratic ballrooms of the Renaissance and baroque eras. Here, by a long refining process of the courtly practice, the formulation of steps, rhythms, gestures, and organized patterns took place. The basic dances, however, seldom originated in these rarefied social surroundings. Most, if not all, found their initial impetus in the energetic expressions of the people. The chaconne, passacaglia, and sarabande, for instance, seem to have originated in the West Indies and Central America, from where they were brought to Spain by the sailors, traders, and colonists who followed in the wake of Columbus. In Spain, they rose to the status of sophisticated art forms. In the hands of composers who supplied the music for aristocratic entertainments, these dances were ultimately accepted in Spanish and French courtly circles.

The Irish jig, in similar fashion, started life humbly as a vigorous folk dance, then was adapted to courtly life under Elizabeth I of England. From there it went to France, where it was glorified at the court of Louis XIV as the gigue. The minuet began as a provincial dance of Poitou. It gradually lost its rustic angularity while working its way up the social ladder, finally gaining hold in princely palaces as the epitome of courtly decorum and ceremonial dignity. Goethe described its further transition from active dance to observed spectacle at the turn of the 19th century: "The minuet in particular is regarded as a work of art and is performed by only a few couples. Such a couple is surrounded by the rest of the company in circles, admired and applauded at the end." Modern composers and choreographers have taken these dances one step further, to the point where concert versions are heard by the audience seated in a hall or seen as stage productions in a theater. The progression from rustic folk dance to sophisticated work of art has once again come full circle.

Dances in instrumental form were played indoors on lutes, on keyboard instruments, and by string ensembles both as dinner music and as chamber music, and outdoors by wind bands as background music for social occasions. When such instrumental dances were taken up by composers of stature, they underwent still further phases of sophistication; and the simple rhythms and regular meters yielded to complicated commentaries on the underlying rhythmic patterns. Instrumental forms such as the suite, partita, *sonata da camera* (chamber sonata) and the later 18th-century serenades and divertimentos are outgrowths of traditions that started in princely ballrooms.

Suites of dances gradually crystallized around four principal types that were presented in sequence—the *allemande, courante, sarabande,* and *gigue.* This relatively stable core could be prefixed at the composer's discretion by a prelude or fantasia; and between the sarabande and final gigue was often inserted the *galanterie,* a group of the lighthearted, elegant dances of the French courtly *style galant*—musettes, minuets, bourrées, or gavottes. As written for instrumental solo and for various ensemble combinations, including the orchestra, these baroque dances in the hands of composers of the caliber of Corelli, Purcell, Handel, and Bach became models of vigorous musical statement and clear structural design. Thus a typical Bach suite, whether scored for keyboard, solo violin, or cello, consisted of an allemande, a sturdy, energetic dance in moderate tempo and 4/4 meter; a courante, a rapid, running patter of eighth notes in triple meter, occasionally complicated with cross rhythms; a sarabande, a slow, stately measured dance in 3/2 meter with a characteristic dotted second beat. At this point came the galanterie, to be followed by a gigue providing the suite with a high-spirited finale.

Even the Viennese sonatas, symphonies, and concertos retained a basic identification with the suite by the inclusion of such movements as minuets. Dance rhythms in disguise also found their way into the structures and textures of fugues and operatic arias. Dance thus pervades virtually all categories of musical form, whether encountered as actual bodily movement or as idealized dances expressed in vocal and instrumental forms for listening only.

Ballet

The earliest documentation on the ballet comes from the lavish courtly entertainments of Renaissance times. *Circé, ou le ballet comique de la reine (Circe, or the Queen's Dramatic Ballet),* performed at the French court in 1581, gives a workable definition of ballet as "a geometrical arrangement of numerous people dancing together under a diverse harmony of many instruments." Thereafter, the development of the French *ballet de cour* (court ballet) proceeded apace and soon became a highly favored form of courtly entertainment. Because of the lavish scale on which they were produced and the attendant expense, these ballets were generally performed only on special occasions, such as courtly weddings or coronations. The ballet de cour and its English equivalent, the court *masque,* consisted of a free combination of costumed pageantry, poetic recitation, dancing, mummery, pantomime, scenic architecture, solo and choral song, and instrumental interludes strung loosely together along the lines of some mythological or allegorical plot.

In England these presentations were the cause of some of the most noble artistic collaborations in history. *The Masque of Blackness,* for instance, was performed at the court of James I at Whitehall in 1605. Shakespeare's younger contemporary, Ben Jonson, wrote the dialogue and poetry. The famous architect Inigo Jones designed the "scenes and machines," which reputedly marked the invention of movable scenery that changed before the eyes of the audience instead of remaining stationary in the manner of the stylized temple facades of classical and Renaissance theaters. And the principal dancers were none other than James I's queen and her ladies. Perhaps the most famous of all masques was John Milton's *Comus* with music by Henry Lawes, written for a performance at Ludlow Castle in 1634. The ballet de cour and the masque were antecedents of opera and ballet in their later, more highly developed forms.

No less notable were the theatrical productions staged at the court of Louis XIV in France. Jean-Baptiste Lully, a ballet master, producer, and composer all in one, supplied abundant dance music for *tragédies lyriques,* theater pieces by the dramatist Racine, and those of the playwright Molière called *comédie-ballets.* The best known of the latter genre is the perennial favorite *Le bourgeois gentilhomme (The Bourgeois Gentleman,* 1670). A *tragédie-ballet* entitled *Psyché* was staged in 1671 with Lully contributing the music, dramatists Corneille and Molière the spoken verses, and the librettist Quinault the prose for the recitatives. All these hybrids were transitional forms on the way to more specific definition as ballets and operas. From the era of Lully on, the ballet has enjoyed a favored place among the arts in France; and to this day classical ballet everywhere still employs a vocabulary dominated by French terms.

Out of such Italian Renaissance entertainments as the carnival pageant, comedy of masks, harlequinade, and intermezzo, out of the French court ballet and ballet-opera, out of the English masque, out of the incidental ballets performed as divertissements and between-the-act interludes, and out of the operatic ballet (whether integrated with or extraneous to the plot and dramatic action), the ballet gradually emerged in the well-defined artistic form practiced today. As always, it retains its close alliance with music.

Ballets can be classified into general types, and they also follow the trends of their respective historical style periods. The *dramatic ballet* employs pantomime and mimetic characterization to carry out a story line, while the *abstract ballet* is concerned more with formal elements than with plot and confines itself principally to the composition of designs and the grouping of dancers and dance movements with an eye to variety and contrast. The *folk ballet* uses ethnic dances as a principal ingredient and can employ plot or not, as the choreographer and composer choose. Needless to say, these classifications represent dominant tendencies rather than fixed rules, and many examples in the repertory fall somewhere in between. It is also usual to classify ballets in style categories such as the *classical ballet,* which follows the formal, stylized steps, gestures, and patterns stemming from the traditions established in the 17th and 18th centuries. *Romantic ballets* and *modern ballets,* on the other hand, are based on the dominant styles of the 19th and 20th centuries, respectively.

THE DRAMATIC BALLET

The *dramatic ballet,* also called the "mimed" ballet, leans heavily on the age-old art of pantomime. The word was coined by the ancient Greeks to mean "all-imitating," and it was used in those times to denote a means of telling a story through gestures: acting out a myth in sign language and symbolic suggestion, presenting tragic or comic situations with mimicry, and communicating with an audience through mimetic dance. In addition to its cultivation in the ballet, the art also survives in the antics of circus clowns and puppet shows, and it flourished in the days of the silent film.

Gesture has always been an eloquent visual language, and styles of acting in the theater and opera owe much to the art of the mime. A shrug of the shoulders or a wave of the hand often tells more than words. Miming also makes use of an extensive vocabulary of bodily movements, varying from those associated with work and occupations to obscure symbolic and allegorical gestures designed to convey meaning only to the initiated. The emotional spectrum encompassed by this visual language is tremendous, ranging from the soaring aspiration expressed by an upward leap to the blackness of despair implied by sinking earthward.

The first dramatic ballet was Gluck's *Don Juan* (1761), which he subtitled "Pantomime Ballet in the Manner of the Ancients." With this ballet, the dance emerged as an art form capable of commanding full attention in its own right as a dramatic spectacle with music, apart from any theatrical or operatic context. Discarding the poetic texts and song elements of the court ballets and ballet-operas, Gluck and his choreographer tell of the licentious lover on his way to perdition. The story unfolds through a combination of expressive gestures, stylized and mimetic dances, and the musical score, which now assumed primary importance.

Like the Greek chorus of old, the orchestra became the principal emotional interpreter of the dramatic action. Continuing through the 19th century with such works as Beethoven's *Creatures of Prometheus* and Delibes' *Coppelia* and *Sylvia,* the dramatic ballet began to take on the color of romanticism, and the plots became fanciful fairy tales liberally populated with assorted mermaids, ondines, elves, and sylphs. Such was the background for Tchaikovsky's essays in the form, and his ballets—*Swan Lake, Sleeping Beauty,* and *The Nutcracker*—remain, either whole or in part, staples in the current repertory.

The dramatic ballet received its greatest impetus in the 20th century from an offshoot of the Imperial Russian Ballet known as the Ballets Russes, which set Paris dance circles ablaze in 1909 under the guiding spirit of Sergei Diaghilev. With rare discernment and creative imagination, this genius among impresarios gathered about him the choreographers Fokine and Massine; the composers Stravinsky, Ravel, and Poulenc; the scenic designers Bakst, Derain, and Picasso; and dancers of such legendary stature as Nijinsky, Pavlova, and Karsavina. The collaboration of these patrons, composers, choreographers, scenic designers, and dancers reflected all the movements that were stirring the world of art at that time—impressionism, neoclassicism, and the mechanical style, to name but three—and led to the creation of many enduring modern ballets.

The scores Igor Stravinsky composed for the Diaghilev company just before World War I made musical as well as ballet history. In a crescendo of creative activity, *The Firebird* (1910), with its lush and colorful orchestration, continued the romantic fairy-tale tradition of Tchaikovsky and Rimsky-Korsakov. *Petrouchka* (1911), with its tragicomic situations and pantomime plot, became a dance drama that re-established the dramatic ballet as a genre among contemporary theater pieces (Plate I). *The Rite of Spring* (1913) then brought about a revolution that changed the entire course of contemporary music. In this solemn evocation of pagan religious rites, Stravinsky's unnerving polyrhythms and savage dissonances created such unforgettable images of brute force and primeval power as to recast the entire rhythmic outlook for the 20th century.

Petrouchka, subtitled "Burlesque Scenes in Four Tableaux," takes place against a kaleidoscopic cross-section of life at a fair in old St. Petersburg at carnival time. The rise of the curtain reveals the hustle and bustle of the carnival crowds milling about amid the merry-go-rounds, booths, and stalls of the fairgrounds. The previously regular rhythmic pulse yields at this point to a polymetrical series of measures (bars 69–77) consisting of such irregular units as 3/4, 2/4, 3/8, 4/8, and 5/8—a highly effective device to describe the irregular movements of the jostling crowds as they go this way then that, as well as to create contrast for the succession of bizarre dances that momentarily command their attention. Stravinsky's orchestra, meanwhile, functions like a gigantic accordion, generating a flood of blatantly raucous but festive music.

In the First Tableau a barrel-organ grinder plays banal hurdy-gurdy tunes while a dancer pivots and pirouettes on the tips of her toes. The piquant instrumentation simulates the barrel organ by combining the piccolo, two flutes, three clarinets, bass clarinet, and triangle. Several competing entertainers on the other side of the stage then distract the fickle attention of the crowds with a music box. Next the Charlatan, a somewhat sinister-appearing showman whom the people regard with superstitious awe, appears before his puppet theater and draws an audience around him with an ingratiating melody on the flute. With a flourish he pulls up the curtain to reveal three marionettes with limp bodies and masklike faces—the Ballerina in the center, with Petrouchka and the Moor on either side. As the strings tighten, their inert, sawdust-filled bodies jerk to attention for the performance of the "Russian Dance." This masterpiece of calculated, mechanical rhythms and percussive, brittle sounds is well adapted for the automaton's dance, but an occasional lyric phrase suggests that even such inanimate creatures are capable of human longings. There is also a rugged peasant vigor in this dance that has nationalistic overtones, as is the case with many of the dances that follow.

The Second Tableau takes us behind the scenes and, beginning with Petrouchka, introduces each puppet individually. Petrouchka is the Russian counterpart of Punch in the Punch and Judy shows, whom Stravinsky himself has characterized as the "immortal and unhappy hero of every fair in all countries . . . the poor, funny, ugly, sentimental and misguided creature, constantly shaken with rebellious rage, whether justified or not, who is known in France as Pierrot, in Germany as Kasperl and in Russia as Petrouchka." Here he also resembles the lovelorn Pierrot of the Italian commedia dell' arte, pining for the fickle affections of the flirtatious Ballerina, who for her part is infatuated with the Moor.

With its sharp, angular movements and dissonant harmonies, "Petrouchka's Dance" expresses the despair of an ardent soul imprisoned in the body of a clown whom no one will take seriously. His dual nature is symbolized in the bitonal chord that accompanies him—a C-major triad followed by or heard together with an F-sharp major "shadow" (Ex. 1-1). Interestingly, the entire ballet was inspired by Stravinsky's conception of this dance. It occurred to him first as a piano concerto; but, as he relates in his memoirs, it eventually shaped up as a picture of a "puppet, suddenly endowed with life, exasperating the patience of the orchestra with diabolical cascades of arpeggios. The orchestra in turn retaliates with menacing trumpet blasts. The outcome is a terrific noise which reaches its climax and ends in the sorrowful and querulous collapse of the poor puppet."

The Third Tableau is in the Moor's room, and the mysterious, slightly menacing music for his dance is at once exotic and evil. He is interrupted by the Ballerina, who enters to the roll of a snare drum and a flourish on the cornet. Mad with jealousy, Petrouchka bursts in and quarrels with the Moor.

Example 1-1. Stravinsky. *Petrouchka.* Part 2, bars 1–4.

The Fourth Tableau returns to the teeming marketplace and shows kaleidoscopic glimpses of the revelry of the crowd as evening approaches. The "Dance of the Nursemaids," based on an old Russian folk tune, is followed by the entrance of a peasant with a trained bear, whose grotesque movements are characterized by an awkward tuba solo sounding against some opaque chords in the lower strings. In turn, there are gypsy dances to the accompaniment of a simulated orchestral accordion, then the "Dance of the Coachmen and Grooms," and finally the appearance of some masqueraders dressed in devil and animal costumes. As the revelry approaches its height, the scene is interrupted by the entrance of Petrouchka, wildly pursued by the Moor. The Ballerina vainly tries to restrain him, but he breaks free and stabs Petrouchka. For the brief death scene Stravinsky devised some remarkably poignant sounds. A melody that recalls "Petrouchka's Dance," with the symbolic bitonal chord as its motif, is carried in turn by the clarinet, violin, bassoon, and piccolo playing solo against the tremolo of muted violins and the harmonics of the violas.

The Charlatan arrives in time to reassure the bystanders that it is all mime and make-believe. He picks up the limp body of Petrouchka, now bleeding sawdust, in order to throw him behind the scenes. While the motley crowd disperses, however, the spirit of Petrouchka reappears above the puppet stage in a kind of mock apotheosis. He grimaces at the Charlatan while the orchestra plays a shrieking dissonance and the curtain is rung down.

ABSTRACT BALLET

Some modern choreographers have tried to move away from what they call the "tyranny of the plot." The abstract ballet is thus not so much concerned with narrative elements as it is with pure dance invention, as well as rhythmic, plastic, and formal movement for its own sake. The dances tend to reflect the abstract aspects of the musical scores that accompany them, and they thus become a species of visible music. Choreographer George Balanchine's ballet *Concerto Barocco,* by way of example, is a dance version of Bach's so-called "Double Concerto" for two violins and orchestra in D Minor *(BWV* 1043). In it, two dancers are the visual equivalent of the concerted solo violins; the rhythmic pulsations correspond to the changes in meter and tempo; the entrances and exits are regulated by musical thematic entries; the visual lines are coordinated with the contours of melodic phrases; and the grouping of dancers is synchronized with the alternation of ensemble and solo passages, contrasts of texture, and dynamic fluctuations in the score.

In other respects, too, modern choreographers have struck out on paths that led away from formal restrictions and restraints. Unimpeded by the traditions of classical ballet, they allow the body to move in any direction, limited only by anatomical considerations. In the expressionistic dances of Isadora Duncan, Mary Wigman, Martha Graham, and the dance group Pilobolus, for instance, a vocabulary of symbolic gestures and movements has developed, giving plastic shape to the secret longings, hidden fears, dark passions, exuberant wit, and wild dreams that emanate from psychological impulses and perceptions both conscious and unconscious. In all these modern phases, music continues its age-old partnership with the dance, and all the choreographic experiments in new rhythmic, dynamic, coloristic, and formal approaches are paralleled by corresponding developments in the scores that composers provide for the ballet.

CHAPTER 2

Art of Song

THE ART OF SONG embraces the simultaneous presentation of a literary text and a musical setting. While poetry and melody have separate existences and independent expressive capacities, song represents a united effort in which each supplements the other, brought into a balance in which neither art dominates completely. As closely related arts, poetry and music share such common elements as melody, meter, rhythm, accentuation, tone color, rhyme structure, and formal organization. They also meet on common ground in matters of phrasing, articulation, and punctuation. Expressively, each or both together can be lyrical, epic, or dramatic as the poet or composer wills. Poetry and song run the entire emotional gamut from the longing of tender love lyrics to the telling of the mighty deeds of rugged warriors in the epic chants of ancient bards.

A complete discussion of song would trace the development of sacred melodies from ancient psalm singing and early Christian canticles to various contemporary religious expressions, and of secular songs from those of medieval troubadours to those of contemporary composers. Socially it would extend from rural folk songs to sophisticated urban art songs. Ethnographically it would point out national differences in such varied forms as Italian Renaissance carnival songs, French chansons, and English catches and carols. Linguistically it would take into account the diverse speech patterns of various countries, as well as such factors as the German declamation of Schubert and Brahms, the French inflections of Debussy and Fauré, and the accented English of Purcell and Sullivan. It could not neglect a variety of media from solo songs with lute accompaniment to such ensemble forms of vocal chamber music as madrigals and rounds. Stylistically the discussion would range from recitatives, opera arias, and song settings, to instrumental songs without words. This discussion will therefore be highly selective and look at some of the principal processes involved when a composer sets a literary text to music.

Prosody

The marriage of word and tone gives birth to *prosody,* which produces our system of metrical structure, or versification. Prosody is a problem child for poet and composer alike, since there are artistic conflicts deeply rooted in such matters as the inflections of the language, stressed and unstressed syllables, rhythmic accentuation, metrical patterns, and versification. A musical melody in some instances may be a simple, straightforward line that follows the natural inflections of the language, thus allowing the word-melody to come to the fore. On the other hand, the musical melody can become a complex, stylized affair, such as an intricate coloratura aria in which the text is for a time completely ignored.

Normally, whether a poem is read or sung, the poetic and melodic accents coincide on syllables that are either stressed dynamically or prolonged lyrically. The composer has alternative modes of expression not available to the poet. Since the singing voice possesses greater sustaining power than the speaking voice, the accented syllable in a song can be prolonged to a much greater extent than in speech. A composer can set words so that each syllable has its allotted note, or stretch a single syllable out over several notes.

Accentuation plays an important role in both speaking and singing. What is said is, of course, important; but how it is said is often even more important. In ordinary speech the meaning of a sentence can be drastically altered by changing the place of the accent. Similarly, a poem or melody suffers no basic change when taken at a slightly faster or slower tempo, or when rendered a little louder or softer. But if the emphasis on certain syllables is changed, or the phrasing altered, the melody will present an entirely different aspect, even though the notes remain the same. Musical designs, by their very nature, usually require more repetition than literary forms, providing a potential source of friction between poets and composers. Tennyson, for instance, complained bitterly that musicians made him say a thing twice when he had said it only once.

In this conflicting marriage of poetry and music, one partner usually dominates. In some instances the words are more prominent, in others the melody. The operatic recitative, for example, is a musical setting of prose that carries the dramatic continuity of the scene. Here the text is most important, the musical line secondary (Ex. 2-1a). In the aria—an operatic song that has a verse text—the situation is reversed and the words are subordinate to the melody. In the aria that follows the recitative (Ex. 2-1b), the emphasis shifts to the melodic potential of the voice. In the world of song, the stronger the poem, the less easily it yields to a musical setting, a fact that accounts for the relatively few successful songs written to Shakespearean texts. In a selection set to the Bard's sonnet "She never told her love," the text remains dominant in spite of the ministrations of a composer of Haydn's stature. On the other hand, Goethe's ballad *Der Erlkönig (The Erlking)* is so completely engulfed in Schubert's setting that the poem seems not to have had separate existence, something that caused the poet considerable annoyance.

Example 2-1. Offenbach. *Tales of Hoffmann.* Act 1.

2-1*a.* Recitative.

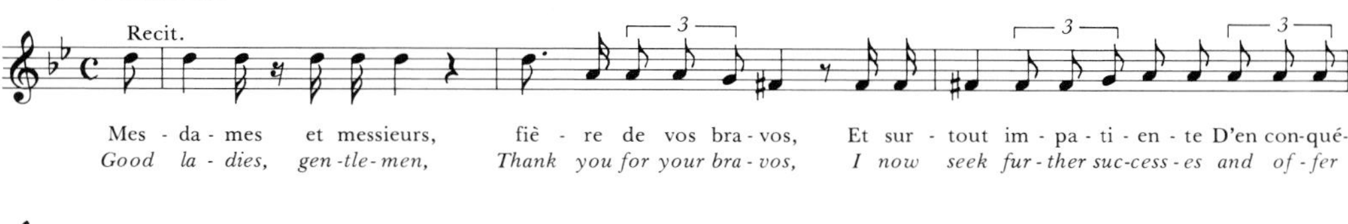

2-1*b.* No. 9, bars 6–10. Aria of Olympia.

Since in actual practice a song usually begins with a poem that inspires a musical setting, the composer is generally the dominant personality in the process. The poet is left in the position of the one who must yield. Exceptions to this rule occur when the poet is also the composer, as was the case with such Elizabethan figures as Thomas Campion and John Dowland, and in the 19th century Richard Wagner. Poets themselves, since theirs is an independent art, quite rightly contend that a good poem justifies its own existence and stands in no need of music. The burden of proof, then, falls on the composer, who must justify the setting of a poem by providing a musical frame to enclose the poetic picture, giving perspective to the poem through the added dimension of music, placing the poetic text in a new light, intensifying the moods and projecting the emotions of the poetry more powerfully, and in general by producing a satisfactory compromise between the often opposing demands of poetry and music.

Types of Song

Songs—folk, popular, or art songs—are usually classified as *strophic* or *through-composed,* according to whether the several stanzas are sung to a single repeated melody, or whether the melody and accompaniment are adapted in each successive stanza to the different meaning of each verse. Most folk, popular, and patriotic songs are of the strophic type, while many art songs—such as those of Schumann, Brahms, and Debussy—are through-composed.

In strophic songs such as *Oh! Susanna* or *Lucy in the Sky with Diamonds*, the melody is repeated over and over to the different stanzas of the poem, and may have a *refrain*—where music and text remain constant—interpolated between the strophic verses. Through-composed songs, contrariwise, are treated with considerable freedom in which successive phrases and sections may be the same or different, symmetrical or asymmetrical, or altered according to the shifts of mood and dramatic necessity. Modified strophic forms are possible, such as in Schubert's *Gretchen am Spinnrade (Margaret at the Spinning Wheel),* in which the melody is the same for each verse, but minor changes are made at the points of climax to produce an unexpected turn or point of emphasis.

In a strophic song the variety lies in the different verses of the poem, while unity is provided by the repeated melody. In a through-composed song the variety manifests itself in both the words and melody, while unity is achieved through a number of sophisticated practices such as recurring rhythmic motifs and melodic figures. Strophic songs are better adapted to simple, forthright verse statements. Through-composed songs serve more fully the needs of narrative (where a sense of progress is maintained as the text and story unfold), and of dramatic poetry (where building toward climaxes is of overriding importance).

Art songs, as opposed to folk songs on the one side and concert or operatic arias on the other, are lyrical or dramatic expressions for voice with instrumental accompaniment. Art songs by known composers survive from as early as the 12th-century troubadours and the songfests of the medieval courts of love. All the great secular composers of the Renaissance contributed liberally to the rich body of vocal literature for solo voice and group songs known in France as *chansons* and in Elizabethan England as airs and madrigals. Most of the literature that the modern listener is likely to encounter goes back no farther than the late 18th century, when such songs were a species of house music. Sung traditionally in the home rather than in public, their style was simple rather than grand, conversational rather than oratorical. They stood in relation to elaborate arias scaled to the proportions of the operatic stage as did short keyboard pieces to concertos for soloist and full orchestra. Even though these art songs are now sung mostly in public, something of this special intimate character associated with their origin still clings to them, and they resist their transplantation from the intimacy of the salon and drawing room to the arena of the large concert hall.

Art songs, representing as they do the union of word and tone, reflect national color by their original language, the special character of the poetry, and the type of musical setting. Songs differ as the languages and literatures of their various countries and the individual approach of the composers who write them. For example, there are widely diverse songs in German by Schubert, Mendelssohn, Hugo Wolf, and Mahler; in Russian by Musorgsky, Tchaikovsky, and Rachmaninov; in French by Berlioz, Debussy, and Fauré; in England by Ralph Vaughan Williams and Benjamin Britten; in America by Stephen Foster, Charles Ives, and Ned Rorem, among many others.

Comparisons of various settings of the same poetic text by different composers can be an illuminating experience in listening. Goethe's *Kennst du das Land (Do you know the land?)* boasts settings by Beethoven, Schubert, Schumann, Liszt, and Wolf. *Nur wer die Sehnsucht kennt (None But the Lonely Heart),* another lyric from Goethe's novel *Wilhelm Meister,* has no fewer than four settings by Beethoven, as well as others by Schubert, Liszt, and Tchaikovsky. One may also compare vocal and instrumental settings of the same melody. Schubert's song *Die Forelle (The Trout)* becomes the subject of a set of variations in his *Trout Quintet,* and Brahms' song *Immer leiser wird mein Schlummer (Ever gentler grows my slumber)* becomes the melody for the slow movement of his Second Piano Concerto.

The German Lied

Out of these various regional art songs, the German *Lied* (plural, *Lieder*) was lifted to the status of a style that transcended national boundaries by a remarkable chain of circumstances in the 19th century. The rising popularity of romantic poetry, the development and general acceptance of the pianoforte as the favored household instrument, and the birth of a number of composers of genius all combined in the early years of that century to bring about the flowering of this special lyrical art. The poetry of Burns, Scott, and Byron, as well as that of Goethe, Schiller, and Heine, was transformed in musical settings by almost every composer in Europe, producing a literature of intensely expressive songs whose artistic and human importance loomed as large as the medium itself was small. These music dramas for voice and piano fulfilled the romantic century's ideal of personal individualism, freedom of form, intimate atmosphere, and the outpouring of emotion.

The piano, with its ability to make dramatic dynamic shifts in crescendos and diminuendos, its capacity for mixing harmonies by means of the sustaining pedal, and its singing power in melodic passages, lent itself well to the expressive demands of the then-new romantic poetry. It was admirably adapted to enact scenes, create atmospheric effects, and reflect the poetic imagery of the text in an instrumental mirror. In prologues the piano could project the mood before the entrance of the voice, while in epilogues it could continue the meaning well beyond the point where the text leaves off. And in these preludes, interludes, and postludes, the piano part could provide the framework for the poetic verses, make occasional commentaries on the text, carry on a running dialogue with the voice on equal terms, and complete the formal design.

In such miniature music dramas the singer as protagonist must declaim the often impassioned lines with an eye on the poetic picture being presented, an ear for the melodic nuances, and a mind alert to the subtle shades of meaning in the text, so as to transform these little lyrical and dramatic designs into engrossing musical and human events. The piano parts, moreover, are raised from the status of mere harmonic accompaniments to full equality with the voice. These are songs "for voice and piano," not songs for voice with piano accompaniments.

Voice and instrument join in the service to the text in a true ensemble sense, and both share the responsibility for interpretative projection. In practice the piano parts may vary—according to the differing demands of the poetry and the conceptions of the composer—from a comparatively minor role, with the piano lending rhythmic and harmonic support to the melody, all the way to the point where the piano bears the full weight of lyrical responsibility as it gives direction to the flow of the vocal commentary.

For the listener, it is as important to understand the text as it is to know the music. English-speaking audiences find no problem with the many art songs set to English-language poetry, but those set to poetry in a foreign language may present a barrier to the full enjoyment of these songs. Under these circumstances, the availability of a good translation is essential. However, German romantic poetry, as well as that of the French symbolists and impressionists, makes special use of the element of word color, which in turn blends with the vocal quality, the word projection, and the instrumental timbre. This so-called onomatopoetic element usually defies translation and often disappears entirely in another language. Some of this verbal color, however, approaches the conditions of the music itself and, when the vowel sounds are treated purely for their color effect, something of this quality comes through even though it is heard in a foreign language. In "Des Baches Wiegenlied" ("Brook's Lullaby"), the concluding song of Schubert's song cycle *Die Schöne Müllerin (The Fair Maid of the Mill),* Wilhelm Müller's poem employs a series of "oo" sounds intended to produce the drowsy effect that lulls one to sleep. The words are appropriate for a lullaby—"Rest well, weary wanderer, at last you are at home." The expressive, soothing tone quality of the German words in this instance comes through in spite of any possible language barrier.

> Gute Ruh', gute Ruh', thu' die Augen zu,
> Gute Ruh', gute Ruh', thu' die Augen zu!
> Wand'rer, du müder, du bist zu Haus.

Schubert, who built his songs on the models provided by his 18th-century predecessors, was perhaps more responsible than any other single figure for raising the rank of the German Lied to universal significance. He provided more than 600 examples from his own inexhaustible creative imagination. Schubert's setting of Matthias Claudius' short poem "Tod und das Mädchen" ("Death and the Maiden") will illustrate his approach to this particular creative problem as well as the solution he devised for it (Ex.2-2). The little drama is crowded into four poetic lines, shared equally by the two characters—the Maiden and Death. The poetic form likewise falls into the two parts allotted to these contrasting personages, and the content reveals a corresponding duality of viewpoint, mood, word, melody, and tempo. If he had started with the Maiden's cry of fear at the entrance of the skeletal form of Death, it would have burst upon the ear too suddenly for its full impact to be felt. To prepare the listener, as well as to round out the form, Schubert therefore opens with the piano part sounding a sustained chorale-like procession of chords in slow march rhythm to warn of the somber, inexorable approach of Death. At one stroke this sets the stage, creates the necessary sinister atmosphere, and leads up to the Maiden's outburst. Technically, it is heard again as a postlude, where it articulates Death's departure with the Maiden, thus framing the through-composed central vocal section.

The terror of the Maiden, too young to yield to Death's embrace, is inherent in the shrill, high-pitched melody. Her illness is apparent in the panting, breathless, broken line irregularly interspersed with gasping rests and reinforced by an agitated piano figure that palpitates in sympathy with her wildly beating heart. The short transition in bars 20 and 21 signifies her resignation and leads to Death's monotonous melody, which now takes on a soothing aspect as he solemnly intones his reassuring words in a line as stiff as rigor mortis itself—that he comes not to punish but to allow her to sleep peacefully in his arms. The final modulation to the major key confirms that all is well. Thus in one short page, and in less than two minutes, Schubert is able to compress an entire drama of life and death, of youth and the desire to live, of pain and deliverance.

Further shades of meaning contained in the song can be discovered in the slow movement of Schubert's D-minor string quartet, where an instrumental version of the song is expanded into a set of variations.

Example 2-2. Schubert. *Death and the Maiden.*

The Song Cycle

With the development of the Lied came the rise of the *song cycle,* a group or series of songs sharing a common thought, theme, or musical treatment, and intended to be sung consecutively. By placing a number of Lieder within a larger context, composers such as Beethoven, Schubert, and Schumann found a more expansive form than is afforded by the more isolated inspirations of single songs. They thus achieved a degree of unity in song composition that compared favorably with the longer instrumental designs of the suite and sonata.

Texts for such song cycles were usually selected by composers with an eye toward narrative continuity, dramatic storytelling, retrospective contemplation, or the exploration of an all-pervading mood. Sometimes the poets themselves grouped their lyrics together for publication around some central idea, thus suggesting the idea of a cycle; or the composer could make a selection from the works of several different poets for his purpose.

In such settings the composers, while allowing themselves ample room for formal freedom, nevertheless sought a semblance of unity in the presentation through such technical devices as sequential key relationships, common thematic substance, recurring motivic material, or smooth modulatory transitions from song to song. In the course of a song cycle, an entire drama can thus be presented in a series of lyrical moments. In performance, they resemble operas involving a single singer in which the dramatic interest is implied rather than overtly acted out, and the emotional content is inwardly rather than outwardly oriented. Many, in fact, exhibit such a high degree of individualism and are so personal and subjective that they seem to be almost autobiographical.

The earliest song cycles are also excellent examples of contrasting types. In *An die ferne Geliebte (To the Distant Beloved,* 1816), Beethoven set a series of six lyrics by A. Jeitteles. Poetically, as the title implies, they express the longing of a lover for his faraway sweetheart. In the setting Beethoven employs marked contrasts of meter and tempo, key and mode, to correspond with the different moods. The unifying factor is found in the modulatory passages between each song as well as in the return of the opening theme for the final song in the manner of a recapitulation. Schubert's first essay in the form, *Die schöne Müllerin (The Fair Maid of the Mill,* 1823), is of the narrative type that tells a tale in a series of episodes (see pp. 243–44). The second, *Die Winterreise (The Winter's Journey,* 1827), is more contemplative in style (see pp. 244–46). In both cycles the composer allows the individual songs a more independent existence within the whole. Unlike Beethoven, Schubert fashions each song with its own beginning and end, and consequently each may be lifted out of its cyclical context and sung separately.

Other cycles from the 19th century include Robert Schumann's *Frauenliebe und -leben (Woman's Love and Life)* and *Dichterliebe (Poet's Love);* see pp. 254–58.

The song cycle since Schumann's time has attracted the attention of an increasing number of composers. Some have gone beyond the confines of the original solo-voice-and-piano combination—for example, Vaughan Williams' *On Wenlock Edge* and Samuel Barber's *Dover Beach,* both of which are scored for voice and string quartet. In his *Das Lied von der Erde (Song of the Earth),* Mahler fuses the form with that of the symphony and scores it for tenor, alto or baritone, and full orchestra. In his *Gurrelieder (Songs of Gurre),* Schoenberg adds elements of the secular cantata to those of the song cycle and scores the work for orchestra, several choruses, vocal soloists, and narrator.

Songs and Art Styles

Each of the postromantic musical styles and literary movements has its quota of examples in song form. Realism and naturalism, for instance, are represented by Musorgsky's *The Nursery;* symbolism and impressionism by Debussy's many settings of the poems of Mallarmé, Baudelaire, and Verlaine; dadaism and surrealism by the songs of Satie, as well as by Francis Poulenc's "profane cantata," *Le bal masque (The Masked Ball),* based on poems by Max Jacob. Neoprimitivism is reflected in Villa Lobos' *Song of the Ox-cart Driver;* neomedievalism in Hindemith's song cycle *Das Marienleben (The Life of Mary);* and neoclassicism in the songs of Stravinsky and Ravel; while expressionism is fully explored in the songs of Richard Strauss, Mahler, Schoenberg, and Alban Berg. Olivier Messiaen's *Poèmes pour mi* combine that 20th-century composer's dictum, "Melody first and foremost," with his commitment to Roman Catholic mysticism, to represent the relationship between man and woman as a symbolic union of Christ and the church.

Contemporary experimentalism is likewise well represented by many novel uses of the speaking voice, such as spoken roles for narrator and musical ensemble as well as that hybrid between song and speech known in German as *Sprechgesang.* An example of the latter is found in Schoenberg's cycle *Pierrot lunaire (Moonstruck Pierrot),* in which vocal inflections are delimited above and below in the score but not defined in precise pitch notation (see pp. 307–8).

Some 20th-century instrumental works include roles for a narrator, as, for instance, in the popular orchestral fairy tale by Prokofiev, *Peter and the Wolf.* The direct collaboration of poet Edith Sitwell and composer William Walton resulted in a work entitled *Façade,* a series of imagistic poems recited to satirical instrumental dances. In the words of her brother Osbert Sitwell, their intentions were in the nature of "inquiries into the effect on rhythm, on speed, and on color of the use of rhymes, assonances, dissonances" and the like, so as to discover "an abstract method of presenting poetry to an audience."

As the century progressed, composers searched for vocal expression that would provide a continuity with the past as well as fresh contemporary experiences. Audiotape recorders and computers have opened up new possibilities for music involving the human voice.

After World War II, the German composer Karlheinz Stockhausen experimented with the voice as a color instrument. Making use of guttural and labial noises, sputters and spurts of sound, cries and screams, he asks the lyric soprano soloist in his composition *Momente* to find new techniques in order to produce new sounds. In his *Gesang der Jünglinge (Song of the Youths),* the prerecorded voices of children are manipulated to produce never-before-heard sounds that extend the listener's view into an imaginary world.

Composers with a scientific orientation have created new sonic adventures, combining the voice with computer-generated tape. In such compositions as Dexter Morrill's *Six Dark Questions for Soprano and Computer,* frontiers have been opened for vocal performers to exercise new freedoms in the decision-making processes, from the planning stages to improvising differences for each performance. Morrill says of his composition:

> This "computer chamber music" is meant to have a reasonable balance of activity between the solo voice and the loudspeaker. The idea of the loudspeaker as a narrator, and as a potential partner in a duet, is initially stated in very simple terms, by rhythmic means, or in a "give and take" texture resembling a conversation. Except for [the soprano's] voice on tape, all the loudspeaker sounds are synthetic.

The art of song thus comes full circle from the medieval troubadour to the modern computer.

CHAPTER 3

Art of Opera

"IN MY OPINION A good opera is nothing but an academy of many fine arts, where architecture, painting, the dance, poetry . . . and above all music should unite to bring about a work of art." So wrote the 18th-century composer Johann Mattheson. The affinity of music for poetry and dance, as seen in the art song and the ballet, also underlies the complex genre of musical theater known as opera. The world of opera is one in which certain dramatic principles and theatrical conventions are modified and enhanced by being set to music. Opera is not, however, a drama set to music, but rather a drama in or through music. Over its life span of some 400 years, it has proven to be a viable vehicle for entertainment, with a faithful following of dedicated admirers.

This coupling of drama and music began in ancient Greece, when the Athenian tragedies unfolded with intoned dialogue interspersed with choral dancing and singing. Music also figured prominently in medieval liturgical and mystery plays. Shakespeare called for songs in his comedies and tragedies and included an entire operalike masque in his last play, *The Tempest.* In the classic and romantic theater, incidental music was an integral part of the performances, as in Goethe's *Egmont,* for which Beethoven composed a lengthy score from overture to finale. In our own time few staged plays or filmed dramas would be complete without at least some background music.

Theatrical and Operatic Conventions

Any work for the theater is first and foremost artifice—that is, a crafted view of the world that presents selective images of reality. The theater of the spoken word has customarily accomplished this artificial process in part through a series of understood *conventions* that help to link the author's intentions with the audience's understanding and appreciation. In a Shakespeare play, for instance, a character can be quite alone on the stage while giving voice to inner thoughts in a convention known as a *soliloquy*. Such conventions have formed an integral part of theater, from the myth-based plays of ancient Greece, through the improvisational Italian *commedia dell'arte* with its stock plots and characters, to 20th-century American western films, in which the hero is identified immediately by the white hat he inevitably wears.

Musical theater also has its own particular conventions. Opera, for example, presupposes a world in which characters communicate mainly in song rather than speech. Some dramatic action and dialogue may employ the spoken word, but in the prevailing repertory it proceeds in sung recitative. Recitative leads into solo arias, duets, and other small ensembles that describe in musical terms the reactions of each character to the dramatic situation at hand.

Also by convention, a specific number of arias may be allotted each of the main characters, and one may count on certain recognizable musical signals to herald the entrance of important personages. In addition, the assignment of operatic character types according to voice ranges is common practice. The hero is nearly always a tenor, the heroine a soprano; altos are often assigned matronly and older women's roles, while baritones and basses become paternal figures.

Opera inevitably stresses emotion over reason, gives credence to outward appearance and artifice over reality. Heroes and heroines dying of suffocation or tuberculosis rise at the last moment to sing impassioned arias and duets in voices robust enough to fill a large opera house. Such behavior is far-fetched when viewed in terms of real life, but to condemn the convention as unnatural would be to confuse life with art. Artificial as such actions are, they serve as conveniences to reveal the dramatic message to the audience.

Opera vs. Play

Opera is far more than just spoken theater with the added dimension of music. It is chiefly a medium designed to express human emotions. With music as the principal communicative force of the drama, the hero and heroine are, quite simply, the music they sing. Their music describes the particular dramatic situation in which they find themselves, and their reactions to it are expressed in words and melodic lines.

Operatic scenes make the most of opportunities to parade heightened levels of emotion—unbridled passion, fierce hatred, frenzied jealousy. The composer Richard Wagner believed that an opera composer must be able to match profound and energetic passion with the talent to express such passion with sweeping gestures. The nature of opera has been such that its characters, and not only those of Wagner, have tended to be larger than life and drawn with bold, broad strokes. This is so partly because the popular mythic subjects called for such characterizations (with settings to match), and partly because many members of the audience in a large opera house are not physically in a position to see and detect intricate subtleties of character portrayal.

Opera has also been an extravagant, often socially exclusive type of theater, frequently an indulgence of the elite. Audiences who expected pomp and spectacle knew its cost and were willing to pay the price. Large-scale operas were customarily produced for courtly circles for such occasions as coronations, royal weddings, and birthdays. Socially prominent audiences reveled in the grandeur of such productions; attending them became a mark of success, rank, and social status.

People from all walks of life frequent the opera today (some dressed in jeans and others in jewels). But a pervasive aura of affluent opulence still surfaces occasionally, on such occasions as the opening of New York's new Metropolitan Opera house in 1966. A fashionable audience of socialites, state and national political figures, and music lovers gathered to experience opera at its grandest: monumental, moving sets, lavish costumes, and internationally famous singers in the the spectacle of Samuel Barber's commissioned opera, *Antony and Cleopatra.*

Words vs. Music

One of the oldest, most persistent questions about lyrics and music is: which is the more important? In the beginning, says the Bible, was the word; and composers have long paid lip service to the concept that music must serve the text. As handmaiden to poetry, music imparts additional intensity and magnified meaning, while directing the listener to particular words and phrases the composer wishes to stress. As the elements of opera were first being defined, one young composer was exhorted to "make it your chief aim to arrange the verse well and to declaim the words as intelligibly as you can, not letting yourself be led astray by the counterpoint like a bad swimmer carried out of his course by the current."

Well over a century later, the great operatic reformer Christoph Gluck expressed his intent "to restrict music to its true office of serving poetry by means of expression." And as late as 1941, Richard Strauss could find enough life left in the old words-vs.-music controversy to fill an entire opera, *Capriccio.* In it, a lovely woman finds herself with two suitors, a poet and a composer.

One writes her a sonnet, the other sets it to music. The choice of suitor gives rise to long arguments on the relative values of the literary and tonal arts. Her final decision is not revealed at the opera's conclusion, though Strauss suggests the outcome, since she leaves the room humming the melody of the composer's sonnet setting.

Understanding the text of an opera in a foreign language may present difficulties for an audience. Even in one's native tongue, high-flying melodic lines do not always allow every word to be heard with absolute clarity by the listener. To deal with this problem, an opera-goer may study the words in advance or follow the practice of 19th-century Italian audiences and read along from the libretto as the opera progresses. A recent development is the use of "supertitles"—texts flashed above the proscenium and timed to coincide with the phrases being sung. But for many listeners, a general outline of the plot is enough to send them into the special world of opera, where the music itself carries the dramatic message.

Components of Opera

When a play is mounted on the stage, the author's text is the principal basis from which the performance is realized. In an opera, the book, or *libretto,* is only the starting point from which the composer produces a *score.* From the score the performance is realized. The situation is similar in the film world, where the book first must be converted into a script. Neither the libretto nor the script can claim independent status as literature, since they are only the agents by which the opera or film is finally realized. They acquire meaning only in the finished work.

Often, the more effective a written work is as pure literature (as with a play by Shakespeare), the more difficult it is to translate it successfully into a musical composition. Similarly, the stronger the poetic values in a play, the more formidable the task of forging it into a good libretto for an opera. It is also true that dramas conceived upon philosophical or aesthetic grounds provide fewer possibilities for operatic setting than those that feature broadly defined characters, strong conflict, and dramatic situations.

Extraordinary craftsmanship is involved in the conversion of a myth, story, novel, or play into a workable vehicle for the musical stage. Refinements of plot and polished characterizations must often yield to the requirements of a broader-ranging musical landscape, in which dramatic points are made in more general and expansive terms than in a novel or play. In addition, the librettist must be aware of up-to-date, ever-changing operatic conventions and be able to provide the major musical moments with poetic styles that communicate meaning to an audience of contemporaries.

Time flow as perceived by an audience is an important element of any theatrical work, and one of the composer's most critical tasks is to control the sense of both real and perceived time on the operatic stage. Opera must of necessity move in a more expansive time frame than that of its spoken counterpart, if only because it is in the nature of melodic utterance to require a longer span of time to sing a text than to speak it. It follows that when narrative time is elongated, an audience must alter its perception of time relationships accordingly. When the composer elects to use additional conventions such as choruses, marches, ballet sequences, and orchestral interludes, operatic time shifts down further into a lower gear. These shifts of perceived time require a corresponding awareness on the part of the audience in order to hold their attention, and they add to the sense of opera as an artificial species.

The main ingredients for controlling dramatic time flow in opera have traditionally been the combination of recitative and aria. Based on natural speech rhythms, the *recitative* (recitation) reinforces stage action and communicates essential plot information to the audience. A recitative may inform viewers and other characters onstage of an event that has already happened, of some current action that has taken place offstage, or of some plan for events to come. While recitatives sometimes move at a carefully measured pace, their main function is to deliver a sizable quantity of information in a short space of time (Ex. 3-1).

Example 3-1. Pergolesi. *The Servant as Mistress.* Recitativo secco.

In baroque and classical times, much of this musically recited action was sung in the style known as *recitativo secco* (dry recitation). The solo voice in secco recitative is accompanied only by a cello and a harpsichord, whose dry, plucked tone gives this recitative its name. The continuo provides a discreet accompaniment, allowing the voice to be heard clearly and supplying chords that give harmonic support and rhythmic punctuation (see Ex. 3-1).

Later, the *recitativo stromentato* (instrumented recitation), sometimes called *recitativo accompagnato* (accompanied recitation), became an alternative. In this type of recitative, the accompanying force is the orchestra, whose extensive resources enable it to draw upon a wider tone-color potential to support and comment upon the text. The recitativo stromentato is reserved for moments of slightly higher drama, involving a short text and leading up to an aria.

An *aria* is a musical declaration, usually in poetic form, representing a reaction to some event or dramatic situation. Time and action stop while a character pours out strong feelings engendered by surrounding events. The aria reveals aspects of an individual's personality and defines relationships with other characters in the drama. Through the device of the aria, the composer may reveal good and evil traits, strengths and weaknesses of character, psychological moods, and highly charged emotional states. At its best, the aria intensifies and enlightens the dramatic situation, but it may also be an excuse for sheer vocalism of high order. At times this vocalism is used in the service of the text; alternatively it may allow the singer to step out of character and simply show off virtuoso skills.

The aria may deliver its message in any of a large number of forms, many of which take virtuosity for granted. Early in the baroque period the strophic, strophic-bass, and ostinato arias became fashionable. In the *strophic* aria, all verses of the aria text were set to the same music, while in the *strophic-bass,* several verses were set in variations over the same bass line. The *ostinato* aria featured a short, repeating bass line, supporting a free-flowing vocal line.

Categories of aria responding to specific dramatic and performance styles were also cultivated—for example, slow and lyrical, fast and brilliant, or broadly declamatory. Later, the *da capo* (A B A) aria became a favorite formal device (Ex. 3-2). In this type of aria, two short texts of comparable meaning are given unrelated musical settings. Once these complementary sections have been sung, a return to the opening (*da capo*) is specified. During the repetition of this section the singer is expected to improvise with imagination and skill. The close of the aria is marked *fine* (end).

In the late 18th century, the recitative-and-da-capo-aria design was expanded to one that began with a recitativo stromentato. The A B A was replaced by a two-part aria, comprising the *cavatina*—a lyrical expression containing the central pronouncement of the emotional state—and the *cabaletta,* a fast finish featuring virtuoso passagework set to a text complementing and extending the cavatina (Exs. 3-3a, b, and c).

Integration of the aria into the dramatic scenario became a prominent practice in the romantic period, when the *scene and aria* functioned as a unit. Characteristic arias of this type deal with strong emotional states brought about by first love, prayers or pleas, and fits of madness.

An opera scenario may call for several characters to reveal emotional reactions simultaneously, and opera from all periods abounds with small vocal ensembles such as duets, trios, and quartets. The challenge of making the operatic text clear to the listener is even more formidable in an ensemble where several individuals sing different words simultaneously. Composers have addressed this problem by allowing single voices to emerge from the ensemble

Example 3-2. Handel. *Julius Caesar.* "I worship your burning eyes." Da capo aria.

on a rotating basis and by means of many repetitions of text phrases. When handled by a composer of Mozart's stature, a trio or quartet can be highly successful in projecting several moods or situations simultaneously.

Operatic dance reflects both the historical period and social-class status depicted onstage. The forest-oriented hunting society in Weber's *Der Freischütz,* for instance, is represented through a rough, stamping clog dance, while a group of Blessed Spirits who dwell in the Elysian Fields of Gluck's *Orfeo* execute a classically refined ballet. Ballet in opera is primarily a means to show pageantry or ceremonial display and seldom involves a real dramatic function,

Example 3-3. Mozart. *Don Giovanni, K 527.* Act 2, No. 25. Recitative and aria.

3-3a. Bars 1–3 and 10–15. Recitative.

as evidenced in the stately processions of sarabandes and minuets in the operas that Lully mounted for the French court of Louis XIV.

The fusion of instrumental music with drama can also be traced back to ancient Greek theater, and by the time opera appeared on the European scene, instrumental music was firmly entrenched as an adjunct to spoken drama. In addition to supporting the human voice, instrumental music has functioned in opera to set the tone at the beginning by means of an overture or prelude; to introduce individual scenes and arias and to provide interludes between scenes; to support dramatic events, such as marches, battle scenes, or hunting scenes; to ornament nondramatic events with dance and ballet music; and to support and underscore spoken dialogue, as in melodrama. Conventions of programme music may also slide into opera, where the tolling

3-3b. Bars 5–12. Aria (cavatina).

3-3c. Bars 9–12 and 20–22. Aria (cabaletta).

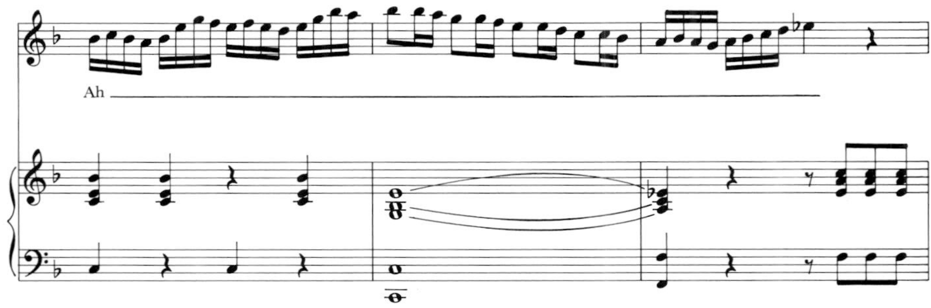

of bells, songs of birds, wildness of storms, and the like are rendered within the context of visual action and sung text.

Mozart's Don Giovanni: *Overture through Act 1, Scene 2*

The musical forms and devices, conventions, and stage business mentioned above come alive only when one is able to see them functioning in combinations, assembled by a master composer working with a skilled librettist. Such

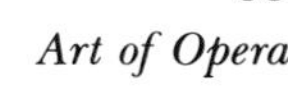

Example 3-4. Mozart. *Don Giovanni.* Act 1.

3-4a. Overture, bars 1–10. "Stone Guest" music.

3-4b. Overture, bars 31–39. Gallant style.

a work is Mozart's *Don Giovanni* (1787), with text by Lorenzo da Ponte, an opera that has been heralded as one of the greatest works of art of all time. It is a sophisticated drama of human relationships, all centering around a fixed point, the title character.

At every stage in an opera the composer has dramatic choices to make. These choices involve the function of the overture, the number and type of arias appropriate for each character, the interweaving of small ensembles into the drama, as well as determining the appropriate type of recitative for given situations.

Mozart's design for the *Don Giovanni* overture is a sonata form with a slow introduction. The introduction states the so-called "Stone Guest" music, which will be heard again near the end of the opera (Ex. 3-4a). Here it serves to forecast the appearance of an avenging spectral statue that will be responsible for the Don's death. The key is D Minor, one that Mozart often chose for the expression of affliction, diabolical ordeals, and terror. Full chords announce the statue's arrival as a premonition of the catastrophe at the opera's close. The main sonata-form component of the overture abruptly shifts to a brisk tempo and into the more genial key of D Major. The character of the music reflects Giovanni's elevated status as a Spanish nobleman through a musical approach known as the *gallant style*, which was appropriate to upper-class circles of Mozart's time (Ex. 3-4b).

Having forecast the future and set the social atmosphere, Mozart chooses to integrate his overture into the drama as a whole. As the curtain rises, he does not bring the overture to a close but instead modulates to the unrelated key of F Major. With the final dominant chord of C Major, Mozart has prepared the audience for the opening of the first act, an aria by the Don's servant, Leporello, in the key of F Major.

It is night. The Don has gone uninvited into the home of a retired Commander to visit the latter's daughter, Donna Anna, confident that she will welcome his nocturnal visit. Leporello, left on watch as usual, is complaining. The opening accompaniment to his aria represents his pacing back and forth, directing him finally forward to address the audience (Ex. 3-4c). Leporello is a type of serio-comic character known as a *basso buffo* (comic bass), and here he is given a buffo aria that is strophic—that is, both verses are set to the same music. The repeated word *no* underscores his irascible nature and cranky disposition (Ex. 3-4d).

3-4c. Scene 1, bars 1–4. Leporello's pacing music.

3-4d. Bars 49–53. Leporello's aria.

As he finishes the last phrase, Don Giovanni and Donna Anna rush on stage. Though he is a social acquaintance of the family, the Don has arrived masked, and at this juncture she has not guessed his real identity (Ex. 3-4e). Her out-and-out rejection of his amorous advances is a real blow to his ego, as she berates him in a high dudgeon. The arrival of her father interrupts her shrieking, which has aroused the entire household. As she retreats into the house, the Commander confronts Don Giovanni, challenging him to a duel. The Don at first demurs, but is goaded into fighting, while Leporello hides nearby, nervously awaiting the outcome. The two duel to explicit directions from the orchestra (Ex. 3-4f), and the Commander falls, mortally wounded.

3-4e. Bars 71–84. Entrance of Don Giovanni and Donna Anna.

3-4f. Bars 168–72. Dueling music.

This desperate action requires an appropriate reaction, and Mozart chooses to allow all three men onstage to recognize its importance in a trio. As the Commander curses the conniving Don, the latter mocks him as a fool, though his music belies his surface bravado and reveals the true effect of the deed on his psyche. From the bushes, Leporello mutters about the sorry state of affairs (Ex. 3-4g). Once the Commander is dead, the definitive event of the drama has occurred. Don Giovanni must now leave the scene with dispatch, and Mozart sends him and Leporello away with a fast-moving secco recitative:

DON GIOVANNI: Leporello, where are you?
LEPORELLO: Here, worse luck; and you?
DON GIOVANNI: I'm over here.
LEPORELLO: Who's dead, you or the old man?
DON GIOVANNI: Foolish question! The old man.
LEPORELLO: Bravo! Two elegant deeds! Ravish the daughter and murder the father!
DON GIOVANNI: He asked to get hurt!
LEPORELLO: And Donna Anna, what did she ask for?
DON GIOVANNI: Shut up and don't bother me. Come along now, unless you want some of the same.
LEPORELLO: I want nothing, master. I'll say no more.

Music has been constant from the opening of the overture until this moment, and much has happened. The audience has been introduced to four major characters in the drama and has learned something of the nature of each. A major event has taken place, providing the impetus for all action to follow. Costume, action, orchestral music, recitative, and aria have been combined into an effective dramatic *mise en scène* (staging, or setting), presenting the audience with a considerable amount of information and setting up crucial tensions that will be resolved only over a longer period of time.

It is only at this juncture that Mozart allows a momentary pause before the re-entry of Donna Anna, who will discover the body, react to the death, and vow to find her father's killer to avenge the family honor. Remarkably, all this action and reaction is telescoped into little more than seven minutes.

Types of Opera

The word *opera* is the plural of the Latin *opus* (work), and the art form has traditionally contained a series of individual works or numbers, among them separate recitatives, arias, duets, choruses, dances, and orchestral interludes. Before Richard Wagner's mid-19th-century reforms demanding that whole acts be performed without pause, traditional operas proceeded in a series of separate arias, duets, and choruses. This convention was known as *number opera*.

As opera became an increasingly popular form of baroque theater, it spread from various Italian centers to Germany and France, and later to England. The French evolved their own approach to the art form by adapting it to the needs and tastes of the court of Louis XIV. *Tragédie lyrique* (lyric tragedy) was a specialized set of conventions meant to indulge the monarch's specific interests in spectacle and the dance. Jean-Baptiste Lully, court composer to Louis XIV, had a shrewd sensitivity to the desires and caprices of the noble class and produced operas that balanced the subtlety of French prosody with

3-4g. Bars 178–83. Trio for male singers.

the grandiose ballets, choruses, and scenic designs that were required to satisfy the desires of a king anxious to prove his power, wealth, and taste to the world (see pp. 169–71).

Out of several national elements of European opera emerged the powerful classical *opera seria* (serious opera), sometimes called *aria opera*. The librettos were designed to give full rein to the recitative and aria as opera's most viable dramatic force. It took as its point of departure a particular *affect* or mood. Postulating that text and music in an aria should project a single, unvarying reaction—pure love, hate, desire, joy—opera seria produced one long succession of action-and-reaction recitatives and arias. Ensembles, dances, and instrumental music were of secondary importance. The great librettists for opera seria were Apostolo Zeno and Pietro Metastasio, who tended to rely exclusively on classical and mythic subjects. Singers took it upon themselves to engage in protracted improvisations, and sometimes actually inserted arias they had prepared for other operas. Among the outstanding composers of opera seria were the Italians Alessandro Scarlatti and Giovanni Pergolesi, and the Germans Johann Hasse, who made his career in Dresden and Vienna, and George Frideric Handel, who studied in Italy and worked mainly in London.

The growing primacy of singers and the manipulative excesses they practiced caused adverse reactions from a number of composers. The first of these led to the creation of the antiserious *comic opera,* discussed below. The second centered on reforms of the opera seria from within, a movement led by Christoph Gluck, who wrote primarily in Vienna. His reform operas *Orfeo* (see pp. 206–10) and *Alceste* retained the essentials of opera seria, but attempted to bring operatic practice once again under the control of the composer.

A lighter type of opera, intermingling serious and comic elements, grew up as a reaction to the heavier forms of opera seria. Opera seria, however, continued its course as the major vehicle for musical tragedy, while comic opera adapted itself to the national styles of popular theater in various countries. Each of these adaptions shared certain common traits—an open and readily understood musical style, the use of stock plots based on aspects of everyday life, an inclination toward worldly and middle-class characters and scenes, and the use of actors who were not necessarily highly trained singers. Some types of comic opera relied on spoken dialogue in place of recitativo secco.

In Italy, two early types of comic opera fused into the more generalized *opera buffa.* There were also the shorter *intermezzi,* designed to be performed between the acts of the longer opera seria. Intermezzi had small casts accompanied by lighter orchestration. The best-known of them is Pergolesi's *La serva padrona (The Servant as Mistress).*

The mature *opera buffa,* with its fast-paced sung recitative, lightweight characters, and sparkling trio and quartet ensembles, became internationally popular with elegant audiences in the 18th century. Opera buffa provided the model for such attractive comical musicals as Cimarosa's *Il matrimonio segreto (The Secret Marriage),* and Mozart's *Le nozze di Figaro (The Marriage of Figaro).*

Early Italian comic operas became the basis for a new approach by the French, some of whose small theaters began to present simple, musically enhanced works at annual Parisian fairs. These coalesced into the company known as the Théâtre de l'Opéra-comique, which combined comedies involving popular tunes with new words and burlesque elements. As it matured the *opéra comique* relied on spoken recitatives, developed stylized plots, and featured light, refined musical settings; Jean-Jacques Rousseau's *Devin du village (The Village Soothsayer)* is a prime example.

England's view of comedy in music was a satirization of opera seria in the form of *ballad opera*. The most famous is *The Beggar's Opera*, by John Pepusch, with a libretto by John Gay. Its cast features a highwayman as hero, beggars, pickpockets, and generally coarse street people. The plot revolves around political and musical satire, with spicy spoken dialogue interspersed with songs of cynical lyrics set to popular ballad tunes.

The success of several English ballad operas in German translations gave some impetus to the development of a national German popular musical called the *Singspiel* (sung play). Folktales told through spoken dialogue, folksong melodies, and rousing choruses characterized the format. Hiller's *Die Jagd (The Hunt)* proved a lasting favorite, while the popularity of plays on folk and magic topics encouraged the Viennese impresario Emanuel Schickaneder to commission Mozart's late opera *Die Zauberflöte (The Magic Flute)*.

A light-hearted cousin to the opera comique, ballad opera, and Singspiel was the *operetta,* populated with amusing characters in sentimental situations; its lyric melodies and jolly choruses supported fluffy plots. Every major European country had its national light-opera style, many of which proved internationally successful. Jacques Offenbach's mythic parodies *Orphée aux enfers (Orpheus in the Underworld)* and *La belle Hélène (The Beautiful Helen)* first charmed Parisian audiences and then the rest of Europe and America. Vienna also had its popular musical theater, with such perennial favorites as Franz Lehár's *Die lustige Witwe (The Merry Widow),* and Johann Strauss's *Die Fledermaus (The Bat)*. In England, the operettas of W. S. Gilbert and Arthur Sullivan (*The Mikado, H.M.S. Pinafore, The Pirates of Penzance*) quickly caught on, and are performed worldwide to this day.

Paris was still the hub of serious opera, and a special type known as *grand opéra* developed there. Comparable in some respects to opera seria, grand opera featured a panorama of violence and passion in heroic proportions. The subjects were tales taken from religious sources, medieval or modern history, and literature. They were presented in settings and music of lofty grandeur. Such thrillers as Halévy's *La Juive (The Jewess)* and Rossini's *Guillaume Tell (William Tell)* featured abundant ensembles, grandiose processions and crowd scenes, sumptuous ballets, and scenes packed with fiery emotion.

The patriarch of grand opera was Giacomo Meyerbeer, who missed few opportunities in his large-scale scores to arouse his audiences with bizarre and gruesome scenarios. Meyerbeer's *Robert le diable (Robert the Devil)* created a sensation with a public caught up in the Gothic horror novel, and he followed it with several passionately romantic views of historical and religious events, including *Les Huguenots (The Huguenots)* and *Le prophète (The Prophet)*. Hector

Berlioz contributed to the grand opera tradition with *Benvenuto Cellini,* based on the life of the Renaissance artist, and *Les Troyens (The Trojans),* a massive drama in five acts after Virgil's *Aeneid.*

Such grandiose operatic conceptions opened the way for the entrance of the German operatic giant Richard Wagner. Wagner's desire to speak out on issues relating to German nationalism and social conditions requiring reform led him to musical theater as the preferred medium for airing his views publicly. After concluding that "By opera alone can our theater be raised again," he proceeded to reject most of opera's traditional conventions. He then initiated a type of musical theater he called the *music drama,* which he conceived as a *Gesamtkunstwerk* (total work of art). Through the Gesamtkunstwerk Wagner sought to control the experiences of his audiences as never before. After writing his own librettos, he then set them to music, designed and built a theater in which to perform them, and oversaw every aspect of their production, even to conducting performances himself.

Wagner and others looked for methods that would free them from what they considered formal distinctions that were too artificial and rigid. With Wagner, the orchestra took on a new role, programmatically providing depths of meaning and commentary on the action that had hitherto been thought possible only through the art of poetry. At the same time, Wagner shifted the emphasis away from the singing voice as the focal point of opera; it now functioned as only one element in a rich musico-dramatic complex. In the new music drama, the functions of recitative and aria were retained up to a point, but they were woven into the whole fabric rather than remaining as separate and distinguishable dramatic components (see pp. 275–82).

The Italian approach to grand opera also attempted to modify longstanding conventions of opera seria by consolidating elements of the previously separate recitative and aria, with the result that the Italian *scena* (scene) became a more carefully integrated unit. Gioacchino Rossini, Gaetano Donizetti, and Vincenzo Bellini based their grand operas on plots akin to those of their French contemporaries. Works such as Rossini's *Moses in Egypt,* Donizetti's *Lucrezia Borgia,* and Bellini's *The Puritans* kept to the Italian tradition, placing greater emphasis on the voice while assigning less value to dance and sensational spectacle.

Wagner's contemporary and Italian counterpart was Giuseppe Verdi, who heated up the stage with his intense portrayals of strong characters placed in compelling dramatic situations. A fervent nationalist and admirer of good literature, Verdi and his collaborators crafted robust librettos from writers of the stature of Shakespeare, Byron, Schiller, Victor Hugo, and Alexandre Dumas the Younger. On occasion Verdi used musical motifs to tighten the drama and alert his audience to dramatic events and elements. In *Rigoletto,* for example, the recurring motif of a curse dominates much of the action. It appears at key moments to foreshadow the doom of some of the major characters, and to remind the audience of the devastating force of fate.

Political revolutions in France, Germany, and Italy were reflected in operatic trends, and there was a renewed sense of national pride in French grand opera, in Wagner's pursuit of a German national theater, and in Verdi's operatic pleas for liberation which helped Italy achieve independence from Austrian oppression. Soon every European country had found the opportunity to give vent to growing ethnic pride through *national opera.*

Russian composers concentrated on Russian history and current literature for their librettos. Political and social conditions in Russia also encouraged a national orientation in opera. Mikhail Glinka's heroic opera *A Life for the Tsar* and the fairy tale *Ruslan and Ludmila* set a trend for the remainder of the 19th century. From the group of composers known as "The Five," cultural subject material was chosen for important statements such as Modest Musorgsky's historical tale of imperial power, madness, and murder in *Boris Godunov,* and Alexander Borodin's *Prince Igor,* based on a medieval epic. The tradition has been continued in our century with works such as Dmitri Shostakovich's *Katerina Ismailova* (see pp. 345–46) and Sergei Prokofiev's setting of Leo Tolstoy's massive *War and Peace.*

Middle Europe and Bohemia felt the pull of nationalism as well. The Czechoslovakian Bedřich Smetana followed the lead with legendary subjects such as *Libuše,* as did his compatriots Antonin Dvořák in *Rusalka* and Leoš Janáček in *The Cunning Little Vixen.* In the north, English nationalism waited until the 20th century to find expression through such Shakespeare-inspired works as Ralph Vaughan Williams' *Sir John in Love* and Benjamin Britten's *A Midsummer Night's Dream.*

Emerging national consciousness in the United States inspired composers to replace traditional European subjects for operas. New England lore inspired Charles Wakefield Cadman in his choice of *A Witch of Salem,* and Douglas Moore's *The Devil and Daniel Webster.* Moore's *The Ballad of Baby Doe* celebrated the pioneering strengths found in the opening of the American West. Successful amalgamation of musical comedy approaches and opera was achieved by Kurt Weill in his biting satire *Threepenny Opera* and by George Gershwin, whose folk-based opera *Porgy and Bess* called for a substantially black cast (see pp. 362–63).

Up-to-date literary currents such as *realism* continued to provide subjects for opera. Alexandre Dumas the Younger, Honoré Balzac, and Emile Zola had opened the world of the middle and working classes to a wide readership. Opera followed suit, when Georges Bizet set Prosper Mérimée's tragedy of love between a strong Gypsy girl and a weak soldier in his ever-popular *Carmen.* Gustave Charpentier's *Louise* attempted to portray the real-life story of a seamstress, while Pietro Mascagni's *Cavalleria rusticana (Rustic Chivalry)* and Ruggero Leoncavallo's *I pagliacci (The Clowns)* purported to show the grim and earthy realities (*verismo*) of the lives of Italian peasants and traveling theatrical players. A persuasive and popular version of verismo was created by Giacomo Puccini, who brought the lives of poor Bohemian poets, painters, and seamstresses to the operatic stage in *La bohème,* and the plight of victims caught up in the machinations of a brutal police state in *Tosca.*

Opera has continued to be closely interwoven with prevailing literary and artistic trends throughout the 20th century. The impressionist and symbolist vocabulary of Maurice Maeterlinck's cloudy, ambiguous play *Pelléas et Mélisande* was set by Claude Debussy as an opera of misty, elusive sonorities (pp. 323–25). Richard Strauss gave voice to violently frenetic emotional outbursts in his operatic setting of Oscar Wilde's *Salome* (pp. 298–99); while Alban Berg chose a few fragmentary scenes by the 19th-century dramatist Georg Büchner on which to construct his grimly powerful opera *Wozzeck* (pp. 316–17).

The vast audience potential for single performances of an opera encouraged occasional productions designed for television. Stravinsky (*The Flood*), Giancarlo Menotti (*Amahl and the Night Visitors*), and Benjamin Britten (*Owen Wingrave*) were all commissioned to design operas for the small screen.

Numerous contemporary musical and stylistic innovations have been incorporated into 20th-century operas—serial writing, minimalism, jazz, unusual vocal effects, and the enlarged tonal spectrum afforded by electronic instruments. The majority of composers have, however, chosen to cling to opera's traditional conventions: the recitative and aria, chorus, orchestral support and commentary, and costumes and scenery still function today as the staples of this vital and living segment of musical theater.

Oratorio and Related Genres

While religious themes were occasionally deemed appropriate, opera has always been mainly a medium directed toward secular subject matter. Religiously oriented parallels to opera are found in such forms as the *cantata* and the *passion,* both designed for performance mainly in Protestant churches, where they became integral parts of religious worship (see pp. 181–83). Scored for organ or orchestra combined with chorus and vocal soloists, they included such components as overtures, recitatives, arias, duets, and choral sections similar to those in opera. The *oratorio,* on the other hand, turned in the direction of the theater, where it was performed as an operalike religious drama without all the scenic and fancy-dress paraphernalia of opera. In some a narrator sets the scene and recounts the action, while soloists and chorus complete the dramatic picture.

Throughout its history, the oratorio style has mirrored contemporary operatic practice, drawing upon the aria, duet, orchestral interludes, and other general style characteristics. Bach, for instance, wrote his passions as sacred oratorios intended for major feast days of the church calendar. His compatriot Handel, on the other hand, composed his oratorios for English audiences as musical entertainments for theater or concert-hall presentation, borrowing liberally from various English and continental, sacred and secular, theatrical and religious traditions. The chorus is central to Handel's oratorios, most of which are highly dramatic, reflecting Handel's operatic style. Outstanding examples contain subjects that are secular, such as *Semele,* and sacred, such as *Israel in Egypt* (see p. 180), *Judas Maccabaeus,* and *Messiah.*

The most frequently performed and popular oratorio of all time is Handel's *Messiah,* composed over a period of only three weeks in 1742. As is sometimes the case with great and enduring works of art, *Messiah* is at once a typical and atypical, conventional and unique example of oratorio. It is Handel's only New Testament oratorio, consisting of a series of meditations (mainly on Gospel texts), appropriate for concert performance in a theater or church. In Handel's time it was clearly recognized as a secular theatrical work on a sacred subject and was described as an "elegant Entertainment."

Built around the tradition of the stately English church anthem, *Messiah* holds listeners in thrall mainly through its exuberant choruses. Critic Paul Henry Lang has captured the sense of audience reaction to the work: "When the Hallelujah Chorus is thundered, its wondrous strains exuding power and pomp, the audience gets to its feet to greet a mighty ruler in whose presence we do not kneel but stand at attention."

The three sections of *Messiah* are organized around major events of the Christian church calendar. Part 1 celebrates Advent with its prophecy of Christ's coming and nativity; part 2 turns to the Passion and Resurrection at Eastertide; while part 3 is concerned with the triumph of the Christian soul over death. Handel's considerable powers of organization produced an architectural scheme similar to that of a typical three-act Italian opera, a type with which he was thoroughly familiar as a composer.

Messiah is in fact a stylistic synthesis of elements that are frequently found in baroque musical practice: the French overture; dance, pastorale, and Sicilian rhythms; the da capo, strophic, and rage arias; and madrigal, fugal, and anthem choruses. Also typical are the inclusion of vocal and instrumental tone painting, as well as reworkings of some of Handel's earlier music.

Like many enduring works of art, *Messiah* has been subjected to numerous "modernizations," from a new orchestration by Mozart, through mammoth spectacle performances in the 19th century, to the present, where the prospective performer may choose from over 50 published versions. All of these it has majestically withstood. Whether performed by Handel's forces—approximately 35 players, 8 soloists, and a chorus of 20—or by a festival array numbering in the thousands, the vitality of *Messiah* remains intact.

Handel's choral descendants included Haydn's *The Seasons* and *The Creation;* Berlioz's *L'enfance du Christ (The Childhood of Christ);* and Mendelssohn's *St. Paul* and *Elijah.* The romantic period produced a number of large-scale choral works in the oratorio tradition meant for public performance, such as the *Stabat mater* of Rossini and the *German Requiem* of Brahms. Continuing interest in the genre in the 20th century has produced extensive concert literature in the choral vein, including compositions on such diverse sacred subjects as Arthur Honegger's *King David,* William Walton's *Belshazzar's Feast,* Olivier Messiaen's *The Transfiguration of Our Lord Jesus Christ,* and Krzysztof Penderecki's *St. Luke Passion.* Greek mythology formed the basis for *Oedipus Rex,* Igor Stravinsky's opera-oratorio, while his *Canticum sacrum* evolved from the structure and unique acoustical properties of St. Mark's Basilica in Venice.

Opera and oratorio remain firmly established as integral components of the musical life in major cities of the world. Through television, live performances from the world's opera stages now reach the teeming millions instead of the favored few, while more listeners hear a single broadcast performance of a Bach cantata or Handel's *Messiah* than the total audiences of their respective composers' lifetimes. Films such as *Amadeus, Carmen,* and *La Traviata* have widened the audience still further, and their availability on videotape makes every home a potential opera house, concert hall, and movie theater.

CHAPTER

4

Art of Programme Music

PROGRAMME MUSIC IS ANOTHER bond that links the tonal art with its companion arts. The term *programme* refers to music reflecting literary or pictorial ideas or specified emotional states. Such music consciously imitates sounds of nature (birdcalls, rain, wind, thunderstorms) or social events (hunting scenes, dances, weddings, funerals); or it may narrate a scenariolike sequence of dramatic episodes derived from literary sources (prose, poetry, theater works).

Programme music, both descriptive and narrative, has its roots in the most ancient musical traditions. The oldest reference to narrative programme music goes back to Greece in 586 B.C., when a piece representing the contest between Apollo and a dragon was performed by an aulos player at the Pythian games. The Roman poet Lucretius, writing in the first century B.C., ascribed the origin of music to the desire of men to imitate "with the mouth the liquid notes of birds":

> The whistling of the zephyr through the hollows of reeds first taught the men of the countryside to breathe into hollowed hemlock stalks. Then little by little they learned the sweet lament, which the pipe pours forth, stopped by the player's fingers, a lament discovered amid the pathless woods and forests and glades, among the desolate haunts of shepherds, and the divine places of their rest.

Lucretius' theory was closely allied with the ancient aesthetic conviction that all the arts—verbal, visual, and musical—are based on the imitation of nature. Such imitative or descriptive effects as the cooing of turtledoves can even be found in medieval plainsong. The 17th-century baroque composer Kuhnau wrote *Bible Stories in Six Sonatas* for the keyboard, one of which depicts the "Combat between David and Goliath," and another, "David Curing Saul by Means of Music." Tone poems that included battle scenes were prime favorites with 19th-century audiences, such as Liszt's *Hunenschlacht (Battle of the Huns)* and the "Battle of the Hero and His Enemies" episode in Richard Strauss's *Ein Heldenleben (A Hero's Life)*. The sounds of modern engines can be heard in Honegger's 20th-century tone poem describing a locomotive, *Mouvement symphonique No. 1: Pacific 231*. Far from being a novelty, programme music is deeply ingrained in the fabric of music's history.

Form and Content

While almost every composer has explored the descriptive capacity of instrumental music, the significance attached to this mirroring by musical means has varied considerably. Such composers as Corelli, Vivaldi, Bach, Haydn, and Mozart put their deepest trust in the ability of music to communicate in more abstract terms, and programme compositions correspondingly hold a lesser place in their total musical output. In the work of Berlioz, Schumann, Liszt, Mahler, and Richard Strauss, on the other hand, the programme commands major attention.

All the arts depend for communication on some association of ideas. In the more abstract phases of any art, this association is less explicit, and the art must rely for its unity more on form than on specific content. The story of programme music has to do with the tensions that arise between these boundaries of form and content, and the extent to which one or the other is allowed to dominate.

Music, in contrast to poetry and painting, cannot convey specific imagery with any particular precision. When a painter wants to represent a rock or a tree, it can be drawn with considerable accuracy. Moreover, when visual art veers toward the abstract, it never completely parts company with nature. Even a so-called nonobjective picture has colors, lines, angles, and surface textures. While these may be quite nonspecific, they are nevertheless concrete to some extent, since color, line, and shape are all present in nature, if in an unrefined state.

Music, on the contrary, is not really a representative art at all, and the sounds of nature can never be imitated with exactitude. A few sounds such as bells and hunting horns, to be sure, can be reproduced, but these are man-made and musical rather than natural. The 18th-century French composer Rameau invested one of his harpsichord pieces with a a cackling theme and called it *La poule (The Hen)*. Lest the listener miss the point, however, the composer found it desirable to inscribe above the notes the syllables "co-co-co-co-co cocodai."

Only when music is coupled with words (as in a song), with pantomime (as in a dance), or with drama (as in opera and oratorio) does this associative process become clear and direct. The "word painting" of the so-called *representative style* as employed by the baroque composers is a case in point. In the aria "Every valley shall be exalted" from his oratorio *Messiah,* Handel uses an exuberant rising line to create and intensify the feeling of exaltation (Ex. 4-1). In *Israel in Egypt* he depicts the plagues with instrumental effects suggesting flies, fire, and hammer blows (Exs. 4-2a, b, and c). For the plague of frogs, he devises a jerky meter with a melodic line that hops along in wide leaps. Without a text, however, no one would know exactly what his intentions were.

Example 4-1. Handel. *Messiah.* "Every valley shall be exalted," bars 15–19.

Example 4-2. Handel. *Israel in Egypt.*

4-2a. No. 6, bars 3–4.

4-2b. No. 7, bars 63–67.

4-2c. No. 9, bars 1–3.

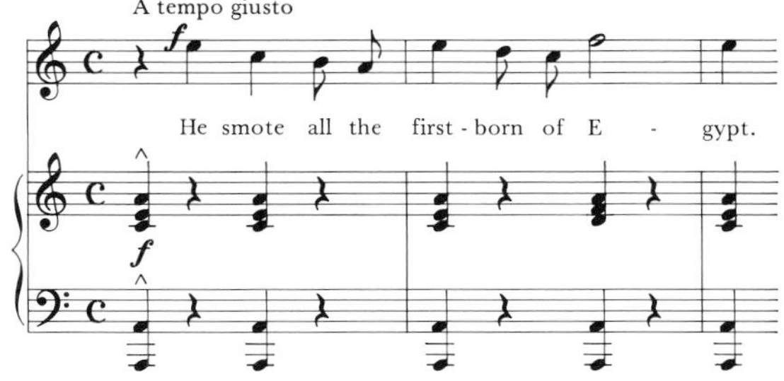

Such descriptive passages are also found in 19th-century music. Schubert's song accompaniment in *To Be Sung on the Water* provides a rippling wavelike figure. Here again, without a guiding text, the accompaniment patterns become subject to a variety of interpretations (Ex. 4-3). Similarly, the rhythmic pattern suggesting the stamping of horses' hooves [♬♪ ♬♪] was identified with cavalry marches in certain instrumental music of the 18th and 19th centuries. When Chopin wanted to suggest horsemen on a battlefield in the central section of his Polonaise in F-sharp Minor, Op. 44, communicative symbols that were perfectly intelligible to his listeners were readily at hand. In general, however, the composer in such cases needs a title, text, or verbal description of some sort so as to avoid obscurity or possible misinterpretation.

Example 4-3. Schubert. *To Be Sung on the Water,* bars 1–3.

The full range of musical literature reveals that programme music exists in every instrumental medium and for all combinations from solo instruments to full orchestra. Since by definition they seek freedom of form, programmatic works bear a bewildering number and variety of titles. In addition to programme symphonies and symphonic poems, there are suites for all instrumental combinations, fantasies for everything from organ to orchestra, as well as programmatic string quartets and concertos.

Imagery and Symbolism

Programme music, as it took shape in the instrumental writing of the 18th and 19th centuries, freely borrowed descriptive images and dramatic devices that were traditionally associated with the opera and oratorio. Certain tonalities were associated with special moods and situations. The key of D Minor was often a storm-and-stress or demonic key for Haydn and Mozart. It is heard in Haydn's "Lamentation" Symphony and Mozart's D-minor piano concerto (*K* 466). Mozart also used the key for the diabolical finale of his opera *Don Giovanni,* when the flames of hell envelop the Don. It again recurs in the fire-and-brimstone, doomsday imagery of the *Dies irae* (Day of Wrath) section in his *Requiem.* In contrast, the tonality of F Major was often used for works of a peaceful, pastoral nature.

Instrumental colors may also carry symbolism, as, for instance, "warlike" trumpets. "Foreboding" trombones were once associated with solemn church festivals or funerals and, in opera, with death; "signaling" French horns with hunting scenes; and "pastoral" woodwinds with bucolic country scenes and landscapes.

Instances of symbolism both obvious and obscure are sometimes found side by side. In Saint-Saëns' *Danse macabre* a general Halloween atmosphere prevails. As harp and pizzicato strings strike the witching hour of midnight, brittle xylophone passages imitate the dancing of skeletons, and an oboe sounds the cock's crow at dawn. The poem on which it is based describes the devil beating time with his heel on a gravestone, while he tunes his fiddle for the forthcoming infernal festivities. The composer also calls for the violin to be retuned by lowering the E string one-half step. With the devil striking a perfect fifth (D and A) in alternation with the diminished fifth (A and E-flat), there is a subtle allusion involved, since the latter is a tritone interval known in medieval times as the *diabolus in musica* (the devil in music).

A vocabulary of such symbols was common musical currency, so that when Mendelssohn wrote a "song without words" intended as a spinning song, he had a ready-made figure at hand that had been used by Schubert before him and would be employed by Wagner and others many times after him (Ex. 4-4).

Example 4-4. Mendelssohn. *Spinning Song,* bars 1–3.

Berlioz wrote his *Harold in Italy* (1834) as an orchestral drama, identifying Harold, his principal character, with a recurring melody assigned to a solo viola. The programme is a free adaptation of Lord Byron's *Childe Harold's Pilgrimage.* In the various episodes this extended theme undergoes a series of adaptations and transmutations associated with the hero's melancholy musings while alone in the mountains, meditating as a religious pilgrimage passes by, participating in a peasant festival, and being kidnapped by outlaws and brigands.

A composer may concoct a programme, as Berlioz did in his *Symphonie fantastique,* or may turn to existent literary sources, as Tchaikovsky did in his *Francesca da Rimini,* based on an episode in Dante's *Inferno.* A composer may go so far as to have a writer publish an "inspired" poem to serve as an authorized interpretation of a composition, as Richard Strauss did with his *Death and Transfiguration.* Most often, composers have some clear programmatic idea in advance of beginning a composition. Spohr and Schumann, on the other hand, said that they gave titles and programmes to their pieces after they were written. In such a case, the music throws far more light on the programme than the programme on the music.

Concrete vs. Abstract Music

A work need not necessarily fall into the category of either *programme* or *abstract* music exclusively. Beethoven's "Pastoral" Symphony is by his own explanation a symphony first and pastoral afterward, while Berlioz's *Symphonie fantastique* might be described as primarily fantastic and secondarily a symphony. Beethoven always knew where to draw the line, and in his own words the "Pastoral" Symphony was "more an expression of feeling than tone painting." It is not, for example, programmatic because of the composer's excursion into ornithology in the second movement, where he imitates the calls of the nightingale, quail, and cuckoo respectively. This passage makes perfectly good sense quite independently, as a transitional passage of contrast near the end of the movement before the main subject is heard as a coda. The symphony is not necessarily programmatic because of a rustic band playing folk dances for peasant merrymaking in the third movement; Beethoven would naturally have called for a dance (scherzo) movement at this point in the overall design in any case. The work is, however, programmatic to the extent that the composer fits the movements into a series of episodes implied by the original heading in his notebook: *Recollections of Country Life*. When published, the various movements were labeled "Cheerful Feelings Aroused on Arrival in the Country," "By the Brook," "Merrymaking of Country Folk," "Storm—Shepherd's Song, Joy and Thanksgiving after the Storm."

Occasionally programmatic hints are found in works that are primarily abstract. The slow movement of Beethoven's A-minor string quartet, Opus 132, bears the superscription "A hymn of thanks to the Deity by a convalescent on his recovery. Feeling of new strength and reawakened sensation." By this reference to a personal episode in his later life, Beethoven indicated to his listeners that he attached more than ordinary significance to this movement. Otherwise the quartet is free of overt programme suggestions.

There are those who are opposed to the concept of programme music, feeling that music should be heard solely as music and should not be subjected to literary, pictorial, or philosophical interpretations. Since music cannot, in any case, convey any very specific imagery (so the argument runs), this fact should become the source of the strength rather than the weakness of the art. The powerful 19th-century Viennese critic Eduard Hanslick, one of the most ardent champions of abstract music, upheld the position that music was a self-contained art having no relation to anything outside itself. Commenting on the bleating of sheep in one section of Richard Strauss's tone poem *Don Quixote,* a practical-minded orchestra conductor once asked why a composer should indulge in the expensive realism of a dozen muted brass instruments, which take ten rehearsals to accomplish what a flock of sheep can do quite naturally. The danger of such frank musical description is that it can all too quickly degenerate into mere sound effects or background music. The poet Goethe once said that "to imitate thunder in music is not art, but the musician who excites in me the feeling as if I had heard thunder would be very estimable."

Ultimately, most people agree that music as a language must be understood on its own terms and is compatible with the other arts only in a matter of degree. Since composers have held very individual views on the extent to which the degree of programmatic latitude may be taken, any attempt to separate music into two opposing camps with one labeled "absolute" and the other "programme" is bound to fail. Some composers may put abstract considerations above concrete ones, formal outlines above emotional content, craftsmanship above description; but fortunately these oppositions are not mutually exclusive. No composer writes without some image in mind. In one case it might be as generalized a notion as a series of tonalities in a sonata movement, in another as particular as a sequence of episodes in a drama; as indefinite as a fleeting mood, or as a precise as a dance rhythm; as subtle as an isorhythm in a medieval motet, or as obvious as the thunderstorm in Rossini's operatic overture to *William Tell.*

When such sounds of nature as birdcalls or gusts of wind do appear in music, they are reproduced as sound patterns rather than represented directly; hence they are always abstract to some degree. Furthermore, all composers, those of the absolute and programmatic persuasion alike, must take cognizance of formal considerations and decide whether they are to be precise and predictable or fluid and free. Regardless of whether the parts are patterned on the principle of variation, recurrence, or development, or are arranged according to adventures, episodes, or dramatic vicissitudes, they are always based on some aspect of human experience—either generalized or particularized, symbolic or actual. It is in fact possible to say that programme music is abstract music in which the composer saw fit to disclose his intentions, while absolute music is programme music in which the composer keeps his intentions to himself.

Since no clear-cut dividing line between musical form and content is possible, a compromise position is generally taken that seems more or less satisfactory to all concerned. No programme, it is conceded, can ever replace the intrinsic structural quality of the music or assure the listener's interest, if the work cannot be launched independently. A bad piece of music, like a leaky vessel at sea, will sink in any case and no literary SOS will keep it afloat. If, however, a composer wants to add a title or reveal some poetic or pictorial idea that he had in mind, it is his privilege as a creative artist to do so. It is also the listener's inalienable right to disregard a poetic programme. Just as an untitled sonata movement may mean more to a person who imagines a story to accompany it, so a programmatic piece may give greater pleasure to another who considers it as abstract music. Richard Strauss himself suggested that "A tone poem must be ship-shape musically considered. Let him who likes look at it merely as a musical work of art. In *Don Quixote,* for instance, I show how a man goes mad over vain imaginings. But I do not wish to compel any listener to think of Don Quixote when he hears it. He may conceive of it as absolute music if it suits him."

Programme Music and the Orchestra

In the main it is the orchestra that carries the principal weight of programmatic output, since the development of the modern symphonic medium in the 19th century coincided so exactly with a growth in popularity of programme music. The constantly increasing numbers in orchestral ranks and the continuously expanding color possibilities during that time confirmed the orchestra as the ideal means for programmatic expression. Many of these orchestral works are classified as overtures, though to all intents and purposes they are the same as tone poems.

Overtures in the beginning were simply "curtain raisers" for the purpose of preparing the audience for what was to follow, whether a play, a ballet, an oratorio, or an opera. As such they were orchestral compositions of a more or less formal type, without any direct connection with the work as a whole. Beginning with Gluck's operatic reforms and continuing with Mozart's contributions, however, overtures began to have a dramatic as well as thematic connection with the opera itself. Examples of this type are Mozart's overture to *Don Giovanni,* Beethoven's "Leonore" overtures to *Fidelio,* all of Weber's overtures, and Wagner's overtures to *The Flying Dutchman* and *Tannhäuser.* Overtures such as Weber's *Euryanthe,* Wagner's *Rienzi,* and Berlioz's *Benvenuto Cellini* still appear on concert programs, but their complete meaning can be garnered only from a knowledge of the lyric dramas with which they were once associated.

Incidental music for plays, such as Beethoven's for Goethe's *Egmont* and Mendelssohn's for Shakespeare's *A Midsummer Night's Dream,* usually included overtures that now survive in the concert repertory. Some overtures were written especially for concert performance; some were based on novels, poems, plays, and sundry other sources that fired the composer's imagination. Examples of this type are Berlioz's overtures to Walter Scott's novels *Waverley* and *Rob Roy;* Mendelssohn's *Calm Sea and Prosperous Voyage* and *Legend of the Lovely Melusina,* based on literary works by Goethe; Wagner's *Faust Overture,* on Goethe's drama; and Brahms' *Tragic Overture,* with only the title as a clue to its content.

After the middle of the 19th century, composers generally followed Liszt's lead, and *symphonic poem,* or *tone poem,* became the commonly adopted designation for these one-movement orchestral works. Their sources of inspiration continued to be highly varied. There were those with literary antecedents, such as Liszt's *The Preludes,* after a poem by Lamartine; Franck's *The Accursed Huntsman,* after a ballad by Bürger; and Richard Strauss's *Don Juan,* after Lenau's dramatic poem. In addition to Musorgsky's *Pictures at an Exhibition* (see pp. 267–70), other examples derive their inspiration from pictorial sources, such as Rachmaninov's *Isle of the Dead,* after the painting of that name by Böcklin. There are also orchestral discourses on philosophy, such as Richard Strauss's *Also sprach Zarathustra (Thus Spake Zoroaster)*, inspired by Nietszche's book of that title; Scriabin's *Poem of Ecstasy,* which reflects the composer's mystical views on theosophy; and Charles Ives' philosophically *Unanswered Question.* Examples fired by national sentiment and patriotism include Liszt's *Hungaria;* Smetana's cycle *My Fatherland,* which includes the descriptive tone poem on the Moldau River; and Sibelius' *Finlandia.*

In addition to the simple designations *overture* and *tone poem,* there are a host of hybrid and fanciful titles by various composers. Tchaikovsky called his *Romeo and Juliet* an overture-fantasy, and his *Hamlet* a fantasy-overture. These, together with his *Ouverture solennelle, 1812 (Solemn Overture, 1812)* and his *Francesca da Rimini,* called an orchestral fantasy, must be charged to the composer's whim, since they differ in no essential respect from other concert overtures. Even more fanciful are some of Debussy's designations, such as his "Clouds," "Festivals," and "Sirens" grouped together as *Nocturnes;* and his "Gigues," "Iberia," and "Spring Roundelays," collectively labeled *Images.*

The suite, originally a series of dance movements, has also been utilized by composers of programme music. In this category are orchestral suites extracted for concert purposes from ballets, from incidental music for plays, and from piano works. Examples include the suite from Tchaikovsky's *Nutcracker* ballet, based on a short story by E. T. A. Hoffmann; Stravinsky's *Firebird* and *Petrouchka* suites, from ballets built on choreographic ideas by Michel Fokine; and Prokofiev's excerpts from his ballet *Romeo and Juliet.* Suites compounded out of incidental music written for plays include Bizet's *Arlésienne Suite,* originally for a play by Daudet, and Grieg's *Peer Gynt Suite* for Ibsen's drama of that name. Ravel orchestrated his *Mother Goose Suite,* originally for piano four-hands.

In another category is the lengthier *programme symphony,* which differs from a symphonic or tone poem in that it is somewhat larger in scope and comprises a cycle of separate movements grouped into a symphonic whole. The history of such symphonies can be traced from Haydn's early series of three called "Morning," "Afternoon," and "Evening" (Nos. 6–8) through the broad tonal landscape of Beethoven's "Pastoral" Symphony. The cornerstone in this category is Berlioz's *Symphonie fantastique;* its successors include Liszt's *Faust Symphony* with its several movements entitled "Faust," "Marguerite," and "Mephistopheles."

More recently in this genre is Hindemith's *Mathis der Maler (Matthias the Painter),* a programme symphony drawn from his opera of the same name. Inspired by the 16th-century painter Matthias Grünewald and his famous Isenheim altarpiece, the three movements bear subtitles after various panels of the great painting: "The Angelic Concert," a subject associated with the Nativity scene, featuring joyful, music-making angels (see pp. 347–48 and

Plate XVII); "The Entombment," a dark, brooding dirge as Christ is laid in the tomb; and "Temptation of St. Anthony," in which diabolical and fantastic apparitions bedevil the saint in his ordeal (see Plate XVIII).

Messiaen's *Turangalîla Symphony* (1948) is described by the composer as "at one and the same time a love song, a hymn to joy, time, movement, rhythm, life and death." Its ten movements have as a foundation the legend of Tristan and Isolde and are woven together with four cyclic themes: a monumental "statue" theme, a "flower" theme, a "love" theme, and a chord progression that "answers the doctrinal formula of the alchemists to 'dissociate and coagulate'."

As it evolved in the 19th century, programme music was essentially dramatic music cast in instrumental forms. In this idiom, the composer could write songs and ballads without words, as did Schumann and Brahms, and librettoless and singerless operas, as did Berlioz and Liszt. With the humanization of musical instruments, a programme symphony or a tone poem becomes a kind of orchestral opera in which the dramatic action is implied in the poetic programme rather than explicitly acted out and sung. In a play, for instance, characters are first presented, then exposed to a series of situations and events in order to reveal their personalities and potentialities. Similarly, in programme music the motif or melody is substituted for a personality and eventually discloses its true nature by evolving through a sequence of qualitative changes. Far from being too concrete (as it is so often accused of being), programme music, by freeing the song from words and liberating opera from librettos, actually becomes the most abstract of all dramatic music.

CHAPTER

5

Art of Architecture

MUSIC IS JOINED WITH rhythmic movement in the dance, with poetry and lyricism in song, with drama in the opera, and with literary and visual imagery in programme music. One further bond remains to be explored: music in its relationship with the architectural, acoustical, and social settings associated with its performance.

Social Occasion and Architectural Setting

To gain insight into the various types and styles of music, one must take into account the architectural setting for which the music was originally designed. To a considerable degree music is conditioned by the place of performance as well as by the occasions on which it is heard. Since music has often been designed for a particular social function, it is naturally conditioned by the environment of the event. Chamber music is different from concert music, theater music from church music, and salon music from outdoor music.

In the baroque period, when worldly music was in the process of emancipating itself from forms connected with religious worship, it was customary to attach the Italian term *da camera* to certain compositions suitable for social entertainment, and *da chiesa* to those intended for church performance. A *sonata da camera* (chamber sonata), with its active, dancelike movements and its secular spirit, could generally be distinguished from a *sonata da chiesa* (church sonata), which displayed rigorously fugal textures and a more contemplative character. In addition to church and chamber sonatas, concertos, and cantatas, various kinds of music have been designated as "music for the home," "table music," and "background music."

This shaping of music to the environment is usually done by the composer, who must take into consideration the space and nature of the place where the music will be played, as well as the type and number of the musicians needed. Haydn's early symphonies, for instance, differ stylistically from later ones depending on the spaces in which they were destined to be performed. Writing for a household orchestra in his patron's salon, where he had to tread lightly with brass and kettledrums, was one thing, while composing for the large-scale public Salomon Concerts in London was quite another. Of Mozart's works in the symphonic form, only the last four (Nos. 38–41) can be called symphonic in the public concert sense. The others remain aristocratic salon pieces conceived for a smaller-scale milieu.

There are parallels in the visual arts. Before the 19th century, works of art were usually commissioned directly from the artist rather than bought through dealers and brokers. Both the patron and the artist knew in advance whether the work of art was to be placed in a church as an altarpiece, in a monastery refectory, in a large palace hall, or in an intimate salon. Consequently the subject matter and dimensions were adjusted to the particular circumstances.

Today, however, works of art are more often seen in the impersonal surroundings of a museum, where they appear completely out of context. On one level the viewer can enjoy the pictures and statuary for their intrinsic qualities, admiring their color, texture, line, and form. But for a fuller understanding one needs to know when they were executed, who was the patron, how they came to be commissioned, where they were meant to be placed. Since it is rarely feasible to take works back to their original locations, an act of the imagination is required to conjure up in the mind's eye how these works would have appeared in their intended settings.

Similarly, hearing great music in a concert hall or played on a recording in the living room requires the listener to envision the initial circumstances that brought the work into being. Was it written for singing or dancing? Was it intended to be performed in a church or palace? The informed listener must strive to recall the setting of a performance by the Sistine Chapel choir at a papal ceremony, or the type of service and ecclesiastical season at which a particular motet or mass setting would have been appropriate. Imagination and knowledge must be summoned to supply the period and style; the social, religious, or economic circumstances of the music's origin; the type of patronage; and the architectural setting for which it was intended. Invoking these frames of reference sets the listener on a path to creative involvement in the musical situation that can bridge the gap between the here and there, the then and now.

The electronic revolution of the 20th century, by which music became so readily available via the transistor, analog and digital disks, film sound track and magnetic tape, has turned every living room into a potential concert hall. Until the advent of recorded sound, however, music was heard only in live performances, where the type and style of the composition were conditioned by its appropriateness to the particular social situation. While home listening has not actually replaced concert-giving and concert-going, nonetheless a music lover's living room today can be as musically active as Carnegie Hall.

In former times it took a princely purse to provide music in palatial surroundings. Only an Esterházy family could maintain a house orchestra frequently used by Haydn, and only a Baron von Swieten could enliven his Sunday mornings with chamber music matinees in which Mozart and Beethoven participated. Musical riches once at the call of kings are now within the reach of everyone. Less than a century ago, a music room was simply a parlor with a piano, and the repertory heard there seldom went beyond simple songs and piano pieces. In today's music room, however, operas and symphony concerts are brought in by radio and television, and masterpieces of all periods can be experienced through various recording media.

A wider variety and range of musical styles are available to the modern listener than ever before. Owing to sound reproduction, many a neglected masterwork by such Renaissance and baroque composers as Josquin Desprez, Palestrina, Monteverdi, and Purcell has been reinstated in the available repertory. What this music of the past loses without the intimate contact of composer, performer, and patron is perhaps compensated for by the expansion of the audience from a few hundred into the millions.

In music a yawning chasm separates the grandeur of the symphony from the more intimate communication of chamber music, the epic pronouncements of grand opera from the tender outpourings of a love song. The process of recording involves a reorientation of the original sound to the decibel level that will fit comfortably into a restricted acoustical space. Massive, brassy climaxes must be suggested without being actually present, faint whispers delivered with a minimum of noisome interference. The chorus of up to a thousand voices, the huge symphony orchestra, and the four brass bands that Berlioz required for his *Requiem* must, in the living room, be reduced to the same dynamic level as that of a classical guitar or clavichord solo. The process is similar to the production of a picture book, in which monumental murals or minute miniatures have to be adjusted to the size of a printed page.

The matter is complicated by the fact that the acoustical qualities a composer had in mind when the music was originally performed must today be realized differently through the recording process. Recording engineers have the capability to overrule both composer and performers, further enlarging the communications gap between composer and listener.

In addition, one must remember that in home listening, recordings and broadcasts on radio and television produce sound that emanates from a narrowly focused space. In an auditorium, however, sound is more spaciously distributed, reaching the ear from many different sources, both directly from performers and indirectly from reflected surfaces. Antiphonal effects, echo nuances, and the building up of cumulative climaxes are correspondingly reduced in effectiveness in the living room. Furthermore, no matter how high the fidelity of the reproduced sound, it is still never quite the same as the original. In this way a recorded symphony is like a photographic portrait, which can serve to recall the image of a familiar face, but can never replace the beaming countenance of the living person.

Thus the disciplined and informed imagination must compensate for the differences in listening environments, conscious engineering enhancements, and the vagaries of reproducing systems.

CHURCH AND CONCERT HALL

Temples and churches were the scenes of large-scale musical activity long before public concert halls and opera houses came into being. The composers who wrote for religious ceremonies were as sensitive to the acoustical possibilities of the building where the work was to be performed as they were to the appropriateness of the music for divine worship. While some early music is still effective in its original or a similar setting, much of it does not easily survive transplantation from its native habitat. The flowing simplicity of a Gregorian chant, for instance, is ideally adapted for intonation in the interiors of basilican churches, where it acquires a vibrant and colorful quality uniquely its own. Removed from these architectural and liturgical surroundings and sung instead in concert halls or recording studios, it loses much of its warmth and resilience.

When Pérotin conceived his grandiose vocal music for the Cathedral of Notre Dame in Paris, he had to take the reverberations of its vast vaulted surfaces into account. In such a Gothic edifice the tones and overtones are enriched and prolonged as they echo through the cavernous interior spaces, and the tones that precede mix with those that follow so that the entire building resounds with their harmony. In other places the frequent empty fifth and octave intervals stay open and exposed, and the harmonies seem barren and hollow in comparison.

Certain conditions and innovations of modern life are responsible for all manner of misconceptions in the minds of composers of church music as well as audiences. Each of the two greatest opera composers of the 19th century, for instance, tried his hand at writing religious music. Verdi's *Requiem,* a setting of the Roman Catholic Mass for the Dead, reflects the increasing secular spirit of its time in both its dramatic treatment and its theatrical grandiloquence. Designed for performance in concert halls rather than in churches, it has been called, with more truth than humor, his "greatest opera." Wagner, for his part, attempted to turn the opera house into a place of worship with his pseudo-Christian mystery drama *Parsifal*. Audiences at the opera house he had built at Bayreuth in Germany are still expected to maintain a reverent hush and to refrain from applause when it is performed.

Palestrina's masses and Bach's cantatas were written as integral parts of church services, while the more ambitious oratorios were conceived as festival offerings during the Advent and Lenten seasons. Today, however, they are as often heard in public halls. When an important 20th-century composer like Stravinsky writes a mass or other religious music, more than likely it will be heard in a concert hall rather than a church. Consciously or unconsciously, he is writing his sacred music for a secular gathering. Music in church, of course, is an adjunct to divine worship, while in a concert hall or opera house it exists as an independent entity and constitutes its own reason for being.

CHAMBER AND CONCERT HALL

A vast amount of music, designated as house music or chamber music, has been written for private performance in middle- and upper-class homes. In Elizabethan England as well as in the northern countries on the Continent, the cult of the home fostered this genial music-making by amateurs. In contrast to southern climates, where much musical activity flourished in the open air, the social life of the English, Dutch, and German people was more strictly an indoor affair. In earlier times a well-equipped home would be furnished with a keyboard instrument such as a spinet, clavichord, or small harpsichord; stringed instruments such as lutes or a chest of viols; and a small library of vocal and instrumental numbers. Groups of singers sat around a table to perform madrigals; singers and instrumentalists gathered around the keyboard for group or solo songs; and string players participated in ensemble numbers.

Bach's keyboard works are written for three different instruments. The compositions for organ are expressly for church use. Those for the clavichord are homelike and informal; in contrast, those for harpsichord were written for more aristocratic, palatial surroundings, thus are more grand and formal. In each case the type of communication as well as the manner of delivery is conditioned by the place where the instrument is normally found.

In the wider sense, chamber music included madrigals and other secular music performed by one voice for each part, instrumental ensembles, and works for vocal and instrumental combinations. In 1776 chamber music was described as "cantatas, single songs, solos, trios, quartets, concertos and symphonies of a few parts." Later, after the turn of the 19th century, it was defined as "compositions for a small concert room, a small band and a small auditorium; opposed to music for the church, theater or a public concert room." Full orchestral and choral music with liberal doubling of parts was thus excluded from the medium, as were solo works of various kinds. More and more, chamber music came to be dominantly instrumental, though voices in combination with instruments are still occasionally used.

Most of the lighter chamber music of the Viennese classical period was conceived and written for intimate entertainments in princely parlors. A poet in such surroundings would tend to read sonnets rather than a high-flown epic; a painter would provide miniatures rather than gigantic canvases; and a composer would introduce sonatas and string quartets rather than symphonies. Music, like the conversation in such elegant and aristocratic surroundings, was expected to be witty but not heavy, energetic but not bombastic.

Because of the growing scope of chamber-music writing from the 18th century on, it became more and more the province of professional performers. Since the players and listeners are in such close proximity, however, and since the audience is more sophisticated, such works are more congenial to smaller rather than larger halls where the auditors are farther away from the source of sound. Chamber music, by remaining the delight of the trained and talented amateur as well as the discerning listener, has managed to retain much of its original warmth and individual character. The particular distinction of the medium lies in its reduced proportions and in the equal weight of each instrument within the ensemble. When the several parts are performed by a multitude of players and singers in an orchestra or chorus, individual responsibility correspondingly declines. Each member of a performing duo, trio, or quartet, however, has an individual sphere of influence and the power to make a particular contribution to the group. Chamber music is thus not crowd entertainment, and its tensions and subtleties can easily be lost in large halls.

INDOORS AND OUTDOORS

Formerly in aristocratic circles, summer musical performances took place in the courtyards and gardens of palaces, and the music was specifically written and designed for the setting in which it was to be heard. When Lully, court composer to Louis XIV, scored his ballets and operas with the outdoor courts and garden pavilions of Versailles in mind, he added woodwinds and brasses to the usual indoor orchestra of 24 strings.

Handel wrote his *Water Music* for performance on a Thames River barge while George I made his royal progress from London to Hampton Court. Handel's *Fireworks Music* was composed for a performance in one of London's public gardens, where the strains of his music formed a prelude to a later display of Roman candles and skyrockets. In each case he chose his instruments—principally woodwinds and brasses—so that they would sound properly in their open-air surroundings.

Nowhere is the adaptation of music to its environment better illustrated than in that genial genre of 18th-century Viennese social music, consisting of informal collections of marches and dances, loosely designated as divertimentos, serenades, and cassations. A definite line of demarcation can be drawn on the basis of instrumentation. Those scored principally for strings point indoors; those with a preponderance of wind instruments, outdoors. For example, Mozart's finely wrought *Eine kleine Nachtmusik (A Little Night Music, K* 525), a small nocturnal serenade as the German title implies, belongs inside, since it is written for strings only. His divertimentos scored for pairs of wind instruments—oboes, horns, bassoons, and, when available, clarinets—were clearly designed for open-air performance. According to contemporary accounts, such ensembles were to be heard in the streets at almost any hour. No matter how late, says the *Vienna Theater Almanac* of 1794, whenever the serenaders struck up, there were "people at their open windows and within a few minutes the musicians were surrounded by a crowd of listeners who rarely departed until the serenade had come to an end."

When Mozart wrote music for weddings, birthdays, garden parties, and the like, he carefully worked within the intended setting and with the instruments that were available. His D-major serenade (*K* 286) is scored for four groups of instruments—designated as principal, first echo, second echo, and third echo orchestras, respectively—each of which contains first and second violins, viola, bass, and horns.

Despite the designation of four orchestras, the effect is that of a single orchestra which is answered by others in triple-echo fashion. In performance the first orchestra plays an entire phrase, the second repeats it exactly, the third plays only the last half of the phrase and the fourth the last measure only. When the respective orchestras are deployed in the four corners of the room, an ingenious round-robin acoustical effect is obtained.

Today it seems taken for granted that music moves out-of-doors in the summer. Concerts and opera performances spring up in city parks and stadiums. Outdoor concerts are, of course, as old as the history of public concert life. In London, where music-making for the general public dates from the 17th century, garden performances achieved enormous popularity. The American colonies during the time of George Washington and Francis Hopkinson also had their share of outdoor performances at such places as the Pennsylvania Tea Gardens in Philadelphia and the Orange Garden in Charleston, South Carolina.

Today, the orchestral repertory remains substantially the same whether played indoors in winter or outside in summer. In the case of outdoor concerts, conductors slow the pace of their fast movements to compensate for acoustical peculiarities of the places where they are performing. Strange instrumental imbalances occur in which the wind and brass sections, playing in their natural element, overwhelm the strings and sometimes make familiar works seem like first-night novelties. Moreover, symphonies and concertos regularly played in these outdoor arenas were never intended by their composers for such surroundings. Subtle features may disappear, leaving only blare and bombast behind. Compositions that stress a festive quality and outsize forces, such as Tchaikovsky's *Ouverture solennelle, 1812* and Berlioz's *Requiem,* fare better in an outdoor atmosphere.

Where a setting can no longer be duplicated or reasonably approximated, informed listeners will call on historical knowledge to aid the imagination in conjuring up the setting and circumstances for which the music was originally created.

Past and Present

Whether written for church or theater, home or concert hall, salon or open air, music is indissolubly associated with its acoustical and social surroundings. Any competent composer is governed to a considerable extent in the choice of style, form, instrumentation, and even expressive content by the spatial environment in which the work is to be performed. A pavane or minuet, whether written by a musician at the time these dances were current or by a contemporary composer as a period piece, belongs in a rarefied courtly atmosphere, while a Laendler is at home in the rustic countryside.

When the music of the past is removed from surroundings approximating those the composer had in mind, an awareness of the environment as well as the occasion for which the work was originally intended is a useful step toward deeper insight into musical styles. This is especially true at the present time, when all types of music are readily accessible through the modern mass media.

Commenting on the prevailing lack of knowledge about the specific purposes and places for which the music of the past was composed, a noted historian wrote, "How barbarous our concert life has become is shown principally by the fact that we no longer feel such distinctions." Since knowledge of form and function is generally limited, the listener must resort to an act of the imagination whereby proper settings are conjured up as part of the listening process. Any serious attempt to fathom music's original function must take architectural, environmental, and social occasion into account.

PART

II

Music and Its Historical Styles

INTRODUCTION

Music in History

MUSIC IS A SOCIAL process, an art addressed to, performed with, and enjoyed in the company of others. In all places and at all times music has been woven into the fabric of community life. And just as a building is incomprehensible except in terms of its place and function, a musical work defies understanding until its nature and purpose are known. The discovery that a particular building was a temple, a theater, or a dwelling does not reveal everything about it, but it does say a good deal. Likewise, knowing that a piece of music was composed for a religious observation, a public spectacle, or a domestic gathering does not explain it completely, but it certainly helps. Like architecture, music in society is a coordinating force. Its function may be as elementary as that of a work song or as exalted as that of a symphony. Music, then, is one of the experiences by which people realize their humanity and create meanings for life.

Patronage

Music has, for the most part, a direct relation to the various social occasions for which it is designed. Like the other arts, it is always addressed to some segment of society. Religious events, civic celebrations, and official functions all call for appropriate music; and, in previous times, special music was usually commissioned for such purposes. This situation immediately pointed to the problem of patronage. According to an old saying, whoever pays the piper calls the tune. There are, of course, as many levels of enlightenment and discernment among patrons as there are levels of competency among composers or any other artists. The application of the proverb by no means implies that the tune will necessarily be either a good or bad one. Music, like all great forces in life, is a double-edged sword. It can ascend to the Olympian heights of great creative art, and it can descend to the depths of blatant propaganda and the commonplace "singing commercial." The important point, always, is whether its control rests in the hands of those who will ennoble the art or debase it.

Since music has so many functions to fulfill, the very diversity of the sources of patronage is one of its special protections. In periods such as the Middle Ages, the church selected, educated, and encouraged the finest available talents. During the Renaissance, the musical direction tended more toward courtly entertainment, and many a princely purse was opened for the training and support of outstanding musicians. In modern times, a vast and anonymous group patron known as the "public" contributes or withholds its support via its patronage, not of the composer, but of the free market—the concert hall, the opera house, and the recording industry—where the composer's products are offered for inspection.

Music as a Social Force

Besides being an organized whole, a piece of music is also a social and historical statement. Beethoven's Ninth Symphony—proclaiming as it does the ideals of liberty, equality, and human brotherhood—is as much a document of the revolutionary years as are the Rights of Man, the Declaration of Independence, or the American Constitution. Thus the soaring aspirations of both individual and collective ideals can be expressed through music, with its own special language of tonal symbols and auditory images, just as through any other form of human expression.

Like other works of art, a piece of music is a bridge between the world of inner experience and the world of external reality. And since it represents the crystallization of a moment in time, it is also a bridge between past and future. Upon such works of art and within such moments in time, composers focus all of their past experience, all of their creative capacities, and all of their present inspiration. The particular event known as the work of art, moreover, does not stand in isolation but is based upon the background of the sum total of experience, both individual and social. The more intense the inner life of the artist and the more vision concentrated into the given moment, the more meaningful will be the particular event that finds its expression in the work of art.

Through the eyes and ears of their artists, then, societies can see and hear aspects of their world they never saw or heard before. By training perceptions and sensitizing eyes and ears, a new and richer world is revealed to the individual observer and listener. The insights of poets and musicians thus become part of a larger world outlook for the individual, and part of a life more intrinsically satisfying.

Composers are as deeply sensitive to their environment as any of their fellow citizens. Robert Schumann wrote to his wife, "Everything touches me that goes on in the world—politics, literature, people. I think after my own fashion of everything that can express itself through music." As articulate members of their respective communities, composers—whether their language is direct or indirect, abstract or concrete—are interpreters of the individual, human, and social issues of their times.

Music moves its mountains slowly, yet it shapes the spirit of humanity as surely as any other force. This may not be open to proof or amenable to the same manner of adducing evidence that would satisfy an inquiry into the impact on human behavior of a mechanical invention like the cotton gin or the automobile. But belief in the truth of the proposition is an article of faith that is found not only among musicians; both Bach and Shakespeare are agreed on it, likewise Monteverdi and Socrates, and Beethoven and the fathers of the early church. Shakespeare marks for suspicion the person whose soul does not respond to music. This a musician can readily understand. A melody communicates a level of experience more immediate and basic than language, for words do not obtrude to distract by their demand for decoding. Composers past and present speak through the abstract inflections that underlie language, and hence their communications cross the borders of time and space and can be understood by all who listen attentively. To be deeply moved by the life experience of another is indeed a profound education for every human being.

Musical Styles

In order to communicate meaning, artists—whether they speak in a verbal, visual, or tonal vocabulary—must do so in a system of symbols, images, and conventions that are, at least for the most part, understood by those to whom the works are addressed. Composers live in the world of tone. Through their tonal perceptions they direct their moving materials, build their sonorous masses, and create their musical shapes. As they put together the sounds that reflect their experiences and reactions to the world, they must obviously do so in terms of a tonal language that their audience can understand.

As in learning one's native tongue, composers first learn the musical language of their cultural environment and, more specifically, the musical speech of their immediate predecessors. Upon reaching maturity as craftsmen and artists, they may have something new and unique to say that entails departures from past precedents. In the process of so doing, composers may find it necessary to add to the existing vocabulary, discover new grammatical syntaxes, and devise new musical symbols that correspond more exactly to their intentions.

The inherited language, the personal usage of that system, the chosen vocabulary, and the conventions composers add to the common currency all add up to a *style*. By definition, then, style is the totality of the symbols, the entire aesthetic system, by which a composer communicates conceptions of order and meaning. It is thus through style that composers make clear their attitudes and comments toward the world around and within them.

When a musical style becomes socially established and universally accepted as it did in the latter part of the 18th century, the demand for new works becomes such that composers can hardly keep up with it. Hence one contemplates with a sense of awe the unparalleled creative activity of a Haydn and a Mozart. During the period when they were composing, a common bond existed between composer and public, so that the music of churches, salons, concerts, and dance halls all spoke in essentially the same language. Even the street musicians of Vienna played the melodies of Gluck, Haydn, and Mozart. Yet within the framework of a common musical language, composers speak in accents that are their own.

Music and History

Music is a many-faceted art, and at various times it presents different aspects to the world. The notion of progress should be promptly dispelled. No one era, such as the romantic period, is necessarily better than any other, but it is certainly different. There is, in fact, no all-embracing art of music, but rather as many musics are there are social orders, historical periods, centers of population, and composers of strong individuality, each speaking a different language with a different syntax, vocabulary, and style. Musical systems rise and fall, come and go; and since there is nothing fixed or immutable about them, a historical and cultural context must be postulated.

By a study of the history of these styles and their common conventions, the listener can master the languages of the musical past sufficiently to establish at least partial understanding. Interpreting the music of the past, of course, presents many problems. Some listeners will inevitably feel a closer kinship with one period than with another. Even so, many subtle meanings of the past will inescapably elude the contemporary ear. One cannot fully hear music from a period of pure melody, such as early medieval music, with ears accustomed to lush orchestral sonorities and rich harmonic accompaniments. Much of the pure, otherworldly beauty of Gregorian melodies, however, is still discernible if the ear is reoriented to this earlier style. Similarly, it would be impossible to hear properly the music of Bach and Mozart without 18th-century ears. Although much of its inner radiance transcends the centuries, some of its meaning is lost unless it is understood as closely as possible within its original cultural context.

The history of the arts is the record of the establishment of types of order. Every individual and every society has a conception of the universal environment and the position of the individual in the general social order. Within a given society, the creative artist conceives order in appropriate symbols and images and gives articulate expression to them. The art that results may be in essential agreement with the established system, may be predicated on some values of the past that the artist seeks to preserve, or may be dedicated to overthrowing the existing order and bringing about a new era. In political life there are those who seek to uphold traditional values, those content to swim along with the tide of their times, and those who want to strike out in new directions. So also in music there are composers who represent various shades of artistic opinion. J. S. Bach, for instance, was a staunch conservative who sought to preserve the values of the grand universal polyphonic style in the face of a movement toward harmonic writing and delicate personal nuances of expression. Mozart, for his part, was quite content to speak in the accents of his own time; and, without fundamentally changing the established language, he contributed his many matchless masterpieces to musical literature. Then there are the revolutionaries—Monteverdi, Wagner, and Schoenberg, for instance—who formulated new theories and forged new musics based on new concepts, and in the process awakened and aroused their contemporaries.

Just as the visual arts can present the visage of a period through portraits, costumes, gestures, attitudes, and scenes from daily life, so music, by dipping deep into the wellsprings of emotional, psychological, and intellectual experience, can also yield understanding of an age. The history of songs reflects the joys and sorrows, the fortunes and misfortunes of the people who sang them. The history of the dance reveals the inner rhythms as well as the outer steps and gestures that mirror the strivings and goals of the individuals and groups who perform them. The history of the lyric stage, including opera, can become a rich source of commentary on the conceptions a society had of itself, its deeds, its manners, and its characteristic attitudes.

The music of a period tells not only of its harmonies but also of its conflicts. In epochs of oppression, music represents the passionate outpouring of the human heart. In periods of religious revival, it sings out with resounding declarations of faith. In ages of reason, it reflects the logical processes of well-ordered minds. In interludes of social upheaval, it rings with revolutionary anthems.

There are those who feel strongly that history is irrelevant to a particular piece of music, because the musical work is essentially a personal document—a record of how one person felt and reacted. In this view all music is self-expression; it is personal autobiography rather than social commentary. There is, to be sure, a measure of truth in this viewpoint. But Lincoln was correct when he said, "No man can escape history," and a personal record becomes universally meaningful only when it reveals more than the individual who created it.

Music history is a special kind of history. It is not a record of the political reasons for a war or of the points of doctrine underlying a religious dispute; but it is a record of how one human being felt during the course of that war, or of one person's reaction to a religious controversy.

Some individuals are by nature more sensitive and more articulate than others. When the depth of their feeling is transmitted through sound, it becomes a measure of the emotions of many of their inarticulate contemporaries, for whom they may be said to speak. Thus Beethoven as a composer may be considered a more profound spokesman for the ideals of his age than either Napoleon or Metternich as statesmen. And Bach may well provide as deep an insight into the faith cherished by the Protestant community as Luther does in his capacity as theologian.

Music must thus be accorded its rightful place in the history of ideas, and when seen in the light of the larger rhythms of human history, its levels of meaning acquire new horizons, new depths, new dimensions. Romain Rolland's manifesto, *On the Place of Music in General History,* is as appropriate today as when it first appeared in the early years of the 20th century:

> Music adapts itself to all conditions of society. It is a courtly art, an art of faith and fighting, an art of affectation and princely pride, an art of the salon, the lyric expression of revolutionaries; and it will be the voice of the democratic societies of the future, as it was the voice of the aristocratic societies of the past. No formula will hold it. It is the song of centuries and the flower of history; its growth pushes upward from the griefs as well as from the joys of humanity.

CHAPTER

6

Ancient Styles

THE GLORY THAT WAS Greece was never more glowing than in the great 5th century B.C., the period that saw the building and carving of the architectural and sculptural marvels on the Athenian Acropolis (Fig. 6-1). High on this hill with its Propylaea gateway, the Athenians could behold the gleaming temples that honored their deities, especially Athena, the goddess of wisdom and patron of the city. Below, on one side, was the Agora, which served as the marketplace and forum where Socrates taught. On the other side was the Theater of Dionysus, where the eager populace experienced works by great playwrights that mirrored their world in poetry, song, and dance. At their annual dramatic festival they chose the prize play by their applause (Fig. 6-2).

Nearby were the gymnasia, where athletes were trained to compete in the Olympic games. In ancient Greek educational practice, however, sound bodies were of no avail unless they were controlled by sound minds. So instruction in the arts formed the basis of the curriculum. In Greek tradition, the sun god Apollo was the patron of a family of nine maidens known as the Muses, who personified the various arts and sciences. Clio stood for history, Thalia and Melpomene for comedy and tragedy, Erato for lyric poetry, Terpsichore for dance, Urania for astronomy, Calliope, Euterpe, and Polyhymnia for various aspects of music and poetry. The traditional seven liberal arts, core of the later medieval and Renaissance university curricula, derive directly from this Greek concept.

According to tradition, Pythagoras' experiments with a vibrating string led to the discovery of the relationship of tones within the musical octave. Espe-

Chronology (all dates B.C.)

PHILOSOPHERS AND THEORISTS	
Pythagoras	c. 582–c. 507
Heraclitus	544–483
Socrates	469–399
Plato	427–347
Aristotle	384–322
Aristoxenus	c. 321 (active)
Euclid	c. 300 (active)
Archimedes	c. 287–231
Lucretius	98–55
Virgil	70–19
Quintilian	A.D. 35–c. 95

DRAMATISTS	
Aeschylus	525–456
Sophocles	496–406
Euripides	480–406
Aristophanes	c. 444–380

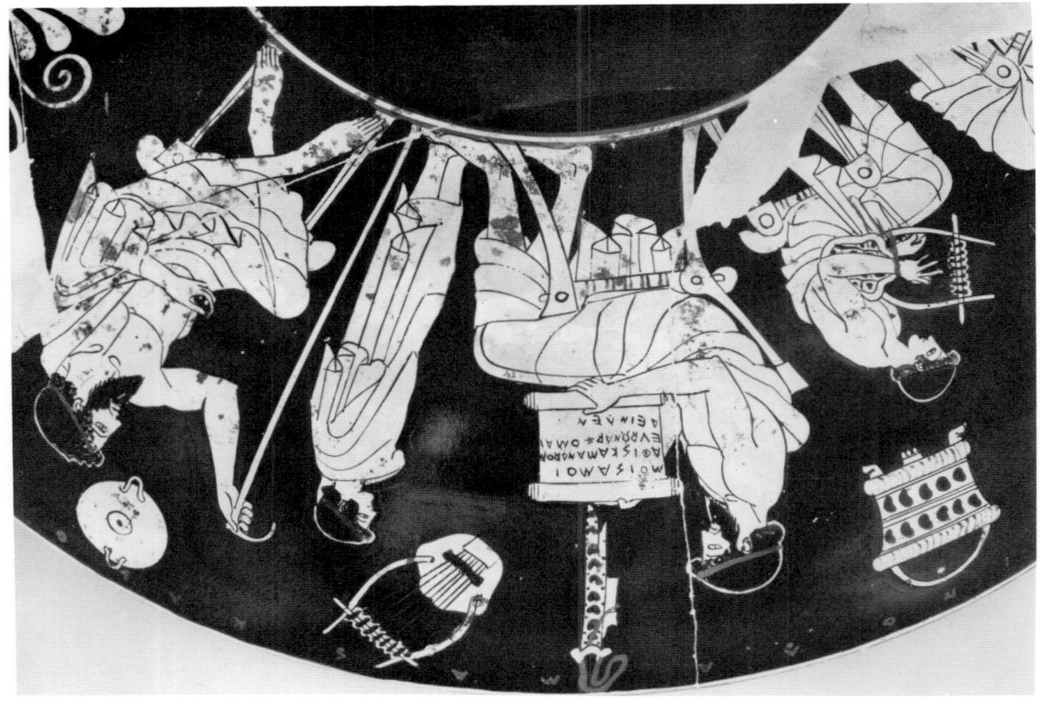

Douris. *Instruction in Music and Grammar in an Attic School.* Red-figured painting on exterior of a kylix, c. 470 B.C. *Courtesy of the Antikenmuseum Berlin, Staatliche Museen Preussischer Kulturbesitz, West Germany.*

cially important were the intervals of the fifth and the fourth (see pp. 457–58). This revelation of the mathematical relationship of musical tones was considered to be the key that would unlock the secrets of the universe. At the end of his *Republic,* Plato recounts the vision of the warrior Er, who was slain in battle but later returned to life to tell of seeing all the heavenly bodies moving together to form one harmony, "and round about, at equal intervals, there is another band, three in number, each sitting upon her throne: these are the Fates, daughters of Necessity, who accompany with their voices the harmony of the sirens—Lachesis singing of the past, Clotho of the present, Atropos of the future."

Greek Musical Instruments

On the more mundane level were the Greek musical instruments: the *syrinx* (panpipes), the stringed *lyre* with its larger cousin, the *kithara,* and the double wind instrument, the *aulos* (Fig 6-3). All were thought to have mythological origins. The nature-demigod Pan, with his goat's horns and hoofs, pursued and was spurned by the wood nymph Syrinx (Fig. 6-4). She fled from him, calling for help from her friends the water nymphs, who transformed her into a tuft of reeds just as Pan was about to seize and embrace her. When he breathed a sad sigh over them, he heard lovely sounds. So he cut some of the reeds of varying lengths, bound them together, and fashioned the instrument he named for her. Ever since, these panpipes have been associated with the bucolic, pastoral aspect of Greek life.

Legend has it that the lyre was invented by Hermes, the fleet-footed messenger of the gods. It was originally fashioned from a tortoise-shell sounding board with a wooden frame attached to hold four stretched strings. Later it

Figure 6-1. Acropolis, Athens, 5th century B.C. View from southwest. Photograph by N. Stovpnapas.

Figure 6-2. Polyclitus the Younger. Theater, Epidaurus, c. 350B.C. Courtesy of the Greek Tourist Office, New York.

became a full-octave instrument associated with Apollo, god of healing and prophecy, of poetry and music, of light and truth. In the educational systems of both Plato and Aristotle, the lyre and the larger kithara were associated with ethical ideals and with a body of melodies thought to uphold the rational element of universal order, as well as the building of human character and the control of emotions. The kithara was also used as the reference instrument for theoretical discussions of music, just as the piano is today.

The discovery of the oboelike aulos, a reed instrument played both singly and in pairs, was attributed to Athena, goddess of wisdom. As she played it to the apparent delight of the Olympians, Eros (Cupid) is said to have laughed, watching her puff out her cheeks to make the instrument sound. Considering such an appearance beneath her dignity, she threw it away and it landed on earth, where mortals might blow away at it. Later it became associated with the worship of Dionysus and was used in the wild, orgiastic Bacchanalian rites of that god of wine and revelry. Since Dionysus was also the patron god of the theater, the aulos had an honored place in all dramatic performances. It is also important to remember that such words as *music, drama, scenery, rhythm, harmony, melody, orchestra,* and *symphony* are all of Greek origin.

Music in Greek Religion

Greek music was closely associated with the religious experience. The worship of the Olympian deities always included hymns sung to the accompaniment of the lyre, the instrument sacred to Apollo. Side by side with the dominant religion, however, were certain secret cults. The Eleusinian mysteries, for instance, flourished among farming communities as they celebrated the change of seasons. When Persephone, daughter of the earth goddess Demeter, descended into the underworld, it was wintertime and the earth was cold and bare. In spring and summer, the rites celebrated her redemption and restoration to the visible world. Such rustic religious rites were closely identified with the fertility and cultivation of the soil. The cult also promised the initiates a more significant afterlife in the Isles of the Blest where the soul could rest from earthly labors and dwell in light rather than in the murky darkness of the Homeric Hades, as projected in the Olympian religion.

More widespread among all classes were the Orphic mysteries, named after the mythical musician Orpheus and honoring Dionysus, god of wine and the hidden sexual urges of the human psyche, as principal deity. He personified the divine spark in human life, but he was also a mercurial god who escaped from his enemies the Titans by changing himself variously into the forms of a bull, lion, or panther. In its earliest forms, the rite of Dionysus involved the sacrifice of a bull, his sacred animal, so that devotees could drink of its blood and ingest its raw flesh. Such divine possession was thought to

Figure 6-3. Ludovisi Throne, showing the kithara and the aulos. Greek, early 5th century B.C. Courtesy of Gabinetto Fotografico Nazionale, Rome.

Figure 6-4. Syrinx (panpipes). Engraving by Arnold van Westerhout, in Bonanni, *Gabinetto Armonico,* 1723. Courtesy of the George Arents Research Library, Syracuse University, Syracuse, New York.

induce a state of ecstasy, literally a stepping out from the body, so that the soul could escape from its prison and attain union with the god himself, hear the music of the spheres, and become one with the infinite.

Later the attainment of ecstasy was induced by the "blood" of the grape, as embodied in wine. The Athenian playwright Euripides describes such a scene, led by Dionysus, in his drama *The Bacchae:*

Him of mortal mother born,
  Him in whom man's heart rejoices,
Girt with garlands and with glee,
First in Heaven's sovranty?
  For his kingdom, it is there,
  In the dancing and the prayer,
In the music and the laughter,
  In the vanishing of care,
And of all before or after;
In the God's high banquet, when
  Gleams the grape-blood, flashed to heaven:
Yea, and in the feasts of men
Comes his crowned slumber; then
  Pain is dead and hate forgiven!

The progressive refinement from animalism and drunken revelry is reflected in the mythic teachings of Orpheus, who held that ecstasy was to be reached through music, which had the power to move both the human soul and the universe itself. Still later, Pythagoras became a real-life reformer of the Orphic cult when he discovered the mathematical principles that formed the basis of the musical experience. Under his teachings Orphism evolved into the philosophically oriented Pythagorean brotherhood which counted Plato himself among its far-flung members. Music was woven into the fabric of the daily life of the Pythagoreans. As recounted by the Roman writer Quintilian in the 1st century A.D., "It was the undoubted custom of the Pythagoreans, when they woke from slumber, to rouse their spirits with the music of the lyre, that they might be more alert for action; and before they retired to rest, to soothe their minds by melodies from the same instrument, in order that all restlessness of thought might be lulled to orderly repose."

For Plato's part, he observed the musical implications inherent in the dialectical give-and-take process exemplified in his dialogues. And in the *Phaedo,* Socrates concludes that "Philosophy is the highest music."

Music and Drama

From all accounts, Greek music reached its highest development in connection with the drama. The great dramatists Aeschylus, Sophocles, and Euripides were also trained in the art and science of music, and the early copies of their plays contained indications of the pitch and mode for the intonation of the poetic lines. In the classical drama, immediately after the *prologue,* the *chorus* appeared in the *orchestra,* a circular area before the *proscenium,* or raised stage (Chart 6-1). Here the leader executed solo dances and songs while the remainder of the players joined in as a single unit or in groups. The chorus could be directed to move about rhythmically in dance steps or remain stationary. The role of the chorus throughout the play was to comment on the action as it unfolded and to provide lyrical interludes between the scenes. Greek drama thus included sequences of choral chanting and dancing, solo singing, and instrumental interludes. The nearest modern equivalent is the opera.

The only surviving fragment of this dramatic music is a small page of thin papyrus with many holes. It is a brief part of a chorus from Euripides' *Orestes,* first performed at Athens in 408 B.C. While it is too sketchy to allow us to form any major generalizations, it nevertheless reveals a coherent metrical pattern and an emotional tone consistent with one of the Greek modes.

Posterity has been more fortunate with the discovery of a short but complete song together with its notation, preserved on a gravestone from the 1st century A.D. It is a touching tribute from Seikolos to the departed Euterpe, with the theme "Eat, drink and be merry, for tomorrow we die." The form

CHART 6-1. GREEK THEATER

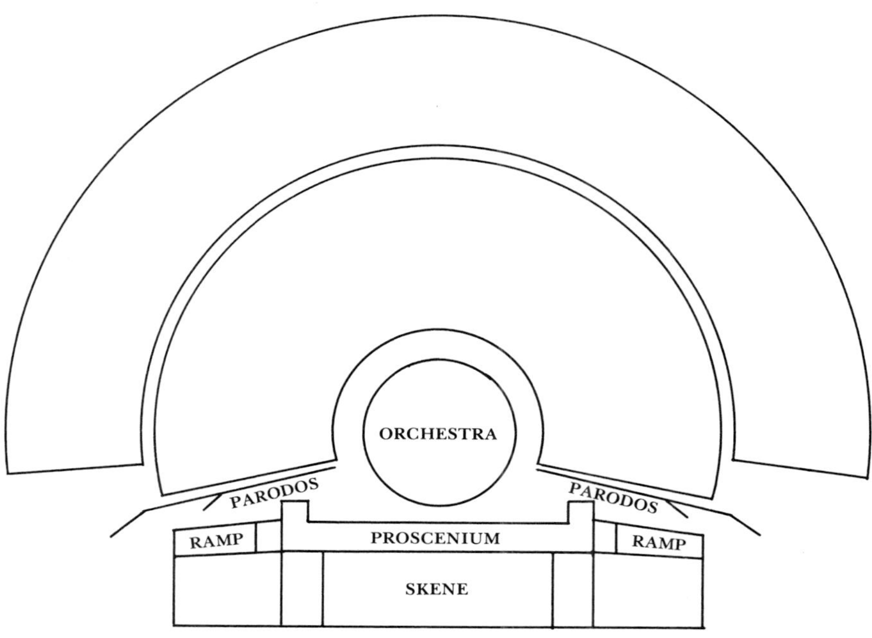

is that of a popular type of drinking song known as a *skolion,* written in the Phrygian mode with the upper and lower notes stretching from the E above middle C to the octave above. The tone that recurs most often is the mid-range A, which becomes a kind of tonal center (Ex. 6-1).

Example 6-1. Skolion of Seikolos. 1st century A.D.

Greek Scales and Modes

From surviving fragments, literary accounts, and musical treatises, it is possible to conclude that Greek music was *monophonic* (single-line) music. When two or more voices or instruments performed together, they did so in unison or at the octave. When Greek writings mention harmony, they refer not to the modern system of combining notes vertically into chords, but to the linear relationship of tones to each other. Plato said in the *Republic,* "Melody is composed of three things, the words, the harmony [by which is meant the relationship of the successive melodic intervals], and the rhythm."

The Greeks had a highly developed system of scales and tunings. The

CHART 6-2. TETRACHORDS

basic unit was a sequence of four notes called the *tetrachord* (Chart 6–2). In normal practice, two tetrachords were placed together to form a scale of seven or eight notes. The tetrachords always encompassed the interval of the perfect fourth, but the two notes within could change, sometimes forming intervals that are not familiar to our ears. The Greeks were trained to be sensitive to intervals smaller than those in common use today, and intervals spanning a quarter-tone and smaller were fairly common.

There were three ways of ordering the intervals in a tetrachord: *enharmonic, chromatic,* and *diatonic.* While much was written of a detailed theoretical nature by the ancients, the Greeks did not specify exactly how the three variants of a tetrachord worked in actual musical practice.

While the theory and the scalar modes do not look particularly complicated in terms of today's harmonic traditions, the picture is made aurally interesting when we remember that the inner notes of the tetrachords (the blackened-in notes) were not of fixed pitch and could be tuned to enharmonic, chromatic, or diatonic intervals as desired. And, since the Greeks did not have harmony as we know it today, individual tones and intervals carried more meaning and substance than they do in later, more complicated musical textures.

Ethical Implications

Since music was based on a system of mathematical ratios, it was considered by the Greeks to be a revelation of the divine order of the universe. In the macrocosmic sense, music mirrored the movement of the planets in their orbits, while on the microcosmic plane it was believed to reflect the motions of the human soul as an entity that could be brought into harmony with the world soul. Music therefore had the quality of *ethos,* or ethical character; and if properly applied to educational and human affairs, it could create a harmonious society. Socrates, Plato, and Aristotle all accorded music a high place in their educational systems.

The Greeks assigned geographical names to their architectural orders and to their music scales. Their earliest temples, for instance, were constructed in the Doric manner according to the ancient name of the northern province —Doria—from which the original inhabitants of the lower peninsula came. The Ionic order derived from the later Greek settlements in Asia Minor, while the Corinthian was named after the people of the city of Corinth. Likewise the modes of music bore the names of the regions where the scale tunings and the types of melody originated. The Dorian mode, associated with stringed instruments and their precise tuning, produced serious, sober, and restrained melodies. Hence it was favored by the philosophers for the education of the young. The Ionian and Lydian, by way of contrast, were considered to be soft and sensuous. The Phrygian, associated as it was with the less stable pitch of the aulos, was looked upon as wild, overly emotional, even orgiastic.

As the system developed, a pattern of seven different modal scales took shape, as seen in Chart 6-3. The Dorian mode is shown on the left, beginning on the note E. Moving upward, the Phrygian starts on F-sharp, the Lydian on G-sharp, and so on up to D-sharp for the Hypolydian. On the right, each of these modes is seen using the tones that result from starting on different notes transferred within the available E to E octave of the kithara. Most melodies were sung or played within the span of an octave. In the center was the *mese* (shown in the chart as an open note) that functioned as the note around which the melody flowed. Each of the seven modes is set out as a scale of seven notes. The Dorian mode was considered the most "pure" and important of the seven modes. Of the other modes, the Lydian and Hypodorian correspond approximately to our major and minor scales. Only these two modes were to remain from the centuries-long modal tradition when the modern harmonic system settled into place during the 17th century.

Roman Music

If the surviving fragments of Greek music are few, those from the Roman Republic and Empire are virtually nonexistent. In the popular field, traditional melodies apparently were passed orally from singer to singer, just as dances were transmitted from player to player without being written down. But the Greek system of pitch notation was apparently still practiced at least up to Hadrian's time, in the early 2nd century A.D. Any manuscripts after that have either disappeared or were destroyed by early Christian iconoclasts.

So for accounts of Roman musical life it is necessary to turn to literary documents and pictorial evidence. These sources show clearly that the Romans enjoyed a lively musical life. On the popular level of experience there were strolling street musicians, professional entertainers who sang at dinner parties and banquets, choral and instrumental music for theatrical performances, and large bands that played in the Colosseum and other sports arenas. On such occasions hundreds of players were said to have taken part, some performing on "lyres as big as chariots." In educated upper-class circles, the Greek tradition continued to hold sway, and the emperors Nero, Hadrian, and Antoninus Pius were reputedly skilled on the kithara and hydraulic organ.

CHART 6-3. THE GREEK MODES

The Classical Heritage

Since the evidence of actual ancient music is so limited, the classical heritage remains largely a legacy of theories and ideas about music, its purpose, and its organization. The comprehensiveness and clarity of Greek musical thought has secured for it a prominent place in all subsequent periods. Greek musical theory was expounded and interpreted in medieval musical treatises, and Greek concepts of music were taught regularly in the universities. In the late Renaissance when a Florentine group attempted to revive dramatic music, they cited ancient Greek drama as a precedent to justify their innovations. In the same era Monteverdi cited Greek musical aesthetics when writing about the principles behind his method of writing madrigals and operas. French baroque drama was replete with Greek gods and heroes, and its forms deferred to Greco-Roman traditions. The operatic reforms Gluck felt obliged to introduce in the 18th century were based directly on an interpretation of Aristotle's observations in the *Poetics*.

These reforms, innovations, and movements are usually labeled *neoclassical,* since the vitality and universality of Greco-Roman thought have compelled each generation, each century, each period, each style to come to terms in some way with the classical heritage. In one case it might be complete acceptance; in another, a topical modification or even an outright rejection; in still another, it becomes a convenient point of departure. In this fashion Greco-Roman ideas and ideals remain a potent intellectual and aesthetic force to this day.

CHAPTER

7

Early Christian and Medieval Styles

THE HISTORY OF WESTERN music effectively begins with the Christian era. At first the Roman followers of Christ had to worship in secret, and Rome's extensive network of subterranean catacombs is ample evidence that the early church began in fact as an underground religion. The Roman emperors as upholders of law and order cast a wary eye on the new cult, just as they did on other mystery religions and Judaism. Some were more tolerant than others, but none was prepared to let the situation get out of hand. When the Roman senator Pliny the Younger reported on the Christians in a letter to Emperor Trajan in the early years of the 2nd century A.D., he wrote: "On certain days they get together before sunrise and sing songs to Christ as if he were God."

With the gradual weakening of Roman power, the growth of Christianity continued until it was recognized as one of several approved state religions in the Edict of Milan, promulgated in the year 313. Eventually various political and economic disasters, as well as threats from barbarian invaders, made Rome's situation so precarious that Emperor Constantine moved his capital and government to the fortified Near Eastern city of Byzantium, which he proclaimed to be Nova Roma (New Rome). His successors renamed it Constantinople in his honor, and that segment of the Roman Empire endured until the year 1453, when it fell to the Ottoman Turks, who renamed it Istanbul. In the West, the decline of Rome continued until its fall to the Ostrogothic invaders under Odoacer and Theodoric, who established a powerful kingdom in the north of Italy at Ravenna. Only briefly was the Empire reunited under

Chronology

RULERS (DATES OF REIGN)

Nero, emperor	r. 54–68
Trajan, emperor	r. 98–116
Hadrian, emperor	r. 117–138
Antoninus Pius, emperor	r. 138–161
Constantine, emperor	r. 323–337
Odoacer, king	r. 476–493
Theodoric, king	r. 493–526
Justinian, East Roman emperor	r. 527–565
Gregory I, pope	r. 590–604
Charlemagne, Carolingian king	r. 768–814
William I, "The Conqueror"	r. 1066–1087
Eleanor, queen of Aquitaine	r. 1152–1173
Richard I, "The Lionhearted"	r. 1189–1199
Thibaut IV, king of Navarre	r. 1201–1253
Clement V, French pope	r. 1305–1314
John XXII, pope	r. 1316–1334

WRITERS, THEORISTS, AND PHILOSOPHERS

Pliny the Younger	61–113
Ambrose	c. 340–397
Jerome	c. 342–420
Augustine	354–430
Boethius	c. 480–c. 524
Benedict	480–543
Cassiodorus	c. 485–c. 580
Guido of Arezzo	c. 991–after 1033
Odo of Cluny	878–942
Thomas Aquinas	c. 1225–1274
Dante Alighieri	1265–1321
Petrarch (Francesco Petrarca)	1304–1374
Gervais du Bus	1313–1338 (active)

MUSICAL FIGURES

Notker Balbulus	c. 840–912
Wolfram von Eschenbach	1170–1220 (active)
Walther von der Vogelweide	c. 1170–c. 1230
Léonin	c. 1163–1201 (active)
Pérotin	c. 1200 (active)
Adam de la Hale	c. 1245–c. 1288
Franco of Cologne	c. 1260 (active)
Philippe de Vitry	1291–1361
Guillaume de Machaut	c. 1300–1377

Matteo. Tympanum, Portico della Gloria, Cathedral of Santiago de Compostela, Spain, 1168–88.

Justinian the Great. Thereafter East and West, except for a few periods of intermittent unity, were more often than not at odds. They would permanently go their separate ways in the Great Schism of 1054, leaving a Greek East and a Latin West.

Before these cataclysmic events, however, Emperor Constantine sponsored an ambitious building program in Rome to accommodate the rapidly growing numbers of the Christian population. Four great basilica complexes were erected, the largest and grandest of which was St. Peter's in the Vatican, the legendary site of the first apostle's martyrdom. In turn, this monumental building became the focal center of Western Christendom. As the power of the Western emperors declined and eventually disappeared, the great structure and power of the papacy came to rule the far-flung centers of Western Christianity and arbitrated all questions of faith and morals. It was also from Rome that missionaries, like the apostles of old, set forth to preach the Gospel northward into France, Germany, England, and Ireland; westward to Spain and Portugal; southward to Africa; and to the various Near Eastern provinces. The Eastern Orthodox church, however, managed to maintain its independence.

Early Christian Worship

The earliest Christian rites were centered around a communal meal in the manner of the Jewish Passover seder. In the Christian sense this was a reenactment of Jesus' last supper with his disciples, when he gave his blessing and broke the bread, saying: "Take this and eat; this is my body." Then, after offering thanks to God, he poured the wine into a cup, saying: "Drink from it, all of you. For this is my blood, the blood of the covenant, shed for many for the forgiveness of sins" (Matt. 26:26–28). The resemblance of this ceremony to the Orphic mysteries and other cults is clear. The idea was that the ingestion of the divine flesh and blood by the worshipers would renew the power of the god in human life (see pp. 76–79).

Early Christian worship gradually crystallized into the celebration of the *mass,* which was then made up of readings from the scriptures, a homily or sermon, the offering of bread and wine by the faithful, prayers of thanksgiving, and finally the communion ceremony. Music in the service was at first confined to the intoning of psalms and the congregational singing of hymns. Any music for its own sake or for pure enjoyment was frowned upon by the stern early church fathers as self-indulgent and sinful. It gradually came to be recognized as a powerful force when channeled for higher purposes in the service of the church and in the praise of God.

Over time the text of the mass came to be sung by the priest or leader in *plainchant.* Plainchant was monophonic and unaccompanied, since in early times the church forbade the use of instruments in worship—church leaders being well aware of the worldly power of instruments to excite the passions. Vocal music, however, received support from several influential church fathers, who realized the power of such utterance to carry the listener toward a divine vision. Saint Augustine wrote in his treatise on music: "When I am moved, not with the singing but with the meaning of that which is sung, I acknowledge the great power of chant. I am inclined to allow the old usage of singing in the church, so that, by the delight taken in at the ears, the weaker minds be roused up into some feeling of devotion."

Gradually, church music was accepted as standard practice, even though its forms and styles varied widely. They included the Byzantine and Syriac rites in the Eastern church, the Egyptian and Alexandrian in North Africa, the Gallican in France, the Celtic in Britain and Ireland, the Hispano-Gallican and Mozarabic in Spain, the Ambrosian in Milan and northern Italy, and the monastic usage in Rome. Church music was transmitted from one center to another largely by oral tradition. This meant that it passed through many voices and that many changes were made along the way. Until early forms of notation began to appear around the mid-9th century, there was no record of exactly how the earliest church music actually sounded.

Outstanding among the early popes was Gregory the Great, whose name is given to a style of music and a collection of monophonic melodies known as *Gregorian chant.* Tending more to strength of organization than to composition, Gregory did much to promote the unification of diverse practices and to standardize the performance of the liturgy. Up to the 7th century, each territory of Christendom had its own mode of performance, its own traditions of texts for worship, and its own melodies for the chant. Gregory supported the training of choir singers in the Roman *Schola cantorum* (school for singers), who could then be sent as teachers to churches and monasteries all over Europe as a step toward unifying worship.

From the time of Gregory to about the year 1000, when the order of the mass and the sequence of the church calendar year were generally settled, a number of liturgical anthologies called *antiphonaries* or *antiphonals* were compiled in European religious centers. These contained texts assigned appropriately throughout the church year, and by the 10th century musical settings were included. The modern publication that provides a reduction of these service forms still sung in some monastic institutions is called the *Liber usualis* (*Book for Common Use*).

Singers sent out from the Schola cantorum in Rome eventually brought about near-universal conformity of the liturgy and music. The process was chronicled during the reign of Charlemagne, early in the 9th century:

> The most pious Charlemagne celebrated Easter, and on the day of the Paschal feast a dispute arose between the Roman and Gallic singers. The

Gauls said that they sang better and more beautifully than the Romans. The Romans said that they articulated the cantilenas most expertly since they had been taught by Pope Gregory himself, and accused the Gauls of singing corruptly and destroying the pure cantilena.

His Lordship the most pious Charlemagne said to his singers, "Which is purer, the living fountain or its streams flowing in the distance?" They all answered that the fountain as the head and source is the purer.

Then His Lordship Charlemagne said, "Return to the fountain of St. Gregory, since you have manifestly corrupted the ecclesiastical cantilena." Thereupon, Charlemagne requested from the pope singers who would correct France in singing.

Practically speaking, plainchant was written, codified, prepared, and performed under fairly strict rules. It was single-line music sung in unison, like all ancient vocal music. An early system of musical staff writing appeared around the year 1000, after a long and complicated history of inexact musical notation (see Plate IV). It had four lines, rather than the more modern five, and the notes that were placed upon it were not standardized. Many scribes produced notation in squares—easily made with a single stroke of a wide-cut quill pen. While this notation gave a more accurate idea of pitch, it was still only a vague indicator of time values. In any case, performance of the chant must have been based more on the rhythms of the text as spoken than on a metrical system of set values. Since the flow of the text was of primary importance, the rhythmic pulse was irregular. Rhythmic vitality came from within, not from without as in modern notation, where the musical flow results from regular beats governed by the bar line.

In the setting of text, plainchant was syllabic, neumatic, or melismatic. In *syllabic chant,* each syllable of text was set to one note, so that an ample amount of text could be performed in a short period of time (Ex. 7-1a).

Example 7-1. Three types of plainchant.

7-1a. Syllabic chant.

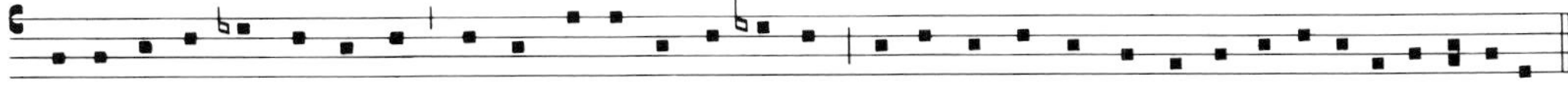

Ae-ter-ne re-rum con-di-tor, Noc-tem di-em-que qui re-gis, Et tem-po-rum das tem-po-ra, Ut al-le-ves fa-sti-di-um:

In *neumatic chant,* some syllables of text were set with groupings of two to five notes. This approach allowed for musical decoration and the highlighting of special words (Ex. 7-1b).

7-1b. Neumatic chant.

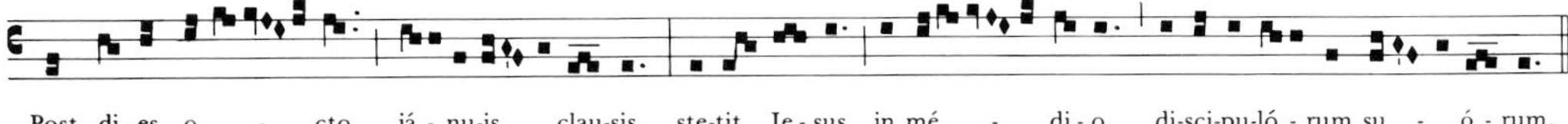

Post di-es o - cto, já - nu-is clau-sis, ste-tit Je-sus in mé - di-o di-sci-pu-ló - rum su - ó - rum,

Melismatic chant was a style suggesting an outburst of spiritual joy, often occurring on such words as *alleluia.* The "ah" syllables might be set to very long decorative passages—sometimes dozens of notes—called *melismas.* It is believed that this ornate singing technique was a carryover from synagogue practice, where the cantor improvised extended, wordless decorated melodies of praise (Ex. 7-1c).

7-1c. Melismatic chant.

Chanting of the psalms occupied a large part of the proper of the mass; both of the two accepted methods followed a statement-and-answer pattern. In *responsorial psalmody,* the priest began chanting the psalm, to which a choir of men and boys responded. In *antiphonal psalmody,* the choir split into two groups, alternately singing the verses of the psalm. The adjective *antiphonal* derives from the early Christian practice of dividing the congregation for alternate chanting; it remains in the vocabulary of church music to this day. It is used to describe the regular alternation of two performing groups, choral and/or instrumental.

In the late 4th century, Ambrose excited congregational interest by encouraging parishioners to sing hymns and antiphonal responses, but as the centuries wore on, the active role of the congregation in the celebration of the mass slowly waned. Gradually, professionally trained choirs—most often monks or minor clergy—began to represent the congregation. This allowed music to attain higher polish in performance. It also inspired composers to write more complex and interesting compositions than could be performed by an untrained laity.

THE MASS AND DIVINE OFFICE

The *ordinary* of the mass contains the core of prayers and statements of belief central to the Roman Catholic faith. These texts are normally included in every mass, solid and unchanging. The *proper* contains those sections of the mass that may vary each day. It is made up of prayers and Bible readings appropriate to the seasons and the special feasts of the church year. Composers made musical settings of the ordinary most often, since it was performed daily.

Five sections of the ordinary were normally sung, while the others were recited. The first and last are pleas for mercy, the second and fourth, statements of joy and praise of God. The central section, the Credo, is a confession of Christian beliefs.

1. *Kyrie eleison* (Lord have mercy) is a threefold call for mercy, the shortest text of the ordinary. It is also the only part to remain in Greek.
2. *Gloria* (Glory) begins with words from the New Testament book of Luke (2:14), recording the birth of Christ: "Glory on high, and, on earth, peace to men of good will." The text continues with a litany of intercession and praise.
3. *Credo* (I believe) is the creed of basic beliefs as codified at Constantine's Council of Nicea.
4. *Sanctus* (Holy) and *Benedictus* (Blessed) derive from Hebrew prayers. The threefold recitation of the word *Sanctus* at the beginning of the prayer parallels the repetition of the Hebrew word for holy, *Kodosh*, at the beginning of that prayer. The sanctus prayer is primarily an expression of praise.
5. *Agnus dei* (Lamb of God) calls upon Christ in his symbolic guise as sacrificial lamb to give mercy and peace to the supplicants who hear the mass. The Agnus dei follows the consecration of the bread and wine and precedes the celebration of the communion.

In addition to their commitment to celebrate the mass, those priests and monks who lived in monasteries also performed eight other services of prayer each day, known as the *Divine Office*, or Liturgical Hours (see below). These services took on new importance as a result of the rise of monastic centers. Increasing numbers of zealous religious converts and those seeking escape from the rigors of a strife-torn world joined newly forming religious communes and monasteries. The most important monastic order was founded by Saint Benedict. Rules for those entering the Benedictine order strictly followed the governing principle "work and pray." Prayer was heightened by singing, and the chanting of the Divine Office became standard in all monastic orders of the Western church from the 6th century.

THE DIVINE OFFICE

Matins	After midnight
Lauds	At daybreak
Prime (1st hour)	6 A.M.
Terce (3rd hour)	9 A.M.
Sext (6th hour)	Noon
None (9th hour)	3 P.M.
Vespers	Early evening
Compline	Before retiring

Music in Education

Formal education in medieval Europe necessarily took place under the aegis of the church. The clergy were among the few literate members of any community, while any learned man who held temporal power was church-trained and often a cleric as well.

Studies of the seven liberal arts (Fig. 7-1) were divided into two major areas, the trivium and quadrivium. The *trivium* was a three-part curriculum we might today label the humanities, for it consisted of grammar, rhetoric, and logic—loosely related to modern studies in linguistics, speech, and philosophy. Grammar was by far the most important of these subjects, encompassing reading, writing, and the study of literature. Scholars of rhetoric studied persuasive speech, and in the philosophical realm they mastered the art of logic and the dialectic mode of give-and-take argumentation.

The *quadrivium*, or four-part curriculum, encompassed the sciences: astronomy, geometry, arithmetic, and music. Music was not then studied as a practical performing art, but as mathematical and philosophical applications of the musical writings of Pythagoras, Plato, and other Greek writers.

Taking the Pythagorean definition of musical intervals according to mathematical ratios as a basis for discussion, university scholars speculated about number and proportion as both representative of and indigenous to the structure of the universe. One medieval writer noted that nothing in the Creator's plan was found to be exempt from musical discipline. In this point of view the writings of pagan Greek and Roman theorists complemented Christian religio-philosophical thinking without contradiction.

Music study in the medieval schools was based primarily on ancient Greek viewpoints as translated and interpreted by two Roman writers—the philosopher known as Boethius and the statesman-historian known as Cassiodorus. Both men served Theodoric, king of the Ostrogoths, who had conquered the Roman Empire in the West. Cassiodorus was secretary to the king and, at his bidding, wrote two important histories: one of the Goths, the other a chronological history of the world from Adam to Theodoric. Cassiodorus lived to age 93 and in later years founded two monasteries, in which he instituted the practice of having monks copy pagan and Christian manuscripts. This practice would continue for several centuries, building up a treasury of ancient literature. Cassiodorus was also instrumental in developing the scholastic curriculum from the Greek sources into the trivium and quadrivium.

Boethius was an aristocratic Roman who served Theodoric as the equivalent of prime minister. In his youth he had studied at the best schools in Athens and Rome, and he spent much time translating into Latin some of the great Greek treatises: mathematics by Nicomachus, mechanics by Archimedes, astronomy by Ptolemy, geometry by Euclid, and logic by Aristotle.

Boethius was read widely by medieval scholars and was well known for his views on music. Some of his writings revived Greek musical concepts, while others deliberated upon the idea of the senses versus reason—that which we hear against that which we know. He also discoursed on the use of arithmetical

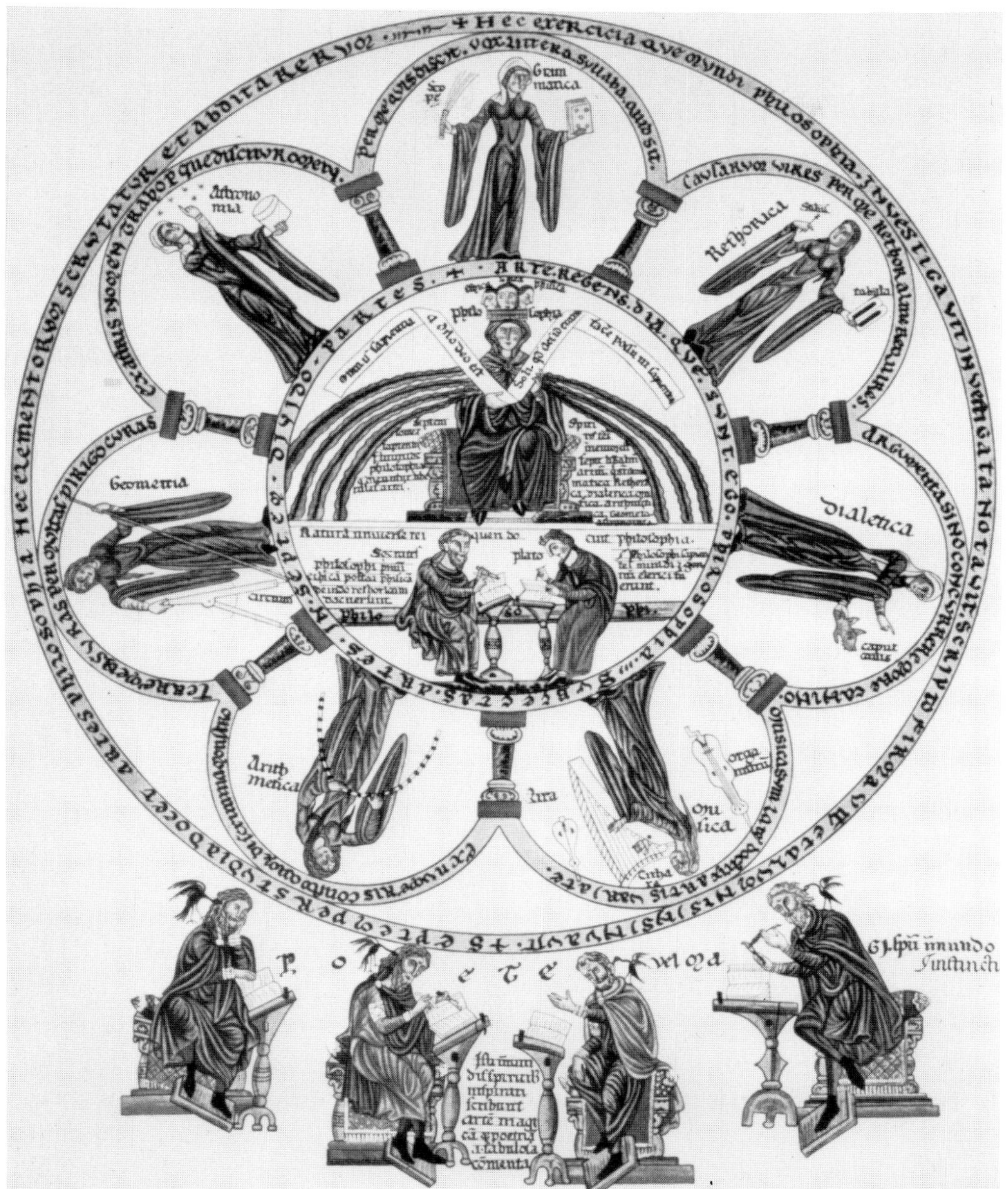

Figure 7-1. The seven liberal arts, from *Hortus Deliciarum,* c. 1180. Illuminated manuscript. By permission of the British Library, London.

methods to achieve musical pitches. Boethius defined three categories of music: *musica mundana* (cosmic music), based on the older Greek ideas of mathematical relationships observable in the behavior of the heavens and the earth; *musica humana* (the music of humanity), the ways in which cosmic musical relationships affect the body and soul of mankind; and *musica instrumentalis* (the realities of audible music), both instrumental and vocal—the music that we actually hear. This last reflects the same principles of acoustical ratios and mathematical laws as the music of the cosmos.

The fact that Boethius placed real music in the third or lowest position indicates that as an educator, he was interested in music more as knowledge and less as actual experience. To him the true musician was not the performer and composer, but the philosopher, theoretician, and critic.

Medieval Modes

The medieval modes, or scales, continued to carry the ancient Greek names, thus creating the connection between music and the Muses (Fig. 7-2); but there the similarity ended. There were eight ecclesiastical, or church, modes; and just as our modern system has two types of modes, or keys—major and minor—theirs had *authentic* and *plagal* modes (Chart 7-1). They were paired, much as are the modern relative major and minor keys. In medieval modes, the most important note was called the *final.* In the four authentic modes, the final was the first note of the scale. In the four plagal modes, it was in the center of the scale, somewhat like that of the Greek *mese.* The second most important note in the medieval mode was called the *reciting tone* or *dominant* (the designation used in present-day terminology). In most authentic modes it was a fifth above the final, as it is in modern seven-tone diatonic scales, while in the plagal modes it was always above the final, though its place varied with the mode.

While medieval modes theoretically had eight notes, it was convenient in practice for singers to think in a series of interlocking six-note scales called *hexachords.* In the 11th century the monk Guido of Arezzo systematized the syllables that we still use to learn the notes of the scale.

Using a hymn to Saint John, Guido assigned the first syllable of each half phrase to the hexachord pitches in ascending order (Ex. 7-2). The syllables that he used—*ut, re, mi, fa, sol* and *la*—are still used today, though we substitute the syllable *do* for *ut* and add *ti* as our seventh tone. Guido's system was used widely during the late medieval period, and a symbolic representation called the Guidonian Hand (Fig. 7-3) appeared in many medieval books on music theory. A syllable was assigned to each joint of the hand, and a student who had memorized it could look at his own hand as a reminder of the pattern of notes in a melody. The practice of using these syllables to memorize music was called *solmization.* It was especially valuable in training singers, who for the first time could develop sight-reading skills.

Until the 11th century, plainchant was a spiritual and intellectual experience for church congregations. It had no pulsating dance rhythms or jolly, rollicking tunes designed to express the worldly aspects of life. Its aim was to serve the inward, searching, contemplative, spiritual orientation of the lit-

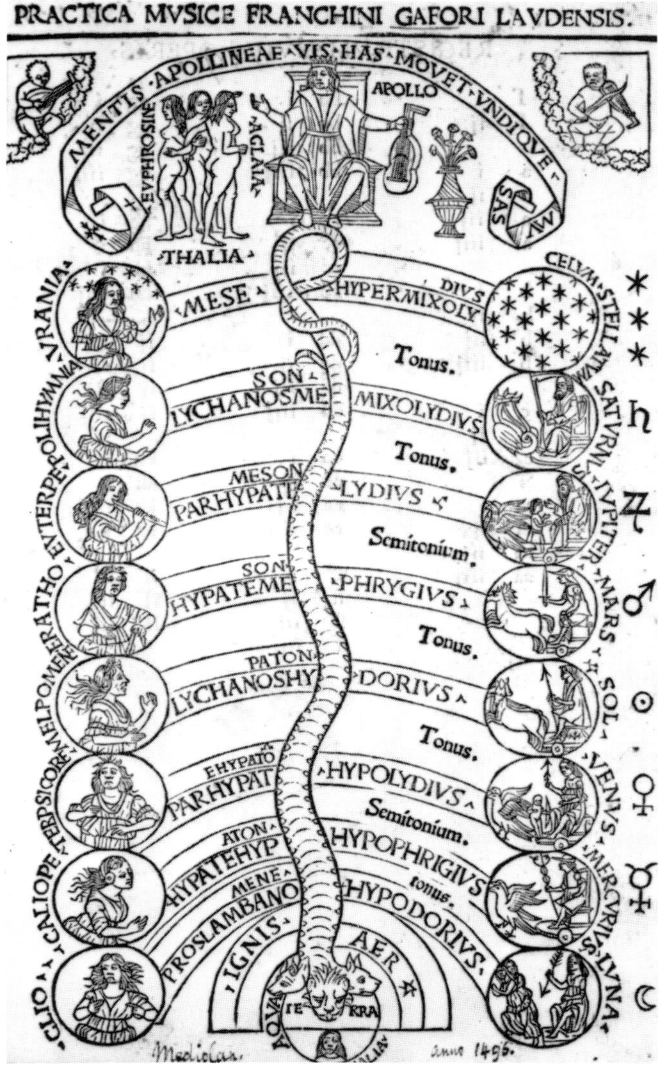

Figure 7-2. Muses, church modes, zodiac, illustrated in Franchinus Gaffurius, *Practica Musice,* 1496. Illuminated manuscript. By permission of the British Library, London.

Example 7-2. Guido of Arezzo. *Hymn to Saint John the Baptist.*

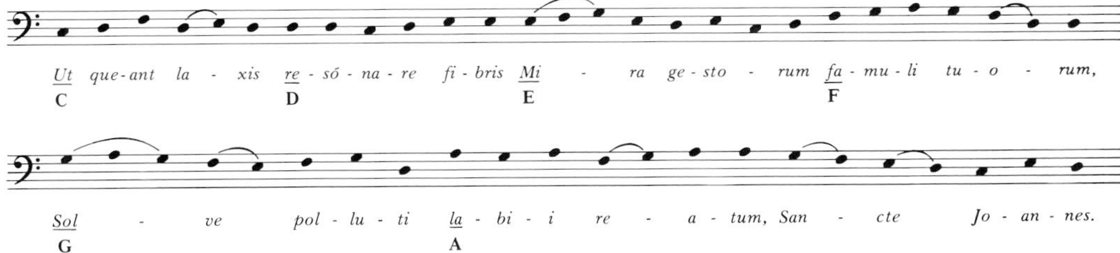

urgy. The church posited that chant was actually a direct gift from God, transmitted through certain chosen monks and clergy; therefore, it was by nature holy and otherworldly. It represented not the world beset by the realities of everyday living, but the world of the spirit, which promised a better life here-

CHART 7-1. THE MEDIEVAL MODES

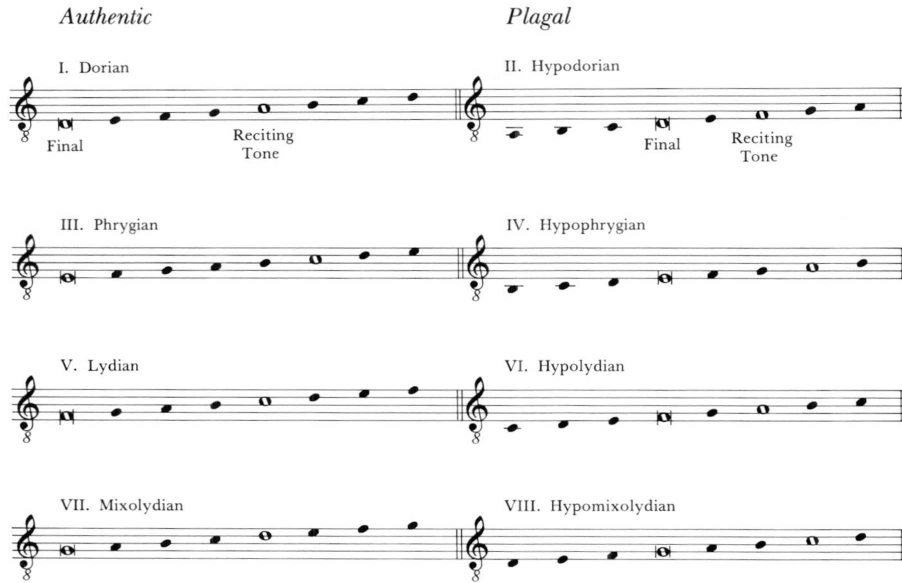

after. It allowed communicants to recommit themselves to the faith each time the sacred texts were intoned by priest, choir, or congregation.

The view of plainchant as otherworldly experience, God-given and sacrosanct, began to change sometime during the 10th century. There is always a dichotomy between the natural conservatism of organizations that represent power, in this case the church, and the individual creative needs of the artist, whether poet, painter, sculptor, architect, or musician. The continuing struggles between conservator and innovator have provided history with some of its most interesting events. The church's view of plainchant as holy, inviolable, and unalterable became a challenge to the creative talents of practicing musician-composers. The innovations that took place from the 10th to the 16th centuries produced major changes within the plainchant, vastly enriching the liturgy of the church in the process. Some of these inventive practices included *troping,* the interpolation of new phrases in the traditional Gregorian chants; *sequences,* which began as words to "fill up" the alleluia melismas and ended by becoming independent hymns; and *organum,* the addition of one or more vocal parts above and below the traditional chant melodies, which may be considered the earliest form of counterpoint.

The Trope

The official church position was that the traditional texts and melodies of plainchant were inviolable. This rule naturally became a major obstacle to the basic human urge for creative expression. Though some ecclesiastical eye-

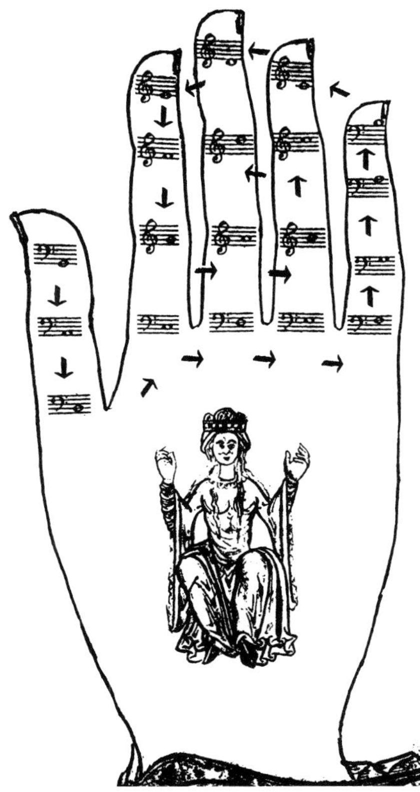

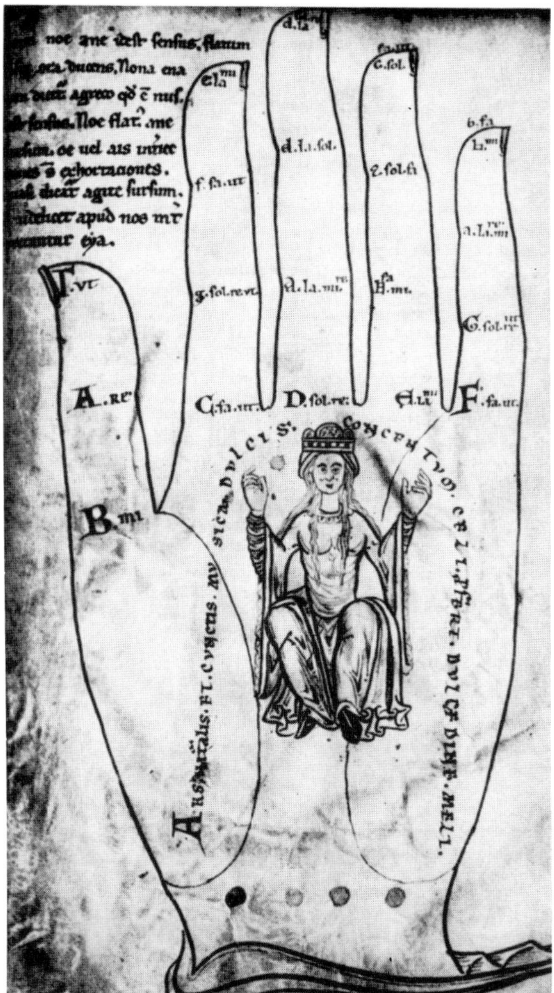

Figure 7-3. Guidonian hand with "Lady Music." Illustrated manuscript, 14th century. Modern notation shown above. Bavarian State Library, Munich. Courtesy of the George Arents Research Library, Syracuse University, Syracuse, New York.

brows were raised, intrepid musicians found an ingenious way around this roadblock that would preserve the old intact while making room for the new. This was the *trope,* a piece of music interpolated into the approved body of plainchant; the term is also used to describe the practice of making such interpolations. Troping became an extension and an enrichment of the chant both in the melodic and in the textual sense. The practice provided a creative outlet for both musicians and poets who had hitherto been shackled by tradition.

Besides amplifying and interpreting the meaning of established texts, the practice of troping was an especially satisfying way to make an individual contribution. Most tropes were applied to the ordinary of the mass, which was chanted every day before a congregation familiar with it. Troping spread rapidly throughout Europe, and these new musical and poetic insights into the religious experience gradually attained respectability. By the 10th century, troping had become so well ingrained in church tradition that all texts of the ordinary except the Credo were subject to interpolation.

The Sequence

Not surprisingly, the word *alleluia* was a favorite for troping, because of its long melismas, following earlier synagogue practice. Before the development of notation, the melismatic melodies were susceptible to improvisation. After much repetition, some of these long, improvised melismas became formalized in the ritual. With so many notes, expanded alleluias were often nearly impossible to remember. It has been theorized that words were therefore added to the melismas as an aid to memory. Words might even be divided, with texts inserted between the two parts, such as "Alle—[new text]—luia."

One of the most arresting characters of medieval music was the monk Notker Balbulus, known as the Stammerer, who was at the Swiss monastery of St. Gall in the late 9th century. He was quite famous as poet and teacher and for writing a history of the life of Charlemagne. In the introduction to a book of sequences, Notker tells his readers that when he was a young man, he often had to commit to memory extremely long melodies (melismas) which he often forgot. Later, a visiting monk came by, bringing his antiphonary, in which he had fitted new verses onto some of the alleluia melismas.

What Notker was describing was his discovery of the *sequence,* the addition of words specifically to the melismas of the alleluia. The practices of interpolating words into the rhapsodic recitations of the alleluias, of writing new words for existing plainchant, and of composing both new poetry and music for the liturgy were all aspects of general troping practice. Notker merely decided he could improve on the quality of the verse settings. His importance lies in his resourceful refining of the process and in his organizing of the alleluia offshoots into clearly patterned syllabic sequences. Though the practice had obviously begun some time before, the term *sequence* first appears in Notker's volume.

As with troping, the practice of sequence writing spread quickly, and the opportunity for individual poet-composers to display their talents provided a strong impetus. By the time of the early Renaissance, well over 4,000 sequences had been written down. These sequences were no longer mere interpolations, having achieved the status of fully independent songs and hymns in their own right, as well as parts of the proper of the mass. Many became the equivalent of popular religious songs, with some sequence melodies serving more than one text. Though standardization was not a fundamental element in so extensive a practice, the pattern of the poetry written for sequences was often characterized by a free line to begin and end, with paired rhyming lines in between (for example, *a bb cc dd e*).

Sacred music popularized by troping probably inspired some secular musical practices. For example, the *lai*—a 12th-century troubadour song—and the instrumental dance *estampie* both utilized a structure similar to that of the sequence.

Organum

By the early 10th century two important treatises dealing with new concepts of music appeared. They were the *Musica enchiriadis* (*Music Manual*), and the *Scholia enchiriadis* (*Commentary on the Manual*). Both introduced the topic of polyphony, the singing of two lines of music simultaneously. To modern eyes and ears, the concept of placing lines in contrapuntal relationships simultaneously seems easy enough. However, music from Greek times to the age of Charlemagne had been largely conceived monophonically, that is, as an unsupported single line.

The opening of the medieval ear to the sound of two voices moving in tandem is perhaps the most decisive change in the history of Western music. For the first time, the attentions of composer, performer, and listener were directed to the appeal of textures woven first by two, then three, then more musical parts. The medieval ear had to be retrained to hear "vertically" as well as "horizontally," and the question of designing sounds that would fall well together became a major issue for centuries. Polyphony would increase the splendor of the church's already imposing liturgy, and music was about to become an art joyously offered *to* God rather than only received as a gift *from* God.

Two types of polyphony are described in the above-named treatises. The first refers to the simplest polyphony that occurs naturally when the voices of men and boys blend in singing at the octave. As described in the treatises, was obviously not a new sound to any 10th-century ear. What was new was the type of polyphony known as *organum* (plural, *organa*), in which the polyphonic element derives from two voice parts moving along in parallel motion at the interval of the fifth (Ex. 7-3a). Specifically, this progression in parallel fifths is known as *parallel organum*, or *strict organum*. Each of the two lines is given a name: the voice holding the plainchant line is the *vox principalis* (principal voice); the line added a fifth above it, the *vox organalis* (organal voice). It is believed that the words *organum* and *organalis* come from Greek and Latin roots pertaining to geometric measurement and to instruments in the generic sense.

Example 7-3. Organum.

7-3a. Strict organum.

Sit glo - ri - a Do - mi - ni in sae - cu - la lae - ta - bi - tur Do - mi - nus in o - pe - ri - bus su - is

For unknown reasons, discussion of organum disappeared from treatises until a century later, when it was mentioned by Guido of Arezzo in his *Micrologus* (*Little Discourse*). In it he described several possible variations in the moving of voices, allowing for intervals other than the octave and the fifth. He was fairly conservative, however, recommending almost exclusively the use of octaves, fifths, and fourths. It was not until the early 12th century that the next major step was taken, in which the lines moved in contrary motion. With the appearance of *counterpoint*—the drama of line against line as well as consonance versus dissonance—an aural giant step was taken. This new organum in contrary motion was called *free organum*. In it the upper, or organal, voice was allowed to move freely in unison at the octave, parallel in fifths or in contrary motion against the plainchant, or principal voice (Ex. 7-3b). The stage was now set for a flood of new sounds and approaches to music. The Western musical ear would never be the same again.

7-3b. Free organum.

Manuscripts from the Spanish pilgrimage center at the Cathedral of Santiago de Compostela and from the Abbey of St. Martial at Limoges in southern France show that while the tones of plainchant (Ex. 7-4a) are still held in the vox principalis, the vox organalis moves more freely with a series of decorative notes above it (Ex. 7-4b). Since the tones of the plainchant have no specific length assigned to them, one cannot determine exactly how the upper line was chanted in relation to it, or precisely how these notes sounded together in the two parts. Both manuscripts, however, show that a new freedom and elasticity was developing within the vox principalis, a practice that came to be known as *St. Martial,* or *melismatic, organum.*

Example 7-4. Organum.

7-4a. Benedicamus domino chant.

7-4b. St. Martial organum.

Be - - - ne - - - - di - ca - mus

The next step in the progress of organum occurred in Paris in the 12th century, and was the achievement of the poet-musician-scholars associated with the Cathedral of Notre Dame (Ex. 7-4c). The most famous of these composers were Léonin, active in the third quarter of the century, and Pérotin, who followed him into the 13th century. Léonin and Pérotin are the major representatives of the so-called *Notre Dame School* of composition, one aspect of which was an extensive elongation of the length of the notes of the chant in the vox principalis. In order to understand their contributions to the music of this period, some knowledge of new developments in rhythmic notation is required.

7-4c. Notre Dame School organum.

With the advance of contrapuntal technique, it became evident that a better way of organizing sounds into coherent performance needed to be found. The result was a concept known as the *rhythmic modes.* Three had been a magic number since ancient times, and for the church it represented the Trinity. The rhythmic modes (Chart 7-2) were formed from various combinations of longs and shorts, always producing triple groupings.

It was this application of recurring metric patterns to the even-flowing, nonmetric plainchant that characterizes the genius of the Notre Dame School. In Example 7–4c, the lower part holding the plainchant (vox principalis), moves in very long, unmeasured notes. Above it the vox organalis is broken

CHART 7-2. THE RHYTHMIC MODES

Mode	Meter		Musical equivalent
1	Trochaic:	long-short	♩ ♪
2	Iambic:	short-long	♪♩
3	Dactylic:	long-short-short	♩. ♪♩
4	Anapestic:	short-short-long	♪♩ ♩.
5	Spondaic:	long-long	♩. ♩.
6	Tribrachic:	short-short-short	♪♪♪

into recurring patterns based on triple measured time, primarily in trochaic meter. This example was composed by Léonin and is taken from an anthology of two-part polyphony he completed sometime before 1180, the *Magnus liber organi* (*Great Book of Organum*). That Léonin's fame survived into the next century is an indication that the prevailing medieval anonymity of great architects, sculptors, painters, and composers was nearing an end.

The new polyphony as practiced by Léonin and other musical clerics was given a special name—*organum duplum*—and the two musical lines were also renamed. The line of plainchant, known for so long as the vox principalis, became the *tenor* part. The word comes from the Latin *tenere* (to hold). It is the line that now contains the plainchant, though in much longer note values than before. The vox organalis became the *duplum,* the second, or "double," line.

Léonin and his successor Pérotin also became responsible for the next step in the history of organum—*clausula* (Ex. 7-5). In clausula, the plainchant appears in the tenor part sung in measured rhythm, aligned rhythmically with the duplum line. This is an innovation that marked the first appearance of *mensural,* or *measured,* music in both voices. Pérotin is also associated with the addition of up to three polyphonic parts in organum. In his time organum was named for the number of lines it contained: *organum duplum* had two lines, *organum triplum* three, and *organum quadruplum* four. By the early 13th century, all of these possibilities had been explored (see Plate IV).

Example 7-5. Notre Dame School. Clausula in organum.

In the Notre Dame School, organa used the same text for all the voices. As settings became more complex, the tenor part with its plainchant in long note values tended to be absorbed into the fabric of the composition, leaving few listeners able either to discover the presence or to follow the meaning of the traditional chant. The addition of new texts heard simultaneously over the plainchant texts opened the way for richer opportunities in composition. While the plainchant remained an obligatory part of the contrapuntal fabric, it now formed but one part of the increasingly complicated tonal web, while the role of the composer became an ever-stronger force.

Conductus and Motet

During the 12th century, certain compositions not prescribed by the liturgy were introduced into church services. Some of these found a place in the church dramas that were reserved for special festivals of the church year. The processional music for such dramas and other music inserted on ceremonial occasions or saints' days fell under the rubric of *conductus.* The theorist Franco of Cologne explained that "he who wishes to write a *conductus* ought first to invent as beautiful a melody as he can." This melody functioned as the tenor part, around which the composer then wrote one or more melodies in organum. The most important aspect of the conductus was that it was not based exclusively on pre-existing material but could be newly conceived music, with parallel rhythms often creating the effect of chordal writing.

Parallel to the conductus, but still partly dependent on the fund of plainchant, was the *motet.* This new approach to the union of music and poetry blossomed in 13th-century France. As words (*mots* in French) were added to the duplum line of a clausula, that part was referred to as the *motetus,* or *motet.* A 13th-century motet, then, is a chant-based composition with one or more newly composed melodies, each with its own text (Ex. 7-6).

Example 7-6. 13th-century motet. Two voices, Latin text.

In the 13th-century motet above, the chant *Benedicamus domino* forms the rhythmic tenor part. In the upper voice, a new text appears in which only the first word coincides with the tenor text. The attention of the listener is directed to the organum (motet) text and the interaction of melodies rather than to the plainchant itself—that is, to the man-made rather than the God-given.

Example 7-7 shows the opening measures of a three-part polytextual motet; note that the duplum and triplum parts have different texts. By the middle of the 13th century, secular texts had begun to infiltrate the motet. The outcome, as this example shows, was a composition in which the tenor part carries the now barely recognizable plainchant, while the duplum and triplum lines declaim contemporary vernacular French poetry.

Example 7-7. 13th-century motet. Three voices, French and Latin texts.

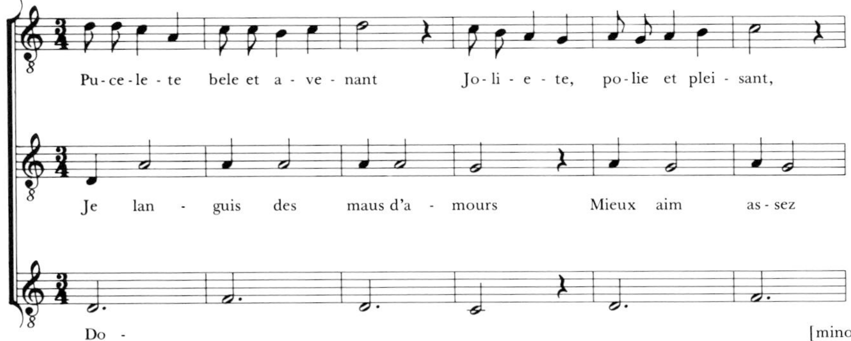

Obviously the average member of the congregation could understand little or none of the several texts that were sung simultaneously. Furthermore, given the extended length of the notes in the tenor part, the ear could not possibly follow the plainchant. The listener could, however, appreciate the interplay of the music, which was exactly what the composers had in mind. And, by including the plainchant within the fabric of the composition, they believed their work would reach the ear of the Almighty as well as those of their clerical colleagues.

Liturgical Drama

Originating in the 10th century, the practice of acting out particular dramatic events during the celebration of the two major Christian holidays became common in the 12th and 13th centuries. Dramatizations of the visitation of the three Marys to the tomb of Christ appeared as additions to the Easter liturgy, as did the Annunciation and sections from the Gospel accounts of the birth of Christ and from favorite biblical stories, such as the Old Testament tale of Daniel in the lions' den, dramatized as *The Play of Daniel.*

The liturgy of the mass is itself high drama about the life, death, and resurrection of Jesus, as well as the redemption of humanity. In the Greek Orthodox service the communion wafer, the symbol of the body of Christ, is literally stabbed in the precommunion preparations before it rises again on the altar at the consecration. The first historical reference to staged liturgical drama is from the late 10th century and pertains to the Easter liturgy. It is a semitheatrical version of some of the events of the first Easter morning, performed in the interests of heightened celebration. When the Marys come to visit the tomb, they find that the stone covering has been removed and an angel stands at the entrance; a dialogue ensues (Ex. 7–8).

Example 7-8. Church drama: dialogue at the tomb of Christ.

In the 11th century, Christmas plays of some complexity found an established place as adjuncts to the prescribed liturgy. Two 12th-century Christmas dramas, *The Representation of Herod* and *The Slaying the Innocents,* are examples of the elaborate staged works that may be considered full-fledged *liturgical drama.* The chanting was monophonic and largely syllabic, without accompaniment; florid passages were reserved for moments of high drama. In the 20th century, samplings of these two types (ancestors of the recitative and aria) have been drawn from a number of sources and merged into a performable combination called *The Play of Herod.* It is concerned with the events surrounding the birth of Christ, including Herod's encounter with the Wise Men, and his order to slay all male children under the age of two to assure that the prophecy of Christ's kingship did not materialize. The lament of Rachel, a bereaved mother, is set in a way that is startlingly modern and affecting (Ex. 7-9).

Example 7-9. Church drama: *The Play of Herod.* "Rachel's Lament."

Rejoice? Alas! Alas! Alas! How could I rejoice, when I am surrounded by severed limbs, the sight of which disturbs my soul and causes my body to shake so violently? Truly, the sight of these dead children will haunt me until the end of my life. O woe! O Gods! Now all mothers' joys are turned to mournful lamentation!

Ars Nova

At the dawn of the 14th century, the fortunes of the Roman church were at a low ebb. After his election, the French Pope Clement V saw fit to move the Holy See from Rome to the southern French town of Avignon, where it became a sumptuous international center of earthly splendor. At the papal court were eminent architects, painters, men of letters, and musicians, gathered from all parts of Christendom. Among them was Petrarch, the renowned Italian poet, who painted a devastating verbal picture of some of the worldly extravagances he beheld around him: "The popes, successors of the poor fishermen of Galilee, are now loaded with gold and clad in purple. I am living in the Babylon of the West, where prelates feast at licentious banquets and ride on snow-white horses. They are decked in gold, fed off gold, and will soon wear gold shoes if the Lord does not check this slavish luxury."

Because they were penned by prominent writers of the time, these exposures of church failings have survived. Christianity, however, was still the sacred mainstream of life in medieval Europe. In spite of critical attacks, satirical burlesques, and bitter bickering, the church remained intact as a vital central force. Religious faith still provided the solace sought by those who needed comfort, healing, and the promise of salvation.

France was still the most progressive center for music at this time. Its adventurous composers felt the need for a method of notating their intentions more clearly, particularly in the area of rhythmic flexibility. A theoretical basis for their innovations was provided in 1316 by Philippe de Vitry, bishop of Meaux, who was both a poet and a composer. His treatise *Ars Nova* (*New Art*) gave its name not only to the "new art" of expanded and flexible rhythmic notation, but to an entire era. Moreover, the difference that Vitry perceived in his music and that which it replaced is indicated by his labeling the latter *ars antiqua* (ancient art). The distinction hinges not so much on theory or history as on the vital practice of music itself.

Composers in 14th-century Europe thought of rhythmic notation basically in terms of rhythmic note groupings and ways in which longer note values could be subdivided. In modern notation, the note relationships are based on the halving of values (whole, half, quarter notes). Vitry, however, inherited a system based on the triple-note relationships inherent in the rhythmic modes.

His new system took a square-note *breve* as the basic note value and a diamond-shaped note, the *semibreve,* as the next smallest note value. The smallest note, called a *minim,* placed a stroke on the semibreve. He set up a 14th-century equivalent of the modern time signature, using the terms *time* and *prolation.* In medieval beliefs, the number three often stood for the Trinity, which in turn implies perfection. So any composition in which the breve equaled three semibreves was in *perfect time* (modern triple meter). Similarly, a composition in which the breve equaled two semibreves was in *imperfect time* (modern duple meter).

Vitry's system carried the subdivision a step further, allowing for the division of the semibreve into note groups of two or three, in a relationship called *prolation.* If the semibreve equaled three minims, the prolation was *perfect;* if two minims, the prolation was *imperfect.* Chart 7-3 shows the four combinations of time and prolation, perfect and imperfect, with an approximation of the way they might appear in modern notation. Also shown is the *Ars Nova* equivalent of the modern time signature, based on combinations of the circle, the half-circle, and the dot.

The new system of notation opened the door to excesses of rhythmic experimentation, and many *Ars Nova* motets abound with rhythmic extravagances (Ex. 7-10a). Among these eccentricities was the practice of alternating notes between voice parts in *hocket,* a term derived from the French word for "hiccup" (Ex. 7-10b). Sometimes the hocket appears as a descriptive device, other times as the interlocking division of a single line requiring great skill on the part of the singers.

This mini-revolution in the history of polyphonic music did not go unchallenged. In 1322 the conservative Pope John XXII took particular exception to the new style, citing specifically the increasing secularization of the new music, the invention of free-flowing, florid melismas and coloratura passages that decorated the melodic lines, and the quickening rhythmic pace of the note values. The pope criticized such practices in a papal bull: "Some disciples of the new school are greatly concerned with the measurement of time values. They introduce new notes, preferring to sing in their own style rather than in the old way. They dissect their melodies with hockets, lubricate them with discants, and sometimes impose on them two upper parts with secular words." Recalling the stately beauties of the plainchant and its "modest ascents and temperate descents," he condemned the new practice, which he described as "completely confused by the multiplicity of notes which run rather than stand still, intoxicate rather than pacify the ear, telling tales as they are uttered." In consequence, "worship, which should

CHART 7-3. TIME AND PROLATION WITH EQUIVALENTS IN MODERN NOTATION

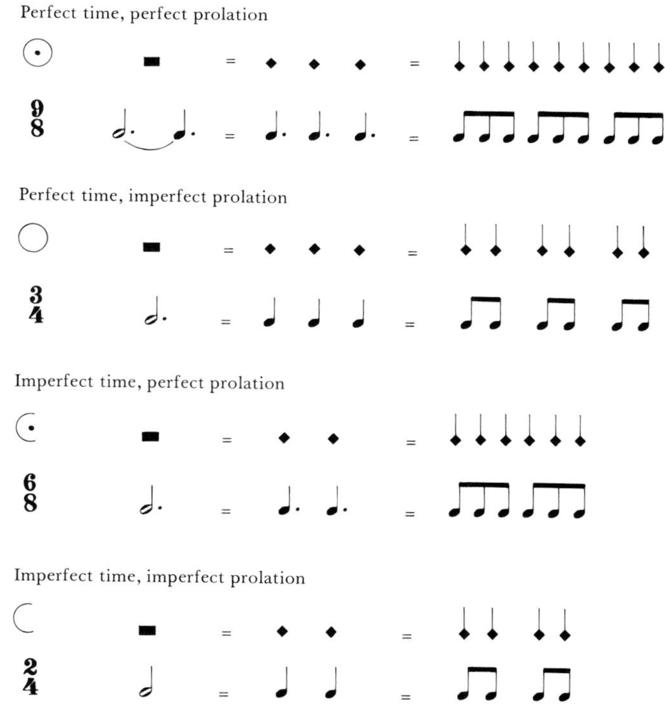

Example 7-10. Ars Nova.

7-10a. Rhythmic notation.

7-10b. Hocket.

be sought after, is disregarded, and frivolity, which should be avoided, is propagated."

The papal ban may have slowed the pace and the spread of the new music, but there was no turning back. The appetite for polyphonic music, once established, eventually swept all before it. Sophisticated music was now well on its way to becoming a recognized secular as well as a sacred art, complete with its own aesthetic laws and standards.

The Roman de Fauvel

A sampling of the 14th-century motet style in secular music may be found in the *Roman de Fauvel* (*Tale of Fauvel*), a long narrative poem by a French royal clerk, Gervais du Bus, dating from about the same time as Vitry's 14th-century *Ars Nova* treatise. Du Bus provided for musical interpolations within the poem, and the manuscript contains a wide variety of music, some of it by Vitry in the new style.

The *Roman de Fauvel* was a satire on the corruptions du Bus saw in both state and church. More freely, the title translates as *Romance of the Fawn-colored Beast.* A "fawn-colored beast" is one that does not look like a human but has some human characteristics—in other words, a donkey. The separated syllables in *fau-vel* translate as "veiled lie." And the letters of the donkey's name form an anagram for six of the deadly sins:

*F*laterie (flattery)
*A*varice (greed)
*V*ilenie (guile)
*V*ariété (inconstancy)
*E*nvie (envy)
*L*âcheté (cowardice)

At the beginning of the poem, Fauvel lives in a stable. He grows ambitious thirsts for wealth and power, sets up residence in the great hall of the master's main house, and has a decorated hay-rack built for himself. Dame Fortune smiles on him and makes him lord of the house (i.e., of the world). Church leaders and worldly rulers come from all over to pay him homage. The term "to curry Fauvel"—that is, to brush down the donkey, or to demean oneself before him—came into modern English as "to curry favor." The obeisances paid to Fauvel by church and state dignitaries are meant to satirize Pope Clement V and the temporal ruler Philip the Fair, suggesting their susceptibility to the deadly sins Fauvel represents (Fig 7-4).

Fauvel finally travels to Macrocosmos, the city of Dame Fortune. Here he finds her with the concentric wheels of fortune and misfortune, mirroring her two countenances, one beautiful and the other ugly. He asks to marry her. She refuses, but offers him as wife a lady-in-waiting, Lady Vainglory. At the wedding, Fauvel's guests—Carnal Lust, Flirtation, Adultery, Wild Desire and Venus—are challenged to a tournament by a group of thirty virtues, led by Virginity. The virtues fight valiantly against the vices and sins, but Dame For-

Figure 7-4. Fauvel crowned by the king and the pope, illustrated in Gervais du Bus, *Roman de Fauvel,* 1314. Illuminated manuscript. Courtesy of the George Arents Research Library, Syracuse University, Syracuse, New York.

tune stops the battle, declaring that the time for a definitive victory on either side is not yet at hand. The work ends with the birth of many baby Fauvels who go out into the world to do misdeeds.

The music of *Fauvel* ranges from monophonic songs to polylingual motets based on plainchant. The motet in Example 7–11 is in three voices with a plainchant tenor. The Latin texts of the upper voices contain references to saints and Old Testament figures, but they are in fact disguised references to the king and the scurrilous characters whom he chose as counselors. Vitry, who composed some of the music, was well acquainted with the excesses of church and state, since he was a trusted official of several royal households, a bishop of the church, and an ambassador on diplomatic missions to the papal court at Avignon.

The motet is organized around a structural time device called *isorhythm,* which was an outgrowth of certain characteristics of the old rhythmic modes. An isorhythm is a rhythmic pattern, usually placed in the tenor (chant) part and then repeated throughout the entire composition. Where the rhythmic modes were uncomplicated groupings of long and short time values grouped in threes, the isorhythm was a pattern of notes and rests spanning several measures. Its presence was known only to the composer and perhaps to the performers. Functioning as a unifying formal device of significance primarily to its creator, it satisfied the personal need of *Ars Nova* composers to create inner order in their compositions. The isorhythm in this *Fauvel* motet is indicated by brackets in the tenor part.

The *Ars Nova* style was adopted by many composers, among them Vitry's younger compatriot Guillaume de Machaut. Although his career paralleled the elder composer's in many ways, Machaut became more famous, especially for his love poems set to his own music. He served as a clerk and secretary to several kings of France and at the time of his death was a canon at the Cathedral of Rheims. A brilliant exponent of the *Ars Nova* style, Machaut was equally distinguished as a poet, composer, and performer, and must be ranked as the most important musician of the 14th century.

Machaut is best known for a unique work first performed at the Notre Dame Cathedral in Rheims most probably in the 1360s, a mass known today as the *Messe de Notre Dame* (*Mass of Our Lady*). While it is unusual for several reasons, its special claim to fame rests on its being the first setting of the ordinary of the mass written by a single composer and designed to be performed during a complete celebration of the mass. Since the parts of the ordinary of the mass are interspersed with those of the proper, there is no practical need for the ordinary to be coordinated musically. But Machaut obviously felt an artistic need to place his personal stamp on each section of the ordinary and to find ways to connect them internally through the music itself. The connecting factor in some movements of his *Mass* is an isorhythm (Ex. 7-12), which always binds the units unobtrusively together.

Example 7-11. Vitry. *Roman de Fauvel.* "Garrit Gallus—In nova fert—Neuma," bars 1–41. Isorhythmic motet.

Triplum: The cock prattles on, lamenting on behalf of all the good servant cockerels (the French), who are betrayed by a crafty fox (Enguerran de Marigne, the king's chief councillor). This sly fox thrives with the cunning of Belial (the devil), and, with the consent of the lion (the king), rules as though he himself were monarch.
Duplum: My purpose is to tell of bodies which have been transformed into shapes of a different kind (Ovid, *Metamorphosis* I, 1). The evil dragon slain by illustrious Michael (lives again as a reigning fox, whose tail the lion obeys).

Example 7-12. Machaut. *Mass of Our Lady.* Isorhythm.

Secular Music

While it has been said with some truth that the history of Western music up to the Renaissance is the history of sacred music, it is also true that a vast amount of secular music was a part of life in the Middle Ages. Since knowledge of medieval music rests almost entirely on written records that were preserved in churches and monasteries over the centuries, quite naturally the preponderance of music that survived was religious. Social music, on the other hand, was primarily passed on by oral tradition, and was only in rare instances written down. All such music for entertainment before the year 1000 has vanished into obscurity, and the number of later surviving examples is tantalizingly small.

Some facts, however, may be gleaned from the available evidence. Almost all medieval music, both sacred and secular, was written in conjunction with verbal texts. In secular music, the texts were in Latin when addressed to the educated few, and in the vernacular for the general populace. Secular music was performed by strolling entertainers who went from town to town and castle to castle. Since communications between such places was sporadic, the wanderers were always welcome for their news and gossip, as well as for the entertainment they provided.

Such strolling players came from varied backgrounds. Many were vagabond clerics who were unable or unwilling to find permanent church positions; often they were less-than-devout dropouts from monasteries. One such group of wanderers were the *Goliards,* whose name is thought to be a composite of *Golia* (Goliath) and *gula* (gullet), referring to their reputation for overindulgence in food and drink. Contemporary illustrations show these unsuccessful scholars spending their time eating, drinking, whoring, and gambling (Fig. 7-5).

Of the other traveling entertainers, the lowest on the social scale were the *jongleurs* (jugglers), who from the 10th century on performed such circus capers as conjuring feats, acrobatics, trained animal tricks, as well as singing, dancing, miming, and the telling of tall tales. The jongleurs were the singers of the 11th-century *chansons de geste* (songs of noble deeds), a type of epic poetry chanted to simple, repetitive melodies. The most famous of these is the *Song of Roland,* written in medieval French—an action-packed story of Charlemagne's campaign against the pagan Moors in Spain, in which he lost his noblest warrior, Roland, in fierce fighting. Contemporary accounts record that a jongleur named Taillefer, a "minstrel whom a brave heart ennobled," accompanied William the Conqueror as he rode into the thick of the Battle of Hastings in 1066. The scribe tells how Taillefer led the men, throwing his sword into the air, catching it again and again, while singing the *Song of Roland.*

A lively collection of earthy social music is found in a large volume of 13th-century music and poetry preserved at a Benedictine monastery in Bavaria. The volume, now known as the *Carmina Burana* (*Songs of Beuron*), contains over 200 gambling, drinking, love-making, satiric, and parody songs, as well as some sacred music. The poetic texts have sporadic musical notation, providing some clues to the sound of popular songs in the Middle Ages.

Medieval musical joyousness is expressed in the playful songs that are found in abundance from the 13th century onward. Many employ a kind of imitative counterpoint that may be considered the ancestor of the canon and fugue. The earliest recorded example is from 13th-century England, *Sumer is icumen in, lhoude sing cuckoo* (Ex. 7-13; see Plate II). The top voice is a *rota,* a single line of music written to be sung with itself at the unison, much like the modern round. Numbers above the score indicate the place where succeeding voices are to enter. The two-voice lower line contains a repeated *osti-*

Figure 7-5. Goliards drinking and gambling, illustrated in *Carmina Burana,* early 13th century. Illuminated manuscript. Courtesy of the George Arents Research Library, Syracuse University, Syracuse, New York.

nato figure that gives harmonic and rhythmic support. Also popular was the related *chace,* in which one part "chases" another in fugal fashion.

Troubadours, Trouvères, and Minnesingers

The high Gothic period is often called the *Age of Chivalry.* In the church the cult of the Virgin Mary venerated her as Queen of Heaven. Many of the great Gothic cathedrals and the chapels within them were dedicated to her, and they were viewed as earthly courts where her devotees could pay her tribute. In secular aristocratic circles women were raised to a lofty level and cherished as her worldly counterpart. This attitude is clearly reflected in the chivalric code of knighthood: "My soul to God, my life to the king, my heart to the ladies, and honor for myself."

Paeans of praise in verse and love songs poured forth to the Virgin Mary as well as to the knight's lady love. Castles, palaces, and chivalric tournaments resounded to the vernacular songs of the *troubadours* in southern France, their *trouvère* counterparts in the north, and the *Minnesingers* in Germany. Such love songs, songs of praise, ballads, and pastoral poems were set to short melodies, unaccompanied or with the accompaniment of the lute. Some of the poetry and music was written by the courtiers themselves, but other important developments came from professionals in their circle and service.

Example 7-13. Sumer is icumen in. English rota.

The most exalted practitioner of the trouvères' art was King Richard the Lionhearted, son of Eleanor of Aquitaine, herself an enthusiastic patroness of poet-singers. As with the troubadours, the art of the trouvères was conceived by the nobility, and the most important surviving examples were actually written by aristocrats and the clergy. For example, one celebrated trouvère was Thibaut de Champagne, king of Navarre; and the last and greatest of the trouvères, Adam de la Hale, was a university scholar in the town of Arras.

Trouvère songs included several intended for dancing—the *rondeau* (plural, *rondeaux*), the *ballade,* and in the 14th century the *virelai.* Each featured a variant of the stanza-and-refrain format.

Adam de la Hale's *pastourelle* (pastoral drama) entitled *Jeu de Robin et Marion* (*The Play of Robin and Marion*) is a small surviving masterpiece of early musical drama. In it the shepherdess Marion loves the shepherd Robin. Complications arise when the knight Aubert appears, and Marion takes his fancy. Adam wrote some of the music for this bucolic fable, but he insured its success with his courtly audience by setting lyrics to popular and folk melodies, which fortunately survive.

German courts from the 12th century onward were not immune to the charms of troubadour and trouvère love poetry, and soon the Germans themselves developed a parallel artistic strain in which the artists were known as *Minnesingers* (singers of courtly love). While love was the central focus of the *Minnesang* (love poem), the experience of the crusades had also left a lasting effect on their poetry.

By common consent, the finest of the Minnesingers were the Bavarian Wolfram von Eschenbach and the Tyrolean Walther von der Vogelweide. Much of their poetry is still extant, but relatively little of their music. A major exception is Walther's song *Palästinalied,* celebrating his first sight of Jerusalem after the long crusade journey. This energetic German Lied, in a military duple meter, represents the outcry of a soldier who is intensely affected by the sight of a long-sought goal. The poetic stanzas, two of which are reproduced below, have seven lines each. The first four lines have an alternating rhyme scheme; the last three rhyme together. The musical setting is strophic with the following lines paired in repetition: 1, 3, and 7; 2 and 4; 5 and 6.

Nu alrest lebe ich mir werde	Now at last my life is worthwhile
Sit min sündic ouge siht	Since my sinful eyes behold
Hie daz land und auch die erde	Here the holy land and soil which
Den man vil der eren giht.	Men hold in such high honor.
Mirst geschehen des ich je bat	I have attained that for which I have so long prayed,
Ich bin kommen an die stat	I have come to the city
Da got mennischlichen trat.	Where God in human form has trod.

Schoeniu lant rich unde here,	What I see has beauty as well,
Swaz ich der noch han gesehen.	A ripe and splendid land.
So bit duz ir aller ere:	Thou art the most glorious land of all;
Was ist wunders hie geschehen!	How wondrous does all appear!
Daz ein magt ein kint gebar her	That here a virgin bore a child
über aller engle schar,	Surrounded by a multitude of angels,
was daz nigt ein wunder gar?	Is it not a wonder to contemplate?

Instrumental Music

An important source of information about medieval instrumental music is to be found in illustrated manuscripts (Plate III). Instruments functioned alone or in unison combinations to accompany songs and dances and to assist choral singers by supplying added color. From an extraordinarily large selection of bowed and plucked strings, flutes, reeds, brass, and percussion instruments, certain favorites emerged. The *rebec* family of bowed strings featured a rounded back and flat front with three strings, while the *fiddles* resembled the later violin family. Plucked instruments included the French *psaltery,* the *harp,* and the *lute.*

A favorite type of flute was the rustic *panpipes,* but there were also many flutes that suggest the later recorder family. The *shawms* comprised a family of extremely loud oboelike instruments, and in the country *bagpipes* were popular. The *cornett,* a wooden trumpet, and the *busine,* a long brass trumpet, played only the overtone series and were reserved for military and courtly fanfares.

A wide variety of nontuned percussion instruments, such as the miniature kettle drums called *nackers* and the over-the-shoulder side drum known as the *tabor,* were the main drums, while the *tambourine, cymbals, triangle,* and *clappers* (called *castanets* in Spain) added spice and color accents. The tuned *chime bells* intoned plainchant in rehearsal and religious ceremonies.

By the 13th century, keyboard instruments had made some inroads into European music. The *organ* had not been welcome in the early centuries of the church, but gradually large pipe organs requiring great physical strength to pump and to play began to appear in some larger cathedrals. By the 12th century they were probably used to double the voice parts in choral music, and some may have substituted for the tenor part in organum compositions where that line was laid out in very long note values. In the 13th century smaller organs were developed—the *positive,* which could be set on a table, and the *portative,* which was placed on the lap and played with one hand while the other hand worked the bellows. Instruments of this type were useful to play along with sacred or secular songs. Immensely popular was the *hurdy-gurdy,* a cranked string instrument with a keyboard, producing a sound resembling that of a bagpipe.

The Middle Ages were above all an age of faith—people's faith in the glory of God and in themselves. The artifacts they created were marvels of inspiration: the great Romanesque abbey churches and monastic complexes, the sculptures that mirrored the medieval world view from the creation of Adam to the Last Judgment, the organization of the fantastic Crusades that brought the peoples of the Christian West and the Moslem East together for the first time, the Gothic cathedrals whose soaring towers rose to pierce the heavens, the philosophical summas that organized all the theological articles of faith into intricate logical systems, the medieval universities that embraced all branches of learning, the drama that grew out of the church festival liturgies, the colorful and fiery miracles of stained glass that transformed natural light into supernatural visions. And of course, the music—the otherworldly sounds and beauties of the plainchant and its transmutations by troping, the adventurous forms of organa, and the intricacies of motet composition.

CHAPTER

8

Renaissance Styles

HISTORIANS HAVE DESIGNATED the developments in the Western world of the 15th and 16th centuries as the Renaissance, a term referring to a rebirth of the spirit of secular humanism, and a reawakening to the beauties and values of the classical Greco-Roman heritage. Many of these developments can also be viewed as the maturation of certain tendencies already present in the later Middle Ages. In any case, it was a time when the otherworldly focus of the medieval mind was yielding to an influence more this-worldly: a feeling that one should experience life here and now to the fullest, rather than wait for promised bliss in the heavenly hereafter.

New forces and fermentations were at work in the body politic. The growth of cities and the increasing wealth among the merchant class challenged the power of the landed aristocracy. The rise of national monarchies, powerful dukedoms, and independent city-states threatened the supranational authority of the Roman papacy. A new openness of inquiry in the universities was rapidly undermining medieval mysticism and superstition. The age of exploration, beginning with the voyages of Columbus and Magellan, broadened human horizons. With so much new wealth now in the hands of self-serving rulers and a strong merchant class, patronage of the arts was no longer dominated by the church. Individual artists developed independent personalities in their own right rather than remaining at the level of members of a craftsmen's guild.

Chronology

MUSICAL FIGURES

John Dunstable	c. 1390–1453
Guillaume Dufay	c. 1398–1474
Johannes Ockeghem	c. 1410–1497
Antonio Squarcialupi	1416–1480
Josquin Desprez	c. 1440–1521
Jacob Obrecht	c. 1450–1505
Heinrich Isaac	c. 1450–1517
Ottaviano Petrucci	1466–1539
Martin Luther	1483–1546
Adrian Willaert	c. 1490–1562
Johann Walter	1496–1570
Jacques Arcadelt	1505–c. 1568
Cipriano de Rore	1516–1565
Gioseffo Zarlino	1517–1590
Thoinot Arbeau (Jehan Tabourot)	1520–1595
Giovanni da Palestrina	1525–1594
Orlande Lassus	c. 1530–1594
Andrea Gabrieli	1533–1585
William Byrd	1543–c. 1623
Giaches de Wert	1535–1596
Tomás Luis de Victoria	c. 1548–1611
Luca Marenzio	1553–1599
Thomas Morley	1557–1602
John Dowland	1563–1626
Giles Farnaby	c. 1563–1640
Thomas Campion	1567–1620
Martin Peerson	c. 1572–1651
John Wilbye	1574–1638
Thomas Weelkes	c. 1576–1623
Orlando Gibbons	1583–1625

LITERATURE AND THEATER

Hans Sachs	1494–1576
Torquato Tasso	1544–1595
William Shakespeare	1564–1616
John Donne	1572–1631
Ben Jonson	1572–1637

ARTISTS AND ARCHITECTS

Filippo Brunelleschi	1377–1446
Leone B. Alberti	1404–1472
Gentile Bellini	1429–1507
Hans Memling	c. 1430–1494
Leonardo da Vinci	1452–1519
Matthias Grünewald	1470–1528
Michelangelo Buonarroti	1475–1564
Titian (Tiziano Vecelli)	1477–1576
Raphael (Raffaelo Sanzio)	1483–1520
Andrea Palladio	1508–1580
Veronese (Paolo Cagliari)	1528–1588
El Greco (Domenico Theotocopuli)	1541–1614
Inigo Jones	1573–1652

HISTORICAL FIGURES

John Huss	1374–1415
Johann Gutenberg	1396–1468
Pope Eugenius IV	r. 1431–1447
Christopher Columbus	1451–1512
Nicolaus Copernicus	1473–1543
Ferdinand Magellan	1480–1521
Martin Luther	1483–1546
Henry VIII (England)	r. 1509–1547
John Calvin	1509–1564
Elizabeth I (England)	r. 1558–1603
Maria de Medici	1573–1642

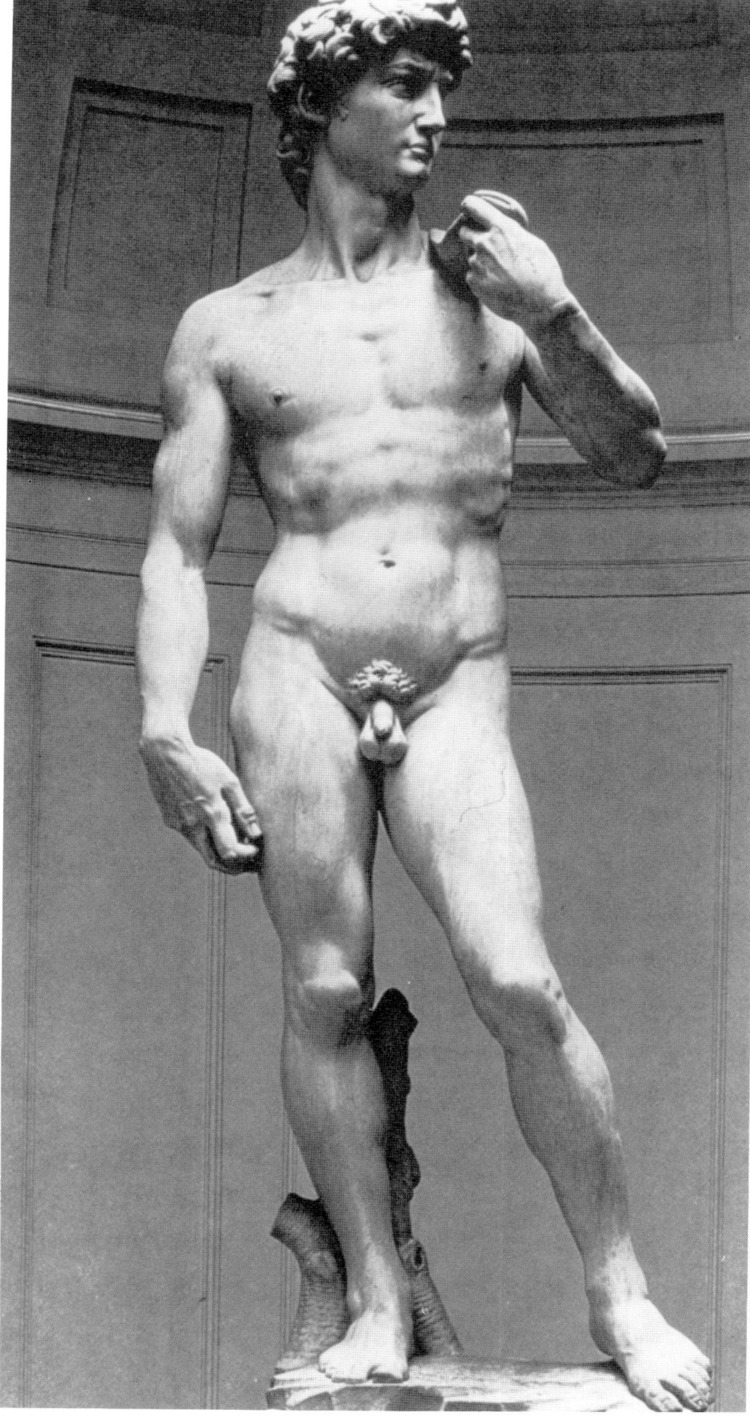

Michelangelo. *David,* 1501–1504. Marble. Galleria dell'Accademia. Courtesy of Gabinetto Fotographico Nazionale, Florence.

Musical and Visual Proportions: Dufay, Brunelleschi

Nowhere was this new spirit more apparent than in the city of Florence in north central Italy. Political and economic power was vested in the Signory, a council made up of representatives of the guilds, most prominently the wool merchants, goldsmiths, and bankers. In the early years of the 15th century the Signory commissioned the young architect Filippo Brunelleschi to crown their late medieval cathedral, Santa Maria del Fiore, with a mighty dome that would dominate the city's skyline. Resting on an octagonal base, the dome soared some 367 feet above the floor of the nave (Plate V).

Sumptuous consecration ceremonies took place in the year 1436. Pope Eugenius IV was present, and in his entourage was a Franco-Flemish musician, Guillaume Dufay, already recognized as the greatest composer of his time. Dufay wrote the dedicatory motet, *Nuper rosarum flores,* a title that alluded to the pope's traditional gift of golden roses placed on the cathedral's altar. Dufay's motet and the other music of the day was rapturously received by the congregation. An eyewitness described it: "The whole space of the building was filled with such choruses of harmony and such a concert of divers instruments, that it seemed as though the symphonies and songs of the angels and of divine paradise had been sent forth from Heaven to whisper in our ears an unbelievable celestial sweetness."

One of the favorite intellectual and architectural pursuits of the Renaissance was the search for concordances of musical and visual proportions, i.e., for ways of achieving in architecture mathematical relationships like those that existed in music. It runs like a thread through the tapestry of Renaissance thought. Both Brunelleschi and Dufay were well versed in the liberal arts, and their awareness of theoretical concepts of design can be seen in the dedicatory celebration of the Florentine cathedral and in the building itself. Brunelleschi based the proportions of his dome on the harmonic principle of the perfect fifth in music (3:2), as expressed in ratios of 6:4:2:3. Elements of the proportions echo throughout the internal structure of the cathedral as well. Dufay chose the same proportions for his musical design. It is not clear whether he did so in order to reflect the architectural proportions, since similar proportional devices were common in much late medieval and Renaissance music. Whether Dufay consciously planned a musical reflection of the building or not, the resulting correspondence reveals the consciousness of numerical harmony that sustains so much Renaissance art and music.

While the modern bar line did not exist in 1436, sections of music are measured out by the regular duration assigned by the symbols for time and prolation. Viewed in this fashion, the composition contains approximately 168 measures set out in four clearly delineated sections; its temporal proportions are shown in the following table.

Proportional scheme of Brunelleschi's cathedral dome	Dufay motet *Nuper rosarum*: Number of measures per section		Beats per measure		Total beats	Proportion of total beats
6:4:2:3	Sec. 1: 56	x	6	=	336	6
	2: 56	x	4	=	224	4
	3: 28	x	4	=	112	2
	4: 28	x	6	=	168	3
	168					

To achieve his chosen proportional scheme, Dufay adjusted the motet text to make musical rather than poetic sense. While the text contains four verses of seven lines each, Dufay divided it into four sections of 13, 8, 3, and 4 lines respectively, with a resultant shift of emphasis which may be seen below.

TEXT: SECTION 1	MUSIC: SECTION 1
Nuper rosarum flores	Despite the winter's bitter cold,
Ex dono pontificis,	Roses arrived a short time ago,
Hieme licet horrida,	To adorn this great Cathedral,
Tibi virgo coelica,	A gift from the Pope,
Pies et sancte deditum	And dedicated in perpetuity
Grandis templum machinae	To thee, heavenly Virgin,
Condecorarunt perpetui.	Holy and sanctified.
TEXT: SECTION 2	
Hodie vicarius	Today the Vicar of
Jesu Christi et Petri	Jesus Christ and the successor to
Successor EUGENIUS	Saint Peter, EUGENIUS,
Hoc idem amplissimum	Will dedicate this
Sacris templum manibus	Mighty temple with
Sanctisque liquoribus	His own hands
	MUSIC: SECTION 2
Consecrare dignatus est.	Using consecrated oils.
TEXT: SECTION 3	
Igitur, alma parens,	Therefore, Gracious Mother,
Nati tui et filia	Daughter of your offspring,
Virgo decus virginum,	Virgin, Thou crown of virgins,

Tuus te FLORENTIAE Devotus orat populus, Ut qui mente et corpore Mundo quicquam exorarit.	Your people of FLORENCE Devoutly pray to you That those pure in mind and body May move you with their entreaties.
TEXT: SECTION 4	MUSIC: SECTION 3
Oratione tua Cruciatus et meritis Tui secundum carnem	Through your prayer Your anguish and merits And those of your Son
	MUSIC: SECTION 4
Nati domini tui Grata beneficia Veniamque reatum Accipere mereatur. AMEN.	Who became man and was crucified, Allow us to receive gracious favor, the benefits of grace and forgiveness of sins. AMEN.

Another Florentine, Leone Battista Alberti, was a truly universal man, renowned both for architectural design and for his highly influential theoretical treatises on architecture, sculpture, and painting. In the first he discourses on the important part the Pythagorean musical proportions and Euclidean geometrical forms play in architectural design. A case in point is his facade for the Florentine Church of Santa Maria Novella. It is a logical system of squares and rectangles, arranged in the proportions of 1:1, 2:1, 3:2, and 4:3, thereby yielding visual parallels to the perfect musical relationships of the unison, octave, fifth, and fourth. It has been noted that if this facade were translated into music, it would sound something like a trumpet fanfare—quite appropriate for the entranceway of a large, richly decorated church. Alberti wrote: "The numbers by which the agreement of sounds affects our ears with delight are the very same which please our eyes and our minds. We shall therefore borrow all our rules for harmonic relations from the musicians to whom this kind of number is extremely well known."

About a century later, the northern Italian humanistic scholar and architect Andrea Palladio published four widely read books on architecture. For his designs, he insisted that harmonic ratios exist within the building as a whole, between each room, and in the length, breadth, and height of the individual rooms. The success of his buildings, he thought, came from experiencing these harmonious relationships, even if the beholder did not consciously perceive them.

The scope of Dufay's career was international, from early proficiency as a choirboy in Cambrai Cathedral to membership in the papal choir in Rome. As a composer, he was active at the courts of Savoy and Burgundy, joining with fellow northern-born composers to forge a style that set new standards of musical mastery. Their intricate manner of writing counterpoint stressed continuous flow of musical sound, equal emphasis on each contrapuntal voice, elegant transparency of choral textures, and a consummate mastery of all the contrapuntal techniques.

Among Dufay's contributions to this high art is the development of the unified mass. The *cantus firmus*, or cyclical, mass was a decisive step toward the control of large-scale musical form. As noted in the discussion of Machaut's *Mass of Our Lady*, there is no liturgical necessity for linking parts of the ordinary of the mass into a unified whole, since they are not sung in continuous sequence. So the usual practice was to organize the movements loosely by a variety of means. Following Dufay's lead, however, composers seized the opportunity to create tighter, more organic works that brought separate parts into a more cohesive musical whole. They also went a step beyond Machaut by extending the choice of unifying materials to include secular song melodies, of which *Se la face ay pale* (*If my face is pale*), *O rosa bella* (*O Lovely Rose*), and *L'homme armé* (*The Armed Man*) were especially popular (Ex. 8–1a).

Example 8-1a. The Armed Man. Medieval folk melody.

The Renaissance cantus firmus mass may be illustrated by Dufay's *L'homme armé* mass (Ex. 8-1b), one of many settings based on this tune. Others who used it included Ockeghem, Josquin Desprez, and Palestrina. Dufay's mass is in four voice parts, and all sections are structurally related by the recurrence of the popular melody in the tenor part of each movement. The presence of such a constant theme justifies the designation *cantus firmus* (fixed part), which served to bring the separated sections into recognizable continuity. While listeners may not have followed the subtle progress of the cantus firmus, composers exploited it endlessly as a reliable building device that was also bound to challenge their individual ingenuity. With the integral unity of its five-section structure, the cyclical mass quickly became the most ambitious form of Renaissance music. The challenge it offered inflamed the imagination of composers to such an extent that mass settings became to Renaissance music what the symphony was to the 18th and 19th centuries.

A common practice of the day should be noted at this point. Especially from the beginning of the *Ars Nova* period, performers had been left on their own to insert accidentals into the music, which resulted in performances that sounded harmonically richer than the score itself indicated. This *musica ficta* (invented music) produced a set of rules in general currency during the 15th and 16th centuries, but individual specific practices differed as widely as individual tastes. Today, performers of Renaissance music study the historical sources and develop their own realizations based on a combination of knowledge and personal judgment.

8-1b. Dufay. "The Armed Man" mass. Kyrie, bars 1–8.

Ars Perfecta: Ockeghem, Josquin Desprez

The most eminent composer of the generation following Dufay was Johannes Ockeghem. A lifetime spent investigating the musical and intellectual fascinations of counterpoint defined and refined his art to an extremely high degree. His analytical mind produced such compositions as the *Missa prolationum (Mass of the Prolations)*. This score displays only two voice parts, but a closer look reveals that each part is to be sung by at least two singers, one in perfect (triple) time, the other in imperfect (duple) time (Exs. 8-2a, b). The resulting composition is a double canon, a connoisseur's music that also speaks through its hidden artifice to the lay listener, for whom the voices float in seemingly effortless balance, the inner intricacies producing alternately states of exalted and suspended animation.

On Ockeghem's death in 1495, many admirers wrote poetic and musical tributes to the memory of the great composer and teacher. Among them was his most famous pupil, Josquin Desprez, who in turn would be praised by his contemporaries as peerless in music. Josquin's tribute, *La déploration sur la mort de Johan Ockeghem* (*Lament upon the Death of Johannes Ockeghem*), was set to a text that expressed mourning not only by the world at large, but by Ockeghem's

Example 8-2. Ockeghem. *Mass of the Prolations.* Kyrie.

8-2a. Original notation.

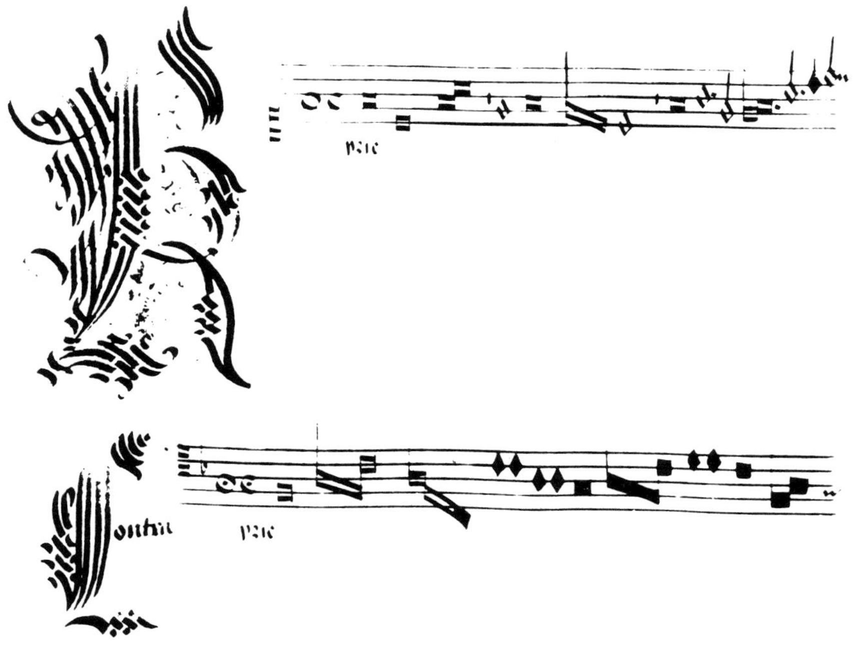

8-2b. Realization in modern score.

musical contemporaries. Some of these were named as specific mourners, representing an entire generation of composers. The tenor line of this five-voice contrapuntal composition is drawn from the plainchant Mass for the Dead, *Requiem aeternam dona eis, Domine* (*Lord, give them eternal rest*). The melding of pagan mythic figures—nymphs and goddesses—with the Christian *Requiem* is typical of Renaissance liberal thinking. Humanism underlies both text and music, and Josquin has movingly captured a sense of deep personal relationships.

All the qualities that some called the *ars perfecta* (perfect art) are present in abundance in the masses and motets of Josquin Desprez—absolute control, balance of voices, and sheer beauty of line for its own sake. He was also at the forefront of the latest developments in secular music (see p. 133). Nearly 50 years after his death, Josquin's reputation as a master was still intact, and a Florentine historian wrote:

> I am well aware that in his day Ockeghem was the first to rediscover music . . . and that Josquin, Ockeghem's pupil, was a prodigy in music, just as our own Michelangelo Buonarroti has been in architecture, painting, and sculpture. For just as Josquin still has to be surpassed in his compositions, so Michelangelo stands alone and without a peer . . . and the one and the other have opened the eyes of all who delight in these arts, now and in the future.

Palestrina, Lassus

The last phases of the "perfect art" produced a music that was at once reserved and highly sophisticated, as is so often the case when a style reaches its culmination. If there were those who feared that the musical art must decline after such masters as Ockeghem and Desprez, their concerns were groundless. The apotheosis of the High Renaissance musical style is to be found in the work of four consummate masters—the Italian Giovanni Pierluigi da Palestrina, the Flemish Orlande Lassus (Orlando Lasso), the Spanish Tomás Luis de Victoria, and the English William Byrd. The music of Palestrina and Victoria is almost exclusively sacred and vocal, characterized by a mystical intensity that has been compared to the metaphysical aspects of El Greco's paintings. The works of William Byrd are marked by an equal mastery of the polyphonic medium, tempered by a tender, intimate lyricism.

The international, eclectic Lassus shared with other Flemish composers an early and profitable sojourn in Italy and thereafter made a distinguished career at the Bavarian court in Munich. As the last major representative of the superb Franco-Flemish school of composers, Lassus invested his music with a healthy emotionality and a love for harmonic experimentation. Comfortable with both sacred and secular idioms, he produced more than 2,000 compositions including Italian madrigals, German polyphonic songs, French chansons, as well as 50 masses and more than 500 sacred motets.

The ultraconservative Palestrina was a choral director at St. Peter's from 1571 until his death. His music exudes a celestial dignity and otherworldly grace. While it had been common practice to allow some instrumental doubling of vocal lines in late medieval polyphonic compositions, helping the singers to stay on pitch and giving added tone color, many choirs of the High Renaissance were noted for singing in the *a cappella* style (without accompaniment). Palestrina's controlled serenity is the epitome of the polyphonic mastery attained in the High Renaissance. Each voice part coolly and cleanly wends its own way, at once separate from and an integral part of the total musical fabric. Faultlessly declaiming the religious text, floating voices extol the church as the haven for all Christian souls who wish to direct their lives heavenward.

Reformation and Rise of Harmony

At the beginning of the 16th century, the Roman Catholic church was still the single most important institution in the Western world. Its universal authority was called into question, however, by strong national monarchs who challenged the pope's authority in secular matters, his intervention in temporal affairs, and his methods of obtaining revenue derived from church property. Christian humanists publicized many of the abuses of church power and began to query the literal interpretation of the Bible, the power of the clergy, and the papal system of indulgences. Soon the solid state of the one, holy, and catholic church was split asunder by various 16th-century reform movements led by Martin Luther in Germany, John Calvin in Switzerland, John Huss in Bohemia, and Henry VIII in England.

Luther believed in the priesthood of all believers and their right to address God through prayer without the mediation of the clergy or the intercession of saints. He also taught that the word of God was to be found only in the Bible itself. So that all the faithful could hear and understand the divine message clearly, he substituted the vernacular German for the Latin of the mass, and devoted years of his life to his monumental translation of the Bible into German so that all his countrymen could read the Scriptures for themselves.

A practicing musician himself, Luther had definite ideas on the function of music in his reformed church. With the participation of the entire congregation in the service, the emphasis on complex counterpoint had to yield to the more straightforward strophic hymn tunes, with or without harmonic accompaniment in simple chordal style. Typically the first hymns, or *chorales,* were sung unaccompanied in unison. Later they were set in four-part harmony with pauses at the end of each phrase so that the congregation could catch a breath before going on to the next line. It is assumed that the congregation sang the tune, while the three lower voices were sung by members of the choir and by congregational members who had the benefit of musical training. Psalm settings also were written with harmonies supporting each note of the melody and with a single note for each syllable of the text.

Luther wrote a number of chorale texts and possibly some of the melodies as well, the most famous of which is *Ein' feste Burg ist unser Gott* (*A mighty fortress is our God,* Ex. 8-3). Some of the chorales were translated directly from Roman Catholic Latin originals. And just as Roman Catholic composers had drawn on secular tunes for their parody masses, Luther formed some chorales by fitting new sacred words onto secular melodies. This practice of using secular tunes as the basis for sacred compositions is known as *contrafactum* (plural, *contrafacta*). As the body of chorales grew and put their roots down in the liturgy and in the consciousness of the congregation, they were woven into other vocal and instrumental segments of the service.

Example 8-3. Luther. *A mighty fortress is our God.*

An example of *contrafactum* is the transformation into a chorale of a German song by Hans Leo Hassler, *Mein Gmüth ist mir verwirret* (*My mental state's in chaos*). In its original 1601 form, it is a strophic song with minimal accompaniment (Ex. 8-4). In 1605 the tune for this Lied became the melody for a chorale based on a poem by Christoph Knoll, *Herzlich thut mich verlangen* (*My heart is filled with longing*). The poem, reportedly written during a plague in 1599, is a prayer from one who rejects earthly fears of death through a series of statements of faith. In 1656, the tune was assigned to a translation by Paul Gerhardt of an 11th-century Latin hymn. Gerhardt's text, *O Haupt voll Blut und Wunden* (*O sacred head now wounded*), describing the sufferings of Christ on the cross, is appropriate for Passion week, and was sung at that period of the church year and incorporated into choral Passion settings by Bach and others. As late as 1973, the tune again appeared, but the process was reversed: in Paul Simon's *American Tune*, the sacred melody became the basis for a popular song (see pp. 483–84).

The chorale became the centerpiece around which the musical components of the Lutheran service revolved, and it provided one kind of opportunity for personal religious expression. As the number of chorales grew, they were carefully assigned to particular Sundays of the church year. Congregations thus gained an invaluable resource of appropriate material with which they could participate actively in the service the year round. In the 17th century, the now-familiar chorale tunes were used as the basis for organ compositions, or *chorale preludes,* which served, among other uses, as instrumental commentaries on the meaning of various chorales when played during the communion service.

Example 8-4. Hassler. *My mental state's in chaos.* German song.

Luther also allowed the chorales to be woven into concertlike art music, which became an integral part of the service. In the 17th century the motet was supplemented by weekly *cantatas*, while *oratorios* and *passions* were written for special holidays. These were orchestrally accompanied choral or solo works, based on texts suitable to the particular Sunday of the church year. Performed before the sermon, they often included appropriate chorales and served to prepare the congregation for the spoken message.

One reaction of the Roman Catholic church to the Reformation was to undertake some house-cleaning of its own. The Council of Trent (1545–63) was called into session to review Catholicism under siege, inaugurating the Counter-Reformation. While the state of church music was a side issue to the main deliberations, nonetheless almost a year was devoted to discussion of music suitable for church services.

The Council reaffirmed that plainchant was the musical foundation of liturgical practice, but ruled that polyphonic music could still be performed if the sacred texts could be heard clearly and if secular melodies were avoided. Only the organ was be used to accompany the music of the mass, and virtuoso musical exhibitions were forbidden. The Council also eliminated hundreds of tropes and sequences from the liturgy. Of the four that remained, the *Dies irae* (Day of wrath) became the most famous (Ex. 8-5). In the 19th and 20th centuries its melody has figured prominently as a metaphor for terror and the demonic in works from Berlioz to Mahler and Rachmaninov. These restrictions were not universally accepted, but they did much to color the official style of the Roman church for the second half of the 16th century and set the tone for the compositions of such conservative church composers as Palestrina.

Example 8-5. Dies irae. Sequence.

Music in Social Circles

Outside church confines, secular music flourished in Renaissance Europe. Courtly lovers and common folk alike raised their voices in song and picked up their skirts in dances that made castles and countryside resound with the joys of music-making. Solo singing to the accompaniment of the lute, group singing of chansons and madrigals, solo and instrumental ensemble music, and an immense variety of dances were everywhere to be heard and seen (Fig. 8-1).

The most popular instrument was the *lute.* More chordal than contrapuntal by nature, the lute was one of the most versatile instruments of the period. It was widely used for solo music, as an accompanying instrument, and in small ensembles. A special *tabulature,* or musical shorthand, was developed for the lute, pointing to the left-hand positions on the frets of the instrument (Plate VI).

The homogeneous sound of the sacred choruses had its counterpart in the secular instrumental *consort.* Instrument making had not only advanced technically; groupings or families of instruments emerged as wordless counterparts to polyphonic choirs. Lute consorts comprised instruments of several sizes, including the larger *theorbo* and the *chitarrone.*

Household keyboard instruments tended toward lutelike, plucked sounds—the *virginals, spinet, clavichord, clavecin,* and *harpsichord.* The thin-sounding medieval strings were being replaced by six-stringed *viols* of various sizes (see Plate VII for some representative Renaissance instruments). The fluty *recorder* and the oboelike *shawm* were joined by light-toned, double-reed *cromornes,* the wooden and ivory *cornetto* (trumpet), and the *sackbut* (trombone). Consorts could combine instruments of a single family such as lutes and viols, or become ensembles of mixed instruments, depending on the occasion and the availability of players. This perspective of ensemble chamber groupings, with a keyboard assisting to coalesce the various instrumental colors, persisted to the end of the 18th century (Fig. 8-2).

On the dance scene, a full-scale ballet was mounted in 1581 for Maria de

Figure 8-1. Simon de Passe. *The Music-makers' Society,* 1612. Engraving. By permission of the Collection Veste Coburg, West Germany.

Medici at the French court, entitled *Circé, ou le ballet comique de la Reine* (see pp. 8–9). It incorporated formal and informal dances, simple strophic as well as more complicated songs, but above all it was elegant. The French court would never again be without the dance as an integral part of its social entertainments.

The French writer Thoinot Arbeau in 1588 published a manual entitled *Orchésographie,* in which he described and gave examples of current dances. The *Orchésographie* contained clear instructions for dance steps and movements, allowing later generations to re-create dances of the 16th century.

Among the favorite dances was the *basse dance* (low dance), so named because the feet glided along the floor. Originally, these dances were written as a single line over which another instrumentalist improvised a contrapuntal obbligato. One of the steps of the *basse dance* was the *branle,* which later developed into an independent dance in its own right.

Paired dances, such as the binary *pavane* and the ternary *galliard,* were staples of any dance collection, as was the *pas de Brabant* (Brabant step), a cousin of the lively Italian *saltarello.* Arbeau included a pavane set to the chanson *Belle qui tiens ma vie* (*Lady, my life is yours*) in his *Orchésographie,* underscoring the close relationship between pavane rhythms (regular dactyl metric patterns, – ◡◡) and those of many chansons. The pavane involved a combination of both single and double steps, as the dancers moved adroitly from left to right (Ex. 8-6).

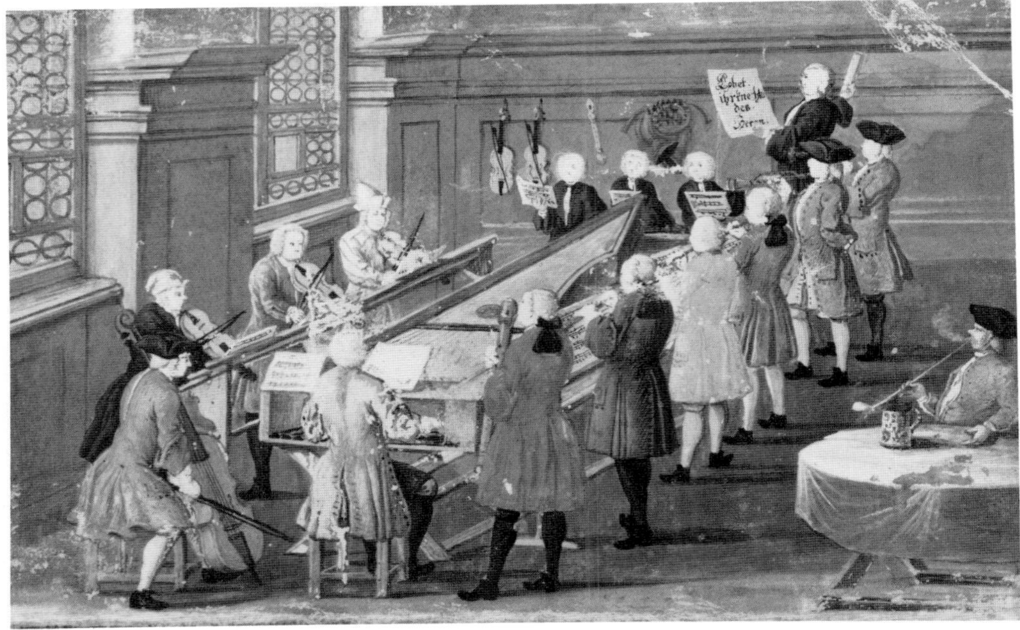

Figure 8-2. Anonymous. *The Cantata Rehearsal,* 1775. Gouache. By permission of the Germanisches National Museum, Nuremberg.

Example 8-6. Arbeau. *Lady, my life is yours.*

While dance music retained wide popularity, a new kind of instrumental literature was beginning to appear, one that reflected an exploration of the specific capabilities of individual instruments. Composers gave special attention to keyboard and plucked stringed instruments, judiciously testing their potential and limitations. The first such compositions were based on music that already existed, namely sacred and secular songs. Composers invented variants on well-known tunes, thus creating a new formal concept, *theme and variations.* Fantasy compositions—*fantasia, fancy, toccata*—encouraged an improvisational style and exploited the possibilities of finger dexterity on keyboard instruments. In their attempt to communicate through compositions without words, composers looked to the contrapuntal *ricercar* and the *fugue,* which explored a new and more serious vein. In addition, they sought subtle methods by which to introduce programmatic imagery into their compositions.

English keyboardists catered to the current taste by publishing numerous sets of varied keyboard pieces. The most famous, *The Fitzwilliam Virginal Book* (1620), contained dance pieces, fantasias, variations on the popular tune *Carman's Whistle,* settings of plainchant melodies, and programme pieces. The latter are mostly charming miniatures, with such diverting titles as *The Fall of the Leafe,* by Martin Peerson, and *The Bells,* by William Byrd.

THE FRENCH CHANSON

The French chanson, a counterpart to the Italian and English madrigal, was the secular outgrowth of some of the contrapuntal skills at work in church music. Those who composed masterful polyphonic mass settings found new successes by directing their talents to the growing groups of amateur performers who took delight in the ingeniously constructed three- or four-part contrapuntal songs. As the chanson developed, the traditional reliance on the borrowed tenor line diminished, and the voice parts were planned to be of equal weight and importance.

Josquin Desprez's late vocal chanson *Mille regretz* (*A thousand regrets,* 1520) shows the master's skills applied to the secular song form. It is a through-composed chanson in which pairs of voices answer each other, individual voices are heard in imitative counterpoint, and stretches of chordal writing are included as well. The text is typical of hundreds of popular "sad to be away from you" songs:

> Leaving you I pine a thousand times over
> departing from your tender countenance,
> I am left with such great gloom and grievous pain
> that my days are clearly numbered.

The four-part setting reveals a high level of skill in part-writing, but also an appropriate sense of lover's longing reflected in the music (Exs. 8-7a, b).

Chansons, like many madrigals and motets, could also be played instrumentally or performed with instrumental substitution for one or more voices. In an instrumental guise, for example, Josquin's *Mille regretz* became a grave and deliberate pavane for a consort of four viols. The chanson is absorbed into the dance structure, transformed into a new composition both purely instrumental and pure dance.

Example 8-7. Josquin Desprez. *A thousand regrets.*

8-7a. Bars 1–9. Chanson.

8-7b. Bars 1–8. Instrumental pavane (arranged by Susato).

THE ITALIAN MADRIGAL

The Italian madrigal was the composite creation of such Franco-Flemish composers as Jacques Arcadelt and Adrian Willaert (active in Rome and Venice, respectively), who were soon joined in trying new techniques by a host of fellow countrymen and native Italians, including Willaert's pupils Cipriano de Rore, Andrea Gabrieli, and Gioseffo Zarlino. Later luminaries were Giaches de Wert, Luca Marenzio, and Carlo Gesualdo, who was prince of Venosa.

Preceded by the simpler, more modest *canzona* and *frottola,* the Italian madrigal was an amalgam of French and Italian influences that gave scope to the Italian native genius for poetry and melody. As the new genre took shape, it was characterized above all by the emphasis on the poetic text. The madrigalists frequently set texts from illustrious writers, ranging from Dante and Petrarch to Tasso and Michelangelo. A contemporary observed that "The notes are the body of the music, but the words are the soul."

The Italian madrigal moved away from the earlier strophic structures of song toward more sophisticated, through-composed, formal procedures. It also capitalized on musical settings that could now freely intermingle polyphonic and chordal textures. Madrigal subjects include the ever-popular pastoral idylls populated by shepherds and shepherdesses, odes to springtime, paeans of praise to feminine and masculine beauty, and love songs both joyous and sad.

Luca Marenzio represents the hyper-refined stylistic ideals of the late Renaissance Italian madrigal, and his writing exhibits extraordinary skill and craftsmanship. In 1591, Marenzio made a musical setting of part of Petrarch's *Io piango* (*I weep*). Petrarch's beloved Laura had died, and his poem recounts her appearance to him in a dream. In this visionary context, Laura brushes away the poet's tears as she berates him for his continued lamentations over her death. The poem ends, "After which she departs as does my sleep." The Marenzio treatment exemplifies the elegant sensitivity for which the composer was renowned. The opening chromaticism describes with graphic word painting the poet's awaking to an illusory vision. As the ghostly Laura wipes away his tears, she sighs and then unexpectedly breaks into a torrent of angry words before disappearing, accompanied by highly descriptive musical treatment (Exs. 8-8a, b, c).

In the examples above, note the treatment on the word "sigh" (*sospira*), the upward-moving line on "grow angry" (*s'adira con parole*), and the dotted rhythm on "break" (*romper ponno*). As seen in this instance, certain pitch alterations have entered the music to give special emphasis in setting emotionally charged words and phrases.

The use of dissonance and chromatic alteration was carried to an extreme by the eccentric Don Carlo Gesualdo, whose melodramatic life was marked by bizarre incidents that were equaled only by his gift for writing violently expressive madrigals. Much as mannerist painters distorted the natural image for expressive purposes, Gesualdo delineated emotion-laden words with picturesque harmonic tone painting. Typical is Gesualdo's madrigal *Io pur respiro* (*Though I breathe*). Intense labored breathing (*respiro,* Ex. 8-9a), stabbing pain inflicted on a heart (*dispietato core,* Ex. 8-9b), the agitated longing for death (*Deh, morte,* Ex. 8-9c)—all are starkly presented through startling experimental harmonies.

The madrigal practices of Marenzio and Gesualdo opened the way for the mature use of chromaticism in the baroque period and such expressive techniques as the so-called *agitated style* of Monteverdi.

THE ENGLISH MADRIGAL

The late Renaissance in England, which produced such formidable personages as Henry VIII, Elizabeth I, Shakespeare, John Donne, and Inigo Jones, also generated a host of fine composers who worked very comfortably within the intimate dimensions of the madrigal. The English madrigal flourished in the transitional decade between the 16th and 17th centuries with the talents of Thomas Morley, John Dowland, Thomas Campion, John Wilbye, Thomas Weelkes, and Orlando Gibbons. The madrigal in England stressed

Example 8-8. Marenzio. *I weep.* Madrigal.

8-8a. Bars 20–21.

8-8b. Bars 24–27.

8-8c. Bars 29–31.

pastoral subjects and was crafted so that music was favored over text. Thomas Morley's collection honoring Queen Elizabeth I, *The Triumphs of Oriana,* featured representative madrigals from nearly all the great English composers of the time.

The English madrigalists were especially fond of poetry that celebrated the beauties of landscapes teeming with amorous nymphs and satyrs, rustic lasses and their swains, and charming flora and fauna. Thomas Weelkes cap-

Example 8-9. Gesualdo. *Though I breathe.* Madrigal.

8-9a. Bars 1–4.

8-9b. Bars 19–22.

8-9c. Bars 29–33.

tured this spirit in a technically difficult madrigal from a 1608 collection of three-voice *Airs or Fantastique Spirits.* One of them graphically reveals the delights of birdsongs as a feathered choir chirps, tweets, twitters, and trills its way through a piece that is easy on the ears, but not on the performers:

The nightingale, the organ of delight,
  The nimble lark, the blackbird, and the thrush,
And all the pretty quiristers of flight,
  That chant their music notes in every bush,
Let them no more content who shall excel;
  The cuckoo is the bird who bears the bell.

Invention of Printing

In the course of Renaissance developments, one technological breakthrough stands out—the invention of printing from movable type, which brought about a revolution in learning, education, religion, music, political life, and social conditions in general. Previously, books had been laboriously copied by hand onto parchment or paper, a slow painstaking process. While there were others who worked independently on movable-type inventions, Johann Gutenberg is generally credited with printing the first book from a press, the beautiful Mazarin Bible in 1456 (Plate VIII). Other craftsmen found ways to manufacture paper inexpensively. Soon the presses were turning out moderately priced editions of the classics; and with this increased availability of knowledge and communication, a momentous social change was under way.

The great port of Venice became a major center for the production and distribution of books. There in 1501 the printer Ottaviano Petrucci published the first movable-type printed anthology of songs with music. It was the *Harmonice musices odhecaton*, a collection of nearly 100 polyphonic compositions by such northern masters as Ockeghem, Obrecht, Heinrich Isaac, and Josquin (Fig. 8-3). The handy-sized volume quickly found wide acceptance among musicians, and soon the works of these composers were known far and wide. Anthologies of madrigals, motets, lute songs, and airs began to appear in all major European cities, and every music-minded household could aspire to own a library of singable, playable music for social entertainment.

Along with printed music came a series of books on social accomplishments and behavior. Their authors always pointed out that every lady and gentleman should be able to sing and play on some musical instrument. Music masters were available to provide instruction in singing and playing the lute, recorder, viols, and keyboard. The strong social pressure to attain musical prowess is reflected in an anecdote by the madrigalist Thomas Morley, who told of a young man at a dinner party, called upon by his hostess after the repast to join the company in singing a part. When he protested that he was unable, everyone raised their eyebrows and wondered how he had been brought up.

The Renaissance, a time when the modern world was young, witnessed the discovery of new worlds overseas; the rise of worldly wealth in the hands

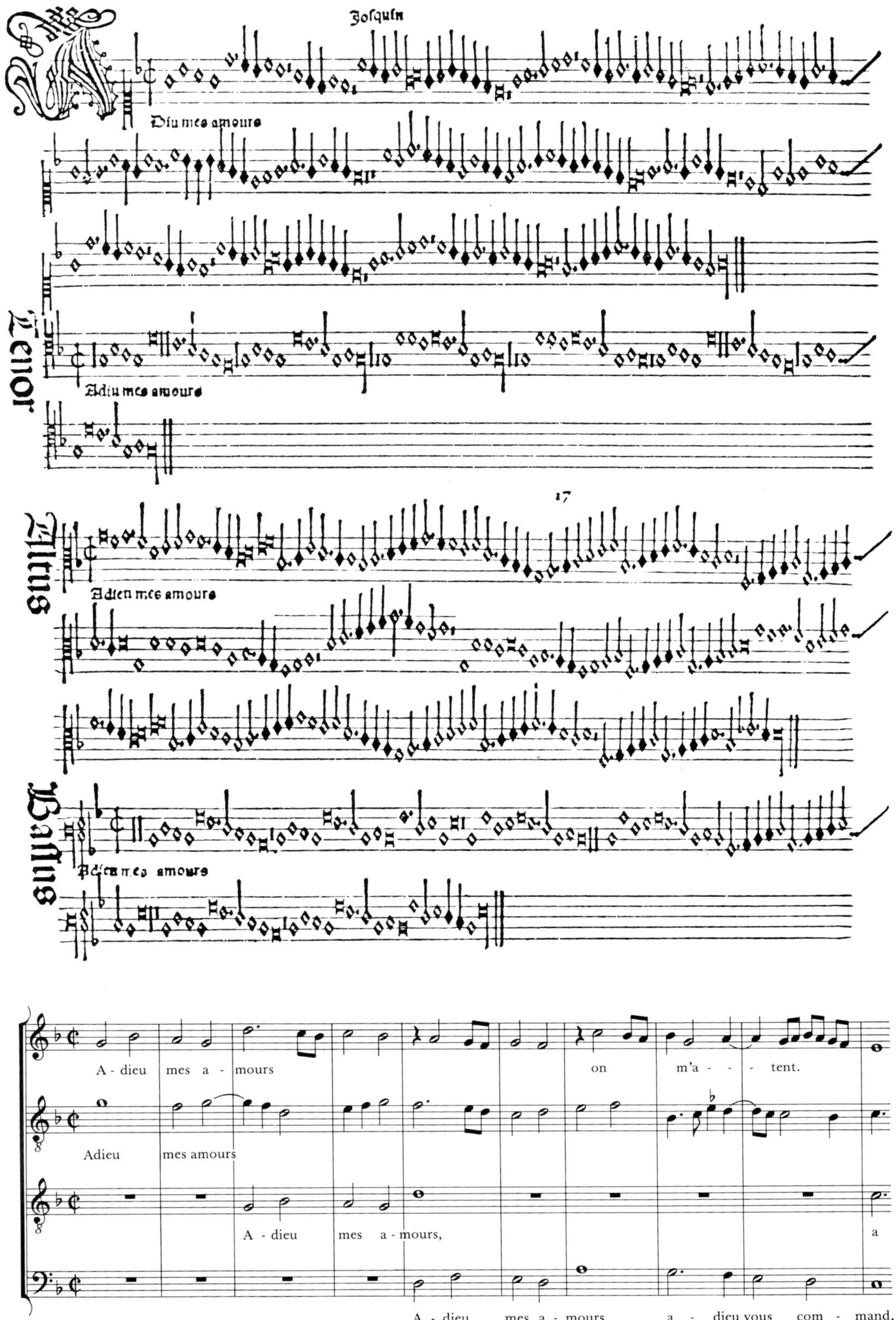

Figure 8-3. Josquin Desprez madrigal *Adieu mes amours (Goodbye, my loves),* in Ottaviano Petrucci, *Harmonice musices odhecaton,* 1501. Courtesy of the George Arents Research Library, Syracuse University, Syracuse, New York.

of the new merchant class and the beginnings of the commercial revolution; the rediscovery of the classics of Greco-Roman literature and art; the development of a new style in the building of churches and palaces, a more naturalistic approach to sculpture, and the discovery of linear perspective in painting; the reformation of the church from without and within; the availability of printed books to spread knowledge and to stimulate the mind, as well as printed scores for domestic music-making; the perfection of the art of musical counterpoint and a new understanding of harmony; and, above all, the affirmation of the joys of life here and now.

CHAPTER 9

Baroque Styles

THE TERM *baroque,* first associated with the visual arts, is now commonly applied to the corresponding style period in music history. Derived from *barocco,* a Portuguese name for a pearl of irregular shape, the word was originally used in a derogatory sense by partisans of the Renaissance ideal of symmetrical design. It indicated their disapproval of buildings, statuary, and paintings that seemed in their eyes grotesquely extravagant, overly ornate, and excessively exuberant.

New Styles and Ideas

The new music likewise sounded somewhat strange to ears accustomed to the balanced choral style of the Renaissance. None, however, was more conscious of the new spirit than the innovators themselves. In 1581 Vincenzo Galilei, father of the famous astronomer, published an argumentative little book entitled *Dialogue on Music, Ancient and Modern.* In 1602 his Florentine compatriot and fellow composer Giulio Caccini brought out a collection of songs, *Le Nuove Musiche* (*The New Music*). Its preface served as the manifesto of the new musical order and its title became the battle cry of the baroque.

Baroque art in all fields was a new and progressive style, the product of a period seeking new religious orientations, new philosophies of life, new geographical discoveries, new scientific knowledge, and new mechanical inventions. The period coincides with the continuing momentum of the Reformation and Counter-Reformation movements; with Descartes' conception of the

Gianlorenzo Bernini. *Apollo and Daphne,* 1622–25. Marble. Galleria Borghese, Rome. By permission of Alinari/Art Resource, New York.

Chronology

MUSICAL FIGURES

Northern Italy

Andrea Amati	c. 1511–1580
Vincenzo Galilei	c. 1520–1591
Giulio Caccini	c. 1545–1618
Jacopo Peri	1561–1633
Marco da Gagliano	1582–1643
Antonio Stradivari	1644–1737
Archangelo Corelli	1653–1713
Giuseppe Torelli	1658–1709
Giuseppe Guarneri "del Gesu"	1698–1744
Giuseppe Tartini	1692–1770
Pietro Locatelli	1695–1764

Rome

Philip Neri	1515–1595
Emilio de' Cavalieri	c. 1550–1602
Girolamo Frescobaldi	1583–1643
Luigi Rossi	1597–1653
Orazio Benevoli	1605–1672
Giacomo Carissimi	1605–1674

Venice

Giovanni Gabrieli	c. 1555–1612
Claudio Monteverdi	1567–1643
Francesco Cavalli	1602–1676
Antonio Cesti	1623–1669
Alessandro Stradella	c. 1644–1682
Antonio Vivaldi	1678–c. 1741
Benedetto Marcello	1686–1739

Naples

Carlo Gesualdo	1561–1613
Alessandro Scarlatti	1660–1725
Francesco Durante	1684–1755
Senesino (Francesco Bernardi)	1717–1740 (active)

North Germany and Holland

Jan P. Sweelinck	1562–1621
Michael Praetorius	1571–1621
Heinrich Schütz	1585–1672
Samuel Scheidt	1587–1654
Heinrich Scheidemann	1595–1663
Dietrich Buxtehude	1637–1707
Johann Kuhnau	1660–1722
Johann G. Walther	1684–1748
Johann S. Bach	1685–1750
Johann Goldberg	1727–1756

South Germany and Austria

Hans Leo Hassler	1564–1612
Johann Froberger	1616–1667
Georg Muffat	1653–1704
Johann Pachelbel	1653–1706
Johann Fux	1660–1741

London

Henry Lawes	1596–1662
William Davenant	1606–1668
Matthew Locke	1621–1677
Pelham Humfrey	1647–1674
John Blow	1649–1708
Henry Purcell	1659–1695
John Pepusch	1667–1752
George F. Handel	1685–1759

France

Jacques Chambonnières	c. 1602–1672
Jean Baptiste Lully	c. 1632–1687
François Couperin "Le Grand"	1668–1733

WRITERS AND DRAMATISTS

Ottavio Rinuccini	1562–1621
Lope de Vega	1562–1635
Pedro Caldéron	1600–1681
William Davenant	1606–1668
Pierre Corneille	1606–1684
Paul Gerhardt	1607–1676
John Milton	1608–1674
Molière (J. B. Poquelin)	1622–1673
John Dryden	1631–1700
Philippe Quinault	1635–1688
Jean Racine	1639–1699
Nahum Tate	1652–1715
Apostolo Zeno	1668–1750
William Congreve	1670–1729
Joseph Addison	1672–1719
Richard Steele	1672–1729
John Gay	1685–1732
Pietro Metastasio	1698–1782
Samuel Johnson	1709–1784

ARTISTS AND ARCHITECTS

Lorenzo Bernini	1598–1680
Rembrandt van Rijn	1606–1669
Louis Le Vau	1612–1670
Jean Lepautre	1618–1682
Elias G. Haussmann	1695–1774

HISTORICAL FIGURES

Philip II (Spain)	r. 1556–1598
René Descartes	1596–1650
James I (England)	r. 1603–1625
Charles I (England)	r. 1625–1649
Oliver Cromwell	r. 1653–1658
Isaac Newton	1642–1727
Louis XIV (France)	r. 1643–1715
Charles II (England)	r. 1660–1685
James II (England)	r. 1685–1688
William III and Mary (England)	r. 1689–1702
George I (England)	r. 1747–1727
Frederick II "The Great" (Prussia)	1712–1786

world as "matter in motion"; with the exploration of the vast new world of the Americas; with Copernicus' theory of a sun-centered solar system in which the earth was no longer static but whirling through space; with Newton's speculation on the laws of gravitational attraction and repulsion; with such inventions as the balloon to probe the upper atmosphere, the diving bell to plumb the depths of the sea, and the telescope and microscope to open human eyes to distant and minute regions of space. The Renaissance ideal of balance and repose, in short, was supplanted by a world in restless motion.

In architecture the love of lavish ornamentation was in the ascendance over restraint and severity, and the angular, symmetrical regularity and clear definition of Renaissance facades gave way to irregular, unbalanced lines, undulating curves, and deep recesses. The sculptured figures of Bernini, such as his *Saint Teresa in Ecstasy* (Plate IX) seemingly defied gravitational limitations as they floated freely on tons of marble clouds. Painters replaced the repose of vanishing-point perspective with restless diagonal accents and broken perspectives, and Rembrandt's dynamics of light and shade dissolved the shapely, clearly defined contours of Renaissance pictures.

It is hardly surprising, then, that musical theoreticians began to speculate on new acoustical possibilities, new methods of tuning instruments, new concepts of key feeling and modulation between tonal centers; or that baroque music started to teem with new energy, that tempos quickened, that complex ornamentation crept in, or that a new interplay between vocal and instrumental forces developed. "Music hath two ends," wrote one of the philosophers of the period, "first to please the senses . . . and secondly to move the affections or excite passion."

The baroque period can be viewed from a variety of angles. Chronologically it extends from the transition time of the late 16th century, throughout the 17th, and into the first half of the 18th century; or, to put it in human terms, from the three great early figures, Giovanni Gabrieli, Girolamo Frescobaldi, and Claudio Monteverdi, through the time dominated by those twin titans, Johann Sebastian Bach and George Frideric Handel.

Geographically the style had its inception in such Italian centers as Venice, Florence, and Rome, and then moved outward into the wider aristocratic orbits of the Spanish crown, the French court of the Sun King, Louis XIV, and the English Restoration rule of Charles II and his successors William and Mary. It then went on to its consummation in Georgian London with Handel and in Protestant Leipzig with Bach.

The new practices of the baroque quickly took on national and regional character. French opera, for instance, was distinguished from Italian opera by its language and dramatic style. Within Italy, differing local preferences accounted for such distinctive types as the Florentine recitative opera, the Roman choral opera, and the Venetian and Neapolitan solo opera. The religious music of Catholic south Germany differed radically from that of Protestant north Germany. Composers everywhere wrote French or Italian overtures, and Bach composed keyboard pieces variously designated as Italian concerto, French suite, and English suite.

Different sources of patronage account for such distinctions as Counter-Reformation, aristocratic, and Reformation aspects of the baroque. Counter-Reformation baroque, for instance, was the art and musical style fostered by the church militant. In a chapel in Rome called the Oratorio (oratory, or place for prayer), allegorical representations and spiritual dramas were set to music and performed, and the building gave its name to one of the important dramatic expressions of the period. Here such social workers as Saint Philip Neri discovered a way of making biblical stories come to life so vividly that the citizens to whom these "dramas" were addressed were both entertained and edified.

The aristocratic baroque, on the other hand, was nurtured in the courts of Italian nobles, where opera performances were literally the spectacle of princes. It was a period of great sovereigns such as Philip II of Spain, Louis XIV of France, and the Stuarts of England, all of whom strived to impress the world with their magnificent way of life, as befitted the cult of the divine right of kings.

Elsewhere in the centers of the Reformation movement, greater frugality, austerity, and industry prevailed, but even in Calvinistic Holland organ music was sponsored by the city of Amsterdam and the Lutheran churches of north Germany all had their professional organists and choirmasters. Baroque composers themselves also differentiated music according to its function in such settings as church, chamber, or theater. Several types of music were thus composed for definite purposes according to the desires of different patrons. Professional composers discriminated between the style of a sonata or concerto written for church use (*da chiesa*) and one composed for chamber performance (*da camera*).

The baroque period was also marked by a new awareness of the expressive possibilities of various vocal and instrumental media. Renaissance composers, for instance, had often merely indicated in their scores that certain passages were "to be sung or played"; the choice of voices or instruments was left to the discretion and convenience of the performers. Whether an Elizabethan composer was writing for a group of voices or a "chest of viols," very little difference in the style of writing could be detected.

During the later Renaissance, the terms *cantata* and *sonata* were used generically to differentiate between compositions to be sung and those to be played, respectively. In the early baroque period, however, these terms began to assume more specific meanings, as composers showed increased sensitivity to various ways of handling small and large choruses, solo and choral situations, and vocal and instrumental combinations.

In this period the construction of stringed instruments, especially violins, reached a peak at the celebrated north Italian center of Cremona, where the finest specimens of the violin maker's art emerged from the workshops of the Amati, Stradivari, and Guarneri families. The impetus for this development was doubtless inspired by the desire for an instrumental counterpart to the human voice—an instrument that would extend the voice's range and increase its dependability while at the same time retaining its sweet singing quality. Stringed instruments were thus established as the nucleus of chamber music groups and the orchestra, from which the trio sonata and the concerto grosso arose.

An idiomatic organ style gradually developed, different from the style of writing for string and wind instruments and largely devised by the organists at St. Mark's Basilica in Venice and by Girolamo Frescobaldi at St. Peter's in Rome. Later, distinctions were drawn between styles of organ music and those suitable for the clavichord and harpsichord. The *toccata* (touch piece) was a composition requiring keyboard technique rather than bowing or blowing. The keyboard pieces called *ricercar* and *canzona,* while related in their early stages to the vocal motet and French chanson, respectively, began to take on a definite instrumental character.

Above all, however, the early representatives of the baroque were very conscious of style, and stylistic rather than formal considerations prevailed early in the period. In the abovementioned books by Galilei and Caccini separating the old from the new music, criticism was directed specifically against the polyphonic principles of Renaissance writing, which emphasized complex contrapuntal manipulations at the expense of projecting and clarifying the dramatic meaning of the text. The experiments of Galilei and Caccini resulted in the formulation of a type of monodic, or single-voiced, form of vocal rhetoric with instrumental accompaniment that they called the *stile recitativo* (reciting style). By intoning the lines of a dramatic text while intensifying the natural inflections of speech, they achieved a manner of declamation suitable for sung drama.

Another early evidence of change comes with the new polychoral practices of the Venetian composers. The breaking up of the unity of Renaissance polyphony by opposing a full choir against a divided one, a chorus against solo singers, and vocal groups against instrumental ensembles pointed toward the development of the *stile concertante* (concerting style). When this principle of opposing larger and smaller forces was applied to purely instrumental music, the result was the concerto grosso and the solo concerto.

While continuing to write church music reminiscent of the Renaissance manner, Monteverdi injected a new tone into his madrigals by emphasizing the dramatic meaning of the text. In the various prefaces to his publications he noted his departure from tradition by coining the term *second practice* as opposed to the older *first practice* of Renaissance polyphony. Summarizing his position in a neat epigram, he pointed out that in the first practice of the Renaissance, "harmony is master of the word," while in his second practice, "the word is master of the harmony." He went on to make still finer distinctions within his second practice, such as the *stile concitato* (agitated style). These new stylistic elements demonstrate how the baroque encompassed a wider emotional spectrum, one that went far beyond the simplicity and restraint of the Renaissance by including such extremes as agitation and joyful abandon.

All these early baroque practices, which will be clarified later—recitative, concertato, concerto grosso, and fugue—are principles or styles of writing rather than forms. Other terms—such as *ritornel,* referring to the principle of repetition or return, *basso continuo* (continuous bass), *basso ostinato* (ground bass), and variation techniques—are to be considered structural devices.

The Basso Ostinato and the Trio Sonata Principle

As the newly polarized counterpoint became a standard feature of vocal and instrumental music in the early 17th century, individualized methods for using it effectively proliferated. In their attempts to find new ways to unify compositions that had no formal basis in a literary text, composers developed various approaches involving repetition and the new variation idea. Two areas of musical texture that would prove especially effective in 17th-century music were the basso ostinato and the trio sonata principle.

The word *ostinato,* like its English equivalent, "obstinate," refers to a stubborn, recurring line in a musical composition. When it is designed to be the recurring motif in the continuo part of a baroque composition, it is known as a *basso ostinato.* By the very obstinacy of its continuous reiteration, the figure encourages the listener to focus on the bass, thereby reinforcing the polarity of the top and bottom lines. The basso ostinato may be as short as two measures (Ex. 9-1) and is found with equal frequency in instrumental and vocal music of the 17th century. In England during the baroque period, basso ostinato was known as *ground bass.*

Example 9-1. Monteverdi. *Return, O Zephyr,* bars 1–3. Basso ostinato.

Two specific types of basso ostinato involving the variation idea are the *chaconne* and the *passacaglia,* closely related procedures in which variations are spun out over a theme that is stated and then repeated in the bass line. The best-known example is Bach's *Passacaglia* in C Minor (*BWV* 582) for organ, in which the eight-bar theme is first heard alone in the pedal. It is then repeated under the several variations as they unfold (Ex. 9-2).

Another popular baroque contrapuntal device was embodied in the *trio sonata* principle. Where the Camerata polarized melodic and bass lines, succeeding baroque composers enriched the texture by pairing two melodic

Example 9-2. Bach. *Passacaglia, BWV* 582, bars 1–16.

voices against the continuo line (Ex. 9-3). The resulting three lines of music provided the "trio" concept, though there were usually four performers, since the continuo required two for realization of the bass line (see p. 470). Many instrumental compositions utilized the term, and the three- to four-movement trio sonata quickly became a standard chamber music vehicle. Upper-voice combinations of two violins, violin and viola, violin and flute, or two oboes were common pairings. But while the "sonata" appellation suggested instruments, the principle was equally at home in vocal music, and vocal duets were equally common in opera and chamber compositions.

In the operas, oratorios, and cantatas of this time, composers were free to choose from any and all of the prevailing vocal, choral, and instrumental practices and styles and adapt them to the particular dramatic or liturgical situation at hand. Only later did such sectional schemes as binary and da capo arias and their instrumental counterparts become standardized.

It was also late in the period before cyclical structures in instrumental combinations crystallized into such relatively predictable series of units as those found in church sonatas, with four movements in slow–fast–slow–fast sequence, and chordal alternating with contrapuntal textures. Other combinations were gradually defined:

Chamber sonatas and dance suites with relatively fixed movements.

The French overture, with a slow harmonic opening in dotted rhythm, then a faster fugal section, and usually a return to a shortened version of the opening slow section.

Example 9-3. Bach. *Musical Offering, BWV* 1079. Trio sonata, bars 1–8.

The Italian overture, with a three-part format in a fast–slow–fast sequence.

The concerto design, with its late consolidation into a three-movement, fast–slow–fast organization.

Two-part combinations such as the prelude and fugue, toccata and fugue, and fantasy and fugue.

Even in this late phase, however, a considerable latitude of choice and formal freedom still prevailed.

Venice and the Concerting Style

Venice, that picturesque city built over the waters of the Adriatic Sea, was the scene of many of the most progressive developments of the early baroque period. A flourishing maritime trade had brought this Most Serene Republic a measure of prosperity unequaled at the time in any other world capital. Among its many enterprises were the famous Aldine Press, which brought inexpensive editions of the classics within the reach of scholars and literate laymen, and Petrucci's early printing of musical anthologies, through which the most important composers of the day found a wider audience (see Fig. 8-3). A crossroads between East and West, Venice had long been a center of wealth and culture and was the site of the first public library in modern Europe, and, in 1637, the first public opera house.

An unusual degree of liturgical freedom prevailed in Venice, since the secular authorities exercised considerable control in the appointments of church officials and clergy. This included the organists and choirmasters of St. Mark's Basilica, which, despite its size, was not a cathedral but the private chapel of the doge, the chief magistrate of Venice (see Plate X). Thus, while Rome remained the bastion of tradition, Venice became the center of progress that charted the course of the musical future.

Voyagers to Venice in the early years of the 17th century encountered music of a grandeur and excellence unsurpassed in their experience. A French visitor, Jean-Baptiste du Val, was as much fascinated by the diversity of musical forces involved in a performance—winds, strings, and organs in addition to voices—as he was astonished by the massive harmony they produced. An English traveler, Thomas Coryate, was even more impressionable, reporting of the music "both vocall and instrumental" that it was "so good, so delectable, so rare, so admirable, so superexcellent, that it did even ravish and stupifie all those strangers that never heard the like." Coryate details the variety in the size of musical ensembles and the diversity of the instruments employed: "Sometimes sixeteene played together upon their instruments, ten Sagbuts, foure Cornets and Viol de gambaes of an extraordinary greatness; sometimes tenne, sixe Sagbuts and four Cornets; sometimes two, a Cornet and a treble violl."

Venice was a city of exuberant splendor, and the music that held the visitors spellbound was an essential ingredient not only in lavish secular entertainments but also in the sumptuous religious celebrations that were an important part of the life of the community. Du Val's impressions were inspired by a vespers service at the Church of the Holy Savior on the eve of the feast of Saint Theodore, while Coryate's observations were based on a "festivitie solemnized to the honour of Saint Roch which consisted principally of Musicke." For Venetians, the borderline that separated the religious from the secular seems frequently to have been blurred. In Venetian painting, Gentile Bellini's *Procession in St. Mark's Square* (Plate X) and Veronese's *Marriage at Cana* (Plate XI) illustrate the infusion of worldly pomp in the sacred pageantry of the Venetians.

St. Mark's, with a central plan that organized all architectural parts under the all-embracing unity of a central dome (Fig. 9-1), lent itself to a type of acoustical experimentation that led to the so-called *polychoral style*. Its ground plan resembled the equal-armed Greek cross; instead of the usual long nave with all the singers concentrated in a single section, the choir of St. Mark's was divided into two groups—hence the term *cori spezzati* (broken choirs)—and placed above the ground level in separate lofts on either side of the central area under the dome. Each choir was a complete four-part unit with its own organ and supporting instruments. When Adrian Willaert was appointed chapelmaster in 1527, he raised this polychoral practice to a high level of accomplishment that commanded the attention of the musical world.

Willaert, a Netherlander, was a practitioner of the complex polyphony associated with his distinguished forebears—Ockeghem, Josquin Desprez, and Isaac—and he consistently worked within the contrapuntal techniques of the older style. By perceiving new potentialities in the acoustical conditions of St. Mark's, however, and by utilizing the opposing choral groups for spatial contrast, he made the first significant departures from the pure polyphony of his predecessors. Through Willaert, the Venetian school began to speak in new accents, while still retaining the traditional Renaissance contrapuntal vocabulary.

In his motets there is a noticeable breaking up of the unity of the chorus, as well as a new way of handling the bass parts almost as if they were conceived harmonically. While his vocal lines still flow smoothly in the Renaissance manner, there is increased awareness of verticality in contrapuntal writing. The dissolution of the unified flow of Renaissance polyphony is likewise seen in the tendency of Willaert and his successors, in both choral and instrumental music, to separate the several sections of their works at certain cadential points. In the older counterpoint, the voice leading had been managed so smoothly, and the beginnings and ends of phrases had overlapped each other so skillfully, that nothing impeded the continuous flow. The Venetian motets and madrigals, as well as the keyboard works of the time, thus definitely began to display a sectional character.

From Willaert through his colleagues and successors—Zarlino, Merulo, Andrea Gabrieli and his illustrious nephew Giovanni Gabrieli—the polycho-

Figure 9-1. Venice, Piazza San Marco. Aerial view. By permission of Underwood and Underwood/Bettmann Archive, New York.

ral style progressed in a continuous line toward its climax. In 1587, with the publication by the Gabrielis of their *Concerti per voci e stromenti (Concertos for Voices and Instruments)*, the new concerting idea, based on the principle of opposing tonal masses of unequal numbers, volume, and density, began to take more definite shape. It culminated with Giovanni Gabrieli's *Symphoniae sacrae* (*Sacred Symphonies*), the first volume appearing in 1597 and the second posthumously in 1615. These collections introduced a new style of music featuring the concepts of *symphony* and *concerto.*

At this time the word *concerto,* together with the verb forms *concertante* and *concertato,* indicated a playing together or a dialogue between contrasting groups. At first this implied an interplay between contrasting forces, such as the opposition of two or more choirs or instrumental groups, or vocal groups versus instrumental ensembles. In addition certain polarities were set up between high and low registers, polyphonic and homophonic textures, loud and soft intensities, between string tone quality and that of wind instruments. Later the procedure took a more purely instrumental turn, emphasizing the contrast between a larger and smaller group of instrumental players, as in the *concerto grosso.*

While St. Mark's was not the only place where music for multiple choirs flourished, it was singularly well adapted to an impressive arrangement of a number of different choral groups. This spatial component seems to have been an especially important part of the aesthetics of Gabrieli's polychoral practice. The architecture of the church where he served as organist may well have provided a source of suggestion and a testing ground for experimentation. Likewise, while the techniques of divided choir treatment neither originated nor ended with Gabrieli, his imaginative and extensive exploitation of these techniques makes his work a veritable compendium of the polychoral style.

More impressive than the techniques, however, is the wide range of expressive purposes to which they are applied. The surface of Gabrieli's music reflects its once functional role as part of the pageantry of the Venetian church ceremonial. But what survives in the modern revival of his music is not merely an impressive relic of a curiously grandiloquent culture, but a completely vital and viable music that had wide popular appeal.

"The grandiloquent man," remarked the English novelist George Eliot, "is never bent on saying what he feels or what he sees, but on producing a certain effect on his audience." Impressing, indeed overpowering an audience was by all means relevant to Gabrieli's purposes. Nonetheless, the ceremonial strut and the pompous processional manner are much ameliorated by moments of eloquent lyricism and by an urgent, inward passion. The splendor of the "Nunc dimittis," a 14-part triple chorus, and the jubilation of "Plaudite psallite," a 12-part triple chorus, both from the 1597 *Symphoniae sacrae,* must be balanced against the gentle purity of "Angelus ad pastores ait," a 12-part double chorus in the 1587 *Concerti,* and the introspection of "O Jesu mi dulcissime," an 8-part double chorus from the 1615 *Symphoniae sacrae.*

This balance in the range of expression marks not only the music of Giovanni Gabrieli but also the compositions of his greatest pupil, the German composer Heinrich Schütz. Schütz's tribute to his master is worth quoting as much for the florid manner that one composer of sacred music uses when writing about another as for evidence of the esteem in which Gabrieli was held in his day: "Gabrieli, immortal gods, how great a man! If loquacious antiquity had seen him, and let me say it in a word, it would have set him above Amphions, or if the Muses had loved wedlock, Melpomene would have rejoiced in no other spouse."

To circumvent Roman control, St. Mark's was designated as the doge's private chapel, so that its musicians could be appointed locally. Those musicians who performed regularly at St. Mark's were thus regarded more as part of one of the most brilliant courts of Europe than as servants of the church. Many of Gabrieli's motets derive their ceremonial character from the fact that they commemorate the great festivals—St. Mark's Day, Ascension, Christmas, Easter.

In the score of his polychoral motet *In ecclesiis,* Giovanni Gabrieli calls for two choirs. Chorus I is to be used either as a whole or with its soprano, alto, tenor, and bass sections singing separately; Chorus II always functions as a unit—vocal soloists, an organ, and an instrumental ensemble consisting of three cornetti, a viola, and two trombones. It is a nonliturgical motet of the processional type apparently intended for performance on some grand civic occasion such as that depicted in Bellini's *Procession in St. Mark's Square* (Figs. 9-2, 9-3). Gabrieli expresses the Venetian love of splendor in a musical realization equal to or even exceeding Bellini's visual pomp and pageantry.

In this motet the sopranos of Chorus I, accompanied by the organ, lead off with the first stanza of the psalmlike text (bars 1–5), while Chorus II chimes in on the alleluia (bars 6–12), which functions as a refrain between verses. The tenors of Chorus I then proceed with the second verse, also with organ accompaniment (bars 13–31), and the alleluia follows once more. The choruses are then silenced for the instrumental sinfonia (bars 32–43), appropriate for a procession (such as that depicted in Figure 9-2) which enters with blazing, brassy sonorities and arresting, festive chordal progressions. The third verse is given to the altos and tenors of Chorus I, accompanied now by the six-part instrumental ensemble rather than the organ. Fullness of sonority increases in the next alleluia (bars 93–99), when the entire Chorus I and the organ join with the other forces. The fifth and final verse brings in the soloists, the complete double choir, the instrumental aggregate and the organ—a total of fourteen independent parts. The accumulation of tonal masses and volumes is then brought to a climax in the concluding alleluia, in which all forces unite in a mighty cadence that projects the full color of the authentic Venetian

Figure 9-2. Detail of Plate X: Chorus. Bellini. *Procession in St. Mark's Square,* 1496. Oil on canvas. Galleria dell'Accademia, Venice. Courtesy of Gabinetto Fotographico Nazionale, Venice.

Figure 9-3. Detail of Plate X: Brass ensemble. Bellini. *Procession in St. Mark's Square,* 1496. Oil on canvas. Galleria dell'Accademia, Venice. Courtesy of Gabinetto Fotographico Nazionale, Venice.

sound in one huge tonal block, and at the same time revels in the wealth of grandiose sonorities for their own sake.

In ecclesiis is an excellent illustration of the *concertato* principle, with its variety of contrasting elements brought together in a harmonious union of opposites. The slower and faster tempos, the polyphonic and homophonic sections, the solo and choral forces, the vocal and instrumental colors, the contrast of soft and loud dynamic levels—all contribute to the total effect. Moreover, a unity is created by the repetition of the alleluia between each verse, as it consistently alternates with the contrasts provided by the intervening sections.

The larger body, represented by the alleluia with its *ritornel* (refrain), contributes unity in its summations and repetitions, while the smaller groups provide the variety. Furthermore, the active progress of the parts, or episodes, reinforced by the prevailing dynamic duple rhythm, can be perceived as moving against the solid background of the whole with its more staid triple rhythm. The throwing back and forth of the unequal tonal volumes and masses thus promotes the feeling of progress through time and space. *In ecclesiis* is a religious expression, to be sure, but one that is infused with sonorous excitement, rich textural contrasts, and material splendor, all projected on an enormous spatial scale.

In Giovanni Gabrieli's *Sonata pian' e forte,* the polychoral style and the concertato principle cross over into the realm of instrumental music. It is a sonata only in the sense that it is meant to be played rather than sung. The work is scored for two unequal ensembles—one consisting of a cornetto and three trombones, and the other of a viola and three trombones—set up in opposition to one another. The *piano* and *forte* announced in the title are true dynamic contrasts of soft and loud levels achieved by combining and separating the two instrumental choirs. Further contrasts are the interplay of high and low registers and the string and wind colors. With this one stroke, Gabrieli cleared the way for the transition of the concertato style to the instrumental medium. This work may be viewed as a prototype, opening the road for the developments that led to the concerto grosso and solo concerto.

Concurrently with their experiments in instrumental ensemble writing, the Venetian composers, beginning with Andrea Gabrieli, developed several types of idiomatic solo pieces for the organ, such as the *intonazione* (intonation), toccata, fantasia, ricercar, and canzona. In each case the early examples were obviously written-out versions of the free improvisation practiced at that time. The intonation, as its name implies, was an introductory warm-up piece functioning as a prelude to the singing of a motet. The organist began with an exhibition of digital dexterity, displaying fast finger-work at the keyboard. The intonation was brought to a close with a chordal cadence establishing the mode and opening pitch for the first choral entrance in the motet.

Toccatas and *fantasias* were usually longer and more elaborate, with the organist scampering over the keyboard in cascades of scales, arpeggios, and broken chords, after which it was customary to settle down to a fuguelike contrapuntal section.

The *ricercar* began its history as an instrumental counterpart to the vocal motet. Derived from the Italian verb meaning "to search" or "to seek again," the name refers to the frequent return of the subject. As each subsequent statement of subject or counter-subject appears, it ushers in a new section in which contrapuntal imitations and rhythmic as well as melodic variation techniques are employed. The ricercar is a prototype of the later fugue.

The *canzona* at first was an instrumental version of the secular French chanson. Compared to the ricercar, it is lighter in texture, more dancelike in spirit, and less strict in its contrapuntal treatment. Both the ricercar and the canzona can be played either at the keyboard or by an instrumental chamber ensemble. In the hands of the Roman organist Frescobaldi, these keyboard types took on a functional character in the liturgy. Such titles as *Toccata per il elevazione (Toccata for the Elevation of the Host)* and *Ricercar dopo il Credo (Ricercar after the Creed)* obviously indicate the points in the mass during which they were intended to be played.

The Camerata

In late 16th-century Florence, meanwhile, a group of intellectuals and music enthusiasts formed a literary and artistic circle they called the Camerata. Together they argued, with considerable heat and in the light of some scholarship, about the need for creating "modern" music by a revival of the spirit of Greek tragedy. Vincenzo Galilei, animated by the spirit of classical antiquity, enthusiastically attributed all music excellence to the ancients. But while he and his Camerata colleagues were relatively well informed on Greek philosophy, poetry, the text of the extant dramas, and the legends attributing miraculous powers to music, their knowledge of Greek music was largely a figment of their lively imaginations. They were aware that the Greek drama incorporated music, that the chorus sang and danced, and that the dialogue was intoned in songlike fashion. But beyond this, they had little idea of how to "revive" ancient music drama.

With the deaths of both Palestrina and Orlande Lassus in 1594, the way was open for a full-fledged attack on the traditions of Renaissance counterpoint. Polyphonic settings of poetic texts, the members of the Camerata felt, were overly concerned with contrapuntal manipulations that tended to obscure rather than illuminate the meaning of the text. Such overemphasis on the perfection of craftsmanship, in their view, limited music's range of expression and precluded concern with its moral and dramatic significance. In order to realize the full meaning of the text, each word and phrase had to be projected with proper emphasis and sufficient force to communicate its full measure of dramatic power. This, they argued, could be done only with a single melodic part supported by appropriate instrumental accompaniment. Hence

Galilei, Giulio Caccini, Jacopo Peri, and Marco da Gagliano composed and published books of secular solo songs they called *monodies.*

The most notable departure from Renaissance polyphony lay in eliminating the homogeneity of the contrapuntal texture. In baroque practice, the upper melodic part was isolated as a solo melody, and the lower voices were absorbed in a bass complex called the *basso continuo,* thus creating an upper and lower line moving against each other. The continuo line, always the bass part, was played by the left hand of the harpsichordist or the organist, or both, and by a melody instrument like the viola da gamba, the equivalent of the modern cello (Fig. 9-4). Between the top and bottom lines, that is, between the melody and the continuo, filler parts were added improvisationally by the keyboard performer. Numbers were often placed above or beneath the continuo bass line to guide the keyboard player in realizing the filler parts in a kind of musical shorthand known as *figured bass.*

Sometimes the continuo part was not melodically conceived, but simply the bass notes of vertical chords. Given the bass notes, the harpsichordist would then fill in the vertical chords to support the melody. Chords were often chosen coloristically, to "paint" the meaning of the text. According to

Figure 9-4. Johann Zoffany. *George, Third Earl Cowper, and the Gore Family,* c. 1775. Oil on canvas. By permission of the Yale Center for British Art, Paul Mellon Collection, New Haven, Conn.

Peri, the vocal part should be maintained at the same pitch level until the meaning of the text called for a change upward or downward. The chord that supported the singer's pitch should also remain the same until the vocal part and the mood dictated a change. In the Camerata conception, chords were thus not organized into harmonic progressions in the modern sense, but were governed more by the mood of the text.

The *stile recitativo* (reciting style) was the Camerata's term for a new type of vocal declamation designed to imitate and intensify the natural inflections of speech. Galilei advised composers to concern themselves less with the intricacies of counterpoint and more with the ways people speak with one another. Observe, he said,

> when one quiet gentleman speaks with another, in what manner he speaks, how high or low his voice is pitched, with what volume of sound, with what sort of accents and gestures, and with what rapidity or slowness his words are uttered. Let them mark a little what difference obtains in all these things when one of them speaks with one of his servants, or one of these with another; let them observe the prince when he chances to be conversing with one of his subjects and vassals, when with the petitioner who is entreating his favor; how the man infuriated or excited speaks; the married woman, the girl, the mere child, the clever harlot, the lover speaking to his mistress as he seeks to persuade her to grant his wishes, the man who laments, the one who cries out, the timid man, and the man exultant with joy. From these variations of circumstance, if they observe them attentively and examine them with care, they will be able to select the norm of what is fitting for the expression of any other conception whatever that can call for their handling.

In the course of the Camerata experiments, the principles of monodic melody and continuo accompaniment, the new musical rhetoric based on the natural inflection of speech—recitative—and the desire to recapture the dramatic impact of Greek tragedy were all combined and applied to the setting of complete dramatic texts. The poet and playwright Ottavio Rinuccini, the principal literary figure of the Camerata, collaborated with the various composing members on a number of these musical dramas.

Chronologically, Peri's *Dafne* (1594–98) came first, though its music is now lost. It was followed by *Euridice* (1600), which survives in versions by both Peri and Caccini; and still another setting of the *Daphne* was made in 1608 by Marco da Gagliano. These productions may be distinguished from the pastoral plays long established in Renaissance tradition. The distinction is drawn, however, on the grounds of their being composed with continuous music throughout, rather than merely with intermittent musical interludes between the sequences of spoken dialogue. Thus in their zeal to re-create Greek tragedy, the Camerata had actually uncovered an entirely new formula, and the momentous result was nothing less than the foundation for the art of opera.

Furthermore, in 1600, when Peri's *Euridice* was performed in Florence, a religious counterpart was produced in Rome—*Rappresentazione di Anima e di Corpo* (*The Story of the Soul and the Body*). Its composer, Emilio de' Cavalieri, whose extended period of residence in Florence coincided with the flourishing of the Camerata, was thoroughly conversant with all the developments and devices employed by his colleagues there. His work, however, had nothing to do with classical antiquity; it was, rather, a religious morality play with such allegorical characters as Time, World, and Life, as well as the Soul and the Body of the title. Its sacred character, its similarity in procedure to the early Camerata opera experiments, as well as its printed publication in 1600, gave it an influence out of all proportion to its actual musical importance.

While the *Rappresentazione* can certainly be considered one of the early prototypes of modern oratorio, that branch of music drama had to await the coming of a more powerful and persuasive advocate than Cavalieri. Giacomo Carissimi became the first great master of the oratorio style, just as Monteverdi was the genius who perceived the dramatic possibilities in the various experiments of his time and went on to become the first great master of the operatic stage.

Monteverdi and Early Opera

The musico-dramatic ideals that were envisaged but far from realized by the Camerata were translated into a viable medium by Claudio Monteverdi, who has aptly been designated the founder of modern music. Early in his career this distinguished musician had not only mastered all the traditional musical techniques but had also assimilated all the current experiments and important innovations of his time. Unlike the Camerata composers, Monteverdi was not so much interested in overthrowing Renaissance polyphony as he was in bringing the art of counterpoint up to date in a way that was more suitable to the spirit of his time.

Seeing that the old and new styles could be made to operate side by side, he separated them partly on a functional basis, retaining the pure choral sound of Palestrina's flowing counterpoint for sacred purposes and calling it the *prima prattica* (first practice). The representative style and other promising experiments of his time he considered better suited to secular music, especially in connection with dramatic presentations, and they therefore became the *seconda prattica* (second practice).

The group of operas that Monteverdi produced at Mantua and Venice, as well as the series of nine books of madrigals that he published, quite literally created the foundation of modern music. In 1607, with his first Mantuan opera, *Orfeo,* Monteverdi in a single stroke determined the future course of lyric drama. For this opera he combined all the styles, ideas, techniques, and devices known to him.

The opening instrumental sinfonia, the prototype of the future opera overture, is an orchestral toccata in the style of the Gabrielis and would have been equally at home in Venice at St. Mark's. The prologue, intoned by a personification of Music, is a strophic song with an instrumental ritornel separating the stanzas. Groups of nymphs and shepherds sing madrigal choruses, while the principals in the cast declaim their lines in a recitative style of deeply expressive character. Orpheus' love song "Rosa del ciel" ("Rose of Heaven") and his desperate outpouring of grief at Eurydice's demise, "Tu se' morta" ("Thou art dead"), are cases in point.

When Orpheus has to summon his most persuasive powers to pacify the infernal furies, he pleads with them in the eloquent aria "Possente spirito" ("Mighty spirit"), a concerted dialogue in the Venetian concertato manner. In a series of strophic variations the voice contends with instruments that personify the shades of Hades, and the vocal part is opposed in turn by two violins, two cornetti, two harps; and, between the fourth and fifth stanzas, by trio combinations including lower strings. As Orpheus is being rowed across the river Styx, the vast spaces of the underworld are suggested by the choral echo effects so typical of baroque dynamics.

The score is also important for its use of a large and varied instrumentation and its primitive but powerful orchestration, since Monteverdi wrote independent parts for instruments instead of following the customary practice of letting them double the vocal lines. He selected the instrumental colors that were most in keeping with the character they accompanied and with the dramatic situation at hand. The choruses of shepherds, for instance, appropriately have a piping obbligato of piccolos and flutes, while the recitatives of the boatman, Charon, are accompanied by lugubrious chords on the organ and spectral tones from the trombones.

Thus, by dramatically contrasting pastoral and infernal elements, by organizing entire scenes with recurrent choral and instrumental ritornels, as well as by combining all the various musical ideas at his command with those of the poetic text—plus scenery, gesture, acting, and ballet sequences—Monteverdi succeeded in making opera effective in both the dramatic and the theatrical sense.

The "Lament" is one of a group of surviving fragments of Monteverdi's opera *Arianna* (1608), the story of Bacchus and Ariadne from classical mythology. It is an eloquent instance of the way he is able to focus on moments of intense human emotion in order to reveal human character within a dramatic context (Ex. 9-4). Upon realizing she has been abandoned by her lover, Theseus, Ariadne gives expression to her overwhelming grief. The downward plunge of the first half phrase encompasses daring melodic dissonance at the outset. Rising emotional tension is portrayed in the chromatically ascending line in bars 4 and 5, as well as the precipitous decline from the upper D to the octave below (bars 5–6). The second and contrasting phrase (bars 7–14) gradually mounts to the poignant climax of bar 14. The exact repetition of the opening phrase (bars 15–19) produces a compact prototype of the three-part da capo aria that was destined to become one of the most important formal designs of the period.

Example 9-4. Monteverdi. *Arianna.* "Lament." Aria in A B A form.

An interesting comparison can be made between this homophonic aria and the polyphonic madrigal setting Monteverdi made of the same melody some years later. His problem was to turn a free-flowing aria with a melody that followed the natural speech rhythms into a contrapuntal composition (Ex. 9-5). In the process the melody is not changed in its essential elements, but is adapted to fit into the contrapuntal texture. The harmonic dissonances within the counterpoint are geared to the meaning of the text, and the result is a good example of the modern harmonic counterpoint that Monteverdi called the second practice.

Monteverdi's early operas, as well as the extant later ones he wrote for Venice—*Return of Ulysses* (1641) and *Coronation of Poppaea* (1642)—were always conceived and executed in terms of the theater. He understood well that the text and the music should be maintained in a balanced relationship, but he also knew that in the final analysis the music had to carry the real dramatic weight. The "Lament," for instance, occurs at a point when Ariadne prepares to bid farewell to life itself, and it became a model for the great *addio* (farewell) scenes of Italian opera. For all its individual melodic excellence, however, it

Example 9-5. Monteverdi. *Arianna.* "Lament," bars 1–8. Madrigal version.

makes no real dramatic sense except with regard to what precedes and what follows. In other words, the audience must witness the heroine's previous hopes and desires so that they will know exactly to what she is bidding farewell. Thus the planning, preparing, and placing of scenes is one of the all-important aspects of opera.

In his effort to widen the range of dramatic music, Monteverdi undertook a series of works in which he experimented with new rhythmic and orchestral devices. Since he used these devices to project specific emotional states, an analysis of such emotional states was requisite. Hence he prefaced his eighth book of madrigals (1638) with a foreword that begins: "I have reflected that the principal passions or affections of our mind are three, namely, anger, moderation and humility or supplication; so the best philosophers declare, and the very nature of our voice indicates this in having high, low and middle registers. The art of music also points clearly to these three in its terms 'agitated', 'soft', and 'moderate'."

The Italian word for "agitated" is *concitato.* Reflecting that the soft and temperate styles were already well known, but that he had never encountered an example of the *concitato* style, Monteverdi undertook to rediscover it by following the precepts laid down for it by Plato. "Take that harmony," he quoted from Plato, "that would fittingly imitate the utterances and the accents of a brave man who is engaged in warfare." Monteverdi further observed that "it is contraries which greatly move our mind," and his eighth book is suitably entitled *Madrigali guerriere ed amorosi* (*Madrigals Warlike and Amorous*).

The most arresting of his concitato works is a curious theater piece entitled *Il combattimento di Tancredi e Clorinda* (*The Combat of Tancred and Clorinda*). It is based on part of the twelfth canto of the famous *Gerusalemme liberata* (*Jerusa-*

lem Delivered), by Torquato Tasso, one of the most impassioned of Italian baroque poets. In a preface to this work, Monteverdi asked the instrumentalists to observe the distinction between the concitato passages and the *molle* (soft) passages, and he further urged that they interpret their parts "in imitation of the passions of the words." The narrator, called *testo* (text part), was enjoined to sing his part clearly, with careful pronunciation of the words, and to refrain from the insertion of ornament except for the one instance where Monteverdi felt it allowable. The singing style likewise was to be "a simulation of the passions of the words."

From the technical point of view, the *Combattimento* is a compendium of the concitato style. Many rhythmic devices are used to mirror the text more realistically—like the figure that represents the galloping of horses. The most famous of the orchestral devices in this score are the string indications *pizzicato* and *tremolando.* The latter in particular is useful to indicate a state of excitement. In a tremolando a note is rapidly repeated many times in one measure, producing a shuddering effect. Monteverdi reported that musicians at first found this device "more ridiculous than praiseworthy," and in simplifying the passage by playing the one note instead of sixteen to a measure, they destroyed "the resemblance to agitated speech" that he intended. He cautioned them to perform such passages in "the manner as written." Monteverdi's tremolando is now one of the clichés of modern orchestration, a stock-in-trade device to represent foreboding, uneasiness, mystery, agitation, or tension of any sort.

Both in his operas and in his madrigals Monteverdi contributed many of the melodic and rhythmic figures that quickly became an accepted part of the vocabulary of baroque operas, oratorios, and cantatas. Baroque psychology conceived the affects as states of mind in the sense of static mental and emotional attitudes, rather than as the more dynamic psychological moods of later times. Specific musical patterns were thus intended, through the process of psychological association, to evoke certain emotional responses in audiences.

Monteverdi's rendering of the poetic imagery of a text is well illustrated by his madrigal setting of Rinuccini's sonnet "Zefiro torna" ("Return, O Zephyr"). The composer invented for it a series of representative-style passages: an undulating melodic figure for the word "waves," *l'onde* (Ex. 9-6a); still another for "murmuring," *mormorando* (Ex. 9-6b); while the scenic profile of the "mountains and valleys high and deep," *da monti e da valli ime e profonde,* is appropriately described with mounting and dipping lines (Ex. 9-6c). For passages of more intense personal expression, Monteverdi rises to the occasion with telling harmonic shifts. To convey the ardent lover's emotional dilemma—"As my fate wills it, now I weep, now I sing," *Come vuol mia ventura hor piango, hor canto*—he employs such contrasts as the downward chromatic descending line and startling dissonance of tremendous intensity for "weep," as well as a festive florid coloratura for "sing" (Ex. 9-6d, 9-6e).

Example 9-6. Monteverdi. *Return, O Zephyr.*

9-6a. Bars 28–31.

l'on - - - - - - - - - - - - - - de

9-6b. Bars 35–38.

e - mor - mo - ran - - - - - - - - - - do

9-6c. Bars 67–73.

e da mon - ti da mon - ti e da val - li da val - li i - me e pro-fan - de

9-6d. Bars 142–45.

pian - - - - - go

9-6e. Bars 148–50.

can - - - - - - - - - - - to

This little chamber duet for two tenors and continuo accompaniment can be described technically as a vocal chaconne with free strophic variations over a steadily repeated ground bass. Since the wealth of melodic and harmonic variety takes place over this insistent basso ostinato, the unity of the composition, despite the freedom of the vocal lines, remains serenely undisturbed.

Monteverdi, as well as the later baroque composers, conceived of an emotion as a psychological disturbance that could be represented by a specific type of dissonance, and the ensuing state of rest by an appropriate resolution and consonance. Melodic figurations could thus be made to correspond to figures of speech. Above all, there was a new concept of musical communication in which an agitated, a restless, or a calm emotional state could be represented with a particular rhythmic pattern.

Baroque as an International Style

While the various Italian centers were the proving grounds of the early baroque, the style was destined to reach its culmination in the great northern centers of Paris, London, Dresden, and Leipzig. The Venetian polychoral practice represented by Gabrieli's large choruses subsequently moved into a stylistic phase known as the *colossal baroque.* In its later manifestations this aspect of baroque style saw the number of choral parts expanded to unprecedented proportions in such works as Orazio Benevoli's mass for the dedication of the Salzburg Cathedral (1628), in which the mighty assembly of musical forces adds up to a total of 53 parts—16 choral, 34 instrumental, plus 2 organs and continuo. A hundred years later, J. S. Bach used such large Venetian double choruses at the opening and close of his *Saint Matthew Passion,* though on a reduced scale. The Venetian concept of terraced dynamics with its contrasting levels of intensity was also adopted in baroque organ music, in the "echo" pieces of Sweelinck and Scheidt in Amsterdam and northern Germany.

The concertato idea, with its dualism that paradoxically produces unity, also became one of the ruling principles of the baroque style. This is manifest through the setting up of polar extremes—larger and smaller groups, solo and orchestral ensembles, soprano and bass registers, slow and fast tempos, regular and irregular rhythms, soft and loud dynamic levels, consonant and dissonant intervals, diatonic and chromatic harmonies, blocked chords and flowing counterpoint—and the maintenance of a continuous interplay between such opposing elements. The principle of supporting the upper melodic lines with the harmonies of basso-continuo accompaniments likewise became a universal practice. From Monteverdi to Bach and Handel, the composers of the period employed the continuo as the foundation of ensemble writing, and baroque music consequently stood solidly on its powerful support.

The early beginnings of the idiomatic treatment of voices and instruments continued throughout the period. Such instruments as the lute, clavier, and lower strings were used mainly in supporting roles; while others, such as the violin, flute, and trumpet, were considered principals in the melodic cast.

Girolamo Frescobaldi, as the foremost organist of the Counter-Reformation, exerted a strong influence on the development of keyboard music, especially in Roman Catholic countries and more particularly through such outstanding pupils as Johann Froberger, who spread Frescobaldi's ideas in Vienna and South Germany. Likewise alert to the instrumental developments in Italy, Jan P. Sweelinck established his reputation as the municipal organist of Amsterdam. He is identified with a type of toccata known as the *fantasy in the manner of an echo,* which represented a transfer of the Venetian polychoral practice to the keyboard. In such pieces a short motif is tossed back and forth from one manual and registration to another with neatly terraced, contrasting dynamic levels. Synthesizing both the Venetian and the English keyboard traditions, Sweelinck's works show the baroque fondness for lively invention, complicated variation techniques, and opulent tonal effects. Sweelinck's fame attracted a host of students, including such important German composers as Samuel Scheidt of Halle and Heinrich Scheidemann of Hamburg. These composers passed on the tradition to the generation of Pachelbel and Buxtehude, who in turn became the principal German influences on Bach and Handel.

During his years at Venice, Monteverdi witnessed the transition of opera from princely court entertainment to public spectacle. Notable also was the toleration by both the Roman Catholic and the Protestant Lutheran churches of the opera idiom in sacred oratorios and cantatas. Secular operas and sacred oratorios were often so close in style as to be indistinguishable, except for the texts and the intended place of performance. Opera thus moved outward from Venice to the cosmopolitan centers of Paris and London, while the oratorio was destined for glory in Italy with Carissimi; in France with Carissimi's pupil Marc Antoine Charpentier; in Germany with Heinrich Schütz, a pupil of Giovanni Gabrieli, a diligent student of the music of Monteverdi, and without doubt the greatest of German composers before Bach; and in England with George Frideric Handel.

The Concerto: Corelli to Vivaldi

In the instrumental field, the concerting style that had originated in Venice soon spread to other Italian centers, Bologna in particular, and thence throughout Europe. The *concerto grosso* format quickly caught on and swept all before it. The basic concept of the concerto grosso is that of contrast between two performing forces of differing sizes and, often, different tone colors. In the 17th century, the larger ensemble, a string group with continuo, was given the name *ripieno* (full), while the smaller contrasting group became known as the *concertino* (small opposition). Played off against each other, the two groups provide contrasting subject materials, tone colors, rhythmic thrusts, and dynamic levels. In fast movements this alternation of larger and smaller groups produces an effect known as *terraced dynamics.*

CORELLI, TORELLI

In Bologna the most important figures in the formulation of the concerto grosso were the violinists Archangelo Corelli and Giuseppe Torelli. Corelli accomplished the marriage of the trio sonata principle with the several-movement sonata da chiesa.

A clear-cut example of Corelli's techniques can be found in the well-known Concerto in G Minor, Op. 6, no. 8, *Fatto per la notte di Natale* (*Written for Christmas night*). Featuring a trio-sonata concertino of two violins and continuo, the concerto is set out in four sections with the following tempo designations:

Vivace–Grave–Allegro
Adagio–Allegro–Adagio
Vivace–Allegro
Largo (Pastorale)

In spite of nine tempo markings, this concerto projects an overall impression of three contrasting fast–slow–fast movements, with the added special fourth pastoral movement, from which the concerto has become known popularly as the "Christmas Concerto."

The first allegro is introduced by two short sections with contrasting tempos, vivace and grave. Its texture is a typical one for Corelli; the concertino plays throughout while the ripieno strings alternately enter and drop out, providing the terraced dynamics and assisting crisp rhythmic motifs to project the necessary energy (Ex. 9-7).

Example 9-7. Corelli. "Christmas Concerto." Allegro, bars 1–5.

The second movement, adagio, has an A B A form, in which the B section is a short, contrasting allegro. The third movement encompasses two fast-moving segments.

Normally, the concerto would end here on a bright, positive note, but this work, assumed to have been written for a holiday performance, contains the added "Christmas" movement. The commemorative element is expressed through the underlying siciliano rhythm, which suggests the pastoral presence of the adoring shepherds (Ex. 9-8).

Torelli investigated the potential of the solo concerto and finally settled on a three-movement format, beginning and ending with an allegro. The

Example 9-8. Corelli. "Christmas Concerto." Pastorale, bars 1–5.

writing of concertos spread throughout Europe in the late 17th and early 18th centuries, but Italy continued to produce a larger and more successful literature for orchestra and solo instruments than the rest of Europe combined.

VIVALDI

The mantle of Corelli and Torelli fell upon the Venetian composer Antonio Vivaldi, a violinist, composer, and cleric who had taken minor orders in the Roman Catholic church. He was associated with the Ospedale della Pietà, a church-sponsored orphanage for girls in Venice. Many of the girls who were cared for and educated by this charitable institution remained to serve the hospice and the church. Musical training was an essential part of their education, and the Ospedale boasted both a fine chorus and probably the first all-girl orchestra in Europe. As violin teacher and composer-in-residence, Vivaldi created for them a superb musical collection of choral and orchestral compositions, and their performances received wide critical acclaim. It was for this orchestra that he wrote most of his more than 600 concerti grossi.

Vivaldi's concertos refined and simplified the three-movement design. His movements were no longer interrupted by sections in contrasting tempos. The outer movements were in a sturdy allegro tempo, the middle movement slow and usually lyrical. While Vivaldi favored a concertino of one to four violins, he also wrote concertos that enlarged the concertino's color potential. The result was an array of solo concertos for such instruments as the lute, guitar, bassoon, and even the piccolo. He also expanded the potential of the concertino as an ensemble device, drawing upon as many as six diverse instruments playing against the ripieno strings.

Vivaldi published several sets of concertos. One of these, *Il cimento dell'armonia e dell'inventione* (*The Contest between the Harmonious and the Inventive,* 1725) contains the famous group known as "The Four Seasons." For this set, Vivaldi wrote four descriptive sonnets, each detailing elements of a season of the year. To illustrate each of the sonnets, he fashioned a three-movement concerto with concertino groups involving from one to three violins.

From the two-volume set of concertos he titled *L'estro armonico (Harmonic Fantasy,* Op. 3, 1712), the A-minor concerto for two violins, No. 8 (*RV* 522), is typical of Vivaldi's compositional procedures. Here the outer movements chug along in quick, energetic tempos, and motifs based on strong rhythms alternate in sequences like well-oiled gears, controlling the inner mechanism to produce a smoothly running operation. The central movement evinces its indebtedness to the baroque opera aria, with an A B A design providing a framework for the two violins singing in reposeful duet.

The voracious mind of Johann Sebastian Bach consumed vast quantities of musical scores by his contemporaries, and among them were many by Vivaldi. Bach thought highly enough of several of Vivaldi's concertos to transcribe them from the original orchestral versions to the organ, and this A-minor concerto was among them. The transcription leaves Vivaldi's music unchanged, and the ability to set different color registrations on the separate manuals and the pedal keyboard allowed Bach to make a clear parallel delineation of orchestral concertino, ripieno, and continuo on the organ.

Lully and French Opera

The internationalization process did not hinder the development of strong national styles. In Paris, opera became indigenously French with Lully. And in Germany the native-born Schütz furthered a national style in his *Passion* oratorios and *Symphoniae sacrae* motets by combining Italian techniques with his unparalleled mastery of German prosody.

Paris had experienced a taste of Italian opera when Cavalli—Monteverdi's younger colleague and successor at the Venetian opera—and Luigi Rossi of Rome were summoned to the French court in the 1640s to write and supervise several productions. Cavalli later received a royal command to stage a spectacular opera for the wedding festivities of Louis XIV in 1662. Since this was the great age of French baroque drama and the heyday of such literary luminaries as Corneille, Racine, and Molière, Cavalli's courtly French audience understandably refused to take his operatic extravaganzas very seriously, either as drama or as music. Instead, to the composer's great indignation, they most admired the sumptuous ballet scenes that concluded each act. In his concern with his singers, Cavalli had not even bothered with the ballet music but had consigned its composition instead to the care of a young ballet master, Jean Baptiste Lully, who consequently emerged as the real hero of the occasion.

Although Italian-born himself, Lully never lost sight of the fact that he was in the service of a French court. To the ambitious young composer, the taste of his patrons always came first. With indefatigable industry and a genius for organization, Lully, as superintendent of the king's music, marshaled all the very considerable resources of the court of Louis XIV. With Molière he wrote a number of *comédie-ballets* (dramatic ballets) including the well-known *Le bourgeois gentilhomme* (*The Bourgeois Gentleman,* 1670), and a series of *tragédies lyriques* (lyric tragedies) in collaboration with the poet-dramatist Quinault.

As conductor and disciplinarian Lully brought the court chamber orchestra known as the Vingt-quatre Violons du Roi (Twenty-four Viols of the King) to a peak of technical precision. Its duties included playing for state dinners, balls, and chamber concerts, and it was also available for theater productions.

If an operatic situation needed a trumpet fanfare for a triumphal entrance or some horns to embellish a hunting scene, Lully could always turn to the king's military band. When he combined them with the string orchestra and the wind band, Lully was in command of the first permanent orchestral ensemble in Europe. He could also draw on the singers and chorus of the court chapel for vocal support. With all of the ingredients of a flourishing operatic organization on hand, he proceeded to make the most of his opportunity. A performance of Lully's *Alceste* took place at the Versailles Palace in the summer of 1674, with the king and his court in attendance. A print was produced celebrating the event, providing us with some idea of the scale of magnificence that set a standard for all the courts of Europe (Fig. 9-5).

Lully opened *Alceste,* as he did all his operas, with an orchestral introduction that soon became a standardized form in the baroque period. Known as the French overture, it had a formal construction based on two contrasting sections, the first of which was dignified in tone and built out of dotted notes advancing in stately measure (Ex. 9-9a). The second section was marked by a change of meter, suggesting a quickening of the tempo, and was usually fugal in texture (Ex. 9-9b). In some of his overtures, Lully added a third section in the same tempo and character as the first (Ex. 9-9c). The *Alceste* overture illustrates this slow–faster–slow design.

After the overture, the proceedings open with the prologue, during which a personification of the Nymph of the Seine River comes forward to make several pronouncements in recitative style. A triumphal march then prepares for the entrance of Glory and the singing of a duet and a solo air. A chorus of pastoral divinities and water sprites, symbolizing the fields and streams of France, enters for song and dance sequences that conclude the prologue.

Following the story line of the Greek myth, the plot unfolds throughout the course of the traditional five acts of classical tragedy. Each act is organized by means of a recurrent choral or orchestral ritornel interspersed with recitative passages, solo songs (usually of the strophic type), vocal duets, and ballet sequences, in the manner of the prologue.

Figure 9-5. Louis Le Vau. Marble Court, Versailles Palace. Engraving by Lepautre showing a performance of Lully's *Alceste,* 1674. By permission of the Metropolitan Museum of Art, New York (Harris Brisbane Dick Fund, 1930).

French audiences always insisted that opera be good drama as well as good music, and they would no more tolerate singing just for the sake of singing than they would accept a text in a foreign language. Lully therefore had to make a thorough study of French prosody, with special attention to rising and falling inflections, word color, and rhythmic flow. His music is capable of rising to considerable expressive power in spite of its baroque grandiloquence.

Addressed to the taste of an aristocratic circle, Lully's operas inevitably reflect the reserve and restraint of a formal way of life based on a rigorous courtly etiquette. As a consequence they failed to develop the broad appeal necessary to assure their survival in the modern repertory. Lully's hand, however, is still felt in the French classical ballet and the standardized series of dances known as the French suite; his overture form, moreover, became the universally adopted French overture; and his approach to the operatic stage influenced French composers for well over two centuries.

Purcell and English Opera

Henry Purcell was born during Cromwell's Commonwealth and bred during the early Restoration, when he served as a singer in Charles II's royal choir. He came to maturity in the turbulent days of the downfall of James II, the Glorious Revolution of 1688, and the wars of William III. French influence

Example 9-9. Lully. *Alceste.* Overture.

9-9a. Bars 1–4.

9-9b. Bars 13–16.

9-9c. Bars 34–36.

had pervaded England under Charles II, who had acquired a taste for continental styles during his long exile at the court of Louis XIV. A chamber orchestra, known as His Majesty's Viols, became the English equivalent of Louis XIV's Vingt-quatre Violons du Roi, and Purcell became its leader in 1677 as well as composer-in-ordinary to the king. Several years later he succeeded his teacher, John Blow, as organist at Westminster Abbey.

Purcell thus found ready outlets for chamber music, which he based principally on Italian models, as well as for his church music, encompassing the organ works, anthems, and sacred songs that account for the preponderance of his output. In addition to his mastery of chamber and church styles, Purcell possessed a good sense of the theater, gained through years of experience in writing incidental music for London stage productions.

A combination of factors augured well for the appearance of an indigenous form of English court opera—Charles II's interest in keeping abreast of the latest international artistic developments, an available wealth of literary and dramatic resources, and a long-established precedent of the court masque (an amalgamation of pageantry, scenic spectacle, dancing, poetic recitation, solo and ensemble singing). However, the slenderness of the royal purse, the steady resistance of English audiences, and the opposition encountered among men of letters were to prove all but insurmountable obstacles.

Several brave and historically important attempts at writing English opera had been made before Purcell's time. *The Siege of Rhodes* (1656), with libretto by William Davenant and music by Henry Lawes and Matthew Locke, for all its masquelike qualities is generally considered the first English opera. Though John Blow still called his *Venus and Adonis* (1682) a "masque," it was really a small but complete chamber opera. Charles II's death in 1685 was followed by several unsettled years; and when Purcell came to write his only opera, it was neither for a royal court nor a London theater, but for an amateur performance at a girls' school of which he happened to be the music master.

Dido and Aeneas (1689), in spite of the curious circumstances of its composition, the obvious weakness of Nahum Tate's libretto, and the smallness of its scale, is nonetheless a masterpiece and still the ranking serious opera by an English composer. With only the older masque tradition, the attempts at opera mentioned above, and the current continental ideas to guide him, Purcell's achievement is all the more impressive. At times with amusing naiveté and at others with profound sophistication, Purcell put together his compact little lyrical drama by selecting what he considered the more promising native and foreign developments of his time.

The story, from Virgil's *Aeneid,* was a popular one with opera audiences all over Europe. After the Trojan war, Aeneas is commanded by the gods to go to Italy to found a great empire on Latium's shores. His ship is blown off course toward the north coast of Africa, where he lands at Carthage. There he is given a royal welcome by Queen Dido, and in due course they fall in love and proceed to go hunting and romancing. Jupiter, however, disapproves and sends his messenger, Mercury, to command Aeneas to sail on to his destination. Dido, thus abandoned, is left to sing her farewell to life in a moving operatic death scene.

The girls' school provided limited theatrical resources, so *Dido* perforce has a small cast, mainly female, and an orchestra consisting only of strings and continuo. The great distinction of the work lies in Purcell's ability to make so much of so little, and in his deft handling of all the complex baroque techniques at his command. The overture, for instance, with its contrasting sections of harmonic and contrapuntal textures, is clearly of the French type established by Lully.

Recitatives, though sparingly used in deference to English taste, nevertheless make vivid use of the Italian representative style to enhance the dramatic projection of the text. The first scene of the opera is set at the court of Dido, and the opening lines are sung by Dido's lady-in-waiting, Belinda. A word such as *shake,* for instance, is rendered by a nervous, fidgety line (Ex. 9-10a), while the word *storms* is represented by a sudden upward, rushing gust of the C-minor scale (Ex. 9-10b). The character of Anchises, the warrior father of Aeneas, is delineated with a positive, martial rhythm; while Venus' voluptuous charms are rendered by heart-melting chromaticisms (Ex. 9-10c); and Aeneas' entrance is heralded by a trumpetlike vocal fanfare (Ex. 9-10d).

Example 9-10a–d. Purcell. *Dido and Aeneas.* Act 1, recitative excerpts.

Dido is not portrayed as the stereotypical mythic figure found in many baroque opera seria treatments. She appears but three times in Purcell's drama and has only fifty lines of text. Yet she emerges as a fully developed character, at once queenly and womanly. Full-scale arias mark her first and last appearances. Both are of the ostinato type, with the singer spinning out her lines over a repeating bass figure.

Dido's aria in the first scene speaks of doubt and desire through the text: "Ah, Belinda, I am prest with torment." At the words "Peace and I are strangers grown," she seems to be relentlessly pursued by fate, as the bass line follows in a series of canonic imitations, and the unbalanced lines of her phrases against their bass support clearly point to her eventual undoing.

The subsequent duet with chorus, "Fear no danger," is a vocal version of the trio-sonata style with the two upper parts bound together and sounding over a continuo, which in turn becomes a concertino to the ripieno of the full choir to make a concerted number. The first scene then ends in the French manner, with a "Triumphing Dance," the music of which is a chaconne in the manner of Lully with free variations soaring over a repeated basso ostinato.

In the second act, the plot thickens. Nahum Tate alters Virgil by moving the focus from godly, noble intervention to earthly, spiteful behavior. This is accomplished through the introduction of a group of witches, the stock-in-trade of many Restoration plays. These "secret, black, and midnight hags" are dedicated to pure evil and take hysterical pleasure in a plot to ruin the queen. In Virgil's story, Jove dispatches his personal messenger, Mercury, to demand that Aeneas abandon Dido and continue his appointed journey. Tate assigns the task to a counterfeit Mercury, who is actually one of the witches in disguise.

To a dark orchestral instrumental introduction, the Sorceress enters, stands in front of a mysterious cave, and calls for her "weird sisters" to appear. When these apparitions materialize, she describes her wicked plan. One of them is then transformed into the Mercury lookalike, and they proceed to stir up a storm. Though the witches' choruses are mainly in the English madrigal style, two of them sing in trio-sonata fashion over a basso continuo. The scene ends with an echo chorus in the Venetian style, with four singers backstage providing the echo from inside the cave, "In our deep vaulted cell" (Ex. 9-11). The scene ends with the "Echo Dance of the Furies," accompanied by on- and offstage strings to produce the desired reverberating effect (see Ex. 18-2).

Example 9-11. Purcell. *Dido and Aeneas.* Act 2, No. 19, "Echo Chorus," bars 1–6.

After the false Mercury has appeared to Aeneas, the scene shifts to a typical English seaport for the opening scene of Act 3. Sailors are dancing the hornpipe and making their customary salty comments as they prepare their ships to sail away. One of them sings an aria that could be a prototype for a song from one of Gilbert and Sullivan's 19th-century operettas. It contains the deathless line "Take a boozy short leave of your nymphs on the shore, and silence their mourning with vows of returning, but never, no never, intending to visit them more."

The rather stiff, stilted libretto by Nahum Tate may have proved a handicap for Purcell. Though he held the post of poet laureate at the time, Tate was once described as "an honest dull man given to fuddling, but a good-natured drinking companion." While Tate's text for *Dido and Aeneas* is typically precious Restoration poetry, the truth of emotional expression in Purcell's music overshadows the problems of a text that is a good deal less than Virgilian or Shakespearean in quality. And there are even moments of poetic power from the pen of this "dull man," as well as moments of honest humor.

As Aeneas' ship disappears on the horizon, Dido is left with the faithful Belinda on the shore. Virgil relates that Dido stabs herself, and her body is placed on a huge funeral pyre. The flames of the pyre consume her body, and the fire spreads, ultimately destroying Carthage. Aeneas sadly views the nocturnal glow of the fire as he sails northward toward Italy. In true operatic tradition, the conclusion of the drama is marked by Dido's moving aria "When

I am laid in earth," a moment that rises musically to true tragic grandeur (Ex. 9-12). Her affecting phrases soar over a chromatically descending basso ostinato, a widely accepted pattern to denote grief and mourning. As she dies, Tate's libretto completes the drama with a chorus that calls for cupids to scatter flowers upon her tomb and keep eternal watch over the queen who was so gentle of heart.

Despite its narrow scope, Purcell's diminutive opera contains practically every baroque operatic convention in capsule form: a French-style overture;

Example 9-12. Purcell. *Dido and Aeneas.* Act 3, No. 35, "When I am laid in earth." Ostinato aria.

a Venetian echo chorus and instrumental dance; representative-style recitatives with their picture writing; choruses that comment on the action; ostinato, strophic, and basso-continuo arias; vocal duets in the trio-sonata manner; and a delightful combination of English and continental dance rhythms.

Though *Dido and Aeneas* was Purcell's only lyric drama without spoken dialogue, he did have one more opportunity to come to grips with the problem of English opera. John Dryden, the primary figure of Restoration drama, invited Purcell to collaborate on *King Arthur* in 1691. Dryden, as well as other contemporary authors, had grave misgivings about the place of music in drama in general and about the recitative style in particular. His solution, a typical English compromise, was to let ordinary mortals discourse in spoken dialogue, and to allow supernatural figures such as gods and goddesses to declaim their lines in what he called a "songish part." Since the play literally abounded in superhuman characters, Purcell had as rich an opportunity as any composer could have desired. Some of Purcell's music for *King Arthur*—the Frost Scene, for instance, with its shivering chorus and realistic tremolando effects—rises to true eloquence.

Purcell, in spite of his continental borrowings, composed with a strong personal style; and whether the surroundings are church, chamber, or theater, his writing always has a clear-cut musical profile.

Handel

An interval of only twenty years separated the collaboration by Purcell and Dryden on *King Arthur* and the first performance in 1711 of George Frideric Handel's opera *Rinaldo*. Attempts to establish a native English opera tradition had withered in the meantime, and Handel's presentations were frankly Italian operas of the type that called forth Dr. Samuel Johnson's famous definition of opera as "an exotic and irrational entertainment." Others, such as Sir Richard Steele, rushed to Handel's defense and pointed out that "an opera is the completest concert" to which one could go. Since public orchestra concerts at this time were nonexistent and concerts of any description were extremely rare, this was a fairly accurate assessment.

This was the golden age of the *bel canto* voice culture, and the singing demanded vocal virtuosity of a high order. The baroque period was also one of great engineering, and the ingenuity expended on complex machinery and scenic architecture contributed to the spectacular aspect of opera.

Handel's early musical training in Germany gave him a good grounding in the style of opera popular in Hamburg, but study in Italy from 1704 to 1710 molded his point of view. By the time he began writing operas for England, it would be in a style closely identified with the Neapolitan opera tradition that flourished during the late 17th and early 18th centuries under the leadership of Alessandro Scarlatti. The chorus is relegated to the background and the texture of the writing is dominated principally by solo arias interspersed with liberal sequences of recitative. According to the tenets of serious opera in general and Handel's procedure in particular, the dramatic continuity is carried on by the freely declaimed recitative in which the irregular metrical organization is adapted to prose speech rhythms. At certain points of the lyrical drama the action is temporarily arrested so that the characters can pour out in song their subjective reactions to the plot situation.

The aria by this time had crystallized into the symmetrical da capo design with its A B A arrangement of parts. In general practice, a single *affect* governed each aria, focusing on one sharply defined emotion such as joy, defiance, rage, or sorrow. The da capo aria, with its ritornel introduction and conclusion, is static by nature. It is, nevertheless, a complete emotional declaration that is made dramatic by what precedes and what follows it. In the hands of a composer such as Handel, it was capable of rising to great expressive power.

Handel's opera company, the Royal Academy of Music, imported many famous Italian singers and the composer wrote nearly 40 examples of Italianate opera seria for London over a period of 30 years. Operas such as *Giulio Cesare* (1724) and *Alcina* (1735) continued to parade larger-than-life historical, mythical, and fictional heroes and heroines. In the first, the part of Caesar was written for the castrato Senesino, who had the pleasure of rendering no fewer than eight arias and one duet, and singing in the final chorus for good measure. Each aria was designed as a static A B A statement, with the character making an exit from the stage at its conclusion. Yet dramatic action of a sort does occur in these operas, in the form of conflicts and interactions among the characters as expressed through their arias; and it was to this internal action that English audiences were most responsive.

Nonetheless, like all audiences, Handel's were fickle and his patrons unreliable. His solid position as a thriving opera impresario foundered at the death of King George I in 1727. In 1728 John Gay's *The Beggar's Opera* opened, scoring a stunning success. It represented a new view of popular musical theater known as *ballad opera,* and gave further evidence that a newly nationalistic English public was increasingly inimical to operas in a foreign language featuring foreign singers. On top of this, the launching of a rival Italian opera company in 1733 dealt another blow to Handel's position, and by the late 1730s his opera career was basically at an end.

When the bottom dropped out of the Italian opera market, Handel turned at age 56 to a genre in which he had been writing intermittently since 1707, the oratorio. His works in this form had been based on biblical and mythic literary sources—for example, his choral oratorios *Israel in Egypt* and *Acis and Galatea.* Now he began to write oratorios that covered a wider spectrum, from the non-narrative, meditative *Messiah* to thinly veiled operas in oratorio guise.

Handel's *Semele,* though technically a secular oratorio, is nonetheless an excellent example of his operatic writing. It has, moreover, the advantage of an English text by the distinguished playwright William Congreve. The plot tells of Jupiter's love for the mortal maiden Semele. This romance arouses the jealousy of the god's Olympian spouse, Juno, who plots the ruin of her rival by playing on Semele's vanity.

Act 2 opens with Juno venting her jealous fury in an impassioned passage of *recitativo stromentato* (accompanied recitative). Semele, by way of contrast, sings a serene solo aria, "Oh sleep, why dost thou leave me?" The eloquent melody rises over a lullabylike continuo accompaniment, revealing the sleeplessness of a woman overwhelmingly in love and longing for her lover—none other than the divine Jupiter. When he appears, their dialogue is carried on in *recitativo secco* (dry recitative), which leads up to one of Handel's most ardent arias, "Where'er you walk."

After lavishing two such masterpieces on a single scene, Handel has still further lyrical revelations in store, such as Semele's aria "Myself I shall adore" (Ex. 9-13). Her vanity, which is to be her downfall, has been cleverly prodded by Juno in disguise, and the aria is sung as she gazes fondly into her mirror. Handel chooses the *concerted aria* for this situation, and Semele's reflection is graphically described by the violins, which reflect her phrases as mirror images in echoing imitations of the vocal line. Through his constant flow of melodic invention, and by using such technical devices as the concerted aria with significant insight into human character, Handel succeeds in drawing dramatic sparks from Congreve's text and in writing most convincingly for the lyric stage.

Example 9-13. Handel. *Semele.* "Myself I shall adore," bars 17–19.

Handel's oratorios were written for public concert halls; and even though they were often settings of sacred subjects and texts, they were nevertheless billed on presentation as "Grand Musical Entertainments." The most familiar of these, the *Messiah,* is at the same time the least typical of the composer's oratorios (see p. 45). Completely without dramatic plot and continuity of action, its three acts are in actuality three independent cantatas comprising an extended commentary and meditation on Christ's messianic mission. It is the only one of Handel's great oratorios written on a New Testament text; both Handel and his London audiences found more ready identification with Old Testament events and characters, in which they saw reflected the heroism of their own empire-building leaders.

The inward orientation and lyrical qualities of the *Messiah* contrast strongly with the sweep of such biblical epics as Handel's *Israel in Egypt.* In this mighty oratorio the chorus represents the collective image of the children of Israel, and it is both the dramatic protagonist and the group narrator. Handel makes liberal use of the representative style, notably in such pictorial passages as those depicting the plagues (see Exs. 4-2a, b, c). A leaping accompaniment figure to a solo aria, for instance, neatly describes the frogs mentioned in the text (No. 5). Further graphic realism is found in the buzzing "Chorus of Flies" (No. 6), as well as in the "Hailstone Chorus" (No. 7). The heavy, lugubrious harmonies of "He sent a thick darkness over all the land" (No. 8) paint a vivid picture of nightfall; while the driving rhythms of "He smote all the firstborn of Egypt" (No. 9) proceed in powerful, hammerlike strokes.

The chorus, not the solo aria, dominates a Handel oratorio, and it is in his complete mastery of the choral medium that Handel's baroque spirit is most vividly revealed. The scope of his choral writing in such a massively designed work as *Israel in Egypt* summarizes and completes the practice of the two prior centuries; Handel always managed to achieve the mightiest of effects seemingly by the simplest possible means. It contains traces of the old motet style, scaled to larger proportions (No. 17, "And with the blast"); the monolithic harmonies of Protestant chorales (No. 5, "And Israel saw," and No. 30, "Who is like unto Thee"); the elemental power of the Venetian polychoral practice (No. 6, "Chorus of Flies," No. 7, "Hailstone Chorus," and No. 33, "The people shall hear"); and the solid eight-part cantus firmus chorus (No. 2, beginning on the words "And their cry came up unto God"). Uniquely Handelian are the "Chorus of Darkness" (No. 8), in which the singers grope their way in harmonic space through a maze of remote keys; the solemn fugal choruses, "They loathed to drink" (No. 4) and "And believed the Lord" (No. 16); concerted choruses in which a solo voice is pitted against the combined forces of the double choir, as in "Sing ye to the Lord" (No. 39); and the ritornel choruses at the beginning of "Moses' Song" (Nos. 17 and 18), which function as gigantic da capo structures.

Handel made his most unforgettable impressions with the power and breadth of the jubilant sounds of his choruses. His operas, for all their inherent beauty, failed to catch on. But his synthesis of his native German polyphony with the Italian operatic practice, the French dance forms that he mastered in his journeyman years, the English choir music of his adopted country, and especially his use of the English language in texts meaningful to the people, succeeded in establishing an oratorio tradition that has continued with undiminished luster to the present day.

Bach and the Reformation Tradition

The universality and all-encompassing art of Johann Sebastian Bach is deeply rooted in the German Reformation. To be sure, he wrote chamber music, instrumental dance suites, and concertos for the pleasure of aristocratic patrons; and he wrote his monumental B-minor Mass for a Roman Catholic prince, who subsequently gave him the title of Royal Polish and Electoral Saxon Court Composer. But the vast quantity of his artistic output is found in the cantatas, oratorios, and organ pieces he wrote for the faithful Protestant congregations of St. Thomas' Lutheran Church in Leipzig.

While the Reformation brought austerity in matters relating to the visual arts, and some pietistic sects even looked askance at professional musicians generally, the Lutheran tradition in the main was very liberal as far as music was concerned. Luther held that every person may address God directly through prayer and that the Bible is the supreme authority in religious matters. Thus Protestant churches were conceived as halls of instruction with a sermon-oriented liturgy, and as gathering places where all good Christians could raise their voices in song to praise God.

The Reformation first found its musical voice in simple, unadorned congregational *chorales,* or hymns, which were sung in family circles and schools as well as in churches. The chorale thus became the nucleus of its musical tradition, with other expressions such as organ chorale-preludes, cantatas, and oratorios developing around it. Martin Luther himself was the reputed author of some of these chorales, though the musical aspects of their creation can be more accurately ascribed to his musical collaborator, Johann Walter. These chorales had tremendous influence, and one of them, *A mighty fortress,* has aptly been called the *Marseillaise* of the Reformation (see Ex. 8-3).

Bach's duties, like those of all Lutheran choirmasters of his time, consisted of providing the music for the church services. In practice this meant officiating as choir director at regular services as well as rehearsing the choir and the band of instrumentalists who served as the orchestra. In addition, he was musical director of the school attached to St. Thomas' Church, where he also taught Latin.

More important for posterity, however, was the creative aspect of Bach's position. He wrote cantatas for Sunday services and large-scale oratorios for Christmas, Passion Week, and Easter, and he supplied music for marriages, funerals, the installation of a pastor, and important civic occasions. Bach's fertile musical imagination and unflagging energy led to his completing no less than five series of cantatas for each Sunday and feast day of the church calendar, some 300 in all, of which about 200 are extant.

The Sunday service was highly musical in orientation; as the sermon was an interpretation of the meaning of the scriptures, so were the chorale and cantata musical commentaries on the day's scriptural lesson. After the organ prelude, one or more motets were sung. Then followed the Kyrie, an intonation at the altar, the reading of the Epistle, and the singing of the Litany. A chorale was sung by the congregation, preceded by an improvisation on the tune by the organist (chorale prelude). After the Gospel reading and another improvisatory prelude, the cantata (with a text related to the Gospel for that Sunday) was performed. After the singing of the Credo, the sermon was delivered. Finally, another chorale was sung and Communion was celebrated, during which more chorale preludes were played and chorales sung. If the occasion warranted music on a larger scale than usual, the cantata might have a second part, which would be performed during the Communion. With a sermon length of one hour, the typical service lasted four hours.

Bach's cantatas vary greatly as to the performers involved. Some feature a single vocal soloist singing recitatives and arias with orchestral accompaniment, while in others the chorus carries the entire vocal burden. Some combine arias and duets with choral numbers, and some include purely instrumental movements. In the following discussion, Cantata No. 140, *Wachet auf, ruft uns die Stimme (Wake, awake, now calls the watchman,* 1731), written for the 27th Sunday after Trinity Sunday, serves as one example of Bach's approach to musical organization for this important element of the church service. It is scored for solo soprano, tenor, and bass; four-part chorus; and an orchestra of strings augmented by a solo violin, two oboes, English horn, French horn, and continuo. The title of the cantata is that of the chorale on which it is based (Ex. 9-14).

Example 9-14. Wake, awake, now calls the watchman. Chorale.

The text reflects the Gospel reading for the day (Matthew 15:1–13) and concerns the parable of the ten wise and foolish virgins. In the story the virgins, awaiting a wedding ceremony, are awakened by the announcement that they must prepare for the impending arrival of the bridegroom (Christ) and the bride (a conventional symbol for the church).

Of the cantata's seven parts, the first five express longing, and the last two, fulfillment. The opening chorus is, appropriately, a busy, festive choral bustling, over which the sopranos announce the hymn of the day as a cantus firmus in clear, high tones.

The sturdy chorale provides the underlying materials for the motifs, themes, and obbligatos as well, and it is thus closely woven into all parts of the cantata's fabric. Italian opera next enters the picture, with a short tenor passage in secco recitative. It leads up to a duet for soprano and bass, also with continuo accompaniment but now with an obbligato for solo violin that embroiders festoons of florid garlands around and over the voice parts.

In the exact center of the design the chorale again appears, this time with the tenors carrying the cantus firmus, supported by the continuo below and the violins and viola above. This number is a typical chorale-prelude, a fact confirmed by Bach's own arrangement of it for organ solo. Now follows an instrumented recitative written for bass voice, continuo, and strings. The penultimate number is a duet for soprano and bass with oboe obbligato and continuo accompaniment. Then finally comes the chorale once more, in this instance as a harmonized hymn in which the choir, orchestra, and congregation all join.

For the great church festivals Bach provided special music on a much larger scale. The origins of such presentations are the mystery, miracle, and passion plays of the Middle Ages, when at Christmas time, for instance, a manger scene (*crèche*) was set up in the church for the re-enactment of the story of the Nativity. In such a liturgical drama choirboys would represent angels; adult choristers, the shepherds; and members of the clergy, Joseph and the Three Wise Men. Bach's illustrious 17th-century predecessor, Heinrich Schütz, wrote a notable example of music for such an occasion called the *Christmas Story;* and Bach himself composed a *Christmas Oratorio* (*BWV* 248) in 1734, consisting of a series of six cantatalike segments that were performed over the period from Christmas Day through Epiphany.

The Passion oratorios, similarly, grew out of the liturgical dramas performed during the week preceding Easter, particularly on Good Friday, and they are the epical counterparts of the more lyrical and intimate Sunday cantatas. Here again Bach had precedents, such as Schütz's *Saint Matthew Passion.*

Bach's own *Saint Matthew Passion* (*BWV* 244), with its unflagging intensity and musical invention, possibly represents his supreme achievement in choral music. In keeping with established tradition, the scriptural passages are intoned by the Evangelist, assigned to a tenor singing in recitative style. In the course of the work, the recitatives, solos, and ensembles represent the dramatic action, which is balanced by the more contemplative choral sections. The solo passages express individual reactions, while the chorus may represent group situations, such as an angry mob or a gathering of faithful Christians. When the congregation joins in singing the chorales, they gain a sense of participation in the events surrounding the life of the Lord. Similarly, episodes in Christmas and Passion music reflect situations in family life—birth, marriage, suffering, and death.

Baroque Synthesis

Bach's mystical worldview, embracing the restless search for ultimate truths as expressed in his religious works, is balanced by his rationalistic and comprehensive approach to composition. Together they combine to make him the universal figure he is. His musical output reflects the rational spirit of a period that witnessed great philosophers formulating monumental systems of religious, moral, mathematical, and scientific thought. Bach's searching mind was always on the alert for possible syntheses, and he systematically explored all the stylistic and technical resources of his age. Each work he undertook, in fact, seems to have been considered not as a single, isolated instance, but rather as part of a larger whole that constituted an encyclopedia of all possibilities known to him. His series of Lutheran cantatas, oratorios, Passions, and the Mass cover a vast scope of religious expression. Within their internal organization are overtures of all types, every variety of recitative and Italian solo and ensemble arias, and a compendium of baroque choral writing.

In the *Clavierübung* (*Keyboard Practice*), which Bach published serially between 1726 and 1742, one encounters an encyclopedic survey of keyboard writing. Part 1 (*BWV* 825–30) presents six carefully diversified partitas, a series of dance suites that Bach described on the title page as "consisting of Preludes, Allemandes, Courantes, Sarabandes, Gigues, Minuets and other Gallantries, Composed for Music Lovers, to Refresh their Spirits." Each partita, furthermore, opens with an introductory piece of a different type variously entitled "Praeludium," "Sinfonia," "Fantasia," "Ouverture," "Praeambulum," and "Toccata."

Part 2 is a keyboard summary of the most characteristic orchestral forms associated with the two major national styles—the "Italian Concerto" (*BWV* 971), in the style of Vivaldi, and the "French Overture" (*BWV* 831), a suite in the manner of Lully.

Part 3 is devoted to organ music presented in a series of chorale preludes (*BWV* 669–89), and the monumental Prelude and Fugue in E-Flat (*BWV* 552), popularly known as the "Saint Anne."

Part 4 returns to the harpsichord for the "Aria with Thirty Variations" (*BWV* 988), better known as the "Goldberg Variations" because they were written for Bach's pupil, J. G. Goldberg. This work is nothing less than a comprehensive synthesis of all contemporary variation procedures. In spite of its seeming spontaneity, Bach methodically arranged within the overall design a series of canons in the third, sixth, and so on up to the twenty-seventh variation, which are canons at each interval from the unison, second, and third, on up to the final canon at the ninth, respectively (see pp. 471–73 for a discussion of canon).

Even the modest two-part *Inventions* (*BWV* 772–801), so familiar to beginning piano students, were originally arranged in a definite logical order of keys: C, d, e, F, G, a, b, B-flat, A, g, f, E, E-flat, D, and c (capital letters standing for major keys and small letters for minor keys).

The series of 48 preludes and fugues entitled *The Well-Tempered Clavier* (*BWV* 846–93) is a veritable catalogue of key relationships in which the keys are arranged in successive steps of the rising chromatic scale. The plan involves pairs of preludes and fugues in each major and minor tonality. Bach's intent was to write a manifesto for the efficacy of the tuning system employing well-tempered or equal temperament—a practical compromise permitting a wide choice of tonalities and expanded freedom of modulation.

Turning to the keyboard concerto, Bach systematically provided examples that featured concertinos consisting variously of one, two, three, and four harpsichords. The concerto grosso found encyclopedic expression in his six *Brandenburg* concertos (*BWV* 1046–51), which not only survey concerto grosso practice from Corelli to Vivaldi, but employ original instrumental combinations that Bach himself envisioned.

During the last five years of his life, Bach continued to search for new musical depths in older formal procedures, resulting in *The Musical Offering*, 1747 (*BWV* 1079), and *The Art of Fugue* (*BWV* 1080), unfinished at his death in 1750.

Das musikalische Opfer (*The Musical Offering*) was the happy result of an invitation to visit King Frederick of Prussia. The king was a knowledgeable musician who played the flute and had for some time employed Bach's son Carl Philipp Emanuel as one of his court musicians (Fig. 9-6). Since J. S. Bach had a reputation as one of the finest keyboard improvisers in Europe, the king designed a theme on which Bach extemporized a three-part fugal composition in the style of the early, conservative ricercar (Ex. 9-15). After his return to Leipzig, Bach devised a series of compositions based on the "royal theme" and sent them as a musical gift to the king.

Example 9-15. Bach. *Musical Offering, BWV* 1079. Royal theme.

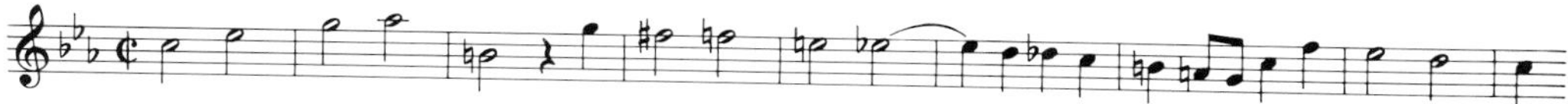

The Musical Offering comprises the following sections: (1) a three-part ricercar, probably a written-out version of Bach's improvisation; (2) a six-part ricercar, which the king had requested as an improvisation, but which Bach had at the time of the visit declined; (3) a trio sonata for flute, violin, and harpsichord in four movements, which flatteringly assumed the king's ability to negotiate the flute part; (4) ten canons.

The composition represents much more than a typical workaday gift from a composer to a patron. Bach especially does honor to the king by presenting him with pieces that may be understood only by a person with a secure knowledge of musical styles. In effect, he placed the king in that elite group who could deal with "musician's music."

With his penchant for musical and literary gamesmanship, Bach placed an acrostic on the word *ricercar* on the first page:

*R*egis *I*ussu *C*antio *E*t *R*eliqua *C*anonica *A*rte *R*esoluta

In Accordance with the King's Order,
the Theme and Remainder are Resolved with Canonic Art

In particular the ten canons provide us with insight into Bach's respect

Figure 9-6. Engraving after Hermann Kaulbach, *Frederick the Great and Sebastian Bach,* 1876. Reproduced by courtesy of the Trustees of the British Museum, London.

for the king's knowledge. They break down into two groups, five employing the royal theme as the subject, and five that are two-voiced with the royal theme inserted as a third line (cantus firmus). In addition to well-known canonic procedures such as augmentation and retrograde, some were specially fashioned for the occasion. One is a canon in inversion at the seventh introduced by the provocative phrase "Seek and you shall find." The contrary motion of the two lines is indicated by Bach, but he leaves it for the performers to puzzle out when the second voice is to enter. There are several possible solutions to this canon, one of which is shown in Example 9-16. The title was meant as a compliment, assuming the king's ability to penetrate this contrapuntal puzzle. On the canon in augmentation, Bach gallantly notes, "May the fortune of the King grow with the length of the notes"; and on the spiral canon, in which each entry modulates up one tone, he expresses the wish that "The glory of the King may rise with the rising modulation."

In their original printed form, these compositions do not suggest the careful sense of order that we expect from Bach. The Bach scholar Karl Geiringer has suggested an organization that seems reasonable: (1) ricercar in three parts; (2) five canons with royal theme as cantus firmus; (3) trio sonata; (4) five canons with royal theme as subject; (5) ricercar in six parts.

As a sequel to the *The Musical Offering,* Bach planned a set of contrapuntal views of a single subject, investigating even further the polyphonic potential of the canon and fugue processes. Bach completed 18 elements of this process, each titled "Contrapunctus," in his *Art of Fugue.* He was at work on the 19th, a four-voice fugue which was to include the notes of his own name—B-flat, A, C, B-natural—when he died (Ex. 9-17a). The subject is pithy, designed

Example 9-16. Bach. *Musical Offering.* "Seek and you shall find." Canon.

9-16a. Original notation.

9-16b. Realization.

as a motif for maximum contrapuntal flexibility (Ex. 9-17b). As was true for the ricercare in the *The Musical Offering,* Bach gives no instructions for realizing the individual "counterpoints" of the *The Art of Fugue.* Realization may be accomplished by a keyboard instrument or by an instrumental ensemble, but as often as not, the work is studied in the abstract.

The Art of Fugue is a didactic work of the highest mastery and intellectual magnitude. Each segment is the product of a lifetime spent contemplating, investigating, and perfecting the contrapuntal process. It was this type of the-

Example 9-17. Bach. *The Art of Fugue, BWV* 1080.

9-17a. B A C H motif.

9-17b. Subject.

oretical work, conceived as much for study and introspection as for performance, that carried Bach's name and reputation through the remainder of the century.

The two towering figures of the later baroque period—Handel and Bach—invite comparison, since, though they were compatriots and exact contemporaries, they were products of different external environments and different individual temperaments. Handel was a cosmopolitan figure accustomed to being a celebrity, while Bach was a provincial personality content with a comparatively modest place in the social scheme of things. Bach's post at Leipzig was an important one, and Leipzig itself was a university town of some standing in Germany. But 18th-century London provided Handel with an environment that vied with Paris for the position of cultural and intellectual capital of Europe. Handel was a free agent completely at home on the operatic and concert stages of a world capital, while Bach worked all his life under direct patronage in relatively small positions principally within the church framework. Handel, as a robust man of the world, had a straightforward, vigorous mind, while Bach was more prone to brooding and introspective contemplation. Handel was more concerned with the joy and beauty of this life, while Bach beheld beatific visions of ultimate truth.

Both were astute students of the Bible, but Handel preferred the Old Testament and the inevitable victory of the righteous cause, while Bach was drawn to the New Testament and issues of death and redemption. Handel, in his choral music, approached a text much more directly and concretely, while Bach's thought ran in a more abstract vein, at times to the complete disregard of the prosody of the text. And it has often been observed that Handel was essentially a vocal composer, while Bach's primary orientation was to instrumental music.

Both, however, were masters of external forms as well as inner expression, and in the end they must be considered complementary rather than comparable figures. In any final evaluation, they must be accorded equal eminence in their respective spheres. Together these twin musical suns of the baroque period sum up two centuries of accumulated creative experience and expression.

CHAPTER

10

The Classical Style

AS THE BAROQUE STYLE gradually began to break up in the early years of the 18th century, it was replaced by many artistic tendencies moving in a diversity of directions. The classical period, usually designated as the latter half of the 18th century and the first quarter of the 19th, includes such intellectual and aesthetic trends as the *rococo, sensibility, Enlightenment,* and *storm and stress.* Whatever consistency there is in the music of this period will be found in the balances and syntheses of the various styles that its great exponents—Gluck, Haydn, Mozart, and Beethoven—were able to achieve, rather than in any underlying unity of philosophical, social, and aesthetic thought. For instance, the rococo style was the final phase of the aristocratic baroque order, as it left the grand avenues and marbled halls of the Versailles Palace on the death of Louis XIV in 1715, and moved to the smaller salons of the urban aristocracy in Paris. It then became the fashion for the ruling class all over Europe. Instead of serving a single sovereign and addressing their creative efforts to a single class at a unified court, writers, artists, and musicians had to take into account a new social order and the tastes of a variety of patrons.

Rococo-Gallant Style

When the baroque architect bowed to the rococo interior decorator, long vistas and spacious chambers were replaced by intimate glimpses and small salons (see Plate XII). The pomp and circumstance of baroque decoration yielded to the delicate ornamentation of the elegant rococo; royal purples and

Antoine Watteau. *The Music Lesson,* 1719. Oil on canvas. Reproduced by permission of the Trustees of the Wallace Collection, London.

Chronology

MUSICAL FIGURES

Vienna and Salzburg

Christoph W. von Gluck	1714–1787
Georg C. Wagenseil	1715–1777
Leopold Mozart	1719–1787
Joseph Haydn	1732–1809
Michael Haydn	1737–1806
Karl Ditters von Dittersdorf	1739–1799
Antonio Salieri	1750–1825
Wolfgang Amadeus Mozart	1756–1791
Ludwig van Beethoven	1770–1827
Johann N. Hummel	1778–1837

Northern Germany

Georg P. Telemann	1681–1767
Johann J. Quantz	1697–1773
Johann Hasse	1699–1783
Wilhelm F. Bach	1710–1784
Carl P. E. Bach	1714–1788
Johann Hiller	1728–1804
Christian Schubart	1739–1791
Johann Reichardt	1752–1814

Southern Germany (Mannheim)

Johann Stamitz	1717–1757
Christian Cannabich	1731–1798

Italy

Domenico Scarlatti	1685–1757
Giovanni Sammartini	c. 1700–1775
Padre Giovanni Martini	1706–1784
Giovanni P. Pergolesi	1710–1736
Francesco Algarotti	1712–1764
Niccolò Piccinni	1728–1800
Giovanni Paisiello	1740–1816
Luigi Boccherini	1743–1805
Domenico Cimarosa	1749–1801

London

Johann C. Bach	1735–1782
Johann Salomon	1745–1815

France

Jean-Philippe Rameau	1683–1764
Louis-Claude Daquin	1694–1772
Louis Guillemain	1705–1770
Johann Schobert	c. 1735–1767
Ignaz Pleyel	1757–1831
Etienne Méhul	1763–1817
Rodolphe Kreutzer	1766–1831

WRITERS AND DRAMATISTS

Samuel Richardson	1689–1761
Henry Fielding	1707–1754
Laurence Sterne	1713–1768
Rousseau, Jean-J.	1712–1778
James Stuart	1713–1788
Raniero Calzabigi	1714–1795
Horace Walpole	1717–1797
Nicholas Revett	1720–1804
Oliver Goldsmith	1729–1774
Gotthold Lessing	1729–1781
Caron de Beaumarchais	1732–1799
Thomas Paine	1737–1809
Matthias Claudius	1740–1815
Marquis de Condorcet (Marie-Jean Caritat)	1743–1794
Gottfried Bürger	1747–1794
Johann W. von Goethe	1749–1832
Lorenzo da Ponte	1749–1838
Friedrich M. von Klinger	1752–1831
Emanuel Schikaneder	1751–1812
Robert Burns	1759–1796
Johann F. von Schiller	1759–1805
Jane Austen	1775–1817

ARTISTS AND ARCHITECTS

Antoine Watteau	1684–1721
William Hogarth	1697–1764
Giambattista Piranesi	1720–1778
Jean-Baptiste Greuze	1725–1805
Hubert Robert	1733–1808
Johann Zoffany	1735–1810
Etienne Aubry	1745–1781

HISTORICAL FIGURES

Isaac Newton	1642–1727
Gottfried Wilhelm Leibniz	1646–1716
Voltaire (François M. Arouet)	1694–1778
Prince Nikolaus Esterházy	1714–1790
Johann Winckelmann	1717–1768
Denis Diderot	1713–1784
Immanuel Kant	1724–1804
Hieronymous Colloredo, archbishop of Salzburg	1731–1803
George Washington	1732–1799
Marie Antoinette	1755–1793
Count Ferdinand von Waldstein	1762–1823
General Jean B. Bernadotte	1763–1844
Napoleon Bonaparte	1769–1821
Joseph Hopkinson	1770–1842
Prince Joseph Lobkowitz	1772–1816
Prince Ferdinand Kinsky	1781–1812
Archduke Johann Rudolf	1788–1831

golds softened into a rainbow of pastel hues. The majestic mural gave place to the precious miniature. Monumental sculpture descended from its pedestal and shrank to the size of a figurine for the mantelpiece. The center of life shifted from the grand ballroom to the boudoir. Heroic passions and grand emotions melted into subtle shades of personalized expression and amorous intrigue. Grandiloquent language modulated its voice and entered into witty, *tête-à-tête* conversations.

In music the transition from the baroque to the rococo, or the *style galant* as the latter is also called, shows many similar changes. From Paris, Rameau in his *Treatise on Harmony* led the way from the tried-and-true polyphony into the new homophony. While the baroque strove for grandiose effects and pompous statements, the rococo tried for elegance and a minimum of material means. Instead of melody appearing at all levels, linear interest shifted to the slender treble register. The ponderous baroque basso continuo was streamlined into the slender *Alberti bass,* a harmonic accompaniment in which a broken chord is spread out in a simple rhythmic pattern (Ex. 10-1). The lofty lyrical tragedy of Lully was engulfed by the rising tide of the theatrical divertissement, the purpose of which was to amuse rather than to edify. The mythological characters and historical figures who struck their heroic attitudes in baroque opera seria were felled by the frivolous coquettes of *opera buffa,* in which amorous swains, jealous suitors, vainglorious guardians, and meddlesome music masters all contended for attention. The old baroque concerto grosso was pared down to the slim proportions of the *sinfonia concertante.* Large cyclical instrumental forms yielded to short separate pieces. The inexorable progress of baroque tempos was interrupted by the capricious contrasts of rubato rhythms.

Example 10-1. Alberti bass with chord equivalents above.

Baroque unity of emotion within single movements dissolved into mercurial fluctuations of mood from phrase to phrase. Instead of such forthright tempo indications as allegro and adagio, the qualifications of *allegro furioso* (furiously fast) and *adagio affettuoso* (affectingly slow) began to appear. The broadly terraced levels of baroque dynamics were discarded in favor of capricious changes, abrupt alternations of forte and piano, as well as the gradual swelling and fading of crescendos and diminuendos. And the long sweeping lines of baroque melody were broken up into a series of undulating melodic curves whose contours were often barely discernible under an excess of embellishments.

Sensibility

While the rococo was restricted for the most part to international aristocratic circles, it had a close relative in a middle-class counterpart known in France as *sensibilité,* in England as *sensibility,* and in Germany as *Empfindsamkeit.* This bourgeois edition of the rococo shunned high-flown histrionics for more down-to-earth statements, amoral eroticism for soulful sincerity, and the frivolous social attitudes of the aristocracy for the sterner virtues approved by solid citizens. In France Denis Diderot declared that the purpose of art was to render "virtue adorable and vice repugnant." The French painter Jean-Baptiste Greuze portrayed homely scenes in pictures variously entitled *Innocence, Family Reading the Bible,* and *Return of the Prodigal Son.* In a similar vein his young contemporary Etienne Aubry expressed warm family feeling and middle-class moral responsibility in *Fatherly Love,* a popular picture of the time (Fig. 10-1).

Jean-Jacques Rousseau called upon one and all to go "back to nature." Suddenly it became fashionable in both aristocratic and bourgeois society to love the simple country life. Pastoral plays were staged and novels about idyllic rural life were devoured by eager readers. In these works a nobleman usually disguises himself as a shepherd in order to commune more closely with na-

Figure 10-1. Etienne Aubrey. *L'amour paternel (Fatherly Love),* 1775. Oil on canvas. Copyright by the Barber Institute of Fine Arts, University of Birmingham, Birmingham, England.

ture. While tending his flock, he meets and falls in love with a charming shepherdess. The reader's heartstrings are gently pulled when the nobleman cannot marry his shepherdess because she is so far beneath his social station. A visit to the fortune teller, however, reveals that the girl, when only an infant, was spirited away from her castle by Gypsies, and in reality she is noble by birth. True love thus finds its way in the end.

Rousseau's influential little pastoral opera, *Le devin du village* (*The Village Soothsayer,* 1752) is a variation of this stock plot, and it became the model for Mozart's first opera, *Bastien et Bastienne* (1768). The Viennese composer Gluck recognized in Rousseau's style a new, more natural emotionalism. Gluck entertained hopes of collaborating with him in order, as he put it, to arrive at "a melody noble, affecting and natural, with an exact declamation according to the prosody of each language and the character of each people."

In England, meanwhile, a series of "sensibility" novels by Samuel Richardson, beginning with *Pamela* (1740), portrayed poor but proud people struggling with the problems of life in modest, middle-class surroundings. Their heroines were genteel women of some education whose circumstances invariably forced them to accept employment as governesses in well-to-do households. The heroine's virtue is inevitably but vainly assailed by the master, who is so impressed that he later decides to marry her and achieve his desires by more honorable means. Henry Fielding, in *Tom Jones* (1749), found that telling his tale in the first person intensified the subjective side of the story and enhanced the feeling of personal participation on the part of the reader. Oliver Goldsmith's *Vicar of Wakefield* (1766) was not far removed from a moral tract, with the saving grace of several plausible characters and the semblance of a plot. Laurence Sterne's *Sentimental Journey* (1768) was recounted in the form of an intimate diary.

As in France and England, the *Empfindsamkeit* movement in Germany was directed in both literature and music toward a new audience made up of members of the increasingly articulate urban middle class, as distinguished from the nobility on one side and the academic groups on the other. Gotthold Lessing established the new genre of the bourgeois drama with his *Miss Sara Sampson* in 1755, and two years later Denis Diderot followed suit in France with *Natural Son.* The cast of Lessing's play is made up of real-life, believable middle-class people. Sara falls in love and strays into an affair with a married man, and the fabric of her life is torn asunder. The drama, however, concludes on a note of understanding and reconciliation.

Rising prosperity was accompanied by the acceptance and acquisition in middle-class households of the new pianoforte as the favored domestic instrument, replacing the more delicate and aristocratic harpsichord. Printed novels as well as engraved songs and keyboard works found a wide public, and compositions poured forth in a steady stream to fulfill the demand.

For the first time, composers were exploring a type of intimate emotional expression based on personalized experience. Honest sentiment, soulful sighs, and a touching melancholy bordering on tearfulness permeated the songs and instrumental works of the time. The new emotional orientation and the new social class to which the works were addressed are strikingly illustrated in some of the titles of the time. A rococo composer such as the Parisian Louis-Gabriel Guillemain subtitled a set of six quartets *Gallant and Amusing Conversations between a Flute, a Violin, a Bass Viol, and Continuo* (1743), while the German composer J. F. Reichardt called one of his song collections *Lullabies for Good German Mothers* (1798), and C. P. E. Bach named a touching tonal keyboard ode *Farewell to My Silbermann Clavier* (1781).

In the music of the sons of J. S. Bach, the new psychology of emotions was catalogued and codified into a new doctrine of affects. As C. P. E. Bach pointed out in his famous *Essay on the True Art of Playing Keyboard Instruments,* music was concerned with the fluctuation and flow of the affects, or feelings. As his colleague J. J. Quantz put it in his *Essay on Playing the Transverse Flute,* "The player should change—so to speak—in every measure to a different affection, and should appear alternately sad, joyous, serious, etc., such moods being of great importance in music."

Leopold Mozart also expressed these sentiments in his tract on violin playing published in 1756, the same year his illustrious son Wolfgang was born. Each piece, he declared, must be played "in accordance with the passion prevailing in it." He further cautioned that the performer "must spare no pains to discover and deliver correctly the passion that the composer has sought to apply and, since the mournful and the merry often alternate, he must be intent on delivering each of these in its own style. In a word, he must play everything in such a way that he will be himself moved by it."

After the turn of the 19th century, Empfindsamkeit became the full-fledged middle-class style that was known in Vienna as the *Biedermeier.* Taking its name from a popular comic cartoon character featured in the Viennese journal *Fliegende Blätter,* the Biedermeier typified a kind of honest Philistine figure, ingenuous and lovable. The art and music that fall into this category were addressed to other good-humored, comfortable burghers, who were self-indulgent but not frivolous, amiable but somewhat self-conscious about their taste for the "higher" things in life. In decoration the Biedermeier style was seen in billowing, rosy garlands and clusters of true lovers' knots; in costume it meant full skirts with liberal ruffles and flounces; in music its voice was heard in tunes that belonged more in the beer garden than in the salon. In short, what had begun in France as a kind of drawing-room rococo was now the undisputed property of the comfortable middle class. The Empfindsamkeit doctrine of affects began to border on affectation, and sensibility was coming perilously close to sentimentality.

The Enlightenment

The philosophy of the Enlightenment was also a powerful stimulus in shaping the spirit of this time. Its central concept was the notion of a mechanical universe in which all physical events could be understood and predicted if only all the facts could be discovered, collected, and collated. All human knowledge could then be clarified in the light of reason. Rational rules could be formulated to govern all aspects of human existence and behavior, from profound thinking to the daily chores of human life, from the structuring of human society to the forms of its government, from the regulation of moral principles to the writing of poetry and music. Translating this cosmic design of a world that ran like a well-regulated clock into philosophical, religious, social, and artistic terms was the object of specialists in each field. In Enlightenment thought, the goal of the arts was to produce beauty in terms of order, clarity, symmetry, and harmonic proportions, all with a high degree of skill and elegance of presentation. These ideals found expression in all media, including city planning (exemplified in a view of central Paris in Figure 10-2).

Sense and Sensibility, the title of one of Jane Austen's novels, typifies two opposing ways of life, one based on reason, the other on intuition. The pure scientific speculation of such baroque intellects as Isaac Newton and Baron Leibniz was now applied to problems that had a direct effect on daily living. Previously discovered principles and the new inventions based on them were

Figure 10-2. Place de la Concorde, Paris. Daguerreotype. By permission of the Hulton Picture Company/Bettmann Archive, New York.

turned to commercial channels and the production of new wealth. This broadening of the base of baroque rationalism spread the spirit of scientific inquiry to the educated classes generally, and it is perhaps best symbolized by the *Encyclopedia, or Classified Dictionary of Sciences, Arts, and Trades,* published serially by Diderot beginning in 1751.

Even though Rousseau wrote the musical articles for Diderot's *Encyclopedia,* Rameau was the chief proponent of the Enlightenment as applied to musical theory. As a disciple of the philosopher Descartes, Rameau's expressed intention was to restore reason to musical thought, speculation, and composition. This rationalism is also reflected in the titles of such political tracts as Thomas Paine's *Common Sense* and *The Age of Reason,* and it reached its political apotheosis in the American and French revolutions of 1776 and 1789, when the rule of the hereditary aristocracy was cast off and the age of republican democracy dawned.

The spirit of sublime optimism engendered by the Enlightenment is best expressed philosophically in Condorcet's *The Progress of the Human Spirit* (1794), which projected ten stages by which the human race had advanced from primitive savagery through centuries of superstition to the point where ultimate perfection was within its grasp. By the free exercise of their rational and moral powers, Condorcet believed, human beings could eventually control their material and spiritual environment. This optimism found its most complete and articulate musical spokesman in Beethoven, who believed implicitly that the creative power of music could enlighten the human spirit and guide it along the pathway toward eternal progress and ultimate perfection.

Storm and Stress

A strong stylistic opposition both to sensibility and to the Enlightenment exploded in the German movement known as *Sturm und Drang* (storm and stress) that began in the 1770s. Taking its apt name from the title of a drama by Friedrich Klinger, this "Enlightenment in reverse" burst the bonds of propriety and politeness that had restricted the emotional range of the gallant style and Empfindsamkeit and embarked on an all-out emotional orgy.

Instead of projecting an enlightened, predictable, and benign universe standing ready to unlock its secrets to the inquiring mind, the storm-and-stress world was obscure, incomprehensible, malignant, mysterious, and elusive in the extreme. *The Nightmare* (Fig. 10-3), a painting from this period by the Swiss-born Henry Fuseli, shows an awakening interest in the subconscious dream world that conjures up a host of diabolical and demonic forces. Shrugging off the artificial etiquette of the rococo as well as the tenets of middle-class morality, the movement recognized only the intellectual and emotional aristocracy of genius.

The most familiar literary representation of storm and stress is found in

Goethe's *Sorrows of Young Werther,* and in his early *Faust,* which was first written during the peak of the storm-and-stress period and published later. Werther finds surcease from the tragedy of life in suicide. In *Faust,* Goethe's stormy-and-stressful hero casts aside the objective detachment of the Age of Reason and gives up searching for nature's secrets in books and tomes. He seeks ultimate truth in the world of experience and emotion. His operatic counterpart is Mozart's Don Giovanni, a kind of Latin Faust, who recognizes no rules of the game except those of his own making. Impetuous and defiant, he storms ruthlessly through life in search of an erotic freedom that turns out to be self-destructive license. In their unrestricted passions, both Faust and Don Giovanni unchain demonic forces that eventually devour them.

The extreme subjectivity of storm and stress perhaps found its most productive and enduring expression when sublimated into instrumental music. Haydn and Mozart in turn were both struck by its emotional lightning. This agitation is manifest in the urgent syncopations of the very opening measures of Haydn's stormy D-minor "Lamentation" Symphony (No. 26) and in the stark, angular unison opening of his E-minor "Mourning" Symphony (No. 44), as seen in Examples 10-2a and b.

Figure 10-3. Henry Fuseli. *The Nightmare,* 1785–90. Oil on canvas. Copyright by the Detroit Institute of Arts. Gift of Mr. and Mrs. Bert L. Smolker and Mr. and Mrs. Lawrence A. Fleischman.

Example 10-2a. Haydn. Symphony No. 26 in D Minor ("Lamentation"). First movement, bars 1–8.

10-2b. Haydn. Symphony No. 44 in E Minor ("Mourning"). First movement, bars 1–12.

The new emphasis on passion and personal individualism brought an increasingly subjective type of expression to Haydn's music, and he was able to infuse the gallant-style symphony with greater emotional depth, thus setting its course toward the dramatic, all-embracing, and appealing musical form that it eventually became. The storm-and-stress movement is also echoed in Mozart's music in his early G-minor symphony (No. 25), where expressive pathos is punctuated with violent outbursts of passionate protest (Ex. 10-3a).

Classicism

Classicism in two of its many guises also appeared in the 18th century, and the impression it made was strong enough to imprint its name on the period. The two sides of the classical coin in this case consisted of an antiquarian head and an academic tail. The visual arts experienced a revival of the classical Greek orders of architecture and the use of classical Greek subject matter in painting. Composers also exhibited an interest in antiquity, as they continued to draw upon Greek myths as the basis for some opera plots. However, the

Example 10-3a. Mozart. Symphony No. 25 in G Minor, *K* 183. First movement, bars 1–12.

10-3b. Mozart. Symphony No. 40 in G Minor, *K* 550. First movement, bars 1–9.

obverse side of the coin found music reaffirming its academic credentials, as composers clung to certain baroque contrapuntal techniques and revealed a clear priority for musical craftsmanship in spite of the increasing popularity of the lighter-textured, more elegant rococo style. The continuation of this academic tradition is often called the "learned" style, and as such it is to be considered as one of the several facets of this type of classicism.

The 18th-century classical movement was accompanied by the codification of new rules and the devising of more modern procedures that made the products of the period models of their kind. Classics in this sense are usually the end result of a long period of trial-and-error experimentation in which the rules of construction are formulated and in which a balance of form and content is established. Whether the medium is verbal, visual, or tonal, such works tend to be humanistic in conception, clear in design, rational in execution, and objective in approach—all qualities that generally lead to their universal acceptance.

Since the works of the Viennese composers qualify as high points in the craftsmanship of musical composition, and also in view of their central position historically, they have become classics in the sense of being classroom models for future generations to study and emulate. It is in this sense that their sonatas, chamber music, concertos, and symphonies are to be considered classical. The "neoclassical" style that crops up in the music of the 20th century thus refers to new versions of the forms and images projected by 18th-century composers. Prokofiev's first symphony, subtitled "Classical," Ravel's bow to the keyboard suite, *Le tombeau de Couperin* (*The Tomb of Couperin*), and Debussy's *Hommage à Rameau* are cases in point.

Antiquarian classicism, on the contrary, finds its expression in such manifestations as the new science of classical archaeology, the revival of Greek and Roman art forms, and the reinterpretation of Aristotle's principles of drama as found in 18th-century plays and operas. The excavations of Herculaneum and Pompeii that began in mid-century led to reverberations in all the arts. Two Englishmen, James Stuart and Nicholas Revett, visited Greece and in 1762 published an influential book, *The Antiquities of Athens.* The German historian Johann Winckelmann took a new look at Greek statuary and found it superior in workmanship to the later Roman models. His book *History of Ancient Art* (1764) became the 18th-century equivalent of a best-seller.

The stalwart patriotism and civic virtues extolled by the ancients served the political purposes of the postrevolutionary French governments, and the spirit of classical stoicism and individual self-sacrifice became the new social creed as well as the bourgeois answer to the wanton waste and reckless self-indulgence of the deposed aristocratic governing class.

In the visual arts a veritable cult of ruins could be seen in the popular prints of Giambattista Piranesi and the picturesque canvases of the French painter Hubert Robert, who has gone down in history by his nickname, "Robert of the Ruins." Architects built replicas of Greek temples and adapted classical motifs for the exteriors and interiors of the town houses they erected for aristocratic and for wealthy middle-class patrons. A literary counterpart of this archaeological orientation is found in the work of the French lyric poet André Chénier, who adopted Greek metrical patterns rather than those of Roman models for his paeans and odes.

A desire to restore the principles and the spirit of Greek drama is apparent in the plays and operas of the period. The new rules were derived from Aristotle's *Poetics* rather than the writings of his Roman successor Seneca. The dramatist Gotthold Lessing, the critic Francesco Algarotti, the librettist Raniero Calzabigi, and the operatic composer Christoph Gluck all embarked zestfully upon dramatic and musical reforms. The ancient ideal of art as the "imitation of nature" was explored and specifically applied to the delineation of characters who were representative of true human nature rather than the stilted and stylized types found in Pietro Metastasio's baroque dramas. Gluck echoed the phrases and sentiments of Winckelmann when he stated that "simplicity, truth, and naturalness are the great principles of beauty in all artistic manifestations."

The key words of the time were always *nature* and *natural*, and they were echoed over and over in the letters of Mozart and his contemporaries. Classicism in this sense, then, means the attempt to recapture some of the glories of Greco-Roman antiquity and, by implication, the establishment of a new art that achieved the ancient ideals of clarity, symmetry, balance, and order.

Vienna, the Crossroads

The stage on which this drama of music was enacted embraced the entire European continent. The scenes in the several acts shifted rapidly from one capital and provincial center to another, until all the dramatic developments eventually converged on Vienna, the capital of the multinational Austro-Hungarian Empire. Here the final climactic act took place from 1750 to 1828, with such players as Gluck, Haydn, Mozart, Beethoven, and Schubert in the leading roles. It is important always to bear in mind that this configuration of great composers represents only the highest peaks in a mountain range of hundreds of talented and well-trained musicians.

PATHS OF HAYDN AND MOZART

Two of the principals achieved their musical pre-eminence by taking diametrically opposite pathways. Joseph Haydn arrived at the peak of his creative powers late in life, while Wolfgang Amadeus Mozart flashed across the musical firmament in a brief but meteoric career. Haydn, until late in life, never ventured farther than a few miles from Vienna and remained for the most part a provincial figure until he set out for London as he was approaching his 60th year. Mozart was internationally prominent from his days as a child prodigy at the age of six, when he and his father began touring the capitals and courts of Europe.

Haydn's ideas took shape only after a long period of gestation. He himself explained, "As a conductor of an orchestra I could make experiments, observe what produced an effect and what weakened it, and was thus in a position to improve, alter, make additions or omissions, and be as bold as I pleased; I was cut off from the world, there was no one to confuse or torment me, and I was forced to become original."

Though he was geographically confined, Haydn was well aware of what was going on in Italy, Paris, and in such German capitals as Mannheim, Berlin, and Hamburg. Colleagues sent him copies of the latest treatises, symphonies, and concertos, while prominent visitors brought him the latest information about the world of music outside the Esterházy estate, his chief place of work. Mozart, however, as the most cosmopolitan of composers, was conversant at first hand with all the contemporary developments of his time. In his native Salzburg he was the apt pupil of his astute and intelligent father, Leopold; and Michael Haydn, musical director to the archbishop of Salzburg and younger brother of Joseph, regularly brought the young Mozart copies of Joseph's latest works to study. Salzburg at this time was a bit of Italy transported to an Austrian province, and here Mozart grew up in an atmosphere of Latin lyricism, in which the singing voice, whether it was human or instrumental, was all-important.

In London, J. C. Bach, the youngest son of the prolific Johann Sebastian, made an indelible impression on the eight-year-old Mozart and instilled in him a lifelong love for the *cantabile,* the singing instrumental style that he later used so freely in his own concertos as well as in his keyboard music. Later, in Naples, Mozart absorbed the principles of opera seria, as well as its more fashionable competitor, opera buffa. In Bologna he studied counterpoint with the famous historian and composer Padre Martini, while in Paris he met the operatic successors of Rameau. He also became acquainted with the free improvisatory keyboard style of Johann Schobert, which was moving away from the tinkling harpsichord confections for the ear concocted by Couperin, Daquin, and Rameau.

Finally, in Mannheim at the court of the discerning patron Duke Carl Theodor, the young Mozart heard the finest orchestra in Europe, and saw opening up before him many new vistas of orchestral playing. The innovations he observed there included the modern method of conducting; the shaping of the new symphonic form with its dramatic dualism of opposing subjects, and important strides in amplifying the development section in sonata-form movements; the idiomatic treatment of various instrumental sonorities, especially in situations involving contrasting groups; the brilliant use of wind instruments, which later assumed such prominence in Mozart's writing; the antiphonal alternation of strings and winds; and above all, the startling new dynamic shadings that ran the gamut of tonal gradations from pianissimo to fortissimo. The German poet Christian Schubart described the Mannheim orchestra: "Their forte is like thunder, their crescendo a cataract, their diminuendo the rippling of a crystal stream, their piano the soft breath of spring."

The paths of Mozart and Haydn crossed in Vienna in 1781. Mozart had left the unsympathetic court of the archbishop of Salzburg to set up shop in the capital city as an independent, free-lance composer; and Haydn had begun to spend more time in his Vienna residence away from his Esterházy patron. This was also the year in which Haydn brought out his series of six quartets, Opus 33, which bore the interesting inscription "In an entirely new and special manner." Also known as the "Russian" Quartets because of their dedication to the Grand Duke Paul, they contain some of Haydn's most profound discoveries in musical craftsmanship (see p. 215). This little revolution of Haydn's, on top of his excursions into new territory in his Opus 20 quartets (see p. 217), made a powerful impression on Mozart's musical thought. His response was a series of six quartets of his own, which he dedicated to Haydn.

Three of Mozart's new quartets were played on a memorable occasion in his house in Vienna in 1785, when his father was a visitor and Haydn the guest of honor. Leopold Mozart wrote home to his daughter in Salzburg, "On Saturday evening Herr Joseph Haydn . . . came to see us and the new quartets were performed. . . . Haydn said to me, 'Before God as an honest man I can tell you that your son is the greatest composer known to me either in person or by name. He has taste, and, what is more, the most profound knowledge of composition'."

The tables were thus turned and the younger master now became a decisive influence on the older. This great musical dialogue lasted for a full and fruitful decade, until Haydn went to London in 1790 and Mozart died the following year.

CULTURAL CULMINATION IN VIENNA

Many circumstances—historical, ethnographical, social, and economic—figured in the confluence of forces that led to the great cultural culmination in Vienna. A broader spread of the sources of patronage, for instance, prevented the imprint of a single standard or personality on the period, thus permitting a wider variety of styles and tastes to develop. While maintaining various court composers on modest stipends, the imperial court nevertheless dispensed only a fraction of the total patronage, preferring a less important role than that played by royal courts elsewhere. As a result composers were gradually emancipated from the restrictions of a single aristocratic employer.

Through the eyes of a contemporary, it is possible to get a picture of the way Vienna appeared to a perceptive observer. Referring to the influx into Vienna of noble provincial families and the landed gentry of central Europe, the composer and writer J. F. Reichardt pointed out:

> Some have established themselves with taste and not infrequently on a grand scale, and live here in great splendor and hospitality. This applies especially to Russians and Poles, who bring the good sociable spirit with them and amal-

> gamate themselves with the Viennese the more easily. Aside from them, the great Bohemian, Moravian, and Hungarian families, like the Austrians, live regularly all winter long in Vienna, giving it the brilliance and magnificence that make it the great splendid imperial city, for the court itself prefers a retired family life to external pomp and show. Yet the court appears also with great dignity and no little brilliance at the few public festivities which it still maintains. The greatest brilliance consists, however, in the rich background provided by the higher nobility of the crown lands.

Thus it was that a Czech nobleman, Prince Lobkowitz, first brought Gluck to Vienna and the Hungarian Prince Esterházy became the patron of Haydn. Even the independent Beethoven, finding safety in numbers, accepted a lifelong pension from a committee of aristocrats that included Prince Kinsky, Prince Lobkowitz, and one member of the imperial family, the Archduke Rudolph.

As noble families vied with one another for cultural prestige, men of ambition and genius were understandably attracted to Vienna by the large number of available commissions and the variety of sources of employment. In addition to the nobility, Reichardt further noted that "The bankers and great landowners and manufacturers are included here; and so on through the bourgeoisie proper down to the well-to-do petite bourgeoisie; in the way that all the great public diversions and amusements are encouraged by all classes without any abrupt divisions or offending distinctions—in these respects Vienna is quite alone among the great cities of Europe." While much of the music-making in Vienna was in private households and accessible by invitation only, there was also a thriving public concert life available to all who cared to participate.

Genius ranked high in prestige in the healthy international atmosphere that prevailed in this Central European crossroads. Men of talent, no matter what their point of origin, were accepted and encouraged for what they could contribute. The streams of folk music and art music met and merged in this polyglot melting pot. In the process folk songs and dances lost their rusticity and roughness, and the musical forms in which they were incorporated lost their artificiality, thereby gaining new vigor and vitality. The country Laendler, for instance, originally had a hop-and-turn step, but when it came to Vienna, the staccato stamping was replaced by a gliding glissando and it became the sliding, whirling waltz. As it rose on the social ladder it could be heard in the trios of the minuets—for instance, in that of Mozart's E-flat symphony, *K* 543. The bourgeois waltz was thus well on its way toward replacing the aristocratic minuet.

The unprecedented demand for the production of works by the contemporary composers of this period prevented Viennese programs from becoming archives made up principally of museum pieces from the past. A new comprehension of the inherent dramatic possibilities of instrumental music, especially in the emerging sonata form, was responsible for its subsequent rise to a position of equality with vocal works such as the opera. As Reichardt summed it up:

> Vienna has everything that marks a great capital in a quite unusually high degree. It has a great, wealthy, cultivated, art-loving, hospitable, well-mannered, elegant nobility; it has a wealthy, sociable, hospitable middle class and bourgeoisie, as little lacking in cultivated and well-informed gentlemen and gracious families; it has a well-to-do, good natured, jovial populace. All classes love amusement and good living, and things are so arranged that all classes may enjoy in all convenience and security every amusement that modern society knows and loves.

Vienna thus experienced a florescence during this period that may well be compared to that of Periclean Athens, Medicean Florence, and Elizabethan England. But while these other eras brought the arts of architecture, sculpture, painting, and literature to unprecedented peaks of perfection, the unique distinction of Vienna was its music.

Gluck: Operatic Reform

The year 1762 was a momentous one in the history both of Vienna and of the lyric theater, as it marked the appearance of the first of Christoph Gluck's reform operas, *Orfeo ed Euridice.* In the operas of the time, as in the products of all aesthetic movements, innovation was liberally mixed with tradition, and the projected brave new operatic world was still populated principally by personifications of the contemporary 18th-century styles as well as by many survivals from the past. Preferring the muses of classical antiquity to some of the more seductive sirens of their own time, the Bohemian-born Gluck and his Italian librettist Raniero Calzabigi were both highly articulate about what they were trying to accomplish.

Heretofore the reigning librettist had been the celebrated and brilliantly successful Italian poet and dramatist Pietro Metastasio. Roman-born but a long-time resident of Vienna, the prolific Metastasio had written the libretti for most of the major composers of his day, including Handel, Alessandro Scarlatti, Giovanni Pergolesi, Haydn, Mozart, and Gluck himself. His rather stiff but stately dramas on historical subjects had begun to pall, however, and Gluck and Calzabigi were intrigued by the newer styles and ideas that were sweeping the late 18th-century scene.

In order to build their lyric dramas on a solid authoritative basis, they hearkened back to the precedents of Greek drama and the pronouncements of Aristotle. As to "unity of action," Gluck's operas have a greater feeling of progress than previous examples because, for the first time in music history, he discarded the dry recitative for a continuous, through-composed orchestral score from beginning to end. He also assigned both the chorus and the orchestra a more prominent position by allowing them to comment on the action and reflect the emotional substance of the text in appropriate musical images. The action is also interrupted less often for long introductory ritornels and static da capo arias.

Gluck further attempted to return to classical clarity and simplicity by banishing coloratura roles and eliminating superfluous vocal virtuosity, though he did not disdain an occasional flourish or cadenza if it suited his dramatic purpose. He also reduced the number of characters in his casts: *Orfeo,* for instance, has only three principals—Orpheus, Eurydice, and Amor. Instead of striking heroic attitudes, strutting about with grandiose gestures, and voicing conventionalized sentiments neatly packaged in standardized da capo arias, his characters behave more in accordance with the Greek "imitation of nature" principle—meaning in this case the representation of human nature. In spite of all his posturing in the classical toga, however, Gluck remained essentially a man of his own times, and a look now at his *Orfeo ed Euridice* will show how his theories worked out in actual practice.

In this retelling of the Orpheus tale, Gluck and Calzabigi chose to begin after Eurydice's death. Once appropriate mourning has taken place, Amor appears to announce that the gods have taken pity on Orpheus. If he will travel to Hades, Eurydice will be restored to him, on condition that he not look at her until they have returned to the world of the living. Orpheus undertakes the journey, and his magic singing convinces the guardians of the gates to the nether regions—the Furies and the three-headed dog Cerberus—to let him pass through. In the Elysian Fields, Eurydice's hand is placed in his, and they begin the ascent earthward. Eurydice, unaware that Orpheus may not look upon her, berates him mercilessly for ignoring her. Orpheus relents, turns to her, and she falls lifeless. After an aria of Olympian grief, Orpheus is once more confronted by Amor. The gods have taken pity a second time and Eurydice is restored once more to life, amid general rejoicing.

In spite of Gluck's announced intention that an overture should prepare the audience for what follows, the *Orfeo* overture is still a mere curtain raiser, establishing a festive atmosphere and sounding a fanfare for the arrival of latecomers. Set in the sunlight key of C Major, it provides both a contrast and a complement to the opening scene, which is set in the somber key of C Minor. The rise of the curtain reveals a chorus mourning at Eurydice's tomb. The statuesque stances of the chorus and the restrained tone are generally representative of the spirit of antiquity, as are many of the well-chiseled arias that follow.

More important in a purely musical sense, however, is the immediate enunciation of a musical motif that appears again and again throughout the opera, changing each time to reflect shifting moods and dramatic progress, yet recognizable enough to bind the work together in a tight motivic unity. After its initial appearance as a grief motif (Ex. 10-4a), the theme recurs in one of its many mutations in an aria after Orpheus reaches the Elysian fields (Ex. 10-4b) where, played by the plaintive oboe, it symbolizes Orpheus' longing for Eurydice. Since Eurydice is about to become his once more, the motif becomes quite buoyant in the following chorus (Ex. 10-4c).

Example 10-4. Gluck. *Orpheus and Eurydice.*

10-4a. No. 1, bars 1–4. Mourning Chorus motif.

10-4b. No. 33, bars 1–3. Aria of Orpheus.

10-4c. No. 34, bars 1–8. Chorus.

After Eurydice and Orpheus are reunited, she becomes convinced that he loves her no more and berates him in the style of a Handelian rage aria. Here, at an allegro tempo, the motif takes a furious turn (Ex. 10-4d). When Orpheus relents and gazes upon her, she falls lifeless, setting the scene for the apotheosis of his grief, expressed in the well-known aria "Che farò senza Euridice" ("How shall I go on without Eurydice," Ex. 10-4e). The motif appears here for the final time, in a transcendent lyric form.

Practically all of the current styles of the time make their appearance in appropriate places. The pantomime ballet in front of Eurydice's tomb in the opera's first scene is an excellent example of the Empfindsamkeit. The sighing, tearful chorus creates gentle dissonances on strong beats of the measure

10-4d. No. 41, bars 1–6. Aria of Eurydice.

10-4e. No. 43, bars 1–4. Aria of Orpheus.

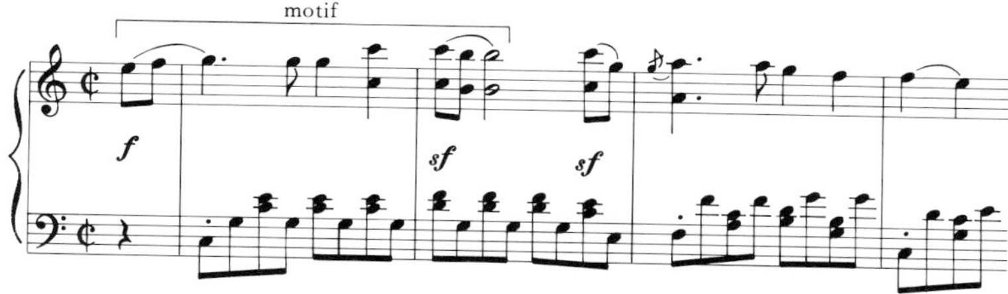

and resolves them on adjacent weak beats, as in bars 2 and 4 of Example 10-4a.

The appearances of Amor, the god of love, are invariably accompanied by rococo music in the best Dresden china figurine tradition. The Sicilian rhythm of the aria No. 15 (Ex. 10-5a) for instance, bespeaks a pastoral character, and Amor gently tugs at our heartstrings with several sighing, gallant-style appoggiaturas (Ex. 10-5b).

As Orpheus descends into the underworld, he is greeted by menacing growls in the double-bass register from the mythological watchdog Cerberus, as each of his three heads barks in turn (Ex. 10-5c). This bit of storm-and-stress demonology is an amusing continuation of the baroque representative style, and Gluck further intensifies the image by letting the five-note rising figure span the diminished fifth, the old medieval *diabolus in musica.*

The "Dance of the Furies" (Ex. 10-5d) continues the storm-and-stress horror music. Orpheus pleads eloquently with the Furies in the most melting Neapolitan-opera manner, and they are moved by the ardor of his music to such unaccustomed emotions as pity and sympathy.

The transition from the terrible abode of the Furies to the serenity of the Elysian Fields is full of dramatic contrast. Orpheus' aria "Che puro ciel" ("How pure the sky"), with its accompaniment describing the chirping of the birds, running rivulets, and radiant sunshine, is a worthy representation of Rousseau's "back to nature" in music. In contrast to the earlier "Dance of the Furies," the "Ballet of the Blessed Spirits" in the Elysian Fields is once again in the elegant gallant style.

Gluck's musical characterizations are drawn with a keen ear for the thematic material that aptly reflects the mental and emotional outlook of his characters; his themes also lend themselves to development as the dramatic action

Example 10-5. Gluck. *Orpheus and Eurydice.*

10-5a. No. 15, bars 8–11. Aria of Amor. Sicilian rhythm.

10-5b. No. 15, bars 25–28. Gallant style.

10-5c. No. 21, bar 15. Chorus.

10-5d. No. 28, bars 1–5. "Dance of the Furies."

progresses. The survival of the artificial male contralto voice in the role of Orpheus is, however, a serious lapse in dramatic truth. Since the roles of Eurydice and Amor are both assigned to sopranos, there is a complete lack of deep male voices except in the choruses, and a corresponding absence of contrast in timbre. This situation later changed when Gluck reworked the opera for a natural tenor in the Paris version, and today audiences may hear the role sung by a female alto, a baritone, or a countertenor.

There are several inconsistencies in Gluck's reform position. While ostensibly he was criticizing Metastasian drama, he nevertheless continued to set librettos by Metastasio whenever he was commissioned to do so, because they were still admired in certain theatrical circles. For all his pious protestations against the "abuses in Italian opera," Gluck was never one to scorn the mainstream of the Italian lyric stage. And despite his declarations about "reducing music to its proper function of seconding poetry," Gluck, like every other successful opera composer before and since his time, was primarily musically minded. Finally, despite his aesthetic and musical authority, Gluck lacked the technical security and compositional craftsmanship of Haydn, Mozart, and Beethoven.

As for his earnest reforms, his operatic successors—Mozart, Beethoven, and Rossini, for instance—paid them little heed; only such romanticists as Berlioz, Liszt, and Wagner officially adopted him as a forerunner. And for all the noble, tragic utterances of his maturity, it is well to remember that in his unreformed days Gluck also wrote some rollicking good comic operas in the French manner.

As an international figure, Gluck often traveled to Paris where he had a friend at court in one of his former pupils—no less a personage than Queen Marie Antoinette, who always stood ready to put in a word for him with opera impresarios at the right moment. The opposing forces of innovation and tradition in his work were bound to clash, and Gluck's ideas led to one of the most heated critical debates of the century. With the Italian composer Niccolò Piccinni as his adversary, the operatic battle of the Gluckists versus the Piccinnists raged. The Parisian performances of *Orfeo* and *Iphigénie en Aulide* in 1774 and *Alceste* in 1776, however, carried the day for Gluck.

As the written preface to *Alceste* makes clear, Gluck sought a "beautiful simplicity" instead of a "useless superfluity of ornaments," and "heartfelt language, strong passions" in place of "florid descriptions . . . and sententious cold morality." In this, Gluck represents that aspect of the Enlightenment that sought to liberate natural man from the veneer of artifice and convention.

Haydn

Unlike the opera specialist Gluck, Joseph Haydn was a universal composer who contributed liberally to all the categories of music popular in his time. Vocal church music in the forms of masses, cantatas, motets, offertories, and sacred arias occupied him from his early years onward and reached a final fruition in his two great concert oratorios, *The Creation* and *The Seasons.* While he wrote a quantity of secular songs and no fewer than 32 operas, he is most remembered as an instrumental composer and was happiest working in the fertile fields of chamber music and the symphony.

SOCIAL MUSIC

Haydn also wrote prolifically in the genial genre of Viennese social music. More than any other composer, he was responsible for the crystallization of the string quartet and the symphony out of such casual ensemble works as the divertimento and the serenade.

Social music of this kind was in demand for such occasions as wedding celebrations, birthdays, anniversaries, garden parties, and the visits of distinguished guests. Light rather than serious in style, it was performed also as dinner or "table" music, dance music, conversation music, and background music in private households as well as in public places and coffee houses. Vast quantities of this social music came from the workshops of every minor and major composer of the time—Dittersdorf and Wagenseil, Leopold Mozart and Michael Haydn, as well as Joseph Haydn with more than 60 examples and Wolfgang Mozart with more than 40.

Variously designated as *divertimento, serenade,* or *cassation,* the titles carry little specific meaning. Leopold Mozart, for instance, called one of his works *Divertimento militare sive sinfonia* (*Divertimento in the Military Manner, or Symphony*). *Divertimento* was generally used as a generic name for all the works of this style, while *serenade* usually indicated a work intended to be played in the evening. Wolfgang Mozart, for instance, entitled several of his early examples by the Italian title *Serenata notturna.* His well-known later serenade bears the German equivalent, *Eine kleine Nachtmusik* (*K* 525), literally "a little night music," figuratively a nocturnal serenade.

Divertimentos could be written for any combination of instruments from three or more of any kind all the way up to a chamber or full orchestra. Sometimes specific instruments were called for, sometimes not. The instrumentation always depended upon what was available for the occasion, since the music was written on demand. Those scored for strings alone were probably intended for the salon; those exclusively for winds would be performed in the garden or park; and the vast quantity, combining a mixture of strings and winds with occasional percussion, could be played indoors or outdoors as the occasion required.

All sorts of odd combinations were possible. Because Haydn's patron Prince Nikolaus Esterházy played the baryton—a large viol about halfway between the viola and cello in size—Haydn wrote a large number of trios and quartets for baryton and strings. They are all divertimentos, however, rather than trios and quartets in the later structural sense.

Divertimentos could include any number of movements from two to ten, the average being around six. Much freer in overall form than the baroque dance suite, the component parts followed no set order. Traditionally beginning with a march, the divertimento could be continued with an instrumental aria, several minuets or rondos, one or more sets of variations, and so on.

Theme-and-variation movements were apparently great favorites, probably because they offered the various members of the ensemble an opportunity for stepping forward as soloists, with each variation featuring another instrumentalist in turn. The casual divertimento-serenade style was fundamental to early classical chamber music and symphony. Haydn's early string quartets are really divertimentos, as are the early symphonies. Echoes of divertimento-serenade idioms are still detectable in his late London symphonies and some choral works.

Divertimentos thus provided composers with frequent commissions. Although the divertimento was always functional music, more alert and ambitious composers used it as an opportunity for experimentation in ensemble writing, trying out various instrumental combinations, and developing new technical ideas. The very fluidity and flexibility of the divertimento was ideal for this sort of trial-and-error composing. All of Haydn's early instrumental music falls into this flexible category, and it was the proving ground of his mature style. It is important to remember that this type of social music was never intended as a vehicle for a composer to make profound statements, nor was it concerned in the slightest with his personal emotions.

By its very nature the divertimento tradition was social, not individual; popular, not serious; designed for easy listening, not concentrated attention. Relying as it did on melodic invention rather than development of ideas, it was occasional rather than permanent, meant for every day rather than the long term. Later, when the string quartet and the symphony came to be works that were meant for repeated performances, composers took into account the need for weightier ideas in addressing a more attentive audience. Much of the total output of social music was the routine product of the time and can be consigned to well-deserved oblivion. In some cases, however, the inventive power and the craftsmanship of execution of a Haydn or a Mozart lift them above their original purpose and make them welcome in today's concert repertory.

CHAMBER MUSIC AND SYMPHONY

From this common source of social music Haydn gradually evolved the ensemble combinations and the cyclical sonata forms that today are classified as duos, trios, quartets, quintets, and so on up to symphonies. His early string quartets, for example, were simply divertimentos for four stringed instruments with a wide variety of short movements. While literally dozens of other 18th-century composers shared in the development of the string quartet—two violins, viola, and cello—Haydn, more than any other composer, shaped the style of string quartet writing on principles that provided the foundation for the work of other composers from his day to the present.

Thus the urge to evolve formal plans that could encompass the cyclical character of the dance suite, the freedom of the fantasia, the lyrical quality of the aria, the opposition of one and several instruments of the concertante style, the dialogue of the concerto grosso, the rationalism of contrapuntal techniques, and the emotionalism of the lyric drama led to the decades of experimentation that culminated in the *sonata* style. Out of the old baroque dance suite, the church and chamber sonatas, the toccata, the Italian overture or opera sinfonia, the aria da capo, and the divertimento emerged the sonata, which, both technically and spiritually, is a composite affair synthesizing the forms, tendencies, styles, attitudes, and ideas of two centuries.

Chamber music is separate from social and dinner music in that the accent is on active, concentrated listening, and its purpose is not to accompany polite conversation or to drown out the clatter of dinner dishes. Chamber music practices moderation in all things and argues using the logic of sweet reason. Each player is assigned an independent part within the whole and there is little doubling. The planes of sound have their separate identities and the parts rarely invade each other's territory by crossing registers. Chamber music is slim and sleek in its lines, its contours are well proportioned, its balances are symmetrical. Each instrumental voice, moreover, is intended to be heard in a give-and-take manner. Unlike large ensembles in which a leader imposes his will upon the orchestral masses, chamber music reflects the democratic image of equals among equals. Shorn of all bombast, it does not shout from the housetops or speak in tones of violent emotionalism. Yet it can loom as large in conception as it is intimate in expression.

Haydn's particular contributions to chamber music are legion, and the bulk of his symphonies are to be considered in this category. But from about 1785, he was sought after by an international audience. The first major commission came from the famous Parisian musical enterprise, the Concert de la Loge Olympique, resulting in the six "Paris" Symphonies (Nos. 82–87) of 1785–86. Six more symphonies for Paris and London increased Haydn's popularity, culminating in the twelve most mature symphonies (Nos. 93–104), written between 1791 and 1795 for the Salomon concerts in London. These are in every sense full-scale symphonic works, and they still form part of the fundamental repertory of the modern symphony orchestra.

There remains, however, a large group of important, superb symphonies whose sonority, tone color, and sound mass are still of chamber rather than of concert-hall dimensions. The high level of soloistic dexterity required of individual performers in some of the early Haydn symphonies indicates that the chamber orchestra of the Esterházy household, for which they were conceived, was small and dexterous enough (about twenty performers) for Haydn to take full advantage of individual talent when it was available to him. In the late concert-hall symphonies this individualization largely disappears.

Much the same is true of Mozart's essays in the form, and only the later symphonies are full-scale concert-hall symphonies in the modern sense. In Haydn's hands, however, both chamber music and the symphony broadened out stylistically from the ultra-refinement and gracefulness of the gallant style to include the unexpected twists and witty turns of the sensibility style, the gaiety and gusto of lusty peasant folk idioms, the impassioned emotional outbursts of storm and stress, and the spiritual loftiness of church music.

THE CYCLICAL SONATA DESIGN

Haydn brought a new and compelling logic to the overall cyclic form of the sonata design. From the loose groupings of the multimovement divertimento he retained just four movements—an opening in sonata form, a lyrical slow movement, a minuet, and a finale that was usually in either rondo or sonata form.

In his hands the rococo minuet and the rondo became full, expressive members of the cycle, reflecting the prevailing mood of the whole composition. In this way the minuet served to bridge the span between the slow movement and the finale. Beginning with the "Russian" Quartets (Op. 33), it lost its last rococo vestiges and was designated as a scherzo, one characteristic of which may be playfulness or jesting. The rondo shed some of its lighthearted character, and all sorts of novel and ingenious ways to reintroduce the recurring opening section were devised.

Above all, Haydn endowed individual sonata-form movements with a new vitality. Taking elements of the design that could be found in Neapolitan opera overtures, in the scintillating keyboard essays of Domenico Scarlatti, in the lighthearted but influential trio sonatas of Pergolesi, in the experiments of the Mannheim composers, and in the keyboard sonatas of C. P. E. Bach, Haydn proceeded to forge the form anew. It was he who divined the latent possibilities of the development section and made it the most important part of the design.

At first the development section had been only a central episode in which the previously presented thematic material was broken up and regrouped, thus creating a sense of suspense before it reappeared as a reassembled whole in the recapitulation. But in the "new and special manner" of the "Russian" Quartets of 1781, as well as in the six "Paris" Symphonies, subject material was reduced to the smallest of musical particles, the *motif,* which now became the most vital unit of the form. It is indeed no accident that the word *motif* is derived from the verb "to move," since it is a tonal fragment that contains within itself an incipient directional tendency and the potential for further melodic, rhythmic, and dynamic motion, and which in turn lends itself to repetition and begs for adventure.

Motivic development and expansion, once confined to the central section, now became a constant and continuous process throughout the composition. All instrumental voices, furthermore, shared prominently in the developmental procedures, and none any longer occupied a subordinate position. Even the bass part, which formerly only filled a place in the harmony, was released from its subservient role and shared equally in the presentation and development of melodic ideas.

Thus it was that Haydn worked out the set of structural and stylistic principles that did not confine but instead brought a new freedom to music. The rare combination of lawfulness and liberty that he achieved in his creative approach and method is unmatched in the annals of music. No one knew as well as he the eternal paradox of art: namely, that freedom lies in the direction of discipline, and that only through the acceptance of limitations can the creative fires be released in such forms that make it possible for the artist to transmit ideas to other minds. His music thus rests solidly on principles of form that progress and evolve rather than crystallize in the final or definitive sense.

Haydn's forms are myriad, since no two works are ever alike, but there is always unity in the underlying principles. The spirit of freedom and flexibility that he breathed into his music thus raised it above the elegant routine products of many of his contemporaries into the rarefied atmosphere of masterpieces with universal appeal.

Storm and Stress: Haydn and Mozart

When the limits of expression within the confines of the gallant style and Empfindsamkeit code of manners had been explored, Haydn searched for greater emotional heights and depths so as to broaden the force and power of his musical forms. This he found in the storm-and-stress style. His E-minor symphony, No. 44 (c. 1771), for instance, bears the designation "Trauer" ("Mourning"). It opens with an abrupt unison gesture, harsh in its angularity and forceful in its sharp forte-piano contrasts (see Ex. 10-2b).

The style is also echoed by Mozart, in his two G-minor symphonies, for example, where expressive pathos is punctuated with violent outbursts of passionate protest (see Exs. 10-3a, b). This is the type of commanding gesture heard again in the opening of Mozart's C-minor piano concerto (*K* 491), composed in 1786 (Ex. 10-6a), as well as in the opening of Beethoven's C-minor piano concerto (Op. 37), composed in 1800 (Ex. 10-6b). The striking similarity between the Mozart and Beethoven works is hardly a coincidence, for this Mozart concerto was one that Beethoven especially admired and played in public.

Example 10-6a. Mozart. Concerto in C Minor, *K* 491. First movement, bars 1–8.

10-6b. Beethoven. Concerto in C Minor, Op. 37. First movement, bars 1–4.

If Haydn points ahead to the heroic idiom of the future in the first movement of the "Mourning" Symphony, its strange minuet movement is a most pointed reversion to the learned style of the past. It proceeds not as courtly and elegant minuets were wont to do, but as a canon at the octave in a minor key, strict in execution and ungracious in style (Ex. 10-7).

In his F-minor symphony, No. 49, "La Passione," we again encounter the duality of a fierce emotional drive controlled by techniques rescued from the

Example 10-7. Haydn. Symphony No. 44 in E Minor ("Mourning"). Third movement, bars 1–16.

past (Ex. 10-8). In the opening of the second movement, a recognizably old-fashioned baroque basso continuo rhythm is used to control a driving tempo—*allegro di molto*—and a ferociously exaggerated distension of intervallic leaps quite modern for its day. Written in 1768, the "Passion" Symphony indicates that Haydn was using the storm-and-stress idiom several years before a number of angry young literary men proclaimed an ideology for it.

Such a blend of radicalism and traditionalism in Haydn's Sturm und Drang music is nowhere more evident than in the Opus 20 series of six string quartets composed in 1772 and revealing his rebellion against the prevailing gallant-style prototypes. Three of these daringly modern quartets, Nos. 2, 5, and 6, end in old-fashioned fugues.

The fifth quartet, in F Minor, is the most somber and searching of the series and has been described as the most nearly tragic work Haydn ever wrote. Its first movement begins with a throbbing figure full of turbulence and deeply felt emotion (Ex. 10-9). The expansive development section contains an impassioned argument moving through a series of key centers while various mutations of the opening theme contend for attention. Eventually it subsides in an abbreviated recapitulation. The prevailing dark mood colors the ensuing minuet movement, also cast in the minor tonality. The pastoral *sicilienne* rhythm of the adagio movement then provides a momentary lyrical respite from the heart-rending outpourings of the two that preceded it.

There follows a rigorous, stern finale, once more in F Minor, which Haydn labels a "fugue with two subjects." The main subject (Ex. 10-10a) had been a traditional favorite in the baroque period. It can be traced back to Kuhnau, Pachelbel, and Buxtehude. Bach used it as a fugue subject in the second book of his *Well-Tempered Clavier,* where it appears in the same F-minor tonality as Haydn's string quartet (Ex. 10-10b). Handel also builds the *Messiah* chorus "And with His stripes we are healed" upon it (Ex. 10-10c).

Example 10-8. Haydn. Symphony No. 49 in F Minor ("Passion"). First movement, bars 1–4.

Example 10-9. Haydn. String Quartet in F Minor, Op. 20, No. 5. First movement, bars 1–5.

Haydn felt the full force of the Sturm und Drang when he reached his early forties, whereas Mozart was still in his teens when this old baroque fugue-subject formula cast its spell on him. The year after Haydn's F-minor quartet, Mozart composed a series of string quartets that show the impact of Haydn's work. Two of them, *K* 168 and *K* 173, have fugal finales. In the slow movement of the first, the instruments are muted and the familiar subject appears, once again in F Minor (Ex. 10-10d), making fugal entries although the movement itself is not a full fugue. The tempo and the quiet dynamic levels help to tone down the emotionality of what is evidently a strongly felt piece of music.

No such reserve, however, marks Mozart's second treatment of this subject in the G-minor symphony of 1773 (*K* 283), sometimes known as the "Little" G-minor Symphony. At the age of seventeen, he proposed as the initial subject of his symphony a more impatient, much stormier and more stressful adaptation of this traditional subject than Haydn had ventured. Nothing better illustrates the differences between Haydn in his forties and Mozart in his teens than the austere, traditional statement of the subject by Haydn and the nervously syncopated, imaginatively altered version of it by Mozart. And while Haydn proceeds contrapuntally, Mozart moves into chromatic harmonic territory (see Ex. 10-3a).

At seventeen, Mozart was closer in age, and his "Little" G-minor Symphony closer in spirit, to the pronouncements of the tempestuous young literary Stürmer und Dränger in the German universities in the 1770s. At the end of his life Mozart once again turned back to this fascinating fugue subject. But as it appears in his *Requiem* (*K* 626), which he was composing at the time of his death, the subject has lost all its fiery impatience and has taken on a magnificent austerity and somberness of tone (Ex. 10-10e).

In *Don Giovanni* (see pp. 34–38) Mozart commences the overture with fortissimo, foreboding, fire-and-brimstone chords in the demonic key of D Minor and follows them with spine-tingling ascending and descending scale passages

Example 10-10a. Haydn. String Quartet in F Minor, Op. 20, No. 5. Fourth movement, bars 1–7.

10-10b. Bach. *The Well-Tempered Clavier II, BWV* 881. Fugue in F Minor, bars 1–4.

10-10c. Handel. *Messiah.* "And with His stripes we are healed," bars 1–5.

10-10d. Mozart. String Quartet in F Major, *K* 168. Second movement, bars 1–5.

10-10e. Mozart. *Requiem, K* 626. Kyrie eleison, bars 1–2.

that blow a cold wind over the waiting audience. He then slips into rollicking gallant comedy music for the main sonata-form section, suggesting the patrician environment in which Don Giovanni operates. The "Stone Guest" opening of the overture functions like a premonition of the final scene, when the Don, having defied all social conventions and man-made laws, is thrown into the flames of hellfire and damnation (see Ex. 3-4).

Mozart: Concerto and Opera

Of all instrumental media, the concerto proved the most congenial outlet for Wolfgang Amadeus Mozart's unique dramatic gifts, and he produced no fewer than 50 works in the form. With a truly Grecian genius for the reconciliation of opposites, Mozart saw the concerto as an ideal means of bringing about a harmonious unity in such dualities as the opposing demands of solo and tutti passages, the personal soliloquy of the soloist and the group orchestral commentary, the improvised cadenza passages and the through-composed sections, and the separate domains of the soloist proper and of the other concertante instruments. He saw each of these as individuals in their own right, yet socially compatible within the performing dimensions of the concerto.

More broadly, he extended this unity-in-duality principle even further by merging the oppositions in the gallant and learned styles; in the emotionalism of sensibility or storm and stress and the rationalism of the Enlightenment; in comic and tragic elements; in capricious and profound attitudes; and in the transitory and the eternal. All these opposites are integrated in specific instances in a masterly manner. This could come about, however, only in the hands of a composer who had immense technical resources and whose workshop was so well stocked with tools of the trade that an almost infinite number of means could be brought to bear on a wide variety of desired ends.

Of Mozart's 50 concertos, about half are for piano. While others before him had written vast quantities of concertos for violin, flute, and harpsichord, Mozart must be regarded as the creator of the piano concerto. Like all composers of his time, Mozart wrote works to order; but the piano concertos, while often commissioned, were nevertheless intended expressly for the occasions when he himself played the solo part. Furthermore, the concertos he wrote for violin and various solo wind instruments occupied him only intermittently, while the piano concertos were a constant preoccupation from his prodigy years onward.

Mozart's serious interest in concertos for single wind instruments probably dates from his visits to Mannheim when he was in his early 20s. Here the most brilliant players of the day were employed, and composers such as Johann Stamitz began to exploit the timbres of the wind instruments as much in their symphonies as in their many solo concertos. Stamitz, for instance, was the composer of one of the earliest concertos for solo clarinet. The prominent role and poetic usage that the woodwinds assumed in Mozart's later concerto, orchestral, and operatic writing was the mature realization of a potential revealed to him at Mannheim.

In his concertos for wind instruments Mozart developed the various timbres in much the same manner in which he delineated dramatic characters in his operas. The two flute concertos, *K* 313 and *K* 314, and several quartets for flute and strings (written on commission for wealthy amateurs) stress the flute's pale pure tone. Mozart seems not to have considered the instrument worthy of serious dramatic treatment, and his flute writing always tended toward rococo gallantry.

Other wind instruments, however, assumed the status of real dramatis personae in his concerted instrumental dramas. Mozart was particularly sensitive both to their color capacities and to their power to evoke mood, divining innate possibilities and using them in idiomatic ways. The bassoon, for instance, chants philosophically in *K* 191, while the French horn in four examples (*K* 412, *K* 417, *K* 447, and *K* 495) exhibits an appropriately masculine outdoor character in keeping with its uses as a hunting instrument and a post horn. The mellow lyrical qualities of the clarinet were particularly favored by Mozart, who featured them in two of his finest works—the Clarinet Quintet *K* 581 and the Clarinet Concerto *K* 622.

The 18th-century concerto, like the string quartet and the symphony, stemmed from the fertile soil of the social music tradition. Indeed, the occasions on which they were usually played coincided with those on which divertimentos were also performed. The concerto style that Mozart inherited from such older contemporaries as J. C. Bach and Georg Wagenseil was a species of social music known as the *sinfonia concertante.* In it the usual festive, forthright, marchlike first movements, the contrasting lyrical slow movements, and the high-spirited rondo finales were very closely related to the divertimento.

Unlike the sprawling multimovement serenades and cassations, however, the sinfonia concertante earlier in the century had crystallized to a traditional three-movement organization. Out of it would grow the Viennese solo concerto which, in contrast to the older baroque concerto grosso, would become predominantly a solo work, reflecting perhaps the higher degree of value given to individual personality. The soloist did not depart from the orchestral crowd as it would in the 19th-century concerto. The individual always operated within the sphere of polite social decorum in the chamber-music tradition.

Haydn, in his preoccupation with other matters, did little to change the basic character of the concerto in spite of his 30 essays in the form. It remained for Mozart to free the concerto from the limitations of rococo gallantry, to lift it out of the social-music tradition, to make it into a serious independent form, and to endow it with a significant new literature. Mozart's development of the latent possibilities inherent in the concerto thus parallels Haydn's contribution in the evolution of the string quartet and the symphony.

Excluding his first four essays, which have proved to be youthful adaptations of solo sonatas by contemporaries, Mozart wrote 23 concertos for piano and orchestra, including one each for two and three pianos. It is also important to note that they were written for the piano, not the harpsichord. In the piano Mozart found the ideal instrument for the balanced antiphony between solo instrument and orchestra. The pitch range of the piano is roughly equal to that of the orchestra. Unlike the violin and the wind instruments, it is capable of airy counterpoints and harmonic densities of its own; but like them, it can also sing lyrically when called upon to do so.

Beginning in 1773 with his first original effort in the form, *K* 175, and continuing with a few intervening works, Mozart arrived at his mature conception in one bold stroke with the E-flat Major concerto (*K* 271), which has been aptly called Mozart's "Eroica." The soloist here occupies a prominent virtuoso position rather than functioning as a chamber musician among equals.

After settling in Vienna in 1781, Mozart attained the peak of his instrumental writing with the 12 great piano concertos he wrote for the series of subscription concerts there. In the Viennese life of Mozart's time the concerto was a more important vehicle for public performance than was the symphony. Only when these concerts ceased as a productive source of revenue did Mozart briefly, in the summer of 1788, turn his attention again to the symphony.

It will suffice here to point out a few of the salient stylistic features of two exceptional piano concerto examples, the only two in minor modes. The D-minor piano concerto (*K* 466) is the best known of all Mozart's works in the form and is notable for its dark moods as well as for its close resemblance, both in tonality and spirit, to the demonic sections of his opera *Don Giovanni.* Storm-and-stress demonic fury marks its impassioned measures, and the duality of orchestral and soloistic elements is never fully reconciled. The soloist is cast in the role of a noble soul battling with the menacing orchestral furies.

Even more dramatic is the C-minor piano concerto (*K* 491), a work which goes completely beyond the confines of social music in the depth of its expressive content, and in which the tragic and lyrical elements are mixed in about equal measure. Significant also is the important role assigned to a full complement of wind instruments, a flute, two oboes, two clarinets, two bassoons, two trumpets and two French horns, which are treated almost as the equals of the piano soloist. The transparency of the part writing, the discreet commentary the wind instruments make on the action, the way they participate in concertante lyrical sections in which they are accompanied by the piano—all mark a new departure and point to a growing kaleidoscope of orchestral color.

This C-minor concerto is a heroic tragedy; and before its epic sweep, anguished outbursts, and granitic strength even Beethoven himself stood in awe. Its heroic outlook, however, is humane enough to make room for some quiet, touching serenade music in both the slow movement and in the final set of variations. This is a finale in the monumental mold, since Mozart was more interested in the emotional vicissitudes available through variation than in a display of wit with the mechanics of art. The variations are alternately majestic, decorative, dramatic, and serene. Some of them work close to the basic subject, others make significant departures from it. The last variation is the most poignant and the most powerful. There is no happy ending here as in the D-minor concerto, but a true climax to a heroic endeavor. Everyone has a personal concept of the heroic. But there is surely something universally apt in Mozart's decision to conclude a concerto of this kind with a set of variations, for intrinsic to a humanistic heroism is an acquaintance with all the emotional climates in the human personality as well as a just regard for all the seasons of the human soul.

Thus it was that Mozart could divine dramatic possibilities in the concerto far beyond anything envisaged by his contemporaries. By writing concerted dialogues for piano and orchestra with both treated as equals in the cast and by ranging from witty repartee to violent conflict, he made the piano the principal protagonist in a symphonic drama. Indeed, the dramatic spirit of Mozart the opera composer is most transparently revealed in these piano concertos. That he conceived them in an operatic manner is evidenced by the many passages that appear first in the concertos and then later in the operas themselves. The music for the entrance scene of Donna Elvira in *Don Giovanni,* for instance, is foreshadowed in the opening movement of the B-flat Major piano concerto (*K* 238), a full decade before the opera was written. Opera buffa elements abound in the frolicking finales and in many instances versions of them appear in the comic scenes of the later operas. Some of the substance of the C-minor episode of the concerto for two pianos (*K* 365), for example, is "borrowed" by Mozart for Papageno's comic-tragic attempt at suicide in *The Magic Flute.* Some of the motifs that accompany Papageno may also be found in the final bars of the C-major piano concerto (*K* 467) and in the presto finale of the G-major piano concerto (*K* 453), where Papageno cavorts once more. This is straight opera buffa, with all the hilarity and slightly hysterical clamor of a comic opera final "curtain" ensemble.

Of all the instrumental music from his Viennese period, Mozart lavished most of his attention and affection on the piano concertos. Fully conscious of the contribution he was making, he commented in a humorous letter to his father that they were "written for all kinds of ears, not just for the long ones." He further informed his father that the new concertos represented "a compromise between the too easy and the too difficult, pleasant to the ear and very brilliant without, of course, sounding empty. Some passages will appeal only to connoisseurs, but others will also be satisfied and enjoy themselves without, perhaps, knowing why." There was thus something for listeners at all levels, and with full justification the piano concerto has been called Mozart's "most characteristic creation."

Mozart's *Magic Flute,* half fairy tale and half allegorical morality play with multiple meanings, shows a similar range of styles. The opera opens with a scintillating overture clearly in the gallant style. Then the delineation of each character is revealed. Tamino is a prince whose love for the heroine, Pamina, leads him (with the aid of his aristocratic magic flute) through tests and trials into the realm of enlightened knowledge. Papageno, his companion, a guileless child of nature as envisioned by Rousseau, plays on rustic panpipes before receiving a set of magic bells.

The Queen of Night is first revealed surrounded by a starry firmament within a mountain, which has opened accompanied by a clap of thunder and musical passages in storm-and-stress D Minor. She appears to Tamino as a grieving mother, whose daughter has been stolen by a sorcerer. Later she proves to be the the villainess of the opera, proclaiming in a series of fiendish fioraturas that the fires of hell rage in her heart. Sarastro, at first a supposed sorcerer, is really a personification of the Enlightenment, advocating the rule of wisdom tempered by social responsibility and the free-masonic ideals of equality and fraternity. Pamina, daughter of the Queen of Night and Sarastro, has been carried away by the latter to save her from her mother's evil ways. Believing herself to be deserted by her hero, Tamino, she sings one of the most affecting Empfindsamkeit arias in the literature, "Ach, ich fühl's" ("Ah, I feel that the joy of love is lost forever"). Thus the gallant style, storm and stress, and sensibility all function effectively side by side within the greater dramatic context as the plot unfolds.

The formal structure of *The Magic Flute* has been likened to that of a large-scale sonata movement based on the unfolding of its plot, character development, and key relationships. The first act then becomes the exposition, with the fairy-tale elements as the first series of events, and the finale with the scene in Sarastro's temple as the second, contrasting subject. The greater part of Act 2 constitutes the development, with its stresses, strains, and processes of growth and change as the forces of darkness and light contend for supremacy. Sarastro's aria "In diesen heiligen Hallen" ("In these hallowed halls") then becomes the harmonic and dramatic turning point, while the finale concerns the reconciliation of opposites, summing up the opera's dramaturgy in the manner of a recapitulation and coda.

Mozart, the greatest dramatist in the history of music, not only assimilated and refined all the contemporary styles of his period, but also delved into the historical past to rediscover some of those that had been forgotten or overlooked by his colleagues. All the stylistic voices of his time are heard in his music—sophisticated rococo gallantry and back-to-nature rusticity, ingenuous naiveté and learned counterpoint, classical calm and tender sensibility, lofty, impersonal statements and intimate confessions in the manner of Rousseau, uproarious opera buffa antics and aristocratic opera seria aloofness, heavenly serenity and demonic storm-and-stress fury, passionate protest and tragic resignation.

Instead of becoming a mere international eclectic, however, he appropriated all this wealth of material, techniques, and ideas, adapted them to his own particular expressive purposes, and emerged within his short life span of 35 years as a composer of powerful individuality. No style or form of his time was left untouched or untransformed by the magic of his musical imagination, and his spirit transfigured and illuminated every page he wrote.

Beethoven

Like a colossus the figure of Ludwig van Beethoven bestrides the turn of two centuries, both in respect to the temporal span of his lifetime and in the scope of the ideas he represented. During his 30 formative years in the late 18th century, he was illuminated by the sun of the Enlightenment, the fire of the social and stylistic crosscurrents of the revolutionary years, and the reflected radiance of the music of his predecessors, C. P. E. Bach, Haydn, and Mozart. All of these influences helped to nurture his art toward its full fruition.

During his remaining 27 years of maturity in the early 19th century, he produced the unique masterpieces that in turn cast their elongated shadow on the entire future course of music. Just as Kant's "Copernican revolution" changed the direction of modern philosophy, so Beethoven's ideas provided the turning point in modern musical thought. Many intellectual, emotional, and aesthetic influences of his time are mirrored in his work, most especially perhaps the rationalism of Enlightenment thought, with its optimistic conviction that men and women could transcend all limitations if only they would exert their innate creative powers. The same force that motivated the American and French revolutions finds its musical counterpart in Beethoven's overriding concern with social, individual, and artistic freedom of expression. This freedom, however, like that of the founding fathers and revolutionary leaders, was governed by an overwhelming sense of self-discipline and stern moral responsibility.

Beethoven's individuality was so powerful that, like Napoleon, he inevitably became the dominating personality who stamped his image not only on his own time but also on the century that followed. Small wonder, then, that he became the adopted godfather of the romanticists, who claimed him as one of their own. In his titanic emotional power, heaven-storming pronouncements, defiance of social convention, and mighty struggle for individual freedom of expression, they saw the ideal of their art. However, the sheer weight of the logical processes he brought to bear on composition and the uncompromising rationalism of his approach to formal problems preclude his containment within the dreamy world of romanticism and seem more consonant with the Enlightenment. It is true that he brought a new subjective power of expression to music, and his music demands to be lived and experienced as well as understood. But even when personal emotional reactions were mirrored in his music, the very objectivity of his approach raised his inner conflicts to the heights of universal significance.

Unlike Haydn and Mozart, Beethoven was not under the constant pressure of one or more imperious patrons to produce a steady stream of workaday scores. His finished products are fewer in number, and as a result they bear the signs of a greater concentration of creative energy. Compared to

Haydn and Mozart, for instance, his symphonies number only 9 to their 104 and 41, respectively. But in his time the symphonic idea had outgrown its divertimento beginnings and had matured both in material resources and expressive power. Compared to Haydn's 83 string quartets, Beethoven's number but 18; against Mozart's 23 piano concertos, Beethoven produced 5; Mozart's 20 operas and 6 violin concertos are matched by only a single Beethoven contribution in each category.

Yet Beethoven, no less than his predecessors, was a universal composer who made major additions to all the current forms of his period. All musicians since his time can claim him as their own. To conductors he is the author of the dramatic overtures and the 9 symphonies with their stormy allegros, sublime slow movements, robust scherzos, and jubilant finales. To pianists he is the composer of the 32 sonatas, those great soliloquies in which he revealed his innermost thoughts. To violinists he is the creator of one of the cornerstones of the concerto repertory, as well as the 10 splendid sonatas for violin and piano. To cellists he has given 5 expressive sonatas. And to choral directors he issues the challenge of the immense *Missa Solemnis,* as well as the choral finale of the Ninth Symphony.

No biography of Beethoven has yet done true justice to him, nor is one ever likely to, because his external life is of little help in understanding his art. The true significance of his music is embodied in his internal life. In order to understand Beethoven, one must approach him on his own terms, and these are musical terms that must be sought in the creative workshop where the mighty monuments were wrought. The notebooks, for instance, show what a fearful struggle it was for Beethoven to forge a chain of notes into the desired melodic and rhythmic shape. Thus only in the great autobiography contained in the musical works themselves can the real creative life and thought of the master be discovered.

As with all artists of stature, the materials, mediums, and forms in which he wrote are not so important in themselves as are the ways he adapted, shaped, and transformed them. The piano sonata and violin-and-piano duo, for instance, were mainly humble species of house music when they came into his hands. By breathing elements drawn from the symphony and concerto into such works as the *Sonata Pathétique* (Op. 13), the "Waldstein" Sonata (Op. 53), and the "Kreutzer" Sonata (Op. 47), as well as readdressing them to a public assembly in a concert hall, he raised the stature of these two comparatively modest genres to heroic size and transformed them into larger mediums with expressive possibilities never before realized.

In spite of Mozart's dramatic treatment, the piano concerto was still a dialogue in which the piano and orchestra discoursed on equal terms. In a work such as Beethoven's Fifth Piano Concerto (Op. 73), however, the virtuoso pianist now possessed a triumphant vehicle for the conquest of vast audiences. From his commanding position, the soloist's proclamations completely dominated the masses of orchestral humanity in an epic panorama that extended from the ringing opening chords to the closing whirlwind of scale passages.

A similar evolution took place within the framework of the symphony. Here as elsewhere the foundation of Beethoven's art was entirely traditional, since both Haydn and Mozart had blazed the trails leading into new fields. But Beethoven was able to extend the frontiers still further and to break through into vast new musical terrain. The first two symphonies were individual in conception although they remained within the boundaries of 18th-century practice. Beginning with his third essay in 1804, the epoch-making "Eroica" Symphony, Beethoven crossed the Rubicon dividing the 18th and 19th centuries. As he continued with the Fifth, Seventh, and Ninth, he cast the symphony in the heroic mold of great human documents in which the symbolic image of the emergence of a free and triumphant humanity was envisaged. Between the scaling of these mountain peaks, he paused for breath in the Fourth and Eighth and managed to recapture once again the clarity and universality of the 18th-century spirit. In the pastoral idyll of the Sixth he explored the antiphony of self and nature in the search for unity between the individual and the divine being.

The appearance of Beethoven's Third Symphony, the "Eroica," was as decisive a moment in the history of music as it was in the history of civilization. It was one man's ringing declaration of independence and of his personal dedication to the revolutionary ideals of liberty, equality, and the brotherhood of all mankind. The idea for this work seems to have germinated in 1798, when General Bernadotte, an emissary from France, visited Vienna on a diplomatic mission. A lover of music, he had the noted violinist Rodolphe Kreutzer in his entourage. He soon sought out Beethoven, who composed for him the famous "Kreutzer" Sonata for piano and violin. At the time Bernadotte also suggested that he write a work dedicated to Napoleon Bonaparte, then first consul of the French government.

The figure of Napoleon was one of strong magnetic power in the early 19th century, and as with any magnet, his personality and actions represented positive and negative poles. His admirers were legion. Goethe, who kept a bust of the leader in his room, wrote, "Napoleon managed the world as Hummel did his piano; both achievements appear wonderful, but we do not understand one more than the other; yet so it is, and the whole is done before our very eyes."

Many intellectuals and artists had great problems reconciling Napoleon's statements with his actions—the ideals of the French Revolution with Napoleon's wars of conquest. Napoleon himself understood this conflict and remarked, "Everybody has loved me and hated me. I was like the sun; as soon as I entered a new territory, I kindled every hope, I was blessed, I was adored; but as soon as I left it, I no longer was understood."

Beethoven had strong feelings for the French and their music early in his career. Elements from a number of French symphonists found their way into his early symphonic style, and for a time he considered moving to Paris. Beethoven also had positive, if ambivalent, feelings about Napoleon. There were times when he considered the French leader to be a defender of oppressed people and the liberator of Europe. During one such period, from 1798 to 1803, he turned over in his mind the idea for a symphony to be titled *Bonaparte,* which finally crystallized into the form of his Third Symphony. At the time of its first performance in 1804, Beethoven still thought of the symphony as his "Bonaparte" Symphony, even though Napoleon had already proclaimed himself emperor. But while he continued to respect Napoleon for his qualities of enlightened leadership, and in spite of plans to dedicate several compositions to him, Beethoven could never bring himself to finalize any of the dedications. It was not until 1806, when the orchestral parts were published, that the title page of the Third Symphony finally read *Sinfonia Eroica,* with the inscription "Composed to Celebrate the Memory of a Great Man."

A tremendous surge of vital energy is unleashed with the two massive opening chords of the first movement. Then come the notes of the germinal first subject, the source of future developments and the cornerstone for the logic of the work's construction (Ex. 10-11a). Like a fanfare it simply confirms the tonal center of E-flat Major while descending and rising to the lower and upper dominant tones of B flat before subsiding chromatically from E flat downward to C sharp. The movement then begins to build upward to colossal proportions. The 245-bar development section itself is longer than some of Haydn's or Mozart's entire symphonies.

Example 10-11. Beethoven. Symphony No. 3 in E-flat Major, Op. 55 ("Eroica").

10-11a. First movement, bars 1–7.

A funeral march, also cast in the heroic mold, appears for the first time in a symphonic context in the second movement. Its stately tread moves inexorably to a crashing climax, then subsides into a sequence of broken fragments with tragic overtones. With such a grand design, the traditional aristocratic minuet would be entirely inappropriate. So Beethoven wrote a robust scherzo to lighten the gloom after the funeral march and to pave the way for the grand finale.

For the themes and ideas of the final movement Beethoven looked to his earlier ballet score, *The Creatures of Prometheus.* In the Enlightenment era, the titanic mythological figure of Prometheus personified the liberation and aspirations of humanity. After Zeus had mistreated the people, it was Prometheus who championed their cause, ascended to Mount Olympus, and stole the divine fire of the arts and sciences from the hearth of the gods. In the ballet, and likewise at the beginning of this movement, Prometheus is heard descending in a precipitous downward-moving passage with the firebrand that is to animate the spirits of all men and women (Ex. 10-11b). The movement then proceeds in a series of free-form variations on a dance tune also taken from the ballet score (Ex. 10-11c). As they unfold, they build up to a pageantlike picture of a liberated humanity. One hears in bars 175–97 the elegant, transparent sonorities that point to the nobility, while the rough-and-ready brass-band music of bars 211–55 gives voice to the popular masses. The fugal textures of bars 117–74 and 266–348 with their sophisticated inversions and segmentations of the theme exemplify the intellectual faculties, while the solemn chorale (bars 249–364) bespeaks religious feeling. In these variations the fugue and chorale join with dancelike and songlike measures to form a procession that climaxes in triumph (bars 381–95) when Beethoven throws all his orchestral forces together to celebrate the achievement of the heroic ideal. A whirlwind presto then terminates the entire awesome spectacle.

10-11b. Fourth movement, bars 1–7.

Whether or not Beethoven realized it, the "Eroica" marked a clear break with 18th-century classicism, for in it he had created a symphony that achieved an inner unity. This contrasted with the 18th-century classical practice, in which individual movements were carefully balanced, but whole symphonies expressed unity only by means of key relationships and tone color.

10-11c. Fourth movement, bars 76–83.

Beethoven's innovative mind now led him to conceive and construct both movements and whole works as organically related, wherein each moment, from the first to the last, is seen as a logical process of growth. In his public music after the "Eroica," he constantly strove to find new methods to control the listening experience, while attempting to enlighten at the same time. As subject material became shorter and more motiflike, he put more stress on immediate development, and all sections of movements became longer.

The "Eroica" was only the first of several works that presented problems for Beethoven's listeners. Audiences were accustomed to concentrating for about 20 minutes over the four movements of a classical symphony. Beethoven's lasted well over twice as long, and while his music was recognized for its great quality by many, the length and concomitant complications of the "Eroica" often proved bewildering. This led to reactions such as a review written a quarter of a century later: "The *Heroic Symphony* contains much to admire, but it is difficult to keep up admiration of this kind during three long quarters of an hour. If this symphony is not by some means abridged, it will soon fall into disuse."

Beethoven continued to experiment with organic unity in his concert music that followed the "Eroica." In the Fifth Symphony, a single motif forms the basic material for each of the four movements (Exs. 10-12a, b, c, d).

Example 10-12. Beethoven. Symphony No. 5 in C Minor, Op. 67.

10-12a. First movement, bars 1–4.

10-12b. Second movement, bars 18–21.

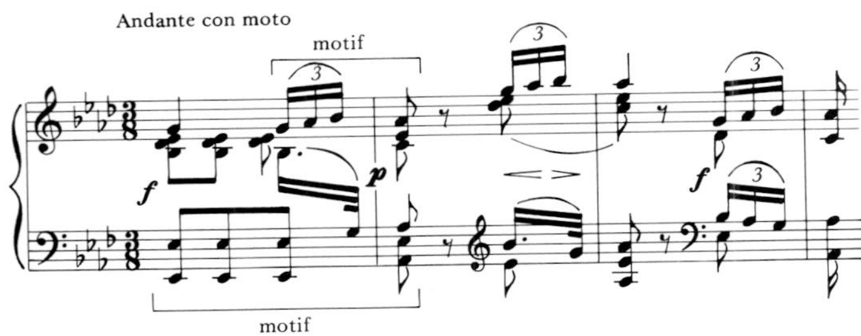

10-12c. Third movement, bars 19–26.

In his Sixth Symphony, the "Pastorale," the concept of nature is threaded programmatically through the five movements via a series of descriptive titles, and further unity is achieved by combining the final three movements so that

10-12d. Fourth movement, bars 45–46.

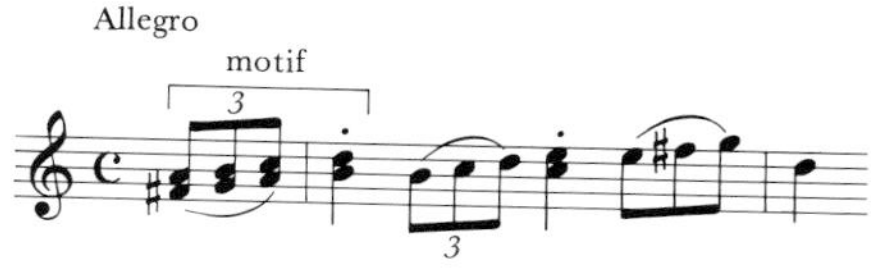

they are played without pause. In the Seventh and Eighth, rhythmic motifs underlie all four movements (Exs. 10-13a, b, c, d). Example 10-13 shows the anapest rhythmic cell from the Seventh Symphony and instances of its development throughout the symphony. Beethoven did not expect his listeners to identify the rhythmic cell as such in all movements, but it is meant to provide an underlying sense of unity and coherence for the listener. In that sense, it functions as did a plainchant tenor in medieval organum, an isorhythm in an *Ars Nova* motet, or a chorale tune woven into the fabric of a Bach organ chorale prelude.

Finally, in the monumental Ninth Symphony, with its introduction of the chorus into the traditional symphony for the first time, Beethoven draws on materials from the first three movements in the choral finale to place his musical setting of Schiller's "Ode to Joy" in a perspective that intertwines abstract, programmatic, operatic, and cantata elements.

Beethoven's interest in the ideals of human brotherhood that inspired the French Revolution was not confined to the symphony or indeed to instrumental music. His single opera, *Fidelio* (first version, 1805), was written about the same time as the "Eroica", while its revision occupied Beethoven on and off until 1814. It is in the popular style of the *Singspiel,* a type of music theater in which most of the story goes forward via spoken dialogue, and music is introduced in moments of high drama. As "people's theater," Singspiel is performed in the language of the audience. *Fidelio* is also an example of a special kind of romantic theater called *rescue opera,* a type of melodrama.

Fidelio extols the qualities of a virtuous wife and condemns the power-hungry tyrants who enslave and imprison the innocent. Its strong-willed heroine, Leonore, is the wife of an unjustly imprisoned Spanish nobleman, Florestan. Leonore has disguised herself as a young man, calling herself Fidelio, and has gone to work in the prison where her husband is held captive, hoping that he is alive and that she may do something to help effect his rescue.

Leonore is a heroine in every sense of the word. Throughout she is unswerving in her loyalty to their marriage, and her heroism takes her to a heart-stopping climax where she leaps in front of her husband to save him from Pizarro's knife. For Beethoven, the horror of the story is not in the specific plight of the hero but in the contemplation of enslavement, whether tangibly expressed by Florestan's chains or symbolically suggested as the ideological chains of a repressive society.

Beethoven takes great musical pains to present his characters and their motives clearly. In the first act, Pizarro, the prison governor, expresses his vio-

Example 10-13. Beethoven. Symphony No. 7 in A Major, Op. 92.

10-13a. First movement, bars 1–8.

10-13b. Second movement, bars 1–10.

10-13c. Third movement, bars 37–43 and 149–52.

10-13d. Fourth movement, bars 5–8.

lent, deranged personality in an aria of sheer malice, "Ha! Welch' ein Augenblick!" ("Ha! What a moment!"). A duet with the prison warden follows, in which Florestan's murder is plotted. Leonore has overheard a part of this scene, which provides the opportunity for her to react in a large-scale aria.

Through this aria, Beethoven sets her upright, moral character in bold opposition to the evil, base character of Pizarro.

The formal pattern of the aria is the popular one of *recitative, cavatina,* and *cabaletta*—preparation, statement, and dramatically virtuoso close. The recitative text—"Abscheulicher! wo eilst du hin?"—proclaims her sense of doubt and concern over the situation: "Despicable man! Whence such haste? To what ends such a wild, angry state?" She pulls herself together for the cavatina, "Komm, Hoffnung," a lyrical and passionate litany to the spirit of Hope, entreating that spirit to sustain her and act as a potent heavenly weapon in her upcoming trials: "Come, hope . . . sweet love, light my goal that I may achieve it." The brilliant cabaletta is in the tradition of virtuoso singing, and as the spirit of Hope floods her being, the intensity of her excitement projects both an emotional and a vocal high pitch: "Ich folg' dem innern Triebe" ("I obey instincts from within and will not waver, I am strengthened by the duty of true married love").

The role of the chorus in *Fidelio* is treated with special sensitivity. For most of the opera, the chorus functions as a group of male prisoners who speak not only for their own unhappy condition but for that of the unjustly accused everywhere in the world. Fidelio persuades the jailer, Rocco, to allow the prisoners out of their cells into the courtyard for a breath of air, secretly hoping to view her husband among them. As they emerge from their dank cells, the prisoners sing with great eloquence of their desire for freedom and sunlight, to a text and music that speak with an eloquence as timely for today's world as for Beethoven's. The same sentiments appear later in Beethoven's Ninth Symphony, for which he chooses as a choral text Schiller's "Ode to Joy."

Love and marriage, truth and heroism triumph in due course. The disguised Leonore whips out her trusty pistol and stays the hand of Pizarro, who is trying to kill Florestan in his dungeon cell. The result is that Pizarro's activities are investigated and he is himself arrested. The prisoners and Florestan are released and Leonore is given the honor of physically removing his chains.

For various productions of *Fidelio,* Beethoven wrote a total of four overtures. Three of them are named for the heroine, Leonore, and draw on music from the opera. The last, known as the "Fidelio Overture," is a conservative curtain-raiser, with no direct musical connection to the opera. Of the others, the third "Leonore Overture" has gained a special place in the symphonic literature. Beethoven, who spent a lifetime investigating and extending the communicative power of the symphony, here explores the potency of the opera overture. Through this single-movement sonata-form composition, Beethoven hoped to offer the listener a distillation of the dramatic character of the entire opera—an "opera without words," so to speak.

In the work of the Viennese composers a maximum of variety emerges from a minimum of material, thus achieving an ideal of composition out of a complete coincidence of matter and form, technique and inspiration. The medium of abstract sound in instrumental music becomes a means of expressing ideas powerfully conceived and forcefully realized. Beginning with Gluck, continuing with Haydn and Mozart, and culminating in Beethoven, the Viennese composers projected through the language of tone a convincing and universal image of humanity that is as valid today as it was in the 18th century.

CHAPTER

11

Romantic Styles

Romanticism

The battlefield for the new artistic, social, and political struggles that were stirring minds in the 1820s was found in the theaters, opera houses, salons, cafés, and eventually in the streets of Paris. While the beginnings of romanticism arose in earlier developments in England and Germany, the style first moved into the international arena in France. Paris at this time was literally teeming with poets and playwrights, painters and composers. Franz Liszt came from Hungary in 1823, Frédéric Chopin arrived from Poland in 1830, and the poet Heinrich Heine from north Germany in 1831. In Paris they brushed shoulders with such native French intellectuals and artists as the painter Eugène Delacroix, the poet Victor Hugo, and the composer Hector Berlioz, who have aptly been called the triumvirate of romanticism.

Romanticism projected a new emotional spectrum that reflected the ways composers interpreted their world, and how they reacted to the revolutionary, literary, dramatic, and pictorial events of their time. The French Revolution of 1789, for instance, had emphasized the ideals of liberty, equality, and fraternity. It had instilled a humanitarian interest in human rights and had given promise of a more liberal social framework in which individuals could realize their personal ambitions.

Théodore Géricault (attributed to). *Artist in His Studio.* Oil on canvas. The Louvre, Paris. By permission of the Musées Nationaux, Paris.

Chronology

MUSICAL FIGURES

Germany and Vienna

E. T. A. Hoffmann	1776–1822
Johann N. Hummel	1778–1837
Louis Spohr	1784–1859
Carl Maria von Weber	1786–1826
Karl Czerny	1791–1857
Ignaz Moscheles	1794–1870
Franz Schubert	1797–1828
Johann Strauss, Sr.	1804–1849
Felix Mendelssohn	1809–1847
Robert Schumann	1810–1856
Richard Wagner	1813–1883
Clara Wieck	1819–1896
Anton Bruckner	1824–1896
Johann Strauss, Jr.	1825–1899
Johannes Brahms	1833–1897

France

Daniel Auber	1782–1871
Frédéric Kalkbrenner	1785–1849
Jacques Halévy	1799–1862
Giacomo Meyerbeer	1791–1864
Hector Berlioz	1803–1869
Frédéric Chopin	1810–1849
Franz Liszt	1811–1886
Jacques Offenbach	1819–1880
César Franck	1822–1890
Camille Saint-Saëns	1835–1921
Leo Delibes	1836–1891
Georges Bizet	1838–1875

Italy

Muzio Clementi	1752–1832
Luigi Cherubini	1760–1842
Gaspare Spontini	1774–1851
Nicolò Paganini	1782–1840
Gioacchino Rossini	1792–1868
Gaetano Donizetti	1797–1848
Vincenzo Bellini	1801–1835
Giuseppe Verdi	1813–1901

England

Johann Cramer	1771–1858
Arthur Sullivan	1842–1900

Czechoslovakia

Bedřich Smetana	1824–1884
Antonin Dvořák	1841–1904

Norway

Edvard Grieg	1843–1907

Russia

Mikhail Glinka	1804–1857
Anton Rubinstein	1829–1894
Alexander Borodin	1833–1887
Nikolai Rubinstein	1835–1881
César Cui	1835–1918
Mily Balakirev	1837–1910
Modest Musorgsky	1839–1881
Peter Tchaikovsky	1840–1893
Nikolai Rimsky-Korsakov	1844–1908
Alexander Glazunov	1865–1936

Spain

Isaac Albéniz	1860–1909

United States

Stephen Foster	1826–1864
Louis M. Gottschalk	1829–1869
John K. Paine	1839–1906
Victor Herbert	1859–1924
Horatio Parker	1863–1919

WRITERS AND DRAMATISTS

Edmund Burke	1729–1797
André de Chénier	1762–1794
Sir Walter Scott	1771–1832
E. T. A. Hoffmann	1776–1822
Thomas de Quincey	1785–1859
Lord Byron (George Gordon)	1788–1824
Alphonse de Lamartine	1790–1869
Eugène Scribe	1791–1861
Wilhelm Müller	1794–1827
Alois Jeitteles	1794–1858
Heinrich Heine	1797–1856
Alexander Pushkin	1799–1837
Honoré de Balzac	1799–1850
Nikolaus Lenau	1802–1850
Alexandre Dumas, Sr.	1802–1870
Victor Hugo	1802–1885
Prosper Mérimée	1803–1870
Edward Bulwer-Lytton	1803–1873
Ralph Waldo Emerson	1803–1882
Nathaniel Hawthorne	1804–1864
Alfred, Lord Tennyson	1809–1892
Alfred de Musset	1810–1857
Georg Büchner	1813–1837
Henry David Thoreau	1817–1862
George Eliot (Mary Ann Evans)	1819–1880
Alexandre Dumas, Jr.	1824–1895
Antonio Ghislanzoni	1824–1893
Henrik Ibsen	1828–1906
Eduard Hanslick	1825–1904
Leo Tolstoy	1828–1910
Louisa May Alcott	1832–1888
Alphonse Daudet	1840–1897
Gerard Manley Hopkins	1844–1889

ARTISTS AND ARCHITECTS

Henry Fuseli	1741–1825
Hokusai	1760–1849
Eugène Delacroix	1799–1863
Moritz von Schwind	1804–1871
Grandville (Jean Gérard)	1803–1847
Arnold Böcklin	1827–1901
Victor Hartmann	1834–1873

HISTORICAL FIGURES

Prince Klemens von Metternich	1773–1859
Arthur Schopenhauer	1788–1860
Abraham Lincoln	1809–1865
Queen Victoria (England)	r. 1837–1901
Friedrich Nietzsche	1844–1900

PARIS, 1820S

Paris in the year 1827 saw many events that presaged a new order of things. An English Shakespearean troop, for instance, created a sensation with its performances of *Romeo and Juliet, Macbeth,* and *Hamlet*; hitherto the Bard had been considered too uncouth and unclassical for the polished French stage. New voices were heard from Germany with the first French translation of Goethe's drama *Faust* and the first performance of Weber's opera *Der Freischütz* (*The Free Shot*), both of which bespoke a new attitude toward man and nature. Victor Hugo published his play *Cromwell,* with a lengthy preface that was to become the manifesto of the romantic movement. A few years later, Hugo's play *Hernani* put the French classical drama into eclipse.

The year 1828 saw the creation of Berlioz's *Eight Scenes from Faust* (Op. 1), a work he later expanded into *The Damnation of Faust.* And this was the year when Daniel Auber once again captured the operatic spotlight in Paris with his *Deaf-Mute of Portici,* the first work to be called a *grand opéra.* It impelled Gioachino Rossini to revise his style completely in the work he was composing for the Paris Opéra, *William Tell* (1829). The case for the grandiose was then settled once and for all by the German expatriate Giacomo Meyerbeer, who became the leading proponent of romantic-historic grand opera with his *Robert the Devil* (1831), *The Huguenots* (1836), and *The Prophet* (1848).

Meyerbeer's formula for such operas included five-act plots liberally bestrewn with powerful melodramatic episodes, dark and devious conspiracies, dashing deeds of derring-do, and pompous cavalry marches led by the hero on his prancing steed. Technically these operas wove together sequences of recitative, passionate arias and duets, large ensemble numbers, frequent stretches of ballet, milling mass choruses, spectacular stage mountings, and a large orchestra. Such extravagant and bombastic goings-on prompted the young Richard Wagner to characterize them as "effect without cause." This sarcasm notwithstanding, Meyerbeer's operas influenced Wagner's own thinking more than he cared to admit, and the cause of grand opera can be seen marching along through the century in Wagner's *Tannhäuser,* Verdi's *Aïda,* and a host of other sumptuous stage spectacles.

ROMANTIC HISTORICISM

Such fanciful flights of the imagination were among the many manifestations of a new psychology of historical nostalgia and escapism, summed up neatly in the slogan "Any time but now and any place but here." Romanticism in this sense amounted to a reaction against rationalism and a withdrawal from reality in order to envision a roseate dream world through the intuitive eye of the artist. In so doing poets, composers, and painters sought to go beyond sense experience and view the world in the light of an ideal.

The Middle Ages, for instance, were seen as a colorful golden age of the past, far removed from the sordid materialistic struggle of the present. In England the reading public had long been conditioned to the so-called Gothic novels such as Horace Walpole's *Castle of Otranto* (1765), to hearing at Covent Garden comic operas with medieval trappings such as *Banditti or Love in a Labyrinth* (1781), and to attending melodramas such as *Raymond and Agnes* and *The Bleeding Nun of Lindenberg* (1797).

This experience prepared the way for the sensational popular success of the novels of Sir Walter Scott, whose influence was felt in France through Victor Hugo's novel *The Hunchback of Notre Dame* (1831), and the works of Alexandre Dumas such as *The Three Musketeers.* Dante became to the romantic movement what Homer had been to the classicists; Shakespeare's popularity eclipsed that of the French tragic dramatists Corneille and Racine; and the poetic stars of Byron and Goethe were in the ascendancy.

PROGRAMME MUSIC

Composers of the time had strong literary interests, and music drew much closer to poetry. Berlioz was busy writing a symphony based on *Romeo and Juliet*; a viola concerto, *Harold in Italy,* based on Lord Byron's *Childe Harold*; and overtures to Shakespeare's *King Lear* and Scott's *Waverley* and *Rob Roy.* Franz Liszt was composing piano pieces after Petrarch's sonnets and symphonies after Dante's *Divine Comedy* and Goethe's *Faust.* Gaetano Donizetti found the story for his most successful opera, *Lucia di Lammermoor,* in Scott's novel *The Bride of Lammermoor.* Richard Wagner was tapping the rich sources of old Celtic sagas and the Arthurian legends of the Holy Grail for the subjects of his *Tristan und Isolde, Lohengrin,* and *Parsifal,* as well as the medieval epics for his operatic cycle *Ring of the Nibelung.*

All this led right to the doorstep of programme music, and the desire for a closer union of literature and music was accompanied by the need for freedom from such traditional forms as theme and variations, rondo, and sonata. If, for instance, a composer set out to base a work on *Romeo and Juliet* or *Mazeppa*—a subject treated by both Byron and Hugo—no ready-made forms were available and no preconceived molds were expected; therefore new patterns had to be devised. Or, to put it the other way round, if a composer abandoned the established forms, he needed the compensation of some degree of literary unity to keep his musical episodes in line and to make them dramatically convincing. Hence literary sources became handy suggestive material; and, since no two literary works unfolded in identical sequence, a symphonic poem became a convenient way for composers to avoid crystallizing their forms, as well as giving them the desired excuse for having each work different from the last.

In general it can be said that while other centuries experimented with programmatic music, it came into its own only in the 19th century. This was particularly true after romantic composers attempted to establish a theory of composition based on the concept of a programme and consequently made this theory the basis of a musical style in its own right.

THE SUBLIME

Another element of the romantic style was the rejection of beauty in the 18th-century sense and the acceptance of the ideals of the sublime, grotesque, and fantastic. Edmund Burke as early as 1756 had admitted the awesome and ugly into the realm of art by distinguishing the two concepts in his *Philosophical Enquiry into the Origin of Our Ideas of the Sublime and the Beautiful.* "The sublime," he wrote, "is vast in dimension, rugged and awesome, dark and gloomy. The sublime embraces vast power including the terrible, and the emotional reaction to it is that of astonishment and even horror, rather than admiration and respect." Victor Hugo went a step beyond Burke, and his preface to *Cromwell* (1828) became the manifesto of the romantic movement:

> The ugly exists beside the beautiful, the unshapely beside the graceful, the grotesque on the reverse side of the sublime, evil with good, darkness with light. . . . The grotesque fastens upon religion a thousand original superstitions, upon poetry a thousand picturesque fancies. It is the grotesque which scatters lavishly in air, water, earth, fire those myriads of intermediary creatures which we find all alive in the popular traditions of the Middle Ages; it is the grotesque which impels the ghastly antics of the witches' revels, which gives Satan his horns, his cloven feet and his bat's wings.

This spirit of the grotesque finds vivid musical expression in the "Wolf's Glen" scene from Weber's *Der Freischütz* and the last two movements of Berlioz's *Symphonie fantastique.*

All this implied a new concept of nature, which to the romanticist did not exist independently but rather as a complement to and reflection of human nature. In this sense nature provided a picturesque and resonant sounding board, reflecting back and at the same time revealing to the self all the complicated states of the tortured human soul—as, for example in "Scene in the Country," the third movement of the *Symphonie fantastique.* The predictable, benign universe of the Enlightenment, in short, had yielded to the capricious, often malignant world of romanticism.

Such forces were beyond human control, and the romanticists personified them in a demonology conjured up from the witchcraft and superstitions of the Middle Ages as well as from their own fevered imaginations. Examples are readily found in the "Invocation to Nature" from Berlioz's *Damnation of Faust,* and in the storm scenes, witches' sabbaths, and macabre dances of many other romantic operas and symphonies.

INDUSTRIAL REVOLUTION AND THE ARTS

The regressive aspects of romanticism as seen in these various escapist pursuits were counterbalanced by the progressive effects of the times, which artists were quick to turn to their advantage. In the wake of the Industrial Revolution, for instance, had come a rapid change from an agrarian to an industrial economy, as well as a shift from a rural to an urban society. The large new city populations became potential patrons of the arts; and, after the French Revolution had drastically curtailed the powers of aristocratic patrons, artists were forced into free-lance work. Music-making consequently moved out of the aristocratic salons into the public concert halls, where a new, largely middle-class audience gathered. This was the culmination of a process that had begun in the 18th century; and, as will presently be seen, this shift to a more democratic base had its effect on both the form and the content of romantic composition.

With the advent of the Industrial Revolution also came greater technical precision and standardization in the manufacture of musical instruments. New valve mechanisms in brass instruments, for instance, made it possible for players to command a wider and more controllable range of instrumental color and to produce effects never before heard; composers consequently had a vastly expanded orchestral color palette at their fingertips. Pianos were improved by the replacement of wooden frames with those made of cast iron. The cost of their manufacture was reduced, they stayed in tune longer, and it became possible for touring virtuosos to ship them safely from place to place.

With the industrialization of printing and the machine manufacture of paper, the circulation of journals, novels, and sheet music grew rapidly. The influence of the press was also reflected in the rise of the modern concept of journalistic music criticism, and composers such as Weber, Berlioz, Schumann, and Liszt took up their pens as critics and propagandists for the romantic cause.

INDIVIDUALISM AND NATIONALISM

In the face of this growing collectivism came a vigorous reassertion of individualism. A new aristocracy of genius replaced that of the hereditary dynasties in the public mind, and the era of the great individual was the result. It was also a time in which a composer's creative work no longer spoke for itself alone. Some composers seemed impelled to be great personalities and to lead fascinating lives that commanded public attention. At the psychological moment, the artist's autobiography, memoirs, or confessions appeared in print—as in the case of Berlioz and Wagner. Liszt wryly commented on this development by observing that he never had time to write about his own life because he was too busy living it.

This romantic individualism, moreover, extended into the sphere of nationalism. A poet or composer was expected to become the voice of the people, shaping their unconscious aspirations toward the conscious goals of self-discovery and self-determination. Byron the poet and Chopin the composer espoused the heroic causes of Greek and Polish independence, respectively, and national self-determination became almost a religion.

The spirit of a people was thought to be reflected in their native language and literature. The new reading and listening audience was often not familiar with the international languages of Italian and French, as the aristocratic 18th-century audience had been. This gave new impetus to the development of a national, indigenous drama and opera for each country. The effect of nationalism was also apparent in the admiration of local color in painting, in the introduction of regional dialects into literature, in the use of native songs and dances in music, and in the popularity of folklore and folk ballads.

New Voices among the Old

It is always fascinating in the overlapping counterpoint of history to observe how new voices arise while the old are still being heard. Franz Schubert and Carl Maria von Weber were both younger contemporaries of Beethoven—Schubert surviving him for a year, Weber succumbing a year before.

SCHUBERT

Of all the great Austrian masters, Schubert was the only one born in Vienna and was the most Viennese of them all. His early symphonies and piano sonatas are closer in style to Mozart than Beethoven, but the inspired lyricism of his songs and short piano pieces are already redolent with the spirit of romanticism. Unlike Mozart and Beethoven and the later romantic virtuosos, Schubert was not a distinguished performer and was almost never in the public eye. He lived out his short span of 31 years completely immersed in a world of sound. So busy was he with composing, his personal life took a background role, and romantic biographers ever since have had a field day inventing fictitious activities to fill the vacuum. What little performing he did took place within an intimate circle of friends. When questioned about his method of composition, he replied simply, "When I finish one piece, I begin the next." Everything was inwardly oriented and took external shape only in the steady stream of scores that flowed from his pen. Schubert's music, then, was his life.

Like his Viennese contemporaries, Schubert was a universal composer in the sense that he wrote in all genres: masses, operas, choral and solo songs, instrumental solos, chamber music of all combinations, and symphonies; but no matter what vocal or instrumental form he touched, it always turned into the gold of song. His pure lyricism and absence of feeling for the theater defeated his repeated attempts at opera, and he completely lacked the overt dramatic flair of Mozart. Yet the inner fire and passion he packed into his miniature music dramas (the Lieder and the song cycles) endowed them with a concentrated intensity unique in music literature.

In Schubert's chamber music, one is hardly conscious of the instruments, only of musical lines; and in his trios, quartets, and quintets, not only the slow movements are lyrical but all the others as well. This lyrical approach was recognized by Schubert's contemporaries. After the first performance of the A-minor string quartet (*D* 804), the painter Moritz von Schwind commented in a letter, "It is very smooth and gentle, but has the kind of melody one associates with songs." Schubert's treatment of the piano sonata is likewise almost purely melodic; and the shorter *Impromptus* and *Musical Moments* are the prototypes of the later genre of songs without words.

Nowhere is this lyrical approach to instrumental music more in evidence than in the numerous instances in which he took motifs and melodies from his own songs and used them as a basis for later, much expanded movements. This happened not only in such obvious instances as the "Death and the Maiden" Quartet, the "Trout" Quintet, and the "Wanderer" Fantasy, but also in more subtle and disguised forms. His song *Die Götter Griechenlands* (*The Gods of Greece*), for instance, appears in the ballet music for *Rosamunde,* in the slow movement of the A-minor string quartet (*D* 804), and once again in the B-flat Major *Impromptu (D* 935) for piano. The rondo finale of the posthumous A-major piano sonata (*D* 959) is based on his song *Im Frühling* (*In Springtime*); and the melody of the opening movement of his last piano sonata in B-flat Major (*D* 960) is closely associated with his setting of one of Goethe's lyrics from *Mignon.*

Whatever programmatic implication, if any, this song material may have had for the composer, he never explained. There can be little doubt, however, that a knowledge of the words, spirit, and mood of the songs can lead both performer and listener to a closer understanding of the instrumental music that is based on them.

The distilled essence of Schubert's art is almost always to be found in his songs, and perhaps nowhere is it more transparently revealed than in his two song cycles. The earlier *Die schöne Müllerin* (*The Fair Maid of the Mill,* 1823), a setting of the poetic cycle of Wilhelm Müller, is an example of the narrative type, which unfolds in a series of 20 lyrical episodes. Songs 1 to 13 represent various stages in the idyllic courtship of the miller's daughter by the young apprentice, ending in the rapture of his being accepted. In Song 14, however, a dashing rival, the huntsman, makes an unwelcome appearance; and Songs 15 to 20 tell of the young miller's rejection and of the unhappiness that leads to his ultimate renunciation of life.

All events are viewed through the hero's subjective eyes, and the other characters never appear from any other point of view. The principal contrast is in the more objective part played by the piano as it personifies the voice of nature, speaking through the symbol of the brook. At various times the brook gurgles cheerfully (Song 1), chatters garrulously (2), slumbers soundly (4), splashes gaily (5), leaps with joy (11), roars angrily (15), and sings sorrowfully (19). In true romantic fashion the voice of nature thus reflects every nuance of the hero's innermost being. The brook is his guide and confidant, sharing his joys and comforting his griefs, and ultimately resolving his sorrows by drawing him to her maternal breast. The transcendental union of man and nature is touchingly symbolized in the piano postlude of Song 19, which in alternate measures weaves together the last phrase of the young miller's song with the final appearance of the brook motif.

The poetic theme of the later *Die Winterreise* (*The Winter's Journey,* 1827), is essentially the same: rejected love, the man wandering alone, the solitary soul seeking solace in nature. But this cycle is of the more contemplative type. The poetry, again by Wilhelm Müller, recalls events that took place in the indefinite past and describes everything in retrospect.

Schubert's setting in this case is a masterly exposition of every conceivable aspect of a single somber mood. With sorrow in joy and joy in sorrow, and with all enveloped in melancholy, each song represents a stage in life's dark journey into the night of death. With Schubert's penetrating power of portraying emotional states in music, the songs begin in sadness; progress through moods of nostalgia, conflict, frustration, self-pity, protest, defiance, illusory hopes, disappointment, courage, despair; and end in eventual resignation.

Inviting his friends to hear the work for the first time, Schubert cautioned them that he was going to sing "a cycle of terrifying songs." He further added, "They have affected me more deeply than has been the case with any other songs." They are indeed so personal and subjective that they seem like an introspective autobiographical statement.

From a compositional standpoint, the unity of the *Winterreise* is contained in what can be called the "wandering" motif, an insistently repeated ostinato rhythmic figure that is present at some point in every song and obviously symbolizes the weary tread of the tired wanderer (Exs. 11-1a, b, c). In the first song, "Good Night," it is heard throughout in the accompaniment figure; it is featured prominently in "Rest" (10); but perhaps is nowhere more poignantly stated than in the climax of "The Guide Post" (20).

The dualism of the major and minor modes also plays an important role in the cycle. The minor predominates, and the occasional excursions and modulations into the major occur at points where they symbolize the recollection of past joys, in "The Linden Tree" (5); the escape into the world of dreams, in "Dream of Springtime" (11); an occasional ray of hope, in "Illusion" (19); or the peace of the graveyard, in "The Wayside Inn" (21).

Plate I. Alexander Benois. *Petrouchka: Backdrop for the Fair,* 1911. Graphite, watercolor, gouache on paper. Courtesy of the Wadsworth Atheneum, Hartford, Connecticut. From the Serge Lifar Collection and the Ella Gallup Sumner and Mary Catlin Sumner Collection.

Plate II. Sumer is icumen in, 13th century. Illuminated manuscript. By permission of the British Library, London.

Plate III. Music and Her Attendants, in Boethius, *De arithmetica,* 14th century. Illuminated manuscript. Center: *Music* playing a portative organ. Clockwise from top center: psaltery, plucked lute, clappers, long trumpets, nackers, bagpipes and shawm, tambourine, fiddle. By permission of the British Library, London.

Plate IV. Pérotin. *Alleluia (Nativitas),* early 13th century. Illuminated manuscript. Herzog August Bibliothek, Wolfenbüttel. Courtesy of the George Arents Research Library, Syracuse University, Syracuse, New York.

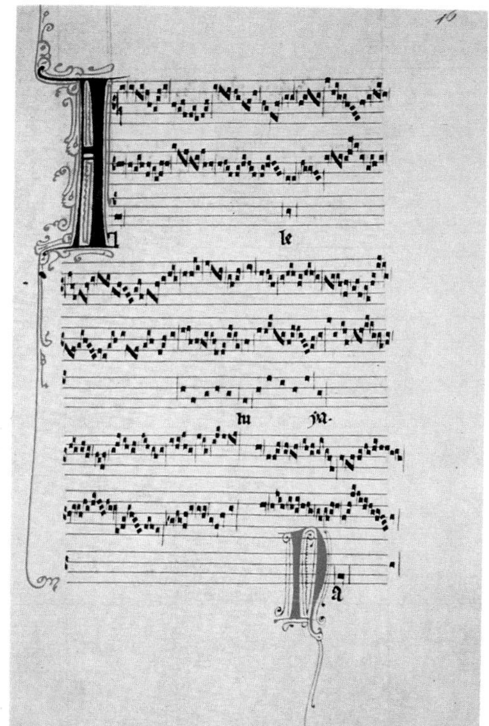

Plate V. Filippo Brunelleschi. Dome, Cathedral of Santa Maria del Fiore, Florence, 1420–36. By permission of Scala/Art Resource, New York.

Plate VI. Vincenzo Capirola lute book. *Pavane in the French manner II,* c. 1519. Lute tablature. Courtesy of the Newberry Library, Chicago.

Plate VII. Hans Memling. *Angel Musicians,* 1480. Oil on wood. Left panel: psaltery, tromba marina (marine trumpet), lute, folded trumpet, tenor shawm. Right panel: busine (long trumpet), folded slide trumpet, portative organ, harp, fiddle. By permission of the Koninklijk Museum voor Schone Kunsten, Antwerp.

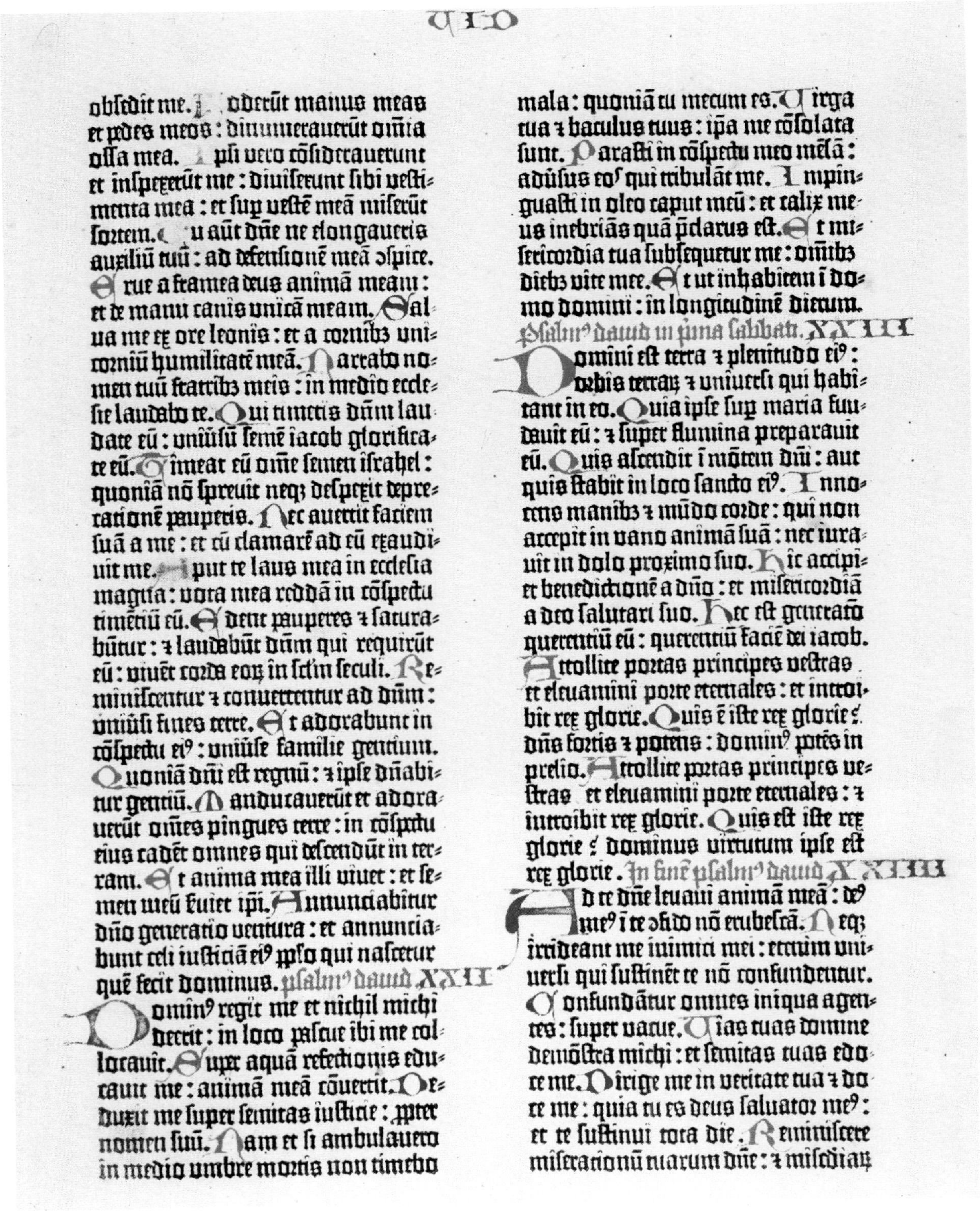

obsedit me. Foderūt manus meas
et pedes meos: dinumerauerūt om̄ia
ossa mea. Ipsi uero cōsiderauerunt
et inspexerūt me: diuiserunt sibi uesti=
menta mea: et sup uestē meā miserūt
sortem. Tu aūt dn̄e ne elongaueris
auxiliū tuū: ad defensionē meā aspice.
Erue a framea deus animā meam:
et de manu canis unicā meam. Sal-
ua me ex ore leonis: et a cornibꝫ uni=
corniū humilitatē meā. Narrabo no=
men tuū fratribꝫ meis: in medio eccle=
sie laudabo te. Qui timetis dn̄m laudate eū: uniūsū semē iacob glorifica=
te eū. Timeat eū om̄e semen israhel:
quoniā nō spreuit neqꝫ despexit depre=
cationē pauperis. Nec auertit faciem
suā a me: et cū clamarē ad eū exaudi=
uit me. Apud te laus mea in ecclesia
magna: uota mea reddā in cōspectu
timentiū eū. Edent pauperes ⁊ satura=
būtur: ⁊ laudabūt dn̄m qui requirūt
eū: uiuēt corda eoꝝ in sclm̄ seculi. Re=
miniscentur ⁊ conuertentur ad dn̄m:
uniūsi fines terre. Et adorabunt in
cōspectu eiꝰ: uniūse familie gentium.
Quoniā dn̄i est regnū: ⁊ ipse dn̄abi=
tur gentiū. Manducauerūt et adora-
uerūt om̄es pingues terre: in cōspectu
eius cadēt omnes qui descendūt in ter=
ram. Et anima mea illi uiuet: et se=
men meū seruiet ipsi. Annunciabitur
dn̄o generatio uentura: et annuncia=
bunt celi iusticiā eiꝰ ppl'o qui nascetur
quē fecit dominus. psalmꝰ dauid. XXII
Dominꝰ regit me et nichil michi
deerit: in loco pascue ibi me col-
locauit. Super aquā refectionis edu=
cauit me: animā meā cōuertit. De=
duxit me super semitas iusticie: ꝑpter
nomen suū. Nam et si ambulauero
in medio umbre mortis non timebo
mala: quoniā tu mecum es. Virga
tua ⁊ baculus tuus: ipa me cōsolata
sunt. Parasti in cōspectu meo mēsā:
aduūsus eos qui tribulāt me. Impin=
guasti in oleo caput meū: et calix me-
us inebriās quā p̄clarus est. Et mi=
sericordia tua subsequetur me: om̄ibꝫ
diebꝫ uite mee. Et ut inhabitem ī do=
mo domini: in longitudinē dierum.
Psalmꝰ dauid in prima sabbati. XXIII
Domini est terra ⁊ plenitudo eiꝰ:
orbis terraꝝ ⁊ uniuersi qui habi=
tant in eo. Quia ipse sup maria fun=
dauit eū: ⁊ super flumina preparauit
eū. Quis ascendit ī mōtem dn̄i: aut
quis stabit in loco sancto eiꝰ. Inno=
cens manibꝫ ⁊ mūdo corde: qui non
accepit in uano animā suā: nec iura=
uit in dolo proximo suo. Hic accipi=
et benedictionē a dn̄o: et misericordiā
a deo salutari suo. Hec est generatio
querentiū eū: querentiū faciē dei iacob.
Attollite portas principes uestras
et eleuamini porte eternales: et introi=
bit rex glorie. Quis ē iste rex glorie?
dn̄s fortis ⁊ potens: dominꝰ potēs in
prelio. Attollite portas principes ue=
stras et eleuamini porte eternales: ⁊
introibit rex glorie. Quis est iste rex
glorie? dominus uirtutum ipse est
rex glorie. In finē psalmꝰ dauid. XXIIII
Ad te dn̄e leuaui animā meā: deꝰ
meꝰ ī te cōfido nō erubescā. Neqꝫ
irrideant me inimici mei: etenim uni=
uersi qui sustinēt te nō confundentur.
Confundātur omnes iniqua agen=
tes: super uacue. Vias tuas domine
demōstra michi: et semitas tuas edo=
ce me. Dirige me in ueritate tua ⁊ do=
ce me: quia tu es deus saluator meꝰ:
et te sustinui tota die. Reminiscere
miserationū tuarum dn̄e: ⁊ misericordiaꝝ

Plate VIII. Gutenberg Bible, 1456. Psalm 23. Courtesy of the George Arents Research Library, Syracuse University, Syracuse, New York.

Plate IX (facing page). Gianlorenzo Bernini. *Saint Teresa in Ecstasy,* 1645–52. Marble and gilt bronze. Cornaro Chapel, Santa Maria della Vittoria, Rome. By permission of Scala/Art Resource, New York.

Plate X. Gentile Bellini. *Procession in St. Mark's Square,* 1496. Oil on canvas. By permission of the Galleria dell'Accademia, Venice.

Plate XI. Paolo Veronese. *Marriage at Cana,* c. 1560. Oil on canvas. The Louvre, Paris. By permission of Scala/Art Resource, New York.

Plate XII. Germain Boffrand. Salon de la Princesse, Hôtel de Soubise, Paris, begun 1732.

Plate XIII. Claude Monet. *Clouds,* 1921. The Louvre, Paris. By permission of the Musées Nationaux, Paris.

Plate XIV. Léon Bakst. *L'après-midi d'un faune: Portrait of Nijinsky as the Faun,* 1912. Graphite, charcoal, watercolor, gouache, gold on cardboard. Courtesy of the Wadsworth Atheneum, Hartford. From the Serge Lifar Collection and the Ella Gallup Sumner and Mary Catlin Sumner Collection.

Plate XV. James McNeill Whistler. *Nocturne in Blue and Gold: Old Battersea Bridge,* c. 1875. Oil on canvas. By permission of the Tate Gallery, London/Art Resource, New York.

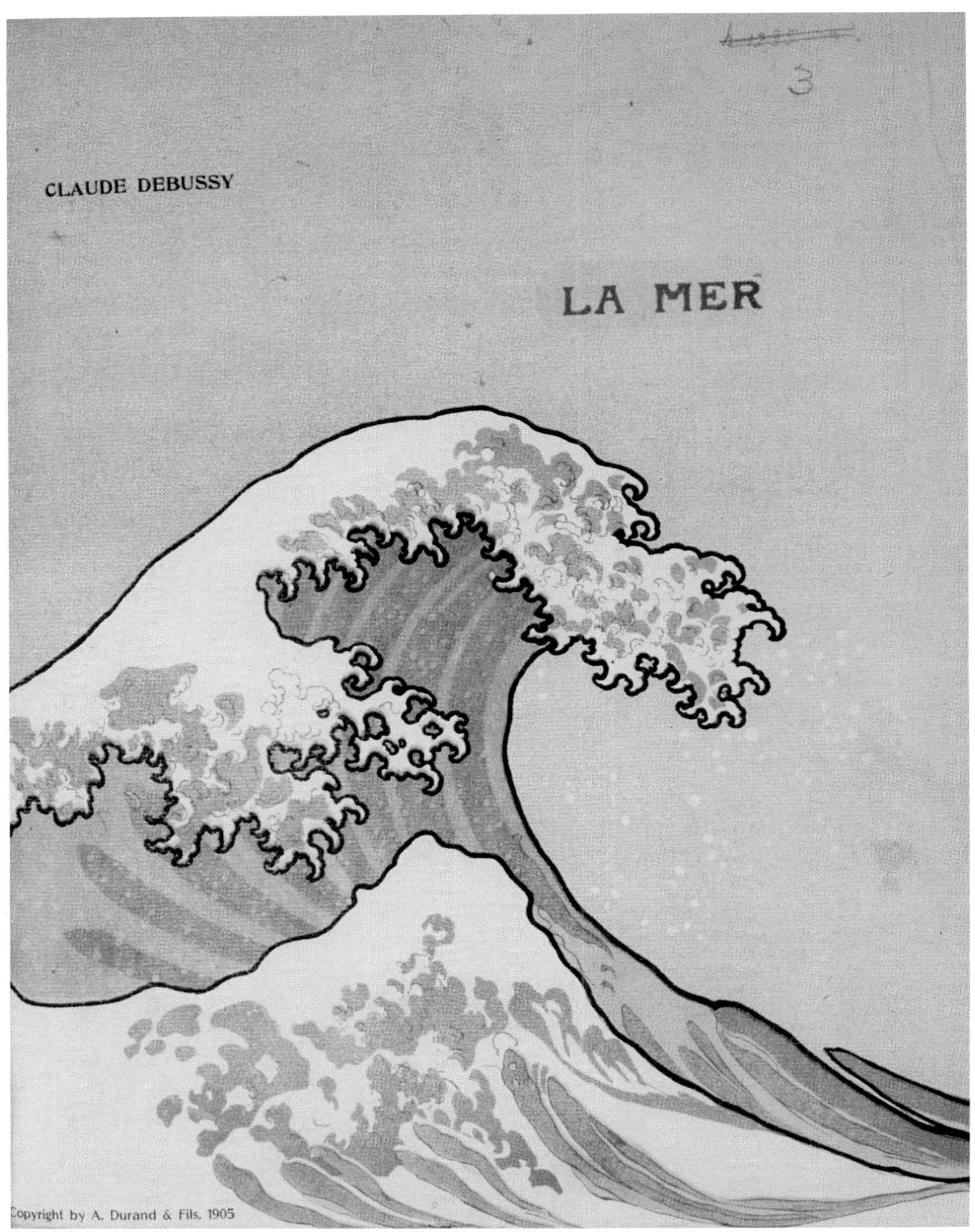

Plate XVI. Claude Debussy. Cover page of *La mer,* 1905. By permission of the British Library, London.

Plate XVII. Matthias Grünewald. *Angelic Concert,* from the Isenheim Altarpiece, c. 1510–15. Panel. Musée d'Unterlinden, Colmar. By permission of Giraudon/Art Resource, New York.

Plate XVIII. Matthias Grünewald. *Temptation of Saint Anthony,* from the Isenheim Altarpiece, c. 1510–15. Panel. Musée d'Unterlinden, Colmar. By permission of Giraudon/Art Resource, New York.

Example 11-1. Schubert. *The Winter's Journey,* Op. 89.

11-1a. No. 1, "Good Night," bars 1–4.

11-1b. No. 10, "Rest," bars 1–6.

11-1c. No. 20, "The Guidepost," bars 34–39.

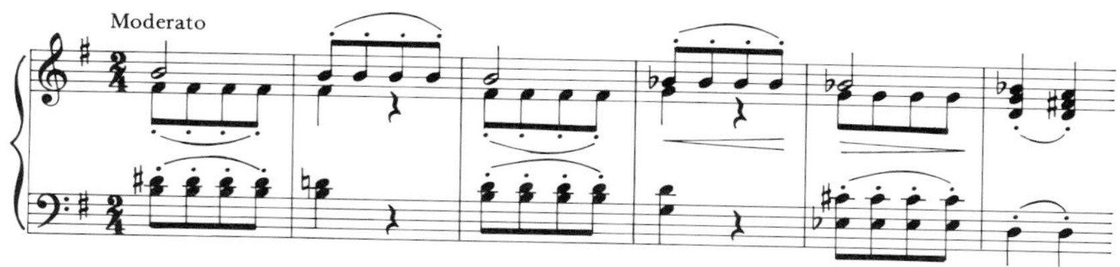

Nature imagery in both the graphic and symbolic sense appears prominently in the piano part. The wind howls in "The Weather Vane" (2); leaves and branches rustle in "The Linden Tree" (5); the pounding of horse's hooves and the sounding of the posthorn are heard in "The Post" (13); dogs snarl and bark in "In the Village" (17); and a storm rages in "The Stormy Morning" (18).

All roads, however, lead to the final song, "The Organ Grinder" (24). Paralleling the barren landscape implied in the text, the melody and accompaniment are reduced to stark simplicity. With the utmost economy of means, the recitativelike voice part alternates with the barrel organ's melancholy melody over a monotonous, droning accompaniment. When Schubert was painting this bleak tonal picture, he may well have seen the reflection of his own last years in the image of the organ grinder whose plate was always empty but whose lyre was never still.

Wunderlicher Alter	Strange old man,
soll ich mit dir gehn?	Shall I go with you?
Willst du meinen Liedern	Will you play my music
deine Leier drehn?	on your organ too?

The organ grinder then becomes the image of death, conveying the premonition that the poet-wanderer's music would be heard only after he was gone.

Example 11-2. Schubert. *The Winter's Journey.* No. 24, "The Organ Grinder," bars 58–61.

The entire song is marked a subdued pianissimo. Only as the song ends, is there a sudden forte to mark the recognition of death's grim visage (Ex. 11-2).

WEBER

Unlike Schubert, Carl Maria von Weber was born to the prominence accorded a concert pianist, conductor, and opera composer in the international capitals of Vienna, Prague, Berlin, and London. Weber's *Der Freischütz,* when first performed at Berlin in 1821, was a real victory for the new style as well as for the cause of German national opera. Subtitled "A Romantic Opera in Three Acts," it departs in significant ways from the mainstream of Italian and French models and strikes out on its own. Weber's sensitivity to orchestral and vocal coloration, as well as the compelling force of his melodic invention, placed him in the vanguard of romanticism. In *Freischütz* he first realized his ideal of opera as an artwork complete in itself, in which related arts blend together, disappear, and in so doing, form a new world.

Like Mozart's *Magic Flute, Der Freischütz* is a union of the folklike and the fantastic, and it became an opera of genuinely popular appeal. The theme is idyllic love and the people's freedom in God's realm of nature. The form is that of the Singspiel, a German song-play with spoken dialogue. Because the sung recitative is always orchestrally accompanied and is so closely connected with the arias or choruses that follow, there is a tendency to break down the rigid distinctions of the old number opera.

The setting is a Bohemian forest, and the tale is one of simple rustic life, without goddesses or heroic personages. The heroine, Agathe, is a gamekeeper's daughter; the hero, Max, a forest ranger. The choruses are sung by peasants, villagers, and hunters. The play, an adaptation from a book of popular ghost stories, was originally entitled *The Huntsman's Bride,* and the somewhat obscure term *Freischütz* can perhaps best be rendered as *free shot.* The huntsman Kaspar has sold his soul to the forest devil Samiel in return for seven magic bullets, six of which are guaranteed to hit the target he designates. The seventh, "free" shot is to be directed by Samiel alone.

Nature is here seen as a force that can either destroy or heal. Its demonic and divine aspects are explored, both the sorcery of black magic and the innocent joy of nature worship. Samiel, the Black Huntsman, is the personification of the Evil One, who commands the malignant elements, while his counterfoil is the old Hermit, who knows the secrets of nature's healing power. Against this play of forces the young lovers grapple with their fate.

The overture, still a staple in the symphonic repertory, is a song of the German forest with the voices of the hunting horns and woodwinds. The principal melodies of the opera are heard, including the sinister Samiel motif with its shuddering orchestral tremolando, pizzicato bass viols, and fatalistic drumbeats. This is the type of music that the German writer, critic and composer E. T. A. Hoffmann described as being "The mysterious essence of nature expressed in sounds; through [music] alone can be understood the divine singing of the trees, of flowers, of animals, of stones, and of waters."

Der Freischütz encompasses a mixture of styles. Agathe's scene and aria in the first act, "Leise, leise" ("Softly, gently"), suggest an Italian opera counterpart, but the aria itself is a folklike ballad with strophic repetitions in the tradition of the German domestic Lied. The influence of French opera is heard in the haunted "Wolf's Glen" scene. However, the "Chorus of Bridesmaids" and the "Huntsman's Chorus" with the sounds of hunting horns are as German as the traditional singing society.

The core of Weber's drama is the weird scene in the Wolf's Glen, to which Kaspar has lured the hero so that they can pronounce an incantation to conjure up the spectral figure of Samiel, an orchestral evocation that runs the gamut of romantic demonology. The foreboding trombones, the clarinet in its dark, low register, and the agitated tremolo string effects vividly describe the fantastic visions involved. The scoring of this terrifying episode has aptly been described as the arsenal of romanticism, from which Berlioz and Wagner freely borrowed some of their most potent orchestral effects. Weber's stage directions delineate the macabre atmosphere his romantic imagination sought to evoke: "A weird, craggy glen, surrounded by high mountains, down the side of one of which falls a cascade. To the left a blasted tree, on the knotty branch of which an owl is sitting. To the right a steep path by which Max comes; below it a great cave. The moon throws a lurid light over all. A few battered pine trees are scattered here and there. Kaspar, in shirt sleeves, is making a circle of black stones; a skull is in the center; near by a ladle, a bullet mold, and an eagle's wing. A thunderstorm is coming on."

Weber's lifetime fell entirely within that of Beethoven, and he died two years before Schubert. Yet he was one of the principal prophets of romanticism. In addition to his place as a major opera composer in his own right, with *Freischütz* as well as with the later *Euryanthe* (1823) and *Oberon* (1826), Weber laid the foundations for the future Wagnerian music drama, just as his bravura piano pieces made him a significant precursor of Mendelssohn, Chopin, Schumann, and Liszt.

Mainstream Romanticists

BERLIOZ

Romanticism, after its beginnings in other centers, first moved onto the international stage in Paris. With the July Revolution of 1830 it became the official French style, and it was destined to remain such until the February Revolution of 1848. The flamboyant figure of Hector Berlioz, with his shock of red hair and burning eyes, illuminated the cafés and concert halls of Paris in 1830, as the red glare of revolutionary rockets lit up the Parisian streets. How far things had come since the days of polite 18th-century social music can be measured by the spectacle of this ardent 26-year-old composer proclaiming his personal passion for an Irish actress to one and all at the top of his symphonic lungs.

The *Symphonie fantastique,* as this orchestral autobiography was called, served as the musical manifesto of the new movement, just as the plays of Victor Hugo and the paintings of Delacroix were its literary and pictorial equivalents. "Bizarre and monstrous," wrote one of the reviewers; but the *Symphonie fantastique* commands such attention that no one to this day can disregard its challenge.

Berlioz's lively imagination was fired equally by the literary and musical directions of the romantic movement. He found inspiration in Gothic novels, Shakespeare revivals, Dante's *Inferno,* Byron's poetry, and Goethe's *Faust.* At the same time, current musical developments fed his literary interests: romantic opera as exemplified in Weber's *Freischütz,* the "grand" style illustrated in Beethoven's "Eroica" Symphony, and the programmatic elements in his "Pastorale" Symphony. Some of Berlioz's works, such as *Roméo et Juliette* (1839) and the *La damnation de Faust* (1846), are made even more explicit in their literary connection by the incorporation of sung texts. Though he called the former a *dramatic symphony* and the latter a *dramatic legend,* both are actually hybrid forms obtained by crossing the oratorio with the symphony.

The *Symphonie fantastique* projected a large-scale design in five movements, and the composer's problem was how to keep such a large, varied work together without letting it dissolve into a loose collection of episodes. Like his fellow romanticists, Berlioz was at his best in quick flashes of inspiration and deft strokes of the dramatic. His solution was typical of his compositional procedures, being half literary and half musical—a poetic programme prefacing a fanciful story line for each of the movements, and a melodic motif he called an *idée fixe* (fixed idea) running through each movement. The technique is not unlike that used by Gluck in *Orfeo* (see Ex. 10-4, p. 208). Berlioz devised a theme to be identified with his heroine and altered it according to the events of each symphonic episode. Later, Liszt and Wagner appropriated this fixed-idea motivic scheme, modifying and expanding it to suit their own purposes.

The first movement, "Reveries, Passions," is the only one that follows the outlines of the classical sonata form. The slow, dreamy largo introductory section, redolent of romantic longing, leads directly into an allegro agitato e appassionato assai in which the fixed idea is first sounded by the flute and violins (Ex. 11-3a). In the development section the motif is exposed to a series of musical experiences, much in the manner of Beethoven. According to Berlioz's rather lurid programme,

> The composer imagines that a young musician sees for the first time a woman who possesses all the charms of the ideal being he has dreamed of, and falls desperately in love with her. By some strange trick of fancy, the beloved vision never appears to the artist's mind except in association with a musical idea, in which he perceives the same character—impassioned, yet refined and diffident—that he attributes to the object of his love.
>
> The transition from a state of dreamy melancholy, interrupted by several fits of aimless joy, to one of delirious passion, with its impulses of rage and jealousy, its returning moments of tenderness, its tears, and its religious solace, is the subject of the first movement.

The literary source in this case was Thomas De Quincey's psychological study *Confessions of an English Opium Eater,* which had appeared earlier in 1830 in a very free French translation by Alfred de Musset.

Example 11-3. Berlioz. *Fantastic Symphony.* Examples of fixed idea.

11-3a. First movement, bars 9–16.

A scene added by Musset serves as the programme for the second movement, in which the musician finds himself musing about a carnival ball. Though the dance floor is crowded, his eye follows one figure, his beloved, as she whirls to the measures of a brilliant concert waltz. The fixed idea, still recognizable, is refashioned within the swirling waltz tempo (Ex. 11-3b).

11-3b. Second movement, bars 302–9.

The hero's wild despair can be assuaged only in the bucolic arms of Mother Nature, and the third movement is a "Scene in the Country." Interrupting the peaceful pastoral dialogue of the English horn and oboe, "*She* appears once more, his heart stops beating, he is agitated by painful presentiments." With the fourth movement the real phantasmagoria begins. According to the programme,

> The artist, now knowing beyond all doubt that his love is not returned, poisons himself with opium. The dose of the narcotic, too weak to take his life, plunges him into a sleep accompanied by the most horrible visions. He dreams that he has killed the woman he loved, and that he is condemned to death, brought to the scaffold, and witnesses his own execution. The procession is accompanied by a march that is sometimes fierce and somber, sometimes stately and brilliant: loud crashes are followed abruptly by the dull thud of heavy footfalls. At the end of the march, the first four bars of the *idée fixe* recur like a last thought of love interrupted by the fatal stroke.

This mock march of triumph, with its raffish rhythms and nightmarish atmosphere, tells much about the relation of the romantic artist to society. The artist-hero is misunderstood by the jeering mobs and marched off to the guillotine, recalling executions such as that of the revolutionary lyric poet André Chénier during the Reign of Terror in 1792. Similarly, in Berlioz's *Harold in Italy* (1834) the noble and sensitive artist is surrounded by uncomprehending savages in the final "Orgy of the Brigands."

The hellfire and brimstone of Dante's *Inferno* and the wild imagery of Goethe's grotesque "Walpurgisnight's Dream" from *Faust* are echoed in Berlioz's fifth movement, the "Witches' Sabbath," and howling demons come to claim the hero's soul. Like Victor Hugo's poem entitled "Witches' Sabbath," this piece seems to be set in a Gothic church at the mystical hour of midnight. The smell of sulfur is in the air, the holy water boils in the fonts, and the fantastic congregation—specters, ghouls, monsters, and, from the graveyard, the souls of the damned—gathers from all directions. Satan himself sings the Black Mass, and the fearsome assembly joins in his mad capers.

The fixed idea appears here in a grotesque version (Ex. 11-3c). The woman who has been bewitching the hero was apparently a witch all along, and with a shriek he recognizes his beloved on her broomstick, just before the doomsday theme is intoned. As Berlioz's programme promises, this is a "burlesque parody" on the *Dies irae,* the ancient chant that has long been part of the traditional Latin Mass for the Dead (see p. 000). This parody on a prayer from the sacred service is one of the many instances of romantic irony characteristic of a period that was enamored of the supernatural, fascinated by the grotesqueries of gothic gargoyles, and beguiled by the demons depicted in medieval Last Judgment scenes. The movement concludes with a fugue based on the witches' dance and the *Dies irae* melody.

The *Symphonie fantastique* contains many of Berlioz's original touches in instrumentation and orchestral tone color. Though the symphony was written only three years after the death of Beethoven, Berlioz called for an orchestra much larger in numbers and wider in tonal resources than any previously.

11-3c. Fifth movement, bars 41–44.

He was destined to expand the orchestra to truly colossal proportions in such later works as the *Grande messe des mortes* (*Requiem Mass,* 1837). Such works called for as many as 800 performers and delivered thunderous sounds, creating such reactions from the public that Berlioz was often the subject of derisive cartoons (Fig. 11-1).

SCHUMANN

Robert Schumann's youthful enthusiasms, like those of Berlioz, were about equally divided between literature and music. And, like Weber and Berlioz, he also turned to musical criticism as a means of giving support for his views. The influence of the fanciful dream world of E. T. A. Hoffmann is felt in Schumann's *Phantasiestücke* (*Fantasy Pieces,* 1837), *Nachtstücke* (*Night Pieces,* 1839), and *Kreisleriana* (1838), the titles and subjects of which are taken directly from Hoffmann's imaginative short stories. The last mentioned, for instance, is based on anecdotes about an eccentric conductor named Kreisler, a wild genius who was the literary prototype of the mad musician.

Without exception Schumann's early published works up to Opus 23 were written for piano. Like his fellow romanticists he placed inspiration first and foremost; and, with the courage of his convictions, he stuck principally to smaller forms. These were, in the main, short lyrical fragments or character pieces that have a spontaneous freshness of approach associated with improvisations. For publication he grouped them into various series, but beneath their fancy-dress titles they bear some resemblance to the older traditional keyboard dance suites.

Carnaval (1835), for solo piano, is a colorful combination of the old dance suite and a fanciful free adaptation of the variation principle. This "rogue's gallery" of romanticism contains the distilled essence of Schumann's early life—his experiences, friendships, literary ideas, feeling for his fellow artists, infatuations, and dreams, transformed into music full of Puckish humor animated by romantic warmth. The organization of the whole structure is definitely subordinated to the parts, and the general impression is that of a collection of miniature scenes, fleeting glimpses, and kaleidoscopic shifts of color.

Schumann added to *Carnaval* the somewhat enigmatic subtitle "Little Scenes on Four Notes," and often referred to it in his letters as the "Masked Ball." It is indeed a masquerade, and as such it reveals the whimsical side of Schumann's nature as well as his love of little mysteries. On one level it ex-

Figure 11-1. Grandville. *A Shell-burst Concert* (Berlioz conducting), 1846. Lithograph. Courtesy of the George Arents Research Library, Syracuse University, Syracuse, New York.

presses a kind of cult romanticism, full of secret allusions known only to the initiated. Only after the eighth piece, and then as a kind of parenthesis in the score, does Schumann reveal the four-note figure on which his variations are built; and even here it is propounded in the form of a riddle entitled "Sphinxes." The device is not unlike the eccentric practices of Schumann's literary idol, Jean Paul Richter, who once put a preface in the middle of one of his novels. The three Sphinxes read S-C-H-A, As-C-H, and A-S-C-H (Ex. 11-4). In German notation these are references to the notes of the scale that form the motivic scheme:

S = E-flat (*Es*)
C = C
H = B-natural
A = A
As = A-flat

The solution of the anagram is found in the fact that Schumann's lady love at this time lived in the small town of Asch, and the letters also happen to be the only musical ones in his surname, SCHumAnn. In the tenth number,

"A.S.C.H.—S.C.H.A.," the letters join hands in a lively dance. Each piece is based on some constellation of this four-note motif, which is varied rhythmically and melodically to suit each instance.

Example 11-4. Schumann. *Carnaval,* Op. 9. "Sphinxes."

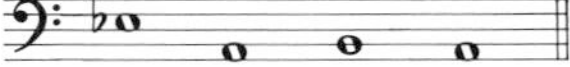

After the "Préamble," a prelude that establishes the festive atmosphere, a series of scenes and portraits are executed with brief bold strokes and often with incisive psychological insight. Many are stock masquerade characters out of the Italian commedia dell' arte. "Pierrot" (2) is ever the ardent but inept lover; "Harlequin" (3), the gaudily dressed acrobatic clown; "Coquette" (7), the frivolous, flirtatious, eternal feminine. Pantalon, the jealous old husband, and the coquettish Columbine are engaged in one of their incessant quarrels in No. 15. Schumann explains in one of his letters that "Reconnaissance" (14) is a scene of recognition; "Aveu" (17), an avowal of love; "Promenade" (18), a walk such as one takes at a German ballroom dance with one's partner.

Concurrent with these general characterizations is a series of particular portraits that reveal much about Schumann's world. "Valse Noble" (4), a title taken from Schubert, is apparently a portrait of the master whom Schumann admired so ardently, and whose instrumental lyricism he emulated. Schubert's short piano pieces, the *Musical Moments,* impromptus, and many series of short dances were models not only for Schumann but for Mendelssohn, Chopin, and Liszt as well. And it was Schumann who discovered the "Great" C-major symphony of Schubert amid a pile of neglected manuscripts.

The titles "Eusebius" and "Florestan" (5 and 6) refer to the pseudonymns under which Schumann published his early works. In these obvious self-portraits he reveals the two sides of his temperament, with the dreamy, reflective Eusebius representing him as a quiet man of contemplation, and the bold, aggressive Florestan as the vehement man of action. In the latter piece there is a quotation from Schumann's highly original youthful work *Papillons* (*Butterflies*), Op. 2.

"Chiarina" (11) with bravura and dash portrays the young pianist Clara Wieck, who was later to become Schumann's wife. The fluency and grace of Chopin's nocturne style can next be heard in No. 12, and one is reminded that Schumann was one of the first to hail the young Chopin in his famous critical review that began, "Hats off, gentlemen, a genius!"

"Estrella" (13) was his affectionate name for his sweetheart at the time, Ernestine von Fricken, the lady who lived in Asch. In the midst of the "Valse Allemande" (16) there is an apparition of Paganini, fiddling with diabolical virtuosity (see Fig. 11-2). Schumann's bedazzled reaction to Paganini also caused him to transcribe some of that composer's violin caprices for the piano.

Just before the finale comes the "Pause" (19), a frantic scene with everyone scurrying around and mounting the barricades to do-or-die for the cause of romanticism. Then ensues the "March of the Davidsbündler against the Philistines," the battle royal of Schumann's self-declared war on the enemies of the modern art and music of his time. The ranks of the latter included the purveyors of dry academic stereotypes, those who upheld outmoded traditions, and the smug middle-class conservatives who were the bulwark of the mediocre and commonplace.

The *Davidsbund*, or David's League, was a mythical society of romantic reformers who banded together to fight the Goliaths of conservative Philistinism, like the biblical David. Schumann acknowledged that it was "a purely abstract and romantic society" and a figment of his own imagination. The officers of this ideal and progressive "organization" included Berlioz, who was never informed of the honor accorded him, and Beethoven, who had been dead nearly a decade. "In every time," remarked Schumann in one of his critiques, "there reigns a secret league of kindred spirits. Tighten the circle, you who belong to it, in order that the truth in art may shine forth more and more brightly, everywhere spreading joy and peace." Schumann's critical articles sometimes assumed the form of minutes of the "meetings" of this society, and his review of a performance of Beethoven's Ninth Symphony began with Florestan climbing onto the piano and haranguing the group. The "March of the Davidsbündler" in *Carnaval* has all the optimistic ring of a crusader's song, and the composer satirizes the academic conservatives by including the old-fashioned "Grandfather's Dance" that traditionally concluded ballroom dances and wedding festivities in Germany.

Only after 1840 did Schumann turn to larger forms, including the song cycle, the piano quintet, the piano concerto, and the symphony. He enriched the literature with numerous Lieder, four symphonies, several song cycles. The *Dichterliebe* (*Poet's Love,* 1840) is a particularly happy example of a com-

Figure 11-2. Johann Lyser. *Dance of Death (Paganini, the Master Entertainer),* 1828. Cartoon. Courtesy of the George Arents Research Library, Syracuse University, Syracuse, New York.

poser finding his true poetic counterpart; for in Heinrich Heine, Schumann found a poet for whose verses he had a real affinity. Selecting 16 poems from the 65 Heine had published under the title *Lyrical Intermezzo,* Schumann combines narrative and contemplative approaches. In the manner of an intimate personal confession, the cycle explores a gamut of emotions ranging from youthful rapture to pathos, morbid feeling to airy fantasy, romantic irony to grim humor.

Musically the settings are equally multidimensional, comprising a variety of types. There are purely lyrical evocations, such as "In the lovely month of May" (1), "Out of my tears" (2), "I will baptize my spirit" (5), "And if the flowers only knew" (8), "I hear an echo singing" (10), and "On a radiant summer morning" (12); folklike songs, such as "A young man loves a maiden" (11) and "From ancient fairy stories" (15); dramatic ballads, such as "I will not mourn" (7), "Beloved, in dreams" (14), and "The songs, so old and bitter" (16); dance songs, such as "The rose and the lily" (3) and "Flutes, violins, and trumpets are sounding" (9); and quasi-operatic recitatives, such as "Whene'er I look into your eyes" (4) and "I wept as I lay dreaming" (13).

One of the most interesting is "In the Rhine" (6), composed in the spirit of Bach, whose music Schumann admired greatly (Ex. 11-5). Like one of the master's organ chorale-preludes, the austere vocal melody is reinforced by resounding octaves in the bass register of the piano, while over it a precipitously descending obbligato figure in a majestic baroque dotted rhythm reflects the imagery of the text:

In the Rhine, that stream of wonder,
The great, the holy Cologne
Is mirrored, and there under
The waves the Cathedral is shown.

Somewhat less lean and angular is the setting for the second verse describing the interior of the cathedral. Rich, organlike chromatic harmonies then fill the widely spaced unison intervals to give a warmer, more personal tone to the third and final verse:

Mid flowers and angels she stands there
Our Lady we bow before.
But the eyes and the lips and the hands there
Are those of the one I adore!

The piano part then takes over in an extensive postlude, and the song ends as austerely and starkly as it began.

Schumann often assigns the principal part to the piano, while the voice functions as a commentary on the action. This procedure, however, always has a clearly defined poetic purpose. For instance, in the ninth song, "Flutes,

Example 11-5. Schumann. *Poet's Love,* Op. 48. No. 6, "In the Rhine."

violins, and trumpets are sounding," the poet describes the scene of his beloved's wedding to another. Instrumentally the "accompaniment" is a complete piano piece in its own right, while the voice part proceeds independently. The general impression is that of the lover looking at the scene from the outside, a clear and effective way to show him and his beloved going their separate ways.

Example 11-6. Schumann. *Poet's Love*. Use of motif.

11-6a. No. 1, "In the wondrous month of May," bars 9–12.

11-6b. No. 16, "The old, spiteful songs." Motif in postlude, bars 53–56.

Schumann also integrates the songs of the *Dichterliebe* by the use of a recurring motif consisting of a simple four-note scalewise figure (Ex. 11-6a). This germinal motif appears first in the opening song in ascending order; later it evolves through a series of mutations beginning with the inverted order in songs 5 and 6; a chromatic variant appears in song 8; and a sequential figure occurs in songs 9 and 10. Toward the end the motif is restored to its original ascending form, as in the close of song 11, and in the accompaniment figures of songs 15 and 16; and finally it reaches its apotheosis in the piano postlude of the cycle (Ex. 11-6b).

MENDELSSOHN

While considering some of the wilder faces of romanticism, Felix Mendelssohn once remarked that Berlioz, in spite of all his efforts to go stark, raving mad, never once really succeeded. Mendelssohn's was a voice of moderation: While his music was in the mainstream of romanticism, it provided a close link and sense of continuity with the voices of his predecessors—Haydn, Mozart, Beethoven, and Schubert.

Unlike Berlioz and Schumann, Mendelssohn shunned a radical departure from the academic tradition that was standard fare in the concert halls of his time. Thus, with the clarity of his forms and the elegance of his craftsmanship, his works found more ready acceptance in musical circles than did those of his more revolutionary colleagues. Unlike Mozart and Schubert, he lived a life free of financial concerns and held important musical posts in Germany, most notably as permanent director of the prestigious Leipzig Gewandhaus Orchestra and as head of the Leipzig Conservatory of Music.

Mendelssohn developed an early interest in the music of the past, especially that of Bach. During the last 12 years of his life he maintained a close connection with the city of Leipzig, where Bach had spent his last 27 years. In 1829 he presented the first public performance in a century of Bach's *Saint Matthew Passion.*

Mendelssohn's compositions show a healthy respect for all his forebears, concentrating on existing forms and styles. A large body of chamber music is joined by works for piano and organ solo that draw liberally on the chorale and prelude-and-fugue traditions of Bach. He wrote many songs, both with and without words. The former are set to poetry by Heine, Goethe, Schiller, Byron, and other romantics; the latter are lyric evocations for solo piano. The concertos include one for violin in E Minor (1844) and two for piano that were written to display his own virtuoso skills. Mendelssohn conducted performances of many of Handel's oratorios, and his own large-scale *Saint Paul* (1836) and *Elijah* (1846) carry the oratorio traditions of Bach, Handel, and Haydn into the middle of the romantic century.

Of Mendelssohn's five symphonies, his travel experiences play a part in the Third and Fourth, which bear the subtitles "Scottish" and "Italian." In the single-movement "Reformation" Symphony (1832), Mendelssohn paid homage to the Protestant faith which he shared with Bach.

Mendelssohn's music projects a Mozartean clarity and transparency in which every line is easily perceived. A no-nonsense composer, he developed the practical programmatic *concert overture* for use with his orchestra in Leipzig. Short and colorful, with clear sonata-form structures, these overtures were designed to act as sturdy, attractive concert openers. Inspiration for his overtures came from such sources as Goethe (*Calm Sea and Prosperous Voyage,* 1828), Shakespeare (*Midsummer Night's Dream,* 1826), and Mendelssohn's own travels (*Fingal's Cave* or *Hebrides,* 1830). The *Midsummer Night's Dream* overture, written when Mendelssohn was sixteen, later became part of an enlarged score of incidental music for the play (1842), which for generations has served to enhance the evocative fairy-tale atmosphere of Shakespeare's drama.

Virtuosity and the Symphonic Poem

The career of the legendary violinist Nicolò Paganini, as well as the careers of his pianistic counterparts Frédéric Chopin and Franz Liszt, created a growing new audience for solo instrumental music. Their emphasis on specialization in composition and performance bespoke the romantic admiration for individuality as expressed by a great virtuoso. Instead of composing and performing for an educated and discriminating elite, the romantic virtuoso had to take into account the wide varieties of taste of a new and enlarged audience. No longer was it possible to win approving nods for subtle, intricate manipulations of formal design. Instead, the composer and performer, in order to stir an enthusiastic response, had to amaze and astonish. The age of the universal composer who was at home with all media was over, and the era of the specialist had begun. Practically the entire creative output of Berlioz, for instance, was cast in the orchestral mold. Paganini composed for the violin; Chopin, for the piano; and Wagner and Verdi, almost exclusively for the operatic stage.

PAGANINI

Nicolò Paganini's meteoric career became a touchstone for the attainment of technical virtuosity, just as he himself became a fantastic legend in his own lifetime. This traveling celebrity was a matchless showman, performing at concerts that drew vast crowds willing to pay fantastic admission fees to hear him. His gaunt figure and feverishly burning eyes quickened the rumor that, like Faust, he had sold his soul to the devil in return for the gift of supernatural skill (Fig. 11-2). His prodigious violinistic feats included mysterious high harmonics—often with the addition of double and triple stopping—and a dancing bow that bounced nimbly off the strings. The sparks he ignited with his left-hand pizzicatos, and the playing of entire pieces on a single string, were but two of the highly inventive effects the majority of his listeners were hearing for the first time.

His breath-taking virtuosity not only captivated the crowds of curiosity seekers but inspired the careers of his younger contemporaries as well. He received the unreserved admiration of Schubert, Rossini, and Berlioz; and Chopin once remarked, "Paganini is perfection." His 24 *Caprices,* one of the few works he actually published, had wide circulation. These short, polished technical and character studies had much to do with increasing the vogue for short aphoristic forms, and they undoubtedly influenced Chopin's corresponding sets of 24 etudes, as well as the many transcriptions for piano by Schumann, Liszt, and others. The vitality and appeal of his melodic invention are likewise confirmed by the choice of the theme of the 24th caprice as the basis for such great sets of variations as Brahms' *Variations on a Theme of Paganini,* and Rachmaninov's *Rhapsody on a Theme by Paganini.*

CHOPIN

Frédéric Chopin, in contrast to Paganini and Liszt, played for others rather rarely, and only for a select few in the elegant salons of Parisian society. He consequently had more time for teaching and composition, and his creative work proves the truth of Goethe's observation that a master reveals himself through his limitations. Except for a few early songs and several chamber compositions, everything he wrote was for the piano. His complete works, moreover, occupy no five-foot shelf; on the contrary, they are small in number, compact in size, fine-grained in texture, lustrous in their polish, masterly in their workmanship. Unlike so many of his more vocal colleagues, he made no fetish of formal freedom; instead, he quietly achieved fluidity of form without sacrificing the clarity of his designs.

If Chopin's piano studies can be considered his reply to Paganini's challenging violin caprices, then his set of 24 *Preludes* (Op. 28) in each of the major and minor keys is his tribute to Bach's two sets of 24 preludes and fugues covering all the tonalities of the "well-tempered" system of tuning. The first in C Major, for instance, unfolds like a sophisticated commentary on the first prelude in the same key from Bach's Book I. Chopin's miniature masterpieces fall in the category of character pieces or mood pictures. They are noted for their inexhaustible invention of pianistic figurations, their subtle chromatic harmonies, and their daring, dynamic contrasts and fluctuations of rhythm.

The *Preludes* are painted with bold strokes and cover a spectrum of emotional states. Some have the brevity of aphorisms, such as the 16-bar No. 7 in A Major, which is like a tiny mazurka, or No. 20 in C Minor, whose short 13 bars move with the stately tread of a funeral march. More expansive are the serene, nocturnelike No. 13, the famous "Raindrop" (No. 15), and the richly harmonized No. 21. Morbid broodings are expressed in No. 2, tender intimacy in No. 6, transparent aerial accents in Nos. 3 and 23, headlong passion in No. 22. Finally there is the grim and tempestuous No. 24 in D Minor, ending with three bass thunderclaps that recall Burke's evocation of the sublime.

In his scherzos Chopin adopts the form that Haydn and Beethoven had evolved out of the old minuet and trio; but while his predecessors positioned theirs within the cyclical sequence of sonata movements, Chopin permits his to stand alone. The essential triple meter and strong formal contrasts (flexible A B A coda) are still present, but these scherzos sometimes suggest the trappings of romantic masquerade, with humor in the vein of romantic irony.

The Scherzo in C-sharp Minor, Op. 39, was written during the composer's winter journey of 1838 to the Mediterranean island of Majorca. The moods expressed in it are also evident in his letters of that period. "Tomorrow," he wrote, "I go to that wonderful [abandoned] monastery of Valdemosa, to write in the cell of some old monk, who perhaps had more fire in his soul than I, and stifled and extinguished it, because he had it in vain." His cell was in "the shape of a tall coffin," and his view overlooked "the most poetic of cemeteries" and a ruined crusaders' church. Thus was the stage set for Chopin to create a scherzo of the ironic type. First, a challenging chromatic introduction ushers in an insistent, whirling-dervish dance in the traditional triple meter. As it subsides, a trio section in the style of a chorale ensues, in which a sober prayer is intoned under pianistic figurations descending like mysterious moonbeams. The macabre dance returns to round out the design, and leads up to the free fantasia of an extended coda.

The idea of a sinister dance in sacred surroundings was a favorite romantic device dating from the shock tactics of Berlioz's parody of the *Dies irae* in the *Fantastic Symphony* and the scandal of Meyerbeer's ballet of nuns in his opera *Robert the Devil.* After the solemnity of the chorale, Chopin indicated in the score that his finale should be played *con fuoco* (with fire); and the sulfurous smoke of the fire-and-brimstone passages leaves no doubt as to its location in the hellish hereafter.

It is hardly accidental that many major and minor romantic composers were pianists. Weber, Mendelssohn, Chopin, Liszt, and Schumann—through his wife, Clara Wieck—could reach their audiences readily through piano recitals and the circulation of printed pieces. The piano as a solo instrument offered certain advantages to romantic composers, being an instrument with a still unexplored spectrum of tone color, and one that provided a convenient, immediate prospect for the performance of new works. It was, furthermore, completely under the control of a single player and was therefore ideal for direct self-expression, intimate soliloquy, and autobiographical confession.

LISZT

Franz Liszt's fabulous pianistic career followed in the path blazed by Paganini (Fig. 11-3). With a trace of good-humored envy, Berlioz describes a Liszt recital in his *Memoirs.* After the grand entrance, he comments,

Figure 11-3. Cartoon of Liszt concert in Berlin, 1841. Courtesy of the George Arents Research Library, Syracuse University, Syracuse, New York.

> The silence speaks; the admiration is intense and profound. Then come the fiery shells, a veritable bouquet of grand fireworks, the acclamation of the public, flowers and wreaths showered upon the priest of harmony as he sits quivering on his tripod, beautiful young women kissing the hem of his garment with tears of sacred frenzy; the sincere homage of the serious, the feverish applause wrung from the envious, the intent faces, the narrow hearts amazed at their own expansiveness! And the next day the inspired young genius departs, leaving behind him a twilight of dazzling glory and enthusiasm. It is a dream; it is one of those golden dreams that come to one when one is named Liszt or Paganini.

Liszt became the first pianist to present public solo recitals. Up to that time, a concert always called for a wide variety of personages, including several singers, assorted instrumental soloists, and often an orchestra. Liszt's programs, however, made up the deficiency by supplying piano versions of Beethoven symphonies, songs by Schubert and others, whole opera scenes and operatic fantasies, and musical travelogues such as his *Années de pèlerinage* (*Years of Pilgrimage*) and *Album of a Voyager.* His programme music drew from the visual arts and literature, including a musical commentary on Raphael's *Sposalizio* (*Marriage of the Madonna*) and Michelangelo's seated statue of Duke Lorenzo de' Medici, *Il penseroso* (*The Thinker*), and Liszt's literary musings *Après une lecture de Dante* (*After Reading Dante*)—all for piano alone. As one contemporary put it,

> Liszt does not merely play the piano. He tells, at the piano, the story of his own destiny, which is closely linked to and reflects the progress of our time. To him the piano becomes an approximate expression of his high mental cultivation, of his views, of his faith and being. How far inquiry has reached into the domain of science; how far speculation has fathomed musical thought; how it goes in the world of the intellect. Such a brain must be rated higher than a piano, and it is an accidental circumstance of no importance that Liszt plays the piano at all.

As with Paganini, there was indeed a seriousness of purpose behind the external glitter, and Liszt envisioned himself as a modern incarnation of Orpheus, high priest of harmony. He actually took minor orders in the Roman Catholic faith. His own literary programme for the symphonic poem *Orpheus* has an authentic autobiographical ring:

> Men's brutal instincts are silenced. The very stones are softened. Hearts, harder perhaps than the stones, are melted to burning but grudging tears. The singing birds, the murmuring waterfalls, suspend their melodies. Laughter and pleasure are hushed at these sweet sounds, which reveal to humanity the beneficent power of Art, its glory and civilizing influence.

Programme music, the attempt to intensify music by incorporating some of the power of the other arts such as drama, poetry, and painting, found its most articulate spokesman in Franz Liszt. Though its basic principles had been worked out long before and many shining examples had been written before his time, it was in Liszt's comments and orchestral compositions that programme music first became an unabashed, self-conscious, stylistic reality. It was he who first coined the term *symphonic poem* to signify the mystical marriage of orchestral music to poetic idea. Later the name was modified by others to *tone poem* to imply that any instrumental combination, large or small, could harvest the fruits of this process of hybridization. "The programme," as Liszt pointed out, "has no other object than to indicate preparatively the spiritual moments which impelled the composer to create his work, the thoughts which he endeavored to incorporate in it."

Liszt's stated objective was thus to infuse music more and more with poetry so as to preserve its circulatory system from a hardening of its formal arteries, a danger he professed to see in composition as it was taught by the academicians in conservatories. He well knew that in music's state of classical health, the design of a sonata was extremely flexible. So he took violent issue with the formulation of a set of "express rules, which are considered inviolable, although the composers who originated them had no other precept for them than their own imagination, and themselves made the formal dispositions which people wish now to set up as a law. In programme music, on the other hand, the return, change, modification, and modulation of the motifs are conditioned by their relation to a poetic idea."

Liszt's principal quarrel with the purists of his time is contained in his statement that "All exclusively musical considerations, though they should not be neglected, have to be subordinated to the action of the given subject. Consequently, the action and subject of this kind of a symphony demand a higher interest than the technical treatment of the musical material."

As such, Liszt's innovations represent a tempering of the cold logic of technique with the warmth of human feeling, as well as a revolt against formal stereotypes. Far from disregarding formal procedures, his method was based on a specialized application of developmental principles as worked out in the sonatas of the Viennese composers from Haydn and Mozart to Beethoven and Schubert. The exposition–development–recapitulation plan of a sonata design is still loosely discernible in his symphonic poems. He studiously avoided exact repetition, however, in favor of continuous variation and development from beginning to end. Since the external outline and the internal arrangement of parts may be adjusted in each case to suit the dramatic necessity of the subject at hand, the symphonic poem can be considered a type rather than a form. The only things that all symphonic poems have in common is that they are continuous rather than divided into separate movements (like the sonata and the symphony) and that they are based on a central motif.

This motivic writing was essentially the same process that the classical composers had considered to be one of the more important devices in the craft of composition. In the 19th century, however, it began to acquire a host of different names. To Berlioz it was the *idée fixe* (fixed idea), and to Wagner the *Leitmotif* (leading motif). Liszt, with one of his characteristic rhetorical flourishes, called it the *metamorphosis of motif* (thematic transformation). All are essentially the same process, with allowances made for the personal idioms and the various methods of the respective composers who used it.

This metamorphosis, or growth principle, permeated much of the scientific as well as the aesthetic thought of the period. It was expressed in a poem Goethe called "The Metamorphosis of Plants" (1789), a prose translation of which reads, "Observe how the plant, little by little progressing, step by step guided on, changes to blossom and fruit. First the seed unfolds itself as soon as the fruitful womb of the earth releases it. Simply slumbers the force of the seed, a germ of the future. Upward then it strives, trusting in gentle moisture; and from the night wherein it dwelt, straightaway ascends to the light." The motif, then, in this natural history of musical composition, is the thematic germ cell containing within itself all the embryonic potentialities of future growth. Each musical seed unfolds differently according to the individual laws of its genus and species, yet each follows in its own way the laws of external harmony.

Liszt's method is perhaps best exemplified in his well-known symphonic poem *Les Préludes,* for which he provided a programmatic point of departure adapted from a poem by Lamartine. "What is life," the poem asks, "but a series of preludes to that unknown song whose first solemn note is sounded by Death?" The basic motif, contained in the first three notes, thus poses the question of the meaning of life with the ascending interval of the fourth (Ex. 11-7a); and the remainder of the first section, andante maestoso, continues with some of the implications and consequences of the motif. "The blissful dawn of every life is heralded by love," continues the programme, and appropriately enough the second section dissolves into the amorous duet of Example 11-7b. In that example, note that the asterisked notes add up to a transformed version of the motif.

Example 11-7. Liszt. *The Preludes.* Motif and transformations.

11-7a. Motif, bar 3.

11-7b. Bars 70–73.

Next, a storm—allegro tempestuoso—interrupts "with a deadly blast that dispels youth's illusions" (Ex. 11-7c). This is followed by an allegretto pastorale interlude (Ex. 11-7d), in which the flute, then the rustic oboe, sound the motif and recall "the memories of the pleasant calm of rural life." Yet one should not linger too long "in the idyllic lap of Nature, but must hasten to his post when the trumpet sounds the warning," and an allegro marziale then begins on a warlike note (Ex. 11-7e). The final section now functions like a symphonic recapitulation, and the various mutations of the motif yield to its triumphant restatement by the full orchestra, signifying victory over the adversities of fate (Ex. 11-7f).

11-7c. Bars 110–12.

11-7d. Bars 260–63.

In this symphonic form, the motif is the vital unit that lends itself to repetition and variation and begs for adventure. After its initial presentation, the

11-7e. Bars 351–54.

11-7f. Bars 370–73.

successive themes and melodic details may be derived directly from this motif or may be closely related to it. Each reappearance is marked by alterations of melody, harmony, rhythm, and texture according to the exigencies of the dramatic scheme. The motif is thus the unifying force, while the surrounding series of episodes provides the variety.

Curiously enough, after the initial flush of formal freedom had time to wear off, composers returned with fanfares and flourishes to the pre-established forms. In the early part of the 19th century romantic composers had largely avoided compositions with specific names such as *rondo* or *theme and variations.* But Richard Strauss would use them in the titles of his tone poems of 1895 and 1897: *Till Eulenspiegel's Merry Pranks, after the old roguish manner, in rondo form*; and *Don Quixote, fantastic variations on a theme of knightly character.* Gustav Mahler, for his part, was to write weighty philosophical discourses for orchestra, bundle several of these metaphysical tone poems together into single cyclical packages, and once again call them symphonies (see pp. 300-305).

Romantic Nationalism

Another of the characteristic expressions of the romantic era was the rise of nationalism. Like programme music, nationalism was by no means a 19th-century phenomenon. Regional differences and ethnic attitudes are common to all historical periods. The particular form that nationalism assumed in the 19th century sprang from the liberating force generated by the French Revolution, which continued in the wake of the Napoleonic wars and inspired ethnic groups to seek national self-determination.

The popular struggles in various countries to throw off the tyrant's yoke were reflected artistically in the efforts of the people to free themselves from foreign influences and importations that hitherto had dominated their cultural life. Writers, artists, and composers were often in the intellectual vanguard of such movements, and the increased interest in folk stories and ballads, national epics, and local color provided them with a powerful stimulus. Those interested in the arts sought indigenous sources and thought in terms of a national art, and they listened for "the voice of the people." In music this meant an awakening to the beauty of folk songs and dances and to the possibility of using them in art music; and it meant a new encouragement of native composers.

The nationalistic movement in the 19th century applied principally to the continental countries previously viewed as tributaries to the main centers: Hungary, Bohemia (Czechoslovakia), the Scandinavian countries, Finland, and Russia. In Italy, France, Germany, and Austria there had been a continuous musical tradition for centuries. While the operas of Weber, Berlioz, Verdi, and Wagner admittedly expressed nationalistic feelings, they were but a minor manifestation within a major movement.

Hitherto, however, there had been no self-conscious body of music and musicians specifically wearing a Hungarian, Bohemian, Scandinavian, or Russian label. Liszt began writing Hungarian rhapsodies, and his 20th-century successors, Béla Bartók and Zoltán Kodály, continued in his footsteps. Poland was handsomely represented by Chopin's polonaises and mazurkas; Bohemia, by such works as Bedřich Smetana's opera *The Bartered Bride* (1866), his collection of six symphonic poems, *My Fatherland,* which includes "The Moldau" (1874), and Dvořák's *Slavonic Dances*; Norway, by Edvard Grieg's incidental music to Ibsen's drama *Peer Gynt.* The nationalistic theme was taken up in England by Sterndale Bennett, Edward Elgar, and more recently Ralph Vaughan Williams; in America by Edward MacDowell and Charles Ives; and in Finland by Jean Sibelius.

THE RUSSIAN FIVE

The noisiest of all the nationalistic movements was probably that of the Russian group known as the Mighty Five, who set out to establish a specifically Russian style of music. Mikhail Glinka had shown them the way with his historical opera *A Life for the Tsar* (1836) and his operatic fairy tale *Russlan and Ludmilla* (1842), based on a play by Alexander Pushkin. The Five—Mily Balakirev, César Cui, Alexander Borodin, Modest Musorgsky, and Nikolai Rimsky-Korsakov—were, with the exception of the last, self-taught amateurs who compensated for their lack of technical training by the freshness and vitality of their ideas. Borodin's opera *Prince Igor* (1869) and Musorgsky's *Boris Godunov* (1874) rank as achievements of the first magnitude; transcending their narrower nationalistic aspects, they are now accepted as masterpieces in the international repertory.

An interesting instance of a composition that has made its mark both in the original piano version and in an orchestral arrangement by Ravel is Musorgsky's *Pictures at an Exhibition.* The work is also one of the few in the repertory that has successfully incorporated the visual arts as the basis of a poetic programme. It is a good illustration of the manners and methods of romantic programme music in general. The exhibition referred to in the title, a retrospective showing of sketches, architectural drawings, and watercolors by the composer's friend Victor Hartmann, was held in St. Petersburg—now Leningrad—in 1874, shortly after the artist's death. These drawings reveal that Russian architects like Hartmann were trying to establish a national art for Russia, just as Musorgsky and his colleagues were searching for national musical idioms. Of the ten drawings that Musorgsky chose for musical settings, all but three are now lost.

To suggest the sauntering gait of viewers in a gallery as they pause occasionally before a picture that attracts their attention, Musorgsky opens with and later interpolates a recurring but variable section called "Promenade" (Ex. 11-8). This device is akin to a ritornel, and it functions in this case as a connecting link in the chain of musical pictures. The general design seems closely related to suites of character pieces for piano like Schumann's *Carnaval,* with the promenades exerting a unifying force as the viewers stroll from picture to picture.

Example 11-8. Musorgsky. *Pictures at an Exhibition.* "Promenade."

"The Gnome" was originally a design for an ingenious little toy nutcracker intended as a Christmas-tree ornament. Musorgsky depicts the gnome as a figure out of Russian folklore, waddling along on bandy legs to an awkward, grotesque rhythm. A variant of the Promenade then leads to "The Old Castle," which, according to the catalogue of the exhibit, portrayed a minstrel singing and strumming in front of a medieval castle. Another version of the Promenade introduces a pair of pictures—"Tuileries," subtitled "Children Quarreling after Play," and "Bydlo," a Polish oxcart lumbering along across the landscape. Over the rumbling wheels soars Musorgsky's fine melodic representation of the driver's song, as robust and stolid as the peasant who sings it.

The Promenade interlude now takes the listener to the "Ballet of the Unhatched Chicks," as they dance in their shells (Fig. 11-4). The drawing in this case was a costume sketch for a fanciful ballet production, with "canary chicks enclosed in eggs as in suits of armor." Next comes "Samuel Goldenberg and Schmuyle," a musical caricature of two Polish Jews, one rich and the other poor, as they haggle and quarrel.

The Promenade returns, changing the scene to France for a glimpse of the bustling "Market Place at Limoges" where the women are furiously disputing with one another; then on to an eerie view of the "Catacombs" in Paris by lantern light. This section, a variation on the Promenade, moves with mysterious harmonies. Above the score appears a cryptic inscription in the composer's hand: "With the dead in a dead language."

Figure 11-4 (above left). Victor Hartmann. *Chicks in Their Shells.* Costume sketches for the ballet *Trilbi.* Institute of Literature, Leningrad. Courtesy of Alfred Frankenstein.

Figure 11-5 (left). Victor Hartmann. *Bronze Clock in the Form of Baba Yaga's Hut.* Institute of Literature, Leningrad. Courtesy of Alfred Frankenstein.

Figure 11-6 (above right). Victor Hartmann. *Project for the City Gate of Kiev.* Institute of Literature, Leningrad. Courtesy of Alfred Frankenstein.

After another statement of the Promenade, "Baba Yaga," the wicked witch of Russian fairy tales, makes an appearance. She lives in a hut that stands on chicken's legs (Fig. 11-5). Musorgsky in this case is translating a design for a clock with medieval Russian decorative motifs into a whimsical witch's dance, and at the end she takes off on the traditional broomstick.

For his finale Musorgsky contrives a massive, majestic musical version of Hartmann's project for "The Great Gate of Kiev" (Fig. 11-6). The catalogue description reads in part, "The archway rests on granite pillars, three-quarters sunk in the ground. Its top is decorated with a huge headpiece of Russian carved designs with the Russian state eagle above the peak. To the right is a belfry of three stories with a cupola in the shape of a traditional Slavic helmet." Hartmann's design is elevated by Musorgsky to a truly monumental piece of musical architecture in which a pageantlike procession of chords, the solemn chanting of monks, and the ringing of bells are all heard in turn, as on a great festive occasion.

The exotic subjects and colorful orchestral scores of the Five found favor with Western audiences, and a lively cultural exchange of composers and performers was soon under way. Such stars as Berlioz and Liszt were popular with Russian audiences, while Anton Rubinstein and Peter Tchaikovsky scored notable successes in Germany, France, England, and America.

TCHAIKOVSKY

In contrast to the Five, Tchaikovsky, as well as his successors Alexander Glazunov, Alexander Scriabin, and Sergei Rachmaninov, stood apart by adhering to the international tradition, though they did not hesitate to utilize folk material when it suited their operatic, symphonic, or instrumental designs. The Five were by choice insular in orientation, and they largely stayed in Russia. Under Balakirev's guidance, the attitude of the group was progressive and pro-East rather than militantly anti-West. They saw the formalistic European tradition as a trend that had passed, while their dedication to new compositional freedoms and their championship of the Russian nationalist cause seemed to them the wave of the future.

Leaders in the conservative camp were the Rubinstein brothers, Anton and Nikolai, who were diametrically opposed to the feisty Five. Anton enjoyed an international reputation as a pianist in the Liszt tradition, and in 1862 he established the first Russian music academy of higher education, the St. Petersburg Conservatory. Following his brother's lead, Nikolai founded the Moscow Conservatory in 1866. Both institutions were modeled on Austrian, German, and French conservatories. They were tuition-free, boasted largely German faculties, and offered curricula that stressed the traditions of academic classicism.

The Five were quick to react. In 1862, Balakirev became a guiding force in the establishment of the St. Petersburg Free Music School, which featured a specifically Russian "progressive" point of view and a curriculum that gave wide latitude for personal expression.

The battle lines were drawn, and in the campaign propaganda for their European point of view, the Rubinsteins fixed on the promising young musician Peter Tchaikovsky. Like most of the Five, Tchaikovsky's early education had led him first into government service, but the Rubinsteins' influence steered him on a course toward a career as a composer and set him apart from the Five.

Tchaikovsky wrote in all the media current in late 19th-century music:

opera, symphony, symphonic poem, ballet, song, concerto. Two of the concertos, Opus 23 (1875), for piano in B-flat Minor, and Opus 35 (1878), for violin in D Major, are today among the most frequently performed works in the literature. He drew as often from Western writers for ideas for symphonic poems—Dante's *Francesca da Rimini,* Shakespeare's *Hamlet, Romeo and Juliet,* and *The Tempest,* and Byron's *Manfred*—as he did from Pushkin and other Russians for opera, song, and choral texts.

While the Rubinstein brothers claimed him for their Western-oriented cause, and his works at least on the surface stemmed from the European tradition, Tchaikovsky was at the same time an ardent admirer of Balakirev and salted his music liberally with quotes from Russian folk songs. As he confided in a letter to his patroness Nadezhda von Meck, "I grew up in the backwoods, saturating myself from earliest childhood with the inexplicable beauty of the characteristic traits of Russian folk song, so that I passionately love every manifestation of the Russian spirit. In short, I am *Russian* in the fullest sense of the word."

Much has been made of the relationship between Tchaikovsky's personal life and his music, since both were characterized by gripping heights and depths of emotional tension contrasting with moments of resolute hope. The vicissitudes of his life led to such a highly charged outpouring of emotional content in his music that it was difficult for him to contain it within the boundaries of traditional form. He wrote:

> All my life I have been much troubled by my inability to grasp and manipulate form in music. I fought hard against this defect and can say with pride that I achieved some progress, but I shall end my days without ever having written anything that is perfect in form. What I write has always a mountain of padding: an experienced eye can detect the stitching in my seams and I can do nothing about it.

As it turned out, his approach to form became more innovative than imitative. Aspects of Western formal principles are always present, but Tchaikovsky looks at such long-standing traditions as sonata form with a fresh eye and ear. As a result, he could say of his Fourth Symphony:

> In certain compositions, such as a symphony, the form is taken for granted and I keep to it—but only as to the large outline and proper sequence of movements. The details can be manipulated as freely as one chooses, according to the natural development of the musical idea. For instance, the first movement of [the] symphony is handled very freely. The second theme, which tradition places in a related major key, is here minor and unrelated. The Finale also deviates from conventional form.

Tchaikovsky consciously disavowed the idea that his music should be viewed programmatically, no matter what his personal involvement had been in writing it. Again, concerning the Fourth Symphony, he confessed in a letter, "Most assuredly my symphony has a programme, but one that cannot be expressed in words: the very attempt would be ludicrous. Should not a symphony reveal those wordless urges that hide in the heart, asking earnestly for expression?"

Always given to theatrical gesture in his music, Tchaikovsky's highly charged symphonic poems and symphonies are matched by several ballets, which for him proved to be a congenial medium in which music and dance combine to create a special theatrical experience. *The Nutcracker,* Op. 71 (1892), and *Swan Lake,* Op. 20 (1876), are an essential part of the international dance repertoire.

The Russian-European synthesis in Tchaikovsky can most easily be discovered in his symphonic works, where the romantic orchestra served him as the ideal vehicle for strong, passionate utterance. For his last effort in the medium, the Symphony No. 6 in B Minor, Op. 74 (1893), Tchaikovsky used the descriptive title "Pathétique," one suggested by his brother Modest for its connotations of suffering. The symphony has a classical four-movement structure, utilizing a typical large-scale, late romantic orchestration. One may assume the existence of at least the skeleton of a programme from notes made a year earlier as the work began to take shape in his mind: "The ultimate essence of the plan of the symphony is LIFE. First movement—all impulsive passion, confidence, thirst for activity. Must be short. Second movement love; third disappointments; fourth ends dying away (also short). (Finale DEATH—result of collapse)."

The symphony is Tchaikovsky's ultimate statement of tragedy, in which the individual is at the mercy of life's fateful forces. It is a work representing continuing struggle, in which musical subjects that give the appearance of inner exertion or of hope (upward movement) are inevitably turned to despair (downward movement). Overall, Tchaikovsky's subject matter is weighted toward the downward-moving motifs, several of which are built on descending adjacent notes, a device for tragic utterance that has been regarded as a teardrop figure since baroque times (see Ex. 11-9f).

The design of the first movement corresponds to that of a sonata form with a slow introduction, but structural clarity is somewhat obscured by Tchaikovsky's merging of subject-statement and developmental sections. The movement opens with a brooding adagio in E Minor, scored for bassoon solo with divided violas and basses. It presents thematic materials that forecast the movement's nervous first subject, which appears in B Minor, allegro non troppo (Ex. 11-9a). After an impassioned treatment of this subject, Tchaikovsky sets his second subject in the traditionally related key of D Major. The combination of a major key with muted strings creates a period of respite (Ex.

11-9b). The tempestuous development is a working out of the first subject, but there is a short quote from a chant taken from the liturgy of the Russian Orthodox Requiem, the text of which refers to blessed rest. After hope once more appears in the guise of a full-orchestra statement of the second subject, the movement dies away quietly in the key of B Major.

Example 11-9. Tchaikovsky. Symphony No. 6 in B Minor, Op. 74.

11-9a. First movement. Allegro non troppo, bars 1–2.

11-9b. First movement. Andante, bars 1–8.

Although the two central movements at first seem to carry on the tradition of the romantic scherzo, neither fulfills the traditional promise. The metric marking for the second movement is an unusual 5/4, and while it moves in a waltzlike manner, the charm and joy of the dance appear only at the surface level (Ex. 11-9c). The third movement contrasts two subjects, the first made from whirling staccato triplets, and the second a sturdy, resolute march (Exs. 11-9d, e). The metric signature of 12/8 allows for rhythms that may be either duple or triple, permitting the composer to intermingle the triplet- and march-rhythms. Combined with a progressive intensification in energy level throughout, this unity from diversity produces a movement that is both exciting and tension-filled. The aftermath of both movements leaves the impression that attempts to escape one's fate via public diversions, such as the ballroom or the parade ground, must in the end be futile.

While these movements express some attempts to face life and join in the struggle to succeed, by the final movement all energy has been spent. Revert-

11-9c. Second movement. Allegro con grazia, bars 1–4.

11-9d. Third movement. Allegro molto vivace, bars 1–4.

11-9e. Third movement, bars 71–74.

ing to the dark mood of the first movement, it presents two melodically related subjects. Both establish an attitude of grief with downward-plunging lines and diminished-seventh harmonies (Exs. 11-9f, g). Mercurial changes of mood are reflected through 28 tempo changes, far more frequent than in any of the other movements. The lugubrious close is marked by a considerable decrease in dynamic level from the passionate full-orchestra statement that immediately precedes it, and it features the same instruments that opened the first movement of the symphony: bassoons with divided violas, cellos, and basses. One by one the lines for violas, basses, and bassoons drop out, leaving only the cellos on a quiet dark B-minor chord. As strength finally drains away, the listener is brought full circle, from despair through hope and resolve, returning ultimately to despair.

11-9f. Fourth movement. Adagio lamentoso, bars 1–4.

11-9g. Fourth movement. Andante, bars 39–46.

In some ways, Tchaikovsky's final symphony may be considered his personal requiem. The "Pathétique" had its premiere in October of 1893, and within two weeks the composer was dead.

Romantic Culmination

WAGNER

Three major figures, each in his own way, led the romantic style to its resounding climactic point—Wagner, Verdi, and Brahms. The art of Richard Wagner matured later than that of his more precocious contemporaries, thereby granting him a fuller perspective of the entire romantic movement. His restless, searching eye and acute critical faculties perceived that, in spite of many inspired ideas and magnificent musical moments, none of the romanticists had yet achieved public acceptance on a broad scale. Neither, from Wagner's point of view, were their works finding permanent places in the concert repertory.

For Wagner, the music-making of Schubert was conducted on much too small a scale, even though his union of romantic poetry, vocal melody, and instrumental collaboration in the Lied contained artistic truth. Beethoven's only opera, *Fidelio,* for all its imposing music and clear-cut social message, had won only critical esteem. *Fidelio*'s four dramatic overtures, as well as those to the plays *Egmont* and *Coriolanus,* however, were orchestral poetry of the highest dramatic intensity; and to Wagner, Beethoven seemed to be on the right track when he brought vocal soloists and a chorus into his heroic Ninth Symphony.

Weber too had made a brave beginning toward establishing a national German opera, but his librettos lacked focus and he was still too close to the outworn idioms of Italian opera. (Nevertheless elements of Weber's *Euryanthe* would find their way into Wagner's *Lohengrin.*) In Wagner's opinion, Berlioz was a noble failure, but his original experiments in hybridizing drama, symphony, and song were commendable; and the themes and the erotic atmosphere of Berlioz's *Romeo and Juliet* were echoed in Wagner's *Tristan and Isolde.*

Schumann's secret-society romanticism, with its hidden meanings revealed only to the initiated, was perhaps too refined and obscure, but the cult idea had a certain attraction for Wagner. The success of Paganini and Liszt as performers had certainly been sensational enough, but personal virtuosity was a highly perishable commodity. Liszt's programmatic principles and symphonic poems, however, seemed sound enough. Chopin's urbane salon style was, for the master of Bayreuth, too restricted, but his chromatic harmony provided worthy colors for the Wagnerian palette. As he peered backward into history, the dramatic sweep of Shakespeare and the colossal baroque qualities of Handel also did not escape his notice.

In Wagner's view no one approach was sufficiently successful in itself, yet all contained enough vital elements to assure success if carefully selected, blended, and combined by him in the proper proportions. The production of those complete works of art, to be known as *music dramas,* was thus Wagner's calling as he saw it; and he set forth on his aesthetic mission with religious fervor and messianic dedication.

In 1840 this self-declared musico-dramatic successor to Shakespeare and Beethoven brought forth *Rienzi, Last of the Tribunes*, an operatic adaptation of Edward Bulwer-Lytton's historical novel. This was followed by *The Flying Dutchman* (1842), based on a poetic ballad by Heinrich Heine. From this point onward, however, Wagner was to be his own poet and playwright as well as composer and producer. *Tannhäuser* (1845) began the procession of national pageants founded on the lives of historical figures; its hero was a medieval Minnesinger, just as the hero of *The Mastersingers of Nuremberg* (1867) was to be the Renaissance cobbler-poet Hans Sachs. Both the early *Lohengrin* (1848) and the late *Parsifal* (1882) have the quasi-religious tone of medieval miracle plays. The four-opera cycle *Ring of the Nibelung* (1853–74) is derived from the early Germanic pagan epic *Nibelungenlied*; and *Tristan and Isolde* (1859) stems from an old Arthurian romance.

Wagner's mature music dramas are closer to symphonic procedure than to Italian operatic conventions, and he transfers the principal lyrical burden to the orchestra. This gives his operas the general effect of vast symphonic poems, augmented by visualized stage spectacle and a verbalized as well as vocalized running commentary on the orchestral action by the singers. Since the music runs on in an unbroken continuity, clearly defined arias, recitatives, and choruses would only interfere with the flow of drama; only rarely does a self-contained aria appear. The orchestra alone can provide unbroken continuity, and the voice parts are often melodically subordinate to this continuous orchestral flow. The vocal parts must necessarily grow out of the symphonic core or else be superimposed upon it. The process requires singers to project within the context of a continuous musical development which may have begun before they arrive on stage, and which may well continue after they have, in operatic parlance, "sung their say" and gone. While individual singers may not be given a "number" to sing, each will have a considerable time share of the drama.

In lieu of aria, recitative, or ensemble numbers, then, the essential convention in Wagnerian music drama is the *Leitmotif* (leading motif). In Wagner's usage, these short aphoristic fragments are designed to characterize individuals, aspects of personality, abstract ideas, or the singular properties of inanimate objects. The entities that can be so characterized are limited only by the composer's ability to conceive convincingly appropriate motifs. Wagner is astoundingly skillful in creating such musical-dramatic characterizations. The forthright, ringing sound of the motif for the invincible sword in the *Ring* cycle, for example, has a martial snap, buglelike melodic intervals, and the sharp, gleaming tone quality of the trumpet, all of which help to convey the image (Ex. 11-10a). The motif assigned to the dauntless Valkyrie Brünnhilde (Ex. 11-10b) differs considerably from the strange, mysterious harmonies that signify her transformation from godhood to womanhood (Ex. 11-10c).

Example 11-10. Wagner. *The Ring of the Niebelungs.* Motifs.

11-10a. Sword motif.

11-10b. Brünnhilde as Valkyrie.

These motifs, moreover, are by no means static entities, for they undergo constant symphonic development. The motif assigned to the hero, Siegfried, is broad and serious by way of its minor key (Ex. 11-10d). He is also represented as a youthful hunter by a jaunty horn call in 9/8 measure (Ex. 11-10e). As he develops into healthy manhood, the motif grows with him (Ex. 11-10f); and when he finally attains true heroic stature, it takes on the characteristics of a march, with full harmonies reinforced by the whole brass choir and roll-

11-10c. Brünehilde as mortal woman.

ing drums (Ex. 11-10g). At the time of his death, the heroic motif, now broken and shattered, appears in a minor key that deteriorates into an ambiguous diminished-seventh chord (Ex. 11-10h).

Given an extended array of motifs, the role of the orchestra as a participant in the drama is vastly enlarged. Furthermore, a motif sounded in the orchestra can recall an earlier event and clarify the motivation behind a given action on the stage. In a grand cycle like the *Ring,* which takes four evenings to unfold, events of the first night (*Das Rheingold*) may be recalled in the subsequent operas. Similarly, the orchestra can anticipate the future for the listener. At the end of the second evening (*Die Walküre*), when Wotan puts Brünnhilde to sleep on a mountain ringed with magic fire, promising that only an intrepid and fearless mortal will awaken and claim her, the orchestra announces for the first time the motif later associated with Siegfried as hero. In fact, at this point in the drama he is not yet born, but in the fatalistic predestination of mythology the musical prediction can safely be made.

Wagner's orchestra can also interpret states of mind not yet revealed by explicit action on stage. Thus when Siegmund and Sieglinde meet (Act 1 of *Die Walküre*), the orchestra makes clear that they are falling in love, though their conversation demonstrates that they themselves are not yet entirely aware of it.

Finally, the leading-motif system shows its particular power at the end of the cycle in *Die Götterdämmerung* (*The Twilight of the Gods*). In Act 3, when the mortally wounded Siegfried recalls his past, and in the subsequent orchestral funeral march, all the motifs previously associated with him pass by in biographical review: fate, his mother Sieglinde, the heroism of his paternal ancestors the Wälsungs, the sword (Ex. 11-10a), Siegfried's own motif (Ex. 11-10d), Siegfried as hero (Ex. 10-11g), and finally the women in his life—Brünnhilde (Ex. 11-10c) and Gutrune. The procedure thus lends itself to storytelling in music and at the same time summarizes the entire dramatic cycle.

If one were called upon to name the two greatest love stories of all time, the answer would surely have to be Shakespeare's *Romeo and Juliet* and Wagner's *Tristan and Isolde.* Wagner's libretto is based on a medieval Celtic legend. In modernizing and mounting it as a music drama, he allowed for a mini-

11-10d. Siegfried motif.

11-10e. Siegfried's horn call.

11-10f. Siegfried's manhood.

11-10g. Siegfried's heroic stature.

11-10h. Siegfried's death.

mum of stage action so that the story could unfold as a true psychological drama within the minds and hearts of its two principal characters. As he himself expressed it, the essence and spirit of the opera is "endless yearning, longing, the bliss and the wretchedness of love; world, power, fame, honor, chivalry, loyalty and friendship all blown away like an insubstantial dream; one thing alone left living—longing, longing unquenchable, a yearning, a hunger, a languishing forever renewing itself; one sole redemption—death, surcease, a sleep without awakening."

The overall form is like a triumphal arch resting on twin columnar supports—the pillar of the opening orchestral prelude on one side, and the concluding "Liebestod" ("Love Death") scene on the other (Exs. 11-11a, b). The connecting thread is the leitmotif, from its opening declaration of ineffable longing to its final pronouncement of spiritual transfiguration. This is one reason that the two have made a successful pairing in the orchestral concert repertory. Enclosed within these extremes, Acts 1 and 3 with their close thematic correspondences provide the framework for the keystone of the arch—the intimate, ecstatic love scene that illuminates the middle of Act 2. The form

Example 11-11. Wagner. *Tristan and Isolde.*

11-11a. Prelude, bars 1–11.

11-11b. End of opera.

thus shapes up in almost perfect symmetry, psychologically as well as musically.

The romance begins in the first act when Isolde, who is pledged to a loveless marriage with the old King Mark, reveals that she is hopelessly in love with Tristan. The high point of Act 2 comes with the lovers' nocturnal tryst and their rapturous love duet, which begins with the stillness of a long embrace, then gradually intensifies over a period of half an hour to an orgasmic climax.

Since the lovers can never be united in the earthly sphere, Wagner turns to a philosophical solution he discovered in Arthur Schopenhauer's book *The World as Will and Idea* (1819). Influenced by Eastern mysticism, Schopenhauer and Wagner saw the insatiable will as the never-ending force of human life. Only in the renunciation of selfhood can true freedom and final fulfillment be found. Tristan intones the inevitable consequences in the love duet:

> But should we die, we would not part,
> Joined forever without end, never waking,
> Never fearing, nameless there, in love unfolding,
> Each to each belonging, with love alone our life source!

Tristan is seriously wounded after King Mark discovers his supposed treachery, and in Act 3 he dies in Isolde's arms. So the true destiny of life becomes death, and the lovers may now be joined forever in a mystic mingling in the great beyond.

Isolde's "Liebestod" then becomes a retrospective re-enactment of their sexual union, which is now transmuted from sensuality to spirituality. As the successive waves of desire and passion mount ever higher and higher toward their consummation and climax, Isolde, completely enveloped by her inner vision, falls transfigured on Tristan's body. The orchestra then finally pronounces the motif of ineffable longing heard at the very beginning of the opera (see Exs. 11-11a, b).

Wagner's decision to shift the dramatic action to the inner emotional spectrum called for a new and unprecedented approach to the techniques of operatic composition. First, the orchestra assumed the dominant role, and *Tristan* accordingly is the most completely symphonic of all Wagner's operas. It has been likened to a monumental, four-hour-long symphonic poem, with the voices becoming an integral part of the orchestral fabric. A second important aspect of the score was the drastic reduction in the number of leitmotifs so that their development could be maximized to reflect all the subtle emotional changes, nuances, and tensions of the principal characters as the drama progresses.

Most important of all, however, the mysterious and metaphysical aspects of the story rendered traditional treatment of tonality and harmony unsuitable. With the diatonic major-and-minor system there is always a clear sense of starting and stopping, departure and return. Chromaticism, however, can suggest continuous transition from one emotional state to another, a constant drift that allows for all manner of subtle ambiguities, evasions, and endless yearnings that can never be satisfied. The nonstop motion and seemingly endless chains of chromatically altered chords keep the listener unsure, anticipating many different possibilities of resolution, while at the same time they provide the composer with a number of tonal directions from which to choose. Wagner thus pushed the tonal system of his century to its utmost limits, and the score of *Tristan* marks a decisive turning point in the history of harmony.

Recognizing the essential symphonic core of Wagner's writing, many composers after him decided to dispense with stage business altogether and wrote their dramatic music in other mediums. Anton Bruckner, Gustav Mahler, and Richard Strauss, for instance, translated the Wagnerian idioms into the programme symphony and symphonic poem. César Franck and Max Reger did the same in their organ and orchestral works. Hugo Wolf's "songs for voice and piano" show Wagner's impact on small-scaled music, and Arnold Schoenberg honored the master's techniques in chamber music like *Verklärte Nacht* (*Transfigured Night*) and orchestral song cycles such as the *Gurrelieder* (*Songs of Gurre*).

VERDI

From his first-produced opera of 1839 to his *Falstaff* of 1892, the incredible creative career of Giuseppe Verdi spanned a full and active 53 years. The principal works in between were: *Ernani,* 1844 (after Hugo); *Macbeth,* 1847, revised in 1865 (after Shakespeare); *Luisa Miller,* 1849 (after Schiller); *Rigoletto,* 1851 (after Hugo); *Il trovatore,* 1853 (after Lope de Vega); *La traviata,* 1853 (after Dumas, Jr.); *A Masked Ball,* 1859 (after Scribe); *Aïda,* 1871 (Ghislanzoni); *Messa da Requiem,* 1874; *Don Carlo,* 1867, revised in 1884 (after Schiller); *Otello,* 1887 (after Shakespeare). As the logical successor to Gioacchino Rossini and Vincenzo Bellini, Verdi quickly established himself as the principal proponent of Italian opera in the 19th century, and no serious challenges ever appeared on the horizon to contest the pre-eminence of his position.

La traviata (1853) will serve to illustrate Verdi's operatic writing. It was one of the first operas on a contemporary subject—thus anticipating Georges Bizet's *Carmen* (1875) by almost a quarter of a century—and its setting and emotional theme were neither historical nor heroic in the usual sense. Violetta, the heroine who has "lost her way," as the title delicately suggests, was in real life a well-known figure of the Paris demimonde. She had died five years before the younger Alexandre Dumas wrote his novel and play *Camille* (*La dame aux camélias*) based on her life. It was, in effect, a domestic tragedy about the conflict between middle-class morality and free love, and was not far removed from a moral tract on the sanctity of the home and family life. Alfredo's father, Germont, describes his son's romance with Violetta as "passion in its most terrestrial and human form," a violation of the prevailing belief that marriages presumably are made in heaven. Inevitably the woman with a past must yield to the woman with a future in holy wedlock. Verdi, however, sees only the poignant human situations amidst the moralistic platitudes.

The prelude to Act 1 of *La traviata* is a lyrical evocation that introduces the various themes to be associated with Violetta and her love for Alfredo. High pianissimo chords, sounded by the divided strings, cast a long, tragic shadow and lead to the shapely, descending melodic line that reveals the tender side of Violetta's nature, that of a lonely spirit longing for true love (Ex. 11-12a). Her more worldly, frivolous side is reflected in the succeeding passage, in which the melody of her inner self is now complemented by a rising staccato counterpoint (Ex. 11-12b), a bubbling, champagnelike obbligato that hints at the gala drinking song soon to follow. After Alfredo's declaration in Act 1, she wonders, in a two-part aria that reflects her mercurial changes of mood, whether it is possible to surrender to true love ("Ah, fors' è lui" ["Perhaps he's the one"]) or whether she should whirl her life away in gay waltzes ("Sempre libera" ["Always free"]). When she overhears Alfredo singing under her balcony window, the insistent, throbbing melody acquires a counterpoint of rising and falling scales, depicting her mounting emotional conflict (Ex. 11-12c).

Example 11-12. Verdi. *La traviata.* Act 1.

11-12a. Prelude, bars 18–25.

11-12b. Prelude, bars 29–31.

The prelude to Act 3 is a complement to that of Act 1, but provides a contrast in attitude. A variant of the warm, ardent opening phrase is now broken up into short, breathless fragments that hint of Violetta's mortal illness and foreshadow the inevitable tragic conclusion. Verdi with his true Latin temper-

11-12c. No. 6. Assai brillante, bars 29–33.

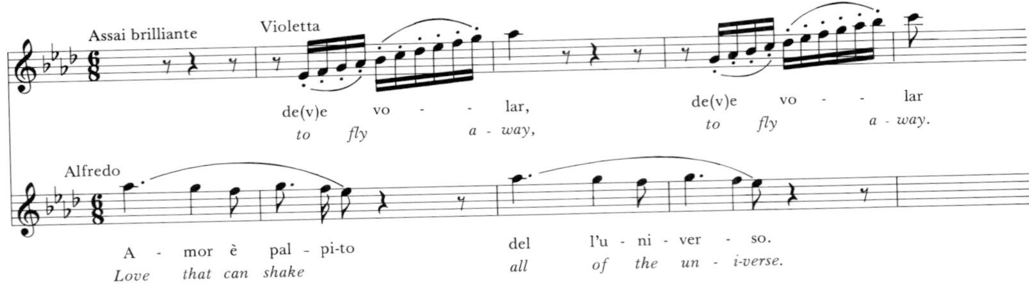

ament here lavishes the utmost care on one of his heroines, who are usually much more complicated characters than his heroes. The way in which he portrays human character through such manipulations of his melodic lines is truly one of the major miracles of music.

Since both Verdi and Wagner were born in 1813, and since they were the two dominant figures of 19th-century opera, their works have inevitably invited comparison. Much more than the Alps divided these two giants. When Verdi was questioned about the contrast between his sunny music and that of his darkly brooding northern colleague, he reportedly answered, "Do you think that under these skies I could have composed *Tristan* or the *Ring*?" Unlike Wagner, it would never have occurred to him to write abstruse philosophical essays or to indulge in abstract aesthetic speculation. "Not theory but music" was always his self-declared motto.

Verdi was also unconcerned with nature as such, and orchestral descriptive landscape interludes like Wagner's "Forest Murmurs" and "Siegfried's Rhine Journey" held little interest for him. As a Latin humanist, he always put human nature first and foremost, and in his operas this concern carries all before it. Since he always deals in basic human types rather than metaphysical personifications, his characters react to their dramatic conflicts with such basic emotions as love and hatred, or rage and repentance, rather than with philosophical discourses and high-flown histrionics. His heroines, moreover, die in bed from accidental or natural causes, not by mysterious "love deaths" or heroic self-immolations on funeral pyres. Verdi, with a long Italian musical tradition behind him, instinctively felt that the essential material of opera should be human voices, not musical instruments. Reacting to Wagner's operatic symphonic poems, he disarmingly observed, "Opera is opera, symphony is symphony." The Wagnerians, of course, likened Verdi's orchestra to an oversized guitar, but it is more articulate and provides more dramatic substance than his critics cared to admit. It is nonetheless true that Verdi's orchestra often plays a supporting role, and the singers invariably shoulder the weight of the drama.

BRAHMS

From his vantage point in the second half of the 19th century, Johannes Brahms, like Wagner, was able to view the strengths and weaknesses, the successes and failures of the earlier generation of romantic composers. Starting his artistic life as an ardent romanticist, and hailed as such by Robert Schumann, he later steered a more conservative middle course between the academic formalism of Louis Spohr and Mendelssohn on one side, and the romantic emotionalism of Schubert and Schumann on the other. From this position Brahms could admire the inspired lyricism of his romantic elders, while realizing at the same time certain limitations in their command of form and technical control. Brahms recognized too that spontaneous lyricism was not sufficient ground on which to base large symphonic edifices. He felt even Wagner had failed in attempting to build his monumental music dramas out of those miniature scraps of material known as leading motifs.

After a careful study of his classical Viennese predecessors—Haydn, Mozart, Beethoven, and Schubert—Brahms built his safe-and-sane style on a return to earlier formal principles. He also tried to escape the bias of the pianistic, orchestral, and operatic specialists by returning to the spirit of universalism that characterized his classic forebears. In his collected works one encounters piano music, songs, chamber music for all combinations from duos to sextets, concertos, orchestral overtures, serenades, symphonies, and a wealth of choral music. Even the modest genre of house music for amateur pianists, as evidenced in his sets of waltzes and the *Hungarian Dances,* was not neglected. Only the opera, in spite of his many projected and rejected plans, was left untouched.

Ein Deutsches Requiem (*A German Requiem*), for chorus and orchestra with soprano and baritone solo voices, is the most extensive and expansive of Brahms' works. It grew slowly and steadily in the mind of the composer for well over a decade, before achieving its final form in 1868. The work probably had a deep personal significance for Brahms, as it was begun shortly after the death of his friend and musical mentor, Robert Schumann, in 1856 and came to full fruition after the loss of his beloved mother in 1865. The *Requiem* is unique among oratorios both in its formal architecture and in its expressive content. In spite of the title, the work bears no resemblance to the traditional Roman Catholic Mass for the Dead. Neither does it have a narrative sequence to hold it together. Instead Brahms depends for unity purely on inner musical necessities and on the meditative and contemplative themes of the text, for which he drew freely from a variety of Old and New Testament sources.

The *Requiem* is the creation of a master composer who knew how to use all the formidable technical devices at his command to reinforce the desired expressive effects at just the right moments. While he was thoroughly conversant with the abstract play of instrumental forms, Brahms did not conceive the *Requiem* symphonically. Instead, he turned to simple song forms for the internal outlines of the individual movements, principally A B A with a coda. A study of the work will reveal his use of a broad range of technical parapher-nalia: pedal points; deceptive cadences; diatonic, modal, and chromatic harmonies; and wide contrasts of choral and orchestral color. These are all used only when needed to illuminate the imagery, intensify philosophical meditations, and deepen the expressive meaning. Fugues, for instance, are reserved for moments of affirmation and paeans of praise. The chorus sings in unison or octaves where proclamations or dire warnings occur. Static pedal points, where harmonic and contrapuntal passages hover over a stationary bass, convey a sense of arrival after moments of doubt, wandering, and searching; while beauty, hope and joy are delineated in highly lyrical phrases.

The orchestral opening raises a handsome melodic and harmonic arch of sound over a pulsating tonic pedal point (Ex. 11-13a). The instrumental hue is deliberately muted by the omission throughout the movement of the violins in favor of the violas, thus creating a somber background to usher in the words "Blessed are the sorrowful, for they shall find consolation" (Matt. 5:4). The theme of promise and aspiration in the melody is realized later as the text continues: "They that sow in tears shall reap in joy." On the word "joy" a quickening of the pulse occurs, as if the sun had suddenly appeared to dispel the clouds of gloom.

The second movement is an architectonic structure of rhythms, melodies, and contrasting tone colors. The text from Peter's First Epistle (1:24) reminds listeners of the certainty of death: "All mortals are like grass; all their splendor like the flower of the field; the grass withers, the flower falls."

Over the slow-motion Austrian Laendler in the bass, Brahms shapes a melodic line in the rhythm of a stately sarabande, while the kettle drums beat an insistent motif derived from military drumrolls that symbolized fate or the force of destiny for 19th-century audiences. The relationship between these rhythms and the text offers a sensitive instance of polyrhythmic procedure (see p. 000). Since the Laendler is a rustic dance, it represents the rank and file of humanity, whose numbers are as the blades of grass on the landscape. Consequently it is placed in the bass line, as befits the foundation of humanity. The 18th-century aristocratic sarabande rhythm, given to instruments on the high end of the score, depicts the textual reference to the grandeur of mankind and to its leaders as the flowers of the field. Finally, in the center of the design the fateful, funereal drumroll brings to completion the intertwining of social strata as they are made one in the face of death's inevitability. The dirgelike atmosphere of the movement is relieved occasionally by a note of tenderness and hopefulness in the choral parts, with their closely contained

Example 11-13. Brahms. *A German Requiem.*

11-13a. Movement 1, bars 1–9.

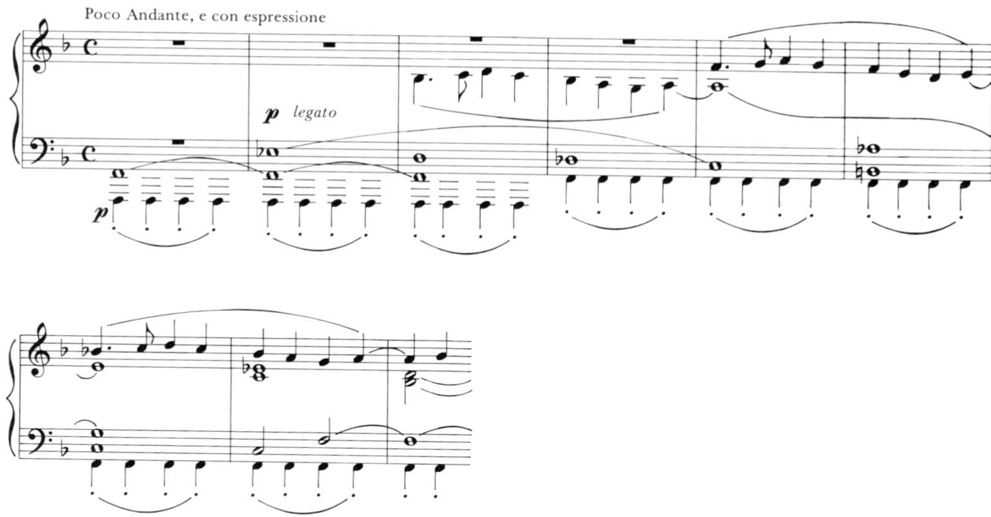

harmonies and stepwise melodic intervals that stand in contrast to the relentlessness and spaciousness of the orchestral sections. The somberness dissipates toward the end, with a buoyant fugue in quickened march time and in anticipation of "everlasting joy."

Questions about the presence of death in the midst of life, the brevity of man's days as measured against eternity, and the limits of human versus divine power are propounded by the baritone in the text of the third movement. Beginning in a bleak D Minor, the fluctuating key structure reflects uncertainty and vacillation by means of a chain of deceptive cadences as the questions are evaded and the answers not forthcoming. The anxiety mounts steadily until the final affirmation comes in the triumphant resolve of a D-major fugue over a pedal point, as the chorus intones the words "But the souls of the just are in God's hand" (Wisdom of Solomon 3:1).

The fourth and central movement is a psalmlike song of praise and longing for the "amiable tabernacles of the Lord." The writing is marked by a poised, symmetrical balance of descending and ascending lines in which the phrases of the orchestra and the chorus answer each other in mirrorlike, interweaving melodic inversions. The heavenly expansiveness appropriate for the "courts of the Lord" is suggested by modulations that move as far afield from the tonic of E-flat Major as the remote D-flat and C-flat Major before eventually returning to the original key.

The lyrical tenderness continues throughout the fifth movement with its idyllic soprano solo, but the gnawing uncertainties return in the sixth, where the groping in the darkness of vague tonalities leads to an allusion to the sound of the doomsday trumpet. Both Berlioz and Verdi in their requiem settings of the *Dies irae* called forth the dead from their graves with fire and brimstone fury, as the saved are separated from the damned amid general weeping and gnashing of teeth. Brahms, using more restrained treatment and brief understatement, achieves just as powerful and dramatic an expression. The brooding darkness of doomsday lifts, and the blinding light of truth and triumph dawns with the great C-major chorus, "Thou art worthy, O Lord, to receive glory and honor and power" (Rev. 4:11), set as a double fugue of Handelian proportions and majesty. This, together with the fugal choruses that conclude the second and third movements, was the style of writing that prompted Wagner's pointed jibe that Brahms was donning Handel's "Halleluia wig."

Following this climax of the grand design, there remain only the compassion and consolation of the seventh movement: "Happy are they who die in the faith of [the Lord]" (Rev. 14:13). A comparison of the first and last parts of the *Requiem* reveals that they are in close partnership. This seventh part opens with a broadly expansive melody derived from a phrase toward the end of the first part (Exs. 11-13b, c); and to underscore the cyclic principle of the work, Brahms closes the *Requiem* with a final statement of comfort and contemplation that is a repetition of the music that ended the first part (Exs. 11-13d, e).

11-13b. Movement 1, bars 145–46.

11-13c. Movement 7, bars 2–5.

In retrospect, the great seven-movement work may be seen to create a noble, majestic archway, in which motivic and textual correspondences constitute a thematic and spiritual linkage between the beginning and the end. Internally, the second and sixth numbers also correspond, in that both begin somberly in the minor mode and end with jubilant fugal choruses in the major. Indeed, some of the material of the second is quoted in the sixth, and both texts are concerned with the transitory nature of earthly life. The third and fifth sections both begin with solo voices and present a poetic link between moods of grief and consolation, the bonds of lamentation and the release of deliverance. The fourth, standing in the exact center of the design, becomes the keystone of the arch, with its lofty, lyrical contemplation: "How amiable are thy tabernacles, O Lord of Hosts!" (Ps. 84:1–2,4).

11-13d. Movement 1, bars 154–58.

11-13e. Movement 7, bars 162–66.

Brahms was a composer who could combine the musical forms of the baroque and classical periods with the progressive harmonies and expressive freedoms of romanticism. As a thinker he was convinced that the masters of the past had a more solid and viable command of their craft and hence could soar to greater heights than the composers of his time. Many of Brahms' most significant works show that he delved deep into the historic past. One notes the influence of Schütz, for instance, at some points in his *German Requiem,* and that of Handel (the large pedal-point choral fugue at the end of the third number) among others. His Double Concerto for Violin, Cello, and Orchestra harks back to the old concerto grosso, while the Fourth Symphony concludes with a masterly set of variations after the manner of baroque chaconnes and passacaglias.

The great shadow of Beethoven fell on Brahms as it did on all the musicians of the century, and set them to wondering who among them would write the "Tenth Symphony." Brahms thus became a lonely and somewhat anachronistic figure, perhaps daunted by the shadow of his great predecessor. His overenthusiastic champions probably hampered his career by mistakenly coupling his name with those of Bach and Beethoven. However, Brahms did succeed in breathing new life into the older forms. Just as Wagner precipitated the harmonic and tonality crisis of the 20th century, Brahms laid the foundation for the neoclassical return to formal clarity.

Romantic Synthesis

In retrospect, the romantic revolution was fought not so much against the classical tradition as against the codification of its principles into academic stereotypes. It was this frozen academicism that was taught in the conservatories, and the majority of bourgeois audiences found it satisfying, predictable, and reassuring. Romantic music was "modern music" to the ears of 19th-century audiences, and was performed infrequently in opera houses and concert halls. The repertory of the time was dominated by such conservative figures as Cherubini, Spontini, Hummel, and Reinecke, as well as a host of now-forgotten composers. Pianists, for their part, played pieces by Clementi, J. B. Cramer, Kalkbrenner, Czerny, and Moscheles, all now remembered principally as purveyors of finger exercises; and the programming of a work by Beethoven, Schubert, or Weber was a comparatively rare event.

Louis Spohr is a case in point. Since his music was always agreeable, well mannered, and at times quite elegant, he enjoyed wide success during his long lifetime. Occasionally he introduced innovations, but his mild-mannered radicalism was always carefully couched in conservative terms so that his audiences were rarely startled. Some of the real romantics—Weber, Berlioz, and Schumann—were at this time the wild men of music. Their revolt was never against genuine inspiration, whether of the past or present, but rather against slavish adherence to the formal stereotypes that the conservatories held up as models.

The romantic artists were capable of recognizing inspiration and genius, whether it appeared in their own or any other century. Berlioz was a lifelong champion of Gluck's cause, Mendelssohn and Schumann ardently admired J. S. Bach, while Weber and Chopin showed great respect for Mozart. However, when the academic mind reduced the works of C. P. E. Bach, Haydn, and Mozart to a series of pedantic textbook prototypes, the ire of the romantics was understandably aroused, and they led the revolt for formal freedom—not against Bach and Mozart, but against academic conventions and clichés.

The obverse side of this romantic coin shows some curious inconsistencies.

For example, an academic approach seems to have been present to some extent even in the most ardent romanticists. Berlioz, for instance, wrote a textbook treatise on orchestration; Mendelssohn was both the director of and a teacher at the Leipzig Conservatory; Chopin projected, but never finished, a "piano method." Robert Schumann, a Ph.D. from the University of Jena, was one of the founding editors of the Bach Society, the group of scholars who prepared the monumental publication of the master's complete works. Wagner was a voluble and verbose writer of didactic, theoretical, and critical essays.

In similar fashion the effusive romantic historical novels foreshadowed the development of modern historiography, just as the popularity of folklore and the ballads of the people led to the new science of philology. Admiration for the artistic monuments of the past pointed toward the solid disciplines of classical and medieval archaeology, while the "back to Bach" movement and the accompanying revival of interest in past musical periods was one of the first steps in building the foundation of modern musicology.

At the same time, the romantic revolt against rational and methodical thinking ushered in a new wave of emotional outpouring. The romantics, in other words, would have altered Descartes' dictum, "I think, therefore I am" to "I feel, therefore I am." Instead of emphasizing the general, universal, and suprapersonal, the romantics stressed the particular, transitory, and personal. Intuition superseded reason; the subjective was valued above the objective; and individual soliloquy replaced social dialogue. Out of this panorama of revivals of the past, the regressive and progressive tendencies of the time, and various evolutionary and revolutionary factors came the constellation of ideas that led to the new emotional spectrum and the new technical vocabulary for its expression.

In their respective ways and from their respective vantage points late in the romantic cycle, both Brahms and Wagner achieved their styles by effecting viable syntheses of the past while mapping out new musical territory for future composers to follow. Brahms, in addition to his prolific output in composition, was an authority on the works of J. S. Bach and an editor of the complete edition of that master's works. He was also a keen student of Handel and other baroque composers, as is revealed in his attraction to their contrapuntal techniques and forms. As a romanticist, he was likewise the logical successor to Schubert, Schumann, and Mendelssohn in his songs, piano pieces, and symphonies. He was hailed in his lifetime along with Bach and Beethoven as one of the "three B's." As both a romantic and a progressive composer, he paved the way for the forthcoming neoclassicism of the 20th century.

Wagner's music dramas brought together such diverse tendencies as romantic nostalgia for the past, Mozart's and Weber's efforts to establish a German operatic style, Berlioz's hybridizations of drama and symphony, the chromatic harmonies exploited by Chopin and Liszt, the modes of thematic transformation stemming from Beethoven's developmental techniques, and Liszt's thematic metamorphoses as exemplified in the symphonic poems. All were forged on the anvil of Wagner's particular genius into large-scale forms highly controlled and integrated, cast in a distinctive dramatic-musical language. He prophetically identified his goals as the "Art Work of the Future."

CHAPTER 12

From Romantic to Modern

Postromanticism

In the closing years of the 19th century, the earlier currents of romanticism had already run their course, and the later composers were casting about for new directions. Richard Wagner's radical musico-dramatic synthesis stood as a monument to progress, while Johannes Brahms satisfied defenders of the more traditional approach. Heated partisanship in public opinion led to a veritable war between radical and conservative styles. The battle line against the academicians was drawn, and the vivid orchestrations and psychological dramas of Richard Strauss's tone poems joined with Gustav Mahler's heaven-storming symphonic proclamations to conquer new territories.

The conflict continued with the expressionistic manner and 12-tone writing of Arnold Schoenberg, Alban Berg, and Anton von Webern. On the French ramparts, the symbolist movement broke new ground in both literature and music, while Claude Debussy's experiments in what he called "musical chemistry" led the vanguard of tonal impressionism.

Mahler once said that he and Richard Strauss were like two construction engineers tunneling into a mountain from opposite sides, planning to meet at some point in the middle. Mahler and Strauss were close contemporaries, colleagues in the musical life of Germany and Austria, and close friends. Both were outstanding exponents of the art song and the symphonic poem, both spoke and wrote in a post-Wagnerian orchestral language, and both had roots

Aubrey Beardsley. *The Dancer's Reward* (Salome with the head of John the Baptist), 1894. Pen and ink drawing. Courtesy of the George Arents Research Library, Syracuse University, Syracuse, New York.

Chronology

MUSICAL FIGURES

Germany and Vienna

Hugo Wolf	1860–1903
Gustav Mahler	1860–1911
Richard Strauss	1864–1949
Franz Lehár	1870–1948
Arnold Schoenberg	1874–1951
Anton von Webern	1883–1945
Alban Berg	1885–1935

France

Claude Debussy	1862–1918
Erik Satie	1866–1925
Maurice Ravel	1875–1937

Italy

Ruggero Leoncavallo	1857–1919
Giacomo Puccini	1858–1924
Pietro Mascagni	1863–1945
Ferruccio Busoni	1866–1924
Ottorino Respighi	1879–1936

Spain

Enrique Granados	1867–1916
Manuel de Falla	1876–1946

England

Edward Elgar	1857–1934
Frederick Delius	1862–1934
Ralph Vaughan Williams	1872–1958
Gustav Holst	1874–1934

Finland

Jean Sibelius	1865–1957

Russia

Alexander Scriabin	1872–1915
Sergei Rachmaninov	1873–1943

ARTISTS AND ARCHITECTS

James M. Whistler	1834–1903
Claude Monet	1840–1926
Léon Bakst	1866–1924
André Derain	1880–1954
Walter Gropius	1883–1969
George Grosz	1893–1959

HISTORICAL FIGURES

Hermann Helmholtz	1821–1894
Alma Mahler Gropius (*née* Schindler)	1879–1964
Manon Gropius	1917–1935

WRITERS AND DRAMATISTS

Jean-Paul Richter	1763–1852
Clemens Brentano	1778–1842
Ludwig J. Arnim	1781–1831
Joseph von Eichendorff	1788–1857
Charles Baudelaire	1821–1867
Stéphane Mallarmé	1842–1898
Paul Verlaine	1844–1896
Oscar Wilde	1854–1900
Albert Giraud	1860–1929
Maurice Maeterlinck	1862–1949
Richard Dehmel	1863–1920
Frank Wedekind	1864–1918
Romain Rolland	1866–1944
Pierre Louÿs	1870–1925
Colette	1873–1954
Hugo von Hofmannsthal	1874–1929
Hans Bethge	1876–1946
Isadora Duncan	1878–1927
E. M. Forster	1879–1970
Michel Fokine	1880–1942
Anna Pavlova	1885–1931
Tamara Karsavina	1885–1978
Mary Wigman	1886–1973
Vaslav Nijinsky	1890–1950

firmly planted in the style and outlook of German romanticism. Both were also aware of the significant developments in the literary and artistic worlds of their day. Strauss began his career as a Brahmsian conservative but soon converted to the Wagnerian spirit that marked his art songs and symphonic poems in the 1880s and 1890s. Mahler was also an early admirer of Brahms, and the master himself complimented Mahler's accomplishments as an orchestral and operatic conductor. At the same time, however, he declared Mahler's compositions to be too "revolutionary" for his taste.

As the careers of Strauss and Mahler progressed, quite as many differences as similarities became apparent. In his orchestral writing, Strauss inclined toward the shorter one-movement design of the symphonic poem, while Mahler extended the classical heritage of the multimovement symphonic design to unprecedented proportions. After mastering the skills of orchestral writing, Strauss allowed his strong theatrical instinct to lead him into the operatic field. Except for a lost youthful effort, Mahler never considered operatic writing. In their lifetimes, it was Strauss who first commanded international acclaim as a composer, while Mahler's reputation rested mainly on his virtuoso conducting. Almost half a century after Mahler's death in 1911, his works finally won a secure place in the regular symphonic repertory.

Composers of the late 19th century faced an aesthetic crisis. In the realm of abstract music, tonality and form had entered new stages of complexity, while instrumental advances and ever-larger orchestras encouraged greater demands on performers and invited the use of literary programmes to exploit elaborate innovations in tone color.

STRAUSS

The Bavarian-born Richard Strauss built his career as composer and conductor around the symphony orchestra, conceived by him as a single, immense virtuoso instrument. Expanding on Liszt's concept of thematic metamorphosis as exemplified in his symphonic poems, Strauss created a series of tone poems in the 1890s that exacted higher levels of instrumental mastery from orchestral players than ever before. A composer with an extraordinary ear for orchestral color, he quickly recruited a large public following, and at age 35 was one of the most celebrated composers in the Western world.

The tone poems of Strauss were scored for as many as 85 performers, and from these vast orchestral palettes he painted subjective programmatic canvases. For his programmes, Strauss drew on a wide range of subjects. Some were tonal depictions of fictional characters, such as *Don Juan* (1888), *Macbeth* (1890), *Till Eulenspiegel* (1895), and *Don Quixote* (1897). Aesthetic and philosophical concepts captured his attention for a period, resulting in *Tod und Verklärung* (*Death and Transfiguration,* 1889) and *Also sprach Zarathustra* (*Thus Spake Zoroaster,* 1896). His home life was the subject of the *Sinfonia domestica* in 1905, and he undertook a mountain travelogue in *Eine Alpensinfonie* 1913. Though designated by Strauss as symphonies, the last two are in fact extended tone poems.

While each of these works represents the composer's personal interpretation of a topic, the tone poem *Ein Heldenleben* (*A Hero's Life,* 1898) shows most clearly the self-involvement of Strauss in his musical works. The tone poem contains six contiguous sections: "The Hero" (1); "The Hero's Adversaries" (2); "The Hero's Lady" (3); "The Hero's Battlefield" (4); "The Hero's Works of Peace" (5); and "The Hero's Retirement from the World and Final Fulfillment" (6).

The hero is introduced as a larger-than-life figure through a broad, sweeping subject in the key of E-flat Major (Ex. 12-1a). Strauss made no secret of the fact that his brand of heroism was akin to that of Beethoven's "Eroica" Symphony, a work built upon that heroic key. The second section provides a strong contrast of subject material, in which the great hero's adversarial critics are presented as nit pickers and grumblers (Ex. 12-1b). The hero's lady now appears (Ex. 12-1c). In the words of the composer, she is "very complex, very feminine, a little perverse, a little coquettish . . . at every minute different from how she had been the moment before." This captivating creature is portrayed by means of a violin solo of virtuoso design, and the section concludes with a love scene between the two protagonists.

Example 12-1. R. Strauss. *A Hero's Life.*

12-1a. Bars 1–9. Hero motif.

12-1b. Etwas langsamer, bars 1–3 and 5. Critics' motif.

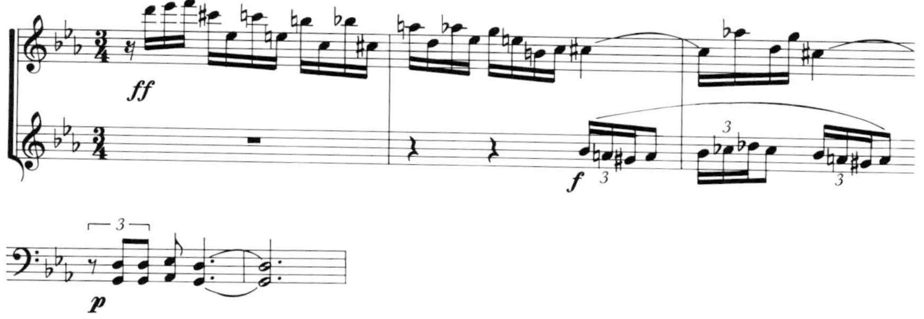

Abruptly, a trumpet signals the hero's call to battle, and he enters the fray against his enemies (the critics from section 2) with bravado. Expanding and alternating previous motifs, Strauss recounts the battle, as the hero's theme

12-1c. Erstes Zeitmass, bars 31–36. Hero's Lady motif.

is submerged beneath that of the critics, only to surge again into the foreground. From time to time the recollection of his love gives him strength, and he finally emerges triumphant through an expanded restatement of the opening bars of the tone poem.

With the defeat of his enemies, the hero is now free to continue along his valiant path, and in a position to do great deeds unimpeded. It is only here that the alert listener discovers the composer's true intent, for the "works of peace" consist of a series of quotations from his own earlier compositions. The hero, then, is none other than Strauss himself; his companion represents Strauss's wife, Pauline; and the hero's enemies are those critics who have dared to find fault with the master's compositions.

In his earlier tone poem *Tod und Verklärung,* Strauss had not only used the word *transfiguration* (*Verklärung*) in the title, but had devoted the last section of the work to a description of the central character's withdrawal from the world after a period of suffering and struggle with death. For the final section of *Ein Heldenleben,* Strauss once again turns to the concept of transfiguration. The hero, having completed his great works, is now free to consider renunciation of the world and retirement. The concluding segment recalls some of the characters and situations of the drama, before drawing to a close with a feeling of fulfillment and a return to the tonic key of E-flat Major.

Strauss himself did not retire from the world on completion of this tone poem; rather, he transferred his activities from the sphere of the concert hall to that of the opera house. In doing so, he did not renounce the extravagant orchestral effects typical of the tone poems, but placed them in the service of singers and of stage action. The operas he wrote during the early years of the 20th century may be regarded as staged and sung tone poems, for which his post-Wagnerian orchestral resources provide the dramatic foundation.

The first important opera Strauss wrote was *Salome* (1905), a faithful setting of the text of Oscar Wilde's grim and grizzly one-act play. In this opera, as well as in *Elektra* (1908), inner emotions drive major characters to actions condemned by society and considered to be against nature and accepted moral values.

Wilde's Salome is a pampered, amoral, egocentric, oversexed adolescent. She is presented as the symbol of a decadent society, and her unconscionable behavior implies an alienation from traditional societal values that can only result in death. With passions running high, relationships between the major characters form a circle of unfulfilled, frustrated desires. Salome's stepfather, the tetrarch Herod, lusts after her, while she in turn exhibits a blind, unholy passion for the prophet John the Baptist. The Baptist, who has been imprisoned by Herod, takes little notice of the daughter because he is preoccupied with Salome's mother, Herodias, whose immoral lifestyle he denounces unceasingly. This weird quartet sets aflame unresolvable conflicts that result in the death of both the Baptist and Salome, while forecasting ruin for Herod and Herodias. Wilde's sensational version of the sketchy biblical story tossed all the elements into a psychological cauldron and served up draughts of sensual desire, death, and horror in a witches' brew that is not for the squeamish. The explosive score by Strauss intensifies the emotional narrative to a point that can bring an audience to a fever pitch.

In both *Salome* and *Elektra,* Strauss was responding to the new interest in psychological abnormality and Sigmund Freud's clinical research. The previously hidden realms of the subconscious mind were being laid bare, revealing dark, devious urges; and new motivations for human behavior were being proposed. In both operas, Strauss pushed the frontiers of music toward *expressionism,* a style characterized by hyperemotionalism, hidden terrors, and hallucinatory images. These traits were to appear in much early-20th-century music, especially in the works of Arnold Schoenberg and Alban Berg.

The sensational, if scandalous, successes of *Salome* and *Elektra* were gratifying, but Strauss felt that he had gone about as far as he wished with violent subject matter and emotionally expressive music. His intuition told him that it was time to re-examine the resources of the past, and his next operatic project attempted to recapture the atmosphere of the golden age of Mozart. Searching for an appropriate vehicle, he joined forces with the German poet Hugo von Hofmannsthal. The result of their labors was a fictional exploration of manners and morals in Vienna of the late 18th century—*Der Rosenkavalier* (*The Cavalier of the Rose,* 1910). For this opera, Strauss curbed the exuberance of his orchestra somewhat and created an admixture of characters representing the old nobility, new bourgeois wealth, and sharp-witted conspirators, resulting in a persuasive confection topped with musical spun sugar and whipped cream.

During the last 40 years of his life, Strauss concentrated on refining his techniques still further. Another series of operas on classical Greek subjects, among them *Ariadne auf Naxos* and *Dafne,* called for chamber-orchestra accompaniments and exquisitely crafted parts for his soprano heroines. Near the end of his life he wrote five "final" songs, four of which were published after his death as *Vier letzte Lieder* (*Four Last Songs*). The concluding song ends with a verse that allowed the world-weary composer to sigh musically with the poet Eichendorff:

> O wide, still peace,
> So deep in the glow of evening,
> How weary we are of wandering—
> Is this perhaps death?

Strauss gives the orchestra the final word. As it serenely intones the main subject from his tone poem of 60 years earlier, *Death and Transfiguration,* the song group drifts quietly to its conclusion.

MAHLER

Liszt, Wagner, and Strauss had all developed conducting skills as a direct means of controlling the medium through which their ideas most effectively reached audiences. Gustav Mahler, however, became the first major composer to make the role of conductor his principal career. Though Viennese-trained in composition, Mahler came up through the ranks as a conductor of opera until he secured the influential post of music director of the Vienna Opera, where he became renowned for his interpretations of Gluck, Mozart, Beethoven, and Wagner. While his international fame rested on his conductorial talents, Mahler composed prodigiously during his summer holidays. Though his scores did not find wide favor in his lifetime, the monumental symphonies and song cycles have now secured a firm place in the international concert-hall repertoire.

Like Strauss, Mahler chose the symphony orchestra as his most sympathetic medium, and he scored his works for massive orchestral forces. Yet the end product surprisingly often focuses on smaller instrumental subdivisions with fine-grained textures that enrich the color palette of the orchestra. While Strauss viewed his symphonic characterizations and situations from without, Mahler wrote psychologically oriented symphonic movements that sprang from his inner experience. For Mahler, the symphony, often including solo voices and chorus, became the one medium that could express the totality of his highly personal universe.

Mahler's music derived from highly diverse sources. In his predilection for folklore, poetry, and song he followed in the footsteps of Brahms, who had arranged a large number of folk songs. Mahler also drew widely for his texts from Arnim and Brentano's 1808 anthology of folklore, *Des Knaben Wunderhorn* (*Of the Boy's Magic Horn*), a collection of poetry covering a four-century period. From these fertile sources Mahler was able to capture a certain sense of the idyllic and innocent in an age when the world was still young. In typical postromantic fashion, Mahler looked to nature for inspiration, and he also introduced religious and metaphysical themes into many of his scores. In his final song cycle, he turned to the Orient, mirroring its rejection of human striving and will in search of a spiritual resolution in a better afterlife.

Tonally, Mahler subscribed to the chromatic idiom of Wagner, with a special melodic-harmonic emphasis placed on the interval of the perfect fourth. Formally, he espoused an expanded application of the traditional four-movement sonata design.

The important groundwork laid by Liszt and Wagner in the methods of transforming musical motifs became the foundation on which postromantic composers shaped their musico-philosophical messages. Mahler's opulently elongated symphonic compositions, conceived programmatically and traversing widely divergent musical paths, stand as prime examples. Moments of quiet mystery alternate with raucous, frenzied outbursts; waltzes and marches are transformed into country Laendler and burlesque funeral processions; while apocalyptic visions conjured up by massive orchestral sonorities are countered by antic street tunes that are often mocking, ironic, or banal. From his First Symphony onward, Mahler continually drew upon song for inspiration. His cantata *Das klagende Lied* (*Song of Lamentation*), as well as certain oratoriolike symphonic movements, give evidence of an evolutionary connection with Beethoven's Ninth and Liszt's *Faust Symphony.*

Mahler's First Symphony (1889), with its forthright programmatic scheme, was initially conceived as an extended five-movement symphonic poem and given the designation "Titan," after a novel by the German romantic writer Jean-Paul Richter. It was originally divided into two sections. The first part contained movements entitled "From Days of Youth," "A Chapter of Flowers (Blumine)," and "Under Full Sail (Scherzo)." The second was made up of "The Hunter's Funeral Procession (Funeral March in the Style of Callot)" and "From Inferno to Paradise (Allegro furioso)." After several revisions, Mahler dropped the "Flowers" movement in favor of a four-movement design with a more generalized program dealing with the life cycle of birth, life, death, and heavenly transcendence.

The symphony took shape at the same time Mahler was working on a symphonic song cycle, *Lieder eines fahrenden Gesellen* (*Songs of a Wayfarer,* 1885). This cycle, with texts chiefly by Mahler himself, paralleled the subject matter of several earlier romantic cycles of Schubert, Schumann, and others, all of which recount the fate of a young man who has loved and lost, then sets out to wander alone in the world seeking solace in nature and ultimately in death.

Mahler's concern with transformation of song into symphony is clearly in evidence. The opening movement of the First Symphony is in sonata form. It begins with the suggestion of awakening spring and introduces several motivic fragments—including birdcalls—that shortly mature into full thematic entities. From one of them grows the main subject, taken from the second song of the abovementioned cycle, "Ging heut' Morgen übers Felds" ("Going this morning into the fields"), giving voice to the joys of a pastoral spring morning (Exs. 12-2a, b). A bright scherzo, "Under Full Sail," follows; it is an extended, waltzlike Laendler with a lilting trio section.

Example 12-2. Mahler.

12-2a. Songs of a Wayfarer. No. 2, bars 3–9.

12-2b. Symphony No. 1 in D Major. First movement, bars 63–69.

Bruno Walter, a conductor and Mahler's friend, described the third movement as "a spiritual reaction to a tragic event translated into music," and referred to the "spectral creeping of the canon." A woodcut by the 19th-century artist Moritz von Schwind, *How the Animals Snared the Hunter,* is thought to have been Mahler's source of inspiration (Fig. 12-1). The rejoicing of animals over the dead hunter is transformed into an ironic funeral march with a lugubrious burlesque of the children's round *Frère Jacques,* expressed as a D-minor canon for bass viol and bassoon (Ex. 12-2c). The central section quotes directly from the fourth of the *Gesellen* songs, "Die zwei blauen Augen" ("The two blue eyes"), a passage in which the poet accepts his fate and bids the world farewell (Exs. 12-2d, e).

The final movement is marked "Stormily agitated" and is concerned with symbolic thoughts of death and resurrection. It also reflects an extreme view of postromanticism, characterized by mercurial changes of mood and successive transformations of motivic materials. Mahler described the introduction as "a clap of thunder followed by a sudden outcry from a deeply wounded heart." Out of this controlled chaos emerges a two-part Day of Judgment motif (Ex. 12-2f) that grows into a fully developed subject (Ex. 12-2g). The subject is worked out in stormy fashion, and as the whirlwind subsides, a few moments of transcendent calm give rise to the second subject, long-lined and lyrical (Ex 12-2h). The development emphasizes the drama between subject materials, alternately stormy and peaceful. The appearance of the motif transformed into D Major signals the Resurrection section (recapitulation), and the introduction of a new subject that is closely related to Handel's *Messiah* chorus "And He shall reign for ever and ever" (Exs. 12-2i, j). Orchestral scoring of the subject suggests the ringing of bells. After a recollection of the spring awakening that opened the symphony, the first and the resurrection subjects are worked into a triumphant close.

Succeeding symphonies and song cycles underscored the composer's continuing concerns with innocence, death, and the afterlife. Mahler's superstitious nature, however, gave him pause after concluding his monumental Eighth Symphony, the "Symphony of a Thousand," since Beethoven, Schubert, Bruckner, and Dvořák had all expired after completing their ninth symphonies. Instead, he produced a symphonic song cycle entitled *Das Lied von der Erde* (*Song of the Earth,* 1909). It is scored for full orchestra with tenor and either alto or baritone soloists. Texts for the six sections are based on 8th-century Chinese poetry rendered into German by Hans Bethge and further modified by Mahler.

For the opening movement the composer chose a poem of three verses, each ending with the words "Life is dark, as is death." In the closing movement, Mahler set two poems, separated by a long orchestral interlude. The first, "In Erwartung des Freundes" ("Awaiting a Friend"), paints a placid landscape at sundown. The solitude is broken by a cry: "Why have you left me alone so long?" After a long orchestral interlude, the tone of "Der Abschied des Freundes" ("A Friend's Farewell") becomes one of resignation: "He asked him where he was going and why it had to be." Recent personal tragedies in Mahler's life lead one to speculate that the poet's answer might have been his own: "I am seeking rest for my lonely heart. . . . Still is my heart, it awaits its own hour. The beloved earth everywhere blossoms with Spring green anew!

Figure 12-1. Moritz von Schwind. *How the Animals Snared the Hunter,* 1850. Woodcut. By permission of the British Library, London.

12-2c. Symphony No. 1 in D Major. Third movement, bars 1–12.

12-2d. Songs of a Wayfarer. No. 4, bars 41–44.

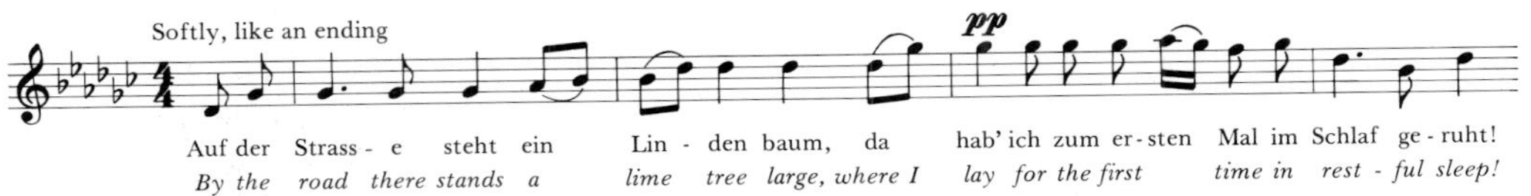

12-2e. Symphony No. 1 in D Major. Third movement, bars 86–89.

Everywhere and forever is a blue-lit vista on the horizon. Ever . . . and forever." The music for this section is based in part on the Oriental pentatonic scale (Ex. 12-3). Harmony, melody, and rhythm are fused, allowing the work to slip off into infinity.

Mahler spent much of the last four years of his life in the United States, first as conductor at the Metropolitan Opera, then as director of the newly reorganized New York Philharmonic Orchestra. During that period he completed his Ninth Symphony; but fate decreed that, like his four great symphonic predecessors, he would die while still at work on his Tenth Symphony.

12-2f. Symphony No. 1 in D Major. Fourth movement, bars 7–8 and 20–21.

12-2g. Symphony No. 1 in D Major. Fourth movement, bars 55–62.

12-2h. Symphony No. 1 in D Major. Fourth movement, bars 176–90.

12-2i. Handel. *Messiah.* "And He shall reign," bars 1–3.

12-2j. Symphony No. 1 in D Major. Fourth movement, bars 679–82.

Example 12-3. Mahler. *Song of the Earth.* "A Friend's Farewell," ending.

Expressionism and the Second Viennese School

The trio of early-20th-century composers in Vienna—Schoenberg, Berg, and Webern—has been called by some historians the Second Viennese School, implying a resurgence of the earlier stellar period of Haydn, Mozart, Beethoven, and Schubert. Collectively the works of this extraordinary artistic trio had decisive consequences for an important phase of 20th-century music: *expressionism.*

SCHOENBERG

Arnold Schoenberg was a serious composer, painter, poet, author, theorist, and teacher, whose music involved him in swirling controversy throughout his lifetime. A deep concern for the future direction of music led him through a carefully calculated series of steps, by which he brought 20th-century listeners to a new experience of tonality.

Throughout his career, Schoenberg acknowledged the influence of two composers who may appear to be at polar opposites of the musical scale: Wagner and Brahms. Wagner, on the one hand, was didactic and revolutionary in his controversial proclamations and his exclusive focus on music in a theatrical context. Brahms cultivated a conservative style of absolute music built on the traditions of Bach and Beethoven, and he wrote no music for the stage. Each in turn was an inheritor of Beethoven's mantle of prophecy, and each found a separate manner of dealing with the Beethovenian legacy. Each, like Beethoven, chose the motif as the basic unit for organic musical growth. This emphasis on controlling motivic structures became the crucial force in Schoenberg's efforts to discover a way to impose order on his materials while allowing for a maximum of expressionistic content. Like Wagner, Schoenberg concentrated on dramatic and programmatic elements in his early works; like Brahms, he emphasized abstract, nonprogrammatic writing in his mature years.

Schoenberg's first important composition appeared in 1899, the string sextet *Verklärte Nacht* (*Transfigured Night,* Op. 4). It was a chamber-music tone poem inspired by the expressionist poetry of Richard Dehmel. Its programmatic basis profited from advanced Wagnerian chromaticism, night imagery, and the idea of transfiguration. It also portrayed the domination of the metaphysical over the physical, and the power of love to transcend nature.

For Dehmel's poem, Schoenberg chose not the multicolored diversity of the orchestra but the intimacy of a string sextet, probing the poet's expressionistic undercore with scalpel-like precision: the cold moonlit night, the inner conflict of a woman whose primal need for motherhood had driven her into the arms of a man she did not love; her sorrow and fear as she reveals to the man she does love that she is with child; and the moving warmth of his reply, suggesting that their love will transfigure the child she carries to make it his offspring as well.

During the following decade Schoenberg covered great distances in his theoretical speculations. In 1911 he published a treatise, *Harmonielehre* (*Study of Harmony*), that represented his current views on the subject of tonality and chromaticism. Specifically disavowing old and new tonal systems, Schoenberg encouraged his contemporaries to avoid all the harmonic devices that audiences had come to expect. These included, of course, the very foundation stones of functional diatonic harmony: the intervals of the octave and fifth, major and minor triads, dominant seventh chords, and tones moving melodically in such a way as to suggest the diatonic scale. Schoenberg considered this point of view less as a rejection of traditional harmonic practices than as a logical step forward, building upon tonal innovations introduced by Wagner. This phase of Schoenberg's career is described as *atonal* (without tonality), i.e., without reliance on diatonic tonality. In his *Harmonielehre* he stipulated:

> We have progressed so far today as to make no more distinction between consonance and dissonance. . . . I believe that in the harmony we modern composers use, the same laws will ultimately be recognized as in the harmony of the old masters, only correspondingly extended, more generally conceived. I believe that a further development of harmonic doctrine is not to be expected at present. In composing I decide only in accordance with feeling, with a feeling for form. Everything else is excluded. Every chord that I set down corresponds to an urge of my need for expression, and also perhaps to an urge of an inevitable but unconscious logic in the harmonic construction.

It is not coincidental that Schoenberg's music from the first decade of the century often relied on psychologically oriented literary sources and seemed to emanate from the subconscious. In the following year, this "need for expression" produced his most important atonal composition, *Pierrot lunaire* (*Moonstruck Pierrot,* 1912). This expressionistic work is a setting of 21 verses from a set of 50 by the Belgian poet Albert Guiraud, grouped into three divisions of seven songs each. Guiraud's poetry is a reflection of the long-standing expressionist interest in the moon, lunatic madness, and the psychological ramifications of dreams. Pierrot, the sadly comic "hero," was a character taken from the old commedia dell' arte, in which the poetic settings neither tell a story nor attempt clear character delineation. Poor Pierrot, as always, is plagued by unfulfilled yearnings and forced into all sorts of adventures against his will. The performing forces are intimate: a vocal part for a singing actress described as "recitation," and a chamber ensemble of eight instruments. Selecting from these, Schoenberg chose a separate combination for each poem in *Pierrot.*

The difficulties in the execution of *Pierrot* were so great that a group led by Schoenberg, who had performed the work in public many times, held 200 rehearsals for the first recording of the work. The stumbling block for performers—and for listeners—was Schoenberg's new and expressionistic use of the human voice, one that he labeled *Sprechstimme* (speaking voice), a type of vocal declamation that combines qualities of both speech and song.

The vocal line of *Pierrot* seems at first glance to consist of traditional melodic phrases. But some notes are written as small circles and others are marked with a small cross in the stem (Ex. 12-4). These notes tell the performer to declaim the text within the general pitch area of the note so marked. The contour of the melodic phrase is to be honored, but the notated pitches need not be sounded as written. This technique opened up a wide interpretive base for the soloist, encouraging the concept of acting with the voice, while simultaneously enhancing the concept of expressionism as planned artistic distortion.

Black, shadowy giant moths
Kill the sun's brightness.
A closed book of magic,
The horizon reclines—secluded.

Expressionist poetry, painting and music often center on terror, and this poem deals with Pierrot's fear of darkness. The subtitle, "Passacaglia," implies regularity of subject pattern. "Night" is scored for cello, bass clarinet, and piano, with the vocal recitation in a low register.

One of Schoenberg's stated aims in atonality was the "emancipation of dissonance" from its role as a point of tension that required consonant resolution, and there is nothing in the musical settings of the *Pierrot* poems that relies on traditions of diatonic consonance. In 1912, Schoenberg's atonal vision shocked many, and there were those who thought him as mad as Pierrot. Time has shown him to be eminently sane, and the songs have taken on classical status and are much admired in contemporary musical circles.

Schoenberg's path to tonal emancipation covered three phases. During his early tonal phase, he immersed himself in the theories and sounds of Wagner and absorbed his predecessor's careful use of dissonance as an emotional device. During the second, the atonal phase, he attempted to remove all outward manifestations of diatonic tonality, but without having a specific plan for its replacement as a generator of form. The third phase introduced one of the most important developments in 20th-century music, that of *12-tone,* or *serial,* composition.

For seven years, Schoenberg worked on the formulation of a new, unified system that would replace the tonal organization of diatonic harmony. That

Example 12-4. Schoenberg. *Moonstruck Pierrot.* No. 8, "Night," bars 1–10.

revolutionary system, through which he hoped to transform 20th-century music, has been variously described as *12-tone, dodecaphonic, serial,* and *tone-row* writing. In his *Method of Composing with Twelve Tones Related Only to Each Other,* Schoenberg proposed several epoch-making concepts. The first was based on his conclusion that, since diatonic tonal relationships within the octave were no longer a viable means on which to build a composition, all 12 tones within the octave must be considered as equals and none was to be given preference. Furthermore, since no diatonic relationships were used, a reliance on chords built on the interval of the third (triadic harmony) was no longer admissible.

In place of one or more subjects for a given composition, a composer could now use all 12 notes within the octave, arranging them in any order. In putting together the series of 12 notes for any given composition, the composer could choose to include elements of melody, harmony, tone color, and rhythm as motifs for expansion and development. This *tone row,* or *series,* providing the core of material for the composition, was to be stated at the outset. From that point onward, the composer drew exclusively upon the row—both as a whole and in parts—as the substance from which the composition was constructed. Harking back to older contrapuntal procedures, certain permutations of the row were encouraged: *retrograde* (backward), *inversion* (upside down), and *retrograde inversion* (backward and upside down; see Chart 12-1).

Schoenberg realized early that his path would not be an easy one either for his or for his listeners, and that his compositions might never reach the average citizen. In his book *Style and Idea,* he wrote: "There are relatively few people who are capable of understanding what music has to say on a purely musical level. There are always many who provide what is suitable for the needs of our time in a much more accessible form than can be offered by someone who already belongs to the future."

As his works became more elusive and difficult for the musical public at large to understand, Schoenberg garnered support from a limited number of dedicated musicians and knowledgeable amateurs who had the training to comprehend his techniques and goals. To assist readers of his complicated scores, Schoenberg introduced the symbols Ɦ and Ɲ . *Hauptstimme* (principal voice) and *Nebenstimme* (subordinate voice) were used to indicate where the focus of the listener or performer should be. Where these designations occurred, other voices were to be considered as accompaniment.

The new method of composition was introduced in a piano work that looked both backward—in Brahmsian fashion to the 18th-century keyboard suite—and forward to the serial future. The *Suite for Piano* (Op. 25, 1924), is a five-movement work utilizing traditional dance forms from the baroque dance suite. Each grows from the same tone row, but no two draw on the same version of the row (Chart 12-1). In Example 12-5, three permutations of the row are shown. Example 12-5a posits the row within the opening two mea-

CHART 12-1. SCHOENBERG: SUITE FOR PIANO, OPUS 25 (TONE ROW)

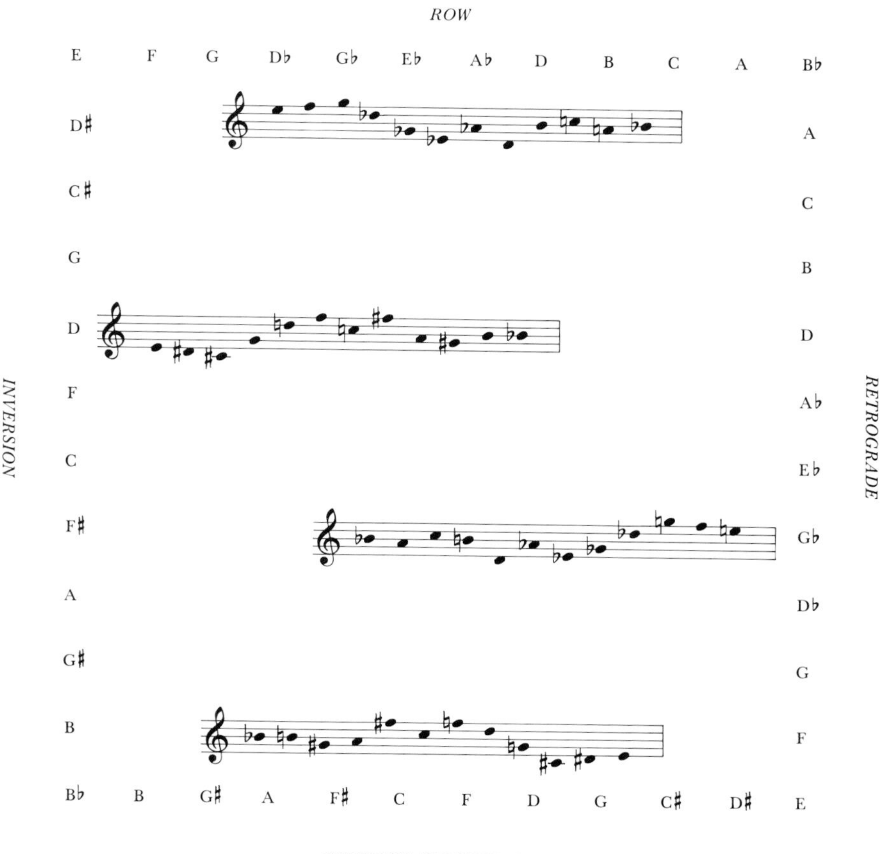

sures, in the order 5, 6, 7, 1, 2, 3, 4, 9, 10, 11, 12. In the trio section of the minuet (Ex. 12-5b) the row is presented in order by the left hand of the pianist, and is followed by its inversion. The right hand plays the row as a mirror canon at the interval of the diminished fifth. For the gigue (Ex. 12-5c) the row is presented in straightforward order, and then at the interval of the diminished fifth. In each movement of the suite, the row is an omnipresent element, providing constant variety.

Schoenberg never strove to break with certain elements of his past. Students who came to him expecting to find a wild-eyed revolutionary encountered instead a perceptive and analytical teacher who expected them to be able to write solid contrapuntal exercises. He also insisted they cultivate a knowledge of Brahms and the classical tradition.

Schoenberg's hope that future listeners might leave the concert hall humming his music was not to be realized; but his prediction that an understanding of his serial methods would someday be an integral part of the study of composition in every music conservatory has been fulfilled. As had happened

Example 12-5. Schoenberg. *Suite for Piano,* Op. 25.

12-5a. Minuet, bars 1–3.

12-5b. Minuet: trio, bars 1–5.

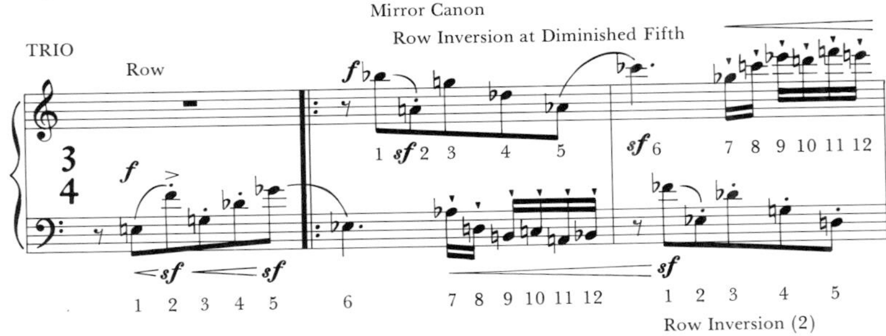

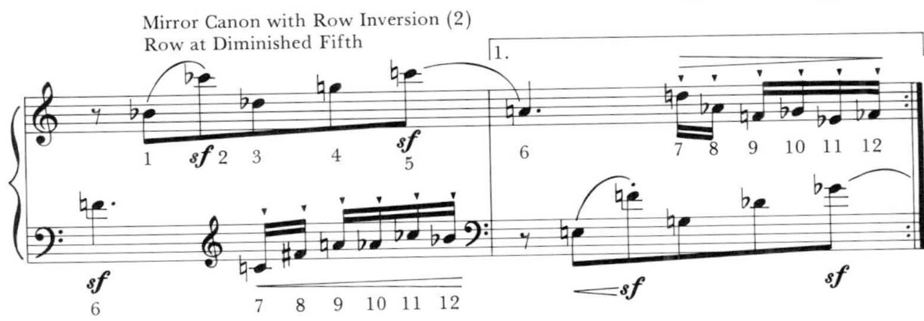

12-5c. Gigue, bars 1–2.

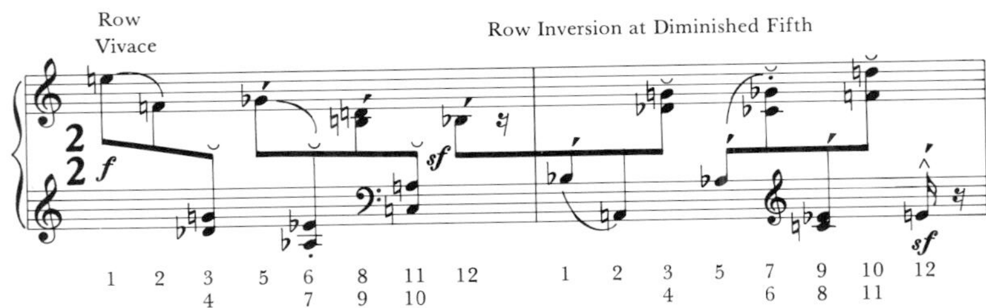

a century earlier with Wagner, younger composers in the decades following World War II found they could not set out on their own individual paths until they had examined, understood, and personally assessed Schoenberg's method.

WEBERN

Of the many pupils of Arnold Schoenberg, two in particular built upon the work of the master, while carving unique places for themselves in the music of the 20th century. The first of these was Anton von Webern, who crystallized Schoenberg's techniques to the point of utmost refinement. Webern was fascinated by the challenge of reducing his musical materials to the absolute minimum. In his scores, he seems to be asking, Why should I write a melody when a single note contains the completeness of a pitch with all its overtones? Why should I use a rhythmic motif when, by virtue of duration, each note stands as the essential element of rhythm? Why should I orchestrate, when a single note carries within itself a special tone color? And, why should I write crescendos and diminuendos, when every note contains its own fluctuating level of intensity?

In his early experimental *Five Orchestral Pieces* (Op. 16, 1909), Schoenberg had chosen one of the movements to probe the tone-color potential of a single chord (Ex. 12-6). In this movement, titled "Farben" ("Colors"), dimensions of time, melody, and formal development disappear. All that the listener perceives is the delicate drift of color tints as single tones of the chord are altered instrumentally. In the *Harmonielehre* of 1911, Schoenberg described the thinking that had produced "Farben": "I find that a note is perceived by its color, one of whose dimensions is pitch. Color, then, is the great realm, pitch one of its provinces. If the ear could discriminate between differences of color, it might be feasible to invent melodies that are built of colors—*Klangfarbenmelodien.* But who dares develop such theories?"

Example 12-6. Schoenberg. *Five Orchestral Pieces.* "Colors" chord.

With his aesthetic concentration on the perfect miniature, Webern dared. For him, the single notes of the series became the equivalent of subjects. This approach produced exquisitely short, jewel-like compositions that whisper rather than shout, that simply breathe the most intense and subtle musical language. While he wrote for varied combinations of instruments and voices, few of Webern's compositions last more than a few minutes (Ex. 12-7).

Example 12-7 shows the fourth of Webern's *Five Pieces for Orchestra* (Op. 10). To perform it takes only 25 seconds, and all five pieces together require just over seven minutes. Wispy, fragmentary, suggestive and intense, it is a work with no repetition of ideas, no hint of traditional form. The whole is a single progressive phrase made up of a row statement and answer.

Webern also adapted the Klangfarbenmelodie idea to music of the past, feeling that contrapuntal music might benefit particularly from this "tone-

Example 12-7. Webern. *Five Pieces for Orchestra,* Op. 10, No. 4.

color-melody" approach (Exs. 12-8a, b). The exposition of Bach's "Six-part Ricercar" from the *Musical Offering* (see pp. 185–86) shows the potential problem for the listener. It is possible for the ear and mind to follow perhaps four simultaneous lines of music, mentally retaining a sense of the separate lines and of their bonding together. But when a fifth and then a sixth line enters, the conscious perception of individual linear relationships quickly declines. Webern took Bach's score and realized it orchestrally, using the techniques of Klangfarbenmelodie. He broke up each line so that a few notes at most are assigned to a single instrument. As the tone color changes, the ear is directed via subtle changes in instrumentation. Webern felt that the listener could, through exposure to continually changing timbres, distinguish Bach's contrapuntal intent with greater ease and clarity.

Example 12-8. Bach. *Musical Offering, BWV* 1079.

12-8a. "Six-part Ricercar," bars 1–14.

12-8b. "Six-part Ricercar," bars 1–14, scored by Webern.

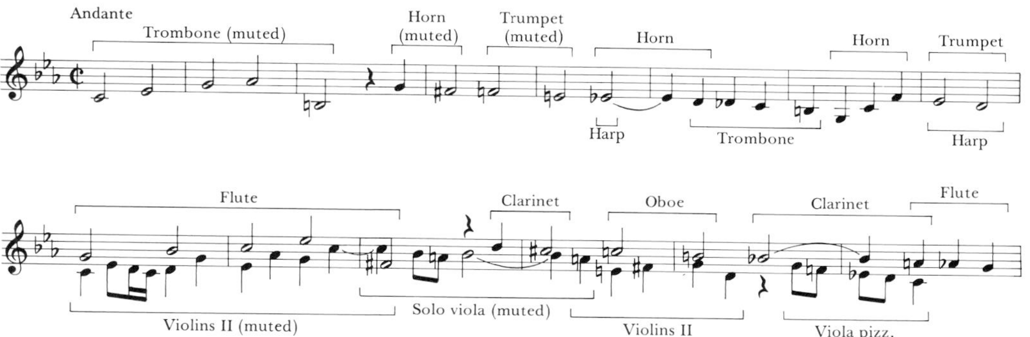

BERG

Schoenberg's other major pupil was Alban Berg, who is often credited with having humanized the cold objectivity of 12-tone construction. Berg's output was largely directed along expressionistic lines that were laden with secret inner symbolism. Like Schoenberg and Webern, Berg was a skilled and subtle craftsman, and his early 12-tone *Lyric Suite* (1926) provides a prime example. Written for string quartet, it alternates between the heights of exalted emotional intensity and the depths of dark desolation. Underneath its expressionistic surface, however, runs a hidden and constant theme of love. Berg's initials and those of his mistress, Hannah Fuchs, are used as a motif intertwined throughout the composition (B F A B-flat; in German notation H F A B). In addition, the working out of the row places essential importance on Berg's assignment of "numbers of fate," 10 and 23. Hannah's two children "appear" in the second movement, play, argue, and are subject to mediation by their mother. Significantly, none of these personal references appear in the score, nor are they explained by Berg. All is a secret game of a type that composers have long enjoyed. In the final movement the appearance of a quotation from the opening of Wagner's *Tristan and Isolde* affirms the underlying motif of love.

Berg's *Wozzeck,* first performed in 1925, is one of the key operas of the century. Written around a selection of loosely connected short scenes from an unfinished play by the early-19th-century author Georg Büchner, *Wozzeck* reflects the postwar European mood of depression. Man's inhumanity to man is reflected in the grim execution scene depicted in George Grosz's drawing *The Lord's Prayer,* which expresses his bitter disillusionment with the hypocritical attitudes of a society that clothes itself in legal and religious garb, without compassion for its victims (Fig 12-2). Berg had seen service in World War I, entering with enthusiasm but emerging with a strong antimilitary bent. *Wozzeck* symbolized his disillusionment with the military and all it represented.

Wozzeck is a career soldier, whose pitiful salary barely pays for the upkeep of his common-law wife and illegitimate child. He allows the quack camp doc-

Figure 12-2. George Grosz. *The Lord's Prayer,* in *Ecce Homo,* 1921. Lithograph. Courtesy of the George Arents Research Library, Syracuse University, Syracuse, New York.

tor to use him for dietary experiments and works as a menial servant for his overbearing captain in order to stretch his small income. Wozzeck is a man alone, with acquaintances and relationships but no friends or true loved ones. Early in the opera he utters the cry of one who has no defense against the ways of the world: "How poor we are! Folk like us are luckless in this world and would be in any other world. If we should go to heaven, we would be forced to help make the thunder!" (Ex. 12-9). Everyone in his life inflicts either physical or psychological injury, gradually crushing his spirit, until in one final mad outburst he kills his wife, Marie, near a small pond outside the town. Fearing he may have left evidence behind, he later returns to the watery scene of the crime and accidentally drowns. As he slips under for the last time, the doctor and the captain happen to pass by on their way to the camp. Hearing Wozzeck's frantic cries, they take fright and rush off into the night.

Example 12-9. Berg. *Wozzeck.* "How poor we are" motif.

Throughout the opera, Berg employs Schoenberg's technique of Sprechstimme, alternating it with more traditional vocal techniques. He also adopts Debussy's practice from *Pelléas et Mélisande* of connecting the five short scenes in each of the three acts by orchestral interludes (see p. 324). Each of the acts is further fashioned from traditional instrumental designs: a symphony, a suite, and a group of inventions. Individual scenes are built around forms such as the sonata, rondo, and passacaglia. The interlude that occurs after Wozzeck drowns (Act 3, scene 4) functions as a symphonic synthesis of the entire drama. Berg draws on subject materials used earlier in the opera, juxtaposing them, thereby tying together individual dark horrors into one bleak tragedy.

While the orchestra has the final word, summing up the central plot of the opera, there is a closing scene that functions as an epilogue. The morning after the deaths of Wozzeck and Marie, their child is found playing outside the house. A boy enters to announce that Marie's body has been discovered by the pond, and all rush out to view the grisly sight. The opera is brought to a poignant close as the child, now alone onstage, too young to understand the situation, follows innocently after them as the orchestra fades away. Like *Pelléas,* this drama suggests that the sins and sorrows of the older generation are fated to be repeated by its children.

Equally bleak was Berg's other opera, *Lulu,* with a libretto based on Frank Wedekind's play *Pandora's Box.* In it love is equated with lust, deviation with normality, charity becomes a vice and self-gratification a virtue. The role of the antiheroine, Lulu, who is ultimately murdered by Jack the Ripper, is written in a throat-wracking Sprechstimme. *Lulu* contains some of the most emotionally powerful orchestral music in the century, and stands as one of the most compelling works of musical expressionism.

Berg's *Violin Concerto* of 1935 summed up much of the essential nature of the Second Viennese School, for it polarized the past and the present, the personal and the objective, the diatonic and the serial, and finally the private and the public. After an introduction in which the violin explores the permutations of its four open strings—G D A E—Berg sets out a row that bridges the gap between diatonic and serial harmony (Ex. 12-10a). The row primarily describes a series of alternating major and minor triads built on the open strings of the instrument. The first three notes outline a G-minor triad and are followed by triads on D Major, A Minor, and E Major. The final four notes are each a whole tone apart. The harmonic potential of the row may be seen in the diatonic qualities of triads built on the perfect fifth intervals inherent in the violin tuning, while the inclusion of all 12 tones provides the substance for serial writing.

Example 12-10. Berg. *Violin Concerto.*

12-10a. Tone row.

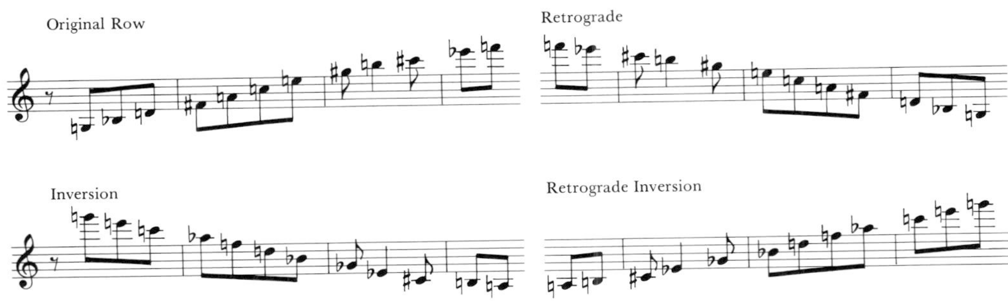

While Berg artfully explored both sides of the harmonic coin in his concerto, the work has an added personal dimension. At the time of its composition, a cherished teenaged friend, Manon Gropius (daughter of Gustav Mahler's widow, Alma, and the architect Walter Gropius), died from complications of polio. Her death was a heavy blow to Berg, and the composer dedicated the concerto "To the Memory of an Angel." To introduce a spiritual tribute to Manon's memory, Berg searched for a chorale with an appropriate text that might be woven into the concerto. He finally found it in *Es ist genug!* (*It is enough!*) from J. S. Bach's Cantata No. 60. The text seemed to Berg to mirror the young girl's suffering and release in death: "It is enough! Now, Lord, take my soul. Loose my bonds and set my spirit free."

The extraordinary fact about the chorale is that it is the only one in the entire literature that has as its opening four ascending tones that are each a whole step apart (Ex. 12-10b). For its appearance in the second part of the concerto, Berg was able to utilize the last four notes from his own row to correspond to the words "It is enough!" The concerto is thereupon guided toward a peaceful ending, in which the soloist brings the listener full circle, once again musing on the open strings of the violin. Berg's own death followed close upon his completion of this concerto.

12-10b. Chorale: "It is enough," bars 1–6.

Symbolism and Impressionism

Meanwhile, in France new styles were taking shape—*symbolism* in poetry and drama, *impressionism* in painting and music. Such writers as Charles Baudelaire, Stéphane Mallarmé, Pierre Louÿs, Paul Verlaine, and the dramatist Maurice Maeterlinck felt that poems were crafted with words more than ideas, with sounds more than reason. They reveled in sense data, the rhythmic flow of lines, and sensuous imagery. The interplay of sights, sounds, scents, tastes, and tactile sensations were explored in the psychological phenomenon known as *synesthesia.* Baudelaire believed that groups of sounds contain the same potential for meaning that words do. He also proposed that sounds are capable of joining other physical and psychic sensations to form correspondences, in which mental images arising from one or more of the senses are in some mysterious way bound up together. Ultimately, all the diverse elements of artistic language act as symbols in a universal hierarchy, each functioning as one aspect of an inevitable transcendent reality.

Baudelaire articulated these ideas in a sonnet entitled "Correspondences," from his poetic cycle *Flowers of Evil* (1857). It neither describes nor narrates, but coolly suggests mysterious links between one type of sense experience and another:

> Nature is a temple, from whose living pillars
> Sometimes perplexing messages escape;
> Between man and nature's shrine lie forests of symbols
> Which watch him with intimate eyes.
>
> Like deep echoes, blending somewhere else
> Into one deep and shadowy unison
> As vast as night's darkness or day's light,
> So sounds, scents, and colors answer each other.

There are perfumes fresh as children's flesh,
Sweet as oboes, green as prairies.
And others, rich, corrupt and triumphant
Possessing the power of infinite things,
Like amber, musk, incense and aromatic resin,
Which intone the ecstasies of the spirit and the senses.

The symbolists saw even the most trivial everyday happenings as a surface play of events that gave symbolic clues to what was actually happening deep in the vast sea of the subconscious mind. Thus they based their poetry on the principles of verbal consonances and dissonances, sensuous sounds, alliterations, onomatopoeia, and rhythmic flow. Subtle suggestions replace objective descriptions, and sense data replace thought. All became the symbolic keys that unlocked the new, uncharted world of transcendent reality.

The impressionist movement got its name from an early work by the painter Claude Monet: *Impression, Sunrise.* The word was immediately seized upon by the critics, who wrote that such seemingly sketchy and unfinished works were indeed impressions rather than paintings. This group of painters were influenced by the scientific discoveries of their time. The invention of the camera had shown that visual images were produced by minute gradations of light intensity as filtered through the lens of the camera or the human eye. They also learned much from Hermann Helmholtz's experiments in optics, which demonstrated that the sensation of color is more the reaction of the retina of the eye to varying reflections of light than a quality inherent in the objects themselves. He also demonstrated that light can be broken down into a prismatic spectrum of separate colors that the eye itself mixes up and perceives as white. Shadows were found not to be gray or black, but composed of the complementary colors of the objects that cast them.

So, in their paintings, the impressionists were more interested in rendering refractions of light than in describing objects. Rather than blend pigments together on the palette, they applied separate colors directly on the canvas and let the eye of the viewer do the mixing. Their subject matter was purposely kept neutral. They told no stories, neither did they allow subjective emotional reactions to intrude on their experiments in light and shadow. Instead of working only in their studios, they often painted outside in natural light and open air. They developed rapid brush techniques to help them catch as much of the momentary effects of the light on their canvases as quickly as possible. Impressionist subject matter ran to landscapes, river scenes, pools filled with water lilies, reflections on water, and airy cloud formations (see Plate XIII).

DEBUSSY

As a young man, Claude Debussy fell under the spell of Wagner and made the obligatory pilgrimage to the Wagnerian shrine at Bayreuth. Like almost all the composers of his generation, Debussy was deeply affected by Wagner's music, and it took him some time to subdue its influence and establish his own individuality. In a letter to the head of the Opéra-Comique in Paris, Debussy wrote:

> Having been an impassioned pilgrim to Bayreuth for several years, I began to cast doubt on the Wagnerian formula; or rather, it seemed to me that it fitted only the peculiar genius of that composer. And without denying him genius one can say that he put the final touch to the music of his time just as Victor Hugo sums up all the poetry written before his age. It was necessary, then, to go beyond Wagner rather than follow in his path.

At the same time, Debussy produced the first composition that asserted his Gallic temperament and ultimately secured his place as a composer of international stature. The orchestral *Prélude à 'L'après-midi d'un faune'* (*Prelude to 'The Afternoon of a Faun'*) was designed as a musical correspondence to Stéphane Mallarmé's symbolist eclogue of the same title. Mallarmé's semierotic poem tells of the sultry afternoon dreams of a mythic faun as he muses over the pursuit of captivating nymphs, whether real or imagined (see Plate XIV). Debussy's equally sensuous orchestral setting creates a similar atmosphere, by means of an insinuating flute solo that evokes the panpipes of ancient Greece. Its luxurious chromatic line liberated his listeners from any expectation of traditional harmony (Ex. 12-11). The phrase becomes the motif for the composition, but it is not used in a typical developmental fashion. Rather, the composer allows the music to fantasize, as the faun does in Mallarmé's poem. As the phrase is in turn repeated, fragmented, and turned in on itself, Debussy uses orchestral instruments in subtle colorations the like of which had never been heard before. The result is the musical equivalent of a sense-correspondence symbolist poem or a series of impressionistic Monet landscapes.

Mallarmé was not the only symbolist poet to attract Debussy's attention. His opera *Pelléas et Mélisande* used a symbolist play by Maeterlinck as its libretto, and he wrote numerous settings of symbolist poetry as art songs. Among them are *Ariettes oubliées* (*Forgotten Songs*) to texts by Verlaine, and *Cinq poèmes de Charles Baudelaire*.

Debussy's selective rejection of diatonic harmony led him on occasion to base his harmonic fabric on the *whole-tone scale*. The whole-tone scale is not capable of representing a key, and since its notes are equidistant from each other, it can suggest none of the traditional diatonic relationships such as tonic

Example 12-11. Debussy. *Prelude to 'The Afternoon of a Faun'*, bars 1–5.

and dominant. All whole-tone scales sound the same, while triads built on any of its degrees produce augmented chords. The musical effect of using such a scale is one of suspended animation, with no solid harmonic floor on which to rest. The scale found musical favor with the impressionists, since the music based on it suggested rather than stated. Debussy's *Afternoon of a Faun* gave a fresh glimpse of an imaginary pseudoclassical landscape, revealed through chromatic and whole-tone harmonies. This development has been widely cited as one of the harbingers signaling the 20th-century overthrow of traditional diatonic music.

Like the impressionist painters, Debussy showed partiality for water imagery, in such piano pieces as "Jardins dans la pluie" ("Gardens in the Rain") and "Reflets dans l'eau" ("Reflections in the Water"), and for a fantasy world, as in *La cathédrale engloutie* (*The Sunken Cathedral*). The most famous example of his water imagery, *La mer* (*The Sea,* 1905), symbolically transforms the orchestra into a large body of water. The work is a series of three aquatic tone poems entitled "From Dawn 'til Noon on the Sea," "Play of the Waves," and "Dialogue of the Wind and the Sea." Debussy achieves a musical correspondence with each of several elements associated with the sea, through his careful control of color nuance, rhythmic motifs, and dynamic levels.

In his earlier *Three Nocturnes for Orchestra* (1899), Debussy had taken a leaf from the notebook of the painter James McNeill Whistler, who had represented night scenes with subtitles indicating their genesis as color studies (see Plate XV). Debussy borrowed Whistler's term, but his nocturnes are not "night pieces." They are nonetheless tone color studies, woven of subtle flecks of aural color where Whistler used beads of paint. Here and in *Images for Orchestra,* Debussy uses instruments as foils for his ideas, and he does not hesitate to demand that instrumentalists forget their old ways of playing and create sounds both new and distinct.

Debussy's musical interests were wide-ranging, and he by no means confined himself to the impressionistic vein. His output embraces a traditional gamut of forms—art song, solo piano music, cantata, opera, ballet, and the orchestral tone poem. Like Bach and Chopin before him, Debussy wrote sets of keyboard preludes. Each of his 24 *Preludes* carries a programmatic title meant to suggest its general atmosphere. The titles, however, appear as suggestions in parentheses at the end of each composition, so that on first perusal of the score, the novice should experience the music purely as music before discovering its programmatic significance. Debussy found the whole-tone scale especially effective for the prelude titled *Voiles* (*Veils*), in which there is a musical correspondence to the delicate, sensuous movement of diaphanous fabric (Ex. 12-12).

Example 12-12. Debussy. *Preludes, Book I.* No. 2, *Veils,* bars 1–5.

Debussy did not forget that music is for the young as well as for adults. His piano suite *Children's Corner,* written for his daughter in 1908, includes a humorous jab at five-finger exercises ("Doctor Gradus ad Parnasum"), and there is a sly quotation from Wagner's *Tristan* in the "Golliwog's Cakewalk." The 1913 ballet *La boîte à joujoux* (*The Toy Box*) he described as "a work to amuse children, nothing more."

Debussy partially succumbed to the spell of 19th-century romantic escapism and to the call of the East. At the Paris Exposition of 1889, he heard a Gamelan percussion orchestra from Java. Later he found ways to translate the hollow melodic-percussive timbres and complicated rhythmic improvisations in several of his compositions. Among them were the piano pieces "Pagodes" from *Estampes* (*Engravings*), and "Et la lune descend sur le temple qui fût" ("And the moon descends behind the deserted temple") from the second set of piano *Images.* Japanese woodcuts, which had inspired Monet to look anew at his art, also had an impact on Debussy. He asked his publisher to use part of the Japanese artist Hokusai's painting *The Great Wave* for the cover of *La mer* (see Plate XVI).

Debussy produced only one opera, *Pelléas et Mélisande,* completed in 1902 after ten years of work. Debussy took Maurice Maeterlinck's drama of the same name and set it almost exactly as it stood, with only minor textual deletions. At first glance, Maeterlinck's play is just another version of the eternal triangle—two brothers in love with the same girl. Beneath the surface, however, lie considerable subtleties, delicate emotional nuances, meaningful pauses, and pregnant dramatic silences. All of these provided Debussy with the material for his operatic masterpiece, which proceeds like a series of tableaux with dreamlike orchestral interludes linking one scene with the next. Maeterlinck's is a symbolist drama, with the weight of the play hanging on suggestion rather than overt statement. He tells his audience almost nothing, and when some rare moment of action takes place, it is carried on in shadowy, delicate dialogue.

The time is an archaic, indeterminately medieval past; the place, the mythic kingdom of Allemonde; the characters, none of them stereotypes, are never clearly delineated, and all are lost in one way or another. Prince Golaud, who has lost his way while hunting, discovers Mélisande weeping by a pond:

> GOL: Why do you cry? Don't be frightened. You've nothing to fear. Why are you crying out here, all alone?
> MÉL: Don't touch me, don't touch me!
> GOL: I won't touch you. Don't be afraid. Has someone done you harm?
> MÉL: Oh, yes, yes, yes.
> GOL: Who was it who harmed you?
> MÉL: All of them! All of them!
>
> . . .
>
> GOL: What is that shining under the water?
> MÉL: Where? Ah, it's the crown he gave me. It fell in when I was crying.
> GOL: A crown? Who gave you a crown? I'll try to retrieve it for you.
> MÉL: No, no. I don't want it. I don't want it any more. I'd rather die, die here and now.
>
> . . .
>
> GOL: I am Prince Golaud, grandson of Arkel, the old king of Allemonde. Will you come with me?
> MÉL: No, I'll stay here.
> GOL: You can't stay here all alone. You can't stay here all night. What is your name?
> MÉL: Mélisande.
> GOL: You can't stay here, Mélisande. Come with me.
> MÉL: Oh, don't touch me.
> GOL: Don't cry out. I won't touch you. But come with me. The night will be very dark and very cold. Come with me.
> MÉL: Where are you going?
> GOL: I don't know. I'm lost too.

Later Golaud and Mélisande marry and return to Allemonde. Over a period of time Mélisande and Golaud's younger half-brother Pelléas drift into love, a love that germinates so subtly that the listener only becomes aware of its flowering as the characters do. In the tragic conclusion, Pelléas comes to a violent end at the hands of Golaud, and Mélisande later dies gently after bearing a child. The drama trails off with the implication that Mélisande's child, like her parents, will lead a lusterless existence lacking any positive life force. Debussy's brand of impressionism melds with Maeterlinck's internally oriented play in a musical drama that communicates through understatement.

Water imagery is depicted throughout the play, and it permeates the entire opera. Golaud discovers Mélisande beside a pool in the opera's first scene. The first stirrings of love between the two protagonists occur symbolically in a scene by a well in the castle park, where Mélisande removes her wedding ring and plays with it until it falls into the water's depths. In the castle dungeons overlooking stagnant waters Golaud frightens Pelléas with veiled threats. Two scenes are set in a grotto by the sea. There are frequent sea views and discussions of a sea voyage, and in the final scene, Mélisande asks that the windows be opened so that she can look at the sea one last time.

The characters do not sing in the usual operatic fashion. There are no arias, as in Italian number opera, nor does the music unfold in the manner of Wagner's music dramas. (Debussy does, however, make use of motifs that are developed throughout the opera, and he owed more to Wagner than he was willing to admit.) The performers simply intone the dialogue in delicate musical nuances that emerge as logical extensions of natural speech. Consequently, the vocal tessituras are not typically operatic, and clear text projection is of the highest importance.

The opera is made up of five acts set out in 14 scenes. To give some unity to this diversity, Debussy connects the internal scenes with orchestral interludes. These interludes relieve the disconnected aspect of the sequence of short scenes and smooth over the time needed for changes of scenery. Most important, they finish off one scene orchestrally while preparing for the next.

Near the beginning of World War I, Debussy turned for a time to abstract music, in an attempt to recall a long-lost French chamber tradition. He had delved into neoclassicism briefly with an earlier string quartet and a piano piece dedicated to Haydn. Now he planned six chamber sonatas in which he decided to forego dependence on his usual literary or visual correspondences. He completed three sonatas, in which he investigated the potential for new sonorities from individual instruments in various chamber combinations (violin and piano; cello and piano; flute, viola, and harp). By now, Debussy was no longer concerned with the notion of continual development, and since diatonic harmony was no longer a factor, the traditional forms based on such harmonic practices no longer had validity. Instead, one finds a reliance on refined, transparent textures, while the constant introduction of new musical materials leaves the listener with an impression of an art ever renewing itself, at once ephemeral and improvisatory. This impression is enhanced through strong, fluid motion and pliant rhythms, transcending Debussy's earlier attempts at water and other imagery.

His final work for orchestra was a ballet commissioned by the impresario Sergei Diaghilev for the Ballets Russes. *Jeux* (*Games,* 1914) sets up a parallel between the game of tennis and the game of love. The action unfolds in an evocative score, in which Debussy's earlier brand of impressionism is superseded by a sensitive play of delicately balanced orchestral forces.

RAVEL

Debussy's successor on the French musical scene was Maurice Ravel. It had been the older master's destiny to carve a new tonal language compatible with the literary ideas developed by the symbolist poets and the visual expressions of the impressionist painters. That Maurice Ravel was completely conversant with Debussy's impressionist vocabulary became apparent from such early pianistic works as *Jeux d'eau* (*Fountains,* 1901, Ex. 12-13) and the orchestral *Rapsodie espagnole* (*Spanish Rhapsody,* 1908). The essence of Ravel's style, however, derives from the neoclassical world of 18th-century French literature, art, and music. While Ravel was influenced by 19th- and 20th-century writers and styles, he stated that his views on composition stemmed from Mozart's declaration that there was nothing that music could not undertake to do, dare, or portray, provided it continued to charm and always remained music.

Example 12-13. Ravel. *Fountains,* bars 1–2.

While Debussy was probing the future of French music, Ravel tried to crystallize the essences of the past by invoking an idealized image of the world of Watteau (see p. 190), and that of his 18th-century musical ancestors, especially the keyboard composers Couperin and Rameau. Ravel once again asserted the role of the artist as craftsman, and proceeded to compose with jewel-like precision. His affinity for a past golden age becomes apparent from piano works that date from the turn of the century, such as *Menuet antique,* the ever-popular *Pavane pour une infante défunte* (*Pavane for a Dead Princess*), and *Menuet sur le nom d'Haydn* (*Minuet on Haydn's Name*). In the suite *Le tombeau de Couperin* (*At the Tomb of Couperin,* 1917) with its prelude, fugue, forlane, rigaudon, minuet, and toccata, Ravel characteristically recalled times past by organizing each segment in ways that were clear, precise, and graceful (Ex.

12-14). It was equally characteristic for him to honor past forms and styles by choosing such recondite dance forms as the forlane and the rigaudon, as well as a dance for the fingers alone in the concluding toccata. Ravel also breathed new life into older classical forms, with the *Sonatine* for piano, a sonata for violin and piano, a trio for piano, violin, and cello, and a string quartet.

Example 12-14. Ravel. *At the Tomb of Couperin.* No. 4, "Rigaudon," bars 1–4.

In addition to his skill as a miniaturist in piano pieces and songs, the composer was a consummate master of orchestration with total command of the medium. Ravel approached both the piano and the orchestra with equal enthusiasm, and he twice combined them in piano concertos. The Concerto in G Major has all the grace, verve, and élan of an 18th-century divertimento in modern attire. Succinct statements, crisp contours, and transparent textures in the outer movements contrast with the somber lyricism of the slow movement to make it a perennial favorite with concert audiences. In an interview at its London premiere, Ravel remarked that he was composing a concerto in the manner of Mozart that was *for* the piano, not *against* it.

Ravel's skills as an orchestrator were also manifest in his colorful setting of Musorgsky's piano work *Pictures at an Exhibition.* In addition, several of Ravel's own piano compositions later appeared in orchestral garb. Among these were two that reflected Ravel's romance with a past time when the Viennese waltz was the height of elegance. His *Valses nobles et sentimentales* (*Noble and Sentimental Waltzes*) are a tribute to Schubert's lilting dance music. His choreographic symphonic poem *La valse,* written in the impressionistic style, evokes the lost dream world of Vienna in the time of Johann Strauss.

Ravel's long-standing love affair with the dance was not limited to the 18th-century suite or the 19th-century waltz. Dance idioms of Spain were displayed in a *Habanera* for piano and the famous *Bolero.* The latter investigated a single rhythmic cell, repeated again and again in ever-increasing crescendos. An examination of what could be done with one subject that remained basically unchanged, Ravel later described it as a "piece for orchestra without music." Neoclassical Greece was resurrected in the ballet based on the myth of Daphnis and Chloe, though Ravel's view of the archaic was one that he admitted bore "fidelity to the Greece of my dreams which is close to that imagined and painted by the French artists of the late 18th century."

Like Debussy, Ravel did not neglect the world of childhood. A suite for piano duet entitled *Ma mère l'oye* (*My Mother Goose*) includes movements titled "Pavane for Sleeping Beauty," "Laideronette, Empress of the Pagodas," "Conversation of Beauty and the Beast," and "The Fairy Garden." It too later became an orchestral work, as a ballet score.

Ravel's surrealist opera *L'enfant et les sortilèges* (*The Child and the Sorceries,* 1925) boasts a libretto by the French novelist Colette. It conjures up a whole world of childhood fantasies, where inanimate objects come to life to teach a naughty boy a series of well-deserved lessons. Pieces of furniture skitter out from under him while they converse and dance. The grandfather clock, having suffered the removal of his pendulum, bemoans his untimely state. Smashed during a fit of temper, the child's beloved Wedgewood teapot and Chinese cup come to life. In their duet the teapot sings in appropriately broken English phrases: "I punch your nose, I knock out you. I box you, I marm'lad' you" (i.e., reduce you to a pulp). The cup in turn articulates a series of nonsense Chinese phrases: "Kengçafou, Mahjong. Sessue Hayakawa!" (a reference to an Oriental film star). After this, the two join in a dance rage of the 1920s, a blues fox-trot with an ironic "wrong-note" accompaniment (Ex. 12-15a).

Example 12-15. Ravel. *The Child and the Sorceries.* Excerpts.

12-15a. Blues fox-trot.

The part of Fire is sung by a coloratura soprano, and as she lashes out of her chimney she threatens to singe the child: "I warm up the good, but I burn the spiteful!" Her vocal line then moves in flamelike leaps (Ex. 12-15b).

In his tantrum, the boy has ripped the wallpaper, and from its rustic design shepherds and shepherdesses now descend. Tattered and torn, they sing a chorus expressing their sadness at being parted from each other. Ravel's affinity for 18th-century French idioms is reflected in his delicate setting for their charming ballet, to the accompaniment of a pipe and tambourine (Ex. 12-15c).

12-15b. Fire.

12-15c. Ballet of shepherds and shepherdesses.

From his favorite fairy-tale book, the boy has torn the picture of the lovely golden-haired princess, and she sings a lyric aria telling him sadly what their future might have been. Suddenly a little old man, the personification of Arithmetic, pops out of a textbook with numbers scattered around him while he spouts the multiplication table with wrong answers: "Four times four make eighteen, ten times six equals twenty, two times nine is thirty."

Next, a black cat and a white cat engage in a playful "meowing" duet (Ex. 12-15d), drawing the child into the garden for the second half of this one-act musical drama. In the summer's night atmosphere, Ravel uses all his orchestral and vocal resources to sketch a rich, colorful mixture of insect and animal sounds. After a series of adventures with them, the boy finally does one good deed. Quite overcome, the garden creatures now sing his praises, and the opera ends in an atmosphere of contentment and reconciliation.

12-15d. Cats' duet.

For *L'enfant et les sortilèges* Ravel chose neither Wagner's style of mythic, through-composed opera, nor Debussy's impressionistic style. Instead he returned to 18th-century number opera and gave the work a few modern twists so that it might be, as he put it, "in the spirit of American musical comedy." The vocal settings display consistent care on the part of the composer to reveal textual meaning with clarity. And, while the opera is scored for a large orchestra, Ravel blends his instruments with a delicacy of touch that matches its constantly varying moods. The elegant eclecticism, minute attention to detail, and refined manner of execution all combine here to present a reflection of Ravel's art as a whole.

As the canons of romanticism receded, they gave place to the fresh approaches of symbolism, impressionism, expressionism, and the new eclecticism. The inspired art of their leading exponents provided a rich variety of stylistic trends that illuminated the pathway from romantic to modern music.

CHAPTER

13

Contemporary Styles I

MUSICALLY, THE STYLES OF a given period are not unlike those of political life. There are staunch conservatives, who cling to the tried and true values of the past; liberals, who try to adapt to changing times and keep up with present-day developments; and radical progressives and revolutionaries, who attempt to transcend the present and clamor for plans that anticipate future needs. So it is with music and all the arts. In the early 20th century, Rachmaninov was content all his creative life to work within the 19th-century romantic style. Then came the more liberal figures Prokofiev and Shostakovich, who adapted to contemporary idioms and spoke in the modern accents of their time. Finally the revolutionaries, such as Schoenberg and Stravinsky, reacted strongly against their romantic heritage and brought radical changes in traditional patterns of thought that launched a sweeping forward momentum in their art.

The more conservative trends of the first part of the 20th century were mainly the neoclassical, neoromantic, and ongoing academic styles. The new progressive breakthroughs included the continuing development of the serialism of Schoenberg, extensions and adaptations of Stravinsky's music built on propulsive rhythmic foundations, the new objective method of Hindemith, and the social-utilitarian approach to the function of music in society. Charles Ives offered fresh views of America's Yankee heritage, while Gershwin and Bernstein combined jazz elements and classical forms.

Fernan Léger. *Propellers,* 1918. Oil on canvas. By permission of the Collection, the Museum of Modern Art, New York. Katherine S. Dreier Bequest.

Chronology

MUSICAL FIGURES

The International Scene

Béla Bartók	1881–1945
Igor Stravinsky	1882–1971
Paul Hindemith	1895–1963
Kurt Weill	1900–1950

France

Nadia Boulanger	1887–1979
Louis Durey	1888–1979
Arthur Honegger	1892–1955
Darius Milhaud	1892–1974
Germaine Tailleferre	1892–1983
Francis Poulenc	1899–1963
Georges Auric	1899–1983

England

William Walton	1902–1983

Russia

Sergei Prokofiev	1891–1953
Dmitri Shostakovich	1906–1975

United States

Arthur Foote	1853–1937
George Chadwick	1854–1931
Edward MacDowell	1860–1908
Charles M. Loeffler	1861–1935
Walter Damrosch	1862–1950
Amy Beach	1867–1944
Charles Ives	1874–1954
John A. Carpenter	1876–1951
Ernest Bloch	1880–1959
Charles W. Cadman	1881–1946
Charles T. Griffes	1884–1920
Deems Taylor	1885–1966
Douglas Moore	1893–1969
Walter Piston	1894–1976
Virgil Thomson	1896–1989
Quincy Porter	1897–1966
George Gershwin	1898–1937
Roy Harris	1898–1979
Aaron Copland	1900–
Marc Blitzstein	1905–1964
Leonard Bernstein	1918–

Jazz and Popular Music

Joe "King" Oliver	1885–1938
Ferdinand "Jelly Roll" Morton	1885–1941
Gertrude "Ma" Rainey	1886–1939
Paul Whiteman	1890–1967
Ferde Grofé	1892–1972
Bessie Smith	1894–1937
Sidney Bechet	1897–1959
Fletcher Henderson	1898–1952
Lotte Lenya	1898–1981
Edward "Duke" Ellington	1899–1974
Louis "Satchmo" Armstrong	1900–1971
Leon "Bix" Beiderbecke	1903–1931
Earl "Fatha" Hines	1903–1983
Coleman Hawkins	1904–1969
Benjamin "Benny" Goodman	1909–
Woodrow "Woody" Herman	1913–1987
Thelonious Monk	1917–1982
John "Dizzy" Gillespie	1917–
Charles "Bird" Parker	1920–1955
Stanley Getz	1927–
Ornette Coleman	1930–
Paul Simon	1941–
Miles Davis	1926–

WRITERS AND DRAMATISTS

Sergei Diaghilev	1872–1929
Gertrude Stein	1874–1946
Max Jacob	1876–1944
Georg Kaiser	1878–1945
Charles F. Ramuz	1878–1947
DuBose Heyward	1885–1940
Edith Sitwell	1887–1964
Jean Cocteau	1889–1963
Charles Chaplin	1889–1977
Elmer Rice	1892–1967
Osbert Sitwell	1892–1969
Dorothy Parker	1893–1967
Martha Graham	1894–
F. Scott Fitzgerald	1896–1940
Leonide Massine	1896–1979
Thornton Wilder	1897–1975
Sergei Eisenstein	1898–1948
Bertolt Brecht	1898–1956
Ernest Hemingway	1898–1961
Tyrone Guthrie	1901–1971
John Steinbeck	1902–1968
Alan Paton	1903–
Moss Hart	1904–1961
George Balanchine	1904–1983
Lillian Hellman	1905–1984
W. H. Auden	1907–1973

ARTISTS AND ARCHITECTS

Henri Matisse	1869–1954
Fernan Léger	1881–1955
Pablo Picasso	1881–1973
Amadeo Modigliani	1884–1920

HISTORICAL FIGURES

Sigmund Freud	1856–1939
Nikolai Lenin (Valdimir Ulyanov)	1870–1924
Winston Churchill	1874–1965
Joseph Stalin (Josif Dzhugashvili)	1879–1953
Joseph Goebbels	1897–1945
Adolf Hitler	1889–1945
Franklin Roosevelt	1882–1945

The International Scene

STRAVINSKY

Igor Stravinsky first catapulted to international fame with the great success of his scores for Russia's Ballets Russes when it traveled to Paris in the first decade of the century. Its legendary impresario and artistic director, Sergei Diaghilev, discovered the young composer studying with the brilliant orchestrator and member of the Russian Five, Nikolai Rimsky-Korsakov. Stravinsky's music for the fairy-tale ballet *L'oiseau de feu* (*The Firebird,* 1910) was an immediate success. Brimming with fantasy and exotic colors, the score unfolds like a late-romantic tone poem, equally at home in the concert hall and the ballet theater. *The Firebird* was the first of a series of works for which Stravinsky drew on Russian cultural traditions and customs. Each was translated into a personal commentary on the practices that had become ritualized in Russian life. The following year Stravinsky provided the Diaghilev ballet with a second score, *Petrouchka* (see pp. 11–13). Whereas *The Firebird* reflected Stravinsky's heritage of colorful orchestration, in *Petrouchka* the composer began to stretch his imagination in the areas of driving rhythms and bold harmonies.

The years 1912–13 saw the appearance of three diverse works that signaled three major directions in which 20th-century music would travel: the quest for a new harmonic orientation in Schoenberg's *Pierrot lunaire,* the search for new formal organization in Debussy's *Jeux,* and the pursuit of new possibilities for rhythmic expression in Stravinsky's *Le sacre du printemps* (*The Rite of Spring*). It should be noted that Freud's *Totem and Taboo* appeared just at this time, a book that delved into the sexual and ritualistic attitudes of the human psyche and the cultural practices of primitive societies.

Le sacre du printemps was Stravinsky's third score for the Ballets Russes. It immediately placed the 30-year-old composer in the forefront of musical innovators and won him world attention overnight. The *Rite* has been called the 20th-century "Eroica," for it threw down the musical gauntlet to composers and audiences alike, as Beethoven's heroic symphony had done in 1804. The subject matter is less narrative than in the fairy-tale *Firebird,* less explicit than in *Petrouchka. The Rite of Spring* tells of auguries and celebrations of spring in ancient pagan Russia, culminating in human sacrifice. It contains some of the most powerful, raw dissonances ever penned. Stravinsky's dissonances, however, are not like the "emancipated" dissonance of Schoenberg; they are powerful, throbbing, neoprimitive dissonances that crawl under the skin. At the first performance of the work, the audience writhed under its spell, reacted viscerally, and erupted into riotous violence (Fig. 13-1).

From the opening bars, Stravinsky presents the listener with a vision of a mysterious primitive past, using powerful accents and bold orchestral colors

(Ex. 13-1). The wailing, seldom-used upper register of the bassoon transports the audience into an unknown time. As ceremonial preparations for the sacrifice are made and the groups dance in mystic rites, the music seems to capture the essence of primitive tribal festivities.

Example 13-1. Stravinsky. *The Rite of Spring,* bars 1–3.

Until the *Rite,* the role of rhythm in Western music had been one of underlying fundamental support for the other musical elements. Here it becomes the primal force of the music, and Stravinsky organizes the various sections of the ballet into highly varied rhythmic cells. The heavy, offbeat rhythms signal a new sense of compositional freedom, and the combination of strong syncopation with polymetric writing confounds the listener's expectations of traditionally repetitive bar lines (Ex. 13-2). Though they are more complex, Stravinsky's rhythmic methods clearly reflect other landmark attempts—like that of Beethoven in the "Eroica"—to put listeners off guard, while at the same time keeping them absorbed in the progress of the work.

Example 13-2. Stravinsky. *The Rite of Spring.* "Spring Rounds," bars 1–6.

The culmination of this relentlessly dissonant and rhythmically vital score is the wild dance of the Chosen Maiden, who must whirl herself to a sacrificial death, moving ever faster and more violently until the final moment when a single flute sounds, and she falls lifeless to earth, to the accompaniment of a crashing chord.

Within a year of the *Rite,* the world was enmeshed in World War I, and Stravinsky found travel between Russia and western Europe difficult. He elected to remain in the West for a time, and for the next decade his works showed a continuing interest in both the folk culture of Russia and in rhythm as the foundational element of composition. Though he was obligated to scale down the size of his performing forces for a time to meet the exigencies of wartime, he continued to write works for the theater and the ballet, and he remained intermittently connected to the world of dance for the rest of his life.

Stravinsky's first three large-scale ballets had been ritualized views of Russian culture. Now, in a series of new works, he moved toward greater economy of means and increasingly abstract tonal designs. The mimed play with music,

Figure 13-1. Jean Cocteau. *Dessins: Stravinsky Playing "The Rite of Spring,"* 1924. Line drawing. Courtesy of the George Arents Research Library, Syracuse University, Syracuse, New York.

L'histoire du soldat (*The Soldier's Tale,* 1918), is representative of this transitional phase. It calls for four actor-dancers and a seven-piece chamber orchestra. One actor functions as narrator, while the Soldier, the Princess, and the Devil mime and dance. Stravinsky's instrumental ensemble is a far cry from the large orchestral forces required for the earlier ballets, but it is crafted with a sensitivity for the individual tone colors of each instrument in its chamber scoring: clarinet, bassoon, cornet, trombone, violin, bass viol, and percussion. This scoring marked a new emphasis for the composer on woodwind and brass instruments. Strings imparted a lushness associated with romanticism, something Stravinsky now sought to avoid.

The satirical libretto by C. F. Ramuz was fashioned from a Russian folktale that to some extent parallels the Faust legend. A soldier, traveling home on leave, meets the devil, who leads him through a series of magical adventures. In folktale fashion, the soldier cures the princess of a mysterious illness and then marries her, but they do not live happily ever after. His naiveté and guilelessness place him in a position where the devil ultimately claims his soul. The music, cleanly dissonant with pungent acidic harmonies, uses several traditional forms: march, waltz, chorale, and concerto, as well as two popular 20th-century dance idioms, ragtime and tango. Parody was to become an intrinsic element in Stravinsky's ritualizing process, and all the above styles are treated satirically.

Stravinsky's Russian-based eclectic period came to an end with *Les noces* (*The Wedding*), subtitled "Russian Choreographic Scenes," which portrayed the ceremonial customs of folk weddings. This work, which occupied him off and on from 1914 to 1923, is a ballet with song, accompanied by four pianos and percussion. The wedding customs treated by Stravinsky had already been ritualized over time, and he further removed them from reality, placing them out of context both in time and space. Stravinsky's unique sense of the ceremonial, which involved removing all the usual sentimental elements from an event, is emphasized by his placing all performers (including the accompanying instruments) on the stage in full view of the audience, and by his eliminating any direct connections between the visual characters (dancers) and the narrating characters (singers).

L'histoire and *Les noces* were watersheds in Stravinsky's musical thinking. He felt that he had said all that he could with a vast panoply of monumental orchestras and full balletic forces, in the three early ballet scores. From this point onward the challenge was to say as much as possible with the utmost economy of means. This period also heralded his departure from the late romantic tradition of his developing years and his movement toward terse statements, economical designs, and the spare aesthetic of neoclassicism. In his treatise *Poetics of Music,* the composer wrote that music should not be concerned with expressing feelings, attitudes of mind, psychological moods, or phenomena of nature. Rather, he says, "music is given to us with the sole purpose of establishing order in things, including, and particularly, the coordination between *man* and *time.*"

This new freedom from romanticism and his own Russian heritage allowed Stravinsky to re-explore the whole field of Western musical literature and to crisscross all styles and periods in order to find the ideas and materials for his prolific output. Ancient Greece was represented with an oratoriolike setting of *Oedipus Rex* (1927), the ballet *Apollo and the Muses* (1928), and the melodrama *Persephone* (1934). The medieval period inspired various choral settings such as the *Mass* (1948) based on 14th-century contrapuntal practices, especially those of Guillaume de Machaut, a composer who commanded Stravinsky's deep admiration.

Dipping into past styles also led him to create works that honored composers both long and recently dead, and consequently to an "updating" of their works or styles. The piano style of Beethoven came under scrutiny in the *Sonata* of 1924, while idioms associated with Tchaikovsky may be heard in the 1929 *Capriccio* for piano and orchestra. He paid homage to some composers through inclusion in his music of excerpts and variants from theirs. These included Tchaikovsky in the ballet *The Fairy's Kiss* (1922), and the 18th-century Pergolesi in *Pulcinella* (1920). From the same year came *Symphonies of Wind Instruments,* written as a memorial to Claude Debussy. Recollections of Bach's concerto style appeared in the *Concerto for Piano and Winds* (1924) and the

Dumbarton Oaks Concerto (1938). Stravinsky transformed Bach's canonic *Chorale-Variations on the Christmas Hymn "Vom Himmel Hoch da komm' ich her"* for organ into a work for orchestra with chorus in 1956. The classical formal clarity of Mozart and Haydn may be discerned in the *Symphony in C* (1940) and the *Symphony in Three Movements* (1945).

With the death of Schoenberg in 1951, Stravinsky had another musical tradition on which to draw. Not surprisingly, he came to terms with Schoenberg's 12-tone method in his own individual fashion, providing inventive and illuminating perspectives on the 12-tone idiom in the ballet *Agon* (1954), the cantata *Abraham and Isaac* (1963), and the orchestral *Variations* (1964).

Agon, subtitled "Ballet for Twelve Dancers," was commissioned by the New York City Ballet and choreographed by George Balanchine. It is scored for large orchestra, including a colorful percussive group consisting of harp, mandolin, piano, timpani, tom-toms, xylophone, and castanets; but the full orchestra is never used as a whole. Rather, Stravinsky's orchestration is a series of chamber-sized combinations that yield a jewel-like delicacy, somewhat reminiscent of Webern. *Agon* progresses in a series of 12 movements arranged in four sections separated by interludes. The title is the Greek word for *contest* and, in place of a plot, the ballet presents opposed groupings of dancers. The stylized dance segments are modeled on 17th- and 18th-century French dance forms—sarabande, galliard, and branle—though the connection is more a symbolic than a literal approach to the actual dance forms. Dance and music connect most basically at the rhythmic level, and Stravinsky once again produced a score in which rhythmic intricacy mirrored human bodily movement. Balanchine's choreographic realization featured the dancers in rehearsal costume, expressing individually through abstract patterns the pulsing energy of the contest.

The music of *Agon* begins and ends diatonically, with excursions into chromatic and 12-tone idioms in the center of the design (Ex. 13-3). The tone rows are largely of chromatic design, and seldom does Stravinsky's technique directly resemble that of Schoenberg. For instance, the row in Example 13-3 is not stated at the outset, but is revealed slowly in the strings and woodwinds.

Example 13-3. Stravinsky. *Agon.* Part 1, No. 2, "Pas de Deux Double." Tone row.

Stravinsky's appetite for variety was inexhaustible. He examined the influence of architecture on music in his cantata *Canticum sacrum* (1956), commissioned by the city of Venice and designed to be performed in the historic St. Mark's Basilica there. He explored aspects of 18th-century art and music in his opera *The Rake's Progress* (1950), based on engravings by William Hogarth and on various style elements from Mozart's opera *Don Giovanni.* He surveyed current jazz trends in the *Ebony Concerto* (1945), written for clarinetist Woody Herman. Whatever the creative problem Stravinsky set for himself, he always carried it out with meticulous and consummate craftsmanship.

The masterpiece of Stravinsky's middle years proved to be the *Symphony of Psalms* (1930), commissioned by the Boston Symphony Orchestra. It is scored for orchestra and chorus of men's and boys' voices. For the text, he chose verses from Psalms 38, 39, and 150, from the Latin Vulgate version of the Bible.

Traditional symphonic form held little attraction for the master. Instead, he declared that he "wanted to create an organic whole without conforming to the various models adopted by custom, but still retaining the periodic order by which the symphony is distinguished." Stravinsky had always expressed a desire to control his musical timing precisely, and he designed the psalm-symphony plan according to the geometrical ratio of 1:2:4. Accordingly, the first movement lasts approximately three minutes; the second, six; and the third, twelve. In the overall plan, the three movements ascend as if in a ritualistic prayer sequence, beginning with the first movement: "Exaudi orationem meam, Domine" ("Hear my prayer, O Lord"). At the outset, a striking chord on pizzicato strings and woodwinds establishes the tonality and leads to the intoning of the text in the manner of plainchant. Melodic emphasis is on the smaller intervals of the second and third, as the chorus and orchestra proceed separately and together.

The second movement points up the need for patience and faith: "Expectans expectavi Dominum" ("I waited, waited for the Lord"). Stravinsky described this movement as "an upside-down pyramid of fugues." The first fugue is for solo instruments, with a subject resembling that of Bach's for the *Musical Offering* (Ex. 13-4a). Following it, "the next and higher stage of the pyramid is the human fugue, which [begins with] instrumental help" (Ex. 13-4b). Finally, "the third stage, the upside-down foundation, unites the two fugues."

As a consequence of the prayer, "The Lord bent down to me and heard my cry" (Ps. 39:1), the third movement opens with reaction to the heavenly intervention: a seraphic phrase on the words "Alleluia. Laudate Dominum" ("Alleluia. O praise the Lord"). The three-part movement contains a central allegro that, according to the composer, was "inspired by a vision of Elijah's chariot climbing to the heavens." Of all the Psalms, the 150th is the most musical, and the composer evokes a verbal orchestra with the biblical words: "Praise him with fanfares on the trumpet, praise him upon the lute and the harp, praise him with tambourines and dancing, praise him with stringed instruments and organs. Praise him with the clash of cymbals." It was typical of Stravinsky to bypass the obvious opportunity to feature the specific instru-

Example 13-4. Stravinsky. *Symphony of Psalms.* Second movement.

13-4a. Bars 1–4.

13-4b. Bars 29–32.

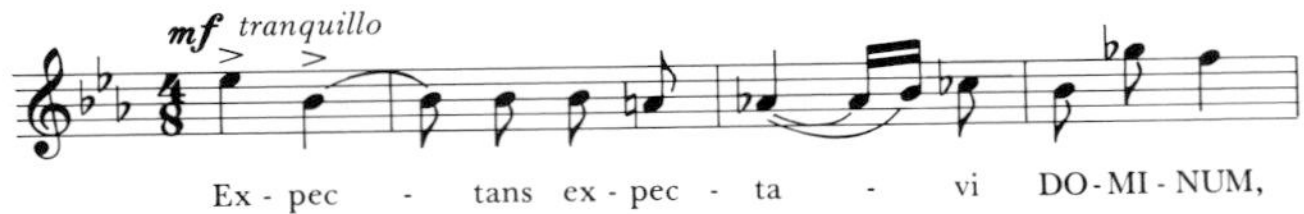

ments mentioned in the text. Nonetheless, the choral text meets and merges with the orchestra, creating an impressive conclusion, and the symphony ends on a sublime basso-ostinato configuration, echoing the close of the first movement.

BARTÓK

The Hungarian-born Béla Bartók was another major figure of international stature who, like Stravinsky, had his musical roots firmly planted in the soil of his native country. Much of his early career was devoted to collecting, recording on Edison cylinders, and cataloguing the folk songs and dances of Hungary and neighboring Balkan countries. Later these folk idioms and scale systems—modal, pentatonic, and whole-tone—found their way into his mature compositions in refined and individualistically cast forms. At first his bold harmonic progressions, unconventional contrapuntal techniques, and vivid scoring startled modern audiences. However, ears previously conditioned by Schoenberg and Stravinsky found his style both piquant and provocative.

To the question asked frequently in contemporary musical circles—Is there life still in the symphony, concerto, string quartet, and sonata?—Bartók's answer was a resounding affirmative. His contribution to these traditional forms, however, were as original, nontraditional, and atypical as his individual genius could make them.

Between 1908 and 1941 Bartók wrote six string quartets that are among the most important 20th-century contributions to that medium. In their exploration and extension of new musical resources, they have been equated in importance with Beethoven's last five quartets. His view of the color potential of the string quartet medium led to the expansion of movements and the relationships between them. One of his quartets is written as a single extended, comprehensive movement. Traditional dramatic values can be found in his work, but Bartók investigated new tone colors and harmonies, and he had his own view of atonality. In his writing for strings there are barbarous dissonances and stunning pizzicato effects, as well as radiant, luminous lyrical moments.

Bartók's *Music for Stringed Instruments, Percussion, and Celesta* of 1936 is a four-movement orchestral, symphonic in character and scope but not a symphony in the traditional sense. In the 20th century, composers had already been attracted to the rhythmic and tone-color resources of an extended group of percussion instruments. However, Bartók's mixture of percussion and strings, omitting the woodwinds, was highly unusual. The work shows an almost baroque interest in spatial relations, and the score contains explicit indications for the orchestral seating arrangement to allow for the particular tonal balances he had in mind.

Bass viol I		Bass viol II	
Cello I	Timpani	Bass drum	Cello II
Viola I	Side drums	Cymbals	Viola II
Violin II	Celesta	Xylophone	Violin IV
Violin I	Piano	Harp	Violin III

Conductor

The opening movement, andante tranquillo, is a contemporary view of fugal process, incorporating a meandering, chromatic subject set within a discreet, shadowy orchestration (Ex. 13-5). Although it is not immediately apparent to the listener, Bartók will use this subject as a motif to unify all four movements. Entries of the subject are introduced, unfolding by fifths alternately above and below each previous entry (A, E, D, B, G, F-sharp, etc.), until all 12 notes of the scale have been utilized. The series of subject entries culminates on E-flat, and the process is then reversed. For the remaining 33 bars, the subject is presented in inversion, with tensions gradually slackening until the movement concludes on the pitch on which it began (the note A). This mirrorlike transposition is a distinctive device on which Bartók drew for several compositions. Sometimes called the *arch form,* it relies on the concept of symmetry accomplished by using the equivalent of mirror images, that is, the repetition of musical sections in reverse (mirror) order.

Example 13-5. Bartók. *Music for Stringed Instruments, Percussion, and Celesta.* First movement, bars 1–4.

The succeeding allegro is set in sonata form with a focus on rhythmic vitality. The third movement, adagio, combines two personal predilections of Bartók. The first is a somewhat eerie, transparent evocation of night imagery, incorporating mysterious birdlike and insectlike sounds. The second is the arch form, described above. After a hollow, ghostly beginning, Bartók proceeds to unfold a delicate study in tone color. At about midpoint, bars 49 and 50 form a near mirror image of bars 47 and 48 (Ex. 13-6). The remainder of the composition is a compressed version in reverse of the first 47 bars. The final movement, allegro molto, is an exuberant, expanded rondo, recalling rustic Magyar guitars tuning up for a riotous village celebration replete with folk-inspired rhythms.

Example 13-6. Bartók. *Music for Stringed Instruments, Percussion, and Celesta.* Third movement, bars 47–50.

Bartók spent the dark days of World War II in the United States, where he concertized, continued his folkloric researches, and lectured at Columbia University. In failing health, he received from the Boston Symphony his last major commission, the *Concerto for Orchestra* (1943). In it he combined the traditions of symphony and concerto, of concerto grosso and solo concerto, while making the most of the performers' capabilities for individual and collective virtuoso performance. It is now one of the most admired and most often performed pieces in the concert repertory. Audiences revel in the kaleidoscope of orchestral colors, and each instrument is allowed its individual moment in the symphonic sun. The concerto is a masterwork that shows Bartók's musical style at its most mature.

The Russian Scene: Government and the Arts

"He who pays the piper calls the tune," says an old adage. Musicians have always had to adapt their music to changing social and political circumstances, whether employed by the church as in medieval times, or by churchly and secular patrons as during the Renaissance. In Louis XIV's France, all the arts were brought into the civil service through an ingenious system of academies whose artists ultimately bowed to the style and taste of the monarch. With the decline of aristocratic means for patronage, sponsorship of the arts spread more broadly in society, involving government, religious organizations, and private individuals. Composers found they often had to take up other activities to support themselves. Some held teaching posts, others wrote journalistic music criticism, still others took to the keyboard and the baton as public concert performers. As the 20th century approached, only a favored few enjoyed regular patronage from affluent benefactors.

In modern times, the Soviet Union has stood alone in assigning official recognition to the composing of music as a professional service to the state and its people, and in placing composers on the government payroll. In 19th-century Russia, several of the group known as the Five held government civil-service positions that had nothing whatsoever to do with music. After the Communist Revolution of 1917, however, music began to be linked to social and political policy. Lenin, the founder of the new Soviet Russia, was an ardent admirer of the music of Beethoven, whom he saw as a partisan of the French Revolution's ideals of liberty, equality, and fraternity in such works as the "Eroica" and Ninth symphonies. Lenin wrote that "art must unite the feeling, thought and will of the masses and inspire them."

Russian art, literature, and music became closely allied to politics with the official Resolution of 1932, which called on writers and artists to "depict reality in its revolutionary development" and to produce "works attuned to the epoch." Shortly thereafter, the Union of Soviet Composers was formed as the official musical wing of the government. The union promoted a policy of "socialist realism," encouraging composers to write music that was "optimistic" and avoided "formalism," a nebulous term that covered most of the current style trends in contemporary music. One of its statutes declared: "The main attention of the Soviet composer must be directed toward the victorious progressive principles of reality, toward all that is heroic, bright, and beautiful. Socialist Realism demands an implacable struggle against folk-negating modernistic directions that are typical of the decay of contemporary bourgeois art, against subservience and servility toward modern bourgeois culture."

This meant that Soviet composers had to adjust to current conditions and write within the restrictions laid down by the government bureaucracy. The two major Russian composers of this period, Sergei Prokofiev and Dmitri Shostakovich, found such sociopolitical constraints both irksome and difficult. Confusion stemmed primarily from two areas: first, that those in the Party responsible for an inhibiting artistic climate regularly published artificial guidelines for production in the arts; second, it was almost impossible for composers to translate these often conflicting directives into sound. How, for example, does one interpret "victorious progressive principles of reality" in sonic terms?

Both Prokofiev and Shostakovich found private solutions to public political pressures. Each composer accepted his Russo-European heritage and continued to write sonatas, string quartets, symphonies, concertos, operas, and ballets. Within these parameters, their styles contained some similar elements, including a ready sense of irony and a sardonic scherzo style in the manner of Mahler; a dedication to the classical tradition in its early and later manifestations; and a partiality for spiky dissonance countered by diatonic melodic writing.

PROKOFIEV

Before the Russian Revolution, Prokofiev was well on his way to a successful career in composition based upon the classical tradition. He celebrated those roots in the charming *Classical Symphony* of 1917, consciously based on the style of Haydn. Shortly after the Revolution, he decided to avoid the problem of government intervention by emigrating to the West, where for 18 years he found favor as a composer and pianist in Europe and the United States. In 1936 he returned to Russia, saying, "I've got to talk to people who are of my own flesh and blood, so that they can give me back something I lack—their songs, my songs." The first compositions on his return to Russia were for children, including *Peter and the Wolf,* the popular symphonic tale for narrator and orchestra.

Always a facile composer, Prokofiev was able to simplify his style to please the Party without sacrificing his musical integrity. He made his compositional style more personal by stressing a combination of neoclassical, neoprimitive, and neoromantic elements. Adept at mixing the grotesque and the ironic in scherzo movements, he could also alternate dissonant passages with hauntingly lovely lyrical moments. His works were generally approved as "optimistic" and less "formalist," and he gained wide popular acceptance with such masterpieces as his Fifth Symphony, Third Piano Concerto, and *Romeo and Juliet,* the latter a ballet score in the lush, romantic style of Tchaikovsky.

Prokofiev also wrote several film scores, beginning with *Lieutenant Kije* in 1933. When government policy was reversed, restoring to favor several historical heroes and past heroic events, he collaborated with the noted Russian director Sergei Eisenstein in two landmark films, *Alexander Nevsky* (1938) and *Ivan the Terrible* (two parts, 1944 and 1945). Some of this music has entered the concert repertory, including the orchestral *Lieutenant Kije Suite* and the *Alexander Nevsky* cantata.

SHOSTAKOVICH

The pressure to write in the so-called social realist style fell most heavily on the shoulders of Dmitri Shostakovich. Though he chose to remain in Russia and rarely went abroad, his music traveled so widely that his fame was as great outside the Soviet Union as it was within. As a young composer, he looked to western Europe for ideas, and many of his compositions in the 1920s and 1930s testify to his knowledge of then-current works by Mahler, Schoenberg, and Stravinsky.

His opera *Lady Macbeth from Mtsensk District* scored a great success at its premiere in 1934. Over a two-year span the taut psychological drama was performed nearly 200 times and was hailed as an opera that "could have been written only by a Soviet composer brought up in the best traditions of Soviet culture." In 1936, however, the dictator Joseph Stalin attended a performance in Moscow and reportedly left in an apoplectic rage. Previously Stalin had stated that the criteria for a "good" Soviet opera must include a libretto built around a socialist topic, realistic music using a national idiom, and a positive hero who exemplified the new socialist age. *Lady Macbeth* offered a libretto filled with criminal greed, licentious eroticism, and brutal homicide, featuring a murderous heroine who was both willful and self-serving.

The next day the official Soviet newspaper *Pravda* published a stinging article entitled "Chaos Instead of Music," believed to have been dictated by Stalin himself. While it was clearly aimed at Shostakovich and his opera, the article also served notice to artists in all fields that they must conform to the officially decreed style of socialist realism and what the Party saw as the needs of the people. The critique read in part: "From the first moment, the listener is shocked by a deliberately dissonant, confused stream of sound. Fragments of melody, embryonic phrases appear—only to disappear again in the din, the grinding, and the screaming. . . . The music quacks, grunts, and growls, and suffocates itself in order to express the amatory scenes as naturalistically as possible."

During the following year Shostakovich reassessed his position. At the last moment, he withdrew the strongly dissonant, Mahler-inspired Fourth Symphony just before its first performance. Then, on November 21, 1937, before an audience that packed the hall of the Leningrad Philharmonic Orchestra, the now-famous Symphony No. 5 in D Minor (Op. 47) received its premiere. The composer later wrote of the symphony: "It may be called a lyrical-heroic symphony. Its basic ideas are the sufferings of man, and optimism. I wanted to convey optimism asserting itself as a world outlook through a series of tragic conflicts in a great inner, mental struggle."

On the surface, the work appeared to be a traditional abstract four-movement symphony: sonata form, scherzo, three-part slow movement, and a closing movement built on sonata-form principles. The composer's stated "lyrical-heroic" views were reflected in an overall impression of sinewy strength, carried out through searing melodic lines and bold rhythms that alternated with quiet passages of introspective pathos. For this work, Shostakovich chose to write for a large, late-romantic orchestra that gave him ample opportunity to demonstrate his mastery of tone color, a practice he continued throughout his career as a symphonist.

The work was pronounced an official success. *Pravda* praised the symphony for its "psychological searching," while Party officials and the world at large viewed the symphony as a statement of triumphant affirmation. Shostakovich was considered "rehabilitated," and he was once again hailed as one of the great Russian composers—for the time being.

But Shostakovich was destined to find himself constantly in and out of official favor, as Russia's political temperature rose or cooled. A composition that was "in" today might as easily be "out" tomorrow. He did, however, live to see *Lady Macbeth,* slightly rewritten and retitled after its powerful heroine, *Katerina Ismailova,* officially endorsed in 1962.

The German Scene

The close of World War I in 1918 was marked by the defeat of Germany by the Allied armies, after which the German monarchy was superseded by a socialist republic and the capital was moved from Berlin to Weimar. For the German people, postwar desolation, deep disillusionment, rampant inflation, and psychological insecurity eventually led to the ascendance of the Nazi Party under the dictatorship of Adolph Hitler in 1933. Before this came about, however, enlightened government sponsorship of the arts under the Weimar Republic turned a brief 15-year interlude into a miniature golden age.

HINDEMITH

The outstanding German composer of this period was Paul Hindemith. He rebelled against the romantic tradition and enthusiastically embraced the movement known as *Die neue Sachlichkeit* (the New Objectivity), which advocated music detached from sentiment, free of pictorial or programmatic suggestion, and expressive of nothing outside itself.

With the idea that music was a practical and useful art, Hindemith became the founder and leading exponent of what was called *Gebrauchsmusik* (literally, utility or workaday music). He noted in a lecture in 1927: "The composer today should write only if he knows for what purpose he is writing. The days of composing for the sake of composing are perhaps gone forever." Hindemith's intention was to make a clear break with the self-conscious, ivory-tower viewpoint of "art for art's sake," as well as the romantic image of the artist starving in a garret while awaiting divine inspiration. Instead, he revived the older notion of composers writing music on commission, citing Bach's position as choirmaster, which entailed writing a cantata for every Sunday of the church year. He also advised younger composers to find a market for their works by writing short pieces for home performance, for schools, for the radio and films, and for various public occasions.

Noting the lack of good playable music for instruments other than the usual chamber combinations, Hindemith projected a series of sonatas that would include all viable modern instruments. He completed sonatas for piano and oboe, bassoon, French horn, trumpet, English horn, and trombone. Hindemith was also one of the foremost contrapuntalists of modern times, and he found formal models in baroque dances, fugue, concerto grosso, and basso ostinato. At the same time he did not hesitate to include jazz idioms when they suited his purpose. After intermittent boycotts of his work by the Nazi Ministry of Culture, Hindemith's music was finally banned in 1937 by Joseph Goebbels as "unbearable to the Third Reich." He came to the United States in 1940. As he matured, he mellowed considerably, stating that "Nothing is more wearisome or more futile than the most antiquated of all manias: the rage to be modern. We should minimize the word *new* in the term *new art* and emphasize rather the word *art.*"

Hindemith's opera *Mathis der Maler* (*Matthias the Painter,* 1934) and the three-movement symphony *Mathis der Maler* were written at about the same time. The opera is based on the famous Isenheim altarpiece by the Renaissance painter Matthias Grünewald. Its libretto, written by the composer, is a multilevel allegory that unfolds in seven tableaux. On the surface, it reveals the artist's need to become politically involved in times of social strife, in this instance the Peasants' Revolt of 1525. At a deeper level, however, the plot becomes a metaphor for the artist's need to express himself through his craft, with the final realization that he can serve society best through art. The revelation comes through a dream-vision, in which the artist becomes the figure of Saint Anthony as represented in the altarpiece. He undergoes violent torment and temptation, carries on a dialogue with Saint Paul (a representation from another panel of the altarpiece), and ultimately returns to the real world to finish his masterpiece.

Throughout both opera and symphony, the harmony is constructed on the tritone (the interval from G to C-sharp), the "devil in music" of medieval theory. The symphony relates closely to the opera, and each of the three movements represents one of the scenes from Grünewald's triptych. The first, "Engelkonzert" ("Angelic Concert"), is a gleaming sonata-form movement, relying mainly on the string section to illustrate a portion of Grünewald's center panel depicting the Nativity (see Plate XVII). One prominent subject is the old anthem "Es sungen drei Engel" ("Three angels sang," Ex. 13-7a). In the opera the music of this movement appears complete as the prelude to the first tableau, and later is woven through the sixth tableau as Matthias describes the painted nativity scene.

The second movement, "Grablegung" ("Entombment"), is characterized by restrained harmonic tension, depicting the lamentation of Saint John and the three Marys as the body of Christ is prepared for the tomb. In the opera it appears as an orchestral interlude in the seventh tableau, a sorrowing com-

Example 13-7. Hindemith. *Matthias the Painter,* symphony.

13-7a. "Three angels sang," bars 9–16.

mentary on the death of a major character. Reference to this music is again made in the accompaniment to Matthias' final monologue, just preceding his own death.

The final symphonic movement, "Versuchung des Heiligen Antonius" ("Temptation of Saint Anthony"), is the longest and musically the richest, as it depicts the corresponding panel of Grünewald's altarpiece (see Plate XVIII). At the beginning of the movement appear the words "Ubi eras bone Jhesu ubi eras, quare non affuisti ut sanares vulnera mea?" ("Where were you, good Jesus, where were you, and why have you not come to heal my wounds?") The phrase, attributed to Saint Anthony at the time of his temptation, appears in the opera in the sixth tableau, during the dream-vision of Matthias as Anthony. The music of the movement is scattered throughout that tableau in the opera. The symphonic score also identifies a quote from the medieval sequence written by Saint Thomas Aquinas for the Mass of Corpus Christi, *Lauda Sion salvatorem* (Praise Zion for salvation), Ex. 13-7b. The passage occurs in the sixth tableau of the opera during a dream of temptation, when a martyr adjures Saint Anthony to "relinquish salvation." The symphony closes with reference to the duet of Anthony and Paul, paralleling the ringing "Alleluia" that closes the operatic tableau.

WEILL

Musical theater became the dominant medium of musical expression for Kurt Weill, after his early exploration of the standard genres of symphony, sonata, and string quartet. He shared with the Marxist-oriented writers Georg Kaiser and Bertolt Brecht a conviction that art could reflect and change contemporary social values. They specifically rejected the complicated, sophisticated theories of Schoenberg, as well as any other music heavy with cerebration, and looked for simpler, more direct avenues of communication.

With Brecht as librettist, Weill's earliest and most enduring success was the cabaretlike Singspiel *Die Dreigroschenoper* (*The Threepenny Opera,* 1928). The plot was based on the satirical *Beggar's Opera* of 1728, which had enjoyed a popular if somewhat scandalous success in London during Handel's time (see p. 178). In that work, John Gay and John Pepusch had ridiculed the mythological divinities and historical heroes that populated opera seria. Their ironic view of society, in which all values seem topsy-turvy, where the beggars rule and the highwaymen are heroes, proved itself an equally appropriate vehicle

13-7b. Lauda Sion salvatorem. Plainsong.

in the 20th century for the biting social commentary of Weill and Brecht.

Weill replaced the baroque orchestra of strings and continuo with a down-to-earth 1920s cabaret ensemble, including banjo, pump organ, piano, trumpet, and saxophone. The prelude, marked maestoso, is a jazzy parody of a baroque French overture, based—as is much of the opera's music—on a kind of "wrong-note" diatonic harmony. As the prelude draws to a close, the Streetsinger comes before the curtain to speak the prologue:

> You are about to hear an opera for beggars. And since this opera was envisioned so splendidly that only beggars could imagine it—and since it needed to be cheap enough that even beggars could pay for it, it is called the *Threepenny Opera.*

In the opera, the role of the Streetsinger functions like a cynical Greek chorus, describing background events and announcing each musical number. The curtain opens on a fair in the Soho district of London. The libretto describes the scene: "Beggars are begging, the prostitutes are prostituting themselves. A penny-dreadful ballad singer is singing a penny-dreadful ballad." The Streetsinger announces the opening song: "First you will hear a penny-dreadful ballad about the bandit Macheath, called Mack the Knife." He then proceeds to sing the seven-stanza ballad, which, like all the "arias" in the opera, is strophic. The music, designed for singing actors who can project the meaning of a song, is small in melodic compass and hypnotically banal in its repetitiveness (Ex. 13-8).

Succeeding verses ironically detail Macheath's "heroic" activities: murder, theft, arson, and rape. Shortly thereafter, Mack marries his sweetheart, Polly, daughter of the King of the Beggars. Once again traditional values are cynically parodied, as they sing a "passionate" love duet to the text: "Love will or won't endure, here or somewhere else."

A typical, cheerless representative of this beggars' society is Jenny, a pathetic, ignorant prostitute in love with Mack. The role was created by Weill's wife, Lotte Lenya, who had been a cabaret performer. Jenny daydreams of escaping into a more exciting, happier life, in the four-stanza "Ballad of Pirate Jenny or Dreams of a Kitchen Maid." In the first three verses, she imagines herself a mysterious, desirable person, somehow connected to "A ship with eight sails and fifty cannons." In the last verse, her frustrations with life and hatred of her station are expressed in a chilling declaration:

Example 13-8. Weill. *The Threepenny Opera.* "Ballad of Mack the Knife," bars 1–15.

And at noon it'll be still by the harbor
  when they ask who will have to die.
And then you'll hear me say: The whole lot!
And when the heads roll, I'll say: Hoop-la!
  And the ship with eight sails
  And fifty cannons
  Will vanish with me.

Over the next five years, increasing Nazi strength and influence made itself felt in German theaters. The first Nazi-inspired riot caused by Weill's outspoken contempt and sarcasm for the regime occurred at the premiere of his next effort with Brecht, *Aufsteig und Fall der Stadt Mahagonny* (*Rise and Fall of the City of Mahagonny,* 1930). Concentrated efforts to stop performances of his works in state-supported theaters finally forced Weill and Lenya to leave Germany in 1933. They reached the United States in 1935, where Weill became a citizen and remained until his death in 1950.

In America he directed his attentions again to a wide public, centering his efforts successfully on the Broadway musical stage and on films. His more notable efforts included the first psychological musical, *Lady in the Dark,* with a libretto by Moss Hart (1941); an opera-musical based on Elmer Rice's telling portrait of life among the lower classes in New York City, *Street Scene* (1947); and *Lost in the Stars* (1949), after Alan Paton's novel *Cry the Beloved Country,* about the encounter of black and white cultures in Africa.

With Brecht, Weill envisioned a type of theater in which plot gave way to narrative, while the audience abandoned its passive state by assuming the active role of the crowd influencing the events taking place onstage. For Weill, music could no longer play the Wagnerian role of heightening and proclaiming text, of illustrating and painting psychological situations. Instead, music was now an art that interpreted text, conveyed a point of view, and depicted attitudes.

The American Scene

American music had always been influenced by that of Europe, not at all surprising in a country that took pride in its "melting pot" image of merging many cultures into one. American composers of art music in the 19th century—George Chadwick, Horatio Parker, Amy Beach, and Arthur Foote—had either studied in Europe or reflected its academic heritage. A bit later, young American composers found themselves under the sway of impressionism, a common influence in the work of several prominent composers at the turn of the century—Charles Martin Loeffler, John Alden Carpenter, Charles Griffes, and Deems Taylor.

Elements indigenous to the culture of America, however, were appearing with increasing frequency. Even the 19th century had seen a few successful attempts to bypass European influence. Stephen Foster gained wide acclaim for songs that had been bred in a minstrel-show environment, and Edward MacDowell delighted a generation with his small-scaled, poetic piano pieces *Woodland Sketches* and *New England Idylls*. By the 1920s, John Alden Carpenter had produced two ballets, *Krazy Kat* and *Skyscrapers,* that were anything but European in their orientation. However, audiences were still predisposed toward music imported from across the ocean. New directions in American music would, for the time being, emerge from its eastern seaboard.

IVES

One American composer who displayed a peppery Yankee temperament, and did so in comparative musical isolation, was Charles Ives. A native of Danbury, Connecticut, Ives reveled in his New England heritage. He attended Yale, where he took a liberal arts degree and studied music with Horatio Parker. Much of his musical training had come not from Parker but from his father, the Danbury town bandmaster. George Ives had extraordinary musical perception. He loved to experiment with "forbidden" sounds—quarter-tones, polytonality, and the like. He instilled in his son a desire to search out new musical resources and in turn to continually stretch the ears of his listeners.

Charles Ives wrote some conservative music during his time at Yale, and titles for compositions from this period include the traditional sonata and symphony. But later, when he was most actively composing, his music recalled the life and musical experiences of his childhood, and this part of his output is remarkably free of the European musical tradition.

Ives was dedicated to a strong, sinewy America rooted in clearly defined moral and religious values. The American experience was for him unity in diversity. The music he wrote came from the land, its people, and their heritage, and he sprinkled it liberally with folk songs, patriotic airs, dance tunes, church hymns, and spirituals.

Ives realized, however, that to be a full-time composer of classical music in America gave no assurance of a living wage. As he wryly observed, "Assuming a man lives by himself and with no dependents, he might write music that no one would play prettily, listen to or buy. But if he has a nice wife and some nice children, how can he let the children starve on his dissonances?" Ives thereupon focused his considerable creative energies on the insurance business, continuing to compose when he had time, mainly at night. By the end of World War I, he was head of the largest insurance company in the country and had suffered his first heart attack.

Ives shared with Beethoven a dissatisfaction with the inherent limitations of musical instruments, and the limitations of performers who played them. His musical vision sent him on forays that more than once resulted in music that was unplayable. Having been often admonished by musicians that his music could not be played on a particular instrument, or that it would "play better" if he were to make changes in it, Ives wrote indignantly:

> My God! What has sound got to do with music! The waiter brings the only fresh egg he has, but the man at breakfast sends it back because it doesn't fit his eggcup. Why can't music go out in the same way it comes in to a man, without having to crawl over a fence of sounds, thoraxes, catguts, wire, wood, and brass? The instrument!—there is the perennial difficulty—there is music's limitation. Is it the composer's fault that man has only ten fingers?

The single work that best sums up Ives' musical philosophy is the *Second Pianoforte Sonata—Concord, Mass., 1840–1860* (1915), better known as the "Concord" Sonata. There was a close affinity between the New England transcendental philosophical movement and Ives' approach to music. Accordingly, the four movements of the sonata bear the names of Ralph Waldo Emerson, Nathaniel Hawthorne, the Alcott family, and Henry David Thoreau, all of Concord, Massachusetts. Under the spell of their writings, music became more than subjective self-expression for Ives, and he sought to capture in the music the essence of transcendent reality. For a privately printed edition of the work in 1920, Ives wrote four "Essays Before a Sonata," plus a prologue and an epilogue. Longer than the sonata itself, the discourse was meant to provide insights into his own thinking and the four musical realizations he had made of the philosophers' thoughts.

Ives' music for this sonata was incredibly diverse. Tonally, it ran the gamut from simple diatonic harmonies with key signatures to jolting atonality; rhythmically, from the familiar pulse of a four-square hymn to wildly complicated polyrhythmic fabrics—including a passage in 4½/4 meter. There were also such instructions on the score as "(quite slowly and as a song) but not too evenly"; "climbing up with rush and action"; "very fast—heavily or in a kind of reckless way"; "From here on, as fast as possible."

His comments on those who inspired the sonata provide some insights into the proper musical treatment.

I. Emerson

> Emerson seems to use the great definite interests of humanity to express the greater, indefinite, spiritual values—to fulfill what he can in his realms of rev-

elation. We see him—standing on a summit at the door of the infinite, where many men do not care to climb, peering into the mysteries of life, contemplating the eternities, hurling back whatever he discovers there—now thunderbolts for us to grasp, if we can, and translate—now placing quietly, even tenderly, in our hands things that we may see without effort; if we won't see them, so much the worse for us. There is an "oracle" at the beginning of the *Fifth Symphony;* in those four notes lies one of Beethoven's greatest messages. We would place its translation above the relentlessness of fate knocking at the door, above the greater human message of destiny, and strive to bring it towards the spiritual message of Emerson's revelations, even to the "common heart" of Concord—the soul of humanity knocking at the door of the divine mysteries, radiant in the faith that it *will* be opened—and the human become the divine!

In the movement itself the elements of sonata form can be discerned. The music is appropriately craggy, strong, and tranquilly thoughtful. The motif from Beethoven's Fifth Symphony enters with the direction "Faster and decisively" and comes back quietly, as the movement begins to fade to a close (Exs. 13-9a, b).

Example 13-9. Ives. *Second Pianoforte Sonata* ("Concord"). Excerpts. Beethoven motif examples indicated by asterisk.

13-9a. From "Emerson."

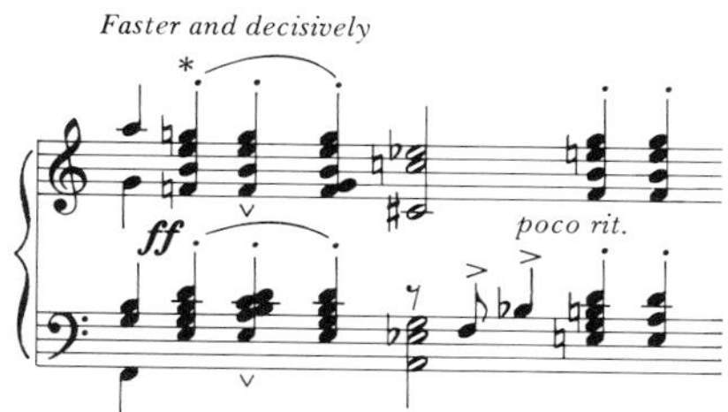

13-9b. From "Emerson."

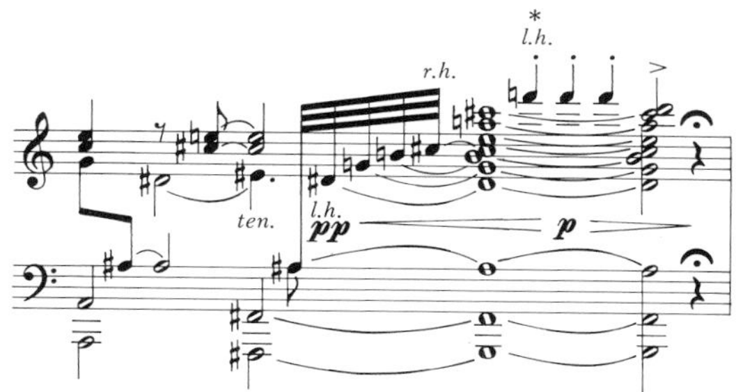

II. Hawthorne

The substance of Hawthorne is so dripping wet with the supernatural, the phantasmal, the mystical, so surcharged with adventures, from the deeper picturesque to the illusive fantastic, that one unconsciously finds oneself thinking of him as a poet of greater imaginative impulse than Emerson or Thoreau. Any comprehensive conception of Hawthorne's, either in words or music, must have for its basic theme something that has to do with the influence of sin upon the conscience. Hawthorne is not attempted in our music which is but an "extended fragment" trying to suggest some of his wilder, fantastical adventures into the half-childlike, half-fairylike phantasmal realms.

Ives' portrait is a fantastic scherzo, with spots of "wrong-note" impressionism, circus big-top music, a drum-and-bugle-corps march, and one of his favorite national tunes, *Columbia, the Gem of the Ocean.* At one point the pianist is directed to take a piece of wood and hold it down silently on all the black or white keys of a two-octave span (Ex. 13-9c). This releases the dampers for those strings, allowing them to vibrate sympathetically when notes are played below, producing a cavernous echo effect. The Beethoven motif appears at the close, followed by the suggestion of a fireworks rocket (Ex. 13-9d).

13-9c. From "Hawthorne."

13-9d. From "Hawthorne."

III. The Alcotts

Old Man Alcott was usually "doin' somthin'" within. An internal grandiloquence made him melodious without; an exuberant, impressible visionary, absorbed with philosophy as such; to him it was a kind of transcendental business, the profits of which supported his inner man rather than his family. [In the Alcott house] sits the little old spinet piano on which Beth played the old Scotch airs, and played at the [Beethoven] *Fifth Symphony.*

In keeping with the preface, the Beethoven motif appears at the beginning of this quiet movement and permeates it throughout (Ex. 13-9e). A lyric section emerges, containing melodically oblique references to "old Scotch airs" such as *Loch Lomond.* The music rises to a climax and a triumphant return of the motif, followed immediately by a short, quiet close.

13-9e. From "The Alcotts."

IV. Thoreau

> Thoreau was a great musician, not because he played the flute but because he did not have to go to Boston to hear "the Symphony." He was divinely conscious of the enthusiasm of Nature, the emotion of her rhythms, and the harmony of her solitude. In this consciousness he sang of the submission to Nature, the religion of contemplation, and the freedom of simplicity. And if there shall be a program for our music, let it follow his thought on an autumn day of Indian summer at Walden—a shadow of a thought at first, colored by the mist and haze over the pond. It is darker—the poet's flute is heard out over the pond and Walden hears the swan song of that "Day"—and faintly echoes. Is it a transcendental tune of Concord?

Ives' musical interpretation stresses the indrawn and deeply introspective aspects of Thoreau's response to universal nature. Near the close, the pastoral atmosphere is enhanced by the introduction of a flute, which sounds the Beethoven motif (Ex. 13-9f). The sonata closes inwardly upon itself with a final rhythmic statement of the motif (Ex. 13-9g).

COPLAND

During the two decades following World War I, young American composers were attracted to the European scene. Following in the footsteps of literary figures such as Gertrude Stein, F. Scott Fitzgerald, and Ernest Hemingway, many musicians went to Paris to study with the prestigious teacher Nadia Boulanger, who helped them find their own individual styles. Among them were Douglas Moore, Walter Piston, Virgil Thomson, Quincy Porter, Roy Harris, Aaron Copland, Marc Blitzstein, and Elliott Carter. Of that group, Aaron

13-9f. From "Thoreau."

13-9g. From "Thoreau."

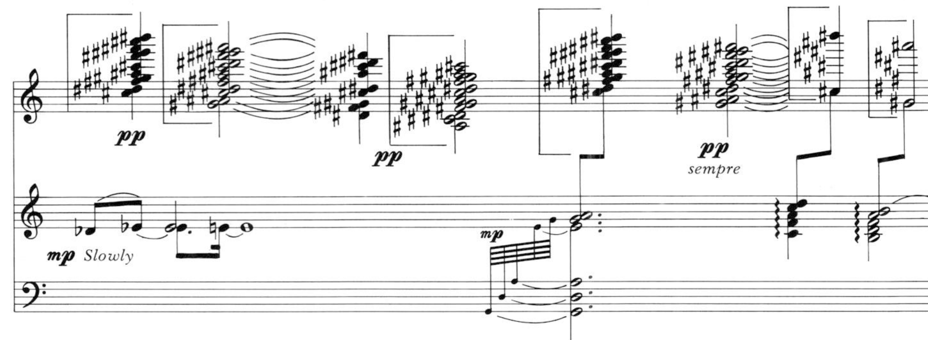

Copland captured the widest public following. His early works, such as the *Piano Variations* (1930) and the *Sonata* (1941), were characterized by astringent dissonances and tight formal control. Thereafter he set out to find a means of musical expression that might communicate the American experience in a broad popular sense.

Not surprisingly, the popularity of jazz here and abroad during that period encouraged fledgling composers to incorporate elements of this uniquely American idiom into their own music. Copland considered jazz the most indigenous expression of American folk music, and his *Music for Theater* (1925) was strongly oriented to the blues and Dixieland traditions. He tried to relate combinations of jazz, diatonic harmonies, and polytonal and polyrhythmic procedures. In the process, he began a search for what he described as "a musical vernacular, which, as language, would cause no difficulties to my listeners," building on "my old interest in making a connection between music and the life about me to see if I couldn't say what I had to say in the simplest possible terms."

Copland found what he sought in the popular music of Latin America (*El salón Mexico,* 1936); in cowboy music of the American Southwest (*Billy the Kid,* 1938); and in the folk religious and dance music of the American eastern seaboard (*Appalachian Spring, 1944*). His ability to reach a wide public was demonstrated in several successful film scores: the documentary *The River* (1937), John Steinbeck's *Of Mice and Men* (1939), Thornton Wilder's *Our Town* (1940), Steinbeck's *The Red Pony* (1948), and *The Heiress,* which won an Academy

Award for best musical score in 1948.

While Charles Ives had been a product of small-town New England, Copland was born and bred in New York City and had studied in Europe. His perception of Americana was wide-ranging, from the formidable *Lincoln Portrait* (1942) for orchestra, speaker, and chorus, to the contemplative art songs in *Twelve Poems of Emily Dickinson* (1950); from the energetic western ballets *Billy the Kid* (1938) and *Rodeo* (1942), to the highly esteemed orchestral suite *Appalachian Spring*.

In its original 1944 form, *Appalachian Spring* was a ballet written for Martha Graham's dance company and scored for 13 instruments. Set in the Pennsylvania hills in the early 1800s, it recounts the courtship and wedding of a young farm couple, as described in the score:

> A pioneer celebration in spring around a newly-built farm house in the Pennsylvania hills in the early part of the last century. The bride-to-be and the young farmer-husband enact the emotions, joyful and apprehensive, aroused by their new domestic partnership. A revivalist and his followers remind the new householders of the strange and terrible aspects of human fate. At the end the couple are left quiet and strong in their new house.

Copland arranged the work for large orchestra in 1945, linking eight scenes without pause. In its way, *Appalachian Spring* is an American counterpart of Stravinsky's ritualizing of Russian wedding traditions in *Les noces*. After an orchestral evocation of spring, Copland's score creates the atmosphere of a hearty and innocent Shaker settlement. His melodic material stresses the "open" intervals of the octave, perfect fourth, and perfect fifth that became one mark of his American musical idiom (Ex. 13-10). Quiet strength is expressed in permutations of the unaffected Shaker tune "Simple Gifts" (Ex. 13-11). An assortment of country dances fills out the remainder of the work, alternately cheery and introspective, raucous and lyrical.

For most of his career as a composer, Copland had little regard for serial writing, feeling that the "12-tone system is the artificial product of an 'overcultured' society and lies outside the main current of music." As he noted, "In my youth I considered Schoenberg as still writing German music, the influence of which I, as an American composer, was trying to escape."

Near the end of World War II Copland discovered that composers such as Pierre Boulez had found ways to use the 12-tone method "without the German esthetic." After long thought and careful consideration, he tried his hand at 12-tone composition in *Piano Fantasy* (1958), in *Connotations for Orchestra* (1962)—written for the opening of New York's Lincoln Center—and in *Inscape* (1967), commissioned for the 125th anniversary of the New York Philharmonic. *Connotations* exploited a variation technique, a "free treatment of the baroque form of the Chaconne." For *Inscape* the composer borrowed his

Example 13-10. Copland. *Appalachian Spring*, bars 84–90.

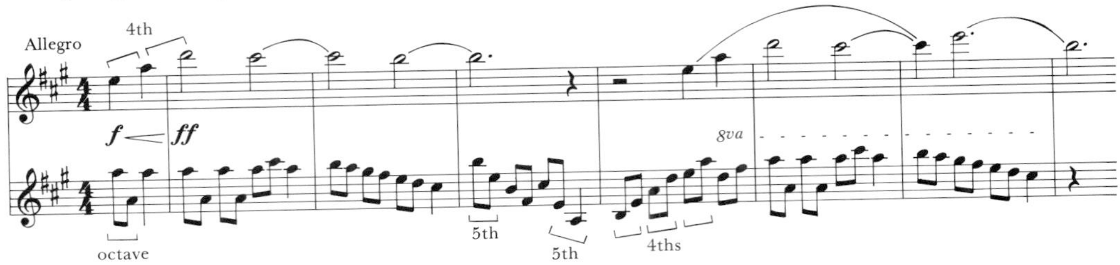

Example 13-11. Copland. *Appalachian Spring.* "Simple Gifts," rehearsal letter 65.

title from the English poet Gerard Manley Hopkins, who explained the term as a "quasi-mystical illumination, a sudden perception of that deeper pattern, order and unity which gives meaning to external forms."

A persuasive writer and commentator on the world musical scene, Copland described these last compositions as reflecting "to some degree, the tenseness of the times in which we live." Audiences have generally tended to prefer the simpler view of American life projected in his ballet scores.

JAZZ

The emergence of jazz as a form of popular dance music that was eventually incorporated into concert music was a major development in both America and the rest of the world. Over the centuries, the arts have consistently reflected certain distinctions of class consciousness, but they have a way of crossing social barriers with comparative ease. Religious composers have a long tradition of transforming popular tunes into hymns, motets, and anthems. Court and concert-hall composers used elements from folk tunes and idioms in their art music. In the 20th century, the popular idiom that most successfully traversed the obstacle course between the dance hall and the concert hall was jazz.

Jazz developed from African musical roots, brought by slaves to the American South and transformed by their descendants. It could also claim ties with the more formal and syncopated ragtime music. Jazz stemmed from no single locale, and had no single ancestor. Like Topsy, it just grew—from long-remembered elements of tribal music, from religious spirituals, from work and prison songs. During the first decade of the century, jazz established itself in New Orleans. Proving to be an easy traveler, it soon found a warm welcome in the working-class dance establishments and bars of Memphis, Chicago, and New York.

Jazz was presented to audiences as a polar opposite to concert music. Since the early 19th century, classical composers had systematically taken stronger control over their published musical scores and had discouraged performers from tampering with their increasingly explicit notation. The published score became the performer's gospel, and improvisation as a lively and vital musical experience virtually disappeared. The notation of a jazz composition, on the other hand, was a point from which to take flight. Jazz composers encouraged highly individual improvisation, giving performers abundant freedom within a contained framework, much like the freedom of the baroque basso continuo line. Performers went on to borrow, improvise upon, or parody the melodies, rhythms, and harmonies. In the process, individual musicians developed their own personal styles. These freedoms at the local level eventually produced performance traditions associated with such jazz centers as New Orleans, Chicago, Kansas City, and New York.

Even when subjected to the scrutiny of scholarship, jazz does not lend itself easily to specific definitions, since the music is by nature one of continuous change and evolution. Moreover, recordings of jazz performances cannot be considered definitive guides from which to draw generalities about performance practice, since jazz is by nature an art of continual transformation in which each performance is unlike those that came before and those that will follow.

In the beginning, jazz stressed a melody over a diatonic harmonic accompaniment, the latter enhanced by chords of the sixth. The jazz sound was also associated with strong melodic lines played by specific instrumental timbres, such as the clarinet or any of a number of brass instruments, the most popular of which were the trumpet, cornet, trombone, and tuba. These were supported by a strong rhythmic complex, consisting of piano, drums, bass viol, and sometimes other plucked instruments.

Rhythmically, early jazz unfolded over a regular beat in duple meter, in a steady tempo (again, like that of the baroque basso continuo). Added to this might be syncopation of the melodic line, unequal subdivisions of the meter, and occasional excursions into triple time. Tempo rubato (literally, "stolen time") is assumed, lending freedom and flexibility of movement (p. 435).

The red-light Storyville district of New Orleans provided a fertile soil for the dynamic new music, and by 1917 its widely varied combinations of stylistic elements were known collectively as *jazz*. The moral climate that produced Prohibition closed down Storyville that year, and many jazz musicians emigrated northward, spreading the new sounds to Chicago and New York. A group from New Orleans, the Original Dixieland Jazz Band, played in New York and made the first jazz phonograph records. In the early 1920s, the saxophone became a regular member of the jazz band. As audiences became familiar with new jazz-band sounds, certain jazz idioms began to infiltrate popular music, and in many dance bands stringed instruments were replaced by clarinets and trumpets.

American soldiers gave jazz a transatlantic boost during World War I, when *le jazz hot* became the rage of Paris. They also brought with them the slightly more formal ragtime and the latest dance styles, the fox-trot and the tango. In war-weary Europe, these dances quickly replaced the waltz in fashionable dance halls. As shaped by the American consciousness, jazz seemed to imitate the restlessness and feverish pace of postwar urban modernity. Those in the European community who had already accepted African-inspired visual neoprimitivism in the works of Picasso, Matisse, and Modigliani were delighted with a new music that reveled in the excitement engendered by its African rhythmic ancestry.

Popular music from other countries also arrived on the European scene. Darius Milhaud, a member of the Parisian group called the Six, was for a time associated with the French Embassy in Brazil. Upon his return to France in 1920, he produced the orchestral *Le boeuf sur le toit* (*The Ox on the Roof,* Op. 58), a title that came from a Brazilian song. Envisioned by the composer as accompaniment for a Charlie Chaplin film, the score included the tango, the samba, and other Hispano-Brazilian dances, all connected by a recurring theme.

Jazz became especially attractive to several younger composers, anxious to distance themselves from a romantic heritage. Stravinsky, working in Paris, tried his hand in *Piano Rag Music* (1919). With its catchy syncopations and polyrhythms, jazz appealed to a number of French avant-garde composers, who incorporated the new craze into their latest efforts at serious music. Erik Satie's entertainment *Parade* (1915) was in part jazz-inspired, and included such modern sounds as a typewriter and a boat whistle.

Darius Milhaud traveled to the United States in 1923. The jazz he heard in Harlem found expression in his ballet *La création du monde* (*The Creation of the World*), which purports to portray an African tribal view of the beginning of the world. The central tradition of jazz with its potential for expansion and elaboration received wider notice in the 1930s, with Schoenberg, Stravinsky, Hindemith, Berg, Milhaud, Copland, and Weill all intermittently inserting jazz-inspired ideas into their compositions.

An early important aspect of jazz was the *blues,* originally a vocal secular lament that stood apart from attitudes expressed in most work songs and spirituals. This style of singing commonly used descending slides and suggestive, guttural throat utterances. In instrumental music these expressive microtones evolved into "blue notes," the melodically lowered third, sixth, and seventh (e.g., E-flat, A-flat, and B-flat introduced into melodies in the key of C Major).

Because of its emphasis on solo improvisation, the history of jazz is studded with star performers, from the early days of "King" Oliver and "Jelly Roll" Morton, through Sidney Bechet, Fletcher Henderson, "Duke" Ellington, Louis Armstrong, "Bix" Beiderbecke, Coleman Hawkins, Earl "Fatha" Hines, Benny Goodman, "Dizzy" Gillespie, Charlie Parker, Thelonious Monk, Miles

Davis, Stan Getz, and Ornette Coleman, to the blues singers Bessie Smith and "Ma" Rainey.

After the 1920s, jazz was most popularly expressed in the softened, commercial *swing,* with a written-out score. For classically oriented composers, jazz had already become a part of the language of contemporary music. It was no longer the latest fashion, and composers turned in other directions to kindle their creative fires.

GERSHWIN

In the United States, jazz was not at first "respectable," and found no welcome in the hallowed halls of serious music. But with its fascinating and complicated rhythms, its opportunities for improvisation, and the strong individuality of many musical personalities who practiced it, a confrontation between jazz and classical music became inevitable.

The American composer who most actively sought a connection between jazz and classical idioms was George Gershwin. Born and raised in Brooklyn, the teenaged Gershwin became a song plugger in Tin Pan Alley and was quickly propelled into the Broadway circuit. He wrote songs for the annual musical extravaganzas *George White's Scandals* during the early 1920s. Soon he was writing musicals that hinted at the urbane, refined Broadway hits to come: *Lady Be Good* (1924), *Oh Kay* (1927), *Strike Up the Band* (1930), and *Of Thee I Sing* (1931). With a gift for melody and a talent for matching it with sophisticated syncopated dance rhythms, Gershwin quickly became an established star on the popular scene.

Gershwin was a fluent pianist, especially playing his own music, but his jazzily popular style had not prepared a public for his aspirations as a classical composer. He became the center of a raging controversy in 1924, when he produced a commissioned work for a special concert planned and led by the popular bandleader Paul Whiteman. Whiteman touted the concert as one that would both demonstrate the great strides jazz had made as a musical idiom in America and present the best in current contemporary music. Gershwin's contribution to the now-famous Aeolian Hall Concert was *Rhapsody in Blue* for piano and jazz band. The mixture of jazz and blues idioms combined with memorable melodies, and all packed in a flexible approximation of Franz Liszt's rhapsody style, made the *Rhapsody* the most talked-about composition of the year. Whiteman was not primarily a jazz musician, but a bandleader who had used certain jazz conventions to popularize his own style of dance music. A purported classical composition that made use of a dance band added one more element to the controversy. Was it classical? Was it popular? Was it jazz?

Rhapsody in Blue was not jazz, since the score does not allow for improvisation, but it unquestionably spanned the gap between jazz and classical idioms through Gershwin's introduction of certain jazz elements. The *Blue* in the title derives from his liberal use of blue notes (see p. 360). These he wove into tapestries in which melodious subjects joined with the tricky polyrhythms and syncopations indigenous to jazz.

Gershwin was 26 at the time of the *Rhapsody* and not yet sufficiently trained in orchestration to complete the task, which was left to Whiteman's arranger, Ferde Grofé. After the premiere of the *Rhapsody,* Gershwin quickly learned enough to handle most of his own future orchestrations. Later he revised the *Rhapsody* twice, and it became a classic in his own lifetime. In an article on the relation of jazz to American music in 1933, he wrote:

> Jazz I regard as an American folk music, not the only one, but a very powerful one, which is probably in the blood and feeling of the American people more than any other style of folk music. I believe that it can be made the basis of serious symphonic works of lasting value in the hands of a composer with talent for both jazz and symphonic music. The great music of the past in other countries has always been built on folk music. This is the strongest source of musical fecundity. America is no exception.

This attempt to amalgamate jazz and classical music, particularly the rhapsodic virtuoso style of Liszt, occupied Gershwin's thinking for the two decades of his maturity.

The *Rhapsody* impressed as many serious musicians as it enraged. In the year following its premiere, Gershwin was given a commission by Walter Damrosch, conductor of the prestigious New York Philharmonic, to write a work for that orchestra. The result was the Concerto in F for Piano and Orchestra, the premiere of which featured Gershwin himself as soloist, with Damrosch conducting.

Even at the height of his fame as a composer of popular music, Gershwin remained dedicated to music for the concert hall, and he continued to try to master its idioms. He approached both Ravel and Schoenberg for composition lessons, but both felt he was on the correct path for his talents and did not need their help. Many in the higher echelons of classical music in the 1930s became his friends and respected his talent. Alban Berg sent Gershwin a portrait of himself with a warm dedication and a quotation from his *Lyric Suite* (Fig. 13-2).

While Gershwin was known to millions for his popular songs and musical comedies, his major contribution to the musical stage was the opera *Porgy and Bess* of 1935. Based on DuBose Heyward's play *Porgy,* the opera was planned as an indigenous American work combining jazz and folk elements from the heritage of the southern black. While it presents a nostalgic view of black lifestyles that never really existed, *Porgy and Bess* is successful in the tradition of the serious Singspiel, operetta, and Broadway musical. Following that tradition of popular musical theater, it contains spoken dialogue and music numbers

Figure 13-2. Photograph of Alban Berg with inscription to George Gershwin and quote from *Lyric Suite,* 1928. Courtesy of the Gershwin Collection, Music Division, Library of Congress, Washington, D.C.

introduced where dramatically appropriate. For Gershwin, "appropriate" meant less dialogue and more music.

The opera found wide popular appeal through its deeply felt arias ("Summertime," "My Man's Gone Now," "I Got Plenty o' Nuttin'"); duets ("Bess, You Is My Woman Now"); and choruses ("Gone, Gone, Gone," "Oh I Can't Sit Down," "Oh, Lawd, I'm on My Way"). *Porgy and Bess* joined the many popular songs, film scores, and the *Rhapsody* to keep Gershwin's name high on the list of best-known and most respected of 20th-century American composers.

BERNSTEIN

The problem that Gershwin attacked—that of keeping a classical tradition healthy for the 20th century—was not solved during his lifetime. One American composer who has continued to grapple with it in his own works is Leonard Bernstein. Born in the year World War I ended, Bernstein was recognized as a child genius. As a teenager he played in a jazz band, and he grew to musical and intellectual maturity at Harvard University, the Curtis Institute in Philadelphia, and the Tanglewood Music Center in Massachusetts. By the age of 25, he was already assistant conductor of the New York Philharmonic Orchestra and had completed his first symphony.

Bernstein's best work has been produced for the theater. During the early years of World War II, he composed the music for the successful Broadway musical *On the Town* (1944), and for nearly two decades after the war's conclusion, he continued to turn out theater works. Eclecticism marked his choice of literary subjects from past and present. He believed that Broadway could accommodate musicals that were serious and purposeful, and in 1957 he wrote *West Side Story,* an updated view of Shakespeare's *Romeo and Juliet* that is by far his most enduring work. Voltaire's 18th-century satire *Candide* was the source for Bernstein's musical of the same name in 1956. *Candide* boasted a book by Lillian Hellman with extra lyrics by Dorothy Parker, staging by Tyrone Guthrie, and an all-star cast. The naive, best-of-all-possible-worlds view of life, treated with such elegant irony by Voltaire, proved an ideal vehicle for Bernstein's sharp, witty "modern" music.

Bernstein's approach to classical music has been similarly eclectic. In several works, he has concerned himself with an issue he perceives as a major contemporary problem: modern society's alienation from traditional values. His three symphonies contemplate the role of religious faith in 20th-century America. The first, *Jeremiah Symphony* (1943), turned to the biblical Lamentations of Jeremiah, which bemoan the loss of a living relationship with the Almighty. The genesis of the third symphony, *Kaddish* (1965), was in the ritual Hebrew prayer for the dead, with interpolated verses by the composer. The result is a revival on the concert platform of the old Judaic concept of God as a personage whom one may question directly and with whom it is possible to engage in dialogue.

In his *Second Symphony* (1949), for piano and orchestra, Bernstein turned to W. H. Auden's poem "Age of Anxiety," about the erosion of moral consciousness in America. Bernstein wrote of this symphony: "The essential line of the poem and of the music is the record of our difficult and problematical search for faith." Bernstein wove jazz elements freely into the the six sections of the poem, dealing with lonely and insecure characters drinking in a New York Third-Avenue bar. Bernstein is at his most provocative in the hectic, scherzo-like "Masque," in which mocking, brittle, jazzy orchestration mimicks the group's unsuccessful attempts to enjoy themselves.

During the past three decades, Leonard Bernstein has allowed other career activities to command his time and energy at the expense of his own commitment to composition. International fame as conductor, writer, and television personality gave him a platform from which he could present his perspective on faith and explore the role of the composer in our society. In a public statement in 1965 he asked, "Are symphonies a thing of the past? Is tonality dead forever? Are the new, staggering complexities of music vital to it, or do they simply constitute pretty *Papiermusik*?" His answer to the first question placed the issue of the future of classical music squarely in focus:

> No, obviously, since they are still being written in substantial quantity. But Yes, equally obviously, in the sense that the classical concept of a symphony, depending as it does on a bifocal tonal axis, which itself depends on the existence of tonality—that classical concept is a thing of the past. A work of art does not answer questions, it provokes them; and its essential meaning is in the tension between their contradictory answers.

Bernstein's place in the history of music is yet to be fully assessed, but whatever the ultimate judgment may be, he represents and illuminates the 20th-century struggle for coexistence between the best of our past and present musical worlds, and the best of the popular and classical traditions.

CHAPTER

14

Contemporary Styles II

IN THE MODERN WORLD, all the cities and countries of the globe are only hours away from each other by jet. Modern communication techniques have brought the world's peoples so close together that events and upheavals in even the smallest and most remote countries are now instantly known through vivid photojournalistic reporting and satellite transmission. The electronic revolution has produced generations of computers that further extend and sharpen the ability of the human mind to structure, coordinate, and collate knowledge. Space exploration has made it possible to watch astronauts walking on the surface of the moon, computer-controlled shovels scooping up soil samples from the surface of Mars, close-ups of the icy rings around Saturn, and raging storms on the surface of Jupiter and Neptune.

Many scientific and technological developments have also enlarged the scope of musical resources. A whole new sonic world, removed from nature and from traditional musical instruments, has emerged in the sounds generated by electronic oscillations that are controlled and manipulated by computer and synthesizer. The new global viewpoint has brought musical systems from far and wide to Western minds and ears. Tribal African rhythms, Indian ragas, Indonesian gamelan orchestras, and the exotic sounds of Chinese and Japanese music have all affected the Western musical experience in one way or another.

From their vantage point in the late 20th century, composers and audiences are more aware of past and present musics than at any other time in history. Through musicological studies and recordings, contemporary com-

Paul Flora. Cartoon of electronic instruments. Courtesy of *The New York Times*.

Chronology

MUSICAL FIGURES

Germany	
Hans W. Henze	1926–
Karlheinz Stockhausen	1928–
France	
Edgar Varèse	1883–1965
Olivier Messiaen	1908–
Pierre Schaeffer	1910–
Pierre Boulez	1925–
England	
Benjamin Britten	1913–1976
Poland	
Krzysztof Penderecki	1933–
Russia	
Alexander Mosolov	1900–1973
United States	
Henry Cowell	1897–1965
George Antheil	1900–1959
Elliott Carter	1908–
John Cage	1912–
Milton Babbitt	1916–
Ned Rorem	1923–
George Crumb	1929–
Robert Moog	1934–
Terry Riley	1935–
La Monte Young	1935–
Steve Reich	1936–
Donald Buchla	1937–
Philip Glass	1937–
Wendy (*né* Walter) Carlos	1939–
John Adams	1947–

WRITERS AND DRAMATISTS

Henry James	1843–1916
Wilfrid Owen	1873–1918
Paul H. Lang	1901–
Samuel Beckett	1906–
René Char	1907–
Chester Kallman	1921–1975

ARTIST

Ad Reinhardt	1913–1967

posers and modern audiences have easy access to the vast literature of music history. Medieval modes, Renaissance counterpoint, baroque dance forms, and 18th-century classical idioms stand as independent material that may be reworked. Through stereo sound, television, audio and video tape, every living room becomes a potential concert hall, ballet theater, and opera house. The range of available musical experiences now extends to an almost unlimited array of choices.

The "modern" movement in the arts has been succeeded in the late 20th century by what critics characterize as "postmodern" styles. Postmodernism is a blanket term covering a host of tendencies, some pushing forward, others pointing backward to premodern times. In architecture, the astringent International style, with its strict functionalism and rigid disdain for decorative devices, has yielded to a variety of styles based on the revival of decorative motifs alluding to the vocabularies of past periods. In painting, "modernism" meant abstraction and various forms of expressionism. After running its course, abstract painting eventually gave way to the postmodern, involving a return to such traditional styles as realism, historicism, neoclassicism, and neoexpressionism. Still life with its accurate description of natural appearances has reasserted itself, along with the expressive power of the human figure.

In music, postmodernism has brought a return to tonality after the mathematical gyrations and gymnastics of atonality and serialism, a renewed emotional expressionism after the excessive cerebration and tight formalism of neoclassicism. Minimalist composers are attempting to win a broader-based following on the evidence that serialism failed to find wide public acceptance. Many of this group incorporate non-Western attitudes and resources into the Western musical experience.

Late 20th-century music still provides the usual range of approaches running from the conservative and middle-of-the-road voices to radical revolutionaries—from the predictability of traditional forms through the theoretical predeterminism of the various techniques of serialism, to unpredictable randomness in aleatory music.

The New Conservative Tradition

BRITTEN

Benjamin Britten, one of the more tradition-oriented contemporary figures, drew his compositional strengths from British culture past and present. His style embodies a personal synthesis of modern idioms mixed with various earlier vocabularies, including the Elizabethan madrigal and Purcell's baroque eloquence. For his song texts and opera librettos he relied on English sources from Shakespeare to Henry James. His extensive output ran a full gamut from songs to symphonies, solo instrumental works to concertos, chamber music to choral anthems and cantatas, incidental music for plays to full-scale operas. Among his best-known works are the perennial favorite *Young Person's Guide to the Orchestra* and the operas *Peter Grimes*, *Billy Budd*, and *A Midsummer Night's Dream*. A striking example of pouring new musical wine into old bottles is his *War Requiem* (1962), written for the consecration of the reconstructed Coventry Cathedral, which had been badly bombed during World War II. Britten sought to create a memorial work that would have specific meaning for a British audience and at the same time would make an antiwar statement transcending place and time.

The dramatic situation that Britten chose for the *Requiem* involves three levels: the physical reality of the war, the world of traditional religion, and the metaphysical, spiritual plane. The ill-fated victims of war speak through the words of the British World War I poet Wilfred Owen, sung by tenor and baritone soloists with chamber orchestra accompaniment. The second level moves outside the horrors of war to mourn the dead through the venerable text of the Catholic Requiem Mass. This level is represented by a soprano soloist, choir, and large orchestra. The third dimension reflects a mystical realm beyond death, represented by a boys' choir and organ placed at a distance from the other participants.

This multileveled plan parallels that which Bach used for the opening of his *Saint Matthew Passion* (see p. 183). Bach set a double chorus watching Christ carrying the cross. The first chorus assumed the role of worldly viewers, posing questions about the scene being enacted before them. The second chorus represented the church as intermediary, providing devoutly acceptable answers. As the double-chorus discourse continued, a distant serene chorus of boys' voices accompanied by organ periodically proclaimed phrases of the Passion Chorale.

The tonal core of Britten's *Requiem* is that of the ancient tritone (C to F-sharp), the medieval *diabolus in musica*. This interval no longer carries "devilish" connotations for modern audiences, and Britten selected it more for its connection to a distant liturgical past. Functionally, the interval forms a basis for diatonic key structures throughout the work (C and F-sharp Major and Minor and their related keys), and it is often played by orchestral chimes as a ritual reference to the death knell.

After a quiet orchestral introduction, a mood of supplication is set by the restrained chant and the tolling of bells, both falling within the tritone interval (Ex. 14-1a). The boys' choir emerges from an ethereal distance, singing its text in unison (Ex. 14-1b), and after a repetition of opening music and text, the chamber orchestra and tenor soloist counter with Owen's poetry:

What passing bells for those who die as cattle?
  Only the monstrous anger of the guns.
  Only the stuttering rifles' rapid rattle
Can patter out their hasty orisons.

Example 14-1. Britten. *War Requiem,* Op. 66.

14-1a. "Requiem aeternam," bars 9–10.

14-1b. Bars 29–32.

No mockeries for them from prayers or bells,
  Nor any voice of mourning save the choirs,
The shrill, demented choirs of wailing shells;
  And bugles calling for them from sad shires.

The choir returns, quietly intoning the traditional prayer from the ordinary of the mass, "Kyrie eleison," reiterating the tritone to close the movement (Ex. 14-1c).

For the fourth section, "Sanctus," Britten assigns that most ancient Latin text to the soprano soloist, whose compelling line is punctuated by clashing percussion, all showering the listener with a resplendence reminiscent of a gleaming Byzantine mosaic. The chorus introduces a contrasting mood, slowly rising from a muttering, muddled mass of voices (Ex. 14-1d), finally joining the soprano and orchestra in an outburst of burnished, brilliant counterpoint. Out of this enormous ensemble the baritone soloist emerges to communicate Owen's quietly reflective lines:

14-1c. Bars 184–86.

14-1d. "Sanctus," bars 12–16.

After the blast of lightning from the East,
The flourish of loud clouds, the Chariot Throne;
After drums of Time have rolled and ceased,
And by the bronze west long retreat is blown,
Shall life renew these bodies?

As the *Requiem* draws to a close, Britten consolidates all three spatial dimensions. Remote and detached, the boys' choir calls for perpetual light to shine on the dead. Supported by both orchestras, the soprano soloist intones a prayer for eternal rest, while the baritone and tenor, representing those killed in battle, entreat, "Let us sleep now." And as Brahms had done in his *German Requiem* (see Exs. 11-13b, 11-13e), Britten concludes the *War Requiem* with the main chorus repeating the final music of the first movement (Ex. 14-1e).

HENZE

Hans Werner Henze is another composer of conservative persuasion. Like Hindemith in prewar Germany, he is one of the most prolific composers on

14-1e. End.

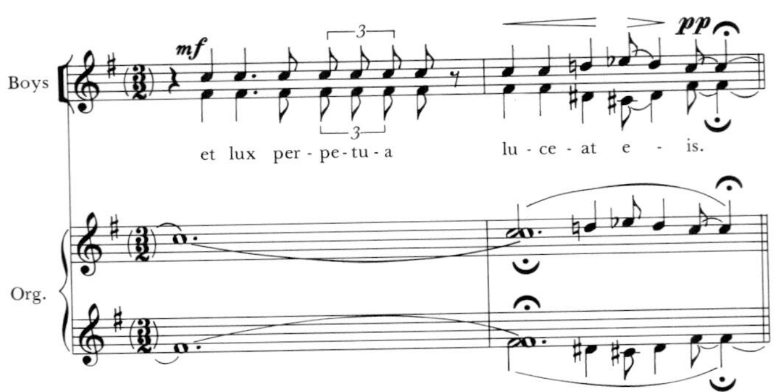
Boys
et lux per-pe-tu-a lu-ce-at e - is.
Org.

(with orchestra)
Sop. Solo
et cum La-za - ro quon-dam pau - pe - re ae - ter-nam ha-be-as re - qui-em.
Ten. Solo
let us sleep now, now. . . . ."
Bar. Solo
let us sleep now, sleep now. . . . ."

Very slow
(Molto lento)
unis.
sustained
rall.
dim.
div.
S
Re - qui - e - scant in pa - ce. A - men, A - - - men.
A
T
B
Bells

the current scene. Whether he is writing symphonies, concertos, or chamber music, he is always thinking in terms of the stage. "Everything," he once commented in a lecture, "moves toward the theater and returns there." Early in his career he was associated with various German opera houses. A steady succession of commissions has resulted in a dozen operas, an equal number of ballets, and as many cantatas. After assimilating the serialism of Schoenberg and Webern, the neoclassicism and the ballet style of Stravinsky, and some of the experimental idioms of the electronic group, Henze turned toward a more conservative style. Who, he asks, can tell which way is forward?

Henze's music shows a clear mastery of form, propulsive rhythmic drive, persuasive lyricism, and a resourceful command of instrumental color. In his five symphonies he bypasses the late 18th and 19th centuries by reverting to such preclassical procedures as the chaconne, the ostinato, and the dramatic recitative style. "In my instrumental compositions," he points out, "there is a constant alternation between counterpoint and a harmonized cantabile line." He attributes this alternation to a strong North German polyphonic temperament that has been modified by long residence in the lyrical warmth of Italy. Each work for him is "a means of clarifying tension and relaxation, severity and freedom. There is no striving after synthesis. From work to work there are different elements of friction."

Henze's full-length ballet *Undine* (1958), written in collaboration with the choreographer Frederick Ashton, first brought him international recognition. Despite its surface play of sophisticated modernity, it is permeated by a nostalgic romanticism. Its form adheres to the clear-cut sectional construction of the classical ballet, with separate dance numbers. Certain motivic themes associated with each of the leading characters are woven into the colorful orchestral fabric. The story tells of the romance between the sea nymph Undine and a mortal man. A tremendous climax is achieved in the storm and shipwreck scene in the second act, and a bizarre "Dance of the Tritons," who are disguised as Neapolitan clowns, enlivens the third act. Henze cleverly works in the amusing "cat fugue" by the Neapolitan composer Domenico Scarlatti as the subject for a brilliant set of dance variations.

In his operatic writing, Henze emulates the Stravinskian style of *The Rake's Progress* by reaching back to 18th-century number opera. Also like Stravinsky, Henze has enjoyed the collaboration of the distinguished poet W. H. Auden. A result of their joint efforts was *Elegy for Young Lovers*, scored for small chamber orchestra and a stylized sextet of singers. The work unfolds in sequences of solo arias, duets, and ensembles. The scene is set at an Alpine inn. Each of the characters is delineated with a leitmotif, and each has an instrumental counterpart in the orchestra. For the aging poet in search of inspiration, it is three brasses; for the visionary coloratura, a flute; for the bumbling physician, a bassoon; for the secretary-factotum, the English horn; for the lovers, a violin and viola.

Confrontation arises because the older characters, completely engrossed in their own problems and pursuits, forbid the union of the young lovers, Elisabeth and Toni. While seeking solace in nature, they are caught up in an ominous Alpine storm, which is mirrored in the orchestra with telling effect. Losing their way, the lovers perish, and the old poet at long last finds his inspiration again in writing an elegy for his daughter Elisabeth and her lover.

CARTER

Elliot Carter also composes in traditional forms with modernized techniques. His ingenious *Double Concerto for Piano, Harpsichord, and Small Orchestra* was hailed by Stravinsky as a masterpiece, while his string quartets have won prizes and international acclaim. "I like music to be beautiful, ordered, and expressive of the more important aspects of life," Carter has observed. "The idea of my music, if it can be considered apart from its expressive and communicative character (which I doubt), could be said to be a constantly evolving series of shapes, like the patterns of choreography." And indeed, for proper access to Carter's work the listener must look to the composer's remarkable rhythmic invention and unique command of the time experience.

Carter points out that a string quartet has four instruments all very much alike in sound, "so in my Second Quartet, I had the idea of composing a piece for string quartet which would be, so to speak, a 'non-string quartet', one in which the instruments were separate in sound and character. This involved composing parts that were much more highly differentiated in pitch, rhythm, and tessitura than those of the Double Concerto because of the similarity in timbres." Each instrument, he says, maintains its own character "in a special set of melodic and harmonic intervals and of rhythms that result in four different patterns of slow and fast tempi with associated types of expression."

Although the Second Quartet seems as closely knit and continuous as a single movement, it nevertheless has clearly defined sections. Between the introduction and conclusion, the four continuous movements are punctuated by three cadenzas that serve as dividers, as well as bring about various instrumental confrontations and oppositions. In the introduction the instruments present themselves as personalities through the rhythms and motifs that define their individual roles and characters. The first violin then takes over the leadership in the opening allegro fantastico by initiating the ideas and their manner of development in a "whimsical and ornate part" that is imitated by the other three instruments, each in its own individual way. In an interlude the viola plays an "expressive, almost lamenting, cadenza to be confronted with the explosions of what may be anger or ridicule by the other three." In the presto scherzando the second violin takes over with characteristically square, regular rhythms. Carter comments that it has here a "laconic, orderly character, which is sometimes humorous."

As a bridge to the third movement, the cello asserts itself with an impetuous virtuoso cadenza in a style approximating that of the first violin. The composer observes, "Its romantic, free way is confronted by the others' insistence on strict time." The viola leads in the andante espressivo. Then the first violin takes off in a rhapsodic cadenza, only to be faced with the stony silence of the other instruments. To show their impatience, they commence the final allegro before the cadenza is over. Cooperation and ensemble teamwork supersede individual leadership as the drive toward a dramatic climax begins. Partly led by the cello, which at one point persuades the other instruments to join in one of its characteristic accelerations, the fourth movement stresses "companionship" rather than "discipleship." The conclusion is a counterpart of the introduction, returning to the "state of individualization of the first part of the work."

New Sounds and Directions

Many composers trying to express the unique qualities of life in the 20th century began to be dissatisfied with the traditional instruments and stereotyped ensembles. How much longer, they asked, can we continue to use the stringed instruments that were perfected in the 18th century? The string quartet and symphony orchestra, they felt, were museum pieces—fine for the music of the past, but having little relevance for the machine age with its mechanical marvels, instant communications, and the fast, ever-changing pace of modern urban life.

Sounds appropriate for the present day were already being heard in the 1920s, in Arthur Honegger's orchestral portrait of a railroad locomotive, *Pacific 231*; in Prokofiev's ballet *Le pas d'acier (Dance of Steel)*; and Alexander Mosolov's factory ballet *Steel.* George Antheil produced a trenchant score to accompany Fernan Léger's silent film *Ballet mécanique.* The instrumentation included eight pianos, eight xylophones, pianola, electric doorbells, and an airplane propeller.

Henry Cowell and others sought to expand the resources of the piano by going beyond the keyboard to scrape and pluck the strings directly. They also experimented with "tone clusters" produced on the keyboard by using the fist, forearm, or wooden blocks of varying lengths to create large blocks of dissonant sound. For John Cage, the piano was primarily a percussion instrument. He developed "prepared" pianos by placing nuts and bolts, screws, and pieces of wood and leather between the strings. Cage's directions called for playing the piano keys part of the time and for applying hammer-like mallets directly to the strings at others. In this way he was able to create unique sound effects and to approximate a purely rhythmic style of composition, consciously avoiding traditional notions of melody and harmony (see Fig. 14-1).

VARÈSE

Edgar Varèse, who had studied mathematics and science as well as music, emerged as one of the most resourceful figures of the pre-electronic phase. His works bear such intriguing titles as *Hyperprism*, *Ionization*, *Intégrales*, *Metal*, and *Density 21.5*. He used percussion instruments to suggest spatial realism and the dissonance of urban noise in *Ionization* (1931), the title referring to one of the complex problems of atomic fission. It was scored for 13 performers playing on 37 different percussion instruments that included tubular gongs, chains, and sirens. They were arranged according to basic qualities of sound—metal and wood, instruments of light texture, and those of heavy texture. In a 1939 article, he heralded the advent of the ultimate musical instrument:

> And here are the advantages I anticipate from such a machine: liberation from the arbitrary, paralyzing tempered system; the possibility of obtaining any number of cycles or, if still desired, subdivisions of the octave, consequently the formation of any desired scale; unsuspected range in low and high registers; new harmonic splendors obtainable from the use of subharmonic combinations now impossible; the possibility of obtaining any differentiation of timbre, of sound-combinations; new dynamics far beyond the present human-power orchestra; a sense of sound-projection in space by

Figure 14-1. Paul Flora. Cartoon of prepared piano. Courtesy of *The New York Times.*

> means of the emission of sound in any part or in many parts of the hall as may be required by the score; cross rhythms unrelated to each other, treated simultaneously—all these in a given unit of measure or time which is humanly impossible to attain.

Varèse's dream was closer to reality than he knew. The appearance of the tape recorder shortly after the end of World War II presented composers with the potential for far greater management of the musical experience than ever before. Suddenly it was possible to control the entire cycle of musical composition from conception, through realization, to performance. The tape recorder, joined later by the synthesizer, could not only capture and preserve sound but could subject it to almost limitless combinations and transformations. With this equipment, composers found they could go beyond Stravinsky's cellular rhythmic procedures, Schoenberg's ear-stretching harmonies, and Webern's miniaturized music, in ways that no longer required either notation or live performance.

The first important tape recorder compositions were created in Europe, where radio broadcasting was under government sponsorship after World War II. Stations such as the Radiodiffusion française in Paris and the Nordwestdeutscher Rundfunk in Cologne were quick to set up recording studios filled with the latest in electronic equipment. These studios became the experimental laboratories of young composers.

A transitory development in taped music was *musique concrète*, the initial example of which was Pierre Schaeffer's *Étude aux chemins de fer (Railroad Study*, 1948). Composers began to tape the sounds of the real world such as the hum of motors, the clashing of metal objects, street noises, and the sound of sirens. This recorded material was subjected to electronic and mechanical processes in which sonic sequences were superimposed on each other, slowed down, speeded up, played backward, snipped into fragments and reassembled. Tape spliced into a loop repeated continuously could create the effect of an ostinato. The primary mechanism for new musical expression was in place, and vast new opportunities for musical experimentation and heightened control were now available.

Expansion of Serialism

Two composers in the forefront of the development of new musical idioms and languages were Pierre Boulez working in Paris and Karlheinz Stockhausen in Cologne. Early on, both absorbed the atonal and serial methods of the Second Viennese School; both attempted to push melody, rhythm, harmony, and counterpoint into previously unexplored territory; both seized upon the new electronic generation of sound, welcoming improvisation and chance elements in musical performance; and both introduced aspects of non-Western traditions in several of their compositions. Both were also conductors, theoreticians, and writers as well as composers.

BOULEZ

Boulez felt that a basic 12-tone row was far too simple a base on which to build a musical style for the new order of complexity that the modern world offered. He argued, however, that such a row is the mandatory starting point for a contemporary composer. This point of view is brilliantly illustrated in Boulez's *Structures* (1952) for two pianos, which attempted to carry serialism to its culmination. In it he designed a row to be presented in 48 separate ways—statement, inversion, retrograde, and retrograde-inversion on each of the 12 notes of the chromatic scale. He assigned to each statement its own unique register, tempo, and dynamic level. Thenceforth, his compositions represented a series of responses to scientific and aesthetic questions about music.

One of Boulez's most approachable works is *Le marteau sans maître (The Hammer Without a Master*, 1954). Here syntax yields to poetry, and serialism to beautiful sequences of sound that call up images of Debussy and Schoenberg. The text is based on a set of three poems by René Char, in which tender and grim moods alternate. Char's dark words evoke the imagery of murder, death, a prison gate, solitude, and "pure eyes weeping in the forest seeking a habitable head."

Le marteau progresses as a series of settings for alto voice surrounded by instrumental commentaries. "The Furious Workshop" is the prelude that sets the mood for the whole. It has a fragmented line recalling Webern's tone-color melodies, with each note sounded by a different instrument. In "Murderers of Solitude" the dynamics are muted, while each sound is delicately shaped and shaded. Its fast-paced middle section contains instrumentation that requires agility from the flutist, a muted quality from the violist, virtuoso abandon from the xylorimba player, and nimbleness from the bongo drummer. In "Fine Structure and Forebodings" tempo changes occur in almost every bar. A commentary on the "Murderers of Solitude" section ensues in a free improvisatory style, while a vigorous canon occurs between the vibraphone and viola. Freedom and strictness are reconciled here much in the manner of the ostinato arias of the baroque period. In the finale, flashbacks to previous movements alternate with repeated fragments of the poetry. The voice and the entire ensemble appear, and the gong is given the last word.

In this remarkable work Boulez manages to temper the strictness of serial formulas with elements of improvisation and unpredictability. He wrote that he wished to communicate the paradox of order and the release from it: "Now rhythm, tone color, and dynamics are organized, all of which serve as fodder for the monstrous polyorganization from which one must free oneself if one is not to be condemned to deafness." In his elegant sound spectrum Boulez includes many subtle allusions to Oriental music. His tone colors invoke both the Balinese gamelan and the Japanese koto, and his deployment of percussion instruments brings African drumming techniques to mind.

STOCKHAUSEN

The compositions of Karlheinz Stockhausen dating from 1952 to 1960 read like a roster of musical resources: counterpoint (*Kontra-Punkte*), improvisation (*Klavierstück XI*, *Refrain*, and *Zyklus*), tempo and space (*Gruppen*), form (*Refrain*), chords (*Carré [Square]*), and timbre (*Kontakte*). In his early electronic works, he manipulated sine-wave tones—pure sounds stripped of their overtones—then synthesized them into new inventive sound spectrums. Rearranging and altering fundamental acoustical elements, he evolved new textures and densities as building blocks for various sound structures. Eventually this led to total manipulation of sound within the acoustical space in which it was performed.

In the *Gesang der Jünglinge* (*Song of the Youths*, 1956), Stockhausen's goal was to bring the human voice into a working relationship with electronic sounds. The text comes from chapter 3 of the Book of Daniel, recalling the story of Nebuchadnezzar, who ordered that three Israelite youths be cast into a furnace because they refused to worship a golden statue he had erected. The vowels and consonants of the text, as sung and spoken by a boy soprano, became Stockhausen's musical materials, which are pulverized into Webernlike pointillistic sounds. They are then superimposed upon electronically pure sonic mixtures of varying density. The effect is airy, spacious, and transparent, as vocal fragments float in and out. Occasionally words are intelligible to the listener, but more often the vocal element is heard as pure sound. Stockhausen first recorded the boy's voice on tape, then realized the whole work spatially through four-channel sound with special antiphonal effects. He intended it to be heard in a large round room in which five speakers throw the tonal materials back and forth, enveloping and surrounding his listeners with the movement of sound waves reverberating through space.

Stockhausen has also experimented with bringing live performers into contact with the electronic medium. He explains, "These known sounds give orientation, a perspective to the aural experience; they function as traffic signs in the unbounded space of the newly discovered electronic sound world." In one instance he used a pianist and a percussionist performing with a prerecorded tape. In *Mikrophonie I* (1965), he used a tam-tam on which performers make various sounds. These sounds are picked up by other performers with microphones, and in turn they are subjected to electronic transformation by a third group operating electronic reproducing equipment.

Although he has invented ingenious notational symbols for scoring electronic sounds, Stockhausen has discarded written scores in his more recent work in favor of composing directly on tape. Producing such a composition begins with defining and delimiting the time dimension—perhaps 20 or 40 minutes—and executing perhaps a dozen "takes." Then the composer, like a film director, edits and chooses what will become the final version. For this approach, Stockhausen has evolved a complicated technique in which he may use performers to produce short motifs, often in the extreme registers of their instruments. He may also call upon them to improvise sequences of grunts and groans, shrieks and squawks, hisses and sighs, in the manner of the theater of the absurd.

Each musician has a contact microphone connected with a central control panel. Here Stockhausen sits as if he were the conductor. Instead of a baton, however, he manipulates a complex of electronic devices: sine-wave generators, potentiometers, and ring modulators. Through a series of takes, he develops the final composition. Developing, as he has commented in the album notes of his recordings, means that sounds are "spread, condensed, extended, shortened, differently colored, more or less articulated, transposed, modulated, multiplied, synchronized."

Stockhausen and Boulez were among the first to challenge the age-old concept of music functioning as a continuous experience of time. They attempted to construct music in which time and space are suspended. In this way the composition has the quality of having already arrived at a state of being instead of reflecting movement in a state of constant becoming. Of his *Momente* (1964), for solo soprano, chorus, two electronic organs, brass, and percussion, Stockhausen has said, "This is no self-contained work with unequivocally fixed beginning, formal structure and ending, but a polyvalent composition containing independent events. Unity and continuity are less the outcome of obvious similarities than of an immanent concentration on the present, as uninterrupted as possible."

Computerized Determinism vs. Aleatory Freedom

BABBITT

Milton Babbitt was a pioneer of computer-controlled determinism in music. In the 1950s and 1960s Columbia and Princeton universities banded together to set up an electronic music center, which boasted an immense synthesizer built for them by the Radio Corporation of America. This RCA machine filled a large laboratory with computerized components capable of generating a vast variety of complex sounds. Babbitt used this as a larger-than-life instrument, drawing upon its sophisticated sound generators and electronic oscillators to fabricate highly controlled musical constructions. By means of the computer-synthesizer, Babbitt was able to extend the technique of serial writing to include rhythm, dynamics, tone colors, and tempos.

About his *Ensembles for Synthesizer* (1964), Babbitt commented: "The title *Ensembles* refers to the multiple characteristics of the work. In both its customary meaning and its more general one signifying 'collections,' the term refers more immediately to the different pitch, rhythmic, registral, textural, and timbral 'ensembles' associated with each of the many so delineated sections of the composition, no two of which are identical, and no one of which is more than a few seconds duration in this ten-minute work."

In the same year, Babbitt produced *Philomel* for soprano and tape, in which the human voice appears as both a live and a recorded instrument. In performance, the part for live soprano is integrated into the stored sounds on the tape, which in turn have been aided by the synthesizer to enhance the moment in Ovid's poem when the mute Philomela is transformed into a nightingale. Musically it is based on a series that incorporates pitch, tone color, rhythm, and dynamics. Babbitt and the live soprano manage to project a certain sense of poetic flow and transparent lightness into what is otherwise a tightly plotted and controlled musical situation.

The space requirements and the cost of such mammoth equipment as the RCA synthesizer meant that it could be available only to a very few. However, the invention in the mid-1960s of smaller, voltage-regulated synthesizers constructed by Robert Moog, Donald Buchla, and others, allowed almost every would-be composer to become an immediate practitioner. As improvements were made, these synthesizers became widely available in recording studios, on the performing stage, and (in the 1980s) in the home (Figs. 14-2, 14-3). Synthesized music reached the popular level in 1968, with the release of Walter Carlos' *Switched-On Bach*, in which the composer reworked several of the baroque master's well-known compositions, presenting them in newly conceived, electronically skewed tone colors.

CAGE

John Cage, as the leader of the movement that turned against both the excessive cerebration of serial music and the carefully controlled predeterminism of computerized compositions, may be considered Babbitt's polar opposite. To describe his approach, he used the word *aleatory*, a term derived from the Latin *alea* (game of dice). In his earlier works he still wrote out a score, but rather than a fixed and predetermining entity, it was to be a document that set up certain situations and circumstances within which the performers had a choice to operate.

Cage was always more concerned with the process of the musical experience itself than with any finite set of instructions by the composer. For example, the score for *Atlas eclipticalis* (1962) contains 86 parts from which the orchestral players choose which they will use, and for how long. Electronic alterations of the parts may be used, but again the performers make the deci-

Figure 14-2. Polyfusion modular analog synthesizer.

sion. The score parts include cryptic patterns based on star charts, encouraging imaginative realization by the performers. Cage's *Variations II* (1961) presents a score of assorted straight lines and points on several transparent sheets. These may be laid over each other in any way the performer wishes. It is described as being written for "any number of players, any sound-producing means."

In Cage's *Concert for Piano and Orchestra* (1958), all 24 instruments plus the solo piano are allowed to rearrange the scored music in any order and omit parts of it as they desire. He also suggested the possibility of performing the piece concurrently with other compositions he had written.

The *Concerto for Prepared Piano and Chamber Orchestra* (1951) points to a nihilistic element in Cage's works. In his notes for a recording of the concerto, Cage stated:

> [In the first movement] I let the pianist express the opinion that music should be improvised or felt while the orchestra expressed only the chart, with no personal taste involved. In the 2nd movement I made large concentric moves on the chart for both pianist and orchestra, with the idea of the pianist beginning to give up personal taste. The 3rd movement had only one set of moves on the chart for both, and a lot of silences. Until that time, my music had been based on the traditional idea that you had to say something. The charts gave me my first indication of the possibility of saying nothing.

This idea led to one composition that literally said nothing. His *4′ 33″* (1952), an allusion to the time span of a 78 rpm record, instructs a pianist to sit in front of the instrument for 4 minutes and 33 seconds without touching it. The audience sits in silence, listening to ambient concert hall sounds, while inwardly "hearing" Cage's soundless music.

Earlier Cage had become aware of certain exotic rhythmic aspects of Balinese music, and he had also studied Zen Buddhism. Both elements have found their way into his compositions. He was also influenced by *I ching*, the Chinese "Book of Changes," which provided him with a mode for what he called "chance operations." Cage's object is to create compositions "free of individual taste and memory in their order of events," so that the composer can "let sounds be themselves in a space of time." A favorite Cage device is the use of multiple radios as aleatory performing instruments. His *Imaginary Landscape No. 4* (1951), for example, uses *I ching* coin-tossing procedures to designate the precise wavelengths, time spans, and volume levels of 12 radios all tuned to different stations.

As ways of coming to terms with the realities of musical experience, Cage's chance happenings and aleatory ramblings are essentially negated the moment they appear as recordings. The composer declares, with justification, that a composition played for a second time is something quite other than it was at first; and that a recording "has no more value than a postcard; it provides knowledge of something that happened, whereas the action was a nonknowledge of something that has not yet happened." He once remarked in a lecture: "I have nothing to say and I am saying it, and that is poetry."

Minimalism

The countercultural minimalist movement of the 1960s and 1970s was the take-off point for an entire generation of American composers including Terry Riley, Steve Reich, Philip Glass, and John Adams. In the visual arts minimalism stressed simplicity, directness, and precision of form and presenta-

Figure 14-3. Algorhythm synthesizer. Yamaha Model DX7 IIFD.

tion. The basic idea behind a work was all-important, and minimalist art was more a process than a finished product. Ad Reinhardt, for instance, sought for the irreducible minimum in such works as his *Ultimate Black Painting.* It was exactly what he claimed for it, a five-foot-square canvas covered with a single color—black. In the theater minimalism meant avoiding the complications of plot and narrative techniques in favor of portraying a sequence of soul states expressed in fragments of speech and inarticulate sounds, without logical organization. Samuel Beckett's late writing, for example, condenses an experience into one essential image or phase. As a musical minimalist, Glass has pointed out that "My background is in the recent tradition of non-literary theater in America in which people draw their inspiration not from a text but an idea, a drawing, a poem, or an image."

After the far-out flights of atonalism, serialism, and computerization, it was only a question of time before rudiments of music would once again appear. The musical version of minimalism is essentially a back-to-basics movement. It stresses a return to tonality, square rhythmic patterns, basic harmonies, elementary counterpoint, and simple repetitive forms. It is concerned not so much with structural principles as with how the music sounds. Minimalists thrive on the use of the commonplace and the musical cliché.

GLASS

Underlying the works of Philip Glass is a system of Eastern ideas and values exotic to Western ears. He attempts to capture the meditative spirit of Oriental religions that involve surrendering the rational approach in order to attain mystical tranquillity, blocking out the conscious mind in order to probe the inner instead of the outer world. In Eastern music repetitive rhythms become the organizing principle; cells grow in additive cycles, such as 1 plus 2, 1 plus 2 plus 3, and so on. The consequence is a compelling music unfolding in a vastly elongated time frame. For the listener it can produce a trancelike, hypnotic spell. This meditative view of life is the outgrowth of a completely different culture. Therefore, the question arises as to what extent Westerners can penetrate beneath the surface play of sound to arrive at a true understanding of a mind-set so foreign to them, or whether the experience is just a kind of musical tourism.

To enter into the spell of Glass's music, listeners must abandon the normal expectation that music progresses through sequential points of tension and release that propel it forward in time. They must also discard the notion of starting at a beginning, continuing with a middle, and arriving at an end. The music of Glass simply starts and stops. He is also concerned with the ascendance of body over mind, and has said that he wants his music to have an "immediate physical appeal." This invitation to physical involvement has elicited a positive response from generations bred on the relentless rhythmic drive of rock and roll played at deafening decibel levels. The minimalist aesthetic may be particularly congenial to the practitioners of transcendental meditation, and to those steeped in the drug-related subcultures. In any case, Glass has a strong appeal for the adventurous and the avant-garde. One critic has dubbed his work "pop music for intellectuals," while another has described him as a composer "who drives musical nails into your soul."

Even though Glass's conventions run contrary to the expectations of the regular opera-going public, he has been hailed as the most original and important figure on the contemporary opera scene. Together with his imaginative collaborators—avant-garde directors, producers, and choreographers—he has managed to create a series of plotless, dreamlike operas featuring visionary tableaux that unfold in harmony with the slow-moving, encircling music. With Glass, emotion always comes first, and reason plays little or no part. The only way to enjoy it is to sit back and let the music surround you like an engulfing wave of shimmering sound.

Einstein on the Beach has proven to be one of the most striking and provocative of his operatic ventures. He chose the discoverer of relativity as the seminal figure in the modern scientific consciousness, a man who has changed our understanding of the universe and whose theories have revolutionized the physics and philosophy of our time. The work forms a trilogy with two other operas: *Satyagraha*, with Gandhi as the figure personifying the social and political aspect of the modern consciousness; and *Akhnaten*, named for the ancient Egyptian pharaoh who was the reputed founder of monotheism, representing the spiritual side.

Einstein, with staging by Robert Wilson, had many European performances before coming to New York's Metropolitan Opera in 1976. The first scene opens like a numerical countdown before a space launching. The choirs sing numbers from one to six, counting forward and backward, with accompanying gestures precisely timed to the second. There are allusions to Einstein's conception of relative speeds, and how the fastest-moving trains and planes seem to crawl in comparison with rockets and the speed of light in outer space. The train motif also refers to the comparative movements of the trolley cars that first crystallized the idea of relativity in Einstein's mind. Einstein himself appears as the leading character with his lion's mane of white hair and bushy mustache. Throughout the performance time of nearly five hours, he fiddles do-re-mi finger exercises and plaintive Hebrew melodies, as the real-life amateur violinist Einstein did.

The tableaux continue with trial episodes, a solar eclipse (alluding to one in 1919 that tended to confirm Einstein's theory), field scenes (possibly a reference to the unified field theory), and a staged protest before an industrial plant with a boy scribbling graffiti equations, including Emc^2, on the walls. In the final scene, a saucer-shaped spaceship floats above the stage as the action shifts to outer space. Astronauts are hibernating in Plexiglas boxes shaped like free-form grandfather clocks, which sail vertically and horizontally all over the stage. There are clocks everywhere, some running faster, others slower, suggesting the theory that time changes as the speed of light is approached. Brilliant fireworks represent passing stars and spiral nebulae, while electric organs shoot off cascades of rising and falling scale patterns.

The choirs intone the text by reciting numerical series with hypnotic incantations. Glass marshals a vast, decidedly nonminimal roster of orchestral instruments ranging from winds to percussion, from saxophones to synthesizers—all powered by rocklike amplification at high-voltage volume. In the final moments, while Einstein is still fiddling away furiously, we return once more to the planet Earth, where a bus driver is telling a tale of two lovers sitting on a park bench in the moonlight. As they embrace, the final words are, "You are my sun, my moon and stars, you are my everything." In this multimedia fantasy, devices that by themselves are simple to the point of banality somehow manage to add up to a structure approaching monumentality. Robert Brustein has noted in a critical article on *Einstein* that Glass and his collaborators have penetrated "deeply into the uncreated dream life of the race. Pulling ecstasy from boredom, finding insight through repetition, alternating mechanical rhythms with pulsing climaxes, *Einstein on the Beach* manages to burrow into your mind and work on you like a wound."

Something Old, Something New

At almost any point in music history, it is common to hear conservative critics deploring the situation in contemporary music. Often they assure us that the state of music has reached the point of self-destruction. In reality all they are telling their readers is that an older conception of music is being replaced by something new. At such a point it is usually difficult for listeners to sort out the lasting from the passing trend, the essential from the trivial, the true genius from the shrewd operator. One composer may rely only on electronic sounds, another on the human voice or traditional instruments. Some may build a style on the chance sounds and silences of aleatory music, while still others choose rigorously computerized formulas.

Eventually one comes back to the basic questions: what is music and what constitutes musical activity? The response admits of no easy answer, since there are always many factors involved in any particular piece of music or in any situation of which music is a part. In one instance a single element may be abstracted and maximized, while traditional components of the musical experience are suppressed or omitted. The mathematical basis of music, for instance, has been established since the time of the Greek philosopher Pythagoras, who discovered the harmonic ratios of the musical intervals. A medieval composer such as Machaut constructed compositions on rigorously calculated isorhythmic principles; mathematical exactitude likewise controls the canons of J. S. Bach's *Musical Offering*. So it is not removed from the scheme of things when 20th-century composers take up 12-tone serialism or turn to computers to express their ideas.

On the other hand, the free play of a composer's creative imagination as expressed in the art of improvisation is also as old as music itself. Therefore, when a modern composer introduces the random sounds of aleatory music, the underlying idea is hardly new. Major composers of the past never regarded the strict and the free as mutually exclusive. They preferred to exercise both options or some combination of them. The logical Bach who wrote canons and fugues is balanced by the Bach who composed the more improvisatory toccatas, fantasias, and preludes. Classical composers such as a Mozart and Beethoven carefully wrote out the contents of their concertos, but there were always places where the solo performer could improvise. Thus, ample precedent exists for the composers of today and tomorrow to introduce random elements into their works. The middle ground and the art of compromise invariably reassert themselves in the annals of history.

Today the electronic media make it possible for composers to produce their works directly on tape without the intervention of a musically notated score. The live performer is thereby eliminated from the process. On the other side, aleatory music minimizes the composer's control by allowing maximum freedom to the random sounds made by performers, whether they are manipulating traditional or electronic instruments. Historically there has always been a struggle for control between composers and performers. The musical notation of a score is at best an approximation of the creator's intentions, yet many composers have resented the liberties taken by performers. The responsible interpreter will always look at the black and white symbols on the printed page and will be properly concerned with the problem of translating them into colorful living sound. As always, the process involves striking a balance between the need for creative interpretation and the obligation to respect the composer's intentions within the framework of the period and style at hand. But no matter how faithfully the performer strives to observe the composer's intentions, there are always elements that call for discretion and the making of choices.

So each performance of a Bach or a Beethoven score becomes a somewhat different composition, however slightly it may vary. In the contemporary world of music-making, it comes down to whether a composer wants to make a final, definitive version of his work on tape to stand forever like a statue in a museum, or whether he wishes to grant the performer some rights to a live, ongoing realization of his music.

Ultimately any musical decision comes down to a sense of critical evaluation and judgment. Composers may develop and bring forth whatever they choose. But any audience may also claim the inalienable right to accept or reject what is being offered, and to judge whether it is worthwhile and rewarding.

PART III

Components of Music

INTRODUCTION

Music and Its Materials

THE BASIC RAW MATERIALS of music are sound and silence. Just as an architect thinks in terms of material masses and voids, so a composer deals with sonorous masses and voids. An architect uses bricks and mortar to enclose space, and a composer arranges tones to articulate the flow of time. An architect defines spatial units, and a composer imposes temporal divisions. An architect tries to make space both useful and meaningful, while a composer endeavors to endow time with significance. An architect communicates his intentions by using lines and spaces on a blueprint, a composer by the notes and rests on a score. And just as an architect must be conversant with the principles of engineering, so must a composer take certain acoustical factors into account. Music, in fact, is a kind of flowing architecture unfolding in time; and the composer is the personal force behind these moving patterns of sound, determining their specific musical content and endowing them with human meaning.

Traditionally a composer needs a performer to transform the symbols in the score into living music, quite as much as an architect needs a builder to translate designs into reality. All the labors of the architect and the builder, however, would come to naught if nobody were there to enjoy the finished structure. The composer and the performer likewise would be working in vain if their efforts did not reach the ears of an audience. So both music and architecture involve planners, builders, performers, viewers, and listeners who are all caught up in the dynamic activity of creating, implementing, and responding.

According to an old proverb, speech is silver but silence is golden. Fortunate is the composer who understands the use of silence, for it is one of the most eloquent means of expression. As in speech, a composer must allow for breathing pauses at the ends of phrases—a literal necessity in the case of singers and wind players, and a figurative necessity for articulation in the case of other instrumentalists. Music also has its innuendos and implied meanings. Sometimes what is left unsaid in a composition or a conversation assumes greater importance than what is actually stated. Composers also employ rhetorical pauses for emphasis that can have dramatic implications when they occur at climactic moments in the build-up of a composition.

The ideal of full employment at all times may be a happy state for a social order, but when the same principle is applied to a musical community, the result is din and confusion. Thinning out the instrumental ranks in an orchestral composition, for example, leaving individual parts silent for periods of time, is one of the necessities of good ensemble writing. Silence as a divider in a formal design is employed to good effect by composers in separating the sections or movements of their compositions. When judiciously used, silence can create a sense of suspense and expectation or allow the listener's imagination to fill in empty musical spaces.

Composer, Performer, Listener

The road to musical understanding begins with the composer projecting ideas from the creative imagination into a work that is fashioned by interlocking sounds and silences. These are then translated by the code of musical notation into a written or printed score that indicates sounds of higher or lower pitch, notes of longer or shorter duration, the rate of speed, and the instruments that are to be played.

Through the processes of selecting, discarding, refining, organizing, and improving, the language of music gradually emerges. The elements of sound are present everywhere, and their possibilities are grasped and forged into art forms that can convey meaning to the minds and hearts of listeners. A composer may find rhythms in the beating of a heart, the drawing of breath, the changing of the seasons, or the periodic revolutions of the planets in their orbits. Chosen mediums are derived from the multiplicity of available sounds, which may include human voices with all their variable qualities, or instruments with their individual ranges and particular timbres. Whether the composer uses them alone or blended with others, each contributes its characteristic color to the work at hand.

Life provides basic experiences that a composer can shape for expressive needs. The encountering of conflicts and difficulties has its counterpart in such points of tension as harmonic dissonances, while the working out of solutions and settlements is reflected in points of relaxation, such as resolutions and cadences. Forms may be based on the universal experiences of recurrence involving both memory and premonition, which together may combine to endow a given musical moment with meaning. As a composition unfolds in time, it is always in transition, and any given tone or group of tones can be at once reminiscent and prophetic. Silences are by no means merely the cessation of sound. Such pauses in the musical progress can arrest the movement temporarily or can suggest continuity of motion, depending on the memory of what came before and the anticipation of what may come after.

Ultimately, tonal relations in music can create their own meaning, and the most abstract aspects of the art can rest on acquired associations and conventions within a given musical context. Composers can thus construct worlds of sound relationships, but they would be powerless to do so if the experiences of pitch, rhythm, intensity, tone color, harmony, counterpoint, dissonance, and consonance did not relate to universal aspects of human experience. The musical tone, then, with its definable qualities and characteristics as well as its capacity for infinite variation, is under the control of the composer. The composer, in turn, functions as an artist endowed with tonal imagination and the power of invention, and as one who lives and works in a world of auditory imagery. Communication through sound is as necessary to the composer as communication through words is to a writer.

The performing musician's task is to translate the silent symbols on the page into living sound. This is usually done under other social circumstances and in a different place, time, and period than those in which the music was first conceived. Since competent interpreters presume to speak for the composer, they are expected to bring to the performance all the skill, good taste, and judgment at their command. Scholarship is summoned to help them come as close as possible to the composer's original intentions. The performance is then received by listeners, who absorb and reinterpret the work in the private world of their personal reactions, imagination, and judgments.

Each listener brings to the music a set of highly individual life experiences. Each member of an audience has an individual life-style, a particular cultural conditioning, a level of musical sensitivity, a private mode of feeling, and a backlog of memories built up from previous musical experiences. This personal context obviously can never be quite the same as those of the composer or the performer. Similarly, no two listeners are going to participate in a musical experience in exactly the same way. Nor will a listener necessarily hear the same piece again in exactly the same way, any more than a musician in successive live performances will perform the music twice in precisely the same manner.

Today, most of our listening is done by means of electronic reproduction rather than through live performance. One of the limitations of recordings is that they fix and freeze a single performance, thereby sacrificing the fluidity, spontaneity, and freedom that any live performance brings to the musical process. On the other hand, recordings and tapes provide far wider listening opportunities than one could ever experience under live circumstances. For example, listeners are now able to study the music and performance practices of past times and learn a historical point of view from artists who have left recordings but are no longer actually performing.

Certain obstacles bestrew the path to musical understanding, but more of them concern the performer than the listener. All musicians, for instance, would agree that the printed score is at best a convenience—a compromise that only approximates the composer's intentions. Pitch notation remains the same as it was in the 18th century, but the actual sounds from these scored notes as heard by J. S. Bach were lower than those of today. Tone qualities have also undergone radical alterations because the construction of instruments has changed much over the years. Bach's trumpet was not the same as the modern valve instrument, nor was Mozart's wooden-framed piano the same as the iron-framed instrument now in use. The size of the orchestra that first performed Beethoven's symphonies was about half that of the orchestras we hear today. Thus the sounds we re-create from musical notation can never be exactly the same as those that earlier composers had in mind.

Yet, however improbable the process may seem on the surface, the system somehow works. Millions of listeners would agree that Beethoven's Fifth Symphony projects an attitude or state of mind that can be described by such words as "epic" or "heroic," which we know the composer actually meant to project. And while each listener will have a somewhat different idea of what is epic or heroic, it has proven possible for listeners of today to understand and share the essential basis of, say, an epic symphony written by a composer born two centuries earlier. We may assume that contact has been made across the time barrier, that the listener and the composer are "in touch," and that some meaningful communication from one to the other has been made.

With changing times and different social and aesthetic outlooks, the musical creations of many composers have been found to lack sufficient vitality and interest to bridge the time gap. Some works that once communicated forcefully and persuasively with the listeners of their day have not retained enough power to remain in today's active repertory. On the other hand, sometimes the works of composers that have lain dormant for previous generations once again establish contact and are revived. A major figure such as Beethoven perpetually communicates all manner of intellectual subtleties and a wide range of emotions, for all ages. Such communication is precious, a minor miracle that performers and listeners may continually experience.

Sounds and Meaning

In Western culture the equation between life experience and musical expression has tended over the centuries to become an increasingly personal one.

Yet there are certain formulas and conventions that are commonly understood by the community. Such a communal relationship between life experiences and sounds occurs, for instance, with the organ. While the instrument has other uses, it is still generally identified with the church, and its music with attitudes appropriate to worship. A composer may choose to convey a religious atmosphere with a blazing brass choir, but the community will still associate the idea of that atmosphere tonally with the organ. Similarly, rock music has become the characteristic secular sound for the life experience of a generation, just as Johann Strauss's waltzes were for an earlier one.

Movement as the sign of life is externalized in space and time. Spatial movement as in dance is visible to the eye, while temporal motion as in a song is audible to the ear. Far from being mere idle motion and dull duration, however, life is made significant by its aims and objectives. Musical motion likewise derives meaning from its direction. From a melodic phrase to a complete form, the musical entity has a beginning, a middle, and an end. With the flow of lines, rhythms, and harmonies and with the recognition of their force and direction, the musical idea becomes apparent and its shape clarified. The form may then be discovered as the musical idea unfolds, and its possibilities are realized in various stages from basic formal units to ever-widening horizons. A basis for understanding the spirit of a work can thus be established.

In his *Poetics of Music,* the composer Igor Stravinsky said: "Natural sounds suggest music but are not yet music. They are promises, but it takes a human being to keep that promise—a human being who is not only sensitive to the sounds of nature, but capable of putting them together. Music can come into being only when there is a mind that can create, organize and construct." Types of musical motion can thus express anything from the image of a simple work song, such as *I've Been Workin' on da Railroad,* to such exalted visions of the emergence of a great and free humanity as the final movement of Beethoven's mighty Ninth Symphony. Furthermore, since each individual composer, each generation, each age expresses itself in its own concepts and formulates its own aspirations and ideals, each musical work becomes the key to understanding the meaning of an individual attitude toward life, the spirit of a creative artist, the essence of an era.

Elements and Textures of Music

When a piano key is struck or a guitar string plucked, a sound is produced. This single tone is at once a psychological and a physical fact. The vibration of the string sets the surrounding air in regular motion, creating waves of sound. The waves in turn set the eardrums vibrating, then move through the auditory nerve until they reach the brain, where they psychologically awaken an auditory response. The effect of a quivering string can be described physically by counting the vibrations, timing their duration, measuring their amplitude, and analyzing the complex system of separately vibrating segments known as harmonics, or overtones. The tone is thus a vibrating, enduring, dynamic, qualitative fact known as the sound wave. Its regularly recurring impulses distinguish it from the unorganized, irregular, confused vibrations of noise. The wave frequency, or number of vibrations per second, of the tone leads to the sensation of *pitch,* its time length to *duration,* its amplitude to *intensity,* and its overtone structure to *tone color.*

The single tone, however, is only a promise of things to come. When two or more tones succeed each other, comparison, change, and movement become possible. If the second tone differs in the number of vibrations per second, the listener hears a movement in pitch. If the next note is longer or shorter, a shift in time values is felt. If the second sound is heavier or fainter, there is a perceived change in intensity. If the next tone is sounded by a different voice or instrument, a transformation in timbre occurs.

Cumulatively, changes in pitch are heard as *line* or *melody;* in duration, as *rhythm;* in rate of speed, as *tempo.* The increase and decrease of intensities become *dynamics,* and the distinction between various timbres produces the spectrum of *tone color.* These musical elements, moreover, are always heard together in the musical experience, never separately. All in all, this four-dimensional linear, rhythmic, dynamic, and qualitative movement is the basic raw material of music, with all its infinite variety and versatility as a medium of expression.

When several tones are combined and heard simultaneously in a *chord,* and several chords succeed each other in progression, *harmony* results. Likewise, when two or more musical lines are heard simultaneously, the combination is known as *counterpoint.* These basic processes are the warp and woof of the musical fabric. Harmony, as the progress of vertically organized chords, and counterpoint, as the horizontal spinning and weaving of combined lines, become the two principal musical *textures.* The contribution of the four elements, the two main textures, and the art of form to the listener's musical experience will be the subjects of the succeeding chapters.

CHAPTER

15

Art of Notation

MUSIC IS A LANGUAGE that uses a system of accepted symbols to translate ideas to paper and thence to sound. As letters, words, and punctuation allow a flow of ideas in literature, so the staff, notes, metric signatures, and accidental function in music. Since the symbols used on the pages of a musical score are so vital to the understanding and communication of the abstract musical idea, the reader may find it useful to review the notation symbols that are used in the examples scattered throughout this book.

Notes and Rests

Music's main symbols are *notes,* representing specific pitches and periods of sonic time (Chart 15-1). While there are theoretically more notes on which a composer may draw—such as breves (double whole notes), 64th, and 128th notes—Chart 15-1 contains the note symbols most often used in everyday practice. The longest note values on the chart are at the top, the shortest at the bottom. Equivalently, then, there are two half notes within each whole note, four quarter notes in each whole note, eight eighth notes in each whole note, and so on. Only the whole and half notes are "open," or not filled in. From the quarter note downward, all the note heads are filled in.

From the half note down, each circle has a *stem,* a straight line that is attached at the right or left, pointing up or down. The direction of the stem does not affect the length, or *value,* of the note, but is placed so as to aid the eye in viewing the music on the staff.

CHART 15-1. NOTE SYMBOLS

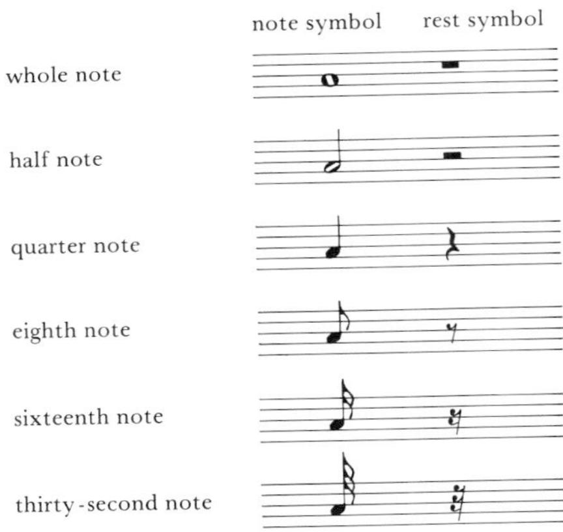

To the eighth note an oblique stroke is appended, known as a *flag*. Each note of shorter value receives an additional flag. The 16th has two, the 32nd has three, and so on. Flags become *beams* when two such flagged notes are joined together (Chart 15-2).

CHART 15-2. FLAGS AND BEAMS

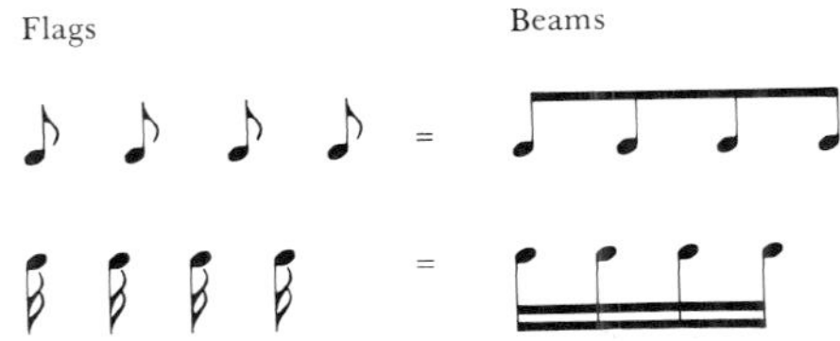

As notes are symbols for pitch and time values, *rests* are the symbols for periods of silence. Chart 15-1 shows the rest symbols that parallel those of equivalent note symbols. The first, hanging down from the line, is a *whole rest;* the second, sitting on top of the line, is a *half rest.* Next down comes a *quarter rest,* and so on.

Chart 15-3 presents the symbols known as the *dot* and the *tie.* A dot placed next to a note lengthens its value by one-half. For example, a dot after a half note gives it the value of a half note plus a quarter note. The curved-line tie over two notes of the same pitch indicates that they should sound their full value, but the second note is not sounded again. A tie over a half note and a quarter note produces the same duration as three quarter notes.

CHART 15-3. DOTTED AND TIED NOTES

The Staff

Chart 15-4 shows a five-line *staff* (plural, *staves*). When notes are higher or lower than those that are inscribed on the staff lines and spaces, they are placed on *ledger lines.* Chart 15-5 details the way notes are placed on the staff lines and in the spaces between them. The lower a note is positioned on the staff, the lower its pitch. Notes are assigned letter names, shown here in ascending order. Pitch names correspond to the first seven letters of the alphabet. Going up the staff, beginning with the note A, letters of the alphabet are used through G, then A begins the cycle again. Another way to refer to these letter-named pitches is to append the word *natural:* A-natural, D-natural, etc.

CHART 15-4. THE STAFF, BARS, AND LEDGER LINES

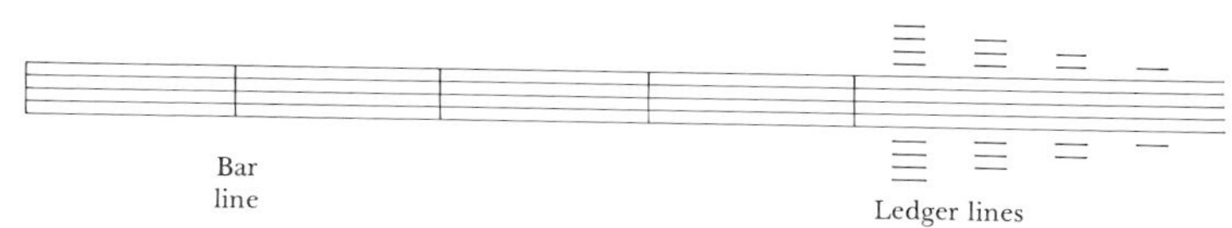

On those occasions when sounds must be notated above or below the staff, ledger lines are provided, as seen on Chart 15-4. While they actually add another line to the staff, they are short because they apply only to a particular note.

Clefs

Chart 15-5 shows the *clef* signs that appear at the beginning of each staff. The sign on the top staff is the *treble clef,* also known as the G clef. The treble clef is built so that it crosses the second line from the bottom four times. A note placed on that line is given the letter name G. In the staff below the clef is a *bass clef,* or F clef. This clef has two dots surrounding the second line from the top. This line is assigned to the pitch name F.

CHART 15-5

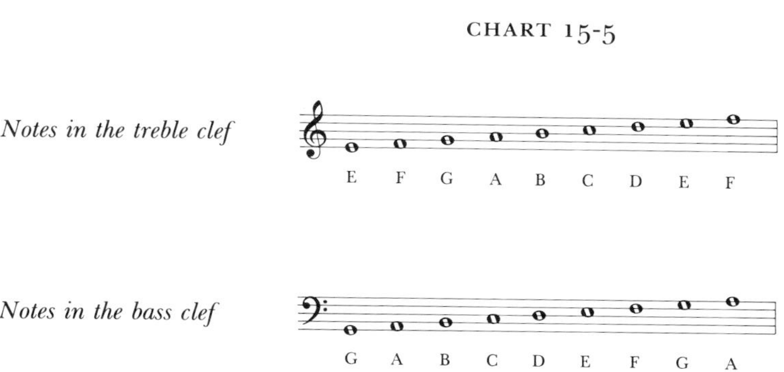

For a long time, the piano has been the basic music-teaching instrument in our culture. Much of the existing printed music uses the piano: solo piano music, vocal music, exercises for instruction, and "piano reductions" of orchestral scores, which allow one to learn at the piano various compositions that were written for many instruments.

Chart 15-6 indicates how piano music uses both the treble and the bass clef with vertical lines joining them at either end of the page and a bracket at the beginning to assist the eye. As a rule, the left hand plays the bass clef, the right hand the treble. The notes listed on the chart are placed consecutively from top to bottom, and it is known as the *grand staff.* Between the two staves the note C is described as *middle C,* indicating its central point here and on the keyboard, where it has the same name.

CHART 15-6. THE GRAND STAFF

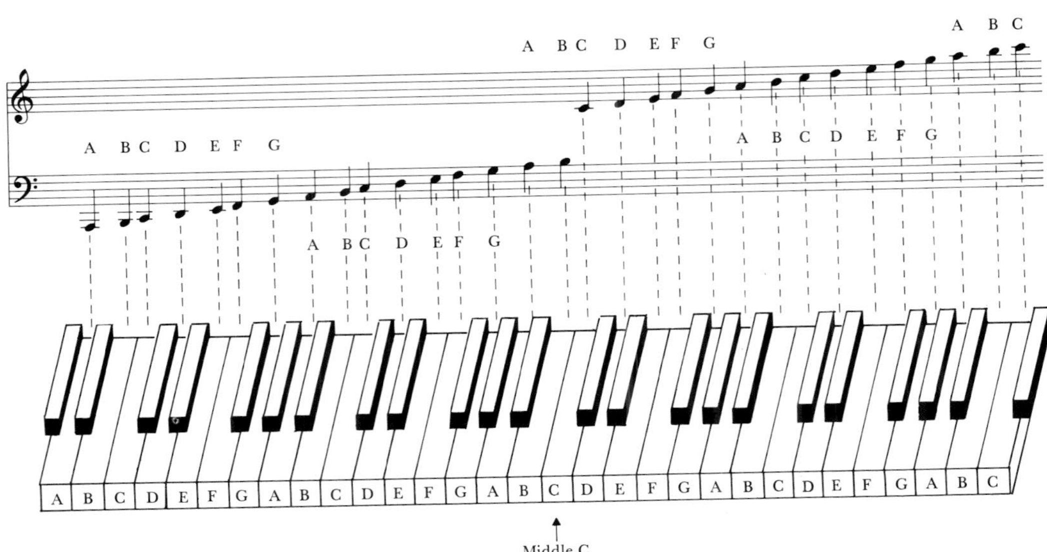

Chart 15-6 also contains a representative piano keyboard with all the white notes named. In any discussion of the keyboard and the note relationships on it, the note C is often chosen as a starting point.

Basic Intervals

The tonal system with which Western ears are most familiar is based on relationships between notes called *intervals.* The smallest interval in regular use is the *half step,* or *half tone*; the next largest interval is the *whole step,* or *whole tone.* We describe our tonal system through *scales,* which comprise formulas of half and whole steps.

By and large, the white notes on the piano are a whole tone apart, the exceptions being between E and F, and between B and C. Therefore, most note relationships that involve adjacent note names on the staff and the keyboard are a whole tone apart: C to D, D to E, F to G, and so on.

Accidentals

Chart 15-7 shows how the smaller relationship, or half tone, is represented on the keyboard by the distance between a white and a black note. Each black note is assigned two names, depending on its relationship to the white note on either side of it. The additional symbol that makes this identification clear is an *accidental.* The *sharp* (♯) accidental is used to refer to the note as it stands "above." For example, the black note between C and D is called C-sharp when we speak of it in relation to the white note C. The *flat* (♭) accidental is used to refer to the note as it stands "below." The black note between C and D is called D-flat when we speak of it in relation to the white note D. The black note above F is F-sharp; the black note below B is B-flat.

CHART 15-7. SHARPS AND FLATS ON THE KEYBOARD

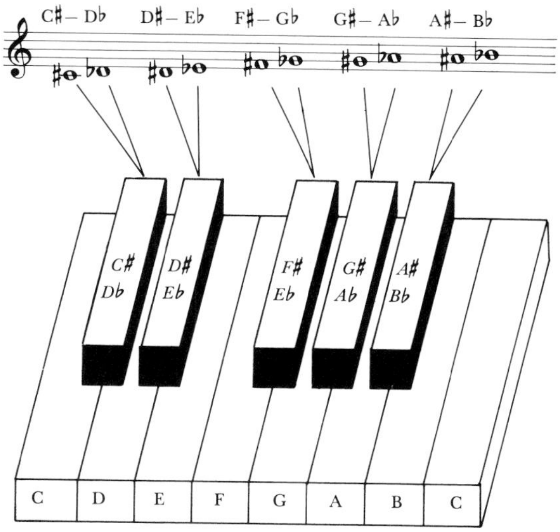

In the case of white notes that do not have a black between them (E-F and B-C), the note immediately adjacent is given the appropriate sharp or flat name. The half step above E is named both F-natural and E-sharp. Note names that are different, but which refer to notes that sound the same—C-sharp and D-flat, for example—are called *enharmonic.*

A third accidental is the *natural* (♮). On the musical staff, a sharp or flat may be "cancelled" with a natural sign.

Key and Metric Signatures

Following the clef sign, the key of the composition is disclosed by means of a grouping of sharps or flats. The function of this *key signature* is to indicate to the performer the notes that should always be performed with sharps or flats, and it implies that all other notes are to be considered natural (see p. 464). Following the key signature, the *metric signature* provides details on the rhythmic grouping of notes within each measure of the composition (see pp. 427–28).

CHAPTER 16

Art of Tone Color

THE WORD *COLOR* IS normally associated with a visual process by which the eye perceives variations in the vibration of light waves and signals these variations to the brain, which in turn interprets them as specific elements of the color spectrum. The intrinsic ability of color to have a psychological effect on the emotions through the eye has been for centuries a matter for study and the basis for many theories. Just as we think we have found the essence of pigment, hue, warm and cool color temperatures, and prismatic relationships, new discoveries lead to new knowledge. Today, laser technology is helping us to know more about what color and light relationships may be.

The parallel phenomenon for the ear, in which sound vibrations are interpreted by the brain, is called *tone color* or, from the French, *timbre*. It too is capable of creating a powerful psychological reaction. It is the quality by which the listener can distinguish the voice of a friend from that of a stranger, the sound of a passing jet plane from that of a truck, the tone of a violin from that of a flute. Each singing voice, each instrument, has its own unique and recognizable timbre. The listener's experience of tone color is rooted in the variations of sound that a single voice or instrument can produce.

With an electronic signal generator, we can today produce in a laboratory an absolutely pure tone with a controlled, measurable number of vibrations per second. However, tones are not pure in their natural state. Instead, they are formed by a complex of vibrations of varying strengths and pitch levels, sounding simultaneously. These complicated tone relationships, from which the sensation of tone color emerges, have been known at least since ancient

Greek times. In the 6th century B.C., the mathematician and philosopher Pythagoras reputedly discovered that the components of sound stand in strict mathematical relationships, and music was for centuries thereafter considered a science as much as an art.

All instruments, including the human voice, produce this complex of sounds, though our ears perceive only a single resulting tone. This unperceived, simultaneously produced sound complex is made up of *overtones,* or *harmonics,* which occur naturally in all instruments and voices. In the human voice the foundation of sound is the vibrating vocal chord; in a wind instrument it is a column of air; in a stringed instrument, a vibrating string; and in a pitched drum, a stretched skin. When any of these is set in motion, it vibrates along its entire length and simultaneously in segments. The result to our ears is a *pitch,* a tone made up of the vibrations of the total length of the vibrating surface. We also perceive that pitch as a specific *color,* depending upon the relative strengths of the overtones. Various combinations of overtone strengths are produced by every instrument and every human voice, thereby allowing our ears to differentiate between a piano, violin, and human voice even when each sounds the same fundamental pitch.

Assume that the vibrating body—a string, for example—produces 110 vibrations per second (vps) when set in motion. The sound that results is known in the sound complex as the *fundamental* pitch, in this case the tone perceived by the ear as the note A. What the listener does *not* consciously hear is the series of mathematically related higher-pitched overtones, for the string is vibrating simultaneously in halves, thirds, fourths, fifths, etc.

The first overtone, derived from the string vibrating in halves, is twice the number of vibrations (220 vps). It produces a tone an octave higher than the fundamental, which we describe as A^1. The second overtone, somewhat weaker, is produced from the string vibrating in thirds, resulting in an interval of the fifth above the first overtone (E, 330 vps). The string vibrating in quarters generates the third overtone, which is two octaves above the fundamental tone (A^2, 440 vps). The fourth overtone, still weaker, finds the string vibrating in five parts, generating a major third above the previous overtone (C-sharp, 550 vps). Each overtone becomes succeedingly weaker in intensity and closer to its predecessor in pitch. If we isolate the separate tones produced by the vibrating string, we find the notes A, A^1, E, A^2, C-sharp. Removing repeated note names, we are left with A E C-sharp, or in another order A C-sharp E, which in Western tonality is a type of chord known as a major triad.

To summarize, every vibrating source produces the same types of tones: fundamental and overtones in set mathematical relationships. Though the overtones are mathematically the same from each vibrating source, their relative strengths differ. We consciously perceive the fundamental tone produced by the source, and we recognize that source—piano, violin, voice—through

CHART 16-1. MUSICAL PROPORTIONS

Vibrations per Second (VPS)	Note Name	Interval	Ratio	Percent of Total Surface Vibrating
110*	A	Unison	1:1	100
121	B	Major Second	9:8	89
128	C	Minor Third	6:5	83
136	C-sharp	Major Third	5:4	80
144	D	Perfect Fourth	4:3	75
161	E	Perfect Fifth	3:2	67
171	F	Minor Sixth	8:5	63
181	F-sharp	Major Sixth	5:3	60
192	G	Minor Seventh	9:16	56
220*	A	Octave	2:1	50

Fundamental and First Four Overtones

110*	A	Fundamental
220*	A^1	Octave
330*	E	Twelfth (Fifth)
440*	A^2	Fifteenth (Octave)
550*	C-sharp	Seventeenth (Third)

*VPS figures ending in o are approximate.

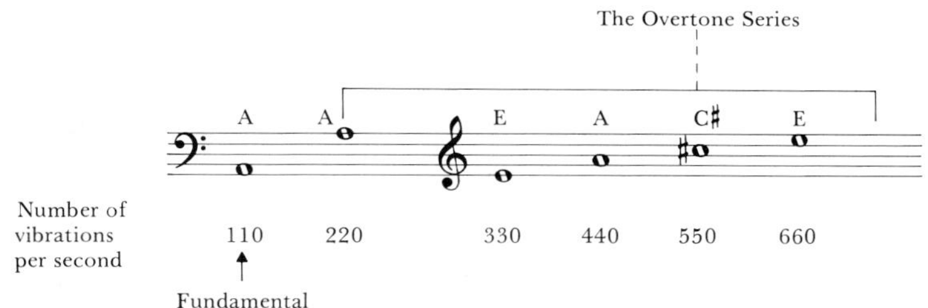

the unconsciously heard relationships of overtones which that source alone produces. On the musical score, the tone colors formed by many instruments and voices alone or in combination constitute a rich palette from which composers may paint varicolored musical canvases.

The Orchestra

The modern orchestra is first and foremost a color phenomenon, a projector of multiple sonorities. Though other types of orchestral communication are important, it is the almost unlimited potential for a kaleidoscope of sound that has kept the symphony orchestra in the forefront with the concert-going pub-

CHART 16-2. A TYPICAL ORCHESTRA

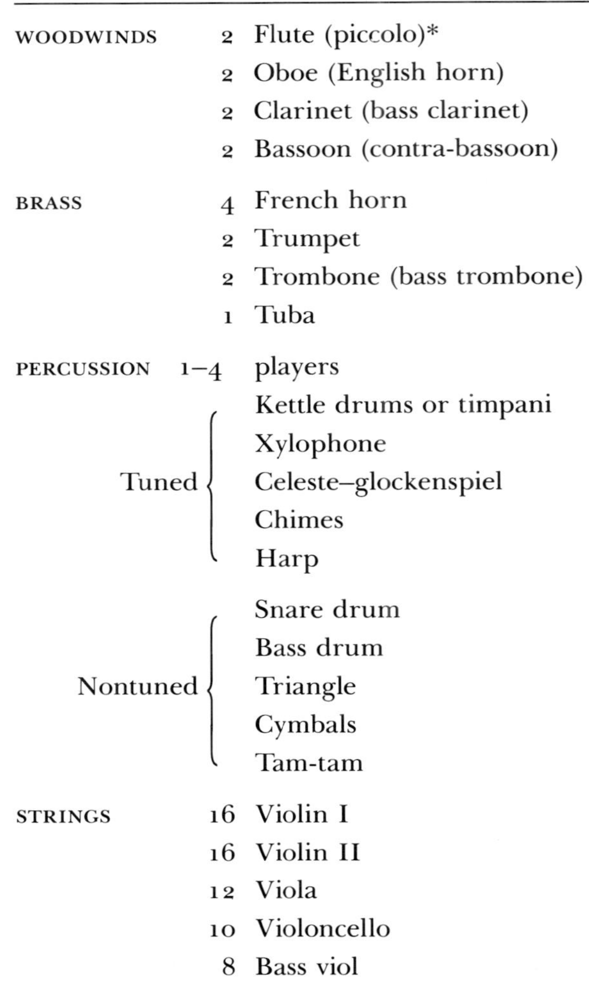

WOODWINDS	2	Flute (piccolo)*
	2	Oboe (English horn)
	2	Clarinet (bass clarinet)
	2	Bassoon (contra-bassoon)
BRASS	4	French horn
	2	Trumpet
	2	Trombone (bass trombone)
	1	Tuba
PERCUSSION	1–4	players
Tuned		Kettle drums or timpani
		Xylophone
		Celeste–glockenspiel
		Chimes
		Harp
Nontuned		Snare drum
		Bass drum
		Triangle
		Cymbals
		Tam-tam
STRINGS	16	Violin I
	16	Violin II
	12	Viola
	10	Violoncello
	8	Bass viol

* "Relative" instruments in parentheses

lic. The burden of musical color in the orchestra rests principally on only 12 basic instruments, plus a group of percussion instruments that varies from composition to composition. There is an additional group of "related" but less frequently used instruments that extend the range and color capabilities of the orchestra.

Musical instruments other than the human voice are customarily divided into classes according to their construction and manner of sound production. Those in which a stretched string is bowed are called the *strings;* those in which an enclosed column of air is set in vibration by blowing are the *woodwinds* and *brasses;* and those in which tightened membranes, metal disks, rods, bars, or the like are struck constitute the *percussion* instruments. In addition to these traditional members of the musical community, an entirely new series of

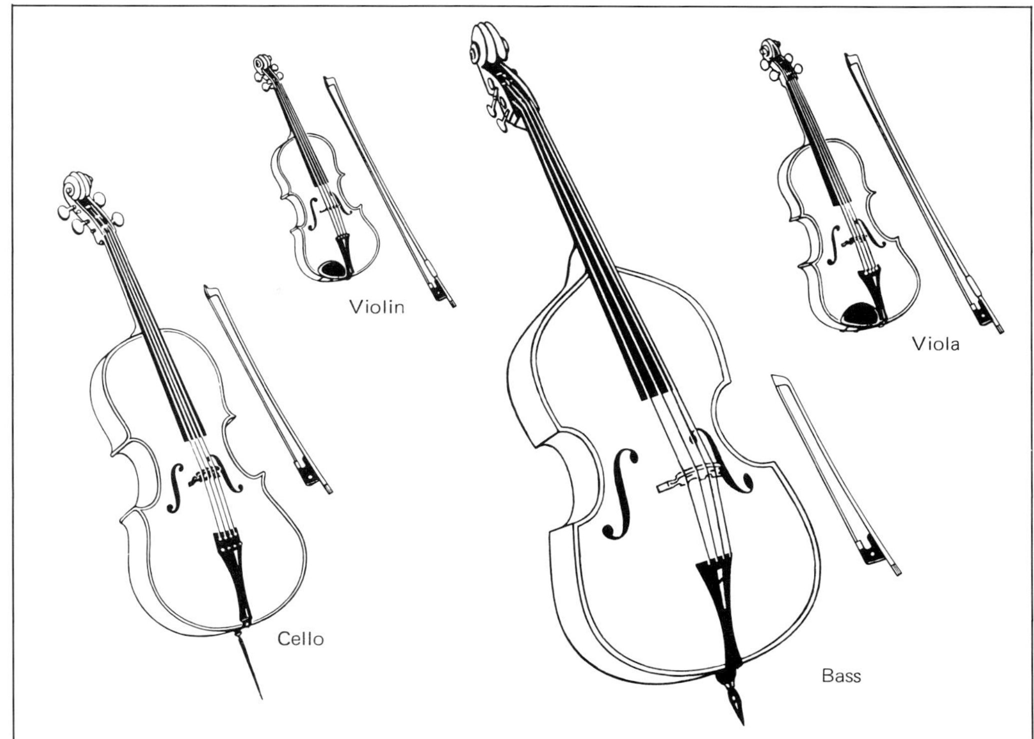

Figure 16-1. String instruments. From *Music: A Design for Listening*, by Homer Ulrich, 3rd ed., copyright 1970 by Harcourt Brace Jovanovich, Inc., reproduced by permission of the publisher.

methods of producing sound is possible through the science of electronics and computers.

Chart 16-2 shows the major instruments with their "relatives," and a small representative list of often-used percussion instruments. Reading from top to bottom, instruments appear as they do in an orchestral score. Note that the orchestra is divided into *choirs,* or *sections*, according to the above classifications. Each of these, in turn, is arranged into registers that correspond roughly to the vocal ranges found in a mixed chorus.

Though the orchestra is constituted from a fairly small number of different instrumental types, most are present in multiple numbers, giving the modern orchestra a personnel of more than a hundred performers. Chart 16-2 indicates one possible numerical combination of instruments.

STRING CHOIR

Those instruments referred to as "strings" in the orchestra are those in which tone is produced by drawing a bow across a stretched string. Appearing at the bottom of the score, the *string choir* contains the largest number of orchestral performers, comprising more than half of its collective ranks (Fig.

16-1). Historically the strings are the senior members of the symphonic society, and string color, coming as it does from a single family of instruments, is more homogeneous in sound than that of the other choirs.

In all choirs of the orchestra, instruments with the highest range appear at the top of the score for that choir, those with the lowest range at the bottom. There are long-standing parallels between orchestral choirs and choirs of human voices, since all melodic instruments are to a degree an extension of or substitute for the voice. The basic division into four parts that is central to the vocal choir is also present in orchestral choirs because of the four basic ranges of the human voice: soprano, contralto (alto), tenor, and bass. The basic quartet of stringed instruments was settled in the early 17th century and has remained more or less unchanged. In the modern orchestra, generally speaking, the violins function as sopranos, the violas as altos, the cellos as tenors, and the bass viols as basses. These parallels must be considered generalizations, since all instruments are called upon to assume a wide range of pitches and colors from time to time.

While bowed string instruments have been in existence since at least early medieval times, it was not until the 16th century that the configuration, number of strings, and generally accepted methods of playing in use today began to be standardized. Italy was the first center for stringed instrument design and manufacture. During the 17th and 18th centuries, the magic names in stringed instruments—Stradivarius, Guarnerius, Amati—were families of highly skilled craftsmen. Their instruments, many of which are still in use today, were assembled from aged wood under carefully controlled conditions. The wood was cut and glued with the greatest care and given several coats of natural protective varnish. Gut strings were then placed under tension, and the instrument was ready to play. The special varnish recipes remained closely guarded secrets, for the varnish on an excellent stringed instrument must be slow to dry and continue to protect the wood, so that it retains its natural vibrating qualities, sometimes for centuries.

In the following discussion of the string section, the *violin* functions as the representative instrument for the entire section. Unless otherwise noted, the same information applies to all other bowed orchestral strings. The principle of violin sound is that of the vibrating string set in motion by drawing a horsehair *bow* across it. The vibrations are transferred through the *bridge,* on which the strings rest, to the body. The body itself vibrates, and the vibrations bounce around inside, where they take on subtle color changes and become somewhat amplified. The sound emerges from the holes on either side of the front of the instrument (see Fig. 16-1). The total sound is a complex of vibrations from three sources: the string, the body of the instrument, and the cavity within the body. The fundamental tone of each of the four strings results from the thickness of the string, the tension upon it, and its length, measured from the *neck* to the bridge of the violin. Depressing the string with the finger onto the *fingerboard* changes the sounding length of the string, and thereby its fundamental pitch.

The size of modern concert halls requires instruments to provide a large volume of sound, and violins are now strung with wire and wire-wound gut strings. While the wire produces a more brilliant and penetrating sound, gut strings produce a more easily balanced, warmer tone. String players who wish to perform, say, 18th-century music as it was originally conceived, often favor gut-strung violins.

A number of color effects are possible on the violin. Under normal playing conditions the bow is drawn across one string in a smooth continuous *legato* or short, detached *staccato,* sounding one pitch at a time. To give the tone a vibrant quality similar to that of the human voice, the player moves his left hand quickly back and forth on the string and fingerboard, thus causing the pitch to waver slightly in the throbbing effect known as *vibrato.*

Other special string effects at the command of composers include *pizzicato* (plucking the strings); *spiccato* (using a bouncing stroke of the bow to produce rapid, detached notes); *tremolo* or *tremolando* (rapidly repeating the same note with upward and downward strokes of the bow); *double* or *triple stopping* (sounding two or three strings at the same time); *harmonics,* (touching the string lightly with the finger, producing high-pitched, ethereal tones); *col legno* (playing with the wooden side of the bow); *glissando* (running the finger rapidly up or down the string to produce a gliding sound). A three-pronged clamp, known as a *mute,* may be inserted on the bridge of the instrument. Its effect is to cancel out some of the overtones, thereby producing a soft, veiled sonority.

It has been said that the *viola* is "a philosopher: sad, helpful, always willing to come to the aid of others but reluctant to draw attention to itself." The viola fulfills the contralto role in the string section. Both the voice type (see p. 422) and the instrument may be described as covered, darker in tone than their soprano and violin counterparts, never quite so dazzling or brilliant. Slightly larger in size and lower in range than the violin, the viola often plays fill-in harmonies, or accompaniment figures for long numbers of measures. When assigned a solo voice, however, it is capable of producing of a husky, robust tone.

The *violoncello,* usually shortened to *cello,* has as its lowest note the C that is an octave below the lowest pitch of the viola (see Fig. 16-1). Because of its size, it is played in a semivertical position and held between the knees. Its lower range has a gutty, vibrant quality; the midrange is smooth; and the high range, which ascends to the middle of violin range, is lean and "pointed." Partly because of its ability to "sing" and partly because it has the most extended range of any of the strings, the cello section is often chosen to articulate broadly sustained melodic lines.

The *bass viol,* or *double bass,* earned the name from its 17th-century assignment of duplicating the cello line an octave lower. Its deep, heavy tone provides not only the string section but the entire orchestra with necessary support. The bass viol is the largest of the orchestral strings and is played in a vertical position with the player standing. In some ways it is also the most ungainly, since the relative distance between tones on a string becomes greater as one moves down the scale. The bass viol, with a range that starts almost two octaves below the cello, requires the player to move distances of up to two inches between adjacent notes, thus making it difficult to create a smooth sense of line. To make the instrument more manageable, its strings are tuned a fourth apart, rather than the normal fifth as for the other strings.

In some instruments with strings, the tone is produced by plucking or striking the strings rather than bowing them; the *harp, guitar, piano,* and *harpsichord* are among them. When these instruments are included as ensemble members in the orchestra, they are placed in the percussion section. Conductors of the 17th and 18th centuries usually sat at the harpsichord playing the bass line and filling in the harmonies while directing the orchestra. In early chamber and orchestral music the harpsichord is often paired with a cello to form the combination known as a continuo (see p. 157).

Plucked instruments like the mandolin and the guitar occasionally appear in chamber and orchestral ensembles. The guitar is an unusually adaptable, convenient, all-purpose instrument. As a successor to the Renaissance lute, it developed an impressive solo literature of its own. In Spain the guitar has long been a standby in the classical repertory, and a favored instrument for flamenco music, and has also found wide acceptance among modern composers. As a solo and accompanying instrument the traditional guitar, as well as the modern electric version, holds a prominent place in the performance of folk and popular music.

WOODWIND CHOIR

At the top of the orchestral score is the *woodwind choir,* which includes the *flutes, oboes, clarinets,* and *bassoons,* whose ranges overlap (Fig. 16-2). When playing as a choir, however, the flutes usually play the soprano role and the bassoons the bass, with the oboes and clarinets in the middle registers. The range of each of these four principals is extended by at least one other member of its own family or by a "relative instrument." The *piccolo,* short for *flauto piccolo* (small flute), is about half the length of the flute and can play an octave higher. The *English horn,* an alto oboe, is the relative instrument that utilizes the register immediately below that of the oboe. The *bass clarinet* and *contrabassoon* sound below their respective namesakes.

The woodwinds are strong individualists in the orchestral community; yet, like good citizens, they can also mix well with their neighbors when necessary. Their family tree has its roots in ancient Greece, where such instruments as the syrinx, or panpipes, were first fashioned out of the hollow stalks of reeds

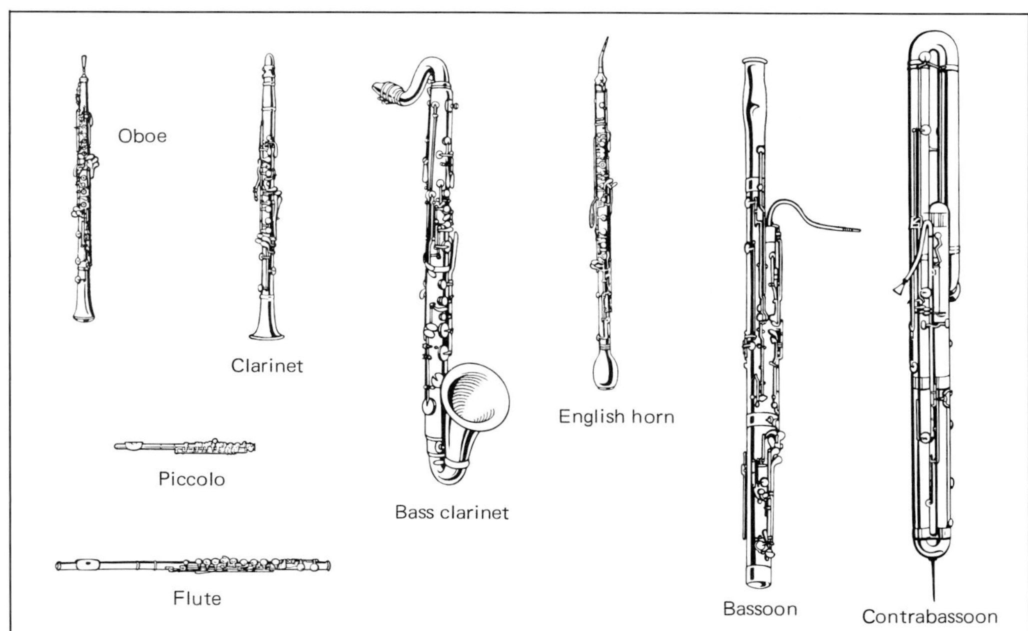

Figure 16-2. Woodwind instruments. From *Music: A Design for Listening,* by Homer Ulrich, 3rd ed., copyright 1970 by Harcourt Brace Jovanovich, Inc., reproduced by permission of the publisher.

of varying length, to become the common ancestor of both the organ and the woodwinds (see p. 75). Over the centuries their contours and mechanisms have varied considerably, and today metal and plastic materials are rapidly replacing the woods that gave them their original generic name. In spite of modern manufacturing methods, however, these country cousins of the orchestra still retain something of their rustic origin and pastoral character.

Most woodwind players color and smooth their tone by using vibrato, in which control of the diaphragm allows for subtle, regular variation in the pitch. As with the strings, a straight tone is used for rapid passage work, and vibrato is brought into play for lyric solo passages as well as for sustained notes. Production of tone in all wind instruments, including the brasses, requires special techniques of controlling the area around the mouth. Such mouth formations are described by the French word *embouchure.*

The *flute,* with its capacity for rapid, agile passage work, is the coloratura soprano of the woodwinds. The tone of the modern flute is produced with an embouchure formed by pursing the lips in such a way that a controlled stream of air is directed over the edge of a lip and into a hole near the top of the instrument.

The musical literature of the flute often stresses the classical background of the instrument as well as its outdoor heritage. The flute has always been extolled for its ability to carry floating, soaring melodies and for its purity of tone, the result of a relatively simple overtone structure.

The other three instruments of the woodwind choir use reeds to initiate the tone. The *oboe,* deriving its name from the French *haut bois* (high wood), is a double-reed instrument. The tone is formed by blowing a stream of air through two shaped pieces of reed which have been bound together. Its distinctive nasal tone has been used for many color effects, one of which is to suggest the Orient, where instruments of the oboe type abound. Our ears are so trained to this snake-charmer sound that an oboe wailing in an Oriental mode is sufficient to conjure up visions of the East in the mind's ear. In Western music, the oboe has long enjoyed a distinguished career in abstract music, where its pointed tone can penetrate the full orchestra. The oboe's distant Greek ancestor was the aulos, a double-reed instrument known for its piercing sound in outdoor spaces (see p. 76). As a result, the oboe from ancient to modern times has been associated with the bucolic, the outdoors, the frolic upon the green.

Because it possesses a pitch stability not found in other instruments, the oboe has long been used as the instrument by which the rest of the orchestra tunes. In modern orchestras, an electronic instrument backstage has replaced the oboe, and basic tuning takes place before the musicians make their appearance.

The *clarinet* is a single-reed instrument, in which the wide reed is fitted into a mouthpiece of glass or hard rubber. The clarinets include a whole family of instruments, most of which are still heard in large military bands. Those that appear in the symphony orchestra have a wider command of dynamic levels from soft to loud than any other wind instrument. The air column, or *bore,* of the instrument is larger than that of the oboe, and its overtone series is particularly rich. Clarinetists did not traditionally use vibrato to keep a sustained tone interesting, but in recent times vibrato has been used successfully by solo artists.

There are three distinct *registers* on the clarinet. The lowest of these is the *chalumeau,* which may be described as rich, velvety, and dark; the middle is bright, strong, and smooth; the top is strongly focused and piercing. The clarinet's ability to "sing" as well as wail has made it a popular instrument in both classical and jazz idioms.

The *bassoon,* a much underestimated musical personality, is the double-reeded bass member of the oboe family. Its Italian name, *fagotto,* means a "bundle" (of sticks), which it somewhat resembles. Like the clarinet, it has distinct registers, the lowest of which is buzzy and has been used to suggest both the humorous and the ironic. The midrange is smoother, with a fine capacity to negotiate lyric passages attractively. The top register produces a wail, sparingly used until this century, when composers seeking new tone-color techniques "rediscovered" it.

The *saxophone* is also a woodwind instrument, though it figures more prominently in dance, marching, symphonic, and military bands than as an orchestral instrument. Saxophones are a family of instruments ranging from a high sopranino to a deep contrabass, but the versions most often heard are the alto and tenor. In the orchestra it ranks as an "extra wind."

BRASS CHOIR

In a way the brass choir (Fig. 16-3) resembles the string section more than any other, since its members are all cut from the same cloth. All are tubes of metal with a mouthpiece at one end and a flared bell to project the tone at the other. Individual characteristics are the result of differences in the length, size of bore, and method of controlling the pitch. When played together, the vigor and virility of the brasses can provide the thunderous sonorities needed for tremendous orchestral climaxes; and when required, they can also sing out with long, sustained, organlike harmonies.

The rich, round resonance of the *French horn* is the essence of sonorous nobility. Socially speaking, the instrument is one of the best mixers in the orchestra. It often deserts its brother brasses to join the woodwinds, where it softens the rough edges of their reedy textures and generally integrates their separate sonorities into a homogeneous group, often without the listener being aware of its presence.

The French horn is a highly versatile instrument with a wide range—about three and a half octaves—and a tone quality capable of great variety. Its original settings were the forest, where it was associated with hunting, and the village, where it appeared as the post horn, signaling the arrival of the mail coach. In the mid-18th century, French horns began to appear in the orchestra, in pairs; today a complement of four to eight is common. Composers often view the French horn section as a choir in itself, since its wide range

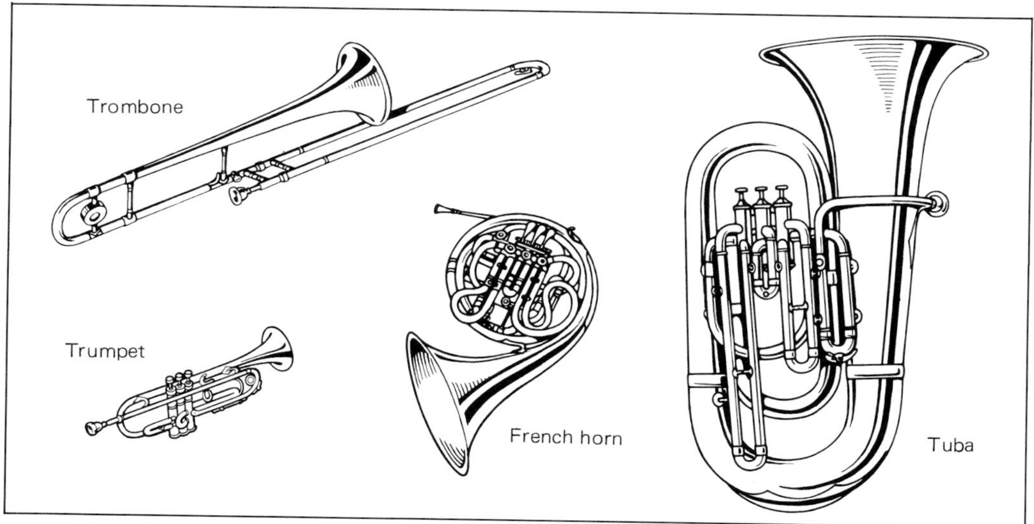

Figure 16-3. Brass instruments. From *Music: A Design for Listening*, by Homer Ulrich, 3rd ed., copyright 1970 by Harcourt Brace Jovanovich, Inc., reproduced by permission of the publisher.

allows four separate performers to function effectively as soprano, alto, tenor, and bass.

The French horn is played in a vertical position with the right hand placed into the bell opening, allowing the hand to regulate both the amount of sound that emerges and to control the pitch to some degree. It has a long-standing reputation as one of the most difficult of wind instruments to play, but its flexibility allows it to blast away impressively or to sing a long legato line. The embouchure requires a very tight lip arrangement, using spurts of air under heavy pressure.

The silvery soprano register of the *trumpet* shines through any orchestral fabric with assurance and ease. Its bright timbre and carrying power have been valued since antiquity, and it joined the baroque orchestra after a long-standing courtly service, in which its function was that of heralding the arrival of important personages. In the classical orchestra, its music recalls its first home in the military, summoning troops to action and relaying battle commands to the troops in the field. Jazz trumpeters have also contributed much to the newer color capabilities of the instrument. In contemporary orchestrations the trumpet's tone is often modified by flutter-tonguing techniques as well as by the insertion into the bell of various mutes made of metal, plastic, or cardboard.

The trumpet works on the same principle as that of the French horn, whereby three valves open and close sections of tubing, thus lengthening or shortening the overall vibrating column of air, and changing both the fundamental pitch and its overtones. Trumpets come in several sizes and are named for the fundamental pitch produced by the full length of the sounding tube. In the orchestra it is normal to find B-flat and C trumpets. For some music of the past, shorter, higher-pitched trumpets in D and F are used.

The *trombone,* with its slide action and stentorian tone, is somewhat similar in sound to the French horn, but with a deeper, more penetrating quality. In his book on orchestration, Berlioz observed: "Directed by the will of a master, the trombones can chant like a choir of priests, threaten, utter gloomy sighs, a mournful lament, or a bright hymn of glory." While the trombone has many passionate adherents, it is seldom heard as soloist either in the orchestra or on the concert platform. Its orchestral role is that of a colleague among the brass group, an accompanist, and strong support in large-scale climaxes.

The *tuba* comes in various sizes to provide the brass section with the heavy tone, broad volume, and deep register needed to complete the choir. The instrument has a very large bore and a flared bell that points upward. It has a close relation in the *sousaphone,* an innovation for outdoor band use designed by the composer John Philip Sousa. He extended the tuba bell upward and outward so that its sound could project more effectively in the open air. The orchestral tuba has a more suave, less gruff voice.

This body of instruments (Fig. 16-4) may be classified as *tuned*—those capable of producing definite pitch, and *nontuned*—those of indefinite pitch. A representative cross-section of tuned percussion instruments includes *timpani* (or *kettle drums*), *chimes, bells, glockenspiel, celesta, xylophone, vibraphone, marimba,* and *harp*. Frequently used nontuned percussion instruments include *snare drum, bass drum, cymbal, triangle, gong* (or *tam-tam*), *castanets,* and *tambourine*.

The nucleus of the tuned percussion group is the *timpani,* the tops of whose shiny copper kettles are covered by a taut skin. The tension of this head can be controlled to produce definite pitches by adjusting screws or pressing on a pedal mechanism. The timpanist can achieve different sonorities by striking the membrane with sticks, the heads of which may be equipped with a variety of soft or hard materials. The timpani can punctuate orchestral statements, give sharp definition to rhythms, make colossal crescendos by the drumroll technique, and point up climaxes.

The tubular *chimes,* a set of metal cylinders hung on a wooden frame, are used to suggest the clangor of bells. More delicacy is possible with the *glockenspiel* (literally, play of bells), in which a set of hard metal bars are arranged in a graduated series based on the keyboard. The bars are contained in a small portable case, and the tone is produced by striking the bars with special wooden sticks. A close relative is the *celesta,* a keyboard version of the glockenspiel. Other percussion instruments that utilize a variety of beaters and a keyboard layout with bars of various lengths are the *xylophone* (wooden bars), its

Figure 16-4. Percussion instruments. Courtesy of Selmer Company, Elkhart, Indiana.

deeper-toned relative, the *marimba*, and the *vibraphone* (electrified with metal bars).

The basic nontuned percussion instruments are the *snare drum,* which crisply displays its assertive military origins; and the *cymbals,* slightly concave disks of brass that intensify orchestral climaxes when clashed together. For popular music they are attached to stands with a foot pedal, where they can more subtly support the rhythmic framework.

There are hundreds of other instruments that may make special appearances in the percussion section of the orchestra. Rattles, sirens, temple blocks, whistles, wind machines, and even chains are occasionally called for in some 20th-century music. Several that are commonly found in orchestral scoring are the *tambourine,* a small half-drum equipped with jingling metal disks and associated with Spanish or Gypsy elements; the *bass drum,* providing the heavy artillery for the percussion section; the tinkling *triangle,* a single hard-metal bar bent into triangular shape, adding sparkle and luster at appropriate moments; and the *tam-tam,* a very large cymbal-like gong of Chinese origin which is hung on a stand. Struck loudly, the tam-tam produces an ominous, diffused sound.

As mentioned above, the piano, harp, and harpsichord are technically percussion instruments. Strings are plucked on the harp and harpsichord, while piano strings are struck by felt-covered hammers.

THE CONDUCTOR

Over this vast, multilayered mechanism presides the *conductor,* who plays no instrument, yet plays them all. While the individual musician in the ranks is concerned with but a single part, the conductor must be responsible for all the complex details of the whole score. Technically the role of the conductor is to provide a clear beat, set and maintain the tempo, signal tempo changes, cue the entrances of various instruments and sections, monitor the precision of the ensemble playing, mold the phrases into shapely melodic entities, adjust the delicate tonal balances, vary the dynamic shading, and build up dramatic climaxes. In this sense the conductor's business is to weld the heterogeneous mass of orchestral players into an organic and responsive instrument through which the composer's ideas, expressed only in notation, may be fully realized in sound. Beyond this, the conductor must provide the authority of knowledge, the personal magnetism of leadership, and the spark of inspiration that ignites the inert pages of the score into musical life.

Thus by the humanization of instrumental personalities, by historical and psychological association, by the suggestion of symbolic meanings, or by stark imitative realism, a composer builds a color vocabulary to communicate individual ideas and to serve particular dramatic designs. The orchestral composer must know not only the limitations and capabilities of each instrument, but also how each sounds in the company of its fellows when conversing in a musical gathering. As in any company, some inevitably attract attention to themselves: the trumpet, E-flat clarinet, and cymbals, for instance, can never appear in disguise. Others, such as the violas and cellos, are essentially good mixers, and their presence would be sorely missed if the composer inadvertently left them off the guest list. Still other instruments, such as the violins, bassoons, and French horns, blend well and tend to merge with the other colors, but they are also able to stand out with pronounced personalities of their own whenever necessary.

Furthermore, to justify using the colossal arsenal of the symphony orchestra with its vast aggregate of strings, reeds, pipes, tubes, and membranes, a composer must match this mighty medium with some correspondingly great ideas. Otherwise, these phalanxes of fiddles and row upon row of performers would be bowing, blowing, and beating in vain.

Electronic Instruments

Modern science has provided the composer with a whole new world of sound. Instead of the vibration of strings or columns of air, sound waves can now be produced by electronic oscillations and microchips. The electronic keyboard is the most visible application of this principle. The impetus to its development was the desire to create an inexpensive instrument that would duplicate some of the capacities of the pipe organ. Once the start had been made, the gates were opened to an almost unlimited scope of sound production.

The tape recorder can capture everyday sounds and store them as raw materials for the composer to manipulate (see p. 377). Another, more sophisticated approach is the use of artificially generated sounds. Employing elaborate, intricate equipment, the composer can produce any conceivable combination of sounds; change their pitch, duration, level of loudness, and tone quality; isolate their components; add reverberations, echoes, and feedback; filter out upper partials (overtones); duplicate conventional instruments; or invent completely new sounds. Electronic sound synthesizers and the computer programming of sounds are still in the developmental stage, as acoustical engineers explore new musical territories. By converting sound waves with their elements of pitch, dynamics, duration, and tone color into digits or number series, the synthesizer and the computer can produce sounds for live performance or store them for later use, in the digital recording process.

Composers who have mastered the techniques of the computer and the synthesizer can dispense with conventional instruments and live musicians if they wish, and record their works directly onto tape or disk for distribution to the listener. The process of producing a musical work on tape is analogous to that of the graphic artist who creates the master plate of an etching or lithograph from which subsequent prints can be made.

Many composers of the past have protested bitterly when singers, instrumentalists, and conductors take what they consider to be unwarranted liberties in the interpretation of their scores. However, the composer who dispenses with the performer by opting for the control of interpretation through electronic means loses the spontaneity of a live performance and the creative insights a skilled and responsible performer can bring to the music. Some have found a compromise by incorporating electronically produced material within a live musical performance. It is also possible to write a symphony in which electronic sound becomes one of the sections of the orchestra, or to compose a concerto for synthesizer and orchestra.

Whatever the case, it should be clearly understood that the medium is not the music. An electronic sound generator is certainly far more complex than a traditional instrument, but ultimately both are only instruments, a means to an end. The electronically oriented composer can work in any desired style. History, however, has shown that each major breakthrough evolves its own vocabulary and exploits areas that are idiomatic and unique to the particular medium. Eventually the composer must summon every ounce of creative imagination so as to produce a valid tonal continuum that is interesting and significant enough to make contact with the listener.

Instrumentation

Instrumentation, or *orchestration,* is the art by which composers organize all the sonic possibilities for their particular expressive purposes—in other words, choosing the right tools and combinations for the job at hand. The process of scoring a work entails problems of a sort that pictorial artists also confront. After they have decided on the scope and size of the design, determined the direction of the lines and the balance of light and shade, artists must then choose the most suitable medium and color scheme. A particular idea, for instance, might best be realized as a black-and-white etching or lithograph, a watercolor, an oil painting, or a large fresco mural.

In much the same manner, composers take into account the various avenues open to them and the nature of the ideas that are to be realized in sound. The variety of tone color available with a single solo instrument, for instance, is somewhat restricted, while an orchestral palette can produce an almost infinite range of hues and instrumental mixtures. And just as a connoisseur of art can recognize instantly the work of a Titian or an El Greco by their color harmonies, so a discerning listener is immediately aware of the characteristic sounds of an orchestration by Beethoven or Wagner. In this way a composer's musical personality is often seen through a characteristic handling of instruments.

Among piano compositions, for example, Beethoven's explosive accentuation, Chopin's florid lyricism, Debussy's mysterious mixtures of tone and overtone, and Stravinsky's brittle, percussive sonorities reveal individual notions of "piano style." In a broader sense, the profile of an entire era is likewise mirrored in the characteristic ways its composers approach the instruments at their disposal. These color images, moreover, are often just as important in the total vocabulary of a composer as melody, rhythm, dynamics, textures, and formal principles.

Clothes, it is often said, make the man; and in similar fashion the choices of instruments make the music. A composer dresses melodies in a variety of sonorities just as a dramatist clothes characters according to the historical periods and situations in which they appear. Whether a melody is conceived in the mind of a composer with or without its unique color, the choice is always dictated by the context, the sequence of colors in a large-scale work, the need for dramatic entries at particular points, and the color that comes closest to realizing the idea in sound.

The Human Voice

The human voice is at once the simplest and the most direct communicative force of all the musical instruments. It boasts a unique and intimate association with speech and verbal communication, and places a minimum of apparatus between the performer and the listener. It is as well the most personal and expressive of all musical instruments. Though styles of singing vary historically and geographically, no other instrument has been so universally employed by composers over such an extended span of time.

The extension of the speaking voice upward and downward for ritual and entertainment purposes is inherent in all societies and cultures. Surviving vocal literature may be traced back to antiquity, while the earliest extant instrumental music dates from a much later period. A considerable quantity of instrumental music has been conceived in terms of the human voice, extending and imitating what the voice can do. The woodwinds in particular have long been considered in relation to the voice. And while the manufacture of instruments has undergone radical changes during the industrial and electronic revolutions, the human voice has remained constant.

Vocal coloration covers a wide spectrum, from the limited range of the untrained singer in the fields or the church congregation, to the characteristic resonance of a traditionally trained opera diva; from the nasal intonations of singers from India to the high, piercing notes of Japanese Noh drama; from the earthy sound of the older Afro-American-inspired blues to the more refined emotionalism of later "soul" singing; and from the sentimental songs and high falsetto head tones of country and western music to the raucous belting of rock songs; from a solo crooner purring into a microphone to the avant-garde singer's virtuoso flights, electronically amplified and altered.

Today we make a distinction between the singing voice that is essentially untrained—the folk and the popular singer—and the one that has undergone rigorous training for the concert and opera stage. Despite such distinctions, there are obviously certain gray areas, since many professionally trained singers choose careers that include popular and folk singing. Likewise, many folk and popular singers elect to undergo the discipline of vocal training. The range of any voice is, of course, restricted. Most commonly, voices fall within the middle ranges of mezzo-soprano and baritone for women and men respectively. With training, voices can be cultivated in their natural placement, pushed upward into soprano and tenor ranges or downward into alto and bass registers. Except in unusual instances, the entire gamut covered by the four principal voices—*soprano, contralto, tenor,* and *bass*—is normally somewhat less than four octaves, extending from A about two octaves above middle C to about two octaves below it.

Vocal training stresses appropriate body support, proper breath control, and a means of tone production that enables the voice to sustain levels of highly charged emotion under physically demanding conditions. Since music in any historical period reflects specific traditions and tastes, the training of the human voice has traditionally attempted to match vocal ability to current needs of expression. For the past 400 years, singers have trained to raise their voices in public—in the opera house, the concert hall, and the church. Naturally, as operatic styles and concepts changed, as the concert hall assumed new functions, and as the church reinterpreted its belief system, singers have reflected new demands to "change with the times."

No two voices have exactly the same overtone structure, just as no two snowflakes are exactly alike. Nonetheless, as there are basic structural correlations common to all snowflakes, certain "color categories" have developed and stabilized in the world of the trained singing voice. In describing specific qualities of voices, it is well to keep in mind that there are no absolutes, and any term used to describe a "type" of voice is a convenience and to an extent a generalization. Therefore, descriptions of vocal tone color must take into account not only the basic quality of an individual voice, but the way it is controlled and directed by the singer at any given moment and the kind of sound the composer envisioned when the musical line was set onto paper.

Voices are categorized into high and low areas for each sex: soprano and alto for women, tenor and bass for men. These terms have already been used to describe the role of some orchestral instruments within their choirs.

FEMALE VOICES

Since opera and oratorio became important public musical genres in the 17th century, composers of serious music have championed the so-called *bel canto* (beautiful singing) vocal style. This is a method in which the open mouth and throat are used to produce a resultant clear and vibrant sound, and it has found special prestige in music written for female voices.

The high female voice is divided by dramatic function and tone color into three categories: coloratura, lyric, and dramatic. *Coloratura* connotes a "decorated" or "ornamented" line of music, one that has many notes and may include fast-moving scale passages and trills. The term is used to describe ornamented lines in both instrumental and vocal music. The *coloratura soprano,* then, concentrates on flexibility and dexterity in the execution of florid passages. Since she sometimes operates at stratospheric heights, whirling and soaring up to two octaves above middle C, and since her music often calls for the performance of rapid, dazzling, cadenzalike passages, the singer must develop great vocal agility.

The physical conditions necessary for the production of very high notes limit the ability of a singer to enunciate words clearly. As a result, much of the high-flying coloratura literature stresses easy-to-project vowel sounds and allows the listener to concentrate on the voice itself. Singing at such heights requires great physical effort and cannot be sustained for long periods. The lower, middle, and upper segments of any singer's range are described as *registers.* Much of the coloratura soprano's music, then, normally lies in her middle register. When a musical passage is placed for a time in a specific voice register, the term *tessitura* is used. Any music that lies particularly high within the composition is said to be in a high tessitura. Even though it is common to associate high tessituras with coloratura sopranos, this need not necessarily be the case. The coloration or decoration of a line of music may occur in any vocal register, and composers such as Rossini routinely wrote coloratura passages and arias even for bass voices.

Closely related in sound to the coloratura soprano is the *lyric soprano,* whose voice possesses a light texture, great warmth, and a capacity for sustained melodic singing. Interpreting texts that express emotions ranging from deep despair to rapturous joy, the lyric voice projects intense drama without sacrificing beauty of tone. As a result, the lyric soprano voice is a popular choice for heroine roles in opera. Where the coloratura sopranos float over a light, somewhat sparse accompaniment, the vocal weight of the lyric soprano may be supported more fully.

Richer and more powerful, with a register extending downward as well as upward, is the *dramatic soprano.* This voice is trained to pour out a great volume of opulent sound that can cut through the fullest orchestral accompaniment, making her most telling musical points with power and splendor. The physique of the dramatic soprano is usually equal to her vocal size, for a formidable sound requires a substantial physical frame. The most famous dramatic soprano roles in opera are those written in the 19th century by Richard Wagner, who commonly required his voices to shine through a complicated orchestral fabric.

The *contralto* (often shortened to *alto*) voice is still deeper and mellower, and the true contralto is a rarer singing bird than the soprano. While the vocal ranges of soprano and contralto overlap appreciably, the latter possesses a quality of sound best described as "covered," not often present in the soprano. It is not only her ability to sing in a lower register than the soprano that sets the alto apart, but also the somewhat duskier sound. An appropriate parallel might be the bright soprano sound of the violin compared to its alto counterpart, the viola. While the soprano is the traditional operatic heroine, the alto usually plays such roles as the mother, the "other woman," or the scheming villain. This female voice has also proven well suited for the expression of great sorrow and pathos.

MALE VOICES

A number of parallels may be drawn between the trained male voice and its female counterpart. The lyric tenor corresponds to the lyric soprano, the dramatic tenor to the dramatic soprano, and the bass to the contralto. Strictly speaking, there is no male voice that is parallel to the coloratura soprano.

The *lyric tenor* is the smooth male counterpart of the lyric soprano, concerning himself as she does with the ability to produce a beautiful tone and to spin out an extended melodic passage. Also in common with her, he is traditionally the operatic hero.

The *dramatic tenor* produces a less smoothly textured sound. Many dramatic tenors have begun their careers as bass-baritones and have found the range of the voice moving upward as training continues. The low-voice quality may remain in the dramatic tenor sound, bringing with it a sandy edge and a slight gruffness. As with the dramatic soprano, this type of tenor is capable of cutting through a large Wagnerian orchestra with ease. The *tenore robusto* (robust tenor) is the Italian equivalent, while in Germany the voice is known as the *Heldentenor* (heroic tenor).

The *bass,* lowest of all voices, can express a range from solemnity and profundity to darkly threatening, foreboding roles. A true bass, like a true contralto, is not an everyday phenomenon. The great basses of the 20th century have often come from Russia and the Balkan countries.

The male anatomy requires that men's voices be trained somewhat differently than those of women. During puberty, when the male voice changes and lowers, vestiges of the higher prepuberty voice remain in the *falsetto* register. This higher range of the voice is not normally used in speaking or singing. As the word implies, the sound is falsely feminine, and it loses strength and power when the voice moves through the break from lower male to falsetto sound. These factors have led composers and singers away from extensive use of this register. It is used on occasion for humorous situations or for distorted and extreme emotional states.

THE CASTRATO, MALE ALTO, AND COUNTERTENOR

One modern school of thought holds that in order to understand the arts of the past, an effort must be made to re-create the conditions in which they were conceived and first performed. In the theater, this leads to productions of Shakespearean plays in which the women's roles are taken by boys, as they were in his time. For opera, performance of vocal music of the 16th and 17th centuries under "original conditions" poses some complications. At this time women were not permitted to sing in the churches of Europe, and boys took the soprano and alto parts in church choirs. "Respectable" women did not appear in any kind of stage production, so women's roles in operas were often sung by young men whose voices had not yet undergone change or by *castrati.*

Castrato singers first appeared in 16th-century Rome in the Sistine Chapel. They were males with a high degree of vocal training who had been castrated as children, so their voices never deepened. They were thus able to devote their ever-high voices to lifelong service in the church. When opera discovered the castrato in the 17th century, this freakish and exciting phenomenon was exploited. Castrati made fabulous reputations for their vocal prowess, matching great sustaining power with the flexibility and brilliance of a female sound. Since the castrato is not a phenomenon of the 20th century, we must rely on earlier written accounts of their abilities. These describe a pure, "white" sound, ethereal and unlike anything else ever uttered by the human throat.

There exists a large amount of music written for these vocal marvels, most of which has not been performed in this century, since the warmer sound of the female soprano or alto is not appropriate for this music. The closest parallels to the castrato that exist in contemporary singing are the *countertenor* and *male alto.* These are voices belonging to normal adult males who train to develop the falsetto register to enable it to project greater power. The male alto and countertenor have perfectly natural speaking and singing voices that are trained to handle the middle and upper registers of the voice in ways that suggest the asexual sound of which 17th- and 18th-century audiences were extraordinarily fond.

VOICES IN CONCERT: CHORUSES AND CHOIRS

When writing for chorus, a composer usually takes care to stay within the comfortable limits of average voices. Though men's and women's voices are often grouped in separate choirs, the most usual and universal choral ensemble is the "mixed" choir, with four sections divided into sopranos, altos, tenors, and basses. Choirs are the oldest and most widespread of the world's musical organizations. In Western music highly skilled professional choruses are known to have existed since the great days of Greek drama some 2,500 years ago. Up to the middle of the 18th century, in fact, the dominant ensemble in musical life—sacred or secular—was the chorus. Only since that time has the star of instrumental ensembles gained ascendancy. Pure *a cappella,* or unaccompanied, choral music represented an abstract ideal of sound associated with the high point of choral writing during the Renaissance.

This perfect blending of a small group of voices into a single choral aggregate, with the resulting quality of disembodied sound, is still capable, when properly performed, of opening up vistas of ethereal beauty. It is interesting to observe in this connection that the great Renaissance choruses seldom used more than about 16 singers, and Bach had a maximum of around 20 at his disposal. Quality rather than quantity was the rule in producing this unity of sound with its resulting clarity of line and shapeliness of proportion. The large chorus is a product of a more gregarious social viewpoint, for which grand collective efforts seem to be more effective in moving large gatherings of people. Choral singing is thus the most democratic of all musical activities, and it still remains the most accessible medium for amateur participation in the music-making process.

CHAPTER

17

Art of Rhythm

FOR THE SAKE OF experiment, imagine an indefinitely sustained tone of constant pitch and unvarying degree of loudness. After a few moments this sound would become uncomfortable; and after endless duration without inflection, variation, pulsation, accent, or recurrence, it would be unendurable. From experience everyone knows that each day has a morning, noon, and night; weeks and months have a repeating procession of days; each successive season has its place in the year; and human life has its periods of childhood, maturity, and old age. So composers and listeners differentiate and measure out sounds into controllable units, create accents to hold interest, shape smaller units into recognizable patterns, and establish a pace for the flow of sound. Finally, they govern this flow by a force that brings the music into being, that looks ahead, that propels it toward some goal that sustains the momentum along the way, so that it eventually arrives at a planned logical conclusion. This force is called *rhythm.*

Rhythm is at once the life's breath that animates the spirit of every musical organism, the life's blood that courses through the arteries and veins of its circulatory system, the heartbeat that pulses throughout the body of a musical composition, and the life cycle that covers the span between the birth of its initial beat and the death of its closing moment. Rhythm articulates the flow of musical time, conveys purposeful movement, and creates a sense of musical progress. Just as motion through space is visible to the eye, so motion through time becomes audible to the ear through the medium of music. Such motion is capable of the widest variety; and rhythm is inextricably intertwined with all the other musical elements and textures—tone color, dynamics, melody, harmony, and counterpoint. The aesthetic experience of rhythm can be as basic as the insistent "oom-pah" beat of the common march, or as exalted as the ethereal trills of a late Beethoven string quartet.

Various types of motion are common to the experience of music. Some, like dance, are concerned with physical action, others with psychological action that arouses feeling. For the dancer, the rhythmic motion supports patterned physical activity that directs the steps and gestures. The listener recalls these bodily movements through the process of what psychologists call kinesthetic imagery or muscular memory. In one case the experience moves the muscular memory, in the other it moves the emotions.

It is no accident that certain single musical forms are called *movements,* referring to sections of a composition that have a certain unity, manifested in recognizable, coherent rhythmic motion. In cyclical forms, a movement is a single unit of a larger whole, like a suite of dances or a multimovement sonata. The aesthetic and psychological considerations of more extended forms demand the contrast of individual movements, thus giving rise to the designations of "allegro movement," "slow movement," "minuet movement," and the like.

One use of the word *rhythm* in music accords with one of the broader meanings of the word in everyday life. The basic experiences of the passage of time underline the overall forces that govern the movement and progress of music. For instance, the daily progression of morning, noon, and night became the inspiration for three related symphonies by Haydn. The sequence of the seasons—spring, summer, autumn, and winter—have been the subjects of many compositions, most notably four concertos by Vivaldi and a Haydn oratorio.

Every era has its own perception of musical movement. Many writers have attempted descriptions of the phenomenon of sound heard in time, and in so doing have used various definitions of certain terms, such as rhythm, meter, and tempo. For purposes of this discussion these terms will be used in a way that takes both historical and present-day views into account. *Rhythm,* then, will refer to the general experience of the time dimension and the overall framework of a musical composition. *Meter* will be seen as the pulse beat of the music and the basic building blocks of its progress in time. *Tempo* functions as the relative rate of speed for the musical time continuum.

Meter

Countering and balancing the chaos and disorder of the life experience is the human preoccupation with order. This phenomenon is clearly evidenced in music throughout the development of rhythmic systems from the ancients to the present; the development of notation is its most pronounced outward sign. In mensural notation, where each bar contains the same physical measurement of time, there is a built-in basic, orderly repetition underlying the pulse that organizes and regularizes the flow of the music. This is called the *meter.* These pulses are combinations of strong and weak beats, accented and unaccented notes, and may be considered the single blocks out of which the rhythmic structures of music are built.

Single beats, as in the case of single tones, have no musical significance. Two or more beats, however, allow for comparative differences. A meter, then, is based on some pattern of two or more equally spaced beats joined together to make a recognizable unit. Meters, by repetition, are grouped into regular patterns that move along in orderly succession.

The mind tends to group separate impulses and experiences together in some pattern. The tick-tock of a clock mechanism, the clickety-clack of a passing railroad train, the drip-drip of a water faucet are each ordered into repetitive patterns of one sort or another. A simple experiment with a metronome will show that the equal clicks quickly resolve themselves into metrical units. Some listeners will think or count ONE-two, ONE-two, others ONE-two-three, ONE-two-three, demonstrating the tendency to infer accented and unaccented beats, even when mechanically the impulses are completely regular. Our perception of meter depends upon the recognition of some sequence of strong and weak pulses, whether actual or implied.

The smallest unit that can be organized consists of two, and the most basic meter is *simple duple meter,* an organization of two pulses, equidistant in time from each other, with alternate pulses receiving a slight accent (Chart 17-1). In this example the overall impression of flow is supported by underlying regular accents in slow, simple duple meter.

CHART 17-1. SIMPLE DUPLE METER

Normally we perceive the meter in a piece of music with ease, a result of certain symbols in the score that act as guides for the performer (Chart 17-2). The most obvious indication is the *time signature,* which looks like a fraction (2/4) but is actually two separate numbers conveying two separate pieces of information to the performer. The upper figure displays the number of basic pulses that underlies each bar (in this case, 2), the lower figure the type of note that represents one of those pulses (in this case 4, the quarter note). It may then be said that the composition is “in 2/4,” or that there will be the equivalent of two quarter notes to each bar.

CHART 17-2. METERS

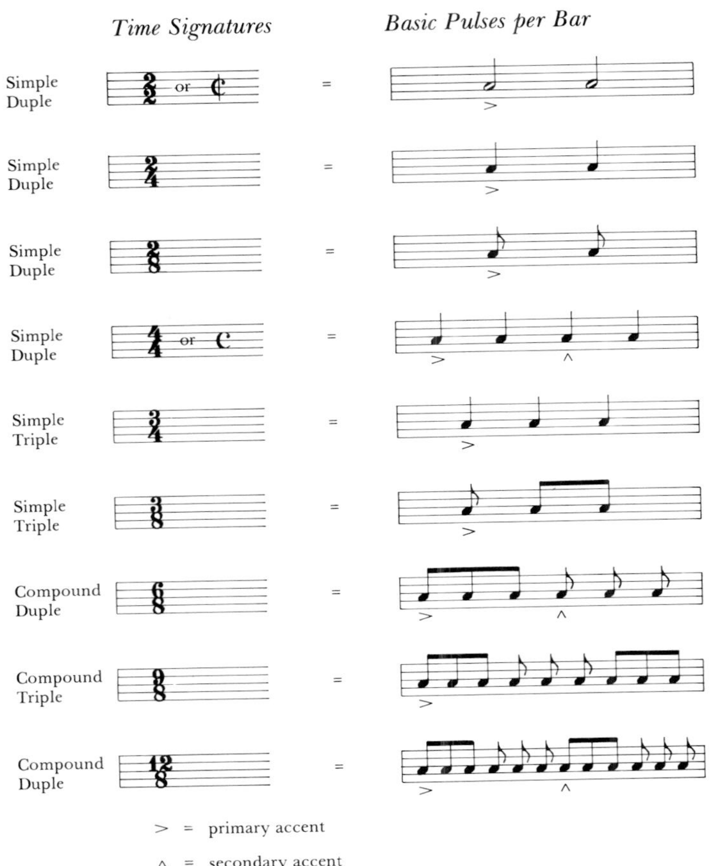

A measure may be broken into units of three as easily as two, in *simple triple meter.* Here our inner clock works on a ONE-two-three, ONE-two-three basis rather than ONE-two, ONE-two (Chart 17-3). A glance at Chart 17-3 tells us that the meter is simple triple, "in 3/4 time." The upper numeral, 3, signifies three basic pulses per measure; the numeral below it, 4, indicates that each quarter note will receive one such pulse.

Many meters were originally based on the step patterns of common dances or organized group movement, such as the march. A march simply alternates a LEFT-right, LEFT-right, ONE-two, ONE-two pattern. Its time signature is 4/4, with an accent pattern like that in Chart 17-2. Likewise, one of the simplest three-step dances is the waltz with its ONE-two-three, ONE-two-three sequence, shown in Chart 17-3 as "simple triple."

These basic metrical arrangements may also be extended, and other time signatures in common use involve multiples of two or three. Any meter with an upper figure divisible by three is called a *compound meter,* shown in the last three examples on Chart 17-2.

CHART 17-3. SIMPLE TRIPLE METER

$\frac{3}{4}$ ♩ ♩ ♩ | ♩ ♩ ♩ ||

POETIC AND MUSICAL METERS

When poetry and music are combined, new formulations of musical meters may occur, based on traditional metric practices in poetry. Ancient Greek and Roman poets used an intricate metrical system consisting of various types of poetic feet whose regular and continuous recurrences determine the poetic rhythm. These meters are made up of units of short and long duration—unstressed and stressed syllables—that closely resemble many of the familiar meters found in music. A bar, or measure, in music usually corresponds to one or two metrical feet in a poem. The grouping of music into half phrases of two or three bars, and phrases of four to six bars, parallels the grouping of meters into poetic lines.

The ancient Greeks' term for *downbeat* was a word that described the stamping of the dance leader's foot, *thesis*; the word for *upbeat*, *arsis*, described the lifting of the foot. Among the most common of these classical meters are the *iamb*, a short-long unit symbolized by ∪ – in poetry, and ♪♩ in music; the *trochee* (long-short) shown by – ∪ or ♩ ♪ ; the *anapest* (short-short-long), shown by ∪∪– or ♫♩ ; and the *dactyl* (long-short-short) shown by – ∪∪ or ♩ ♫ . Some splendid lines of iambic pentameter, five iambs per line, can be found in Shakespeare's Sonnet 23:

∪ – ∪ – ∪ – ∪ – ∪ –
O learn / to read / what si- / lent love / hath writ:
To hear / with eyes / be- longs / to love's / fine wit.

Example 17-1a shows an ebullient example of the iamb converted to a musical rhythmic motif. The trochee is the meter associated with strong-weak alternation of the common march step as well as with the gentle, sleep-inducing motion of a rocking chair (Ex. 17-1b). Anapest rhythms are sometimes used to illustrate specific movement, such as the gait of a horse (Ex. 17-1c); but they may also be used as abstract metric patterns (Ex. 17-1d). Dactyl meters appear diversely in the dance in the triple-meter waltz (Example 17-1d, bass clef), and to underscore the poetic description of water movement in song (Ex. 17-1e).

In ancient Greece the term *mode* applied to a system of scales and also to a system of meters, each of which had a distinctive character and a particular mood associated with it. Just as poetry has the strict rhythms of scanned lines and the wild rhapsodic outburst of free verse, so music too has its regular

Example 17-1. Rhythmic types.

17-1a. J. Strauss. *Artist's Life,* Op. 316. Waltz No. 3, bars 1–8.

17-1b. Brahms. *Ever gentler grows my slumber,* Op. 105, No. 2, bars 1–3.

17-1c. Rossini. *William Tell.* Overture. Allegro vivace, bars 18–21.

17-1d. J. Strauss. *The Beautiful Blue Danube,* Op. 314. Waltz No. 2, bars 7–10.

17-1e. Schubert. *Love's Message,* bars 6–9.

and irregular metrical groupings. The words *mood, mode,* and *meter,* as well as *motion* and *emotion,* are all derived from related root words. The terms *movement* and *motion* still indicate action and progress, while *emotion* now applies to a psychological state.

Rhythmic Figures and Specific Rhythms

Out of this variety of materials—meter, iamb, trochee, anapest, and dactyl—the composer makes a series of choices from which to weave his rhythmic fabric. The examples above show poetic meters transferred to the musical sphere on a short-term basis, usually appearing once or at most a few times. These poetic meters, alone or in combination, may also be extended to provide a unifying factor throughout a musical composition. Such is the case with the anapest in the first movement of Mozart's Symphony No. 40 (see Ex. 17-1c). As the measures of this movement continuously unfold, the listener becomes

Example 17-2. Beethoven. Symphony No. 7 in A Major, Op. 92. Second movement, bars 3–10.

aware of two rhythmic levels. The basic level is the basic metric pulse of two; the second level comprises the repeated anapest figure. Though it was not his regular practice to do so, Mozart unified this entire movement rhythmically through reiteration of this anapest figure.

Mozart's choice of such a short figure makes the movement more accessible, acting as a focal point to draw the listener rhythmically into the composition. As a formal device, composers may also utilize longer, more complicated rhythmic motifs. Rhythmic organization around such motifs takes the form of repeated patterns of long and short notes, which are known as *rhythmic figures.* For the second movement of his Seventh Symphony, Beethoven devised such a rhythmic figure, encompassing two measures (Ex. 17-2). The duration of notes within each two-bar phrase is as follows: bar 1—quarter note followed by two eighth notes; bar 2—two quarter notes. As the pattern becomes established in the listener's ear, the expected repetitions produce a sense of stability and security that continues throughout the movement. The rhythmic figure, along with his chosen subject materials, tone color, dynamics, and form, is an important element of the total organizational scheme.

Over the centuries certain rhythmic figures have gained in strength and popularity, and have gained the status of being known as *rhythms* in their own right. In such cases the term is used in a specific rather than broad sense. Most of these began as rhythmic figures associated with the dance. The assignment of particular forms and rhythmic patterns to particular dances was reasonable, since the pattern is a useful guide that tells the dancer what steps to execute and when to change them. When we see titles on compositions such as *sarabande, gigue, waltz,* or *habanera,* we can assume that the composition features a certain rhythmic pattern, for example a "sarabande rhythm" or a "waltz rhythm."

Symmetry of repetition is naturally not the only procedure by which a composer may direct metric patterns. For every composition that moves with the regular, clocklike precision of Example 17-2, there is an asymmetrical rhythmic organization, such as that in the fugue subject of Beethoven's String Quartet in C-sharp Minor, Op. 131, in which no two measures are rhythmically alike (Ex. 17-3).

Example 17-3. Beethoven. String Quartet in C-sharp Minor, Op. 131. First movement, bars 1–11.

Tempo

The term *tempo* indicates the pace, or relative speed, by which metrical units proceed. Among the several ways by which the passage of music's time-flow is measured, tempo represents the more general experience of time, defines the rate of speed at which rhythmic groups progress, and is closely identified with the expressive spirit of a piece. While internal rhythmic relationships provide variety, tempo promotes the continuity of a musical movement and preserves its basic identity and integrity. A proper tempo should be felt as natural movement welling up from within a musical work rather than an arbitrary pace imposed on it from without. In this way a tempo becomes an effective means of activating static tonal masses, of bringing elasticity to the metrical and rhythmic organization, of breathing life into the formal structure, and of animating the manner of motion and emotion of the musical organism.

This perception of the passage of musical time is not based so much on quantitative measurements (clock time, for instance) as it is on the qualitative flow of events within a given temporal unit. In addition to using mechanical devices, everyone is naturally equipped with various physiological clocks that articulate the flow of time—the beating of the heart, the inhaling and exhaling of breath, sleeping and wakeful states, recurrence of mealtimes, and the like. Psychological factors are also pertinent. When a person is participating in pleasurable activities, time seems to pass more quickly than it does in boring or disagreeable occupations. When events occur in rapid succession, time seems to fly, but when little happens, it lags. As Shakespeare notes in *Othello:* "Pleasure and action make the hours seem short." Similarly, in a state of agitation a person will talk more quickly and walk more hurriedly, while in calmer moments speech is slower and one saunters rather than runs.

Reflections of all these variable physiological and psychological states are to be found in musical tempos. Heightened emotional tension is usually accompanied by a faster heartbeat and faster breathing. An emotional climax in music is often achieved in this same way—that is, by an *accelerando,* or quickening of the pace, or with a *stretto,* a narrowing or shortening of the temporal intervals between beats. Similarly, with a slowing of the pace by means of a *ritardando,* or a broadening of the time span between tones in an *allargando,* a feeling of relaxation and repose is achieved. Tempos are based on these general experiences of ebb and flow in the temporal dimension, and they give important clues to the individuality and special character of a musical work.

The wide range of tempos from slow to fast can best be understood when a norm is assumed. Such a normal tempo would correspond to the average pulse or breathing rate, though allowance has to be made for individual variations. The 18th-century philosopher and composer Jean-Jacques Rousseau called this average pace *tempo giusto,* a "just" progress. *Andante* (going or walking) is a more commonly used term; it also implies a comfortable pace without holding back or forging ahead. The range of moods in this case would be no stronger than those of ease, moderation, and relaxation. Any slackening of this normal rate implies a certain restraint associated with dignified or solemn occasions. The moods suggested by slower tempos extend from peaceful contemplation and serenity to gentle melancholy, dejection, and despair. A quickening of the pulse, on the other hand, indicates agitation, excitement, or joy.

Dances written for group participation must take certain physical limitations into account. Marches, for instance, have many possible tempos, each of them connected with a particular function, pace, and mood. If a military march is accepted as a "normal" march tempo, a graduation, wedding, coronation, or triumphal march would then be in varying degrees slower, with the heavy, measured tread of a funeral march at the bottom of the scale. On the brisker side are quick-step marches and still livelier cavalry marches. For practical purposes, however, none can be so slow that it is impossible to maintain physical balance, none so fast that it is impossible to keep pace.

Other barriers likewise set limitations on the range of tempos in concert music. If the time interval between successive tones becomes so great that the sense of coherence and continuity is lost, the tempo is obviously too slow. On the other hand, when tones succeed each other so rapidly that all articulation between them is lost and the rhythmic relationships become an indistinct jumble, then the tempo is clearly too fast. Within these two extremes fall the various possible concert tempos.

In the distant past, composers either gave no tempo indications at all or made only general suggestions. In the 17th century, for example, performance tradition was part of a singer's or instrumentalist's musical education. When looking at a piece of music, they could ascertain its basic tempo from the way it was written, and seldom required suggestions from the composer. During the 18th century, composers began to make more use of tempo markings, and a number of Italian terms were adopted as standard. It may be seen from Chart 17-4 that these one-word tempo designations are quite general in nature.

CHART 17-4

Tempo Indication	Translation	General Meaning
Grave	Solemn	As slowly as possible
Largo	Very slow	Broad, spacious
Adagio	Quite slow	At ease
Lento	Slow	Slowly
Andante	Walking, going	Medium
Moderato	Moderate	Moderately
Allegretto	Moderately fast	Jolly, rather lively
Allegro	Fast	Cheerful, lively
Vivace	Quite fast	Brisk, spirited
Presto	Very fast	Quickly, fast
Prestissimo	As quickly as possible	Quickest, fastest

In addition to these terms, many qualifying adjectives can be used, depending upon various modifications and unusual moods. The names of older dances—gavotte, sarabande, gigue—are often sufficient to indicate the proper pace and character of a piece. Similarly, concert numbers patterned after dance forms often bear such indications as *tempo di marcia* (in march time) and *tempo di menuetto* (in minuet tempo). Further directions that allow for gradual quickening or slowing of the tempo are in common usage: *accelerando* (accelerating), *ritardando* (slowing), and *allargando* (becoming broader).

The range of tempos is not so great as might be imagined. If a largo sostenuto or a molto adagio is taken as the slowest possible tempo, a prestissimo at the other extreme will be only about eight times faster. Several factors must be borne in mind, since these tempos are relative rather than absolute; sometimes they are better understood simply as negative indications. An allegro can be paced more or less briskly, but never slowly; an adagio can be slow in varying degrees, but never fast.

For a long time, these short tempo suggestions sufficed. Placed at the beginning of a score, they allowed performers to form a general notion for a rate of speed. Yet they were and are symbolic indications at best. If *allegro* means "fast," just how fast is fast? It is a question that every performer answers only after careful study, and a decision that may change according to the circumstances of the time and place of each individual performance.

By the early 19th century, composers were attempting to exercise stronger control over performers. As a consequence, they began to give more explicit indicators for the tempos they preferred. Modifying adverbs such as *molto* (very), *meno* (less), *poco* (a little), and *non troppo* (not too much) came into play. The Beethoven string quartet in Example 17-3 contains the following tempo instructions at the beginning of the slow movement: *Adagio ma non troppo e molto espressivo* (Slow, but not too slow, and very expressive). This is still a cloudy guide as a speed indicator, and may further complicate matters by using the tempo marking as a mood setter.

Ever since the early 19th century, composers have tried to introduce more control into the process of setting tempos by using Maelzel's metronome, a mechanical device that clicks off a specified number of beats per minute. When set at 60, for instance, it ticks off the number of seconds in a minute, like the second hand of a clock. For example, a brisk march time may be indicated in a score as ♩ = 120, thus marking two steps per second, a tempo that corresponds roughly to a concert allegro.

The metronome has proved a mixed blessing, however, since straight metronomic time tends to be mechanical and lifeless; a good tempo always needs a little hurrying here and some lingering there to give it elasticity and room to breathe. Every generation reinterprets the music of the past, and every performer still must find the right tempo based on knowledge, taste, and judgment. Modern-day performers may check the metronome markings to determine the composer's intent; but more often than not, they then interject their own thought and will into the re-creative process.

It should be noted that modern musical editors sometimes add metronome markings to early music to assist performers. They do not always indicate that they are making personal judgments for the composer, who is not in a position to be heard on the matter. Such markings found in music written before the early 19th century should be viewed as modern editorial changes. How, then, should one set a tempo in music before that period? There is no easy answer. Tempo is an area in which all may become instant critics, and it remains a personal, often private decision of musical interpretation.

Fortunately the choice is not between the extremes of mechanical regimentation on the one side and rhythmical chaos on the other. Tempos have a tendency to vary from the comparatively strict to those of a freer type, the difference being one of style. In the final analysis, tempo should always be an outgrowth of the inner character and the individual expressive quality of the musical work.

TEMPO RUBATO

The invention of the metronome has not only given us a positive indication of what the composer thought was the correct tempo for a particular composition; it has given us the negative musical term *metronomic.* When a performance is so described, it means that the performance was mechanical, without inner rhythmic life. To avoid being metronomic, the performer has the prerogative of taking a rhythmic approach meant to assure that the music will convey a sense of life and vitality. It is here that *tempo rubato* enters the picture, a term that describes a rhythmical robbing of Peter to pay Paul.

In tempo rubato, the performer alternately pushes ahead and pulls back the tempo within some musical phrases to give a sense of lifelike breathing to the performance. Normally this is accomplished within the confines of a bar or a phrase. Tempo rubato is a very personal decision for each performer, since it is not usually indicated in the musical score. At its best, tempo rubato gives a flexibility and elasticity to the musical flow through a subtle underscoring of the musical materials.

As we have seen, one must strike a balance between strictness and freedom, bearing in mind that adhering too closely to the metronome can lead to mechanical rigidity and too much freedom can lead to chaos. Minor accelerations and retardations may occur, but such changes in momentum should never be so drastic as to drift from one tempo to a radically different one. The choice between a stricter or freer approach to tempo depends on the performer, who must decide whether the composition seems to call for an objective or subjective attitude. This decision is based in part on historical and stylistic considerations.

Finally, tempos vary somewhat with physiological and psychological conditions, with differences of interior and exterior temperature, with youth and age, and even with the time of day. Moreover, they are subject to acoustical conditions and the capacities of various musical instruments, as well as the temperamental differences of performers. Even with the same performer, however, tempos may vary from performance to performance, depending on mood, state of relative tension or relaxation, and a host of other aesthetic and psychological factors.

Accentuation

Stress and counterstress is an important part of rhythm at all levels. *Accent* in music simply means an added point of energy or stress. A small carat mark is used to indicate accent (see Chart 17-2). It is expected that an accent will normally occur at the beginning of every bar, and these are not usually indicated on the score. Secondary accents may occur later in the measure in compound meters—for example, on the third beat of a bar in 4/4 time. If a composer chooses to indicate such secondary accents on the score, the carat mark is placed in an upright position rather than on its side.

While regularity and repetition are central to the long history of Western musical rhythm, we would tire quickly if we heard rhythmic movement that continued unchanged for an extended period. The mind's ear likes to be reminded of what it has heard, but it also requires change in order to continue to pay attention. Methods by which composers have sought to maintain this interest through rhythmic surprise are legion. The three most common procedures are syncopation, nonstandard meters, and combining rhythms.

SYNCOPATION

Many techniques are employed by composers to insure rhythmic variety. Frequency of stressed beats can make a rhythm strong and stirring, while infrequency of accent in slow and songlike movements can promote a feeling of inactivity and tranquillity. When either of these is too regular, however, the effect often becomes monotonous. In order to create an element of rhythmic interest, the composer may place accents on pulses within the measure other than where they are normally expected.

In Example 17-4, the simple triple meter that underlies the waltz may be seen flowing unimpeded on the lower staff, allowing the listener's inner clock to move along with the music in rational, undisturbed order. The melodic line, however, contains an accent pattern in which some accents fall on the expected first beat, while some do not. The rhythmic interest arises from the use of unexpected accents in the melodic line on the treble staff, simultaneously breaking the easy metric flow. The fact that the unchanging meter and the ever-changing rhythmic patterns are present simultaneously provide the listener with a sense of variety within the overall unity.

Example 17-4. J. Strauss. *The Beautiful Blue Danube,* Op. 314. Waltz No. 3, bars 1–8.

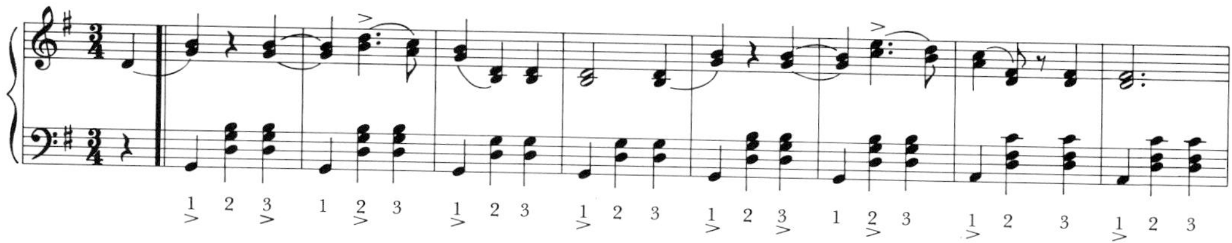

POLYMETER AND POLYRHYTHM

Thus far our discussion of rhythm has centered around even, or regular, metric movement, based on duple or triple units. However, departures from metrical regularity are alternatives used by all good composers. Many compositions, mainly from the 19th and 20th centuries, are based on meters that are neither duple nor triple. A usual choice for such meters is any odd number of five or more pulses per measure.

The 19th-century Russian composer Modest Musorgsky used a series of drawings by the artist Victor Hartmann as the basis for a piano composition he called *Pictures at an Exhibition* (see pp. 267-270). To create the musical equivalent of strolling about in a gallery of paintings, Musorgsky wrote a "Promenade" consisting of a two-bar phrase of 5/4 and 6/4 meters (see Ex. 11-8). No accent, however, falls on the first beat of the second bar, so that the total is in fact a phrase of eleven quarter note beats with no real stressed notes. The listener is given an impression of somewhat casual movement. This is an example of *polymeter,* or *polymetric procedure.* The term literally means "several meters" and refers to the changing of the metric signature several times, often in quick succession, within the composition.

Stravinsky's *Soldier's Tale* introduces a military nonhero as he trudges home on furlough. The soldier is so well trained that he marches even when on leave, out of habit (Ex. 17-5). Through the device of polymeter, Stravinsky gives the impression of a controlled march slightly out of control, leaving the listener somewhat uncomfortable. This discomfort arises naturally, since we are trained to think of a march as ever-even, never-changing in rhythm. The polyrhythmic procedure also functions as a clever device to reflect the soldier's uncertain state of mind.

Example 17-5. Stravinsky. *The Soldier's Tale.* "March," bars 13–18.

In 20th-century music, it is quite common to encounter sudden shifts of meters as the music progresses (see Ex. 13-2). It is less usual to find different meters moving along simultaneously. But a common practice to achieve variety is that of combining two or more rhythms so that they are heard simultaneously, as in *polyrhythm,* or *polyrhythmic procedure.*

This technique is highly developed in the music of the Orient, where work songs are characterized by complicated sounds resembling the clicking, clattering pestle play of rice-pounding women in the Malay Archipelago as they grind their flour. Such complexities are also heard in the gamelan orchestras of Java, in which each percussion instrument plays its own rhythm in concert with the others. In Africa also, tribal drummers, each with an independent rhythm, often coordinate their efforts with a leader in extremely intricate polyrhythmic patterns. Compared with such rich rhythmic fabrics as these, the rhythms of pre-20th-century European music seem comparatively simple and straightforward.

In Western culture, every embryonic pianist has struggled with the problem of playing three beats with the left hand while the right hand plays two, a simple example of polyrhythm (Ex. 17-6). An interesting illustration is in Chopin's Waltz in A-flat Major, Op. 42, which has a melody in duple time riding along over a conventional waltz bass in triple time (Ex. 17-7). Upon analysis it breaks down into the two principal ways of dividing a rhythm of six beats in a bar. In the middle voice the six eighth notes flow along quite smoothly, while above them the melody proceeds in pairs of quarters, equaling three eighth notes each. Below them the bass moves in groups of three regular quarters equaling two eighth notes each. The resulting effect of this interplay

Example 17-6. Brahms. Intermezzo in A Minor, Op. 116, No. 2, bars 14–16.

Example 17-7. Chopin. Waltz in A-flat Major, Op. 42, bars 9–12.

of the two rhythms is one of conflict and some turbulence. A more complex instance of polyrhythmic writing occurs in Brahms' *German Requiem* (Ex. 11-13).

The 20th century has come full circle in returning to notational concepts of earlier times. Composers eager to find new ways to express themselves find this traditional metric notation confining. They complain of the "tyranny of the bar line" and seek ways to free themselves from it. Earlier in the century Stravinsky, who continued to use bar lines, weakened their role by changing meters and using syncopation to upset and surprise his audience's rhythmic expectations (Ex. 17-8).

Both motional and emotional changes in music can be effected by creating shifts of rhythmic relations within the general rhythmic structure. Since the rhythmic structure reveals so much of the ultimate significance of a musical work, it is pertinent to inquire: In what direction is the rhythmic motion striving? Does the rhythmic motion tend toward balance or imbalance? Does the motion tend toward rest or create the demand for further motion? Toward what high point is the rhythmic progress leading? What is the goal of the musical phrase and the overall form?

It must always be borne in mind that rhythm is not bound by the points or notational symbols on the printed page. The dial of a clock, for instance, has marks for minutes and hours, but time itself is measured by the constant movement of the hands through and past these points. Rhythmic movement likewise is felt as the continuous passage of energy between tones as it progresses toward some goal. Thus instead of becoming a series of stops, as the notes in a score might seem to indicate, rhythm actually flows, moves in various directions, and suggests continuous life. Rhythms are based on patterns

Example 17-8. Stravinsky. *The Rite of Spring.* "Dance of Adolescents," bars 1–8.

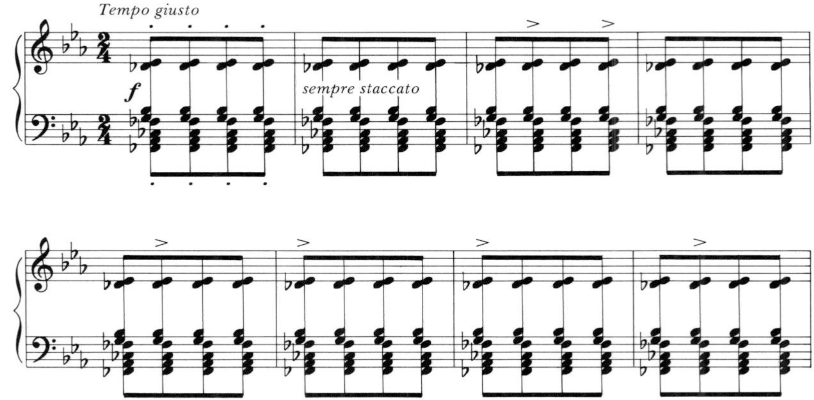

of repetition, variation, and combination; and the experience and perception of rhythm are based on memory and anticipation. When the expected always comes to pass, it can be monotonous and even boring. When the unexpected transpires, it can be interesting and surprising; but when this happens too frequently, it can become disconcerting and confusing. So it is up to the composer to find a happy medium.

Rhythmic concepts vary from country to country geographically, and from period to period historically. According to 17th-century mathematicians, rhythm was "unconscious counting," while to the romantics, it was "subject to moods and emotions, to rapture and depression." In some periods symmetry and regularity of metrical pattern were more prominent, in others asymmetry and irregularity were dominant. Strong body rhythms and explosive accentuation, as well as flow of rhythm toward points of stress, are characteristic of certain styles; while weak body rhythms and a minimum of accentuation, as well as directional flow away from stressed points, are a feature of others. In some centuries tempos tended to be strict, rational, and objective; in others, they were free, irrational, and subjective. The stately measures of a sarabande or the graceful steps of a minuet, for instance, bespeak the rigid etiquette and formal predictability of courtly life, while the nervous syncopations of certain jazz and rock idioms reveal the tensions and constantly changing pace of contemporary times. Rhythms thus can reflect and reactivate patterns of motion both present and past, as well as recapture some of the living substance and ideals of the individuals, generations, and ages from which they spring.

CHAPTER

18

Art of Dynamics

THE ELEMENT OF DYNAMICS is concerned principally with the psychological experience of musical energy at various levels. This general category includes: the various intensity levels from soft to loud; the fluctuation of the flow of sound in one direction or the other; types of accentuation more powerful or exceptional than those normally associated with rhythmic factors; and the volume or amplitude of sonorities that impart to them a sense of size and space. Dynamics is the musical element most concerned with energy, force, and power.

Intensity and Volume

The terminology used in dynamics may seem somewhat perplexing, since it is a mixture drawn from acoustical science, musical usage, and everyday speech. *Intensity* refers to the relative degree of softness or loudness of sound. An acoustical engineer might describe intensity as the energy, force, amplitude, size, or volume of the sound wave. Everyone is familiar with the volume control on a stereo set; technically, this knob would be called the "intensity control." Musicians, however, tend to group all aspects of loudness and softness, the gradations between levels of intensity, and accentuation under the general heading of *dynamics.*

By increasing or decreasing levels of intensity, the composer is able to suggest such effects as proximity and distance, light and dark, emotional tension and relaxation. By the use of dynamic accents a melodic line can become sharp and jagged, a rhythm can be rendered restless and vehement, a dissonance intensified, or a chord progression transformed into a series of explosive outbursts.

The experience of dynamics depends to some extent upon the pitch and duration of sounds, as well as the tone qualities of various instruments. It also embraces gradations all the way from the threshold of audibility to the earsplitting point at which sounds become actually painful. While melody and rhythm remain the more important musical materials, the range of dynamic devices from sudden, breathless pianissimos to sweeping orchestral crescendos, the occurrence of surprise accents, and the contrasting of tonal levels can all produce certain sure-fire reactions.

The expressive possibilities of dynamics take on added significance when combined with other aspects of the tonal art. By the placement of accents at certain places in the melodic line, for instance, a composer can clarify the directional tendency and point up a melodic climax (Exs. 18-1a, b). By varying the degree of stress on particular rhythmic beats, or by vigorous accentuation of downbeats where they normally occur on the first beat of a bar, rhythms can acquire a surging character that imparts to them an impelling sense of forward momentum. By shifting the dynamic accent to a normally weak beat, the resulting syncopation causes the rhythm to take on an assertive, forceful character. As shown in Examples 18-1a and 18-1b, when an accelerating tempo is accompanied by a *crescendo,* the simultaneous effect of becoming both faster and louder heightens the climactic impact. Similarly, when a retard is coupled with a *decrescendo,* the dual device of growing slower and softer at the same time produces the effect of dying away. Many other expressive effects are possible when dynamic devices are coupled with instrumental combinations and contrasting tone qualities.

Example 18-1. Beethoven.

18-1a. Piano Sonata in A-flat Major, Op. 26. First movement, variation 1, bars 1–3.

18-1b. Piano Sonata in E-flat Major, Op. 27, No. 1. Fourth movement, bars 13–16.

A sense of size is also associated with sounds. A low organ tone, for instance, comes from a larger pipe than does a high tone and hence may seem broader and greater in volume. Such big tones are quite accurately associated with large-sounding bodies such as the long, thick bass strings of the piano, the huge bass viol, or the great tuba in the brass section of an orchestra. Pipe organs and orchestras as instruments of massive size are also associated with large architectural spaces, where their ponderous sonorities are capable of filling the vast interiors of a cathedral or a large hall.

Dynamic Indications

Musical scores can impart only relatively imprecise dynamic indications; yet such dynamic and accentuation marks in the score are as important to proper musical performance as any other. In contrast to the indications for pitch, those for dynamics are subject to many modifications, depending on the size and acoustics of the room, the capacities of the instruments, the musical context in which they occur, the style of the period out of which the composition comes, the personal idiom of the composer, and above all the interpretive capabilities and insights of the performer.

Historically, dynamic markings are of fairly recent origin, dating from the latter half of the 18th century, and most particularly in the work of C. P. E. Bach, Haydn, and Mozart. Before that time, baroque dynamics were conceived as *terraced dynamics,* functioning broadly on different levels without individual tones singled out for emphasis. Bach and Handel, for instance, took care of such considerations by their use of instrumentation. In a concerto grosso, for example, they alternated their full orchestra with a smaller group of one to four instruments. Dynamic changes were thus effected by the addition or subtraction of instrumental forces.

Another favorite baroque device that produced terraced dynamic levels was the echo, which can be heard to good effect in the "Echo Chorus" and "Echo Dance of the Furies" from Purcell's opera *Dido and Aeneas.* These numbers achieve spatial effects through the use of onstage and offstage choruses and string orchestras, respectively (Ex. 18-2; and see Ex. 9-11).

Example 18-2. Purcell. *Dido and Aeneas.* Act 2, No. 21, "Echo Dance of the Furies," bars 1–3.

When *graded dynamics,* involving a more gradual increasing and decreasing of sound levels, came into general use in the latter part of the 18th century, composers were less inclined to leave dynamics entirely to the caprice of the performer. Thenceforth, they often used specific dynamic symbols, such as the terms *crescendo* and *decrescendo* or their wedge-shaped counterparts (< and >).

The two principal accent symbols by which individual tones are singled out from their neighbors for emphasis are *sf* and the sign > above or below the note (see Chart 18-1). The first derives from the Italian *sforzando* or *sforzato* (forcing or forced); it is sometimes abbreviated as *sfz*. The amount of force used for an accent must be suitable to the musical context and in keeping with the overall level of dynamics. The *sf* sign in a pianissimo passage, for instance, would be relatively light; while the same indicator in a fortissimo context would be correspondingly heavy.

CHART 18-1. DYNAMIC TERMS

Term	Abbreviation	Definition
pianissimo	*pp**	Very soft
piano	*p*	Soft
mezzo piano	*mp*	Medium soft
mezzo forte	*mf*	Medium loud
forte	*f*	Loud
fortissimo	*ff**	Very loud
sforzando	*sf*	Heavy accent
crescendo	*cresc.*	Become gradually louder
decrescendo	*decresc.*	Become gradually softer
diminuendo	*dim.*	Diminishing
smorzando	*smorz.*	Dying away

Sign for *cresc.* <
Sign for *decresc.* >
Accented note
Heavily accented note *sf*

**ppp* and *fff*, and on occasion even four or five letters, are used to indicate exaggerated dynamic levels.

Accents are further altered by durational and tone color factors, as well as by style considerations. Some accents are accompanied by a shortening, others by a lengthening or sustaining of the accented tone. Some accents are of the sharp percussive type, others have spread-out, diffused sound. Some accents demand special variations of tone quality to set the note apart from its unaccented neighbors. Such accents are produced by enriching the tone color in keeping with the characteristic capacities of particular instruments, which usually means an increased warmth, vibration, or expressive impact.

In his *Pathétique* Sonata, Beethoven indicates by the sign *fp* (*forte piano*) that the initial chords of the first three bars are to receive an extra heavy accent (Ex. 18-3). After this momentary point of emphasis, the remainder of each measure is soft. The middle chord of the third measure is marked *sf*, indicating a sharp accent. The first chord of the fourth bar is similarly marked and is followed by a wedge-shaped symbol calling for a gradual decrease in tone down to the level of *p* (*piano*). The abbreviation *cresc.* (*crescendo*) calls for a gradual increase of volume, culminating in the accented A-flat above and B-flat below, thus preparing the way for a precipitous scalewise descent and implied decrescendo to the *p* (*piano*) of the fifth bar. In this and the next measure, soft and very loud intensity levels alternate with each other as noted by the symbols *p* and *ff* (*fortissimo*). A mounting crescendo is indicated in bar 8, moving toward the climax in the ninth measure. The melody remains momentarily suspended in bar 10 until the chromatic descent begins. On the final beat, Beethoven suddenly arrests the downward rush by reversing his direction on the accented A-flat, thus terminating the introduction and providing a moment of suspense before the beginning of the allegro movement, which is to be "attacked suddenly."

Imagery in Dynamics

The use of graded dynamics to suggest distance and proximity, light and dark, has been employed by composers with striking effect. The mounting of emotional excitement followed by its lessening and relaxation becomes the psychological counterpart of forward and backward movement in space. The faint sounds of distant events leave listeners relatively unaffected, whereas they inevitably become involved in a vibrant swirl of sound at a high level of intensity.

Debussy's second orchestral *Nocturne*, entitled "Fêtes" ("Festivals"), uses only graduated dynamic levels to evoke the vision of a band approaching the listener from a distance. The composer first creates a festive, carnival-like atmosphere full of animated anticipation and dancing rhythms. Suddenly the sound ceases in midair at a fortissimo level. Low drums, harps, and plucked strings (marked *ppp,* "very, very softly") are followed by muted trumpets. As the procession advances, various instrumental groups are added until the saturation point is reached with the addition of the full weight of the brass and percussion sections. After "passing in review," the mood changes, and a long tapering-off process leads finally to a *pp* 14 bars from the end, where the score is marked "retreating ever more into the distance." The festival ends as the parade began, *ppp,* with the revelers far away.

In a symbolic sense, softness can suggest darkness, loudness light. In the prelude to his opera *Lohengrin,* Wagner employed dynamic imagery to invoke the illusion of a luminous vision. The composer revealed his poetic plan, describing it as the "sensuous conception of this supersensuous idea, invested with a wonderful form . . . yet unapproachably far off." An opening of soft shimmering strings suggests rays of light as the Holy Grail is unveiled. The sound is then intensified through the addition of woodwinds, and the cup

Example 18-3. Beethoven. Piano Sonata in C Minor, *Pathétique,* Op. 13. First movement, bars 1–10.

seems to descend from the heights of heaven as if carried by a band of angels (Ex. 18-4a). As the gleaming Grail is bathed in brilliant light, Wagner completes his orchestral picture by the gradual addition of the brass choir. At the climax, the metallic sound of crashing cymbals is heard (Ex. 18-4b), and the vision gradually fades over the final 20 bars to near darkness.

Example 18-4. Wagner. *Lohengrin.* Prelude to Act 1.

18-4a. Bars 1–8.

18-4b. Bars 50–55.

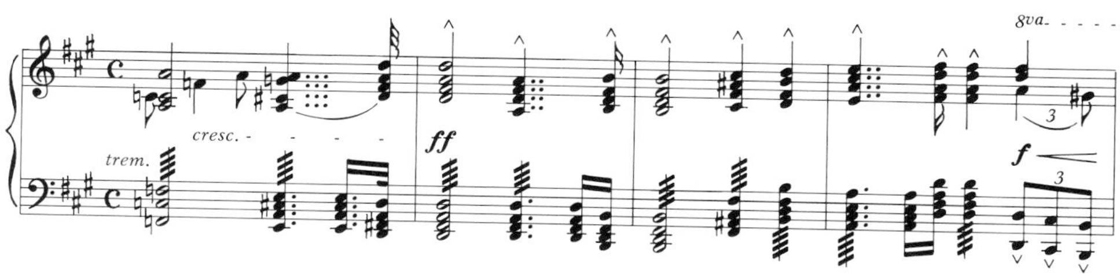

The effect of emotional tensions can also be produced by increasing tonal intensities. In dramatic music, operatic overtures frequently terminate with impressive crescendos designed to prepare the audience for the rising of the curtain. Within the opera itself, vocal and orchestral dynamics may compound the dramatic potential of a scene. A striking use of violent dynamic fluctuations and accents marks the horrifying climax in a scene from Alban Berg's opera *Wozzeck.* Crazed with jealousy, the soldier Wozzeck leads Marie, his unfaithful wife, to a pool in the forest. As dusk falls, the moon rises "like a blood-red iron," and Wozzeck pulls out a knife. Marie's apprehension is gradually revealed to the listener as through a giant stethoscope. A single kettledrum becomes a palpitating heart, at first *pp,* then growing through a three-bar fatalistic crescendo to *fff* at the moment Wozzeck plunges the blade into her throat. As life ebbs from her, the heartbeat wanes, and there is a quick decrescendo to the *pp* level. When the heart stops and Wozzeck begins to realize the enormity of his crime, the full orchestra reinforces the emotional situation with two dissonant, ear-shattering crescendos.

Dynamics are thus among the most important means of eliciting powerful emotional responses from listeners. However, of all the basic elements of music, dynamics loses its effectiveness most noticeably in the recording process and in radio and television transmission. This is even true with modern developments such as digital recording and stereo sound for television. Only under actual live-performance conditions can the whole dynamic range and its expressive possibilities be experienced to the fullest.

CHAPTER 19

Art of Melody

IF TONE COLOR GIVES music its hues, rhythm its heartbeat, and dynamics its energy, then melody is music's speaking voice. Tone colors and dynamics represent measurable and discernible properties of sound, while rhythms generally represent accepted patterns, qualities that open these areas to discussion and definition via the spoken and written word. Melody, on the other hand, is more mysterious, since it depends upon the inspiration of the composer and the intuition of the listener. The composer Richard Strauss once commented that the ability to conceive melodic ideas was "the greatest of divine gifts, not to be compared to any other."

Though much has been written about melody over the centuries, its essence has eluded translation into concrete verbal or literary description. The effects of melody on the listener are apt to be equally elusive. Attempts to describe a melody's effect may result in such adjectives as "beautiful," "strong," "lilting," "energetic," "heavenly," or "demonic." Yet the use of such words can express only individual reactions, and a melody that transports one listener will leave another unmoved. Some melodies sing their way straight into the heart and endure over the years, while others quickly fade.

Because of the elusive qualities and inner meanings of melodic ideas, and the absence of a generally accepted, standardized terminology, we will attempt in this discussion to establish a set of terms that will be both adequate and understandable. First, we may assume that an effective melody is more than a series of notes strung together. Composers design their melodic material with care, intending either to reflect textual meaning or to provide the basis on which to build a formal structure. Several important factors in examining the phenomenon of melody are its relationship to speech patterns, its directional tendencies, its contours, and its place in musical form.

Melody and Speech

Melodic statements, like those in spoken or written language, assume definite forms and occur in certain sequences in order to be intelligible. As words in prose and poetry are grouped into phrases, clauses, sentences, and paragraphs, so tones in a melody are grouped into half phrases, phrases, and sections. The terms *period* and *sentence* are borrowed from language studies to describe certain units of musical form in which two phrases are joined together, much as two independent clauses combine grammatically into a single compound sentence. Melodies may also have occasional pauses in their progress that approximate those after commas, semicolons, and periods. Such musical punctuation points, occurring as they do at the ends of phrases and sections, become convenient breaks for breathing and bowing. Then, by dividing a long line into shorter segments, it becomes possible to clarify complex statements as an aid to understanding.

Inflection in melody is also analogous to that in speech, although a a composer has more specific control over pitch relationships heard by the listener than a writer has over pitch inflections inferred by the reader. In speech, for instance, a sentence often contains an idea set off in two parts: a first phrase introducing an idea and ending in a suspension followed by a concluding phrase that brings the idea to fulfillment: "If music be the food of love, play on." When a half phrase in music shows a similar sense of suspension, it is sometimes called a question, while the succeeding complementary half phrase constitutes the answer (see Ex. 19-2a, bars 1-8).

Emphasis in public address finds a speaker progressively raising the voice to make each point more emphatic than the last. At the ends of sentences and paragraphs, however, the voice will generally fall. Similarly, a melody achieves its climaxes by successive waves moving toward high points, after which it declines at the cadences.

Linear Contours

A line of any kind, whether visual or tonal, has contours, or direction, as one of its basic characteristics. This direction may be downward, upward, or converging toward a center. The perception of this linear movement upward or downward is rooted in the experience of singing, since the lower register of the human voice lies in the deeper chest tones and the higher register in the head tones. Added to these spatial connotations is the feeling of mounting muscular tension as the voice rises, and a corresponding relaxation as it falls. In the 4th century B.C., the philosopher and theorist Aristoxenus wrote in his treatise on harmonics: "Tension is the continuous transition of the voice from a lower position to a higher; relaxation, that from a higher to a lower. Height of pitch is the result of tension, depth of relaxation."

This tendency of motion in melodic lines also has a psychological counterpart. Inflections of the voice in ordinary speech follow emotional states of various sorts. Grief and despair give one a "sinking feeling," accompanied by a slumping of the body and a lowered pitch of the speaking voice. In song, a parallel downward movement of musical line is often employed to suggest sadness (Ex. 19-1a). Exciting or uplifting emotional situations, such as great joy, may produce an opposite upward tendency in bodily movement and vocal pitch. Musical settings often reflect such moods with a concomitant rise of melodic line (Ex. 19-1b).

Example 19-1. Schubert.

19-1a. A Child's Funeral Wreath, bars 11–14.

19-1b. The Shepherd on the Rock. Allegretto, bars 9–12.

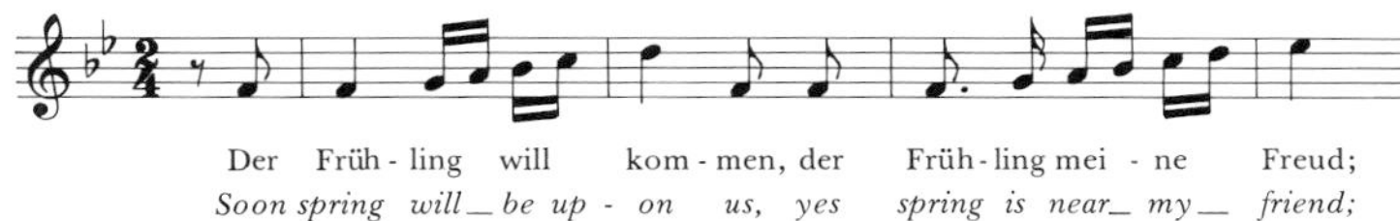

When we think of the chiming of bells, of religious devotion, of quiet meditation, or of death, we may imagine conditions ranging from slavish repetition to complete lack of motion. Melodic lines used to suggest such conditions may concentrate on a central tone without pronounced movement in either direction (Ex. 19-1c; see also Ex. 21-2, p. 470).

19-1c. Swansong. "The Ghostly Double," bars 5–12.

The fashioning of melodic lines requires that the notes in them proceed either by steps or by skips. In stepwise, or conjunct, motion, succeeding notes are placed close to each other on the scale and may produce a calm and peaceful hymnlike atmosphere (Ex. 19-2a). This type of line is easy for musically untrained singers, so the melodies of many national anthems and hymn tunes move in a stepwise manner. Skipwise, or disjunct, motion may spread the line out harmonically along the notes of a chord (Ex. 19-2b), producing a line that is more active, expansive, and energetic.

Example 19-2a. Beethoven. Symphony No. 9 in D Minor, Op. 125. Fourth movement, bars 92–115.

19-2b. Mozart. Violin Concerto No. 5 in A Major, *K* 219. First movement, bars 1–5.

Melodic lines written for the dance are apt to be influenced by the specific mood to be projected. In scenes projecting greater action, melodic lines are dominated by skipwise motion, while those of a more contemplative nature tend to be represented by music featuring stepwise movement.

The ability of instruments to move quickly between tones that are some distance apart may also influence the writing of melodic lines, as seen in Example 19-2c. Composers in the 20th century have often challenged both traditional tonality and melodic writing, and some of them have relied on widely disjunct melodic materials in effective ways (Ex. 19-2d).

The disparate ranges of voices and instruments is another consideration in melodic writing. The average human voice seldom extends to more than an octave and a half, while the piano, for example, encompasses more than seven octaves.

Melodic Forms

Melodic lines that are designed as a basis for restatement and development provide continuity in the unfolding of musical forms. Such lines are described variously as subjects, figures, motifs, and themes.

The broadest concept of these is the *subject.* A subject, to quote Aaron Copland, "is generally what the piece is about." The subject provides an introduc-

19-2c. Mozart. Symphony No. 35 in D Major, *K* 385. First movement, bars 1–5.

19-2d. Boulez. *The Hammer Without a Master.* No. 7, "After 'The furious artist'," bars 1–5.

tion to the musical materials that will grow and be repeated throughout the composition (Ex. 19-3a). Inherent in the concept of a subject is that its design includes elements which allow for flexibility and growth potential. These include melodic, harmonic, rhythmic, and color elements. Subjects are normally stated at or near the beginning of the composition or a movement. As can be seen in other chapters, various formal patterns will automatically contain characteristic numbers and kinds of subjects (see chapters 21 and 22).

A *figure* is a part of a subject that may be detached from it for purposes of repetition, variation, or development (see Ex. 19-3a). When a figure is restated several times or is repeated on different pitch levels, it functions as a *sequence,* as seen in Example 19-3b.

A *motif* is a short subject that is designed with specific important rhythmic and melodic implications. It functions as a germ cell that expands over time into a larger musical organism (Exs. 19-4a, b, c).

A *theme* is a subject that becomes part of a specific formal process known as theme and variations (see pp. 487–89).

Finally, it must be remembered that any melody worthy of the name is always much more than a collection of tones, motifs, themes, and phrases; and the whole will therefore always exceed the sum of its parts. While melodies are primarily products of a composer's creative imagination, a number of rational procedures must come into play as the material is molded into shape and given spatial as well as temporal organization. Composers remain consciously aware that they are manipulating lines as they go upward and downward in direction, as well as forward in time. As the moving material acquires momentum, it must continue in some direction until it reaches its destination or encounters some obstacle in its path. Whether these linear goals are points of high tension or relative repose, moments of comparative excitement or calm, the composer must exercise control to give the melody a sense of purpose as well as direction.

Example 19-3. Beethoven. Symphony No. 3 in E-flat Major, Op. 55 ("Eroica"). First movement.

19-3a. Subject with figure, bars 1–5.

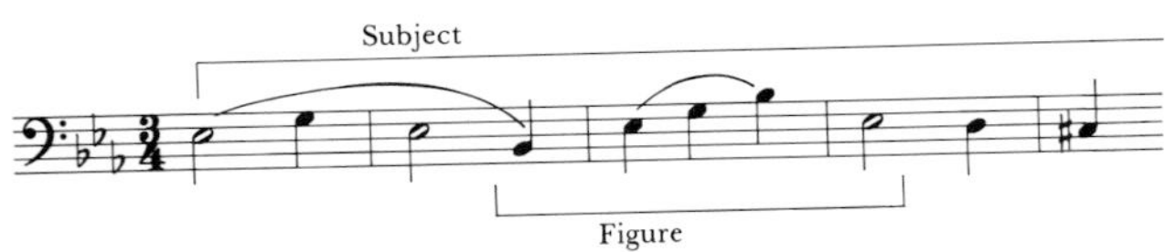

19-3b. Sequence, bars 311–17.

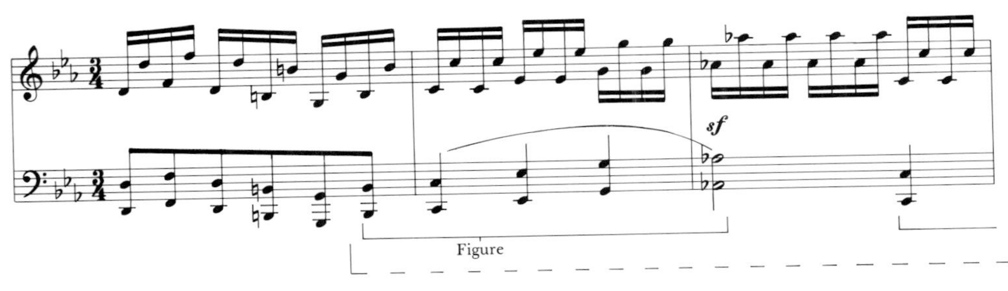

Composers are also aware of the power of moving lines to communicate meaning—whether tangible or intangible, definite or indefinite, literal or symbolic—because they are connected with such universal human experiences as the inflections of speech, linear imagery, muscular memory, and emotional tension. They also know that musical lines move through the temporal dimension, where they are free from gravitational limitations and can more effctively express the soaring aspirations of the human spirit.

As composers ready a melody for presentation to the listener, they must take into consideration such factors as scale organization and harmonic system, the steps and skips of the intervals between notes, the possibilities and limitations of the various voices and instruments, and the placement of melody in the overall structure that is being created. Furthermore, a melody can appear alone, in the contrapuntal company of other melodies, or highlighted against a harmonic background. And since it must always be sung or played either singly or in concert with other voices or instruments, it can take on an

Example 19-4. Franck. Symphony in D Minor.

19-4a. First movement, bars 1–4.

19-4b. Second movement, bars 17–23.

19-4c. Third movement, bars 7–10.

individual coloration, which can vary from the plaintive sound of a solitary voice to the surging power of the entire symphony orchestra. In such ways as these, composers control their melodic lines, shape them in significant directions, and command their moving material to achieve expressive ends.

CHAPTER

20

Art of Harmony

UP TO THIS POINT the various materials at the composer's command have been treated in the main as elements. Detaching them for separate consideration has been for purposes of clarity and convenience. As elements, however, they never exist in isolation, but only in combination with one another in various textures. A melody, for instance, can never appear apart from the presence of some rhythmic pattern, nor can it be heard except through some vocal or instrumental medium. Furthermore, melodies are rarely heard apart from combined sounds such as accompanying chord progressions or in combination with other melodies. These combinations represent textures described as harmonic and contrapuntal.

Music has texture and, like any woven fabric, a warp and a woof. If it is viewed horizontally, as a linear art, it is categorized as *contrapuntal,* and the listener's consciousness is directed to the various lines as they are woven together. If, on the other hand, the listening perception is vertical, as columns of chords march across the page, that music is said to be *homophonic,* or *harmonic.* The two concepts—horizontal and vertical—are not mutually exclusive any more than they are in a piece of cloth. That is, in contrapuntal music, notes from the various lines fall together to make harmony, while in homophonic music certain linear relationships may be easily discernible.

However, it is usual to make a general distinction between the basic methods of writing, and the textures of harmony and counterpoint will be treated here as they function in the Western tonal tradition.

Harmony in its most fundamental sense refers to two or more sounds produced simultaneously. More broadly, the term implies a succession of such experiences, and in its fullest meaning, harmony is concerned with the study of the logical relationships that can exist within a complex of sounds. A mastery of harmony is essential for any composer, and an understanding of some of its underlying theoretical concepts can enliven the listening experience.

The natural mathematical relationships existing between tones has been known since ancient times. As mentioned in the discussion of tone color, Western music has been governed harmonically for many centuries by the relationship between a fundamental tone and its first overtone—an octave (eight tones) above—as well as the relationships of tonal intervals within that octave.

Intervals

In our tonal system, intervals are described by two words, one general and one specific. The general descriptive word gives the basic relationship between the two note names and is stated as a numerical relationship: C to F is the interval of a *fourth,* as is C to F-sharp and C-sharp to F. Any interval that contains the note names C and F is a kind of fourth, simply because there are four note names encompassed by the sequence: C D E F. The specific descriptive word narrows down the type of relationship that exists between actual notes in the interval: C to F is a *perfect* fourth, C to F-sharp is an *augmented* fourth, C-sharp to F is a *diminished* fourth. In traditional Western harmony, the unison, fourth, fifth, and octave are normally perfect intervals, while the intervals of the second, third, sixth, and seventh are normally designated as either major or minor intervals. Further expansion or contraction of interval size results in intervals that are augmented or diminished. Though general interval names larger than the octave are used, this discussion will be limited to intervals within the octave.

To Western-trained ears, certain notes within the confines of the octave seem more settled or stronger than others as they relate to a fundamental tone. These notes are the octave and the fifth, which are the first and second overtones of any fundamental tone. The first overtone of the note C is its octave, C. The second is a fifth above that, G. In addition to the fourth, these intervals in their natural state within the octave are described as *perfect* intervals. Other intervals are considered to have variously weaker characteristics, and from stronger to weaker they are the third, sixth, second, and seventh. In their natural state within the octave they are described as either *major* or *minor.*

Composers have accepted the three perfect intervals as being of almost equal aural weight and have consequently used the octave, fifth, and fourth melodically to suggest ideas of strength (Ex. 20-1). Conversely, certain weaker interval relationships have traditionally been used to suggest vulnerable states of mind. In Example 20-2, the dropping major seventh at the beginning is meant to suggest the lonely, yearning heart to which the text refers.

Example 20-1. Handel. *Messiah.* "Rejoice greatly," bars 1–3.

Example 20-2. Tchaikovsky. *None But the Lonely Heart,* bars 1–2.

As part of their melodic and harmonic functions, intervals may be enlarged or reduced in size. In their natural diatonic state, unisons, fourths, fifths, and octaves are perfect. When any perfect interval is enlarged by a half step, it becomes augmented (Chart 20-1a). When reduced by a half step, it becomes diminished (Chart 20-1b).

CHART 20-1. EXPANDING AND CONTRACTING INTERVALS

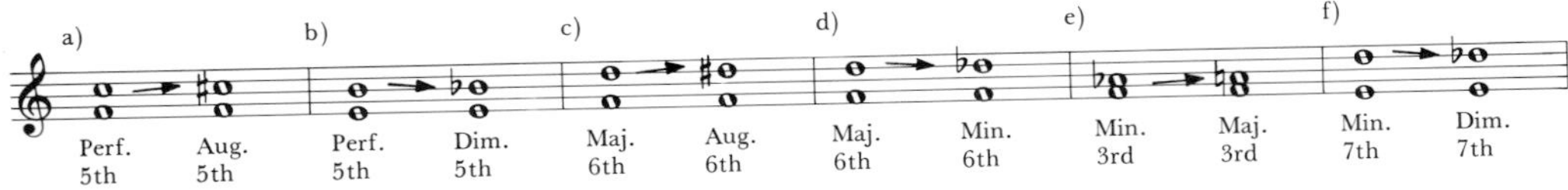

Intervals that are major or minor in their natural diatonic state are seconds, thirds, fifths, sixths, and sevenths. When a major interval is enlarged, it becomes augmented (Chart 20-1c); when it is reduced, it becomes minor (Chart 20-1d). When a minor interval is enlarged, it becomes major (Chart 20-1e); when it is reduced, it becomes diminished (Chart 20-1f).

Chords

Western harmony is based not only on melodic intervals, but on the simultaneous sounding of groups of notes called *chords.* A chord may be described as any combination of notes heard at one time. Traditional tonality has grown from chords made up of three or four notes, built on intervals of a third. Various types of chords are identified through particular combinations of *major* and *minor* thirds, such as C to E or C to E-flat.

Though chords of as many as eight different notes can be found in some music, the foundation from which most tonal music springs is that of the traditional three-note chord known as the *triad.* Triads are made of various combinations of major and minor thirds, and are named in somewhat the same manner as intervals. In a *major triad,* a major third is constructed and a minor third placed on top of it.

G
} minor third
E
} major third
C

In a *minor triad,* a minor third is constructed and a major third placed on top of it.

G
} major third
E-flat
} minor third
C

Each of the three notes of a triad has a functional name. The lowest note, that on which the triad is based, is called the *fundamental,* or *root.* The middle note is the *third,* since it is three tones above the root. The top note is known as the *fifth,* since it is five tones above the root.

G fifth
}
E third
}
C fundamental, or root

CHART 20-2. TRIADS ON THE STAFF

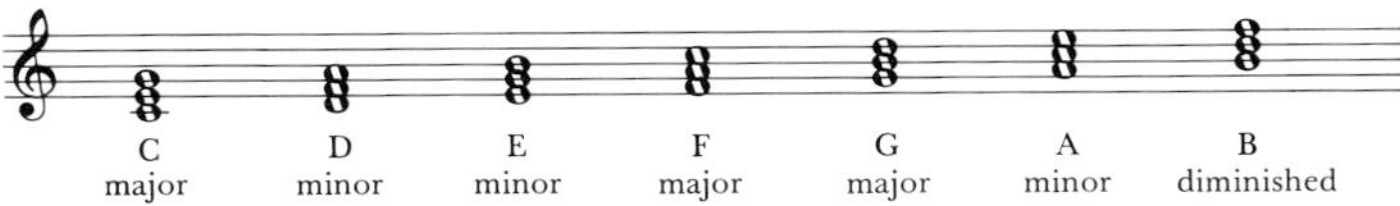

When a triad appears on the score as shown above, it is said to be in *root position.*

The three notes of a triad may appear in any order on the score (Chart 20-3). If the third is on the bottom, the triad is said to be in *first inversion;* with the fifth on the bottom, it is in *second inversion.*

CHART 20-3. TRIAD INVERSIONS

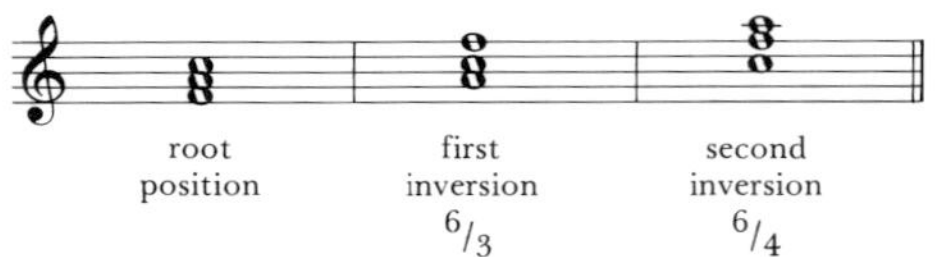

Major and minor triads fulfill strong and less strong roles within the octave. Triads constructed from two major or two minor thirds, *augmented* and *diminished* triads, are extremely weak and are used less frequently.

Scales

The third building block of harmony is the *scale.* Beginning students are usually given scales as exercises to increase and solidify their technical prowess. Within the confines of the octave, there are twelve notes. In Western tonality seven notes are selected in a specific order to form the *scale,* which in turn provides a key center used by composers to build tonal structures in their compositions. The word *scale* has its genesis in the Italian *scala* (ladder), and in fact a scale is actually a ladder of notes climbing or descending the staff. The generic type of scale used in most Western music is called *diatonic.*

There are two types of diatonic scales that govern most traditionally based Western music—*major* and *minor.* This designation is logically related to major and minor intervals, as well as to major and minor triads. Major and minor scales each have seven notes. The first note is sometimes repeated an octave higher at the end of the scale to give a sense of completeness.

Chart 20-4 shows the scale of C Major on a treble staff. It is shown moving ladderlike in an upward direction. As in all scales, all note names (A through G) are used. Within the scale each note, or *degree,* of the scale is assigned a number as well as a letter name. Notes may be described by letter name (F) or by position within the scale (fourth degree).

CHART 20-4. C-MAJOR SCALE ON THE STAFF

Scales are designed around a formula of tone relationships, each type having a series of whole and half steps. In the *major scale* on C in Chart 20-4, relationships are all whole steps except between the third and fourth degrees and between the seventh and eighth degrees.

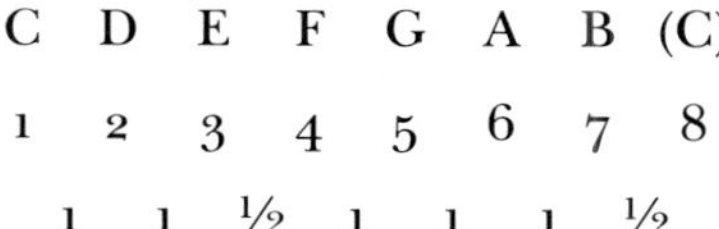
C D E F G A B (C)

1 2 3 4 5 6 7 8

1 1 ½ 1 1 1 ½

This formula pattern of whole and half steps is the same for all major scales built on any pitch. The *natural minor* scale is built on the same principles, except that the half steps are placed between the second and third degrees and fifth and sixth degrees of the scale.

A B C D E F G (A)

1 2 3 4 5 6 7 8

1 ½ 1 1 ½ 1 1

In the 18th century it became common practice to make a small adjustment to the natural minor scale, raising the seventh degree by a half step. This is still popularly employed today, and is known as the *harmonic minor* scale.

A B C D E F G-sharp (A)

1 2 3 4 5 6 7 8

1 ½ 1 1 ½ 1½ ½

It may be useful to know that when the seventh degree of a harmonic minor scale contains an accidental—a sharp in the above example—the accidental does not appear in the key signature, but is placed next to the appropriate note—G in this example—whenever it appears on the score.

Two other scales occur in Western music, the *whole tone* and *chromatic* scales (Charts 20-5a, b). In the case of the first, all tones are a full step apart; in the second, tones are a half step apart. These scales are not employed as the basis for harmony in compositions based on traditional tonality, since it is not possible to build triads on the chromatic scale, and triads built on any note of a whole tone scale produce the weak, augmented variety.

Key and Mode

In the field of harmony, scales act as representatives for two major aspects of Western tonality, key and mode. Without a grasp of these key components, it is not possible to understand the music of our society. Of the two terms, *mode* is the more general concept. It is a word used to describe the basic structure of any tonal system of the past or present. When speaking of past cultures whose music was not built on the same scale systems that we use, we describe their tonal systems as modal (see pp. 80–81, 94).

Our modern and more specific concept of *key* encompasses the totality of relationships possible using the notes of our major or minor scales. The key of C Major, then, represents the potential of every combination of notes present in the C-major scale, including all the notes of the scale as they may be used in melodic configurations and in chordal combinations.

CHART 20-5a. WHOLE TONE SCALES

CHART 20-5b. CHROMATIC SCALES

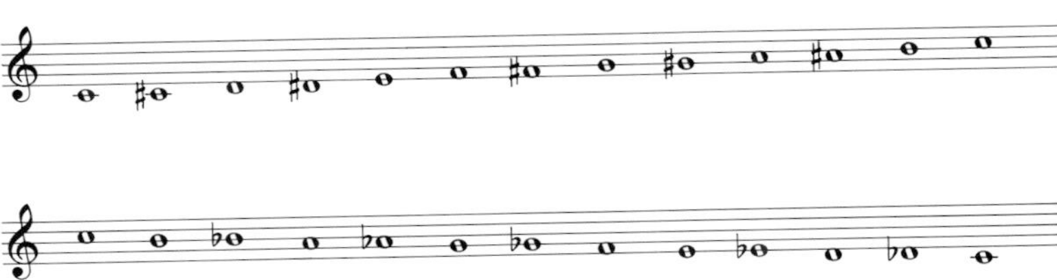

With the chromatic division of the octave into 12 tones, 24 different key centers become possible. These include the possibility of a major and a minor key based on each note of the scale—C Major and C Minor, C-sharp Major and C-sharp Minor, and so on.

Our key system is governed by a sort of musical law of gravity. Western ears have been trained to react to certain notes in the scale as well as the triads built on those notes, as though they had tonal weight or strength. The first note of any scale carries the most weight for the ear, and the same is true of the triad built on that note. In the key of C Major, then, the note C and the major triad built on the note C are for the ear the strongest note and chord. We describe them as *tonic:* the note C is the tonic note, and the C Major triad is the tonic triad. Since both the tonic note and triad are so important within the key, our system of tonality is known as *diatonic,* meaning a system built around a tonic.

Each of the degrees of the scale has its own name:

I	II	III	IV	V	VI	VII
Tonic	Supertonic	Mediant	Subdominant	Dominant	Submediant	Subtonic
Do	Re	Mi	Fa	Sol	La	Ti

The subtonic is also known as the *leading tone.* As may be seen above, singing syllables are also assigned to various degrees of the scale.

The most important notes and triads within the system are I, tonic (do); V, dominant (sol); and IV, subdominant (fa). Each of the triads built on these degrees of the scale will be of the same type (major in a major scale and key, minor in a minor scale and key). Note that in harmonic shorthand, Roman numerals are used for the numbered degrees of the scale.

For Western ears, the tonic note and triad become the tonal center of the key. As a rule, a composer sets the tonality of the tonic triad at the beginning of the composition to give the ear a sense of "home base." Our ears accept this tonal center quickly. The composer may then feel free to move away from it, and the harmonic flow of the composition results from the alternation of strong and weak notes, chords, and keys throughout. It is normal practice to employ the tonic key to close off individual sections in a composition, to return to the tonic at various points during that composition, and to end on it.

These various returns to the tonic are accomplished by means of a *cadence,* a word derived from a Latin root meaning "to fall." A cadence is a literal falling from a triad on an upper degree of the scale to rest on the tonic triad. The movement of triads toward the tonic is known as a *progression* (Chart 20-6).

CHART 20-6. CADENCES

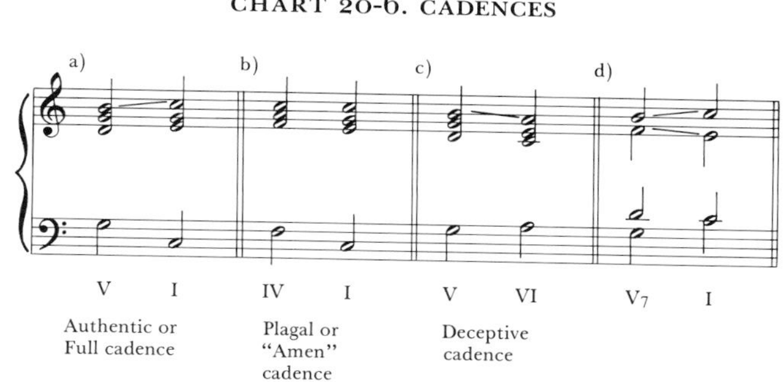

The most compelling cadence progression is from the dominant (V) to the tonic (I), from one strong triad to a stronger one. This is known as an *authentic,* or *full,* cadence. An authentic cadence is expressed as V I. A second cadence often used to close compositions is from the subdominant (IV) to the tonic (I). This is called a *plagal* cadence or an "Amen" cadence (because it is commonly used at the end of hymns).

Even though the triad is the chord that forms the basis of harmonic progressions, chords containing more than three notes are extensively used in Western harmony. Such chords are built by adding intervals of the third. Our ears are conditioned to hear chords of more than three notes as weaker than triads.

Composers may wish to strengthen the sense of a cadence, and one way of doing so is to make the first chord in the progression weaker. For example, the addition of another note to a dominant triad weakens the sound of that chord, and the movement to the tonic is thereby strengthened. A chord so constructed is known as a *dominant seventh* or V^7 chord.

From time to time, a composer may decide to delay the conclusion of a section temporarily. A progression from the dominant (V) to the submediant (VI), known as a *deceptive* cadence, is a useful device to accomplish this. The deceptive cadence "fools the ear" for the moment, and the composer can then move through another set of triads before finishing with an authentic or plagal cadence.

Key Signatures

On the score, the key center is represented by a *key signature* (Chart 20-7). The sharps or flats placed at the beginning of the score are those found in the scale of the key in question. Any line or space on the staff that does not have an accidental is automatically assumed to be a natural (a white note on the keyboard). The key of C Major, for instance, shows no sharps or flats, since it has none in its scale. That of G Major has one sharp in the scale (on the note F), and that sharp is placed on both the treble and the bass staves of the score.

Modulation

A composition of any length would be aurally stultifying if it were to remain in one key for its entirety. Therefore, composers change keys from time to time to assure that the ear retains its freshness and often to signal the beginning of a new section. In the latter case, there may be new melodic and rhythmic materials and a possible change of tone color. A change of key with its

CHART 20-7. KEY SIGNATURES

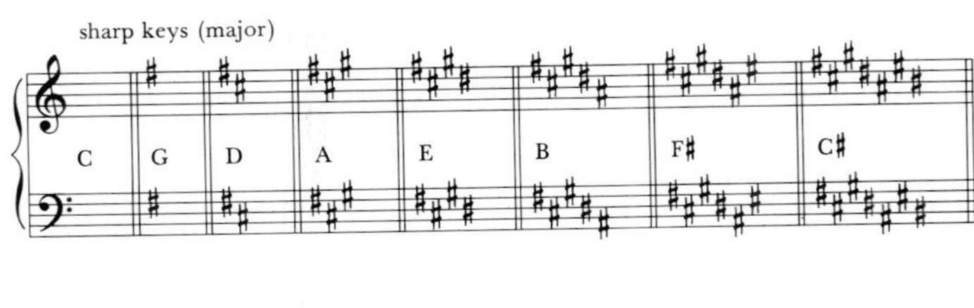

flat keys (major)

F B♭ E♭ A♭ D♭ G♭ C♭

new tonal center functions as one more clue to the listener that something new is imminent. The practice of moving from one key to another is known as *modulation.*

There are a number of ways to modulate between keys. It is the composer's decision whether key changes will function to jolt the listener by interrupting the music's flow, or to provide a smooth transition. One traditional way to modulate is to move to a key that has its tonic a perfect fifth away from the current key.

Chart 20-8 shows the set of traditional diatonic key relationships that is known in the study of harmony as the Circle of Fifths. Outside the circle at the top, the tonic note for C Major is shown; no accidentals are shown below it, since the C-major scale contains none. Moving clockwise, the first representative key shown is G, a perfect fifth from C. This key has one sharp in its scale and key signature. The notes of these two keys are exactly the same with one exception. The listener's ear finds it easy to deal with a shift of key in which only there is only one note difference, and in which the tonal centers are already in strong relationship (tonic C and dominant G).

Progressing clockwise around the circle, each of the succeeding key representations is a fifth above the previous one, and each adds one sharp. Modulation between any two adjacent keys here is comfortable for the ear. The last clockwise listing is C-sharp Major, with seven sharps. Keep in mind that while its tonic note, C-sharp, is immediately adjacent to C on the keyboard, the key it represents is a vast tonal distance away, since all the notes and triads are different. Conservative composers would not modulate from C Major to C-sharp Major, for such a modulation could be conceived only as a distinct shock to the ear.

Returning to the top of the circle and moving counterclockwise, we see key relationships using intervals of the perfect fifth in a downward direction. From C down to F is a perfect fifth, with only one note of the scale different (B-flat). A modulation from C to F leaves the listener perfectly at ease. Further movement around the circle shows additional flats in each succeeding key, arriving finally at D-flat Major. As with its enharmonic cousin C-sharp Major, this key is aurally distant from C Major and is not suitable for normal modulation.

Another easy way to modulate involves moving mode as well as key. On the Circle of Fifths, lower-case letters are placed inside the circle adjacent to the capitals. These represent minor keys, specifically those minor keys that have the same notes in their scales as the major keys shown above them. At the top, then, C Major and A Minor both have the same notes in their scales, though they are set out in a different order. Scales and keys that have the same notes are said to be *relative.* C Major is therefore the *relative major* of A Minor; A Minor is the *relative minor* of C Major. Such scales always have their tonic note and triad a minor third apart.

CHART 20-8. THE CIRCLE OF FIFTHS

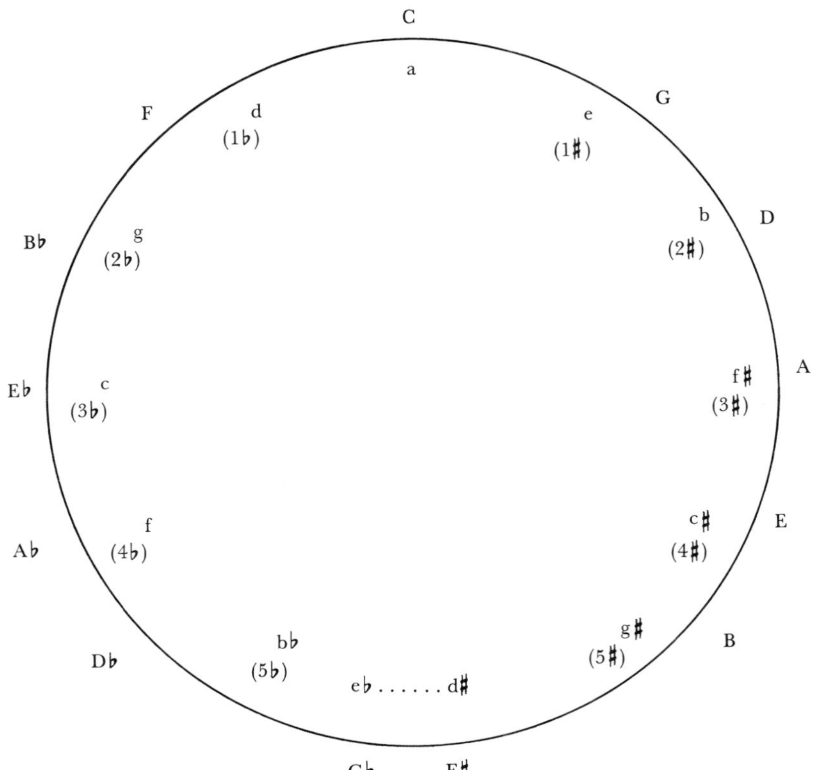

Consonance and Dissonance

If music moves through time via rhythmic and melodic energies, it also moves with harmonic energy. Energy results from tension and opposition, from pulse against pulse, from line against line, from strength against weakness. Harmonic flow can create a sense of energy passing through alternations of consonance and dissonance.

In music, *consonance* is synonymous with resolution or rest. A tonic triad is a consonance; a cadence progression that has as its result a tonic resolution is a *consonant movement.*

Dissonance in music represents tension. Tension is achieved through the use of notes and chords that are outside the boundaries of the diatonic harmony. A popularly held view of dissonance is that it is unpleasant or jarring to the ear, while consonance is sound that is aurally easy and pleasant. While both views contain some truth, the function of consonance and dissonance is often much more subtle. Musical tensions may be mild or strong and are generated by the introduction of notes outside the harmony, by sounding notes that are very close together (smaller intervals than triadic thirds). Just as dynamic levels may be soft or loud, as tempos may be slow or fast, consonances and dissonances may be strong or weak, mild or astringent, pleasant or unpleasant. It is in the balancing and juxtaposition of these opposing forces that musical interest and excitement for the ear is created.

CHAPTER

21

Art of Counterpoint

WHILE HARMONY IS CONCERNED mainly with vertical organization and chordal progressions, counterpoint deals with linear movement in horizontal directions with two or more musical lines sounding simultaneously. The word *counterpoint* and its adjective *contrapuntal* derive from the Latin phrase *punctus contra punctum* (note against note). The concept originated in the Middle Ages at a time when the long-standing practice of performing music in unison was giving way to the new concept of sounding two musical lines at the same time. The term referred specifically to the process of setting every note against a corresponding note in another melodic line, but today we apply the term generally to the simultaneous sounding of two or more lines of music. Careful attention to the disciplines of contrapuntal music is one of the most rewarding experiences available to the serious listener. An ear trained to follow the inner clarity and complexity of well-written counterpoint will be sensitive to the subtlety of detail and the refinements of workmanship contained in every major musical masterpiece.

In common usage, the terms *polyphony* (several voices or parts), and *counterpoint* are interchangeable, as are their adjectival forms, *polyphonic* and *contrapuntal*. These terms designate the kind of texture in which several lines of music progress together. The composer shapes each line individually so that it may be clearly articulated and given its own distinctive character. Then the separate strands are woven into a unified musical fabric.

While contrapuntal music has played a role in every era since medieval times, baroque composers found the most ingenious ways of dealing with its potential and complexities. For this reason most of the examples on the following pages have been selected from works of that period.

Part Writing

While harmonic and contrapuntal music are distinguished by their contrasting textures, their functions often overlap to a certain extent. Chordal progressions that are organized vertically nevertheless move in linear directions. Contrapuntal lines move horizontally, yet they have harmonic implications, since they sound against each other. Thus harmony and counterpoint are related, and they may in some ways be considered as two different ways of looking at the same situation. Consider, for example, the chordal view, in which the sense of a progression of verticals is paramount, and compare it with the contrapuntal view of the same situation (Exs. 21-1a, b). In Example 21-1b, it will be seen that the chordal sense is weakened, and each note tends to be heard primarily as a component of the horizontal line to which it belongs.

Example 21-1a. Chordal texture.

21-1b. Contrapuntal texture.

As noted above, the texture of any chordally conceived composition must also be considered from the linear perspective. For example, a hymn tune may be harmonized for an ensemble of sopranos, altos, tenors, and basses, as shown in Example 21-2. The setting is essentially vertical—a chord succession supporting the melody. Each chord, however, is composed of four separate voice parts, and each part sustains a note in the vertical alignment. The soprano part contains the tune, so its course is predetermined. As each of the remaining voices sustains a note in the supporting harmony, interest for both performer and listener is provided by the introduction of additional passing notes. The effect is to linearize the parts, to give each line a sense of separate existence within the limits of the whole. The result is a shift in emphasis from the purely chordal to the semicontrapuntal, by virtue of its *part writing.*

Example 21-2. Linear harmonization.

Contrapuntal Procedures

Several common procedures are used to help give special definition to lines in a contrapuntal fabric. *Ostinato* (obstinate, unchanging) refers to the process of repeating a musical figure over and over again. Often it is a purely rhythmical device and by the very obstinacy of its reiteration, it sets up a level within the music against which other lines may be played off in a type of rhythmic counterpoint.

Usually the ostinato figure is a melodic motif or line, and it often appears as the bass line. This obstinate bass, technically known as *basso ostinato* or *ground bass,* becomes a floor over which the contrapuntal structure is raised. Implicitly, there is always a contrapuntal relationship, an interplay between distinguishable levels, whenever a ground bass is in operation. A favorite device with baroque composers, extended ground-bass figures appear frequently in the works of Purcell and Bach.

The ostinato principle appears as central to two related types of variation design. The *passacaglia* and the *chaconne* are continuous variation forms, constantly evolving fresh musical material with each variation over the same repeating bass line. The ostinato provides the ground stability and unity, while the simultaneous variations provide variety as they continually revitalize and invigorate the ostinato subject (see pp. 147–48).

Continuo is a contrapuntal concept allied with that of the basso ostinato, and it was similarly favored by composers of the baroque period. Its full name is *basso continuo* (continuous bass). As the name implies, it is the bass line, emphasized in such a way as to become a focus for the listener's attention (see p. 00). Since the continuo line need not involve repetition, it is a freer and more general view of the baroque bass complex than the basso ostinato.

A favorite medium for chamber music among baroque composers was the *trio sonata,* an instrumental composition of several movements composed in three separate contrapuntal parts. In such a trio sonata, the two upper parts were bound together as a contrapuntal duet over the continuo. The two upper voices might be matched (two violins or two sopranos) or contrasting (violin and flute or soprano and tenor; see pp. 147–48).

CANON

When a composition is designed so that various lines echo each other with some immediacy, the term *imitation* is used to describe them. If the design further exposes the listener to a texture in which the lines are perceived to be in formal relationship to each other, the process is called *imitative counterpoint.* The practice of using immediate repetition of musical lines as a unifying factor in musical form has been an accepted device for several centuries. It was central to the high Renaissance style of composition, and baroque composers refined the practice into the specific processes found in the contrapuntal styles known as *canon* and *fugue.*

The *canon* is a process in which a composition is developed by building layers of separate lines, each of which derives from a single seminal voice. A definition of canon might be "a composition in which all parts are realized out of one." If we assume the musical meaning of the term *realize* (to make complete through performance), the definition tells us that the canon starts with only a single line. This line is designed to be performed in some fashion with itself. On the page it is incomplete, but in performance the canon line is "realized," or completed, and becomes a finished composition.

The simplest kind of canon is the *round,* the formal name for which is *canon at the unison* (Ex. 21-3). In this type, a single melodic line is performed over and over with itself, each performer entering successively at a prescribed distance in time, each beginning on the same pitch. Well-known examples are *Row, Row, Row Your Boat* and *Three Blind Mice.* Example 21-4 is a more sophisticated approach to the round, in which the concept of sleep as a shorter death and death as a longer sleep is reflected in the shortening and lengthening of the words *kurzer* and *langer.*

Canons may also be realized at intervals other than the unison, for example a canon at the fourth or a canon at the sixth. In addition, common procedures in designing canon lines include: canon in *inversion,* or *mirror* canon (to be performed both as written and upside down); *cancrizans,* or *crab* canon (to be performed both as written and backward); canon in *augmentation* (to be realized with note values double those of the original line); canon in *diminution* (to be realized with note values half as long as those of the original line).

The discipline required in writing canons places these often complicated compositions within the category of works conceived by musicians primarily for other musicians. Since the intricate linear relationships and nuances of a realized canon may be difficult for the listener to follow, understanding of canonic practice is facilitated by studying the score. Where the eye leads, the ear follows.

Figure 21-1 shows a portrait of J. S. Bach in which he is holding the score of a canon. Bach designed this canon as a musical puzzle for the viewer to

Example 21-3. *Row, row, row your boat.* Round (canon at the unison).

Example 21-4. Haydn. *Death is a longer sleep.* Round (canon at the unison).

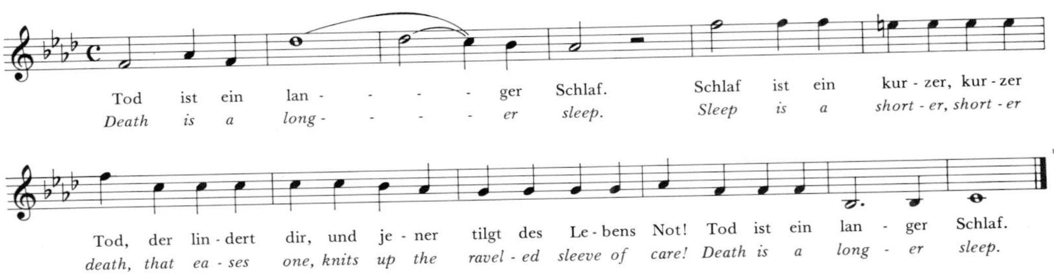

solve (Ex. 21-5a). Three lines are shown, and it is up to the viewer to discover how to join them together to realize the canon into a finished composition (Ex. 21-5b). The example is actually three canons in one, each of which is a canon in inversion. The top canon line is realized at the interval of the fourth, the line in the center at the fifth, and the bottom line at the interval of the third. All three are to be realized simultaneously to form a six-part composition.

While a canon is derived from a single line, it is possible to create a canon that is part of a more complex texture. The canon in Example 21-6 appears in the two upper voices, realized at the interval of the sixth. It is placed over a bass line, the rhythmic and harmonic implications of which complete and add a certain solidity to the composition as a whole.

The foregoing discussion is not meant to be a complete catalog of canonic procedures. Its purpose is simply to show that the parts of any canon tend to display underlying similarities because they are all created from a single source.

FUGUE

If the canon may be conceived both by and for musicians, the *fugue* may be approached on a broader level. Maturing in the 17th century out of the older *ricercar* (literally, "to seek"), the fugue with its imitative "seeking" lines

Figure 21-1. Elias Haussmann. *J. S. Bach,* 1748. Oil on canvas. Courtesy of the Collection of William Scheide, Princeton, New Jersey.

Example 21-5a. Detail of Figure 21-1.

21-5b. Bach. Portrait puzzle canon in six parts, *BWV* 1076. Realization.

Example 21-6. Bach. "Goldberg" Variations, *BWV* 988. No. 18, canon at the sixth, bars 1–4.

became a major musical force in baroque and later music. It is still so today. The fugue is not so much a form as it is a series of principles of organization allowing the composer a good deal of freedom within certain set rules.

A fugue opens with an *exposition,* in which the most important musical statement, the *fugue subject,* is first presented as a single line. The subject is then restated serially and imitatively, each time appearing at a different level, as successive "voices" enter. A fugue in four voices or parts would therefore contain four separate musical lines, and its exposition would present four imitative statements of the subject (Ex. 21-7).

Example 21-7. Bach. *The Art of Fugue, BWV* 1080. No. 4, bars 1–19.

The fugue subject itself is designed to present a clear set of characteristics—intervallic, tonal, and rhythmic—which will help the listener to recognize it whenever and wherever it may later appear. Additionally, a fugue subject may be designed so that it can be combined with other subjects. When such other subjects are introduced, they are known as *countersubjects.* A good fugue subject must act as the basic brick from which the fugal edifice will be constructed, giving substance and life to the finished product. Fugue subjects usually appear in a predictable order—for example, soprano, alto, tenor, and bass (see Ex. 21-7). A fugue subject may, however, begin in any voice, with succeeding entries appearing in adjacent voices (Ex. 21-8).

In the exposition of the four-voice fugue in Example 21-8, the order of entries of the subject is alto, soprano (in bar 2), bass (in bar 5), and tenor (at the end of bar 6). A *countersubject* occurs in the alto line in bar 3. Alternate entries of the subject are called *answers.* In this fugue, then, the alto carries

Example 21-8. Bach. *The Well-Tempered Clavier I.* Fugue 16, *BWV* 861.

the statement of the subject, the soprano the answer, the bass the subject statement again, and the tenor the answer once more.

Subject statements and answers may be in the same or in related keys. If the answer is an exact repetition of the statement or contains exactly the same interval relationships in a different key, it is a *real answer.* If the answer resembles the statement in contour but does not exactly follow the statement, it is a *tonal answer.* The answers in Example 21-8 are tonal.

With the last introduction of the subject, here in the tenor, the exposition of the fugue is complete. The composer then proceeds to manipulate the subject and countersubject with some degree of freedom, stating them either wholly or in parts. During this stretch of "middle entries," subject materials may be placed in any voice, *figures* may be excerpted from them (bars 9 and 10), and may be tossed from voice to voice. It is usual to make much of the *sequence,* a short motif taken from the subject and repeated, moving up or down the scale (bars 18 and 19). Sections may be designed that make no reference to the subject at all. These free-form *episodes* serve to set apart reworkings of subject materials (bars 24–27).

When the composer has completed this developmental process, the fugue is then brought to a close. This ending is often signaled by one or more full statements of the subject in the tonic key (bar 28, beginning in the soprano line).

The practice of fugue composition is equally valid for instruments or voices. Like the canon, the fugue may be designed to fit within larger musical textures. For the close of his Mass in B Minor, Bach wrote a fugue on the text *Dona nobis pacem* (Grant us peace). This example of a vocal fugue with instrumental accompaniment presents the subject entries in a manner we have not seen before (Ex. 21-9). Here the subject entries appear in *stretto,* in which answers enter before the subject statements have been completed. The first subject statement is in the bass voice. Beginning with a real answer, the other voices enter quickly, overlapping one another.

Example 21-9. Bach. Mass in B Minor, *BWV* 232. "Grant us peace," bars 1–6.

Fugues may appear in almost any musical medium—solo keyboard, string quartet, symphony, concerto, opera. And while the serious and noble fugue was indigenous to and particularly popular in the baroque period, the fugal process has continued through the intervening years to the present time. Along the way, the fugue has taken on the stylistic characteristics of each period—classical, romantic, and modern. In the 19th century, for example, the Italian opera composer Verdi wrote a comic opera based on and named after the Shakespearean character Falstaff. At the end of the opera, Falstaff projects onto the entire world his own experiences and character, and leads the cast in a rollicking 14-voice fugue. The fugue subject is set to the text "The whole world's a joke and all men buffoons," and as each voice enters the musical texture becomes further enriched, propelling the opera to a frolicsome close.

In this century, the fugue has tempted many composers to adapt this old process to speak to new audiences. For the second movement of his *Symphony of Psalms* Stravinsky wrote two fugues, one for orchestra, one for chorus. Each has its own separate subject. The two are heard separately, then merged, producing an impressive demonstration of the composer's contrapuntal powers (see pp. 339–40).

Since the fugue has been a popular formal procedure for such a long time, the fugal experience is one with which many listeners are now quite at home. Some composers have taken advantage of this familiarity and on occasion have inserted the equivalent of fugal expositions into larger compositions such as the symphony. When such an exposition appears within a composition written in another form, that section is described as *fugato* or *in fugue.*

As the phenomenon of counterpoint with all its technical paraphernalia passes in review, the reader's reactions may vary from wonder and bewilderment to amazement. It is well to keep in mind that, like all other aspects of music, counterpoint is just another reflection of a fundamental life experience. It can be compared to a social situation, with each line becoming a metaphor for a personality or point of view, expressed concretely in words (in a choral work), or abstractly (in an instrumental composition). Musical personalities may clash and opposing viewpoints may be expressed. They are then settled by argumentation and reconciliation, just as social differences can be resolved in free give-and-take within the context of a democratic society.

CHAPTER

22

Art of Musical Form

AS THE PHILOSOPHER ARISTOTLE observed long ago, a work of art should have a beginning, a middle, and an end. Within these boundaries it should also have an inner logic in the relationship of its parts to the whole and of the whole to its parts. Formal patterns in a musical work, just like those in the visual arts and literature, must also aim to strike a balance between unity and variety, between repetition and invention, between the expected and the unexpected, between the reassurance of the old and the adventure of the new. Put in scientific terms, it becomes a matter of controlling the constants and variables. It is important to approach musical form more as a fluid process than as a rigid mold.

While music is essentially a time-oriented art, it also has spatial and visual dimensions as well. So do the essentially spatial arts have certain temporal aspects. When viewing a painting, for instance, the eye needs time to move about so that the various parts can be seen in relation to the whole. In the case of architecture, the exterior length, breadth, and height of a building require time for people to view it in all its aspects, as well as to walk around it so that all angles may be seen. The spatial aspects of music become evident when one considers its architectural surroundings such as church, concert hall, or opera house, where acoustics play an important part.

Music is also partially a visual art, since the printed score must be read by the performer, and the listener can see the performers in action at a live concert. Occasionally this visual aspect occurs in ways that carry a graphic symbolism, as when a canon or a round is inscribed in a circular design (Fig. 22-1).

Principles of Recurrence: Sectional Structures

Music has developed its own specific formal principles through which its unique communicative power may unfold. In the history of Western music, formal principles have largely been based on the principle of recurrence. This is not surprising, since the perception of any time-oriented art requires that the listener or reader occasionally be given reminders of what has gone before and intimations of what is to come. Of the many possibilities for musical recurrence, several have gained wide favor over the past several centuries. The most important are *immediate repetition,* as in canon and fugue (see pp. 471–79); *repetition after contrast,* with designs such as simple three-part form and rondo; the *variation principle,* in theme and variations; and the principle of *development,* as found in sonata form.

Naturally, communication through musical forms requires that composers couch their ideas within a formal framework that may be grasped by the per-

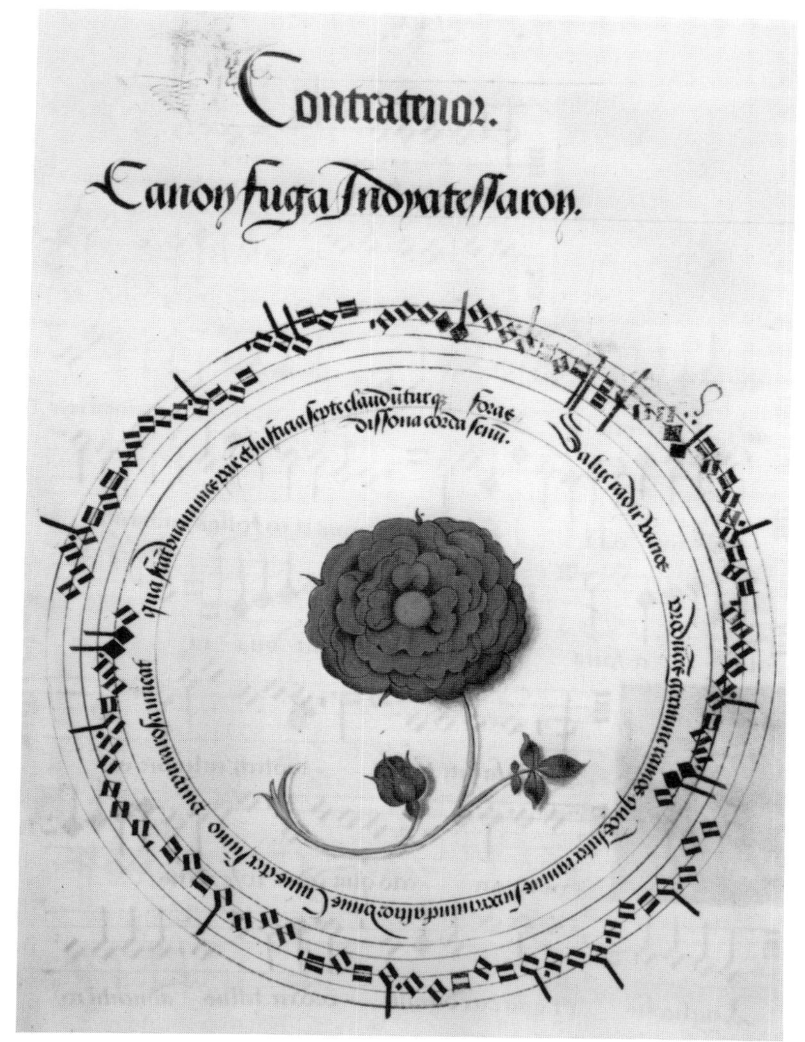

Figure 22-1. Anonymous. Canon in a circle with a rose "for Henry VIII," 16th century. By permission of the British Library, London.

former and the listener. At the same time, the musically creative mind seldom tolerates the constraints of a predetermined design, and composers are constantly testing and stretching forms to their limits. Most formal plans possess an inherent flexibility, which gives the composer the freedom to use repetition tempered with inventiveness.

To develop a sure approach to musical form, then, the listener should regard the formal design as a set of guiding principles and contact points between composer and listener. The fact that no two symphonies, sonatas, songs, or fugues are conceived in exactly the same formal terms should not be a deterrent to understanding. On the contrary, every composition may indeed be a fresh experience for the listener, if the composer mixes the formally innovative and unexpected with the known and expected. Within the self-imposed limitations of a formal outline, the composer discovers creative opportunities that in turn become an important component for listeners as they assess the communicative power of that composition.

SIMPLE SECTIONAL STRUCTURES

The two-part, or binary, form (designated by the letters A B) is based on sufficient resemblances between the two halves so that they come together in a recognizable whole. If the two sections are too radically different, they will fail to cohere. If they are too much alike, they will be dull and repetitious. So a balance between unity and variety must be maintained. Binary form is familiar from everyday songs such as *My Country 'Tis of Thee* and *London Bridge Is Falling Down.* It was also a pattern favored by such composers as François Couperin and J. S. Bach for the various dances that made up their keyboard suites. A viable example of two-part construction is provided by the theme Handel wrote for a set of variations, the so-called "Harmonious Blacksmith" (Ex. 22-1). Note that the A and B sections have sufficient differences to provide interest without disturbing the fundamental unity of the rhythmic and melodic patterns.

Equally familiar is the three-part, ternary, or A B A form. It is also frequently referred to as *song form,* and in the case of opera as *da capo* aria form. The underlying principle is that of statement–contrast–restatement, or statement–departure–return. The pattern appears in such well-known folk songs as *Twinkle, Twinkle, Little Star* and *Old Man River.* Monteverdi's aria "Lasciatemi morire" (see pp. 160–61) shows that the A B A design is also a worthy vehicle for profound and moving emotional expression.

More complex examples of the A B A design are common. In the 17th and 18th centuries, for instance, the *minuet* was a popular aristocratic dance. The form later became established as the third movement of instrumental sonatas, string quartets, and symphonies, where it functioned as a stylized, abstract art form. The formal plan of any dance must be practical, since it is

Example 22-1. Handel. "Harmonious Blacksmith" Variations. Air (theme).

meant to tell the dancers when to change steps or partners. The form of the minuet is one of the tightest and most terse in the history of music.

Minuet	Trio	Minuet
A	B	A
aa baba	cc dcdc	aba
‖:a:‖:ba:‖	‖:c:‖:dc:‖	

The dance is made up of two larger sections, the minuet and the trio, followed by a repeat of the minuet. As seen above, each of the larger A sections has a substructure, to which are assigned small letter designations. In the case of the minuet the substructure has a particular repeat pattern—shown here in both a fully written-out version and a shorthand version with repeat signs. The minuet and trio sections have the same substructure, though the musical materials are not the same. At the end of the trio section the instruction *da capo* (from the top) tells the performers to return to the beginning of the composition and play the minuet (A) section again but without repeats.

The A B A formal plan is far from new. It is still in active use today, where it may extend past the inner design of individual verses. A recent example in the popular field is *American Tune,* by Paul Simon (Ex. 22-2). The tune on which the song is based is not, in fact, an American tune at all. Its ancestry goes back to the 17th century, when it was a Lutheran hymn tune called in English *O sacred head now wounded.* In Simon's version, there are four verses. Verses 1, 2, and 4 constitute the A sections, while the third verse is the contrasting B section. A *modified A B A* form—A A B A—results.

Example 22-2. Simon. *American Tune.* A B A design.

RONDO

Another frequently encountered sectional form is the *rondo,* basically an extension of the A B A idea. Reduced to letter terms, a typical rondo may be described as A B A C A. The rondo carries the principle of statement and contrast one step further, giving one more extension of the contrast–statement pattern. A rondo may actually continue in this fashion indefinitely (D A, E A, F A, etc.), but the five-part formal division is the most common. Notice that the extension from three to five parts produces a shift in emphasis:

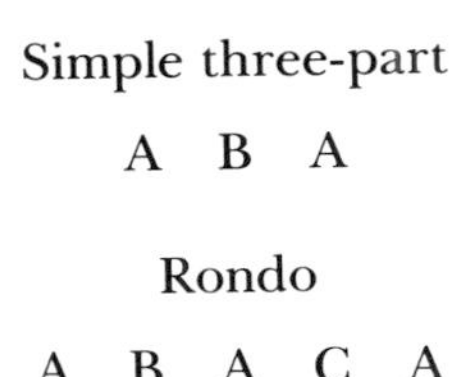

In both forms, the A sections stand as supporting pillars of the design at the beginning and the end, but in the rondo the A section also stands in the important central position.

The presto finale of Haydn's Piano Sonata in D Major, *Hob.* XVI:37, provides a concise, clear-cut example of simple rondo form. Set in the tonic key, the A section provides a clear instance of binary form in which each part is repeated (Ex. 22-3a). The B section, also an example of binary organization, plunges abruptly into the key of D Minor (Ex. 22-3b). Haydn repeats the A part verbatim, then sets the C section in the closely related key of G Major (Ex. 22-3c). To conclude both the movement and the sonata, Haydn varies the last appearance of the A section by quickening the bass part with running 16th notes.

Example 22-3. Haydn. Piano Sonata in D Major, *Hob.* XVI:37. Third movement.

22-3*a*. Bars 1–8.

22-3*b*. Bars 22–25.

22-3*c*. Bars 42–45.

The rondo has been important historically as the final movement of many sonatas, string quartets, concertos, and symphonies. The closing movement from Beethoven's Piano Concerto No. 2 in B-Flat Major, Op. 19, may serve as an example of a more expansive rondo practice, here on a somewhat larger scale. Throughout, the reader should be alert to the fact that this is only one very specific example of a practice that allows for inexhaustible permutations.

As with any large-scale example of a popular form, the composer seeks to provide listeners with a mixture of the expected and the unforeseen. The outline of this rondo is easily discernible, though it is of a type known as an *extended rondo* design.

Normal rondo: A B A C A

Extended rondo: A B A C A B A

The extended rondo modifies the conventional design by appending a further B and A section to the basic form, a practice favored by Beethoven in many of his rondos. In so doing, the central focus is moved from the A to the C section, which is surrounded with two A B A "pillars" (Chart 22-1).

CHART 22-1. BEETHOVEN: PIANO CONCERTO NO. 2 IN B-FLAT MAJOR, THIRD MOVEMENT (RONDO OUTLINE)

A	Bridge	B	Bridge	A	Bridge	C	Bridge	A	Bridge	B	Bridge	A		Close
Bar 1		Bar 49		Bar 96		Bar 126		Bar 173		Bar 221		Bar 262	Bar 270	
B♭ major piano, then orchestra		F major piano, then orchestra		B♭ major piano, then orchestra		G minor		B♭ major piano, then orchestra		B♭ major piano, then orchestra		G major piano	B♭ major orchestra	

The composer of any concerto seeks to strike a dramatic balance between soloist and orchestra and to create an atmosphere in which each may function comfortably as either soloist or accompanist. The listener is made immediately aware of a sense of equilibrium in this movement, as Beethoven opens his rondo in the tonic key with a statement of the A subject by the pianist (Ex. 22-4a). This is immediately followed by an orchestral repetition. The opening subject area contains a *bridge,* which provides continuity to the B section. As the name suggests, a bridge provides a smooth transition and often serves as a device to modulate into a contrasting key.

The piano soloist then embarks upon the jaunty B subject (bar 49, Ex. 22-4b) in the dominant key of F Major, with the orchestra joining in shortly thereafter. A second bridge leads to a repeat of the A subject, introduced again by the piano (bar 96) with the orchestra blending in a few measures later. Another bridge impels the music toward the central C section, introduced by the piano (bar 126, Ex. 22-4c) in the relative minor key (G Minor).

Once more a bridge conducts the listener to a reassessment of the earlier A, B, and A sections (bars 173, 221, and 262 respectively), unified through the shared tonic key of B-flat Major. The ear is given a mild jolt when the piano introduces the final A subject in the somewhat remote key of G Major. The orchestra quickly puts things to harmonic rights, however (bar 270), and a lively close brings both the movement and the concerto to an end in the tonic key.

Principle of Development

THEME AND VARIATIONS

Composers have often used easily recognized popular songs as a basis for instrumental experimentation and innovation. In the early 16th century, at-

Example 22-4. Beethoven. Piano Concerto No. 2 in B-flat Major, Op. 19. Third movement, "Rondo."

22-4*a*. Bars 1–9.

22-4*b*. Bars 49–52.

22-4*c*. Bars 127–32.

tempts to discover an instrumental potential in such vocal works crystallized into the form known as *theme and variations.* In this formal procedure, the known (song) becomes a point of departure for a journey into the unknown (instrumental variations), and along the way old bottles of song are filled with new musical wine.

Originally, variations followed the form of the song chosen as the theme. Later, as composers began to produce their own themes, they settled on the two-part form AA BB. All themes are, in fact, crafted from the basic elements of music: melody, harmony, rhythm, dynamics, and tone color. To display resourcefulness in revealing the new contained within the old, composers center on one or more of these elements for each variation on the theme.

As the final movement of his keyboard Suite in E Major, Handel wrote

Example 22-5. Handel. "Harmonious Blacksmith" Variations.

22-5*a*. First double (variation), bars 1–3.

22-5*b*. Second double, bars 1–3.

22-5*c*. Third double, bars 1–3.

22-5*d*. Fourth double, bars 1–3.

22-5*e*. Fifth double, bars 1–3.

an "Air with Variations" that is known popularly as the "Harmonious Blacksmith" variations. The theme—labeled an *air* by Handel—is conceived with melodic simplicity, clearly outlining tonic and dominant harmonies (see Ex. 22-1). Handel constructed each of the five variations with a slightly more complicated texture than its predecessor, but left the basic harmonic and metric relationships unchanged. This set provides a prime example of the baroque "air with doubles," a set of varied repetitions in which each variation doubles the number of notes of the previous one. Starting with the theme's sturdy 8th notes, the pace is progressively quickened with 16ths, then triplet 16ths, and finally with scampering 32nd notes (Exs. 22-5a through 22-5e).

The first variation breaks up the theme with an added note between each of the notes of the original. In the second, this technique is further explored by turning it upside down. In the third, the theme disappears within triplet figures, which in turn move to the left-hand bass line for the fourth variation. The final variation finds both hands running against each other contrapuntally in lines of 32nd notes, to provide a showy finish.

As a popular formal pattern in later instrumental music, the theme and variations appears in works by all major composers. A few examples are: the second movement of Haydn's Symphony No. 94, the fourth movement of Mozart's Clarinet Quintet, the fourth movement of Beethoven's "Eroica" Symphony, Brahms' orchestral variations on themes by Haydn and Handel, Rachmaninov's *Rhapsody on a Theme of Paganini,* Schoenberg's and Webern's *Variations for Orchestra,* Op. 31 and Op. 30 respectively, the second movement of Stravinsky's *Octet,* and the second movement of Bartók's Second Violin Concerto.

SONATA FORM

Over the past four centuries the term *sonata* has acquired a variety of meanings and has appeared in different guises over many style periods and in many musical situations. Two of these meanings are germane to the present discussion. In the first instance the noun *sonata,* as it appears on the title page of a score, indicates an instrumental composition of several movements. In the second, as an adjective, *sonata form* refers to the pattern or plan of a single movement, usually the first movement of a cyclical design.

Sonata form is perhaps best considered a process rather than a set mold. In its infancy, at the time of some of Haydn's early efforts, it was an extension of the A B A form. The A became a subject area, the B became an expanded view of A, and repetitions were introduced:

CHART 22-2. EARLY SONATA FORM

A	B	A
:Subject I:	:Subject I expanded	Subject I close:

With C. P. E. Bach and the young Mozart, the form took on new dramatic characteristics: a contrasting subject area, bridge passages, and closing sections. As they reshaped the form, it resembled the following:

CHART 22-3. SONATA FORM IN DEVELOPMENT

(A) Statement	(B) Working Out	(A) Return
: Subject I & bridge / Subject II & close :	: Subject I expanded	Subject I & bridge / Subject I & close :

As sonata form evolved through the vision and continued experiments of these and lesser composers, it assumed its mature classical configuration:

CHART 22-4. MATURE SONATA FORM

	Exposition				*Development*	*Recapitulation*			
Slow Intro*	Subject I Area		Subject II Area	Close		Subject I Area		Subject II Area	Close
	: Subject I statement	bridge	Subject II statement	closing : material		Subject I statement	bridge	Subject II statement	closing material
	Tonic key		Dominant or relative key			Tonic key		Tonic key	Tonic key

*Optional

Repetition of the last two sections became optional and gradually disappeared.

The main distinctions between sonata form and those sectional structures that had preceded it lay in the new concept of subject expansion, or *development,* and in the concern to construct subject materials so that they could offer the potential for such development. Sonata form became widespread during the latter half of the 18th century and has continued to be a major formal procedure well into the 20th. The procedure was not named sonata form by the composers who developed it, but by theoreticians who later sought to explain it. Its three sections are commonly called *exposition, development,* and *recapitulation.*

The *exposition* section opens with a *first subject* area in the tonic key, which announces the principal tonal center. A transition (bridge) leads to the *second subject* area in a related key. This is followed by a passage that concludes the section. The exposition is then repeated.

The *development,* or working-out section, makes use of a wide variety of procedures and techniques, during which the composer enlarges the scope and probes the depths of materials presented in the exposition. In the process, the subject materials may be segmented, dissected, expanded, contracted, transposed to near or remote keys, manipulated contrapuntally, subjected to sequential and episodic treatments, or placed in dramatic conflict with each other. The development section is, in fact, the dramatic proving ground, the portion of the form in which a musical power struggle of sorts takes place.

Eventually the development works its way back to the tonic key, and the original materials are presented again in the *recapitulation.* Here the previous subjects, having gone through the crucible of the development, now appear in a new refining light, transformed by the psychological processes of memory and anticipation. The recapitulation is seldom an exact repetition of the exposition because, as the ancient philosopher Heraclitus once observed, "in the flow of time one cannot step into the same river twice." Beethoven, for example, often followed the recapitulation with a "terminal development," providing further adventures for the listener.

Chart 22-4 shows the essential process of sonata form. It is evident that contrast is one of the fundamental devices in the designing of succeeding sections, subject materials, and keys. Like all viable formal processes, sonata form provides the composer with certain freedoms and restrictions. One of the freedoms is the option to place a slow introduction at the beginning of an otherwise fast movement. When a composer chooses this option, it is primarily to provide further contrast, and the musical materials in such an introduction may or may not appear later.

One of the accepted conditions of many forms is that of key relationships, and sonata form is no exception. A change of key signals a new subject or section, and key relationships provide an overall balance between contrast and recurrence. When such relationships are kept within the boundaries of diatonic harmony—tonic-dominant, tonic-relative major or minor—a further sense of unity is established without impeding a sense of motion and progress.

The character of the exposition should allow the listener to grasp the materials presented without difficulty. Therefore, the first subject is often bold and arresting. It may be designed so that figures or motifs may be excerpted from it for use in the development. The bridge functions to provide a smooth continuity, while modulating to a new key center, preparing the listener for the entry of the second subject. This subject is usually designed as a contrast to the first subject in both key and character. It may be lyrical, quiet, or contrapuntal, for example, so long as it provides an effective dramatic foil to the musical materials that have preceded it. Following the statement of this new subject, the composer ends the exposition with closing material. The music for this section is often like that of a bridge, except that it must point in two directions—backward, leading to the repetition of the exposition, and forward to the development section. The composer has the option at this point to introduce a *third subject,* though this practice was less favored by classical composers.

The ear remembers less well than the eye, and a listener cannot review subject materials during the performance of a musical work in the way a reader can turn back a few pages in a book. In sonata form it became standard procedure to repeat the entire exposition, partly as an aid to the memory of the audience, and partly to familiarize listeners with details of the musical materials that might slip by unnoticed on a first hearing. This allows them to become comfortable with materials from the exposition before they are subjected to the development process. Hence, in Chart 22-4 a repeat sign appears at the end of the exposition. This repetition solidifies the "first chapter" of this musical novel so that the listener is in a better position to judge what is to come.

The development has no assumed structure for the listener to follow. The shape of the development is different in each and every sonata form, and this section offers the composer a prime opportunity to show creative mastery. At this point the composer chooses materials from the exposition and treats them as a whole or in part, taking up the challenge to show these materials in new and interesting ways. Keys and tone colors may be changed frequently, while sequences, imitative entries, and isolated rhythmic figures may be sprinkled liberally throughout. There is no predetermined length for the development; but in general, the earlier the date of the composition, the shorter the development section will be.

Once a composer is satisfied that the subject materials have been sufficiently investigated, preparation for a return to the first subject is made. The recapitulation opens with that first subject stated more or less as it was heard at the beginning of the movement. Once listeners know where they are in terms of subject and key, the composer may decide to present the remainder of the exposition materials as originally heard, or to continue the developmental procedure and provide the listener with further ramifications of this now-familiar material. In the recapitulation, unity is provided through the tonal strength of the tonic key on which the remainder of the movement rests, with the bridge, second subject, and closing material all appearing in that now-familiar tonality. Finally, a *coda* may be affixed to give finality to the movement.

The essence of sonata form lies in the balance of discipline with fluidity and flexibility, and its ultimate destiny thus lies in the direction of constant and continuous development as it reflects the course of human life and growth. Of all musical designs, the sonata form is the most dramatic, constituting one part of an overall plan that may be likened to a three- or four-act play. The individual sonata-form movement then becomes a play within a play. Subjects, like characters, make their entrances and exits in the first act, the exposition. Then their interactions and their reactions to each other occur during various events and situations, as the plot thickens in the development. The dénouement follows, with an appropriate reconciliation of opposites and relaxation of tensions. After the characters are transformed in the light of their experiences, the play concludes with the recapitulation.

For the first (sonata form) movement of his Symphony No. 40 in G Minor,

K 550, Mozart plunges immediately into the first subject (Ex. 22-6a). This subject expands into a full melody with the restless, throbbing character that Mozart associated with the key of G Minor. The unifying factor within the subject is the use of an anapest figure, a short-short-long figure that will impart unity to the entire movement.

With an outburst from the music on a chord of B-flat Major (bar 28), the bridge begins its course through a group of sequences to the second subject (bar 44, Ex. 22-6b). In the expected relative major key of B-flat, the character of this subject is in direct contrast to that of the first. It is much more relaxed, providing a tone-color contrast of clarinets and flutes against the strings.

With the reappearance of the anapest figure (bar 72), the closing material begins. Its 29 bars are held together by this figure. Mozart was fond of long closing sections, and this is no exception. At its conclusion, a repeat sign indicates a return to the beginning of the composition.

Example 22-6. Mozart. Symphony No. 40 in G Minor, *K* 550. First movement.

22-6a. Bars 1–8.

22-6b. Bars 44–47.

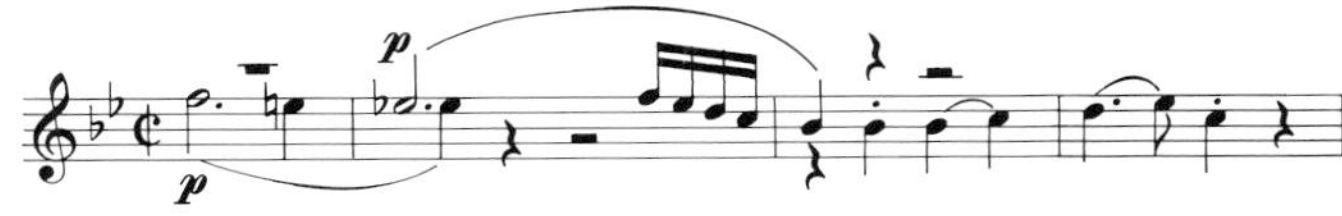

Two sharp chords signal the onset of the development, which opens with a reference to the first subject (bar 104, Ex. 22-6c). Mozart's decision to draw exclusively upon the anapest first subject during the development leads to rapid changes of key and tone color for purposes of contrast.

Toward the end of the development section, the orchestra becomes hushed in preparation for the return of the first subject in the tonic G-minor key, to signal the start of the recapitulation (bar 165). Here the subject is heard as it was at the beginning of the movement, but while Mozart retains its initial outlines, he makes some changes. These result primarily from the fact that the final section of the movement is heard in the tonic key throughout. The bridge no longer functions as a modulating component, and it is longer than its counterpart in the exposition by several bars.

The second subject in the recapitulation now makes its appearance under quite dramatically different circumstances (Ex. 22-6d). In the exposition, it was in a contrasting major key. Here, after a measure of rest for the entire orchestra (bar 226), it makes its entrance in the darker mood of the tonic minor.

22-*6c*. Bars 104–7.

22-*6d*. Bars 227–30.

The close and coda give a final, intensified summation of the material previously heard at the end of the exposition. Here, however, it serves to bring the movement to a vigorous climax and conclusion.

Multimovement Designs

As mentioned above, the sonata form is most often found in the company of other formal plans in multimovement structures, such as sonatas, symphonies, concertos, duos, trios, quartets, and quintets.

During the last half of the 18th century, certain fundamental conventions involving instrumental music were established. They involved the formulation of the principles that would guide the types of composition known variously as the *sonata,* the *string quartet* and diverse related chamber ensembles, the *symphony,* and the *classical concerto.*

As established by Haydn, Mozart, Beethoven, and others, these four instrumental categories became formally related, with the major difference between them largely one of instrumentation. Except for the first movement, this standardized scheme relied for the most part on formal designs and principles that already existed in other contexts. First movements were set in the new and original, briskly moving sonata form. Second movements had their roots in the opera aria, providing an unhurried lyrical or poignant statement in contrast to the first allegro movement. The third movement was a stately minuet taken from the dance suite. In the early 19th century, the minuet was replaced by the somewhat freer scherzo. The last movement presented further contrast through a sprightly theme and variations, an exuberant rondo, or another sonata-form movement.

CHART 22-5. TYPICAL FOUR-MOVEMENT INSTRUMENTAL FORMS

	Form	*Tempo*
First movement	Sonata form	Fast
Second movement	A B A	Slow
Third movement (18th-cent.)	Minuet and trio	"Minuet tempo"
(19th-cent.)	Scherzo	Fast
Fourth movement	Sonata form, Theme and variations, or Rondo	Fast

Under such a scheme, a typical sonata may be seen as a composition in four movements, comprising the formal designs in Chart 22-5 and usually scored for one or two instruments. Standard instrumental sonatas were written for piano and for such combinations as piano and violin, piano and flute, or piano and French horn. By extension, a string quartet is a "sonata" for two violins, viola, and cello, containing the same ordering of movements and forms; while a symphony is a "sonata" for orchestra. The four-movement configuration of forms in Chart 22-5 is to be regarded as a norm, with adjustments (made at the composer's discretion) allowing for three-movement sonatas or five-movement symphonies, as well as changing the inner order of movements.

The classical concerto with its dramatic opposition of soloist and orchestra grew out of the baroque concerto grosso and retained its three-movement design (see pp. 166–69). New formal designs supplanted those of the older concerto, and the classical concerto introduced a standard pattern of sonata form, an A B A slow movement, and an energetic rondo close. The inherent duality of soloist and orchestra also encouraged some alteration of inner formal details, including separate expositions for orchestra and soloist in the first movement and the opportunity for solo improvisation in a cadenza. This three-movement formal scheme has remained an expected norm for listeners well into the 20th century.

In the overall cyclical sense, the outer movements of any sonatalike composition frame the structure with more sophisticated formal contours and serious, searching declarations. The inner components then explore a more intimate spectrum with songlike lyricism, as in a slow second movement, and through dancelike measures, as in a third-movement minuet or scherzo. In the process the sonata form, with its capacity to shape and contain an infinite variety of musical thought and invention, becomes a miniature world in itself.

Like a self-revealing mirror it reflects the visage of the life, times, and ideas of an era, as well as the searching, expressive revelations of an individual composer.

As a final point, it should be apparent that the form of a musical composition is a rational ordering of its component parts. It is also the principle that gives coherence and oneness to two or more sections of the piece. Form, whether symmetrical or asymmetrical, is the guiding force that achieves an adjustment of balances and a sense of togetherness. While form is not an end in itself, knowledge of the logic of relationships within a musical composition assures the listener of understanding it at a deeper level. In the past, music criticism has suffered much by the false dichotomy that form and content were opposites—one ruled by reason, the other by emotion. When properly understood, form and content are just two ways of talking about the same thing. Rather than functioning as immutable sculptured shapes, musical forms provide living flexible principles for musical construction that furnish convenient points of orientation and illumination for the listener.

SUGGESTED READING

Music and the Other Arts: General Sources

Fleming, William. *Arts and Ideas*. 8th ed. New York: Holt, Rinehart and Winston, 1991.

Fleming, William. *Concerts of the Arts*. Pensacola, Fla.: University of West Florida Press, 1990.

Janson, H. W., and Joseph Kerman. *A History of Art and Music*. New York: Abrams, 1968.

The New Grove Dictionary of Music and Musicians. Edited by Stanley Sadie. 20 vols. New York: Macmillan, 1980. Individual biographies of major composers from this dictionary available in paperback from Norton.

The Norton/Grove Concise Encyclopedia of Music. Edited by Stanley Sadie. New York: Norton, 1988.

Sadie, Stanley, ed. *History of Opera*. New York: Norton, 1990.

Medieval, Renaissance, and Baroque Music

Fenlon, Iain. *The Renaissance*. Englewood Cliffs, N.J.: Prentice-Hall, 1978.

Geiringer, Karl. *Johann Sebastian Bach: The Culmination of an Era*. New York: Oxford University Press, 1966.

Hogwood, Christopher. *Handel*. London: Thames and Hudson, 1984.

Hoppin, Richard. *Medieval Music*. New York: Norton, 1978.

Classical, Romantic, and Contemporary Music

Boucourechliev, André. *Stravinsky*. New York: Holmes and Meier, 1987.

Brown, David. *Tchaikovsky*. 3 vols. New York: Norton, 1978, 1983, 1986.

Budden, Julian. *The Operas of Verdi*. 3 vols. New York: Oxford University Press, 1984.

Del Mar, Norman. *Richard Strauss: A Critical Commentary on His Life and Work.* 3 vols. Philadelphia: Chilton, 1978.

Griffiths, Paul. *Modern Music: The Avant-Garde Since 1945.* London: Dent, 1981.

Hildesheimer, Wolfgang. *Mozart.* New York: Farrar, Straus, and Giroux, 1982.

Hilmar, Ernst. *Franz Schubert in His Times.* Portland, Or.: Amadeus Press, 1988.

Holoman, D. Kern. *Berlioz.* Cambridge: Harvard University Press, 1989.

Landon, Harold Robbins. *Mozart: The Golden Years, 1781–1791.* New York: Schirmer Books, 1989.

Landon, Harold Robbins, and David Wyn Jones. *Haydn: His Life and Music.* Bloomington: Indiana University Press, 1988.

Lockspeiser, Edward. *Debussy.* London: Dent, 1980.

Machlis, Joseph. *Introduction to Contemporary Music.* New York: Norton, 1979.

Mellers, Wilfred. *Music in a New Found Land.* New York: Oxford University Press, 1987.

Orenstein, Arbie. *Ravel: Man and Musician.* New York: Columbia University Press, 1975.

Perle, George. *Serial Composition and Atonality: An Introduction to the Music of Schoenberg, Berg and Webern.* Berkeley: University of California Press, 1972.

Pestelli, Giorgio. *The Age of Mozart and Beethoven.* Cambridge: Cambridge University Press, 1984.

Plantinga, Leon. *Romantic Music.* New York: Norton, 1984.

Schuller, Gunther. *Early Jazz* and *The Swing Era: The Development of Jazz, 1930–1945.* New York: Oxford University Press, 1968 and 1989.

Solomon, Maynard. *Beethoven.* New York: Schirmer, 1977.

Watkins, Glenn. *Soundings: Music in the Twentieth Century.* New York: Schirmer, 1988.

White, Chappell. *An Introduction to the Life and Works of Richard Wagner.* Englewood Cliffs, N.J.: Prentice-Hall, 1967.

INDEX

This index also functions as a glossary; technical terms are listed with reference to pages on which they are defined in context. Individual works are indexed under their titles, not composer's or author's names.

Designed by Larry Leshan
Composed by European-American Graphics
in Baskerville
Music set by Johanna Baldwin
Halftone photography by Palm Offset
Printed and bound by Walsworth Publishing
on Mead Matte